PZ
7
S9513
As

Sullivan, Charles
As tomorrow becomes
today.

DATE DUE

DEC 8 72			

AS
TOMORROW
BECOMES
TODAY

AS TOMORROW BECOMES TODAY

edited by

Charles Wm. Sullivan III

University of Oregon

Prentice-Hall, Inc., *Englewood Cliffs, New Jersey*

Library of Congress Cataloging in Publication Data

Sullivan, Charles William, 1944–   comp.
  As tomorrow becomes today.

  SUMMARY: An anthology of science fiction stories designed to be utilized in the instruction of English composition and literature at the high school level.
    Bibliography: p.
    1. Science fiction. [1. Science fiction]
  I. Title.
  PZ7.S9513As   [Fic]   73–17416
  ISBN   0-13-050039-9
  ISBN   0-13-050021-6 (pbk.)

10 9 8 7 6 5 4 3 2 1

Prentice-Hall International, Inc., *London*
Prentice-Hall of Australia, Pty. Ltd., *Sydney*
Prentice-Hall of Canada, Ltd., *Toronto*
Prentice-Hall of India Private Limited, *New Delhi*
Prentice-Hall of Japan, Inc., *Tokyo*

ACKNOWLEDGMENTS

BACKTRACKED, Burt Filer, copyright © 1968 by Mercury Press, Inc.; reprinted by permission of the author.

ALL YOU ZOMBIES—, Robert Heinlein, copyright © 1960 by Mercury Press, Inc.; reprinted by permission of the author's agent, Lurton Blassingame.

THE MEN WHO MURDERED MOHAMMED, Alfred Bester, copyright 1958 by Mercury Press, Inc.; reprinted by permission of the author.

RANDOM QUEST, John Wyndham, copyright 1961 by John Wyndham; reprinted by permission of the author and the author's agents, Scott Meredith Literary Agency, Inc., 580 Fifth Avenue, New York, New York 10036.

THUS WE FRUSTRATE CHARLEMAGNE, R. A. Lafferty. First appeared in *Galaxy,* Feb., 1969; copyright © 1970, by R. A. Lafferty, in *Nine Hundred Grandmothers* (Ace). Reprinted by permission of the author and his agent, Virginia Kidd.

THE MONSTER FROM NOWHERE, Nelson Bond, copyright 1939 by Ziff-Davis Publishing Co.; reprinted by permission of the author and the author's agent Scott Meredith Literary Agency, Inc., 580 Fifth Avenue, New York, New York 10036.

THE NEW REALITY, Charles L. Harness, copyright, 1950, by Standard Magazines, Inc.; reprinted by permission of the author and the author's agents, Scott Meredith Literary Agency, Inc., 580 Fifth Avenue, New York, New York 10036. Printed as it appears in *The Rose,* published by Berkley Publishing Corp.

NO-SIDED PROFESSOR, Martin Gardner, copyright 1946 by Martin Gardner; reprinted by permission of the author.

—AND HE BUILT A CROOKED HOUSE—, Robert Heinlein, copyright 1940 by Street and Smith Publications, Inc.; reprinted by permission of the author's agent, Lurton Blassingame.

THE FUN THEY HAD, Isaac Asimov, copyright 1951 by NEA Service, Inc.; reprinted by permission of the author.

PRIMARY EDUCATION OF THE CAMIROI, R. A. Lafferty. First appeared in *Galaxy,* Dec., 1966; copyright © 1970 by R. A. Lafferty in *Nine Hundred Grandmothers* (Ace). Reprinted by permission, the author and his agent, Virginia Kidd.

HEMEAC, E. G. Von Wald, copyright© 1968, Galaxy Publishing Corp.; reprinted by permission of the author and the author's agents, Scott Meredith Literary Agency, Inc., 580 Fifth Avenue, New York, New York 10036.

PERSONAL, Tuli Kupferberg, copyright© 1966 by East Side Press, Inc.; reprinted by permission of the author.

A BOY AND HIS DOG, Harlan Ellison, copyright© 1969 by Harlan Ellison. Originally published in *The Beast that Shouted Love at the Heart of the World* by Harlan Ellison, Avon Books. Reprinted by permission of the author and the author's agent, Robert P. Mills, Ltd.

RUNAROUND, Isaac Asimov, copyright 1942 by Street and Smith Publications, Inc.; copyright renewed, 1969, by Isaac Asimov; reprinted by permission of the author.

CALLING DR. CLOCKWORK, Ron Goulart, copyright © 1965 by Ziff-Davis Publishing Co.; reprinted by permission of the author.

MASKS, Damon Knight, copyright © 1958 by HMH Publishing Co., Inc.; reprinted by permission of the author.

SPECIALIST, Robert Sheckley, copyright© 1953 by Robert Sheckley; reprinted by permission of Sterling Lord Agency, Inc.

THE SENTINEL, Arthur C. Clarke, copyright© 1951 Avon Periodicals, Inc.; reprinted by permission of the author and the author's agents, Scott Meredith Literary Agency, Inc., 580 Fifth Avenue, New York, New York 10036.

THE GAME OF RAT AND DRAGON, Cordwainer Smith, copyright© 1955 by Galaxy Publishing Corp.; reprinted by permission of the author's Estate and their agents, Scott Meredith Literary Agency, Inc., 580 Fifth Avenue, New York, New York 10036.

THE DECISION MAKERS, Joseph Green, copyright © 1965 by Galaxy Publishing Corp.; reprinted by permission of the author's agent, Lurton Blassingame.

for my sons
Jason and Aaron
whose future is now
being built

Contents

Preface

Reality caught up with science fiction before ninety-nine percent of the American public was aware that such a process was going on. Men on the moon are science fiction; Mars and Venus probes are science fiction; orbiting communications and spy satellites are science fiction; guided missles, jet planes, and atomic and nuclear bombs are science fiction. At some point in this list, many people did become aware that reality was merging with the earliest visions of twentieth century science fiction authors—that tomorrow was becoming today. But it was before any of the events on that list that reality caught up with science fiction. It happened during World War II when science fiction descriptions of atomic research and atomic power were realistic enough to arouse the attention of the government. Federal investigators could find no evidence that any secrets had been leaked for indeed none had been. Science fiction writers were extrapolating into the future on paper in much the same way as government scientists were in the laboratory. Science fiction had portrayed the immediate future with almost incredible accuracy, and science fiction may still be doing it.

At the very least, then, science fiction deserves attention because it describes some of the possible tomorrows. But more important, while most people were reading it for escape, adventure, or imaginative stimulation, science fiction became a respectable literary genre, and it is now beginning to get the serious critical and scholarly attention it has long deserved. In *The Nature of Narrative,* Scholes and Kellogg discuss science fiction and note that educational institutions and professional men of letters have been slow and possibly reluctant to come to terms with speculative literature but that they will soon have to adjust. Marjorie Hope Nicolson, in *Science and Imagination* and in *Voyages to the Moon,* discusses science and literature in general as well as science fiction in particular. And in *Future Shock,* Alvin Toffler suggests that the widespread reading of science fiction could help man prepare for the changes to come. Besides these and other critics, mainstream authors such as Anthony Burgess, Saul Bellow, John Barth, and Vladimir Nabokov have given credit to science fiction as a literary genre. In recent years, these authors have used science fiction premises in their novels. Finally, science fiction is beginning to appear in the university, college, and high school classroom. In 1971, science fiction author Jack Williamson estimated that there were perhaps more than 150 science fiction courses being offered on the university level. Moreover, science fiction novels and short stories are being used in courses dealing with economics, sociology, history, and anthropology. But critics, mainstream authors, and university courses bear, after all, only secondary witness to the stature of science fiction; the primary evidence is the literature itself.

As Tomorrow Becomes Today is designed to present the literature and to examine its relationship to the imagination and to the future. For some readers, this book may serve as an introduction to science fiction, but for all it should serve to indicate one method of organizing this literature. This method encourages imaginative attention to the future so that, by gaining a view of some of the possibilities, man can assert some control over his destiny.

As Tomorrow Becomes Today is divided into two sections: Science Fiction and the Imagination, and Science Fiction and the Future. The first section contains nine stories under the headings Time Travel, Parallel Worlds, and Mind Stretchers. These stories attempt to present theoretical speculations as realities and call for the most intense suspension of disbelief of any literature except, possibly, pure fantasy. The second section contains twenty stories and one poem under the headings Education, World War III, Robots, Man: Himself and Aliens, Technology, and Population. Each of these stories focuses the imagination on a particular area of the future and attempts to make the reader believe that it could come about. The first section of the book, then, exercises the imagination by presenting it with logically constructed "impossibilities" while the second section directs the imagination toward a consideration of facets of today's existence which could become tomorrow's problems or crises.

Each of the nine major divisions of the book is introduced by a headnote in which some of the main topics under that heading are discussed, several pertinent novels are mentioned, and some possible approaches to each of the short stories which follows are suggested. In addition, in various instances, I have tried to comment on the order in which the stories are presented, highlight a few of the literary qualities, and discuss some of the thematic questions which the authors raise. I have not posed all of the questions which it is possible to pose nor have I tried to provide all of the answers—those must be left, by and large, to the readers of this book if science fiction is to function with the imagination in the manner I have suggested above.

A bibliography of critical works on science fiction and nonfiction studies concerning the future concludes the volume.

Many thanks go to authors Harlan Ellison, Martin Gardner, Tuli Kupferberg, and andrew j. offutt; and to Mrs. Lewis F. Glaser, executrix of the estate of Alice Glaser, for kindnesses shown me. Special thanks go to Edward M. Jennings III, State University of New York at Albany, whose suggestions and encouragement were wise and timely. And special thanks also go to my wife, Ann, a most patient aide.

Charles Wm. Sullivan III

AS
TOMORROW
BECOMES
TODAY

Introduction

A quick check of the shelves of any local bookstore will reveal that science fiction novels and short story anthologies are frequently grouped separately under the heading "Science Fiction." However, they are almost as often placed in a section with such works of pure fantasy as J. R. R. Tolkien's *The Lord of the Rings.* A more serious complication arises, though, when such novels as Kurt Vonnegut's *The Sirens of Titan* or Walter M. Miller's *A Canticle for Liebowitz* are found under a sign which reads "Best Sellers."

It would seem, therefore, that there is some ambiguity about what is to be defined as science fiction. Donald Wollheim, in *The Universe Makers,* suggests:

> Science fiction is that branch of fantasy, which, while not true to present-day knowledge, is rendered plausible by the reader's recognition of the scientific possibilities of it being possible at some future date or at some uncertain point in the past.

Other definitions abound, and no two are alike. Significant definitions are presented by Sam Moskowitz in *Seekers of Tomorrow* and Robert Heinlein in Basil Davenport's *The Science Fiction Novel.*

If getting people to agree on a definition of science fiction is difficult, establishing the point of science fiction's origin is equally arduous. L.

Sprague de Camp, in *Science Fiction Handbook,* traces science fiction to the writings of Aristophanes and Plato; Marjorie Hope Nicolson, in *Voyages to the Moon,* believes that science fiction may have begun with Lucian of Samosata (born about 125 A.D.) and his *Icaromenippos, Or a Journey Through the Air* and *A True Story.* Harlan Ellison, in the introduction to *Dangerous Visions,* offers a choice between the Bible and Walt Disney's *Steamboat Willie* (1928) as the origin of science fiction—take Mr. Ellison at your peril. It is also possible to see the works of H. G. Wells and Jules Verne as the beginnings of science fiction. And, of course, the roles of two prominent editors of science fiction magazines, Hugo Gernsback and John W. Campbell, Jr., are not small ones, and either might well be considered as the father of modern science fiction.

Those who wish to investigate the historical and definitional aspects of science fiction should consult the bibliography. The critical works listed at the end of this volume provide a much more complete examination of the nature and history of science fiction than could any introduction of reasonable length. The focus of this introduction, then, moves to a consideration of some of the implications of science fiction as an academic discipline.

Ever since man began to think further ahead than his next meal and plan for more than his next hunt, he has wanted to know something about what the future—the next day, year, or decade—would bring. The knowledge of what was coming would give man some control of the present so that he might have, perhaps, some control of how or even if that future was to be. But as a long line of gypsies, shamans, witch doctors, and prophets will attest, predicting the future is more of an art than a science. First, it is the art of wording prophecies so that a large number of varied occurrences will fulfill them; and second, it is the art of knowing what today means and how today will affect tomorrow. This second art has been employed by rainmakers and Wall Street investors alike. But as the rate of change increases tremendously in every facet of our lives, we need something which is more specific than the method of the old fortune tellers and of much longer range than tomorrow's weather or stock market trends.

Science fiction is the literature to help us look into and prepare for tomorrow because of an essential difference between it and any other form of fiction. The fiction we are most acquainted with in academic and social environments, mainstream literature as well as classical literature, presents us with familiar people and situations. This fiction appeals to us because we can identify with most aspects of it and, more importantly, because we can experience through it a depth of involvement to which we may not have access or experiential referents in our own lives. And this is good in so far as it extends our understanding of ourselves and those around us, but it is, unfortunately, primarily oriented toward the past or the present. The present, however, is less and less a stable situation in our Western civilization. Holden Caulfield, in J. D. Salinger's *The Catcher in the Rye,* is out of date today. The society of which Holden is a part and a product is rapidly disappearing, if it is not already gone. Certainly there may be a core of the human character which remains constant, but concomitant with the vast and rapid changes going on in the social, political, economic, and religious structures in which a person must exist and with which he must deal if not relate, there must be changes in character. And if one is not ready for or able to meet this challenge, he will suffer; Alvin Toffler's *Future Shock* explores this problem in great detail.

Science fiction can help man prepare for tomorrow because unlike mainstream and classic fiction, science fiction presents recognizably human characters in quite unfamiliar situations. The characters are human and have the basic wants, needs, and drives common to man. But that is not to say they are simple; they can be as psychologically, intellectually, socially, and politically complex as any literary analyst could ask. The recognizable and indeed identifiable humans are necessary for the reader since the situation in which he finds them may be as vaguely familiar as a few years in the future, or as totally un-familiar—again, except for the people or what they have become—as thousands of years away. These situations are primarily based upon what we know of our civilization today and upon speculation as to how a facet of this civilization might, if emphasized, continued, or negated, affect things at some point in the future. This facet, now portrayed in terms of its possible effects, is then able to be more accurately evaluated as to what we will do with it now in order to control its possible impact on the future. And there is enough good science fiction available so that we can have separate and even opposing views on the possible results of any one such extended component. Changes in education, the effects of robots, the nature of man himself, the role of technology, and the problem of population control are perhaps the more obvious components to be considered as to their impact on the future, but they are not the only topics which are examined in science fiction.

The examination of possible futures is not science fiction's only strong point. Futurology groups, such as that run by the Rand Corporation, can extrapolate into the future and propose possible courses of action, but science fiction also exercises the imagination. We have for too long, especially under the watchful eyes of the sciences, been concerned with the reasoned approach. In literature, this has meant that we analyzed until a work of art was broken down into its various components, examined, and then reassembled, having gained, hopefully, a greater understanding of the whole and what the writer is trying to say through the work. This type of thorough analysis is not a bad thing, just over-emphasized. And these analytical techniques, when applied to quality science fiction, yield the same result as when applied to the works of Dickens, Conrad, or Bellow. But science fiction also exercises the imagination by presenting it with and making it believe in situations which have no exact correlation with anything which exists today. Certainly fantasy exercises the imagination in the same way, but fantasy does not have the same connection with the world around us. Science fiction, then, not only exercises the imagination but channels it in certain directions. And it requires a judicious reader to examine the plausibility of the possibility offered. In other words, the proposed situation must be examined not only as to its likelihood but also as to the validity of the interrelation of its various parts as affected by the primary components of the civilization extrapolated in the work.

Science fiction and its directed exercise of the imagination now becomes important in two distinct applications. First, a community of imaginative people will be ready to meet the future. They will be ready not so much because they have seen and chosen from among all possible futures but because they will have seen so many possibilities that they will be ready to accept or reject, modify or work within the future that they actually find even if it is not like one of the futures foreseen in literature. Their viable imaginations will aid them in opening their minds to the coming changes and thus allow them to avoid the serious consequences to their sanity which Toffler describes in *Future Shock*. We must, in other words, be open to even the wildest possibilities in every facet of existence. The second application is in problem recognition and solving. The internal combustion engine has been spewing pollution into the atmosphere for decades, but it is only very recently that the consequences of that pollution have been explored. Not that someone should have been on Henry Ford's back when he began to mass produce, but when the two-cars-in-every-garage politicians came along, the problem was obvious. Unfortunately, no one was looking. Few people at that time thought in terms of long-range consequences of such things as automobile engines. We are just now acquiring the ability to formulate statements of the problems; we must continue with this and with formulating long-range solutions. As our technology grows, we must increasingly think in terms not just of the direct consequences of technological developments but of various and long-range side effects as well.

This sort of directed imaginative thinking, sorely needed in the higher planning circles of the world, is what science fiction can help provide; and if we cannot know exactly what the future will bring, we at least should have some idea of what certain inputs may bring, choose carefully from among them, and be ready for the expected and unexpected results.

C. W. S.

SCIENCE FICTION
AND THE IMAGINATION

Time Travel

If you could travel in time, would you go into the future with impatience to know what is in store for mankind? Would you go into the past with an idealistic desire to prevent the assassination of an Abraham Lincoln or to assassinate an Adolf Hitler? And what would those changes, if you could effect them, mean to the time from which you came? Why, indeed, would (or should) one travel in time?

In *The Time Machine* (1895), H. G. Wells not only invented the concept of a device which would enable men to travel through time, but he made impressive use of science fiction as extrapolation into the future for the purpose of social criticism. And in spite of histories of science fiction which begin with Lucian of Samosata, it is Wells' "scientific romances" that much of today's science fiction, or speculative fiction, must regard as its origin. Wells, like most authors who have since written about time travel, accepts the possibility that a man might travel through time and concentrates on what happens after that trip has been made.

Wells was intent on developing the philosophies of his mentor, T. H. Huxley, and on commenting on the nature of his fellow Englishmen by showing what they could be like in the future if they kept on as they were. Subsequent authors, however, have tended to focus on sending a man back through time or on receiving something which has been sent to the present from the future. In the former category, the traditional viewpoint is that a man might travel back through time and change something in the past. The effects of that change would then ripple down through the centuries, and the final effects would substantially alter the age which the time traveller left. Also in this category are stories in which a man goes back in time and meets himself. One danger for the man who travels into the near past is that he may get caught in a time loop. In a time loop, the person lives forward in time to point A, then travels back in time to point B, and is then doomed to continue repeating the cycle. In the latter category, items from the future arrive in the present and are used or misused by those who find them.

In John Brunner's *Times Without Number,* which is also a fascinating parallel-worlds novel, a society possessed of time travel is endangered by one individual who attempts to use time travel as a means of revenge. Karl Glogauer, the protagonist of Michael Moorcock's *Behold the Man,* travels back in time to Judea in search of Jesus Christ and, in a way, finds him twice. Ian Wallace's *Croyd* and *Dr. Orpheus* depict a hero who can travel backward or forward through time by the power of his mind. A war involving the manipulation of events in time is the main conflict in Fritz Lieber's *The Big Time,* a novel told from the point of view of a girl who is a hostess at a rest and recreation center suspended outside the flux of time.

Each of the three stories in this group is based on the premise that a man can travel back in time, and these trips are examined in terms of the paradox created for the present when someone travels back in time and changes something in the past. This paradox is represented for all of the stories in Robert Heinlein's use of the Worm Ouroboros in "All You Zombies—." The stories are also united in that each is primarily personal in theme rather than being concerned with larger issues of a possible social, political, or military nature. In Burt Filer's "Backtracked," a man motivated by love travels back in time to get the second chance for which one always wishes. The irony of the story's conclusion is an interesting comment on this use of time travel. Robert Heinlein's main character in "All You Zombies—" travels back in time and meets his younger self with rather complex results. In "The Men who Murdered Mohammed," Alfred Bester depicts a jealous husband who travels into a particular kind of past which may be the only one into which man will ever travel.

BACKTRACKED

Burt Filer

The first thing he saw was Sally staring at him. She was sitting up in the big bed and had four fingers of her left hand wedged in her mouth. For some reason she'd drawn the sheet up around her and held it there with the other arm, as if caught suddenly by a stranger. Fletcher sat up.

"What's the matter? What time is it?" He felt odd and a little woozy. His voice sounded rough and both legs hurt, the good one and the other one.

"You've backtracked," Sally said. She gritted her teeth and gave that quick double shake of hers. The long brown hair fell down, and a curler came out.

Fletcher looked down at the arm he'd hooked around his good knee. It was sunburned and freckled the way August usually made it, but the August of what future year had done this? The fingers were blunter, the nails badly bitten, and the arm itself was thicker by half than the one he'd gone to bed with.

Sally lay back down, blinking, on the verge of tears. "You're older," she said, "a lot older. Why'd you do it?"

Fletcher tossed off the sheet and swung his legs to the floor. "I don't know, but then I wouldn't. It wipes you out completely, they say." Hurrying across the old green rug they'd retired to the bedroom after long service downstairs, he stared at himself in the dressing mirror. At first he didn't believe it.

Gone was the somewhat paunchy but still attractive businessman of thirty-six. The man in the mirror looked more like a Sicilian fisherman, all weatherbeaten and knotty. Fletcher looked for several long seconds at the blue veins which wrapped his forearms and calves like fishnets. Both calves. The left, though still as warped as ever, was thick now. It looked strong, but it ached.

Fletcher's face was older by ten years. Etched in the seams about his eyes was the grimness that age brings out through a lifetime of forced smiles. And though the hair on his chest was sunbleached, he could easily see that a good deal of it was actually white. Fletcher shut his eyes, turned away.

Walking around to Sally's side of the bed, he sat down and dropped a hand to her shoulder. "I must have had a good reason. We'll find out soon enough."

It was only six o'clock but sleep was out of the question, naturally. They dressed. Sally went down the stairs ahead of him, still slim and lithe at thirty-four, and still desirable. The envy of many.

She turned left into the kitchen and he followed, but continued past into the garage. His excuse for privacy was the bicycles just as hers was breakfast. *Leave me alone and I'll get used to it,* Fletcher thought. *Leave her alone and she can handle it too.*

He edged around the bumper of their car to the clutter of his workbench and switched on the light. The bicycles gave him a momentary sense of rightness, gleaming there. They were so slender and functional and spare. Flipping his own over on its back, he checked tension on the derailleur. Perfect.

He righted the thing and dropped the rear wheel into the free rollers. Mounting it, he pedaled against light resistance, the way he'd always dreamed the roads would be.

Maybe they would be now, with these legs. Why had he spent ten years torturing spring into the muscles of a cripple? Sheer vanity, perhaps. But at the cost of wasting those ten years forever, it seemed unreasonable.

Fletcher was sweating, and the speedometer on the rollers said thirty. He was only halfway through the gears, though, so he shifted twice. Fifty.

Maybe he should call Time Central? No, they were duty bound to give him no help at all. They'd just say that at some point ten years in the future he had gone to them with a request to be backtracked to the present—and that before making the hop his mind had been run through that CLEAR/RESET wringer of theirs.

Sorry, Mr. Fletcher, but it's the only way to minimize temporal contamination and paradox. Bothersome thing, paradox. Your mind belongs to Fletcher of the present; you have no knowledge of the future. You understand, of course.

What he understood was that the body of Fletcher-forty-odd had backtracked to be used by the mind of Fletcher-thirty-six, almost as a beast of burden.

And Fletcher-thirty-six could only wonder why.

A lot of people did it to escape some unhappiness in their later years. It seldom worked. They inevitably became anachronistic misfits among their once-contemporaries. But ten years at Fletcher's age wasn't really that much, and he guessed they'd all get used to him. But would Sally?

Sixty, said the dummy speedometer. Fletcher noted with some surprise that he'd been at it for fifteen minutes. Better slow down, and save some for the trip. What strength! Maybe he'd learn to play tennis. He could see himself trouncing Dave Schenk, Sally looking on from the sidelines— Fletcher was smiling now, Sally would come around. She had a powerful older man in place of a soft young one, a cripple at that. Polio. He'd been one of the last. Other men had held doors open for him ever since, and he'd learned to smile. . . .

Up to fifty again, slow down. And where was breakfast? This body of his hungered. And what had it done, this body? Knowing from bitter experience how slowly it responded to exercise, Fletcher decided that the lost ten years must have been devoted almost exclusively to physical development.

But for what? Some kind of crisis, that he might meet with superior strength on the second go-around? And why had he decided to backtrack to this particular morning?

"Fletch, breakfast," Sally called. The voice was lighter and steady. Dismounting, Fletcher stood with his hands in his pockets and watched the silver wheel whir slowly to a stop.

She wouldn't want to discuss it. Not for a while, anyhow. It'd been the same with his leg, back before they were married. He switched the light off and went in.

"It'll be nice after that burns off," he said, nodding out the window. The bench in the breakfast nook felt hard as he sat on it. Less flesh there now. Sally handed down two plates and joined him. Not across the table but at his side. A show of confidence. They ate slowly, silently.

Fletcher looked over at her profile. With her hair tied back like that she was very patrician. Straight nose, serious mouth. Like Anastasia, Dave Schenk had said, a displaced princess. She caught him looking at her, began to smile, changed her mind, put down her fork.

She faced him squarely. "I think I'll make it, Fletch." She lowered her forehead a fraction, waiting for a reassuring peck, and he gave it to her.

He turned out to have been right about the weather. Within an hour they were pedaling in bright sunlight and had stopped to remove their sweaters. Sally seemed cheerful. For perhaps the third time, Fletcher caught her gazing with frank wonder at his body, especially his leg. He glowed inwardly. Aloud he said, "Forward, troops," and swooped off ahead.

They wound their way up Storm King Mountain. Occasionally a car would grind past them on the steep grades, but soon the two bicycles left the road. They had the clay path which led up to the reservoir all to themselves. May-pale sumacs on the left, and a hundred feet of naked air on the right.

"Hey," said Sally, "slow down." Dismounting, they sat under a big maple. She leaned her head on his shoulder and slid one hand cosily between his upper arm and his ribs. "Oh," she said, and raised her eyebrows.

They sat there for some time. Over them the branches reached across the path and out beyond the cliffs. Below, the Hudson wound in a huge ess, a round green island at one end. It was a wide old river, moving slowly. A tug dragged clumped barges upstream in an efficient line that cut off most of the curves. In the distance a few motorboats buzzed like flies, little white wakes behind them. Crawling along the far shore was a passenger train headed for New York.

It smelled like spring. Rising, Sally went over by the bicycles and bent to pick a white umbrella of Queen Anne's lace. She came back twirling the stalk between her fingers. "Ready," she said.

He set her an easy pace, but did it the hard way himself, not using the lower gears. One of Dave Schenk's subtler tricks. Fletcher wished he was with them today.

At about eleven o'clock they reached the top. Between the power company's storage reservoir and the bluffs was a little park that no one else ever seemed to use. Sally spread most of their food on a weathered wooden picnic table. Then she went over and sat on a broad granite shelf. Fletcher set about starting a fire.

It was taking him quite a while, as he'd forgotten the starter and had to whittle some twigs for tinder. He nicked his thumb, frowned, sucked it, looked up.

Sally was on her feet again, picking more flowers. She paused from time to time to gaze out over the river. The view was even more spectacular here, Fletcher knew, even though too far back to see it himself. They were three or four hundred feet straight above the water.

Running a few feet beyond the main line of the bluff was a grassy promontory. Several bunches of Queen Anne's lace waved above the wild hay and creepers. He wished she'd get away from here and took a breath to tell her to.

Sally screamed as her legs slid out of sight. Twisting midair, she clutched two frantic handfuls of turf.

She was only sixty feet away, but the fireplace and the big old table lay directly between them. Fletcher planted both hands on the smoking stone chimney and vaulted it. The thing was four feet high, but could have been five and he'd still have made it. A dozen running steps, each faster and longer than the last, carried him to the table. He yanked his head down and his right leg up to hurdle it, snapping the leg down on the other side and swinging the weaker one behind. Pain shot through it, and Fletcher nearly sprawled. It took him four steps to straighten out, and in four more he was there.

He hurled himself at the two slender wrists that were falling away, and got one.

Sally screamed again, this time in pain. Fletcher hauled her up to his chin, both sinewy hands around her small white one. Edging backward on his knees, he drew her fully up. Fletcher stood shakily and attempted to help her to her feet. His left leg gave way.

Falling beside her, he lay on the warm granite and tried to catch his breath. It was difficult for some reason. Her face swam before him, and as he lost consciousness he heard himself repeating, "So that's why, that's why—"

Fletcher's eyelids were burning, so he opened them, to look directly into the sun. He must have been lying there an hour. Sally—his mind leapfrogged back and the breath stopped in his throat. But no, it was over, she lay here beside him now. Fletcher rose to an elbow. His leg throbbed between numbness and intolerable pain, and it looked as if someone had taken an axe to it.

But Sally's wrist looked just as bad. The drying scum near her lips attested to that. As he moved her head gently away from the puddle, she moaned.

It took him ten minutes to crawl over to the table and return with a bottle of wine. They'd brought no water. He sprinkled some on her forehead, then held it to her lips. She came around, fainted, came around again.

Sally had made it about halfway down to the road when she ran into some picnickers. The jeep came at three, and at four they were both in the orthopedic ward at Rockland State.

Fletcher was still dopey with anesthetic and delayed shock. As he told the reporter what had happened, the little man nearly drooled. Their episode had occurred on Saturday. When they were released from the hospital and sent home on Wednesday, their story was still up on page four. On the front porch was a yellow plastic wastebasket full of unopened telegrams and letters.

They hadn't had much privacy at the hospital. So after Sally had made the coffee she sat down opposite Fletcher at the kitchen table and asked, "How've you been?"

"Okay. Still a little disoriented, maybe."

"Yes." She stared into her cup. "Fletch, I guess the first time we went though that, I fell?"

Fletcher nodded. "I'd never have made it to you, the old way." He stared down at the cast on his leg. "Ten years of mine, for all of yours. I'd do it again."

"It wasn't cheap," she said.

"No, it wasn't cheap."

They made love that night. Fletcher had been worried about that, and found his fears justified to some extent. Ten years made a difference. But Sally held him long afterward and cried a little, which was the best with her. He fell asleep feeling reassured for then, but knowing what was to come.

Fletcher dyed his hair and had some minor facial surgery done to smooth out his eyes and throat. He gained ten pounds. He looked pretty much like the Fletcher of thirty-six. A certain amount of romance was attached to his reputation now, and when he changed jobs his salary almost doubled.

His broken left leg never healed solidly, though, and for all intents and purposes he was back to where he'd started. He and Sally remained childless right up until their divorce two years later. She was later married to David Schenk, but Fletcher remained alone.

"ALL YOU ZOMBIES—"

Robert Heinlein

2217 Time Zone V (EST) 7 Nov 1970—NYC-"Pop's Place": I was polishing a brandy snifter when the Unmarried Mother came in. I noted the time—10:17 P.M. zone five, or eastern time, November 7th, 1970. Temporal agents always notice time and date; we must.

The Unmarried Mother was a man twenty-five years old, no taller than I am, childish features and a touchy temper. I didn't like his looks—I never had—but he was a lad I was here to recruit, he was my boy. I gave him my best barkeep's smile.

Maybe I'm too critical. He wasn't swish; his nickname came from what he always said when some nosy type asked him his line: "I'm an unmarried mother." If he felt less than murderous he would add: "at four cents a word. I write confession stories."

If he felt nasty, he would wait for somebody to make something of it. He had a lethal style of infighting, like a female cop—one reason I wanted him. Not the only one.

He had a load on and his face showed that he despised people more than usual. Silently I poured a double shot of Old Underwear and left the bottle. He drank it, poured another.

I wiped the bar top. "How's the 'Unmarried Mother' racket?"

His fingers tightened on the glass and he seemed about to throw it at me; I felt for the sap under the bar. In temporal manipulation you try to figure everything, but there are so many factors that you never take needless risks.

I saw him relax that tiny amount they teach you to watch for in the Bureau's training school. "Sorry," I said. "Just asking, 'How's business?' Make it 'How's the weather?' "

He looked sour. "Business is okay. I write 'em, they print 'em, I eat."

I poured myself one, leaned toward him. "Matter of fact," I said, "you write a nice stick—I've sampled a few. You have an amazingly sure touch with the woman's angle."

It was a slip I had to risk; he never admitted what pen-names he used. But he was boiled enough to pick up only the last: " 'Woman's angle!' " he repeated with a snort. "Yeah, I know the woman's angle. I should."

"So?" I said doubtfully. "Sisters?"

"No. You wouldn't believe me if I told you."

"Now, now," I answered mildly, "bartenders and psychiatrists learn that nothing is stranger than truth. Why, son, if you heard the stories I do—well, you'd make yourself rich. Incredible."

"You don't know what 'incredible' means!"

"So? Nothing astonishes me. I've always heard worse."

He snorted again. "Want to bet the rest of the bottle?"

"I'll bet a full bottle." I placed one on the bar.

"Well—" I signaled my other bartender to handle the trade. We were at the far end, a single-stool space that I kept private by loading the bar top by it with jars of pickled eggs and other clutter. A few were at the other end watching the fights and somebody was playing the juke box—private as a bed where we were.

"Okay," he began, "to start with, I'm a bastard."

"No distinction around here," I said.

"I mean it," he snapped. "My parents weren't married."

"Still no distinction," I insisted. "Neither were mine."

"When—" He stopped, gave me the first warm look I ever saw on him. "You mean that?"

"I do. A one-hundred-percent bastard. In fact," I added, "No one in my family ever marries. All bastards.

"Oh, that." I showed it to him. "It just looks like a wedding ring; I wear it to keep women off." It is an antique I bought in 1985 from a fellow operative—he had fetched it from pre-Christian Crete. "The Worm Ouroboros . . . the World Snake that eats its own tail, forever without end. A symbol of the Great Paradox."

He barely glanced at it. "If you're really a bastard, you know how it feels. When I was a little girl—"

"Wups!" I said. "Did I hear you correctly?"

"Who's telling this story? When I was a little girl— Look, ever hear of Christine Jorgenson? Or Roberta Cowell?"

"Uh, sex-change cases? You're trying to tell me—"

"Don't interrupt or swelp me, I won't talk. I was a foundling, left at an orphanage in Cleveland in 1945 when I was a month old. When I was a little girl, I envied kids with parents. Then, when I learned about sex—and, believe me, Pop, you learn fast in an orphanage—"

"I know."

"—I made a solemn vow that any kid of mine would have both a pop and a mom. It kept me 'pure,' quite a feat in that vicinity—I had to learn to fight to manage it. Then I got older and realized I stood darn little chance of getting married—for the same reason I hadn't been adopted." He scowled. "I was horse-faced and buck-toothed, flat-chested and straight-haired."

"You don't look any worse than I do."

"Who cares how a barkeep looks? Or a writer? But people wanting to adopt pick little blue-eyed golden-haired morons. Later on, the boys want bulging breasts, a cute face, and an Oh-you-wonderful-male manner." He shrugged. "I couldn't compete. So I decided to join the W.E.N.C.H.E.S."

"Eh?"

"Women's Emergency National Corps, Hospitality & Entertainment Section, what they now call 'Space Angels'—Auxiliary Nursing Group, Extraterrestrial Legions."

I knew both terms, once I had them chronized. We use still a third name, it's that elite military service corps: Women's Hospitality Order Refortifying & Encouraging Spacemen. Vocabulary shift is the worst hurdle in time-jumps—did you know that "service station" once meant a dispensary for petroleum fractions? Once on an assignment in the Churchill Era, a woman said to me, "Meet me at the service station next door"—which is not what it sounds; a "service station" (then) wouldn't have a bed in it.

He went on: "It was when they first admitted you can't send men into space for months and years and not relieve the tension. You remember how the wowsers screamed?—that improved my chance, since volunteers were scarce. A gal had to be respectable, preferably virgin (they liked to train them from scratch), above average mentally, and stable emotionally. But most volunteers were old hookers, or neurotics who would crack up ten days off Earth. So I didn't need looks; if they accepted me, they would fix my buck teeth, put a wave in my hair, teach me to walk and dance and how to listen to a man pleasantly, and everything else—plus training for the prime duties. They would even use plastic surgery if it would help—nothing too good for Our Boys.

"Best yet, they made sure you didn't get pregnant during your enlistment—and you were almost certain to marry at the end of your hitch. Same way today, A.N.G.E.L.S. marry spacers—they talk the language.

"When I was eighteen I was placed as a 'mother's helper.' This family simply wanted a cheap servant but I didn't mind as I couldn't enlist till I was twenty-one. I did housework and went to night school—pretending to continue my high school typing and shorthand but going to a charm class instead, to better my chances for enlistment.

"Then I met this city slicker with his hundred-dollar bills." He scowled. "The no-good actually did have a wad of hundred-dollar bills. He showed me one night, told me to help myself.

"But I didn't. I liked him. He was the first man I ever met who was nice to me without trying games with me. I quit night school to see him oftener. It was the happiest time of my life.

"Then one night in the park the games began."

He stopped. I said, "And then?"

"And then *nothing!* I never saw him again. He walked me home and told me he loved me—and kissed me good-night and never came back." He looked grim. "If I could find him, I'd kill him!"

"Well," I sympathized, "I know how you feel. But killing him—just for doing what comes naturally—hmm . . . Did you struggle?"

"Huh? What's that got to do with it?"

"Quite a bit. Maybe he deserves a couple of broken arms for running out on you, but—"

"He deserves worse than that! Wait till you hear. Somehow I kept anyone from suspecting and decided it was all for the best. I hadn't really loved him and probably would never love anybody—and I was more eager to join the W.E.N.C.H.E.S. than ever. I wasn't disqualified, they didn't insist on virgins. I cheered up.

"It wasn't until my skirts got tight that I realized."

"Pregnant?"

"He had me higher 'n a kite! Those skinflints I lived with ignored it as long as I could work—then kicked me out and the orphange wouldn't take me back. I landed in a charity ward surrounded by other big bellies and trotted bedpans until my time came.

"One night I found myself on an operating table, with a nurse saying, 'Relax. Now breathe deeply.'

"I woke up in bed, numb from the chest down. My surgeon came in. 'How do you feel?' he says cheerfully.

" 'Like a mummy.'

" 'Naturally. You're wrapped like one and full of dope to keep you numb. You'll get well—but a Caesarian isn't a hangnail.'

" 'Caesarian' I said. 'Doc—*did I lose the baby?*'

" 'Oh, no. Your baby's fine.'

" 'Oh. Boy or girl?'

" 'A healthy little girl. Five pounds, three ounces.'

"I relaxed. It's something, to have made a baby. I told myself I would go somewhere and tack 'Mrs.' on my name and let the kid think her papa was dead—no orphanage for *my* kid!

"But the surgeon was talking. 'Tell me, uh—' He avoided my name. '—did you ever think your glandular setup was odd?'

"I said, 'Huh? Of course not. What are you driving at?'

"He hesitated. 'I'll give you this in one dose, then a hypo to let you sleep off your jitters. You'll have 'em.'

" 'Why?' I demanded.

" 'Ever hear of that Scottish physician who was female until she was thirty-five?—then had surgery and became legally and medically a man? Got married. All okay.'

" 'What's that got to do with me?'

" 'That's what I'm saying. You're a man.'

"I tried to sit up. *'What?'*

" 'Take it easy. When I opened you, I found a mess. I sent for the Chief of Surgery while I got the baby out, then we held a consultation with you on the table—and worked for hours to salvage what we could. You had two full sets of organs, both immature, but with the female set well enough developed for you to have a baby. They could never be any use to you again, so we took them out and rearranged things so that you can develop properly as a man.' He put a hand on me. 'Don't worry. You're young, your bones will readjust, we'll watch your glandular balance—and make a fine young man out of you.'

"I started to cry. 'What about my *baby?*'

" 'Well, you can't nurse her, you haven't milk enough for a kitten. If I were you, I wouldn't see her—put her up for adoption.'

" *'No!'*

"He shrugged. 'The choice is yours; you're her mother—well, her parent. But don't worry now; we'll get you well first.'

"Next day they let me see the kid and I saw her daily—trying to get used to her. I had never seen a brand-new baby and had no idea how awful they look—my daughter looked like an orange monkey. My feelings changed to cold determination to do right by her. But four weeks later that didn't mean anything."

"Eh?"

"She was snatched."

" 'Snatched?' "

The Unmarried Mother almost knocked over the bottle we had bet. "Kidnapped—stolen from the hospital nursery!" He breathed hard. "How's that for taking the last a man's got to live for?"

"A bad deal," I agreed. "Let's pour you another. No clues?"

"Nothing the police could trace. Somebody came to see her, claimed to be her uncle. While the nurse had her back turned, he walked out with her."

"Description?"

"Just a man, with a face-shaped face, like yours or mine." He frowned. "I think it was the baby's father. The nurse swore it was an older man but he probably used makeup. Who else would swipe my baby? Childless women pull such stunts—but whoever heard of a man doing it?"

"What happened to you then?"

"Eleven more months of that grim place and three operations. In four months I started to grow a beard; before I was out I was shaving regularly . . . and no longer doubted that I was male." He grinned wryly. "I was staring down nurses' necklines."

"Well," I said, "seems to me you came through okay. Here you are, a normal man, making good money, no real troubles. And the life of a female is not an easy one."

He glared at me. "A lot you know about it!"

"So?"

"Ever hear the expression 'a ruined woman'?"

"Mmm, years ago. Doesn't mean much today."

"I was as ruined as a woman can be; that bum *really* ruined me—I was no longer a woman . . . and I didn't know *how* to be a man."

"Takes getting used to, I suppose."

"You have no idea. I don't mean learning how to dress, or not walking into the wrong rest room; I learned those in the hospital. But how could I *live?* What job could I get? Hell, I couldn't even drive a car.

I didn't know a trade; I couldn't do manual labor—too much scar tissue, too tender.

"I hated him for having ruined me for the W.E.N.C.H.E.S., too, but I didn't know how much until I tried to join the Space Corps instead. One look at my belly and I was marked unfit for military service. The medical officer spent time on me just from curiosity; he had read about my case.

"So I changed my name and came to New York. I got by as a fry cook, then rented a typewriter and set myself up as a public stenographer—what a laugh! In four months I typed four letters and one manuscript. The manuscript was for *Real Life Tales* and a waste of paper, but the goof who wrote it sold it. Which gave me an idea; I bought a stack of confession magazines and studied them." He looked cynical. "Now you know how I get the authentic woman's angle on an unmarried-mother story . . . through the only version I haven't sold—the true one. Do I win the bottle?"

I pushed it toward him. I was upset myself, but there was work to do. I said, "Son, you still want to lay hands on that so-and-so?"

His eyes lighted up—a feral gleam.

"Hold it!" I said. "You wouldn't kill him?"

He chuckled nastily. "Try me."

"Take it easy. I know more about it than you think I do. I can help you. I know where he is."

He reached across the bar. *"Where is he?"*

I said softly, "Let go my shirt, sonny—or you'll land in the alley and we'll tell the cops you fainted." I showed him the sap.

He let go. "Sorry. But where is he?" He looked at me. "And how do you know so much?"

"All in good time. There are records—hospital records, orphanage records, medical records. The matron of your orphanage was Mrs. Fetherage—right? She was followed by Mrs. Gruenstein—right? Your name, as a girl, was 'Jane'—right? And you didn't tell me any of this—right?"

I had him baffled and a bit scared. "What's this? You trying to make trouble for me?"

"No indeed. I've your welfare at heart. I can put this character in your lap. You do to him as you see fit—and I guarantee that you'll get away with it. But I don't think you'll kill him. You'd be nuts to—and you aren't nuts. Not quite."

He brushed it aside. "Cut the noise. *Where is he?*"

I poured him a short one; he was drunk but anger was offsetting it. "Not so fast. I do something for you—you do something for me."

"Uh . . . what?"

"You don't like your work. What would you say to high pay, steady work, unlimited expense account, your own boss on the job, and lots of variety and adventure?"

He stared. "I'd say, 'Get those goddam reindeer off my roof!' Shove it, Pop—there's no such job."

"Okay, put it this way: I hand him to you, you settle with him, then try my job. If it's not all I claim—well, I can't hold you."

He was wavering; the last drink did it. "When d'yuh d'liver 'im?" he said thickly.

"If it's a deal—*right now!*"

He shoved out his hand. "It's a deal!"

I nodded to my assistant to watch both ends, noted the time—2300— started to duck through the gate under the bar—when the juke box blared out: "I'm My Own Grandpaw!" The service man had orders to load it with Americana and classics because I couldn't stomach the "music" of 1970, but I hadn't known that tape was in it. I called out, "Shut that off! Give the customer his money back." I added, "Storeroom, back in a moment," and headed there with my Unmarried Mother following.

It was down the passage across from the johns, a steel door to which no one but my day manager and myself had a key; inside was a door to an inner room to which only I had a key. We went there.

He looked blearily around at windowless walls. "Where is 'e?"

"Right away." I opened a case, the only thing in the room; it was a U.S.F.F. Co-ordinates Transformer Field Kit, series 1992, Mod. II—a beauty, no moving parts, weight twenty-three kilos fully charged, and shaped to pass as a suitcase. I had adjusted it precisely earlier that day; all I had to do was to shake out the metal net which limits the transformation field.

Which I did. "What's that?" he demanded.

"Time machine," I said and tossed the net over us.

"Hey!" he yelled and stepped back. There is a technique to this; the net has to be thrown so that the subject will instinctively step back *onto* the metal mesh, then you close the net with both of you inside completely—else you might leave shoe soles behind or a piece of foot, or scoop up a slice of floor. But that's all the skill it takes. Some agents con a subject into the net; I tell the truth and use that instant of utter astonishment to flip the switch. Which I did.

1030-VI-3 April 1963—Cleveland, Ohio-Apex Bldg.: "Hey!" he repeated. "Take this damn thing off!"

"Sorry," I apologized and did so, stuffed the net into the case, closed it. "You said you wanted to find him."

"But—you said that was a time machine!"

I pointed out a window. "Does that look like November? Or New

York?" While he was gawking at new buds and spring weather, I reopened the case, took out a packet of hundred-dollar bills, checked that the numbers and signatures were compatible with 1963. The Temporal Bureau doesn't care how much you spend (it costs nothing) but they don't like unnecessary anachronisms. Too many mistakes, and a general court-martial will exile you for a year in a nasty period, say 1974 with its strict rationing and forced labor. I never make such mistakes; the money was okay.

He turned around and said, "What happened?"

"He's here. Go outside and take him. Here's expense money." I shoved it at him and added, "Settle him, then I'll pick you up."

Hundred-dollar bills have a hypnotic effect on a person not used to them. He was thumbing them unbelievingly as I eased him into the hall, locked him out. The next jump was easy, a small shift in era.

7100-VI-10 March 1964—Cleveland-Apex Bldg.: There was a notice under the door saying that my lease expired next week; otherwise the room looked as it had a moment before. Outside, trees were bare and snow threatened; I hurried, stopping only for contemporary money and a coat, hat, and topcoat I had left there when I leased the room. I hired a car, went to the hospital. It took twenty minutes to bore the nursery attendant to the point where I could swipe the baby without being noticed. We went back to the Apex Building. This dial setting was more involved, as the building did not yet exist in 1945. But I had precalculated it.

0100-VI-20 Sept 1945—Cleveland-Skyview Motel: Field kit, baby, and I arrived in a motel outside town. Earlier I had registered as "Gregory Johnson, Warren, Ohio," so we arrived in a room with curtains closed, windows locked, and doors bolted, and the floor cleared to allow for waver as the machine hunts. You can get a nasty bruise from a chair where it shouldn't be—not the chair, of course, but backlash from the field.

No trouble. Jane was sleeping soundly; I carried her out, put her in a grocery box on the seat of a car I had provided earlier, drove to the orphanage, put her on the steps, drove two blocks to a "service station" (the petroleum-products sort) and phoned the orphanage, drove back in time to see them taking the box inside, kept going and abandoned the car near the motel—walked to it and jumped forward to the Apex Building in 1963.

2200-VI-24 April 1963—Cleveland-Apex Bldg.: I had cut the time rather fine—temporal accuracy depends on span, except on return to zero. If I had it right, Jane was discovering, out in the park this balmy spring night, that she wasn't quite as "nice" a girl as she had thought. I grabbed a taxi to the home of those skin-flints, had the hackie wait around a corner while I lurked in shadows.

Presently I spotted them down the street, arms around each other. He took her up on the porch and made a long job of kissing her good-night—longer than I thought. Then she went in and he came down the walk, turned away. I slid into step and hooked an arm in his. "That's all, son," I announced quietly. "I'm back to pick you up."

"*You!*" He gasped and caught his breath.

"Me. Now you know who *he* is—and after you think it over you'll know who you are . . . and if you think hard enough, you'll figure out who the baby is . . . and who *I* am."

He didn't answer, he was badly shaken. It's a shock to have it proved to you that you can't resist seducing yourself. I took him to the Apex Building and we jumped again.

2300-VIII-12 Aug 1985—Sub Rockies Base: I woke the duty sergeant, showed my I.D., told the sergeant to bed my companion down with a happy pill and recruit him in the morning. The sergeant looked sour, but rank is rank, regardless of era; he did what I said—thinking, no doubt, that the next time we met he might be the colonel and I the sergeant. Which can happen in our corps. "What name?" he asked.

I wrote it out. He raised his eyebrows. "Like so, eh? *Hmm*—"

"You just do your job, Sergeant." I turned to my companion.

"Son, your troubles are over. You're about to start the best job a man ever held—and you'll do well. *I know.*"

"That you will!" agreed the sergeant. "Look at me—born in 1917—still around, still young, still enjoying life." I went back to the jump room, set everything on preselected zero.

2301-V-7 Nov 1970—NYC-"Pop's Place": I came out of the storeroom carrying a fifth of Drambuie to account for the minute I had been gone. My assistant was arguing with the customer who had been playing "I'm My Own Grandpaw!" I said, "Oh, let him play it, then unplug it." I was very tired.

It's rough, but somebody must do it and it's very hard to recruit anyone in the later years, since the Mistake of 1972. Can you think of a better source than to pick people all fouled up where they are and give them well-paid, interesting (even though dangerous) work in a necessary cause? Everybody knows now why the Fizzle War of 1963 fizzled. The bomb with New York's number on it didn't go off, a hundred other things didn't go as planned—all arranged by the likes of me.

But not the Mistake of '72; that one is not our fault—and can't be undone; there's no paradox to resolve. A thing either is, or it isn't, now and forever amen. But there won't be another like it; an order dated "1992" takes precedence any year.

I closed five minutes early, leaving a letter in the cash register telling my day manager that I was accepting his offer to buy me out, so see my lawyer as I was leaving on a long vacation. The Bureau might or might not pick up his payments, but they want things left tidy. I went to the room back of the storeroom and forward to 1993.

2200-VII-12 Jan 1993 —Sub Rockies Annex-HQ Temporal DOL: I checked in with the duty officer and went to my quarters, intending to sleep for a week. I had fetched the bottle we bet (after all, I won it) and took a drink before I wrote my report. It tasted foul and I wondered why I had ever liked Old Underwear. But it was better than nothing; I don't like to be cold sober, I think too much. But I don't really hit the bottle either; other people have snakes—I have people.

I dictated my report; forty recruitments all okayed by the Psych Bureau—counting my own, which I knew would be okayed. I was here, wasn't I? Then I taped a request for assignment to operations; I was sick of recruiting. I dropped both in the slot and headed for bed.

My eye fell on "The By-Laws of Time," over my bed:

Never Do Yesterday What Should Be Done Tomorrow.
If at Last You Do Succeed, Never Try Again.
A Stitch in Time Saves Nine Billion.
A Paradox May Be Paradoctored.
It Is Earlier When You Think.
Ancestors Are Just People.
Even Jove Nods.

They didn't inspire me the way they had when I was a recruit; thirty subjective-years of time-jumping wears you down. I undressed and when I got down to the hide I looked at my belly. A Caesarian leaves a big scar but I'm so hairy now that I don't notice it unless I look for it.

Then I glanced at the ring on my finger.

The Snake That Eats Its Own Tail, Forever and Ever . . . I *know* where *I* came from—but *where did all you zombies come from?*

I felt a headache coming on, but a headache powder is one thing I do not take. I did once—and you all went away.

So I crawled into bed and whistled out the light.

You aren't really there at all. There isn't anybody but me—Jane—here alone in the dark.

I miss you dreadfully!

THE MEN WHO MURDERED
MOHAMMED

Alfred Bester

There was a man who mutilated history. He toppled empires and uprooted dynasties. Because of him, Mount Vernon should not be a national shrine, and Columbus, Ohio, should be called Cabot, Ohio. Because of him the name Marie Curie should be cursed in France, and no one should swear by the beard of the Prophet. Actually, these realities did not happen, because he was a mad professor; or, to put it another way, he only succeeded in making them unreal for himself.

Now, the patient reader is too familiar with the conventional mad professor, undersized and overbrowed, creating monsters in his laboratory which invariably turn on their maker and menace his lovely daughter. This story isn't about that sort of make-believe man. It's about Henry Hassel, a genuine mad professor in a class with such better-known men as Ludwig Boltzmann (*see* Ideal Gas Law), Jacques Charles and André Marie Ampère (1775–1836).

Everyone ought to know that the electrical ampere was so named in honor of Ampère. Ludwig Boltzmann was a distinguished Austrian physicist, as famous for his research on black-body radiation as on Ideal Gases. You can look him up in Volume Three of the *Encyclopaedia Britannica,* BALT to BRAI. Jacques Alexandre César Charles was the first mathematician to become interested in flight, and he invented the hydrogen balloon. These were real men.

They were also real mad professors. Ampère, for example, was on his way to an important meeting of scientists in Paris. In his taxi he got a brilliant idea (of an electrical nature, I assume) and whipped out a pencil and jotted the equation on the wall of the hansom cab. Roughly, it was: $dH = ipdl/r^2$ in which p is the perpendicular distance from P to the line of the element dl; or $dH = i \sin \phi \, dl/r^2$. This is sometimes known as Laplace's Law, although he wasn't at the meeting.

Anyway, the cab arrived at the Académie. Ampère jumped out, paid the driver and rushed into the meeting to tell everybody about his idea. Then he realized he didn't have the note on him, remembered where he'd left it, and had to chase through the streets of Paris after the taxi to recover his runaway equation. Sometimes I imagine that's how Fermat lost his famous "Last Theorem," although Fermat wasn't at the meeting either, having died some two hundred years earlier.

Or take Boltzmann. Giving a course in Advanced Ideal Gases, he peppered his lectures with involved calculus, which he worked out quickly and casually in his head. He had that kind of head. His students had so much trouble trying to puzzle out the math by ear that they couldn't keep up with the lectures, and they begged Boltzmann to work out his equations on the blackboard.

Boltzmann apologized and promised to be more helpful in the future. At the next lecture he began, "Gentlemen, combining Boyle's Law with the Law of Charles, we arrive at the equation $pv = p_0v_0 (1 + at)$. Now, obviously, if $_aS^b = f(x)dx (a)$, then $pv = RT$ and $S f (x,y,z) dV = O$. It's as simple as two plus two equals four." At this point Boltzmann remembered his promise. He turned to the blackboard, conscientiously chalked $2 + 2 = 4$, and then breezed on casually doing the complicated calculus in his head.

Jacques Charles, the brilliant mathematician who discovered Charles' Law (sometimes known as Gay-Lussac's Law), which Boltzmann mentioned in his lecture, had a lunatic passion to become a famous paleographer—that is, a discoverer of ancient manuscripts. I think that being forced to share credit with Gay-Lussac may have unhinged him.

He paid a transparent swindler named Vrain-Lucas 200,000 francs for holograph letters purportedly written by Julius Caesar, Alexander the Great, and Pontius Pilate. Charles, a man who could see through any gas, ideal or not, actually believed in these forgeries despite the fact that the maladroit Vrain-Lucas had written them in modern French on modern notepaper bearing modern watermarks. Charles even tried to donate them to the Louvre.

Now, these men weren't idiots. They were geniuses who paid a high price for their genius because the rest of their thinking was other-world. A genius is someone who travels to truth by an unexpected path. Unfortunately, unexpected paths lead to disaster in everyday life. This is what happened to Henry Hassel, professor of Applied Compulsion at Unknown University in the year 1980.

Nobody knows where Unknown University is or what they teach there. It has a faculty of some two hundred eccentrics, and a student body of two thousand misfits—the kind that remain anonymous until they win Nobel prizes or become the First Man on Mars. You can always spot a graduate of U.U. when you ask people where they went to school. If you get an evasive reply like: "State," or "Oh, a fresh-water school you never heard of," you can bet they went to Unknown. Someday I hope to tell you more about this university, which is a center of learning only in the Pickwickian sense.

Anyway, Henry Hassel started home from his office in the Psychotic Psenter early one afternoon, strolling through the Physical Culture arcade. It is not true that he did this to leer at the nude coeds practicing Arcane Eurythmics; rather, Hassel liked to admire the trophies displayed in the arcade in memory of great Unknown teams which had won the sort of championships that Unknown teams win—in sports like Strabismus, Occlusion and Botulism. (Hassel had been Frambesia singles champion three years running.) He arrived home uplifted, and burst gaily into the house to discover his wife in the arms of a man.

There she was, a lovely woman of thirty-five, with smoky red hair and almond eyes, being heartily embraced by a person whose pockets were stuffed with pamphlets, microchemical apparatus and a patella-reflex hammer—a typical campus character of U.U., in fact. The embrace was so concentrated that neither of the offending parties noticed Henry Hassel glaring at them from the hallway.

Now, remember Ampère and Charles and Boltzmann. Hassel weighed one hundred and ninety pounds. He was muscular and uninhibited. It would have been child's play for him to have dismembered his wife and her lover, and thus simply and directly achieve the goal he desired—the end of his wife's life. But Henry Hassel was in the genius class; his mind just didn't operate that way.

Hassel breathed hard, turned and lumbered into his private laboratory like a freight engine. He opened a drawer labeled DUODENUM and removed a .45-caliber revolver. He opened other drawers, more interestingly labeled, and assembled apparatus. In exactly seven and one half minutes (such was his rage), he put together a time machine (such was his genius).

Professor Hassel assembled the time machine around him, set a dial for 1902, picked up the revolver and pressed a button. The machine made a noise like defective plumbing and Hassel disappeared. He reappeared in Philadelphia on June 3, 1902, went directly to No. 1218 Walnut Street, a red-brick house with marble steps, and rang the bell. A man who might have passed for the third Smith Brother opened the door and looked at Henry Hassel.

"Mr. Jessup?" Hassel asked in a suffocated voice.

"Yes?"

"You are Mr. Jessup?"

"I am."

"You will have a son, Edgar? Edgar Allan Jessup—so named because of your regrettable admiration for Poe?"

The third Smith Brother was startled. "Not that I know of," he said. "I'm not married yet."

"You will be," Hassel said angrily. "I have the misfortune to be married to your son's daughter, Greta. Excuse me." He raised the revolver and shot his wife's grandfather-to-be.

"She will have ceased to exist," Hassel muttered, blowing smoke out of the revolver. "I'll be a bachelor. I may even be married to somebody else . . . Good God! Who?"

Hassel waited impatiently for the automatic recall of the time machine to snatch him back to his own laboratory. He rushed into his living room. There was his redheaded wife, still in the arms of a man.

Hassel was thunderstruck.

"So that's it," he growled. "A family tradition of faithlessness. Well, we'll see about that. We have ways and means." He permitted himself a hollow laugh, returned to his laboratory, and sent himself back to the year 1901, where he shot and killed Emma Hotchkiss, his wife's maternal grandmother-to-be. He returned to his own home in his own time. There was his redheaded wife, still in the arms of another man.

"But I *know* the old bitch was her grandmother," Hassel muttered. "You couldn't miss the resemblance. What the hell's gone wrong?"

Hassel was confused and dismayed, but not without resources. He went to his study, had difficulty picking up the phone, but finally managed to dial the Malpractice Laboratory. His finger kept oozing out of the dial holes.

"Sam?" he said. "This is Henry."

"Who?"

"Henry."

"You'll have to speak up."

"Henry Hassel!"

"Oh, good afternoon, Henry."

"Tell me all about time."

"Time? Hmmm . . ." The Simplex-and-Multiplex Computer cleared its throat while it waited for the data circuits to link up. "Ahem. Time. (1) Absolute. (2) Relative. (3) Recurrent. (1) Absolute: period, contingent, duration, diurnity, perpetuity—"

"Sorry, Sam. Wrong request. Go back. I want time, reference to succession of, travel in."

Sam shifted gears and began again. Hassel listened intently. He nodded. He grunted. "Uh huh. Uh huh. Right. I see. Thought so. A continuum, eh? Acts performed in past must alter future. Then I'm on the right track. But act must be significant, eh? Mass-action effect. Trivia cannot divert existing phenomena streams. Hmmm. But how trivial is a grandmother?"

"What are you trying to do, Henry?"

"Kill my wife," Hassel snapped. He hung up. He returned to his laboratory. He considered, still in a jealous rage.

"Got to do something significant," he muttered. "Wipe Greta out. Wipe it all out. All right, by God! I'll show 'em."

Hassel went back to the year 1775, visited a Virginia farm and shot a young colonel in the brisket. The colonel's name was George Washington, and Hassel made sure he was dead. He returned to his own time and his own home. There was his redheaded wife, still in the arms of another.

"Damn!" said Hassel. He was running out of ammunition. He opened a fresh box of cartridges, went back in time and massacred Christopher Columbus, Napoleon, Mohammed and half a dozen other celebrities. "That ought to do it, by God!" said Hassel.

He returned to his own time, and found his wife as before.

His knees turned to water; his feet seemed to melt into the floor. He went back to his laboratory, walking through nightmare quicksands.

"What the hell is significant?" Hassel asked himself painfully. "How much does it take to change futurity? By God, I'll really change it this time. I'll go for broke."

He traveled to Paris at the turn of the twentieth century and visited a Madame Curie in an attic workshop near the Sorbonne. "Madame," he said in his execrable French, "I am a stranger to you of the utmost, but a scientist entire. Knowing of your experiments with radium— Oh? You haven't got to radium yet? No matter. I am here to teach you all of nuclear fission."

He taught her. He had the satisfaction of seeing Paris go up in a mushroom of smoke before the automatic recall brought him home. "That'll teach women to be faithless," he growled . . . "Guhhh!" The last was wrenched from his lips when he saw his redheaded wife still— But no need to belabor the obvious.

Hassel swam through fogs to his study and sat down to think, While he's thinking I'd better warn you that this is not a conventional time story. If you imagine for a moment that Henry is going to discover that the man fondling his wife is himself, you're mistaken. The viper is not Henry Hassel, his son, a relation, or even Ludwig Boltzmann (1844–1906). Hassel does not make a circle in time, ending where the story begins—to the satisfaction of nobody and the fury of everybody— for the simple reason that time isn't circular, or linear, or tandem, discoid, syzygous, longinquitous, or pandicularted. Time is a private matter, as Hassel discovered.

"Maybe I slipped up somehow," Hassel muttered. "I'd better find out." He fought with the telephone, which seemed to weigh a hundred tons, and at last managed to get through to the library.

"Hello, Library? This is Henry."

"Who?"

"Henry Hassel."

"Speak up, please."

"HENRY HASSEL!"

"Oh. Good afternoon, Henry."

"What have you got on George Washington?"

Library clucked while her scanners sorted through her catalogues. "George Washington, first president of the United States, was born in—"

"First president? Wasn't he murdered in 1775?"

"Really, Henry. That's an absurd question. Everybody knows that George Wash—"

"Doesn't anybody know he was shot?"

"By whom?"

"Me."

"When?"

"In 1775."

"How did you manage to do that?"

"I've got a revolver."

"No, I mean, how did you do it two hundred years ago?"

"I've got a time machine."

"Well,. there's no record here," Library said. "He's still doing fine in my files. You must have missed."

"I did not miss. What about Christopher Columbus? Any record of his death in 1489?"

"But he discovered the New World in 1492."

"He did not. He was murdered in 1489."

"How?"

"With a forty-five slug in the gizzard."

"You again, Henry?"

"Yes."

"There's no record here," Library insisted. "You must be one lousy shot."

"I will not lose my temper." Hassel said in a trembling voice.

"Why not, Henry?"

"Because it's lost already," he shouted. "All right! What about Marie Curie? Did she or did she not discover the fission bomb which destroyed Paris at the turn of the century?"

"She did not. Enrico Fermi—"

"She did."

"She didn't."

"I personally taught her. Me. Henry Hassel."

"Everybody says you're a wonderful theoretician, but a lousy teacher, Henry. You—"

"Go to hell, you old biddy. This has got to be explained."

"Why?"

"I forget. There was something on my mind, but it doesn't matter now. What would you suggest?"

"You really have a time machine?"

"Of course I've got a time machine."

"Then go back and check."

Hassel returned to the year 1775, visited Mount Vernon, and interrupted the spring planting. "Excuse me, Colonel," he began.

The big man looked at him curiously. "You talk funny, stranger," he said. "Where are you from?"

"Oh, a fresh-water school you never heard of."

"You look funny too. Kind of misty, so to speak."

"Tell me, Colonel, what do you hear from Christopher Columbus?"

"Not much," Colonel Washington answered. "Been dead two, three hundred years."

"When did he die?"

"Year fifteen hundred some-odd, near as I remember."

"He did not. He died in 1489."

"Got your dates wrong, friend. He discovered America in 1492."

"Cabot discovered America. Sebastian Cabot."

"Nope. Cabot came a mite later."

"I have infallible proof!" Hassel began, but broke off as a stocky and rather stout man, with a face ludicrously reddened by rage, approached. He was wearing baggy gray slacks and a tweed jacket two sizes too small for him. He was carrying a .45 revolver. It was only after he had stared for a moment that Henry Hassel realized that he was looking at himself and not relishing the sight.

"My God!" Hassel murmured. "It's me, coming back to murder Washington that first time. If I'd made this second trip an hour later, I'd have found Washington dead. Hey!" he called. "Not yet. Hold off a minute. I've got to straighten something out first."

Hassel paid no attention to himself; indeed, he did not appear to be aware of himself. He marched straight up to Colonel Washington and shot him in the gizzard. Colonel Washington collapsed, emphatically dead. The first murderer inspected the body, and then, ignoring Hassel's attempt to stop him and engage him in dispute, turned and marched off, muttering venomously to himself.

"He didn't hear me," Hassel wondered. "He didn't even feel me. And why don't I remember myself trying to stop me the first time I shot the colonel? What the hell is going on?"

Considerably disturbed, Henry Hassel visited Chicago and dropped into the Chicago University squash courts in the early 1940's. There, in a slippery mess of graphite bricks and graphite dust that coated him, he located an Italian scientist named Fermi.

"Repeating Marie Curie's work, I see, *dottore?*" Hassel said.

Fermi glanced about as though he had heard a faint sound.

"Repeating Marie Curie's work, *dottore?*" Hassel roared.

Fermi looked at him strangely. "Where you from, *amico?*"

"State."

"State Department?"

"Just State. It's true, isn't it, *dottore*, that Marie Curie discovered nuclear fission back in nineteen ought ought?"

"No! No! No!" Fermi cried. "We are the first, and we are not there yet. Police! Police! Spy!"

"This time I'll go on record," Hassel growled. He pulled out his trusty .45, emptied it into Dr. Fermi's chest, and awaited arrest and immolation in newspaper files. To his amazement, Dr. Fermi did not collapse. Dr. Fermi merely explored his chest tenderly and, to the men who answered his cry, said, "It is nothing. I felt in my within a sudden sensation of burn which may be a neuralgia of the cardiac nerve, but is most likely gas."

Hassel was too agitated to wait for the automatic recall of the time machine. Instead he returned at once to Unknown University under his own power. This should have given him a clue, but he was too possessed to notice. It was at this time that I (1913–1975) first saw him—a dim figure tramping through parked cars, closed doors and brick walls, with the light of lunatic determination on his face.

He oozed into the library, prepared for an exhaustive discussion, but could not make himself felt or heard by the catalogues. He went to the Malpractice Laboratory, where Sam, the Simplex-and-Multiplex Computer, has installations sensitive up to 10,700 angstroms. Sam could not see Henry, but managed to hear him through a sort of wave-interference phenomenon.

"Sam," Hassel said, "I've made one hell of a discovery."

"You're always making discoveries, Henry," Sam complained. "Your data allocation is filled. Do I have to start another tape for you?"

"But I need advice. Who's the leading authority on time, reference to succession of, travel in?"

"That would be Israel Lennox, spatial mechanics, professor of, Yale."

"How do I get in touch with him?"

"You don't, Henry. He's dead. Died in '75."

"What authority have you got on time, travel in, living?"

"Wiley Murphy."

"Murphy? From your own Trauma Department? That's a break. Where is he now?"

"As a matter of fact, Henry, he went over to your house to ask you something."

Hassel went home without walking, searched through his laboratory and study without finding anyone, and at last floated into the living room, where his redheaded wife was still in the arms of another man. (All this, you understand, had taken place within the space of a few moments after the construction of the time machine; such is the nature of time and time travel.) Hassel cleared his throat once or twice and tried to tap his wife on the shoulder. His fingers went through her.

"Excuse me, darling," he said. "Has Wiley Murphy been in to see me?"

Then he looked closer and saw that the man embracing his wife was Murphy himself.

"Murphy!" Hassel exclaimed. "The very man I'm looking for. I've had the most extraordinary experience." Hassel at once launched into a lucid description of his extraordinary experience, which went something like this: "Murphy, $u - v = (u^{1/2} - v^{1/4})$ $(u^a + u^x v^y + v^b)$ but when George Washington $F(x)y^2 dx$ and Enrico Fermi $F(u^{1/2}) dx dt$ one half of Marie Curie, then what about Christopher Columbus times the square root of minus one?"

Murphy ignored Hassel, as did Mrs. Hassel. I jotted down Hassel's equations on the hood of a passing taxi.

"Do listen to me, Murphy," Hassel said. "Greta dear, would you mind leaving us for a moment? I— For heaven's sake, will you two stop that nonsense? This is serious."

Hassel tried to separate the couple. He could no more touch them than make them hear him. His face turned red again and he became quite choleric as he beat at Mrs. Hassel and Murphy. It was like beating an Ideal Gas. I thought it best to interfere.

"Hassel!"

"Who's that?"

"Come outside a moment. I want to talk to you."

He shot through the wall. "Where are you?"

"Over here."

"You're sort of dim."

"So are you."

"Who are you?"

"My name's Lennox. Israel Lennox."

"Israel Lennox, spatial mechanics, professor of, Yale?"

"The same."

"But you died in '75."

"I disappeared in '75."

"What d'you mean?"

"I invented a time machine."

"By God! So did I," Hassel said. "This afternoon. The idea came to me in a flash—I don't know why—and I've had the most extraordinary experience. Lennox, time is not a continuum."

"No?"

"It's a series of discrete particles—like pearls on a string."

"Yes?"

"Eash pearl is a 'Now.' Each 'Now' has its own past and future. But none of them relate to any others. You see? If $a = a_1 + a_2\,ji + \phi ax(b_1)$—"

"Never mind the mathematics, Henry."

"It's a form of quantum transfer of energy. Time is emitted in discrete corpuscles or quanta. We can visit each individual quantum and make changes within it, but no change in any one corpuscle affects any other corpuscle. Right?"

"Wrong," I said sorrowfully.

"What d'you mean, 'Wrong'?" he said, angrily gesturing through the cleavage of a passing coed. "You take the trochoid equations and—"

"Wrong," I repeated firmly. "Will you listen to me, Henry?"

"Oh, go ahead," he said.

"Have you noticed that you've become rather insubstantial? Dim? Spectral? Space and time no longer affect you?"

"Yes."

"Henry, I had the misfortune to construct a time machine back in '75."

"So you said. Listen, what about power input? I figure I'm using about 7.3 kilowatts per—"

"Never mind the power input, Henry. On my first trip into the past, I visited the Pleistocene. I was eager to photograph the mastodon, the giant ground sloth, and the saber-toothed tiger. While I was backing up to get a mastodon fully in the field of view at f/6.3 at 1/100th of a second, or on the LVS scale—"

"Never mind the LVS scale," he said.

"While I was backing up, I inadvertently trampled and killed a small Pleistocene insect."

"Aha!" said Hassel.

"I was terrified by the incident. I had visions of returning to my world to find it completely changed as a result of this single death. Imagine my surprise when I returned to my world to find that nothing had changed."

"Oho!" said Hassel.

"I became curious. I went back to the Pleistocene and killed the mastodon. Nothing was changed in 1975. I returned to the Pleistocene and slaughtered the wild life—still with no effect. I ranged through time, killing and destroying, in an attempt to alter the present."

"Then you did it just like me," Hassel exclaimed. "Odd we didn't run into each other."

"Not odd at all."

"I got Columbus."

"I got Marco Polo."

"I got Napoleon."

"I thought Einstein was more important."

"Mohammed didn't change things much—I expected more from *him*."

"I know. I got him too."

"What do you mean, you got him too?" Hassel demanded.

"I killed him September 16, 599. Old Style."

"Why, I got Mohammed, January 5, 598."

"I believe you."

"But how could you have killed him after I killed him?"

"We both killed him."

"That's impossible."

"My boy," I said, "time is entirely subjective. It's a private matter—a personal experience. There is no such thing as objective time, just as there is no such thing as objective love, or an objective soul."

"Do you mean to say that time travel is impossible? But we've done it."

"To be sure, and many others, for all I know. But we each travel into our own past, and no other person's. There is no universal continuum, Henry. There are only billions of individuals, each with his own continuum; and one continuum cannot affect the other. We're like millions of strands of spaghetti in the same pot. No time traveler can ever meet another time traveler in the past or future. Each of us must travel up and down his own strand alone."

"But we're meeting each other now."

"We're no longer time travelers, Henry. We've become the spaghetti sauce."

"Spaghetti sauce?"

"Yes. You and I can visit any strand we like, because we've destroyed ourselves."

"I don't understand."

"When a man changes the past he only affects his own past—no one else's. The past is like memory. When you erase a man's memory, you wipe him out, but you don't wipe out anybody else. You and I have erased our past. The individual worlds of the others go on, but we have ceased to exist." I paused significantly.

"What d'you mean, 'ceased to exist'?"

"With each act of destruction we dissolved a little. Now we're all gone. We've committed chronicide. We're ghosts. I hope Mrs. Hassel will be very happy with Mr. Murphy. . . . Now let's go over to the Académie. Ampére is telling a great story about Ludwig Boltzmann."

Parallel Worlds

The idea of a parallel world is based on the premise that there are a number of parallel worlds, all of them Earths, which exist in a different space, time, or dimensional continuum from the one in which our Earth exists. Usually these other Earths have the same history as ours up to a crucial point such as the Battle of Waterloo or the settlement of the North American continent. Then the historical patterns diverge, and the author extrapolates a new history for the parallel world.

The construction of a parallel world allows the author, if he wishes, to examine differing value systems and compare them, explicitly or implicitly, with our own. Mainstream novelist Vladimir Nabokov has used the parallel-world concept in *Ada,* a novel envisioning a North America which had been discovered and colonized by the Russians. In *Times Without Number,* John Brunner depicts what might have been if Spain had defeated England in the famous naval battle of 1588. Finding oneself in a parallel world can be the beginning of a heroic adventure as it is for Tarl Cabot in John Norman's *Gor* series. These novels are set in a counter Earth of incredible male orientation. The premise of the counter-Earth theory is that Gor is a planet which has the same orbit as our earth, but Gor revolves around the sun at such a speed that the sun is always between it and our Earth. A strict definition might exclude the counter Earth from the parallel-worlds category, but because Norman is consciously working with a value system which so closely represents that of Western man and because he chooses to set his action on a counter Earth rather than on any other planet in or out of the solar system, Gor deserves consideration as a parallel world.

The struggles of a hero in his attempt to cope with a parallel world can be quite humorous. In L. Sprague de Camp and Fletcher Pratt's *The Carnelian Cube,* Arthur Finch finds himself shunted from world to world by the power of the carnelian cube. Pratt and de Camp's *Harold Shay* stories are set in parallel worlds based on mythology or fantasy which, of course, have their own logic and reality for anyone in them. Mr. de Camp, incidentally, is one of the masters of the parallel-world tale, and such volumes as the appropriately entitled *The Wheels of If* present some intriguing Earths parallel to our own.

The parallel worlds presented in this volume are, generally speaking, rather traditional in nature. John Wyndham's British style, in "Random Quest," makes for a lengthy story, but it should not cloud the reader's eye to the parallel world concept developed therein. Besides being a love story and rather good fiction in any sense of the word, "Random Quest" is satisfying science fiction as it presents an exact description of what a parallel world is, how one might get to a parallel world, and in what ways a parallel world relates to the one we know. Both the love-story action and the science fiction concepts are handled so well that each compliments rather than intrudes upon the other. In "Thus we Frustrate Charlemagne," R. A. Lafferty presents the parallel world as a result of changing the past—the paradox referred to in the Time Travel headnote. Lafferty's humorous and ironic examination of the results of the paradox only serve to reaffirm the essential paradoxical nature of altering the past. Wyndham introduces and explains the parallel world concept, Lafferty comments on it, and Nelson Bond, in "The Monster from Nowhere," presents a variation. Bond explores a parallel world of which we are already well aware in theory—the parallel world of the fourth dimension. As E. A. Abbot discussed the three-dimensional world from the point of view of a two-dimensional world in *Flatland,* Nelson Bond speculates about the existence of a fourth dimension as yet almost totally unknown to the people of the three-dimensional world of "The Monster from Nowhere."

RANDOM QUEST

John Wyndham

The sound of a car coming to a stop on the gravel caused Dr. Harshom to look at his watch. He closed the book in which he had been writing, put it away in one of his desk drawers, and waited. Presently Stephens opened the door to announce: "Mr. Trafford, sir."

The doctor got up from his chair, and regarded the young man who entered, with some care. Mr. Colin Trafford turned out to be presentable, just in his thirties, with brown hair curling slightly, clean-shaven, a suit of good tweed well cut, and shoes to accord. He looked pleasant enough though not distinguished. It would not be difficult to meet thirty or forty very similar young men in a day. But when one looked more closely, as the doctor now did, there were signs of fatigue to be seen, indications of anxiety in the expression and around the mouth, a strained doggedness in the set of the mouth.

They shook hands.

"You'll have had a long drive," said the doctor. "I expect you'd like a drink. Dinner won't be for half an hour yet."

The younger man accepted, and sat down. Presently, he said:

"It was kind of you to invite me here, Dr. Harshom."

"Not really altruistic," the doctor told him. "It is more satisfactory to talk than to correspond by letter. Moreover, I am an inquisitive man recently retired from a very humdrum country practice, Mr. Trafford, and on the rare occasions that I do catch the scent of a mystery my curiosity urges me to follow it up." He, too, sat down.

"Mystery?" repeated the young man.

"Mystery," said the doctor.

The young man took a sip of his whisky.

"My inquiry was such as one might receive from—well, from any solicitor," he said.

"But you are not a solicitor, Mr. Trafford."

"No," Colin Trafford admitted, "I am not."

"But you do have a very pressing reason for your inquiry. So there is the mystery. What pressing, or indeed leisurely, reason could you have for inquiries about a person of whose existence you yourself appear to be uncertain—and of whom Somerset House has no record?"

The young man regarded him more carefully, as he went on:

"How do I know that? Because an inquiry there would be your natural first step. Had you found a birth certificate, you would not have pursued the course you have. In fact, only a curiously determined person would have persisted in a quest for someone who had no official existence. So, I said to myself: 'When this persistence in the face of reason addresses itself to me I will try to resolve the mystery.' "

The young man frowned.

"You imply that you said that *before* you had my letter?"

"My dear fellow, Harshom is not a common name—an unusual corruption of Harvesthome, if you are interested in such things—and, indeed, I never yet heard of a Harshom who was not traceably connected with the rest of us. And we do, to some extent, keep in touch. So, quite naturally, I think, the incursion of a young man entirely unknown to any of us, but persistently tackling us one after another with his inquiries regarding an unidentifiable Harshom, aroused our interest. Since it seemed that I myself came low on your priority list I decided to make a few inquiries of my own. I—"

"But why should you judge yourself low on a list," Colin Trafford interrupted.

"Because you are clearly a man of method. In this case, geographical method. You began your inquiries with Harshoms in the central London area, and worked outwards, until you are now in Herefordshire. There are only two further-flung Harshoms now on your list: Peter, down in the toe of Cornwall, and Harold, a few miles from Durham—am I right?"

Colin Trafford nodded, with a trace of reluctance.

"You are," he admitted.

Dr. Harshom smiled, a trifle smugly.

"I thought so. There is—" he began, but the young man interrupted him again.

"When you answered my letter, you invited me here, but you evaded my question," he remarked.

"That is true. But I have answered it now by insisting that the person you seek not only does not exist, but never did exist."

"But if you're quite satisfied on that, why ask me here at all?"

"Because—" The doctor broke off at the sound of a gong. "Dear me, Phillips allows one just ten minutes to wash. Let me show you your room, and we can continue over dinner."

A little later when the soup was before them, he resumed:

"You were asking me why I invited you here. I think the answer is that since you feel entitled to be curious about a hypothetical relative of mine, I feel no less entitled to be curious about the motives that impel your curiosity. Fair enough?—as they say."

"Dubious," replied Mr. Trafford after consideration. "To inquire into my motives would, I admit, be not unreasonable if you knew this person to exist—but, since you assure me she does not exist, the question of my motives surely becomes academic."

"My interest *is* academic, my dear fellow, but none the less real. Perhaps we might progress a little if I might put the problem as it appears from my point of view?"

Trafford nodded. The doctor went on:

"Well, now, this is the situation: Some seven or eight months ago a young man, unknown to any of us, begins a series of approaches to my relatives. His concern, he says, is to learn the whereabouts, or to gain any clues which may help him to trace the whereabouts, of a lady called Ottilie Harshom. She was born, he believes, in 1928, though it could be a few years to either side of that—and she may, of course, have adopted another surname through marriage.

"In his earlier letters there is an air of confidence suggesting his feeling that the matter will easily be dealt with, but as one Harshom after another fails to identify the subject of his inquiries his tone becomes less confident though not less determined. In one or two directions he does learn of young Harshom ladies—none of them called Ottilie, by the way, but he nevertheless investigates them with care. Can it be, perhaps, that he is as uncertain about the first name as about everything else concerning her? But apparently none of these ladies fulfills his requirements, for he presses on. In the face of unqualified unsuccess, his persistence in leaving no Harshom stone unturned begins to verge upon the unreasonable. Is he an eccentric, with a curious obsession?

"Yet by all the evidence he was—until the spring of 1953, at any rate —a perfectly normal young man. His full name is Colin Wayland Trafford. He was born in 1921, in Solihull, the son of a solicitor. He went to Chartowe School 1934. Enlisted in the army 1939. Left it, with the rank of Captain 1945. Went up to Cambridge. Took a good degree in Physics 1949. Joined Electro-Physical Industries on the managerial side that same year. Married Della Stevens 1950. Became a widower 1951. Received injuries in a laboratory demonstration accident early in 1953. Spent the following five weeks in St. Merryn's Hospital. Began his first approaches to members of the Harshom family for information regarding Ottilie Harshom about a month after his discharge from hospital."

Colin Trafford said coldly:

"You are very fully informed, Dr. Harshom."

The doctor shrugged slightly.

"Your own information about the Harshoms must by now be almost exhaustive. Why should you resent some of us knowing something of you?"

Colin did not reply to that. He dropped his gaze, and appeared to study the tablecloth. The doctor resumed:

"I said just now—has he an obsession? The answer has appeared to be yes—since sometime last March. Prior to that, there seems to have been no inquiry whatever regarding Miss Ottilie Harshom.

"Now when I had reached this point I began to feel that I was on the edge of a more curious mystery than I had expected." He paused. "I'd like to ask you, Mr. Trafford, had you ever been aware of the name Ottilie Harshom before January last?"

The young man hesitated. Then he said, uneasily:

"How can one possibly answer that? One encounters myriad names on all sides. Some are remembered, some seem to get filed in the subconscious, some apparently fail to register at all. It's unanswerable."

"Perhaps so. But we have the curious situation that before January Ottilie Harshom was apparently not on your mental map, yet since March she has, without any objective existence, dominated it. So I ask myself, what happened between January and March . . . ?

"Well, I practice medicine. I have certain connections, I am able to learn the external facts. One day late in January you were invited, along with several other people, to witness a demonstration in one of your company's laboratories. I was not told the details, I doubt if I would understand them if I were: the atmosphere around the higher flights of modern physics is so rarefied—but I gather that during this demonstration something went amiss. There was an explosion, or an implosion, or perhaps a matter of a few atoms driven berserk by provocation. In any case, the place was wrecked. One man was killed outright, another died later, several were injured. You yourself were not badly hurt. You did get a few cuts, and bruises—nothing serious, but you were knocked out—right out . . .

"You were, indeed, so thoroughly knocked out that you lay unconscious for twenty-four days . . .

"And when at last you did come round you displayed symptoms of considerable confusion—more strongly, perhaps, than would be expected in a patient of your age and type, and you were given sedatives. The following night you slept restlessly, and showed signs of mental distress. In particular you called again and again for someone named Ottilie.

"The hospital made what inquiries they could, but none of your friends or relatives knew of anyone called Ottilie associated with you.

"You began to recover, but it was clear you had something heavily on your mind. You refused to reveal what it was, but you did ask one of the doctors whether he could have his secretary try to find the name Ottilie Harshom in any directory. When it could not be found, you became depressed. However, you did not raise the matter again—at least, I am told you did not—until after your discharge when you set out on this quest for Ottilie Harshom, in which, in spite of completely negative results, you continue.

"Now, what must one deduce from that?" He paused to look across the table at his guest, left eyebrow raised.

"That you are even better informed than I thought," Colin said, without encouragement. "If I were your patient your inquiries might be justified, but as I am not, and have not the least intention of consulting you professionally, I regard them as intrusive, and possibly unethical."

If he had expected his host to be put out he was disappointed. The doctor continued to regard him with interested detachment.

"I'm not yet entirely convinced that you ought not to be someone's patient," he remarked. "However, let me tell you why it was I, rather than another Harshom, who was led to make these inquiries. Perhaps you may then think them less impertinent. But I am going to preface that with a warning against false hopes. You must understand that the Ottilie Harshom you are seeking *does not exist and has not existed.* That is quite definite.

"Nevertheless, there *is* one aspect of this matter which puzzled me greatly, and that I cannot bring myself to dismiss as coincidence. You see, the name Ottilie Harshom was not entirely unknown to me. No—" He raised his hand. "—I repeat, no false hopes. There *is* no Ottilie Harshom, but there has been—or, rather, there have in the past been, two Ottilie Harshoms."

Colin Trafford's resentful manner had entirely dropped away. He sat, leaning a little forward, watching his host intently.

"But," the doctor emphasized, "it was all long ago. The first was my grandmother. She was born in 1832, married Grandfather Harshom in 1861, and died in 1866. The other was my sister: she, poor little thing, was born in 1884 and died in 1890 . . ."

He paused again. Colin made no comment. He went on:

"I am the only survivor of this branch so it is not altogether surprising that the others have forgotten there was ever such a name in the family, but when I heard of your inquiries I said to myself: There is something out of order here. Ottilie is not the rarest of names, but on any scale of popularity it would come a very long way down indeed; and Harshom *is* a rare name. The odds against these two being coupled by mere chance must be some quite astronomical figure. Something so large that I can not believe it *is* chance. Somewhere there must be a link, some cause . . .

"So, I set out to discover if I could find out why this young man Trafford should have hit upon this improbable conjunction of names—and, seemingly, become obsessed by it.—You would not care to help me at this point?"

Colin continued to look at him, but said nothing.

"No? Very well. When I had all the available data assembled the conclusion I had to draw was this: that as a result of your accident you underwent some kind of traumatic experience, an experience of considerable intensity as well as unusual quality. Its intensity one deduces from your subsequent fixation of purpose; the unusual quality partly from the pronounced state of confusion in which you regained consciousness, and partly from the consistency with which you deny recollecting anything from the moment of the accident until you awoke.

"Now, if that were indeed a blank, why did you awake in such a confused condition? There must have been some recollection to cause it. And if there was something akin to ordinary dream images, why this refusal to speak of them? There must have been, therefore, some experience of great personal significance wherein the name Ottilie Harshom was a very potent element indeed.

"Well, Mr. Trafford. Is the reasoning good, the conclusion valid? Let me suggest, as a physician, that such things are a burden that should be shared."

Colin considered for some little time, but when he still did not speak the doctor added:

"You are almost at the end of the road, you know. Only two more Harshoms on the list, and I assure you they won't be able to help—so what then?"

Colin said, in a flat voice:

"I expect you are right. You should know. All the same, I must see them. There might be something, some clue . . . I can't neglect the least possibility . . . I had just a little hope when you invited me here. I knew that you had a family . . ."

"I *had*," the doctor said, quietly. "My son Malcolm was killed racing at Brooklands in 1927. He was unmarried. My daughter married, but she had no children. She was killed in a raid on London in 1941 . . . So there it ends . . ." He shook his head slowly.

"I am sorry," said Colin. Then: "Have you a picture of your daughter that I may see?"

"She wasn't of the generation you are looking for."

"I realize that, but nevertheless . . ."

"Very well—when we return to the study. Meanwhile, you've not yet said what you think of my reasoning."

"Oh, it was good."

"But you are still disinclined to talk about it? Well, I am not. And

I can still go a little further. Now, this experience of yours cannot have been a kind to cause a feeling of shame or disgust, or you would be trying to sublimate it in some way, which manifestly you are not. Therefore it is highly probable that the cause of your silence is fear. Something makes you afraid to discuss the experience. You are not, I am satisfied, afraid of facing it; therefore your fear must be of the consequences of communicating it. Consequences possibly to someone else, but much more probably to yourself . . ."

Colin went on regarding him expressionlessly for a moment. Then he relaxed a little and leaned back in his chair. For the first time he smiled faintly.

"You do get there in the end, don't you, Doctor? But do you mind if I say that you make quite Germanically heavy-going of it? And the whole thing is so simple, really. It boils down to this. If a man, any man, claims to have had an experience which is outside all normal experience, it will be inferred, will it not, that he is in some way not quite a normal man? In that case, he cannot be entirely relied upon to react to a particular situation as a normal man should—and if his reactions may be nonnormal, how can he be really dependable? He may be, of course—but would it not be sounder policy to put authority into the hands of a man about whom there is *no* doubt? Better to be on the safe side. So he is passed over. His failure to make the expected step is not unnoticed. A small cloud, a mere wrack, of doubt and risk begins to gather above him. It is tenuous, too insubstantial for him to disperse, yet it casts a faint, persistent shadow.

"There is, I imagine, no such thing as a normal human being, but there is a widespread feeling that there ought to be. Any organization has a conception of 'the type of man we want here,' which is regarded as the normal for its purposes. So every man there attempts more or less to accord to it—organizational man, in fact—and anyone who diverges more than slightly from the type in either his public, or in his private, life does so to the peril of his career. There is, as you said, fear of the results to myself: it is, as I said, so simple."

"True enough," the doctor agreed. "But you have not taken any care to disguise the consequence of the experience—the hunt for Ottilie Harshom."

"I don't need to. Could anything be more reassuringly normal than 'man seeks girl'? I have invented a background which has quite satisfied any interested friends—and even several Harshoms."

"I dare say. None of them being aware of the 'coincidence' in the conjunction of 'Ottilie' with 'Harshom.' But I am."

He waited for Colin Trafford to make some comment on that. When none came, he went on:

"Look, my boy. You have this business very heavily on your mind.

There are only the two of us here. I have no links whatever with your firm. My profession should be enough safeguard for your confidence, but I will undertake a special guarantee if you like. It will do you good to unburden—and I should like to get to the bottom of this . . ."

But Colin shook his head.

"You won't, you know. Even if I were to tell you, you'd only be the more mystified—as I am."

"Two heads are better than one. We could try," said the doctor, and waited.

Colin considered again, for some moments. Then he lifted his gaze, and met the doctor's steadily.

"Very well then. I've tried. You shall try. But first I would like to see a picture of your daughter. Have you one taken when she was about twenty-five?"

They left the table and went back to the study. The doctor waved Colin to a chair, and crossed to a corner cupboard. He took out a small pile of cardboard mounts and looked through them. He selected three, gazed at them thoughtfully for a few seconds, and then handed them over. While Colin studied them he busied himself with pouring brandy from a decanter.

Presently Colin looked up.

"No," he said. "And yet there is something . . ." He tried covering parts of the full-face portrait with his hand. "Something about the setting and shape of the eyes—but not quite. The brow, perhaps, but it's difficult to tell with the hair done like that . . ." He pondered the photographs a little longer, and then handed them back. "Thank you for letting me see them."

The doctor picked up one of the others and passed it over.

"This was Malcolm, my son."

It showed a laughing young man standing by the forepart of a car which bristled with exhaust manifold and had its bonnet held down by straps.

"He loved that car," said the doctor, "but it was too fast for the old track there. It went over the banking, and hit a tree."

He took the picture back, and handed Colin a glass of brandy.

Colin swirled it. Neither of them spoke for some little time. Then he tasted the brandy, and, presently, lit a cigarette.

"Very well," he said again. "I'll try to tell you. But first I'll tell you what *happened*—whether it was subjective, or not, it happened for me. The implications and so on we can look at later—if you want to."

"Good," agreed the doctor. "But tell me first, do we start from the moment of the accident—or was there anything at all relevant before that?"

"No," Colin Trafford said, "that's where it *does* start."

It was just another day. Everything and everybody perfectly ordinary—except that this demonstration was something a bit special. What it concerned is not my secret, and not, as far as I know, relevant. We all gathered round the apparatus. Deakin, who was in charge, pulled down a switch. Something began to hum, and then to whine, like a motor running faster and faster. The whine became a shriek as it went up the scale. There was a quite piercingly painful moment or two near the threshold of audibility, then a sense of relief because it was over and gone, with everything seeming quiet again. I was looking across at Deakin watching his dials, with his fingers held ready over the switches, and then, just as I was in the act of turning my head towards the demonstration again, there was a flash . . . I didn't hear anything, or feel anything: there was just this dazzling white flash . . . Then nothing but black . . . I heard people crying out, and a woman's voice screaming . . . screaming . . . screaming . . .

I felt crushed by a great weight. I opened my eyes. A sharp pain jabbed through them into my head, but I struggled against the weight, and found it was due to two or three people being on top of me; so I managed to shove a couple of them off, and sit up. There were several other people lying about on the ground, and a few more picking themselves up. A couple of feet to my left was a large wheel. I looked further up and found that it was attached to a bus—a bus that from my position seemed to tower like a scarlet skyscraper, and appeared, moreover, to be tilted and about to fall on me. It caused me to get up very quickly, and as I did I grabbed a young woman who had been lying across my legs, and dragged her to a safer place. Her face was dead white, and she was unconscious.

I looked around. It wasn't difficult to see what had happened. The bus, which must have been traveling at a fair speed, had, for some reason got out of control, run across the crowded pavement, and through the plate-glass window of a shop. The forepart of the top deck had been telescoped against the front of the building, and it was up there that the screaming was going on. Several people were still lying on the ground, a woman moving feebly, a man groaning, two or three more quite still. Three streams of blood were meandering slowly across the pavement among the crystals of broken glass. All the traffic had stopped, and I could see a couple of policemen's helmets bobbing through the crowd towards us.

I moved my arms and legs experimentally. They worked perfectly well, and painlessly. But I felt dazed, and my head throbbed. I put my hand up to it and discovered a quite tender spot where I must have taken a blow on the left occiput.

The policemen got through. One of them started pushing back the gaping bystanders, the other took a look at the casualties on the ground.

A third appeared and went up to the top deck of the bus to investigate the screaming there.

I tried to conquer my daze, and looked round further. The place was Regent Street, a little up from Piccadilly Circus; the wrecked window was one of Austin Reed's. I looked up again at the bus. It was certainly tilted, but not in danger of toppling, for it was firmly wedged into the window opening to within a yard of the word "General," gleaming in gold letters on its scarlet side.

At this point it occurred to me that I was supernumerary, and that if I were to hang around much longer I should find myself roped in as a witness—not, mind you, that I would grudge being a witness in the ordinary way, if it would do anyone any good, but I was suddenly and acutely aware that this was not at all in the ordinary way. For one thing I had no knowledge of anything whatever but the aftermath—and, for another, what was I doing here anyway . . . ? One moment I had been watching a demonstration out at Watford; the next, there was this. How the devil did I come to be in Regent Street at all . . . ?

I quietly edged my way into the crowd, then out of it again, zigzagged across the road amid the held-up traffic, and headed for the Café Royal, a bit further down.

They seemed to have done things to the old place since I was there last, a couple of years before, but the important thing was to find the bar, and that I did, without difficulty.

"A double brandy, and some soda," I told the barman.

He gave it to me, and slid along the siphon. I pulled some money out of my pocket, coppers and a little small silver. So I made to reach for my notecase.

"Half a crown, sir," the barman told me, as if fending off a note.

I blinked at him. Still, he said it. I slid over three shillings. He seemed gratified.

I added soda to the brandy, and took a welcome drink. It was as I was putting the glass down that I caught sight of myself in the mirror behind the bar . . .

I used to have a mustache. I came out of the army with it, but decided to jettison it when I went up to Cambridge. But there it was—a little less luxuriant, perhaps, but resurrected. I put up my hand and felt it. There was no illusion, and it was genuine, too. At almost the same moment I noticed my suit. Now, I used to have a suit pretty much like that, years ago. Not at all a bad suit either, but still, not quite the thing we organization men wear in E.P.I. . . . .

I had a swimming sensation, took another drink of the brandy, and felt, a little unsteadily, for a cigarette. The packet I pulled out of my pocket was unfamiliar—have you ever heard of Player's "Mariner" cigarettes—No? Neither had I, but I got one out, and lit it with a very unsteady match. The dazed feeling was not subsiding; it was growing, rapidly . . .

I felt for my inside pocket. No wallet. It should have been there —perhaps some opportunist in the crowd round the bus had got it . . . I sought through the other pockets—a fountain pen, a bunch of keys, a couple of cash receipts from Harrods, a check book—containing checks addressed to the Knightsbridge branch of the Westminster Bank. Well, the bank was all right, but why Knightsbridge?—I live in Hampstead . . .

To try to get some kind of grip on things I began to recapitulate from the moment I had opened my eyes and found the bus towering over me. It was quite vivid. I had a sharp recollection of staring up at that scarlet menace, with the gilded word "General" shining brightly . . . yes, in gleaming gold—only, as you know, the word "General" hasn't been seen on London buses since it was replaced by "London Transport" in 1933 . . .

I was getting a little rattled by now, and looked round the bar for something to steady my wits. On one table I noticed a newspaper that someone had discarded. I went across to fetch it, and got carefully back onto my stool before I looked at it. Then I took a deep breath and regarded the front page. My first response was dismay for the whole thing was given up to a single display advertisement. Yet there was some reassurance, of a kind, at the top, for it read: "*Daily Mail,* London, Wednesday 27 January 1954." So it was at least the right day—the one we had fixed for the demonstration at the labs.

I turned to the middle page, and read: "Disorders in Delhi. One of the greatest exhibitions of civil disobedience so far staged in India took place here today demanding the immediate release of Nehru from prison. For nearly all the hours of daylight the city has been at a standstill—" Then an item in an adjoining column caught my eye: "In answer to a question from the Opposition front bench Mr. Butler, the Prime Minister, assured the House that the Government was giving serious consideration——" In a dizzy way I glanced at the top of the page: the date there agreed with that on the front, 27 January 1954, but just below it there was a picture with the caption: "A scene from last night's production of *The Lady Loves,* at the Laughton Theatre, in which Miss Amanda Coward plays the lead in the last of her father's many musical plays. *The Lady Loves* was completed only a few days before Noel Coward's death last August, and a moving tribute to his memory was paid at the end of the performance by Mr. Ivor Novello who directed the production."

I read that again, with care. Then I looked up and about, for reassurance, at my fellow drinkers, at the furniture, at the barman, at the bottles: it was all convincingly real.

I dropped the paper, and finished the rest of my brandy. I could have done with another, but it would have been awkward if, with my wallet gone, the barman should change his mind about his modest price. I glanced at my watch—and there was a thing, too! It was a very nice watch, gold, with a crocodile strap, and hands that stood at twelve-thirty, but I had never seen it before. I took it off and looked at the back. There was a pretty bit of engraving there; it said: "C. forever O. 10.x.50." And it jolted me quite a little, for 1950 was the year I was married—though not in October, and not to anyone called O. My wife's name was Della. Mechanically I restrapped the watch on my wrist, and left.

The interlude and the brandy had done me some good. When I stepped out of Regent Street again I was feeling less dazed (though, if it is not too fine a distinction, more bewildered) and my head had almost ceased to ache, so that I was able to pay more attention to the world about me.

At first sight Piccadilly Circus gave an impression of being much as usual, and yet a suggestion that there was something a bit wrong with it. After a few moments I perceived that it was the people and the cars. Surprising numbers of the men and women, too, wore clothing that looked shabby, and the flower girls below Eros seemed like bundles of rags. The look of the women who were not shabby took me completely aback. Almost without exception their hats were twelve-inch platter-like things balanced on the top of their heads. The skirts were long, almost to their ankles, and, worn under fur coats, gave an impression that they were dressed for the evening, at midday. Their shoes were pointed, overornamented, pinheeled, and quite hideous. I suppose all high-fashion would look ludicrous if one were to come upon it unprepared, but then one never does—at least one never had until now . . . I might have felt like Rip van Winkle newly awakened, but for the dateline on that newspaper . . . The cars were odd, too. They seemed curiously high-built, small, and lacking in the flashy effects one had grown accustomed to, and when I paid more attention I did not see one make I could readily identify—except a couple of unmistakable Rollses.

While I stood staring curiously a plate-hatted lady in a well-worn fur coat posted herself beside me and addressed me as "dearie" in a somewhat grim way. I decided to move on, and headed for Piccadilly. On the way, I looked across at St. James's Church. The last time I had seen it it was clothed in scaffolding, with a hoarding in the garden to help to raise funds for the rebuilding—that would have been about a fortnight before—but now all that was gone, and it looked as if it had never been bombed at all. I crossed the road to inspect it more closely, and was still more impressed with the wonderful job they had made of the restoration.

Presently I found myself in front of Hatchard's windows, and paused to examine their contents. Some of the books had authors whose names I knew; I saw works by Priestley, C. S. Lewis, Bertrand Russell, T. S. Eliot, and others, but scarcely a title that I recognized. And then, down in the front, my eye was caught by a book in a predominantly pink jacket: *Life's Young Day,* a novel by Colin Trafford.

I went on goggling at it, probably with my mouth open. I once had ambitions in that direction, you know. If it had not been for the war I'd probably have taken an Arts degree, and tried my hand at it, but as things happened I made a friend in the regiment who turned me to science, *and* could put me in the way of a job with E.P.I. later. Therefore it took me a minute or two to recover from the coincidence of seeing my name on the cover, and, when I did, my curiosity was still strong enough to take me into the shop.

There I discovered a pile of half a dozen copies lying on a table. I picked up the top one, and opened it. The name was plain enough on the titlepage—and opposite was a list of seven other titles under "author of." I did not recognize the publisher's name, but overleaf there was the announcement: "First published January 1954."

I turned it over in my hand, and then all but dropped it. On the back was a picture of the author; undoubtedly me—and with the mustache . . . The floor seemed to tilt slightly beneath my feet.

Then, somewhere over my shoulder, there was a voice; one that I seemed to recognize. It said:

"Well met, Narcissus! Doing a bit of sales promotion, eh? How's it going?"

"Martin!" I exclaimed. I had never been so glad to see anyone in all my life. "Martin. Why we've not met since—when was it?"

"Oh, for at least three days, old boy," he said, looking a little surprised.

Three days! I'd seen a lot of Martin Falls at Cambridge, but only run across him twice since we came down, and the last of those was two years ago. But he went on:

"What about a spot of lunch, if you're not booked?" he suggested.

And that wasn't quite right either. I'd not heard anyone speak of a *spot* of lunch for years. However, I did my best to feel as if things were becoming more normal.

"Fine," I said, "but you'll have to pay. I've had my wallet pinched."

He clicked his tongue.

"Hope there wasn't much in it. Anyway, what about the club? They'll cash you a check there."

I put the book I was still holding back on the pile, and we left.

"Funny thing," Martin said. "Just ran into Tommy—Tommy Westhouse. Sort of blowing sulphur—hopping mad with his American agent. You remember that godawful thing of Tommy's—*The Thornèd Rose*—kind of Ben Hur meets Cleopatra, with the Marquis de Sade intervening? Well, it seems this agent—" He rambled on with a shoppy, anecdotal recital full of names that meant nothing to me, but lasted through several streets and brought us almost to Pall Mall. At the end of it he said: "You didn't tell me how *Life's Young Day's* doing. Somebody said it was oversubscribed. Saw the Lit Sup wagged a bit of a finger at you. Not had time to read it myself yet. Too much on hand."

I chose the easier—the noncommittal way. It seemed easier than trying to understand, so I told him it was doing just about as expected.

The club, when in due course we reached it, turned out to be the Savage. I am not a member, but the porter greeted me by name, as though I were in the habit of dropping in every day.

"Just a quick one," Martin suggested. "Then we'll look in and see George about your check."

I had misgivings over that, but it went off all right, and during lunch I did my best to keep my end up. I had the same troubles that I have now—true it was from the other end, but the principle still holds: if things are *too* queer people will find it easier to think you are potty than to help you; so you keep up a front.

I am afraid I did not do very well. Several times I caught Martin glancing at me with a perplexed expression. Once he asked: "Quite sure you're feeling all right, old man?"

But the climax did not come until, with cheese on his plate, he reached out his left hand for a stick of celery. And as he did so I noticed the gold signet ring on his little finger, and that jolted me right out of my caution—for, you see, Martin doesn't have a little finger on his left hand, or a third finger, either. He left both of them somewhere near the Rhine in 1945 . . .

"Good God!" I exclaimed. For some reason that pierced me more sharply than anything yet. He turned his face towards me.

"What on earth's the matter, man? You're as white as a sheet."

"Your hand—" I said.

He glanced at it curiously, and then back at me, even more curiously. "Looks all right to me," he said, eyes a little narrowed.

"But—but you lost the two last fingers—in the war," I exclaimed.

His eyebrows rose, and then came down in an anxious frown. He said, with kind intention:

"Got it a bit mixed, haven't you, old man? Why, the war was over before I was born."

Well, it goes a bit hazy just after that, and when it got coherent again I was lying back in a big chair, with Martin sitting close beside, saying:

"So take my advice, old man. Just you trot along to the quack this afternoon. Must've taken a bit more of a knock than you thought, you know. Funny thing, the brain—can't be too careful. Well, I'll have to go now I'm afraid. Appointment. But don't you put it off. Risky. Let me know how it goes." And then he was gone.

I lay back in the chair. Curiously enough I was feeling far more myself than I had since I came to on the pavement in Regent Street. It was as if the biggest jolt yet had shaken me out of the daze, and got the gears of my wits into mesh again . . . I was glad to be rid of Martin, and able to think . . .

I looked round the lounge. As I said, I am not a member, and did not know the place well enough to be sure of details, but I rather thought the arrangement was a little different, and the carpet, and some of the light fittings, from when I saw it last . . .

There were few people around. Two talking in a corner, three napping, two more reading papers; none taking any notice of me. I went over to the periodicals table, and brought back *The New Statesman*, dated January 22, 1954. The front-page leader was advocating the nationalization of transport as a first step towards putting the means of production into the hands of the people and so ending unemployment. There was a wave of nostalgia about that. I turned on, glancing at articles which baffled me for lack of context. I was glad to find Critic present, and I noticed that among the things that were currently causing him concern was some experimental work going on in Germany. His misgivings were, it seemed, shared by several eminent scientists, for, while there was little doubt now that nuclear fission was a theoretical possibility, the proposed methods of control were inadequate. There could well be a chain reaction resulting in a disaster of cosmic proportions. A consortium which included names famous in the arts as well as many illustrious in the sciences was being formed to call upon the League of Nations to protest to the German government in the name of humanity against reckless research . . .

Well, well . . . !

With returning confidence in myself I sat and pondered.

Gradually, and faintly at first, something began to glimmer . . . Not anything about the how, or the why—I still have no useful theories about those—but about *what* could conceivably have happened.

It was vague—set off, perhaps, by the thought of that random neutron which I knew in one set of circumstances to have been captured by a uranium atom, but which, in another set of circumstances, apparently had not . . .

And there, of course, one was brought up against Einstein and relativity which, as you know, denies the possibility of determining motion absolutely and consequently leads into the idea of the four-dimensional space-time continuum. Well, then, since you cannot determine the motions of the factors in the continuum, any pattern of motion must be illusory, and there cannot be any determinable consequences. Nevertheless, where the factors are closely similar—are composed of similar atoms in roughly the same relation to the continuum, so as to speak—you *may* quite well get similar consequences. They can never be identical, of course, or determination of motion would be possible. But they could be very similar, and capable of consideration in terms of Einstein's Special Theory, and they *could* be determined further by a set of closely similar factors. In other words although the infinite point which we may call a moment in 1954 *must* occur throughout the continuum, it *exists* only in relation to each observer, and *appears* to have similar existence in relation to certain close groups of observers. However, since no two observers can be identical—that is, the same observer—each must perceive a different past, present, and future from that perceived by any other; consequently, what he perceives arises only from the factors of his relationship to the continuum, and exists only for him.

Therefore I began to understand that *what* had happened must be this: in some way—which I cannot begin to grasp—I had somehow been translated to the position of a different observer—one whose angle of view was in some respects very close to my own, and yet different enough to have relationships, and therefore realities, unperceived by me. In other words, he must have lived in a world real only to him, just as I had lived in a world real only to me—until this very peculiar transposition had occurred to put me in the position of observing *his* world, with, of course, its relevant past and future, instead of the one I was accustomed to.

Mind you, simple as it is when you consider it, I certainly did not grasp the form of it all at once, but I did argue my way close enough to the observer-existence relationship to decide that whatever might have gone amiss, my own mind was more or less all right. The trouble really seemed to be that it was in the wrong place, and getting messages not intended for me; a receiver somehow hooked into the wrong circuit.

Well, that's not good, in fact, it's bad; but it's still a lot better than a faulty receiver. And it braced me a bit to realize that.

I sat there quite a time trying to get it clear, and wondering what I should do, until I came to the end of my packet of "Mariner" cigarettes. Then I went to the telephone.

First I dialed Electro-Physical Industries. Nothing happened. I looked them up in the book. It was quite a different number, on a different exchange. So I dialed that.

"Extension one three three," I told the girl on the desk, and then, on second thoughts, named my own department.

"Oh. You want extension five nine," she told me.

Somebody answered. I said:

"I'd like to speak to Mr. Colin Trafford."

"I'm sorry," said the girl. "I can't find that name in this department," the voice told me.

Back to the desk. Then a longish pause.

"I'm sorry," said the girl. "I can't find that name in our staff list."

I hung up. So, evidently, I was not employed by E.P.I. I thought a moment, and then dialed my Hampstead number. It answered promptly. "Transcendental Belts and Corsets," it announced brightly. I put down the receiver.

It occurred to me to look myself up in the book. I was there, all right: "Trafford, Colin W., 54 Hogarth Court, Duchess Gardens, S.W.7. SLOane 67021." So I tried that. The phone at the other end rang . . . and went on ringing . . .

I came out of the box wondering what to do next. It was an extremely odd feeling to be bereft of orientation, rather as if one had been dropped abruptly into a foreign city without even a hotel room for a base—and somehow made worse by the city being foreign only in minor and personal details.

After further reflection I decided that the best protective coloration would come from doing what *this* Colin Trafford might reasonably be expected to do. If he had no work to do at E.P.I., he did at least have a home to go to . . .

A nice block of flats, Hogarth Court, springy carpet and illuminated floral arrangement in the hall, that sort of thing, but, at the moment no porter in view, so I went straight to the lift. The place did not look big enough to contain fifty-four flats, so I took a chance on the five meaning the fifth floor, and sure enough I stepped out to find "54" on the door facing me. I took out my bunch of keys, tried the most likely one, and it fitted.

Inside was a small hall. Nothing distinctive—white paint, lightly patterned paper, close maroon carpet, occasional table with telephone and a few flowers in a vase, with a nice gilt-framed mirror above, the hard occasional chair, a passage off, lots of doors. I paused.

"Hullo," I said experimentally. Then a little louder: "Hullo! Anyone at home?"

Neither voice nor sound responded. I closed the door behind me. What now? Well—well, hang it, I was—am—Colin Trafford! I took off my overcoat. Nowhere to put it. Second try revealed the coat closet . . . Several other coats already in there. Male and female, a woman's overshoes, too . . . I added mine.

I decided to get the geography of the place, and see what home was really like . . .

Well, you won't want an inventory, but it was a nice flat. Larger than I had thought at first. Well furnished and arranged; not with extravagance, but not with stint, either. It showed taste too; though not my taste—but what is taste? Either feeling for period, or refined selection from a fashion. I could feel that this was the latter, but the fashion was strange to me, and therefore lacked attraction.

The kitchen was interesting. A fridge, no washer, single-sink, no plate racks, no laminated tops, old-fashioned-looking electric cooker, packet of soap powder, no synthetic detergents, curious light panel about three feet square in the ceiling, no mixer . . .

The sitting room was airy, chairs comfortable. Nothing spindly. A large radiogram, rather ornate, no F.M. on its scale. Lighting again by ceiling panels, and square things like glass cakeboxes on stands. No television.

I prowled round the whole place. Bedroom feminine, but not fussy. Twin beds. Bathroom tiled, white. Spare bedroom, small double bed. And so on. But it was a room at the end of the passage that interested me most. A sort of study. One wall all bookshelves, some of the books familiar—the older ones—others not. An easy chair, a lighter chair. In front of the window a broad, leather-topped desk, with a view across the bare-branched trees in the Gardens, roofs beyond, plenty of sky. On the desk a covered typewriter, adjustable lamp, several folders with sheets of paper untidily projecting, cigarette box, metal ashtray, clean and empty, and a photograph in a leather frame.

I looked at the photograph carefully. A charming study. She'd be perhaps twenty-four—twenty-five? Intelligent, happy-looking, somebody one would like to know—but not anyone I did know . . .

There was a cupboard on the left of the desk, and, on it, a glass-fronted case with eight books on it; the rest was empty. The books were all in bright paper jackets, looking as new. The one on the right-hand end was the book that I had seen in Hatchard's that morning—*Life's Young Day;* all the rest, too, bore the name Colin Trafford. I sat down in the swivel chair at the desk and pondered them for some moments. Then, with a curious, schizoid feeling I pulled out *Life's Young Day*, and opened it.

It was, perhaps, half an hour, or more, later that I caught the sound of a key in the outer door. I decided that, on the whole, it would be better to disclose myself than wait to be discovered. So I opened the door. Along at the end of the passage a figure in three-quarter length gray suede coat which showed a tweed skirt beneath was dumping parcels onto the hall table. At the sound of my door she turned her head. It was the original of the photograph, all right; but not in the mood of the photograph. As I approached, she looked at me with an expression of surprise, mixed with other feelings that I could not identify; but certainly it was not an adoring-wife-greets-husband look.

"Oh," she said. "You're in, what happened?"

"Happened?" I repeated, feeling for a lead.

"Well, I understand you had one of those so-important meetings with Dickie at the BBC fixed for this afternoon," she said, a little curtly I thought.

"Oh. Oh, that, yes. Yes, he had to put it off," I replied, clumsily.

She stopped still, and inspected me carefully. A little oddly, too, I thought. I stood looking at her, wondering what to do, and wishing I had had the sense to think up some kind of plan for this inevitable meeting instead of wasting my time over *Life's Young Day*. I hadn't even had the sense to find out her name. It was clear that I'd got away wrong somehow the moment I opened my mouth. Besides, there was a quality about her that upset my balance altogether . . . It hit me in a way I'd not known for years, and more shrewdly than it had then . . . Somehow, when you are thirty-three you don't expect these things to happen—well, not to happen quite like that, any more . . . Not with a great surge in your heart, and everything coming suddenly bright and alive as if she had just switched it all into existence . . .

So we stood looking at one another; she with a half-frown, I trying to cope with a turmoil of elation and confusion, unable to say a word.

She glanced down, and began to unbutton her coat. She, too, seemed uncertain.

"If——" she began. But at that moment the telephone rang.

With an air of welcoming the interruption, she picked up the receiver. In the quiet of the hall I could hear a woman's voice ask for Colin.

"Yes," she said, "he's here." And she held the receiver out to me, with a very curious look.

"Hullo," I said. "Colin here."

"Oh, indeed," replied the voice, "and why, may I ask?"

"Er—I don't quite——" I began, but she cut me short.

"Now, look here, Colin, I've already wasted an hour waiting for you, thinking that if you couldn't come you might at least have had the decency to ring me up and tell me. Now I find you're just sitting at home. Not quite good enough, Colin."

"I—um—who is it? Who's speaking?" was the only temporizing move I could think of. I was acutely conscious that the young woman beside me was frozen stock-still in the act of taking off her coat.

"Oh, for God's sake," said the voice, exasperated. "What silly game is this? Who do you *think* it is?"

"That's what I'm asking," I said.

"Oh, don't be such a clown, Colin. If it's because Ottilie's still there—and

I bet she is—you're just being stupid. She answered the phone herself, so she *knows* it's me."

"Then perhaps I'd better ask her who you are," I suggested.

"Oh—you must be tight as an owl. Go and sleep it off," she snapped, and the phone went dead.

I put the receiver back in the rest. The young woman was looking at me with an expression of genuine bewilderment. In the quietness of the hall she must have been able to hear the other voice almost as clearly as I had. She turned away, and busied herself with taking her coat off and putting it on a hanger in the closet. When she'd carefully done that she turned back.

"I don't understand," she said. "You aren't tight, are you? What's it all about? What has dear Dickie done?"

"Dickie?" I inquired. The slight furrow between her brows deepened.

"Oh, really, Colin. If you think I don't know Dickie's voice on the telephone by this time . . ."

"Oh," I said. A bloomer of a peculiarly cardinal kind, that. In fact, it is hard to think of a more unlikely mistake than that a man should confuse the gender of his friends. Unless I wanted to be thought quite potty, I must take steps to clarify the situation.

"Look, can't we go into the sitting room? There's something I want to tell you," I suggested.

I took the chair opposite, and wondered how to begin. Even if I had been clear in my own mind about what had happened, it would have been difficult enough. But how to convey that though the physical form was Colin Trafford's, and I myself was Colin Trafford, yet I was not *that* Colin Trafford; not the one who wrote books and was married to her, but a kind of alternative Colin Trafford astray from an alternative world? What seemed to be wanted was some kind of approach which would not immediately suggest a call for an alienist and it wasn't easy to perceive.

"Well?" she repeated.

"It's difficult to explain," I temporized, but truthfully enough.

"I'm sure it is," she replied, without encouragement, and added: "Would it perhaps be easier if you didn't look at me like that? I'd prefer it, too."

"Something very odd has happened to me," I told her.

"Oh, dear, again?" she said. "Do you want my sympathy, or something?"

I was taken aback, and a little confused.

"Do you mean it's happened to him before?" I asked.

She looked at me hard.

"Him? Who's him? I thought you were talking about you? And what I mean is last time it happened it was Dickie, and the time before that it was Frances, and before that it was Lucy . . . And now you've given Dickie a most peculiar kind of brushoff . . . Am I supposed to be surprised . . . ?"

I was learning about my *alter ego* quite fast, but we were off the track. I tried:

"No, you don't understand. This is something quite different."

"Of course not. Wives never do, do they? And it's always different. Well, if that's all that's so important . . ." She began to get up.

"No, please . . ." I said anxiously.

She checked herself, looking very carefully at me again. The half-frown came back.

"No," she said. "No, I don't think I do understand. At least, I—I hope not . . ." And she went on examining me, with something like growing uncertainty, I thought.

When you plead for understanding you can scarcely keep it on an impersonal basis, but when you don't know whether the best address would be "my dear," or "darling," or some more intimate variant, nor whether it should be prefaced by first name, nickname, or pet name, the way ahead becomes thorny indeed. Besides, there was this persistent misunderstanding on the wrong level.

"Ottilie, darling," I tried—and that was clearly no usual form, for, momentarily, her eyes almost goggled, but I plowed on: "It isn't at all what you're thinking—nothing a bit like that. It's—well, it's that in a way I'm not the same person . . ."

She was back in charge of herself.

"Oddly enough, I've been aware of that for some time," she said. "*And* I could remind you that you've said something like that before, more than once. All right then, let me go on for you; so you're not the same person I married, so you'd like a divorce—or is it that you're afraid Dickie's husband is going to cite you this time? Oh, God! How sick I am of all this . . ."

"No, no," I protested desperately. "It's not that sort of thing at all. Do please be patient. It's a thing that's terribly difficult to explain . . ." I paused, looking at her. That did not make it any easier. Indeed, it was far from helping the rational processes. She sat looking back at me, still with that half-frown, but now it was a little more uneasy than displeased.

"Something *has* happened to you . . ." she said.

"That's what I'm trying to tell you about," I told her, but I doubt whether she heard it. Her eyes grew wider as she looked. Suddenly they avoided mine.

"No!" she said. "Oh, *no!*" She looked as if she were about to cry, and wound her fingers tightly together in her lap. She half-whispered:

"Oh, no! . . . Oh, please God, no! . . . Not again . . . Haven't I been hurt enough? . . . I won't . . . I won't . . . !"

Then she jumped up, and, before I was halfway out of my chair, she was out of the room.

Colin Trafford paused to light a fresh cigarette, and took his time before going on. At length he pulled his thoughts back.

"Well," he went on, "obviously you will have realized by now that *that* Mrs. Trafford was born Ottilie Harshom. It happened in 1928, and she married *that* Colin Trafford in 1949. Her father was killed in a plane crash in 1938—I don't remember her ever mentioning his first name. That's unfortunate—there are a lot of things that are unfortunate: had I any idea that I might be jerked back here I'd have taken notice of a lot of things. But I hadn't . . . Something exceedingly odd had happened, but that was no reason to suppose that an equally odd thing would happen, in reverse . . .

"I did do my best, out of my own curiosity, to discover when the schism had taken place. There must, as I saw it, have been some point where, perhaps by chance, some pivotal thing had happened, or failed to happen, and finding it could bring one closer to knowing the moment, the atom of time, that had been split by some random neutron to give two atoms of time diverging into different futures. Once that had taken place, consequences gradually accumulating would make the conditions on one plane progressively different from those on the other.

"Perhaps that is always happening. Perhaps chance is continually causing two different outcomes so that in a dimension we cannot perceive there are infinite numbers of planes, some so close to our own and so recently split off that they vary only in minor details, others vastly different. Planes on which some misadventure caused Alexander to be beaten by the Persians, Scipio to fall before Hannibal, Caesar to stay beyond the Rubicon: infinite planes of the random split and resplit by the random. Who can tell? But, now that we know the Universe for a random place, why not?

"But I couldn't come near fixing the moment. It was, I *think,* somewhere in late 1926, or early 1927. Further than that one seemed unable to go without the impossible data of quantities of records from both planes for comparison. Something happening, or not happening, about then had brought results which prevented, among other things, the rise of Hitler, and thus the Second World War—and consequently postponed the achievement of nuclear fission on this plane of our dichotomy—if that is a good word for it.

"Anyway, it was for me, and as I said, simply a matter of incidental curiosity. My active concerns were more immediate. And the really important one was Ottilie . . .

"I have, as you know, been married—and I was fond of my wife. It was, as people say, a successful marriage, and it never occurred to me to doubt that—until this thing happened to me. I don't want to be disloyal to Della now, and I don't think she was unhappy—but I am immensely thankful for one thing: that this did not happen while she was alive; she never knew, because I didn't know then, that I had married the wrong woman—and I hope she never thought it . . .

"And Ottilie had married the wrong man . . . We found that out. Or perhaps one should put it that she had not married the man she thought she had. She had fallen in love with him; and, no doubt, he had loved her, to begin with—but in less than a year she became torn between the part she loved, and the side she detested . . .

"Her Colin Trafford looked like me—right down to the left thumb which had got mixed up in an electric fan and never quite matched the other side—indeed, up to a point, that point somewhere in 1926–27 he *was* me. We had, I gathered, some mannerisms in common, and voices that were similar—though we differed in our emphases, and in our vocabularies, as I learnt from a tape, and in details: the mustache, the way we wore our hair, the scar on the left side of the forehead which was exclusively his; yet, in a sense, I was him and he was me. We had the same parents, the same genes, the same beginning, and—if I was right about the time of the dichotomy—we must have had the same memory of our life, for the first five years or so.

But later on, things on our different planes must have run differently for us. Environment, or experiences, had developed qualities in him which, I have to think, lie latent in me—and, I suppose, vice versa.

"I think that's a reasonable assumption, don't you? After all, one begins life with a kind of armature which has individual differences and tendencies, though a common general plan, but whatever is modeled on that armature later consists almost entirely of stuff from contacts and influences. What these had been for the other Colin Trafford I don't know, but I found the results somewhere painful—rather like continually glimpsing oneself in unexpected distorting mirrors.

"There were certain cautions, restraints, and expectations in Ottilie that taught me a number of things about him, too. Moreover, in the next day or two I read his novels attentively. The earliest was not displeasing, but as the dates grew later and the touch surer, I cared less and less for the flavor; no doubt the widening streaks of brutality showed the calculated development of a selling point, but there was something a little more than that—besides, one has a choice of selling points . . . With each book, I resented seeing my name on the title page a little more.

"I discovered the current 'work in progress,' too. With the help of his notes I could, I believe, have produced a passable forgery, but I knew I would not. If I had to continue his literary career, it would be with my kind of books, not his. But, in any case, I had no need to carry over making a living: what with the war and one thing and another, physics on my own plane was a generation ahead of theirs. Even if they had got as far as radar it was still someone's military secret. I had enough knowledge to pass for a genius, and make my fortune if I cared to use it . . ."

He smiled, and shook his head. He went on:

"You see, once the first shock was over and I had begun to perceive what must have happened, there was no cause for alarm, and, once I had met Ottilie, none for regret. The only problem was adjustment. It helped in general, I found, to try to get back to as much as I could remember of the prewar world. But details were not difficult: unrecognized friends, lapsed friends, all with unknown histories, some of them with wives, or husbands, I knew (though not necessarily the same ones); some with quite unexpected partners. There were queer moments, too—an encounter with a burly cheerful man in the bar of the Hyde Park Hotel. He didn't know me, but I knew him; the last time I had seen him he was lying by a road with a sniper's bullet through his head. I saw Della, my wife, leaving a restaurant looking happy, with her arm through that of a tall legal-looking type; it was uncanny to have her glance at me as at a complete stranger—I felt as if both of us were ghosts—but I was glad she had got past 1951 all right on that plane. The most awkward part was frequently running into people that it appeared I should know; the other Colin's acquaintanceship was evidently vast and curious. I began to favor the idea of proclaiming a breakdown from overwork, to tide me over for a bit.

"One thing that did not cross my mind was the possibility of what I took to be a unique shift of plane occurring again, this time in reverse . . .

"I am thankful it did not. It would have blighted the three most wonderful weeks in my life. I thought it was, as the engraving on the back of the watch said: 'C. forever O.'

"I made a tentative attempt to explain to her what I thought had happened, but it wasn't meaning anything to her, so I gave it up. I think she had it worked out for herself that somewhere about a year after we were married I had begun to suffer from overstrain, and that now I had got better and become again the kind of man she had thought I was . . . something like that . . . but theories about it did not interest her much—it was the consequence that mattered . . .

"And how right she was—for me too. After all, what else did matter? As far as I was concerned, nothing. I was in love. What did it matter *how* I had found the one unknown woman I had sought all my life.

I was happy, as I had never expected to be . . . Oh, all the phrases are trite, but 'on top of the world' was suddenly half ridiculously vivid. I was full of a confidence rather like that of the slightly drunk. I could take anything on. With her beside me I could keep on top of that, or any, world . . . I think she felt like that, too. I'm sure she did. She'd wiped out the bad years. Her faith was regrowing, stronger every day . . . If I'd only known—but how could I know? What could I do . . . ?"

Again he stopped talking, and stared into the fire, this time for so long that at last the doctor fidgeted in his chair to recall him, and then added:

"What happened?"

Colin Trafford still had a faraway look.

"Happened?" he repeated. "If I knew that I could perhaps—but I *don't* know . . . There's nothing *to* know . . . *It's* random, too . . . One night I went to sleep with Ottilie beside me—in the morning I woke up in a hospital bed—back here again . . . That's all there was to it. All there is . . . Just random . . ."

In the long interval that followed, Dr. Harshom unhurriedly refilled his pipe, lit it with careful attention, assured himself it was burning evenly and drawing well, settled himself back comfortably, and then said, with intentional matter-of-factness:

"It's a pity you don't believe that. If you did, you'd never have begun this search; if you'd come to believe it, you'd have dropped the search before now. No, you believe that there is a pattern, or rather, that there were two patterns, closely similar to begin with, but gradually, perhaps logically, becoming more variant—and that you, your psyche, or whatever you like to call it, was the aberrant, the random factor.

"However, let's not go into the philosophical, or metaphysical consideration of what you call the dichotomy now—all that stuff will keep. Let us say that I accept the validity of your experience, for you, but reserve judgment on its nature. I accept it on account of several features—not the least being as I have said, the astronomical odds against the conjunction of names, Ottilie and Harshom, occurring fortuitously. Of course, you *could* have seen the name somewhere and lodged it in your subconscious, but that, too, I find so immensely improbable that I put it aside.

"Very well, then, let us go on from there. Now, you appear to me to have made a number of quite unwarrantable assumptions. You have assumed, for instance, that because an Ottilie Harshom exists on what you call *that* plane, she must have come into existence on this plane also. I cannot see that that is justified by anything you have told me. That she *might* have existed here, I admit, for the name Ottilie is in my branch of the family; but the chances of her having no existence at all are considerably greater—did not you yourself mention that you recognized friends who in different circumstances were married to different wives—is it not, therefore, highly probable that the circumstances which produced an Ottilie Harshom there failed to occur here, with the result that she could not come into existence at all? And, indeed, that must be so.

"Believe me, I am not unsympathetic. I do understand what your feelings must be, but are you not, in effect, in the state we all have known—searching for an ideal young woman who has never been born? We must face the facts: if she exists, or did exist, I should have heard of her, Somerest House would have a record of her, your own extensive researches would have revealed *something* positive. I do urge you for your own good to accept it, my boy. With all this against you, you simply have no case."

"Only my own positive conviction," Colin put in. "It's against reason, I know—but I still have it."

"You must try to rid yourself of it. Don't you see there are layers of assumptions? If she did exist she might be already married."

"But to the wrong man," Colin said promptly.

"Even that does not follow. Your counterpart varied from you, you say. Well, her counterpart if she existed would have had an entirely different upbringing in different circumstances from the other; the probability is that there would only be the most superficial resemblance. You must see that the whole thing goes into holes wherever you touch it with reason." He regarded Colin for a moment, and shook his head. "Somewhere at the back of your mind you are giving houseroom to the proposition that unlike causes can produce like results. Throw it out."

Colin smiled.

"How Newtonian, Doctor. No, a random factor is random. Chance therefore exists."

"Young man, you're incorrigible," the doctor told him. "If there weren't little point in wishing success with the impossible I'd say your tenacity deserves it. As things are, I advise you to apply it to the almost attainable."

His pipe had gone out, and he lit it again.

"That," he went on, "was a professional recommendation. But now, if it isn't too late for you, I'd like to hear more. I don't pretend to guess at the true nature of your experience, but the speculations your plane of might-have-been arouses are fascinating. Not unnaturally one feels a curiosity to know how one's own counterpart made out there—and failing that, how other people's did. Our present Prime Minister, for instance—did both of him get the job? And Sir Winston—or is he not

Sir Winston over there?—how on earth did he get along with no Second World War to make his talents burgeon? And what about the poor old Labour Party . . . ? The thing provokes endless questions . . ."

After a late breakfast the next morning Dr. Harshom helped Colin into his coat in the hall, but held him there for a final word.

"I spent what was left of the night thinking about this," he said, earnestly. "Whatever the explanation may be, you must write it down, every detail you can remember. Do it anonymously if you like, but do it. It may not be unique, someday it may give valuable confirmation of someone else's experience, or become evidence in support of some theory. So put it on record—but then leave it at that . . . Do your best to forget the assumptions you jumped at—they're unwarranted in a dozen ways. *She does not exist.* The only Ottilie Harshoms there have been in this world died long ago. Let the image fade. But thank you for your confidence. Though I am inquisitive, I am discreet. If there should be any way I can help you . . ."

Presently he was watching the car down the drive. Colin waved a hand just before it disappeared round the corner. Dr. Harshom shook his head. He knew he might as well have saved his breath, but he felt in duty bound to make one last appeal. Then he turned back into the house, frowning. Whether the obsession was a fantasy, or something more than a fantasy, was almost irrelevant to that fact that sooner or later the young man was going to drive himself into a breakdown . . .

During the next few weeks Dr. Harshom learnt no more, except that Colin Trafford had not taken his advice, for word filtered through that both Peter Harshom in Cornwall and Harold in Durham had received requests for information regarding a Miss Ottilie Harshom who, as far as they knew, was nonexistent.

After that there was nothing more for some months. Then a picture postcard from Canada. On one side was a picture of the Parliament Buildings, Ottawa. The message on the other was brief. It said simply: "Found her. Congratulate me. C.T."

Dr. Harshom studied it for a moment, and then smiled slightly. He was pleased. He had thought Colin Trafford a likable young man; too good to run himself to pieces over such a futile quest. One did not believe it for a moment, of course, but if some sensible young woman had managed to convince him that she was the reincarnation, so to speak, of his beloved, good luck to her—and good luck for him . . . The obsession could now fade quietly away. He would have liked to respond with the requested congratulations, but the card bore no address.

Several weeks later there was another card, with a picture of St. Mark's

Square, Venice. The message was again laconic, but headed this time by a hotel address. It read:

"Honeymoon. May I bring her to see you after?"

Dr. Harshom hesitated. His professional inclination was against it; a feeling that anything likely to recall the young man to the mood in which he had last seen him was best avoided. On the other hand, a refusal would seem odd as well as rude. In the end he replied, on the back of a picture of Hereford Cathedral:

"Do. When?"

Half August had already gone before Colin Trafford did make his reappearance. He drove up looking sunburnt and in better shape all around than he had on his previous visit. Dr. Harshom was glad to see it, but surprised to find that he was alone in the car.

"But I understand the whole intention was that I should meet the bride," he protested.

"It was—it is," Colin assured him. "She's at the hotel. I—well, I'd like to have a few words with you first."

The doctor's gaze became a little keener, his manner more thoughtful.

"Very well. Let's go indoors. If there's anything I'm not to mention, you could have warned me by letter, you know."

"Oh, it's not that. She knows about that. Quite what she makes of it, I'm not sure, but she knows, and she's anxious to meet you. No, it's—well, it won't take more than ten minutes."

The doctor led the way to his study. He waved Colin to an easy chair, and nimself took the swivel chair at the desk.

"Unburden yourself," he invited.

Colin sat forward, forearms on knees, hands dangling between them.

"The most important thing, Doctor, is for me to thank you. I can never be grateful enough to you—never. If you had not invited me here as you did, I think it is unlikely I ever would have found her."

Dr. Harshom frowned. He was not convinced that the thanks were justified. Clearly, whoever Colin had found was possessed of a strong therapeutic quality, nevertheless:

"As I recollect, all I did was listen, and offer you unwelcome advice for your own good—which you did not take," he remarked.

"So it seemed to me at the time," Colin agreed. "It looked as if you had closed all the doors. But then, when I thought it over, I saw one, just one, that hadn't quite latched."

"I don't recall giving you *any* encouragement," Dr. Harshom asserted.

"I am sure you don't, but you did. You indicated to me the last, faintly possible line—and I followed it up—No, you'll see what it was later, if you'll just bear with me a little.

"When I did see the possibility, I realized it meant a lot of groundwork that I couldn't cover on my own, so I had to call in the professionals. They were pretty good, I thought, and they certainly removed any doubt about the line being the right one, but what they could tell me ended on board a ship bound for Canada. So then I had to call in some inquiry agents over there. It's a large country. A lot of people go to it. There was a great deal of routine searching to do, and I began to get discouraged, but then they got a lead, and in another week they came across with the information that she was a secretary working in a lawyer's office in Ottawa.

"Then I put it to E.P.I. that I'd be more valuable after a bit of unpaid recuperative leave——"

"Just a minute," put in the doctor. "If you'd asked me I could have told you there are *no* Harshoms in Canada. I happen to know that because——"

"Oh, I'd given up expecting that. Her name wasn't Harshom—it was Gale," Colin interrupted, with the air of one explaining.

"Indeed. And I suppose it wasn't Ottilie, either?" Dr. Harshom said heavily.

"No. It was Belinda," Colin told him.

"The doctor blinked slightly, opened his mouth, and then thought better of it. Colin went on:

"So then I flew over, to make sure. It was the most agonizing journey I'd ever made. But it was all right. Just one distant sight of her was enough. I couldn't have *mistaken* her for Ottilie, but she was so very, very nearly Ottilie that I would have known her among ten thousand. Perhaps if her hair and her dress had been——" He paused speculatively, unaware of the expression on the doctor's face. "Anyway," he went on. "I *knew*. And it was damned difficult to stop myself rushing up to her there and then, but I did just have enough sense to hold back.

"Then it was a matter of managing an introduction. After that it was as if there were—well, an inevitability, a sort of predestination about it."

Curiosity impelled the doctor to say:

"Comprehensible, but sketchy. What, for instance, about her husband?"

"Husband?" Colin looked momentarily startled.

"Well, you did say her name was Gale," the doctor pointed out.

"So it was, Miss Belinda Gale—I thought I said that. She was engaged once, but she didn't marry. I tell you there was a kind of—well, fate, in the Greek sense, about it."

"But if—" Dr. Harshom began, and then checked himself again. He endeavored, too, to suppress any sign of skepticism.

"But it would have been just the same if she had had a husband," Colin asserted, with ruthless conviction. "He'd have been the wrong man."

The doctor offered no comment, and he went on:

"There were no complications, or involvements—well, nothing serious. She was living in a flat with her mother, and getting quite a good salary. Her mother looked after the place, and had a widow's pension—her husband was in the R.C.A.F.; shot down over Berlin—so between them they managed to be reasonably comfortable.

"Well, you can imagine how it was. Considered as a phenomenon I wasn't any too welcome to her mother, but she's a fair-minded woman, and we found that, as persons, we liked one another quite well. So that part of it, too, went off more easily than it might have done."

He paused here. Dr. Harshom put in:

"I'm glad to hear it, of course. But I must confess I don't quite see what it has to do with your not bringing your wife along with you."

Colin frowned.

"Well, I thought—I mean she thought—well, I haven't quite got to the point yet. It's rather delicate."

"Take your time. After all, I've retired," said the doctor, amiably.

Colin hesitated.

"All right. I think it'll be fairer to Mrs. Gale if I tell it the way it fell out.

"You see, I didn't intend to say anything about what's at the back of all this—about Ottilie, I mean, and why I came to be over in Ottawa—not until later, anyway. You were the only one I had told, and it seemed better that way . . . I didn't want them wondering if I was a bit off my rocker, naturally. But I went and slipped up.

"It was on the day before our wedding. Belinda was out getting some last-minute things, and I was at the flat doing my best to be reassuring to my future mother-in-law. As nearly as I can recall it, what I said was:

" 'My job with E.P.I. is quite a good one, and the prospects are good, but they do have a Canadian end, too, and I dare say that if Ottilie finds she really doesn't like living in England——'

"And then I stopped because Mrs. Gale had suddenly sat upright with a jerk, and was staring at me open-mouthed. Then in a shaky sort of voice she asked:

" '*What* did you say?'

"I'd noticed the slip myself, just too late to catch it. So I corrected: 'I was just saying that if Belinda finds she doesn't like——'

"She cut in on that.

" 'You didn't say Belinda. You said Ottilie.'

" 'Er—perhaps I did,' I admitted, 'but, as I say, if she doesn't——'

" 'Why?' she demanded. '*Why* did you call her Ottilie?'

"She was intense about that. There was no way out of it.

" 'It's well, it's the way I think of her,' I said.

" 'But why? *Why* should you think of Belinda as Ottilie?' she insisted.

"I looked at her more carefully. She had gone quite pale, and the hand that was visible was trembling. She was afraid, as well as distressed. I was sorry about that, and I gave up bluffing.

" 'I didn't mean this to happen,' I told her.

"She looked at me steadily, a little calmer.

" 'But now it has, you *must* tell me. What do you know about us?' she asked.

" 'Simply that if things had been different she wouldn't be Belinda Gale. She would be Ottilie Harshom,' I told her.

"She kept on watching my face, long and steadily, her own face still pale.

" 'I don't understand,' she said more than half to herself. 'You *couldn't* know. Harshom—yes, you might have found that out somehow, or guessed it—or did she tell you?' I shook my head. 'Never mind, you could find out,' she went on. 'But Ottilie . . . You *couldn't* know that—just that one name out of all the thousands of names in the world . . . *Nobody* knew that—nobody but me . . .' She shook her head.

" 'I didn't even tell Reggie . . . When he asked me if we could call her Belinda, I said yes; he'd been so very good to me . . . He had no idea that I had meant to call her Ottilie—nobody had. I've never told anyone, before or since . . . So how *can* you know.'

"I took her hand between mine, and pressed it, trying to comfort her and calm her.

" 'There's nothing to be alarmed about,' I told her. 'It was a—a dream, a kind of vision—I just knew . . .'

"She shook her head. After a minute she said quietly:

" 'Nobody knew but me . . . It was in the summer, in 1927. We were on the river, in a punt, pulled under a willow. A white launch swished by us, we watched it go, and saw the name on its stern. Malcolm said' "—if Colin noticed Dr. Harshom's sudden start, his only acknowledgment of it was a repetition of the last two words—" 'Malcolm said: "Ottilie—pretty name, isn't it? It's in our family. My father had a sister Ottilie who died when she was a little girl. If ever I have a daughter I'd like to call her Ottilie." ' "

Colin Trafford broke off, and regarded the doctor for a moment. Then he went on:

"After that she said nothing for a long time, until she added:

" 'He never knew, you know. Poor Malcolm, he was killed before even I knew she was coming . . . I did so want to call her Ottilie for him . . . He'd have liked that . . . I wish I had . . .' And then she began quietly crying . . ."

Dr. Harshom had one elbow on his desk, one hand over his eyes. He did not move for some little time. At last he pulled out a handkerchief, and blew his nose decisively.

"I did hear there was a girl," he said. "I even made inquiries, but they told me she had married soon afterwards. I thought she—— But why didn't she come to me? I would have looked after her."

"She couldn't know that. She was fond of Reggie Gale. He was in love with her, and willing to give the baby his name," Colin said.

After a glance towards the desk, he got up and walked over to the window. He stood there for several minutes with his back to the room until he heard a movement behind him. Dr. Harshom had got up and was crossing to the cupboard.

"I could do with a drink," he said. "The toast will be the restoration of order, and the rout of the random element."

"I'll support that," Colin told him, "but I'd like to couple it with the confirmation of your contention, Doctor—after all, you are right at last, you know; Ottilie Harshom *does not exist*—not any more. And then, I think, it will be high time you were introduced to your granddaughter, Mrs. Colin Trafford."

THUS WE FRUSTRATE
CHARLEMAGNE

R. A. Lafferty

"We've been on some tall ones," said Gregory Smirnov of the Institute, "but we've never stood on the edge of a bigger one than this, nor viewed one with shakier expectations. Still, if the calculations of Epiktistes are correct, this will work."

"People, it will work," Epikt said.

This was Epiktistes the Ktistec machine? Who'd have believed it? The main bulk of Epikt was five floors below them, but he had run an extension of himself up to this little penthouse lounge. All it took was a cable, no more than a yard in diameter, and a functional head set on the end of it.

And what a head he chose! It was a sea-serpent head, a dragon head, five feet long and copied from an old carnival float. Epikt had also given himself human speech of a sort, a blend of Irish and Jewish and Dutch comedian patter from ancient vaudeville. Epikt was a comic to his last para-DNA relay when he rested his huge, boggle-eyed, crested head on the table there and smoked the biggest stogies ever born.

But he was serious about this project.

"We have perfect test conditions," the machine Epikt said as though calling them to order. "We set out basic texts, and we take careful note of the world as it is. If the world changes, then the texts should change here before our eyes. For our test pilot, we have taken that portion of our own middle-sized city that can be viewed from this fine vantage point. If the world in its past-present continuity is changed by our meddling, then the face of our city will also change instantly as we watch it.

"We have assembled here the finest minds and judgments in the world: eight humans and one Ktistec machine, myself. Remember that there are nine of us. It might be important."

The nine finest minds were: Epiktistes, the transcendent machine who put the "K" in Ktistec; Gregory Smirnov, the large-souled director of the Institute; Valery Mok, an incandescent lady scientist; her overshadowed and over-intelligent husband Charles Cogsworth; the humorless and inerrant Glasser; Aloysius Shiplap, the seminal genius; Willy McGilly, a man of unusual parts (the seeing third finger on his left hand he had picked up on one of the planets of Kapteyn's Star) and no false modesty; Audifax O'Hanlon; and Diogenes Pontifex. The latter two men were not members of the Institute (on account of the Minimal Decency Rule), but when the finest minds in the world are assembled, these two cannot very well be left out.

"We are going to tamper with one small detail in past history and note its effect," Gregory said. "This has never been done before openly. We go back to an era that has been called 'A patch of light in the vast gloom,' the time of Charlemagne. We consider why that light went out and did not kindle others. The world lost four hundred years by that flame expiring when the tinder was apparently ready for it. We go back to that false dawn of Europe and consider where it failed. The year was 778, and the region was Spain. Charlemagne had entered alliance with Marsilies, the Arab king of Saragossa, against the Caliph

Abd ar-Rahmen of Cordova. Charlemagne took such towns as Pamplona, Huesca and Gerona and cleared the way to Marsilies in Saragossa. The Caliph accepted the situation. Saragossa should be independent, a city open to both Moslems and Christians. The northern marches to the border of France should be permitted their Christianity, and there would be peace for everybody.

"This Marsilies had long treated Christians as equals in Saragossa, and now there would be an open road from Islam into the Frankish Empire. Marsilies gave Charlemagne thirty-three scholars (Moslem, Jewish and Christian) and some Spanish mules to seal the bargain. And there could have been a cross-fertilization of cultures.

"But the road was closed at Roncevalles where the rear-guard of Charlemagne was ambushed and destroyed on its way back to France. The ambushers were more Basque than Moslems, but Charlemagne locked the door at the Pyrenees and swore that he would not let even a bird fly over that border thereafter. He kept the road closed, as did his son and his grandsons. But when he sealed off the Moslem world, he also sealed off his own culture.

"In his latter years he tried a revival of civilization with a ragtag of Irish half-scholars, Greek vagabonds and Roman copyists who almost remembered an older Rome. These weren't enough to revive civilization, and yet Charlemagne came close with them. Had the Islam door remained open, a real revival of learning might have taken place then rather than four hundred years later. We are going to arrange that the ambush at Roncevalles did not happen and that the door between the two civilizations was not closed. Then we will see what happens to us."

"Intrusion like a burglar bent," said Epikt.

"Who's a burglar?" Glasser demanded.

"I am," Epikt said. "We all are. It's from an old verse. I forget the author; I have it filed in my main mind downstairs if you're interested."

"We set out a basic text of Hilarius," Gregory continued. "We note it carefully, and we must remember it the way it is. Very soon, that may be the way it *was*. I believe that the words will change on the very page of this book as we watch them. Just as soon as we have done what we intend to do."

The basic text marked in the open book read:

"The traitor Gano, playing a multiplex game, with money from the Cordova Caliph hired Basque Christians (dressed as Saragossan Mozarabs) to ambush the rear-guard of the Frankish force. To do this it was necessary that Gano keep in contact with the Basques and at the same time delay the rear-guard of the Franks. Gano, however, served both as guide and scout for the Franks. The ambush was effected. Charlemagne lost his Spanish mules. And he locked the door against the Moslem world."

That was the text by Hilarius.

"When we, as it were, push the button (give the nod to Epiktistes), this will be changed," Gregory said. "Epikt, by a complex of devices which he has assembled, will send an Avatar (partly of mechanical and partly of ghostly construction), and something will have happened to the traitor Gano along about sundown one night on the road to Roncevalles."

"I hope the Avatar isn't expensive," Willy McGilly said. "When I was a boy we got by with a dart whittled out of slippery elm wood."

"This is no place for humor," Glasser protested. "Who did you, as a boy, ever kill in time, Willy?"

"Lots of them. King Wu of the Manchu, Pope Adrian VII, President Hardy of our own country, King Marcel of Auvergne, the philosopher Gabriel Toeplitz. It's a good thing we got them. They were a bad lot."

"But I never heard of any of them, Willy," Glasser insisted.

"Of course not. We killed them when they were kids."

"Enough of your fooling, Willy," Gregory cut it off.

"Willy's not fooling," the machine Epikt said. "Where do you think I got the idea?"

"Regard the world," Aloysius said softly. "We see our own middle-sized town with half a dozen towers of pastel-colored brick. We will watch it as it grows or shrinks. It will change if the world changes."

"There's two shows in town I haven't seen," Valery said. "Don't let them take them away! After all, there are only three shows in town."

"We regard the Beautiful Arts as set out in the reviews here which we have also taken as basic texts," Audifax O'Hanlon said. "You can say what you want to, but the arts have never been in meaner shape. Painting is of three schools only, all of them bad. Sculpture is the heaps-of-rusted-metal school and the obscene tinker-toy effects. The only popular art, graffiti on mingitorio walls, has become unimaginative, stylized and ugly.

"The only thinkers to be thought of are the dead Teilhard de Chardin and the stillborn Sartre, Zielinski, Aichinger. Oh well, if you're going to laugh there's no use going on."

"All of us here are experts on something," Cogsworth said. "Most of us are experts on everything. We know the world as it is. Let us do what we are going to do and then look at the world."

"Push the button, Epikt!" Gregory Smirnov ordered.

From his depths, Epiktistes the Ktistec machine sent out an Avatar, partly of mechanical and partly of ghostly construction. Along about sundown on the road from Pamplona to Roncevalles, on August 14th of the year 778, the traitor Gano was taken up from the road and hanged on a carob tree, the only one in those groves of oak and beech. And all things thereafter were changed.

"Did it work, Epikt? Is it done?" Louis Lobachevski demanded. "I can't see a change in anything."

"The Avatar is back and reports his mission accomplished," Epikt stated. "I can't see any change in anything either."

"Let's look at the evidence," Gregory said.

The thirteen of them, the ten humans and the Ktistec, Chresmoeidec and Proaisthematic machines, turned to the evidence and with mounting disappointment.

"There is not one word changed in the Hilarius text," Gregory grumbled, and indeed the basic text still read:

> "The king Marsilies of Saragossa, playing a multiplex game, took money from the Caliph of Cordova for persuading Charlemagne to abandon the conquest of Spain (which Charlemagne had never considered and couldn't have affected); took money from Charlemagne in recompense for the cities of the Northern marches being returned to Christian rule (though Marsilies himself had never ruled them); and took money from everyone as toll on the new trade passing through his city. Marsilies gave up nothing but thirty-three scholars, the same number of mules and a few wagonloads of book-manuscripts from the old Hellenistic libraries. But a road over the mountains was opened between the two worlds; and also a sector of the Mediterranean coast became open to both. A limited opening was made between the two worlds, and a limited reanimation of civilization was affected in each."

"No, there is not one word of the text changed," Gregory grumbled. "History followed its same course. How did our experiment fail? We tried, by a device that seems a little cloudy now, to shorten the gestation period for the new birth. It would not be shortened."

"The town is in no way changed," said Aloysius Shiplap. "It is still a fine large town with two dozen imposing towers of varicolored limestone and midland marble. It is a vital metropolis, and we all love it, but it is now as it was before."

"There are still two dozen good shows in town that I haven't seen," Valery said happily as she examined the billings. "I was afraid that something might have happened to them."

"There is no change at all in the Beautiful Arts as reflected in the reviews here that we have taken as basic texts," said Audifax O'Hanlon. "You can say what you want to, but the arts have never been in finer shape."

"It's a link of sausage," said the machine Chresmoeidy.

" 'Nor know the road who never ran it thrice,' " said the machine Proaisth. "That's from an old verse; I forget the author; I have it filed in my main mind in England if you're interested."

"Oh yes, it's the three-cornered tale that ends where it begins," said the machine Epiktistes. "But it is good sausage, and we should enjoy it; many ages have not even this much."

"What are you fellows babbling about?" Audifax asked without really wanting to know. "The art of painting is still almost incandescent in its bloom. The schools are like clustered galaxies, and half the people are doing some of this work for pleasure. Scandinavian and Maori sculpture are hard put to maintain their dominance in the field where almost everything is extraordinary. The impassioned-comic has released music from most of its bonds. Since speculative mathematics and psychology have joined the popular performing arts, there is considerably more sheer fun in life.

"There's a piece here on Pete Teilhard putting him into context as a talented science fiction writer with a talent for outre burlesque. The Brainworld Motif was overworked when he tackled it, but what a shaggy comic extravaganza he did make of it! And there's Muldoom, Zielinski, Popper, Gander, Aichinger, Whitecrow, Hornwhanger—we owe so much to the juice of the cultists! In the main line there are whole congeries and continents of great novels and novelists.

"An ever popular art, graffiti on mingitorio walls, maintains its excellence. Travel Unlimited offers a ninety-nine day art tour of the world keyed to the viewing of the exquisite and hilarious miniatures on the walls of its own rest-rooms. Ah, what a copious world we live in!"

"It's more grass than we can graze," said Willy McGilly. "The very bulk of achievement is stupefying. Ah, I wonder if there is subtle revenge in my choice of words. The experiment, of course, was a failure, and I'm glad. I like a full world."

"We will not call the experiment a failure since we have covered only a third of it," said Gregory. "Tomorrow we will make our second attempt on the past. And, if there is a present left to us after that, we will make a third attempt the following day."

"Shove it, good people, shove it," the machine Epiktistes said. "We will meet here again tomorrow. Now you to your pleasures, and we to ours."

The people talked that evening away from the machines where they could make foolish conjectures without being laughed at.

"Let's pull a random card out of the pack and go with it," said Louis Lobachevski. "Let's take a purely intellectual crux of a little later date and see if the changing of it will change the world."

"I suggest Ockham," said Johnny Konduly.

"Why?" Valery demanded. "He was the last and least of the medieval schoolmen. How could anything he did or did not do affect anything?"

"Oh no, he held the razor to the jugular," Gregory said. "He'd have severed the vein if the razor hadn't been snatched from his hand. There is something amiss here, though. It is as though I remembered when things were not so stark with Ockham, as though, in some variant, Ockham's Terminalism did not mean what we know that it did mean."

"Sure, let's cut the jugular," said Willy. "Let's find out the logical termination of Terminalism and see just how deep Ockham's razor can cut."

"We'll do it," said Gregory. "Our world has become something of a fat slob; it cloys; it has bothered me all evening. We will find whether purely intellectual attitudes are of actual effect. We'll leave the details to Epikt, but I believe the turning point was in the year 1323 when John Lutterell came from Oxford to Avignon where the Holy See was then situated. He brought with him fifty-six propositions taken from Ockham's Commentary on the Sentences, and he proposed their condemnation. They were not condemned outright, but Ockham was whipped soundly in that first assault, and he never recovered. Lutterell proved that Ockham's nihilism was a bunch of nothing. And the Ockham thing did die away, echoing dimly through the little German courts where Ockham traveled peddling his wares, but he no longer peddled them in the main markets. Yet his viewpoint could have sunk the world if, indeed, intellectual attitudes are of actual effect."

"We wouldn't have liked Lutterell," said Aloysius. "He was humorless and he had no fire in him, and he was always right. And we would have liked Ockham. He was charming, and he was wrong, and perhaps we will destroy the world yet. There's a chance that we will get our reaction if we allow Ockham free hand. China was frozen for thousands of years by an intellectual attitude, one not nearly so unsettling as Ockham's. India is hypnotized into a queer stasis which calls itself revolutionary and which does not move—hypnotized by an intellectual attitude. But there was never such an attitude as Ockham's."

So they decided that the former chancellor of Oxford, John Lutterell, who was always a sick man, should suffer one more sickness on the road to Avignon in France, and that he should not arrive there to lance the Ockham thing before it infected the world.

"Let's get on with it, good people," Epikt rumbled the next day. "Me, I'm to stop a man getting from Oxford to Avignon in the year 1323. Well, come, come, take your places, and let's get the thing started." And Epiktistes's great sea-serpent head glowed every color as he puffed on a seven-branched pooka-dooka and filled the room with wonderful smoke.

"Everybody ready to have his throat cut?" Gregory asked cheerfully.

"Cut them," said Diogenes Pontifex, "but I haven't much hope for it. If our yesterday's essay had no effect, I cannot see how one English schoolman chasing another to challenge him in an Italian court in France, in bad Latin, nearly seven hundred years ago, on fifty-six points of unscientific abstract reasoning, can have effect."

"We have perfect test conditions here," said the machine Epikt. "We set out a basic text from Cobblestone's *History of Philosophy*. If our test is effective, then the text will change before our eyes. So will every other text, and the world.

"We have assembled here the finest minds and judgments in the world," the machine Epiktistes said, "ten humans and three machines. Remember that there are thirteen of us. It might be important."

"Regard the world," said Aloysius Shiplap. "I said that yesterday, but it is required that I say it again. We have the world in our eyes and in our memories. If it changes in any way, we will know it."

"Push the button. Epikt," said Gregory Smirnov.

From his depths, Epiktistes the Ktistec machine sent out an Avatar, partly of mechanical and partly of ghostly construction. And along about sundown on the road from Mende to Avignon in the old Languedoc district of France, in the year 1323, John Lutterell was stricken with one more sickness. He was taken to a little inn in the mountain country, and perhaps he died there. He did not, at any rate, arrive at Avignon.

"Did it work, Epikt? Is it done?" Aloysius asked.

"Let's look at the evidence," said Gregory.

The four of them, the three humans and the ghost Epikt who was a kachenko mask with a speaking tube, turned to the evidence with mounting disappointment.

"There is still the stick and the five notches in it," said Gregory. "It was our test stick. Nothing in the world is changed."

"The arts remain as they were," said Aloysius. "Our picture here on the stone on which we have worked for so many seasons is the same as it was. We have painted the bears black, the buffalos red and the people blue. When we find a way to make another color, we can represent birds also. I had hoped that our experiment might give us that other color. I had even dreamed that birds might appear in the picture on the rock before our very eyes."

"There's still rump of skunk to eat and nothing else," said Valery. "I had hoped that our experiment would have changed it to haunch of deer."

"All is not lost," said Aloysius. "We still have the hickory nuts. That was my last prayer before we began our experiment. 'Don't let them take the hickory nuts away,' I prayed."

They sat around the conference table that was a large flat natural rock, and cracked hickory nuts with stone fist-hammers. They were nude in the crude, and the world was as it had always been. They had hoped by magic to change it.

"Epikt has failed us," said Gregory. "We made his frame out of the best sticks, and we plaited his face out of the finest weeds and grasses. We chanted him full of magic and placed all our special treasures in his cheek pouches. So, what can the magic mask do for us now?"

"Ask it, ask it," said Valery. They were the four finest minds in the world—the three humans, Gregory, Aloysius and Valery (the *only* humans in the world unless you count those in the other valleys), and the ghost Epikt, a kachenko mask with a speaking tube.

"What do we do now, Epikt?" Gregory asked. Then he went around behind Epikt to the speaking tube.

"I remember a woman with a sausage stuck to her nose," said Epikt in the voice of Gregory. "Is that any help?"

"It may be some help," Gregory said after he had once more taken his place at the flat-rock conference table. "It is from an old (What's old about it? I made it up myself this morning) folk tale about the three wishes."

"Let Epikt tell it," said Valery. "He does it so much better than you do." Valery went behind Epikt to the speaking tube and blew smoke through it from the huge loose blackleaf uncured stogie that she was smoking.

"The wife wastes one wish for a sausage," said Epikt in the voice of Valery. "A sausage is a piece of deer-meat tied in a piece of a deer's stomach. The husband is angry that the wife has wasted a wish, since she could have wished for a whole deer and had many sausages. He gets so angry that he wishes the sausage might stick to her nose forever. It does, and the woman wails, and the man realized that he had used up the second wish. I forget the rest."

"You can't forget it, Epikt!" Aloysius cried in alarm. "The future of the world may depend on your remembering. Here, let me reason with that damned magic mask!" And Aloysius went behind Epikt to the speaking tube.

"Oh yes, now I remember," Epikt said in the voice of Aloysius. "The man used the third wish to get the sausage off his wife's nose. So things were the way they had been before."

"But we don't want it the way it was before!" Valery howled. "That's the way it is now, rump of skunk to eat, and me with nothing to wear but my ape cape. We want it better. We want deer skins and antelope skins."

"Take me as a mystic or don't take me at all," Epikt signed off.

"Even though the world has always been so, yet we have intimations of other things," Gregory said. "What folk hero was it who made the dart? And of what did he make it?"

"Willy McGilly was the folk hero," said Epikt in the voice of Valery, who had barely got to the speaking tube in time, "and he made it out of slippery elm wood."

"Could we make a dart like the folk hero Willy made?" Aloysius asked.

"We gotta," said Epikt.

"Could we make a slinger and whip it out of our own context and into—"

"Could we kill an Avatar with it before he killed somebody else?" Gregory asked excitedly.

"We sure will try," said the ghost Epikt who was nothing but a kachenko mask with a speaking tube. "I never did like those Avatars."

You *think* Epikt was nothing but a kachenko mask with a speaking tube! There was a lot more to him than that. He had red garnet rocks inside him and real sea salt. He had powder made from beaver eyes. He had rattlesnake rattles and armadillo shields. He was the first Ktistec machine.

"Give me the word, Epikt," Aloysius cried a few moments later as he fitted the dart to the slinger.

"Fling it! Get that Avatar fink!" Epikt howled.

Along about sundown in an unnumbered year, on the Road from Nowhere to Eom, an Avatar fell dead with a slippery-elm dart in his heart.

"Did it work, Epikt? Is it done?" Charles Cogsworth asked in excitement. "It must have. I'm here. I wasn't in the last one."

"Let's look at the evidence," Gregory suggested calmly.

"Damn the evidence!" Willy McGilly cussed. "Remember where you heard it first."

"Is it started yet?" Glasser asked.

"Is it finished?" Audifax O'Hanlon questioned.

"Push the button, Epikt!" Diogenes barked. "I think I missed part of it. Let's try it again."

"Oh, no, no!" Valery forbade. "Not again. That way is rump of skunk and madness."

THE MONSTER
FROM NOWHERE

Nelson Bond

One nice thing about the Press Club is that you can get into almost any kind of wrangle you want. This night we were talking about things unusual. Jamieson of the *Dispatch* mentioned some crackpot he had heard of who thought he could walk through glass. "Snipe" Andrews of the *Morning Call* had a wild yarn about the black soul of Rhoderick Dhu, who, Nova Scotians claim, still walks the moors near Antigonish. The guy named Joe brought up the subject of Ambrose Bierce's invisible beast.

You remember the story? About the diarist who was haunted, and pursued, by a gigantic thing which couldn't be seen? And who was finally devoured by it?

Well, we chewed the fat about that one for a while and Jamieson said the whole thing was fantastic; that total invisibility was impossible. The guy named Joe said Bierce was right; that several things *could* cause invisibility. A complete absence of light, for one thing, he said. Or curvature of light waves. Or coloration in a wavelength which was beyond that of the human eye's visual scope.

Snipe Andrews said, "Nuts!" Winky Peters, who was getting a little tight, hiccoughed something to the effect that "There are more things under Heav'n and Earth than are dreamed of in your Philosophy—" and then got in a hell of a fuss with the bartender who said his name *wasn't* Horatio.

I said nothing, because I didn't know. Maybe that is the reason why this stranger, a few minutes later, moved over beside me and opened a conversation.

"You're Harvey, aren't you?" he asked.

"That's me," I agreed. "Len Harvey—chief errand boy and dirt scratcher-upper for the *Star Telegram*. You've got me, though, pal. Who are you?"

He smiled and said, "Let's go over in that corner, shall we, Harvey? It's quieter over there."

That made it sound like a touch, but I liked something about this guy. Maybe it was his face. I like tough faces; the real McCoy, tanned by Old Sol instead of sunlamp rays. Maybe it was the straightness of his back; maybe the set of his shoulders. Or it could have been just the way he spoke. I don't know.

Anyway, I said, "Sure!" and we moved to the corner table. He ordered, and I ordered, and we just sat there for a moment, staring at each other. Finally he said,

"Harvey, your memory isn't so good. We've met before."

"I meet 'em all," I told him. "Sometimes they are driving Black Marias, and sometimes they're in 'em. Mostly, they're lying in the Morgue, with a pretty white card tied to their big toe. Or, maybe—Hey!" I said, "You're not Ki Patterson, who used to write for the Cincinnati *News*?"

He grinned then.

"No, but you're close. I'm Ki Patterson's brother, Burch."

"Burch Patterson!" I gasped. "But, hell—you're not going to get away with this!" I climbed to my feet and started to shout at the fellows. "Hey, gang—"

"Don't, Len!" Patterson's voice was unexpectedly sharp. There was a note of anxiety in it, too. He grabbed my arm and pulled me back into my seat. "I have very good reasons for not wanting anyone to know I'm back—yet."

I said, "But, hell, Burch, you can't treat a bunch of newspaper men like this. These guys are your friends."

Now that he had told me who he was, I could recognize him. But the last time I had seen him—the only time I had ever met him, in fact—he had been dressed in khaki shirt and corduroy breeches; had worn an aviator's helmet. No wonder I hadn't known him in civvies.

I remembered that night, two years ago, when he and his expedition had taken off from Roosevelt Field for their exploration trip to the Maratan Plateau in upper Peru. The primary purpose of the trip had been scientific research. The Maratan Plateau, as you undoubtedly know, is one of the many South American spots as yet unexplored. It was Burch Patterson's plan to study the region, incidentally paying expenses *à la* Frank Buck, by "bringing back alive" whatever rare beasts city zoos would shell out for.

For a few weeks, the expedition had maintained its contact with the civilized world. Then, suddenly—that was all! A month . . . two months . . . passed. No word or sign from the explorers. The United States government sent notes to the Peruvian solons. Peru replied in smooth, diplomatic terms that hinted Uncle Sam would a damn sight better keep his nutsack adventurers in his own backyard. A publicity-seeking aviatrix ballyhooed funds for a "relief flight"—but was forbidden the attempt when it was discovered she had already promised three different companies to endorse their gasoline.

The plight of the lost expedition was a nine-days' wonder. Then undeclared wars grabbed page one. And the National Air Registry scratched a thin blue line through the number of pilot Burchard Patterson, and wrote after his name, "Lost."

But now, here before me in the flesh, not lost at all, but very much alive, was Burch Patterson.

I had so many questions to ask him that I began babbling like a greenhorn leg-man on his first job.

"When did you get back?" I fired at him. "Where's your crew? What happened? Did you reach the Plateau? And does anyone know you're—"

He said, "Easy, Len. All in good time. I haven't told anyone I'm back yet for a very good reason. Very good! As for my men—" He stared at me somberly. "They're dead, Len. All of them. Toland . . . Fletcher . . . Gainelle . . ."

I was quiet for a moment. The way he repeated the names was like the tolling of a church-bell. Then I began thinking what a wow of a story this was. I could almost see my name by-lining the yarn. I wanted to know the rest so bad I could taste it. I said,

"I'm sorry, Burch. Terribly sorry. But, tell me, what made you come here tonight? And why all the secrecy?"

"I came here tonight," he said, "searching for someone I could trust. I hoped no one would remember my face—for it *is* changed, you know. I have something, Len. Something so great, so stupendous, that I hardly know how to present it to the world. Or even—if I should.

"I liked the way you kept out of that crazy argument a few minutes ago—" He motioned to the bar, where a new wrangle was now in progress. "—because you obviously had an open mind on the subject. I think you are the man whose help and advice I need."

I said, "Well, that's sure nice of you, Patterson. But I think you're overrating me. I kept my yap shut just because I'm kind of dumb about scientific things. Ask me how many words to a column inch, or how many gangsters got knocked off in the last racket war, but—"

"You're the man I'm looking for. I don't want a man with a scientific mind. I need a man with good, sound common-sense." He looked at his wrist watch. "Len—will you come out to my home with me?"

"When?"

"Now."

I said, "Jeepers, Burch—I've got to get up at seven tomorrow. I really shouldn't—"

He leaned over the table; stared at me intently.

"Don't stall, Len. This is important. Will you?"

I told you I was snoopy. I stood up.

"My hat's in the cloak-room," I said. "Let's go!"

Patterson's estate was in North Jersey. A rambling sort of place, some miles off the highway. It was easy to see how he could return to it, open it up, and still not let anyone know he had returned. As we drove, he cleared up a few foggy points for me.

"I didn't return to the States on a regular liner. I had reasons for not doing so—which you will understand in a short time.

"I chartered a freighter, a junky little job, from an obscure Peruvian port. Pledged the captain to secrecy. He landed me and my—my cargo—" He stumbled on the word for a moment. "—at a spot which I'm not at liberty to reveal. Then I came out here and opened up the house.

"That was just two days ago. I wired my brother, Ki, to come immediately. But he—"

"He's working in L. A.," I said.

"Yes. The soonest he could get here would be tonight. He may be at the house when we arrive. I hope so. I'd like to have two witnesses of that which I am going to show you."

He frowned. "Maybe I'm making a mistake, Len. It is the damnedest thing you ever heard of. Maybe I ought to call in some professor, too. But—I don't know. It's so utterly beyond credibility, I'd like you and Ki to advise me, first."

I said, "Well, what the hell is it, Burch?" Then I suddenly remembered a motion picture I'd seen some years ago; a thing based on a story by H. G. Wells. "It's not a—a monster, is it?" I asked. "Some beast left over from prehistoric ages?"

"No; not exactly. At least, I can assure you of *this*—it is not a fossil, either living or dead. It's a thing entirely beyond man's wildest imaginings."

I leaned back and groaned. "I feel like a darned kid," I told him, "on Christmas Eve. Step on it, guy!"

There were lights in the house when we got there. As Burch Patterson had hoped, Ki had arrived from California. He heard us pull up the gravel lane, and came to the door. There was a reunion scene; one of those back-clapping, how-are-you-old-fellow things. Then we went in.

"I found your note," Ki said, "and knew you'd be right back. I needn't tell you I'm tickled to death you're safe, Burch. But—why all the secrecy?"

"That's what *I* asked him," I said. "But he's not giving out."

"It's something," Ki accused, "about the old work shop behind the house. I know that. I was snooping around back there, and—"

Burch Patterson's face whitened. He clutched his brother's arm swiftly. "You didn't go inside?"

"No. I couldn't. The place was locked. Say—" Ki stared at his brother curiously. "Are you feeling okay, guy? Are you sure you're not—"

"You must be careful," said Burch Patterson. "You must be very, very careful when you approach that shed. I am going to take you out there now. But you must stand exactly where I tell you to, and not make any sudden moves."

He strode to a library table; took out three automatics. One he tucked into his own pocket. The others he handed to us. "I'm not sure," he said, "that these would be any good if—if anything happened. But it is the only protection we have. You *might* be lucky enough to hit a vulnerable spot."

"A vulnerable spot!" I said. "Then it *is* a beast?"

"Come," he said. "I shall show you."

He led the way to the work shop. It lay some yards behind and beyond the house; a big, lonesome sort of place, not quite as large as a barn, but plenty big. My first idea was that at some time it must have been used as a barn, for as we approached it, I could catch that animal odor you associate with barns, stables, zoos.

Only more so. It was a nasty, fetid, particularly offensive odor. You know how animals smell worse when they get excited. Or when they've been exercising a lot? Well, the place smelled like that.

I was nervous, and when I get nervous I invariably try to act funny. I said, "If they're horses, you ought to curry them more often."

I saw a faint blur in the black before me. It was Ki's face, turning to peer back. He said, "Not horses, Len. We've never kept horses on this estate."

Then we were at the door of the shed, and Burch was fumbling with a lock. I heard metal click; then the door creaking open. Patterson fumbled for a switch. The sudden blaze of light made me blink.

"In here," said Burch. And, warningly, "Stay close behind me!"

We crowded in. First Burch, then Ki, then me. And as Ki got through the door, I felt his body stiffen; heard him gasp hoarsely. I peered over his shoulder—

Then I, too, gasped!

The thing I saw was incredible. There were two uprights of steel, each about four inches in diameter, deeply imbedded in a solid steel plate which was secured to a massive concrete block. Each of these uprights was "eyed"—and through the eyes ran a third steel rod which had been hammered down so that the horizontal bar was held firmly in place by the two uprights.

And on this horizontal rod was—a *thing!*

That is all I can call it. It had substance, but it had no form. Or, to be more accurate, it had every form of which you can conceive. For, like a huge, black amoeba, or like a writhing chunk of amorphous matter, it *changed!*

Where the steel rod pierced this blob of *thing* was a clotted, brownish excrescence. This, I think, accounted for some of the animal odor. But not all of it. The whole shop was permeated with the musty scent.

The *thing* changed! As I watched, there seemed to be, at one time, a globular piece of matter twisting on the rod. An instant later, the globe had turned into a triangle—then into something remotely resembling a cube. It was constantly in motion; constantly in flux. But here is the curious part. It did not change shape slowly, as an amoeba, so that you could watch the sphere turn into an oblong; the oblong writhed into a formless blob of flesh. It made these changes instantaneously!

Ki Patterson cried, "Good God, Burch! What unholy thing is this?" and took a step forward, past his brother's shoulder.

Burch shouted, "Back!" and yanked at Ki's arm. He moved just in time. For as Ki quitted the spot to which he had advanced, there appeared *in the air* right over that spot, another mass of the same black stuff that was captured on the bar. A blob of shapeless, stinking matter that gaped like some huge mouth; then closed convulsively just where Ki had stood a moment before!

And now the fragment on the rod was really moving! It changed shape so rapidly; twisted and wriggled with such determination, that there was no doubt whatsoever about the sentiency governing it. And other similar blobs suddenly sprang into sight! A black pyramid struck the far wall of the shed, and trembling woodwork told that here was solid matter. An ebon sphere rose from nowhere to roll across the floor, stopping just short of us. Most weirdly of all, a shaft of black jolted down *through* the floor—and failed to break the flooring!

That's about all I remember of that visit. For Ki suddenly loosed a terrified yelp; turned and scrambled past me to the door. I take no medals for courage. He was four steps ahead of me at the portal, but I beat him to the house by a cool ten yards. Burch was the only calm one. He took time to lock the work-shed door; then followed us.

But don't let anyone tell you *he* was exactly calm, either. His face wasn't white, like Ki's. Nor did his hand shake on the whisky-and-splash glass, like mine. But there was real fear in his eyes. I mean, *real* fear!

The whisky was a big help. It brought my voice back. "Well, Burch," I said, "we've seen it. Now, what in hell did we see?"

"You have seen," said Burch Patterson soberly, "the thing that killed Toland, and Fletcher, and Gainelle."

"We found it," said Burch, "on the Maratan Plateau. For we did get there, you know. Yes. Even though our radio went bad on us, just after we left Quiché, and we lost contact with the world. For a while, we considered going into Lima for repairs, but Fletcher thought he could fix it up once we were on solid ground, so we let it ride.

"We found a good, natural landing field on the Plateau, and began our investigations." He brooded silently for a minute. Then, reluctantly, "The Maratan is even richer in paleontological data than men have dared hope. But Man must never try to go there again. Not until his knowledge is greater than it is today."

Ki said, "Why? That *thing* outside?"

"Yes. It is the Gateway for that—and others like it.

"Some day I will tell you all about the marvels we saw on the Plateau. But now my story concerns only one; the one you have seen.

"Fletcher saw it first. We had left Gainelle tending camp, and were making a field survey, when we saw a bare patch in the jungle which surrounded our landing field. Fletcher trained his glasses on the spot, and before he even had time to adjust them properly he was crying, 'There's something funny over there! Take a look!'

"We all looked then. And we saw—what you saw a few minutes ago. Huge, amorphous blobs of jet black, which seemed to be of the earth, yet not quite of it. Sometimes these ever-changing fragments were suspended in air, with no visible support. At other times they seemed to rest naturally enough on solid ground. But ever and ever again—they changed!

"Afire with curiosity, we went to the open spot. It was a mistake."

"A mistake?" I said.

"Yes. Fletcher lost his life—killed by his own curiosity. I need not tell you how he died. It was, you must believe me, horrible. Out of nowhere, one of the jet blobs appeared before him . . . then around him . . . then—he was gone!"

"Gone!" exclaimed Ki. "You mean—dead?"

"I mean gone! One second he was there. The next, both he and the *thing* which had snatched him had disappeared into thin air.

"Toland and I fled, panic-stricken, back to camp. We told Gainelle what we had seen. Gainelle, a crack shot and a gallant sportsman, was incredulous; perhaps even dubious. At his insistence, we armed and returned to the tiny glade.

"This time, it was as if the *thing* expected us—for it did not await our attack. It attacked us. We had barely entered its domain when suddenly, all about us, were clots of this ever-changing black. I remembered hearing Toland scream; high and thin, like a woman. I dimly recall hearing the booming cough of Gainelle's express rifle, and of firing myself.

"I remember thinking, subconsciously, that Gainelle was a crack shot. That he never missed anything he aimed at. But it didn't seem to matter. If you hit one of those fleshy blobs, it bled a trifle—maybe. More likely than not, it changed shape. Or disappeared entirely.

"It was a rout. We left Toland behind us, dead, on the plain. A black, triangular *thing* had slashed Gainelle from breast to groin. I managed to drag him half way out of the glade before he died in my arms. Then I was alone.

"I am not a good pilot, under the best conditions. Now I was frantic; crazed with fear. Somehow I managed to reach the plane. But in attempting to take off, I cracked up. I must bear a charmed life. I was not injured, myself, but the plane was ruined. My expedition, hardly started, was already at an end."

I was beginning to understand, now, why Burch Patterson had not wanted the world to know of his return. A tale as wild and fantastic as this would lead him to but one spot—the psychopathic ward. Had I not seen the *thing* there in the shed, I would never have believed him myself. But as it was—

"And then?" I asked.

"I think there is a form of insanity," said Burch, "which is braver than bravery. I think that insanity came upon me then. All I could comprehend was that some *thing*—a *thing* that changed its shape—had killed my companions.

"I determined to capture that *thing*—or die in the attempt. But first I had to sit down and figure out what it *was!*"

Ki licked his lips. "And—and did you figure it out, Burch?"

"I think so. But the result of my reasoning is as fantastic as the *thing* itself. That is why I want the help and advice of you two. I will tell you what I think. Then you must say what it is best to do."

I poured another drink all around. It wasn't my house, or my liquor, but nobody seemed to mind. Ki and I waited for Burch to begin. Burch had picked up, and was now handling with a curiously abstract air, a clean, white sheet of notepaper. As he began, he waved this before us.

"Can you conceive," he said, "of a world of only two dimensions? A world which scientists might call 'Flatland'? A world constructed like this piece of paper—on which might live creatures who could not even visualize a third dimension of depth?"

"Sure," said Ki. I wasn't so sure, myself, but I said nothing.

"Very well. Look—" Burch busied himself with a pencil for an instant. "I draw on this sheet of paper, a tiny man. He is a Flatlander. He can move forward or backward. Up or down. But he can never move *out* of his world, into the third dimension, because he has no knowledge of a dimension angular to that in which he lives. He does not even dream of its existence."

I said, "I see what you mean now. But what has that to do with—"

"Wait, Len." Patterson suddenly struck the paper a blow with one finger; piercing it. He held the sheet up for our inspection. "Look at this. What do you see?"

"A sheet of paper," I said, "with a hole in it."

"Yes. But what does the *Flatlander* see?"

Ki looked excited. "I get it, Burch! He sees an unexpected, solid object appear before him—out of nowhere! If he walks around this object, he discovers it to be crudely round!"

"Exactly. Now I push the finger farther through the hole—"

"The object expands!"

"And if I bend it?"

"It changes its shape!"

"And if I thrust another finger through Flatland—"

"Another strangely shaped piece of solid matter materializes before the flatlander!" Ki's eyes were widening by the moment. I didn't understand why.

I said, "I told you I didn't have a scientific mind, Burch. What does all this mean?"

Burch said patiently, "I have merely been established a thought-pattern, Len, so you can grasp the next step of my reasoning. Forget the Flatlander now—or, rather, try to think of *us* as being in his place!

"Would we not, to a creature whose natural habitat is a higher plane than ours, appear much the same sort of projection as the Flatlander is to us?

"Suppose a creature of this higher plane projected a portion of himself into *our* dimension—as I projected my finger into Flatland. We would not be able to see *all* of him, just as the Flatlander could not see all of us. We would see only a tri-dimensional cross-section of him; as the Flatlander saw a bi-dimensional cross-section of us!"

This time I got it. I gasped:

"Then you think that *thing* in the work-shed is a cross-section of a creature from the—"

"Yes, Len. From the Fourth Dimension!"

Patterson smiled wanly.

"That is the decision I reached on the Maratan Plateau. There confronted me the problem of capturing the *thing*. The answer eluded me for weeks. Finally, I found it."

"It was—" Ki was leaning forward breathlessly.

"The Flatlander," said Burch, "could not capture my finger, *ever*, by lassooing it. No matter how tight he drew his noose, I could always withdraw my finger.

"But he *could* secure a portion of me, by fastening me to his dimension. Thus—" He showed us how a pin, laid flat in Flatland, could pierce a small piece of skin. "Now if this pin were bolted securely, the finger thus prisoned could not be withdrawn.

"That was the principle on which I worked, but my task had just begun. It took months to effect the capture. I had to study, from afar, the amorphous black *thing* which was my quarry. Try to form some concept of what incredible Fourth Dimensional beast would cast projections of that nature into the Third.

"Finally I decided that one certain piece of black matter, occurring in a certain relationship to the changing whole, was a foot. How, it is not important to tell. It was, after all, theory, coupled with guesswork.

"I constructed the shackle you have seen. Two uprights, with a third that must pierce the *thing;* then lock upon it. I waited, then, many weeks. Finally there came a chance to spring my trap. And—it worked!"

Ki said, "And then?"

"The rest is a long and tiresome story. Somehow I found my way to a native village; there employed natives to drag my captive from the Plateau. We were handicapped by the fact that we could never get too near the trap. You see, it is a *limb* we have imprisoned. The head, or eating apparatus, or whatever it is, is still free. That is what tried to reach you, Ki, there in the shed.

"Anyway, we made an arduous trek to the coast. As I have told you, I chartered a vessel. The sailors hated my cargo, and feared it. The trip was not an easy one. But I was determined, and my determination bore fruit. And—here we are."

I said, "Yeah—here we are. Just like the man who grabbed a tiger by the tail; then couldn't let go. Now that you've got this *thing*, what are you going to do with it?"

"That's what I want you to tell me."

Ki's eyes were glowing. He said, "Good Lord, man, is there any question in your mind? Call in the scientists—the whole damned brigade of them! Show them this thing! You've got the marvel of the age on your hands!"

"And you, Len?"

"You want it straight?" I said. "Or would you like to have me pull my punches?"

"Straight. That's why I asked you out here."

"Then get rid of it," I said. "Kill it. Set it on fire. Destroy it. I don't know just how you're going to do it, but I do know that's the thing to do.

"Oh, I know what you're thinking, Ki—so shut up! I'm a dope. Sure. I'm ignorant. Sure. I don't have the mind or the heart of a true scientist. Okay—you win! But Burch said I had common sense—and I'm exercising it now. I say—get rid of that damned thing before something happens. Something horrible that you will regret for the rest of your life!"

Ki looked a little peeved. He said, "You're nuts, Len! The thing's tied down, isn't it? Dammit man—you're the kind of guy who holds back the progress of the world. I bet you'd have voted to kill Galileo if you'd been alive in his day."

"If he'd trapped a monster like this," I retorted, "a monster who'd already killed at least three men, I'd have voted just that way. I'm not superstitious, Burch. But I'm afraid. I'm afraid that when Man starts monkeying with the Unknown, he gets beyond his depth. I say—kill it, now!"

Burch looked at me anxiously.

"That's your last word, Len?"

"Absolutely my last," I said. I rose. "And just to prove it, I'm going home now. And I'm not even going to write a damned word about what I've seen tonight. I don't care if this is the best story since the Deluge—I'm not going to write it!"

Ki said, "You give me a pain, Len. In the neck."

"Same to you," I told him, "only lower down. Well, so long guys." And I went home.

I kept my word. Though I had the mimsies all night, tossing and thinking about that crazy, changing black *thing*, I didn't put a word concerning it on paper. I half expected to hear from Burch Patterson some time during the next day. But I didn't. Then, the following morning, I saw why. The *Call* carried a front page blast, screaming to the astonished world the news that, "the missing explorer, Burch Patterson, has returned home," and that "tonight there will be a convocation of eminent scientists" at his home to view some marvel brought back from the wilds of upper Peru.

All of which meant that brother Ki's arguments had proven more persuasive than mine. And that tonight there was to be a preview of that damned *thing*.

I was pretty sore about it. I thought the least they could have done was give me the news beat on the yarn. But there wasn't any use crying over spilt milk. Anyway. I remembered that Ki's paper had a tie-up with the *Call*. It was natural he should route the story that way.

And then I went down to the office, and Joe Slade, the human buzz saw who calls himself our City Editor, waved me up to his desk.

"You, Harvey," he said, "I'm going to give you a chance to earn some of that forty per we're overpaying you. I want you to represent us tonight out at Patterson's home in Jersey. He's going to unveil something mysterious."

I said, "Who—me? Listen, chief, give it to Bill Reynolds, won't you? I've got some rewrites to do—"

"You, I said. What's the matter? Does New Jersey give you asthma?"

"Chief," I pleaded, "I can't cover this. I don't know anything about science or—"

"What do you mean—science?" He pushed back his eyeshade and glared at me. "Do you know what this is all about?"

That stopped me. I didn't want to go, but if I ever admitted that I'd known about Patterson's changeable what-is-it, and not beaten the *Call* to the streets with the story, I would be scanning the want ads in fifteen seconds flat. So I gulped and said, "Okay, boss. I'll go."

Everybody and his brother was there that night. I recognized a professor of Physics from Columbia U., and the Dean of Paleontology from N.Y.U. Two old graybeards from the Academy of Natural History were over in a corner discussing something that ended in —zoic, and the curator of the Museum was present, smelling as musty as one of his ancient mummies.

The Press was out in force. All the bureaus, and most of the New York papers. Ki was doing the receiving. Burch had not yet put in an appearance. I found a minute to get Ki aside, and told him what a skunky trick I thought he'd pulled on me, but he merely shrugged.

"I'm sorry, Len. But you had your chance. After all, I had to think of my own paper first." Then he smiled. "And besides, you were in favor of destroying the *thing.*"

"I still am," I told him dourly.

"Then what are you here for?"

It was my turn to shrug. "It was either come or lose my job," I said. "What do you think?"

Then Burch put in an appearance, and the whole outfit went genteelly crazy. Flash bulbs started blazing, and all my learned *confrères* of the Third Estate started shooting questions at him. About his trip, the loss of his comrades, his experiences. I knew all that stuff, so I just waited for the big blow-off to follow.

It came, at last. The moment when Burch said:

"Before I tell my entire story, I prefer that you see that which I brought back with me," and he led the way out to the work-shed.

Ki and Burch had fixed up the place a little; put chalk lines on the floor to show the visitors where they might stand.

"And I warn you," Burch said, just before he opened the shed door, "not to move beyond those lines. Afterward you will understand why."

Then the crowd began to file in. From my vantage point in the rear, I could tell when the first pair of eyes sighted that *thing*—and when every subsequent visitor saw it, as well. Gasps, exclamations, and little cries of astonishment rippled through the crowd as one by one they moved into the room.

The *thing* was still suspended on its imprisoning rod. As before, it was wriggling and moving; changing its shape with such rapidity that the human eye could scarcely view one shape before that turned into another. In view of what Burch had told me, I could comprehend the *thing* better now. I could understand how, if that black blob of flesh captured by the bar were *really*—as Burch presumed—a leg of some ultra-dimensional monster, the movements of that limb, as it sought to break free, would throw continually changing projections into our world.

I could understand, too, why from time to time we would see *other* bits of solid matter appear in various sections of the room. Though these seemed disassociated with that chunk hanging on the trap, I knew it was really separate portions of the same beast. Because if a *man* were to thrust four fingers, simultaneously, into Flatland, to the Flatlander these would appear to be four separate objects; while in reality they were part of a single unit in a dimension beyond his powers of conception.

The astonishment of the professors was something to behold. I began to feel a little bit ashamed of myself, there in the background. Perhaps I had been wrong to give Burch the advice I had. Perhaps, as Ki had said, this was one of the greatest discoveries of all time. It belonged to the world of science.

One of the photographers was dropping to his knee, levelling his Graflex at the shifting, changing *thing* on the rod. I caught myself thinking, swiftly, "He shouldn't do that!" Evidently Burch had the same idea. He took a swift step forward; cried, "Please! If you don't mind—"

He spoke too late. The man's finger pressed. For an instant the room was flooded with light.

And then it happened. I heard a sound like a thin, high bleating that seemed to come from far, far away. Or it may not have been a sound at all, in the true sense of that word. It may have been some tonic wave of supernal heights; for it tortured the eardrums to hear it.

The thing on the rod churned into motion. Violent motion. It grew and dwindled; shifted from cube to hemisphere; back to cube again. Then a truncated pyramidal form was throbbing, jerking, churning on the steel. Where I had once noticed an old, ugly healed wound, ichor-clotted; now I saw ragged edges of black break open. Saw a few, fresh gouts of brownish fluid well from what seemed to be raw edges in that changing black.

Burch's horrified voice rose above the tumult.

"Get out! Get out—all of you! Before it—"

That was all he found time to say. For there came a horrible, sucking sound, like the sound of gangrenous flesh tearing away; and where there had been a changing black shape swirling on an imprisoning steel rod—now there was nothing!

But with equal suddenness, several of the shapeless blobs of matter from various parts of the room seemed to rush together with frightful speed. Someone, screaming with terror, bumped against me then. I fell to my hands and knees in the doorway, feeling the flood of human fear scramble over me.

But not until I had seen a scimitar-shaped blob of black flesh reach out to strike at Ki Patterson. Ki had not even time to cry out. He went down, dead, as though stricken by the sickle of Chronos.

I cried, "Burch!"

Burch had turned to face the coalescing monster. A revolver in his hand was filling the little room with thunder. Orange gouts of flame belched from its muzzle; and I knew he was not missing. Still the thing was closing in on him. I saw what seemed to be four jet circles appear in a ring over the head of Burch Patterson. Saw the circles expand; and a wider expanse of black—flat and sinister—appear directly over his head. They came together with a clutching, enveloping movement. Then—he was gone!

Somehow I managed to struggle out of that work shed. Not that it made any difference. For with the disappearance of Burch Patterson, the *thing* itself disappeared.

I won't try to describe the frightened group of news men and scientists who gathered at the Patterson house. Who trembled and quaked, and offered fantastic reasons for that which had transpired. Who finally summoned up courage enough to return to the shed cautiously; seeking the mortal remains of Burch Patterson.

They never found anything, of course. Ki was there, but Ki was dead. Burch was gone. The air was still putrid with that unearthly animal stench. Beneath the steel "trap" Patterson had built for his *thing*, there was a pool of drying brownish fluid. One of the scientists wanted to take a sample of this for analysis. He returned to the house for a test-tube in which to put it . . .

Maybe it was the wrong thing for me to do. But I thought, then, that it was best. And I still think so. If he had taken that sample; made that analysis; sooner or later another expedition would have set out for the Maratan Plateau in search of that *thing* whose blood did not correspond to that of any known animal. I didn't believe this should happen. So, while he was gone, I set fire to the work shed. It was an old place; old and dry as tinder. By the time he had returned, it was a seething cauldron of flame. It made a fitting pyre for the body of Ki Patterson . . .

But—I don't know. I have wondered, since. Somehow, I have a feeling that Burch Patterson may not be dead, after all. That is—if a human can live in a dimension of which he cannot conceive.

The more I think of it; the more I try to reconcile that which I saw with that which Burch told me; the more I believe that the thing which descended upon Burch, there in the shed, was not a "mouth"—but a gigantic paw! You know, I saw four circles appear . . . with a flat black spot above. It could have been four huge fingers . . . with the palm descending to grasp the daring tri-dimensional "Flatlander" who had the audacity to match wits with a creature from a superior world. If that be so . . . and if the *thing* were intelligent . . . Patterson might still be alive . . .

I don't know. But sometimes I am tempted to organize another expedition to the Maratan Plateau, myself. Try to learn the truth concerning the *thing* from beyond the Gateway. The truth concerning Burch Patterson's fate.

What would *you* do?

Mind Stretchers

Stories of time travel and parallel worlds could easily be called mind stretchers, but the term as used here covers stories in which scientific, philosophical, or mathematical theories become reality. For example, the theoretical possibility of attaining the speed of light and the subsequent effects on humans who travel at or near that speed would be included in this category as would stories which involve the powers of the mind—telepathy, ESP, and teleportation. Theories concerning the possibility of such phenomena can be found in university courses and in professional publications for scientists, philosophers, psychologists, and mathematicians. It should come as no surprise, then, that it is this category of science fiction which consistently requires the greatest command of technical and theoretical knowledge on the part of the author and the reader.

A great deal of science fiction involves mind-stretching concepts, but the works which use those concepts as the primary focus of the story are fewer in number than those stories which accept the ideas and concentrate on something else. A. E. Van Vogt's *The World of Null–A* attempts to explore the concept of non-Aristotelian logic by confronting it from our world of Aristotelian logic. Van Vogt's inspiration for this novel was Alfred Korzybski's introduction to non-Aristotelian logic and semantics, *Science and Sanity*. Samuel R. Delaney's *The Einstein Intersection* depicts the results when this world, which operates according to Einsteinian laws, intersects a universe which operates according to a different set of rules. Piers Anthony, after spending a great deal of time setting things up, explores the idea of a macroscope, a doorway which leads to all space and time, in his recent novel, *Macroscope*. The macroscope is the ultimate nexus. In *The Triumph of Time,* the fourth book of *Cities in Flight,* James Blish portrays the end of the universe in the collision of matter and anti-matter. Arthur C. Clarke has edited an anthology entitled *Time Probe* in which there is a science fiction story for each of eleven sciences.

While much science fiction of the mind-stretching variety tends to be weak on plot, there are some exceptions. Charles L. Harness' "The New Reality" heads this group of stories because its strong plot-line and attention to detail, in both science and fiction, make it a good story with which to move from familiar to unfamiliar concepts. "The New Reality" is about ontology, and in the course of the story, the reader discovers that the characters literally determine the structure of their world. Moreover, this story also involves existential concepts of identity and order. "The New Reality" operates on several levels, one of which does not become obvious until the archetypes are revealed at the end making the reader wonder why he didn't see what was going on all along.

The next two stories have several things in common. Both are humorous in tone, have a theory-made-reality, and have plots which are subordinated to concepts. Martin Gardner's "The No-Sided Professor" is an almost whimsical use of topological theory; in fact, the humor may obscure the mind-stretching concepts Gardner presents. The balance is achieved in the footnotes, and the reader should follow the directions —make a Moebius strip, experiment with it as suggested, and become enlightened concerning its "impossible" characteristics. Suddenly the humorous enjoyment is equalled if not surpassed by the implications of the topological phenomenon discussed in the story. There is, by the way, a sequel to this story entitled "The Island of Five Colors" in which the professor vanishes again by falling into a klein bottle.

Theoretical geometry is the reality in Robert Heinlein's "—And he Built a Crooked House—" (required reading in some graduate mathematics courses) in which an architect designs a house in the shape of an unfolded tesseract. During an earthquake, the house is able to assume its natural or "folded" shape, and the complications begin. The characters in this story provide some additional interest as the "progressive" architect is contrasted to the rather "traditional" husband and wife for whom he designs the house. This contrast is basically a contrast of imaginations as each of the three characters deals with the house in a different manner, illustrating not only attitudes toward but abilities to deal with something of drastic newness.

THE NEW REALITY

Charles L. Harness

Prentiss crawled into the car, drew the extension connector from his concealed throat mike from its clip in his right sleeve, and plugged it into the ignition key socket.

After a moment he said, "Get me the Censor."

The seconds passed as he heard the click of forming circuits. Then: "E speaking."

"Prentiss, honey."

"Call me 'E,' Prentiss. What news?"

"I've met five classes under Professor Luce. He has a private lab. Doesn't confide in his graduate students. Evidently conducting secret experiments in comparative psychology. Rats and such. Nothing overtly censorable."

"I see. What are your plans?"

"I'll have his lab searched tonight. If nothing turns up, I'll recommend a drop."

"I'd prefer that you search the lab yourself."

A. Prentiss Rogers concealed his surprise and annoyance. "Very well."

His ear button clicked a dismissal.

With puzzled irritation he snapped the plug from the dash socket, started the car, and eased it down the drive into the boulevard bordering the university.

Didn't she realize that he was a busy Field Director with a couple of hundred men under him fully capable of making a routine night search? Undoubtedly she knew just that, but nevertheless was requiring that he do it himself. Why?

And why had she assigned Professor Luce to him personally, squandering so many of his precious hours, when half a dozen of his bright young physical philosophers could have handled it? Nevertheless E, from behind the august anonymity of her solitary initial, had been adamant.

A mile away he turned into a garage on a deserted side street and drew up alongside a Cadillac.

Crush sprang out of the big car and silently held the rear door open for him.

Prentiss got in. "We have a job tonight."

His aide hesitated a fraction of a second before slamming the door behind him. Prentiss knew that the squat, asthmatic little man was surprised and delighted.

As for Crush, he'd never got it through his head that the control of human knowledge was a grim and hateful business, not a kind of cruel lark.

"Very good, sir," wheezed Crush, climbing in behind the wheel. "Shall I reserve a sleeping room at the Bureau for the evening?"

"Can't afford to sleep," grumbled Prentiss. "Desk so high now I can't see over it. Take a nap yourself, if you want to."

"Yes, sir. If I feel the need of it, sir."

The ontologist shot a bitter glance at the back of the man's head. No, Crush wouldn't sleep, but not because worry would keep him awake. A holdover from the days when all a Censor man had was a sleepless curiosity and a pocket Geiger, Crush was serenely untroubled by the dangerous and unfathomable implications of philosophical nucleonics. For Crush, "ontology" was just another definition in the dictionary: "The science of reality."

The little aide could never grasp the idea that unless a sane world-wide pattern of nucleonic investigation were followed, some one in Australia—or next door—might one day throw a switch and alter the shape of that reality. That's what made Crush so valuable; he just didn't know enough to be afraid.

Prentiss had clipped the hairs from his nostrils and so far had breathed in complete silence. But now, as that cavernous face was turned toward where he lay stomach-to-earth in the sheltering darkness, his lungs convulsed in an audible gasp.

The mild, polite, somewhat abstracted academic features of Professor Luce were transformed. The face beyond the lab window was now flushed, the lips were drawn back in soundless amusement, the sunken black eyes were dancing with red pinpoints of flame.

By brute will the ontologist forced his attention back to the rat.

Four times in the past few minutes he had watched the animal run down an inclined chute until it reached a fork, chose one fork, receive what must be a nerve-shattering electric shock, and then be replaced in the chute-beginning for the next run. No matter which alternative fork was chosen, the animal always had been shocked into convulsions.

On this fifth run the rat, despite needling blasts of compressed air from the chute walls, was slowing down. Just before it reached the fork it stopped completely.

The air jets struck at it again, and little cones of up-ended gray fur danced on its rump and flanks.

It gradually ceased to tremble; its respiration dropped to normal. It seemed to Prentiss that its eyes were shut.

The air jets lashed out again. It gave no notice, but just lay there, quiescent, in a near coma.

As he peered into the window, Prentiss saw the tall man walk languidly over to the little animal and run a long hooklike forefinger over its back. No reaction. The professor then said something, evidently in a soft slurred voice, for Prentiss had difficulty in reading his lips.

"—when both alternatives are wrong for you, but you *must* do something, you hesitate, don't you, little one? You slow down, and you are lost. You are no longer a rat. Do you know what the universe would be like if a *photon* should slow down? You don't? Have you ever taken a bite out of a balloon, little friend? Just the tiniest possible bite?"

Prentiss cursed. The professor had turned and was walking toward the cages with the animal, and although he was apparently still talking, his lips were no longer visible.

After relatching the cage-door the professor walked toward the lab entrance, glanced carefully around the room, and then, as he was reaching for the light switch, looked toward Prentiss' window.

For a moment the investigator was convinced that by some nameless power the professor was looking into the darkness, straight into his eyes.

He exhaled slowly. It was preposterous.

The room was plunged in darkness.

The investigator blinked and closed his eyes. He wouldn't really have to worry until he heard the lab door opening on the opposite side of the little building.

The door didn't open. Prentiss squinted into the darkness of the room.

Where the professor's head had been were now two mysterious tiny red flames, like candles.

Something must be reflecting from the professor's corneas. But the room was dark; there was no light to be reflected. The flame-eyes continued their illusion of studying him.

The hair was crawling on Prentiss' neck when the twin lights finally vanished and he heard the sound of the lab door opening.

As the slow heavy tread died away down the flagstones to the street, Prentiss gulped in a huge lungful of the chill night air and rubbed his sweating face against his sleeve.

What had got into him? He was acting like the greenest cub. He was glad that Crush had to man the televisor relay in the Cadillac and couldn't see him.

He got to his hands and knees and crept silently toward the darkened window. It was a simple sliding sash, and a few seconds sufficed to drill through the glass and insert a hook around the sash lock. The rats began a nervous squeaking as he lowered himself into the darkness of the basement room.

His ear-receptor sounded. "The prof is coming back!" wheezed Crush's tinny voice.

Prentiss said something under his breath, but did not pause in drawing his infra-red scanner from his pocket.

He touched his fingers to his throat mike. "Signal when he reaches the bend in the walk," he said. "And be sure you get this on the visor tape."

The apparatus got his first attention.

The investigator had memorized its position perfectly. Approaching as closely in the darkness as he dared, he "panned" the scanner over some very interesting apparatus that he had noticed on the table.

Then he turned to the books on the desk, regretting that he wouldn't have time to record more than a few pages.

"He's at the bend," warned Crush.

"Okay," mumbled Prentiss, running sensitive fingers over the book bindings. He selected one, opened it at random, and ran the scanner over the invisible pages. "Is this coming through?" he demanded.

"Chief, *he's at the door!*"

Prentiss had to push back the volume without scanning any more of it. He had just relocked the sash when the lab door swung open.

A couple of hours later the ontologist bid good-morning to his receptionist and secretaries and stepped into his private office. He dropped with tired thoughtfulness into his swivel chair and pulled out the infrared negatives that Crush had prepared in the Cadillac darkroom. The page from the old German diary was particularly intriguing. He laboriously translated it once more:

As I got deeper into the manuscript, my mouth grew dry, and my heart began to pound. This, I knew, was a contribution the like of which my family has not seen since Copernicus, Roger Bacon, or perhaps even Aristotle. It seemed incredible that this silent little man, who had never been outside of Koenigsberg, should hold the key to the universe—the *Critique of Pure Reason*, he calls it. And I doubt that even he realizes the ultimate portent of his teaching, for he says we cannot know the real shape or nature of anything, that is, the Thing-in-Itself, the Ding-an-Sich, or *noumenon*. He holds that this is the ultimate unknowable, reserved to the gods. He doesn't suspect that, century by century, mankind is nearing this final realization of the final things. Even this brilliant man would probably say that the earth was round in 600 B.C., even as it is today. But *I* know it was flat, then—as truly flat as it is truly round today. What has changed? Not the Thing-in-Itself we call the earth. No, it is the mind of man that has changed. But in his preposterous blindness, he mistakes what is really

his own mental quickening for a broadened application of science and more
precise methods of investigation—

Prentiss smiled.

Luce was undoubtedly a collector of philosophic incunabula. Odd
hobby, but that's all it could be—a hobby. Obviously the earth had never
been flat, and in fact hadn't changed shape substantially in the last couple
of billion years. Certainly any notions as to the flatness of the earth
held by primitives of a few thousand years ago or even by contemporaries
of Kant were due to their ignorance rather than to accurate observation,
and a man of Luce's erudition could only be amused by them.

Again Prentiss found himself smiling with the tolerance of a man
standing on the shoulders of twenty centuries of science. The primitives,
of course, did the best they could. They just didn't know. They worked
with childish premises and infantile instruments.

His brows creased. To assume they had used childish premises was
begging the question. On the other hand, was it really worth a second
thought? All he could hope to discover would be a few instances of
how inferior apparatus coupled perhaps with unsophisticated deductions
had oversimplified the world of the ancients. Still, anything that
interested the strange Dr. Luce automatically interested him, Prentiss,
until the case was closed.

He dictated into the scriptor:

"Memorandum to Geodetic Section. Rush a paragraph history of ideas
concerning shape of earth. Prentiss."

Duty done, he promptly forgot it and turned to the heavy accumulation
of reports on his desk.

A quarter of an hour later the scriptor rang and began typing an
incoming message.

> To the Director. Re your request for brief history of earth's shape. Chal-
> deans and Babylonians (per clay tablets from library of Assurbanipal), Egyp-
> tians (per Ahmes papyrus, ca. 1700 B.C.), Cretans (per inscriptions in
> royal library at Knossos, ca. 1300 B.C.), Chinese (per Chou Kung
> ms. ca. 1100 B.C.), Phoenicians (per fragments at Tyre ca. 900 B.C.), Hebrews
> (per unknown Biblical historian ca. 850 B.C.), and early Greeks (per
> map of widely-traveled geographer Hecataeus, 517 B.C.) assumed
> earth to be flat disc. But from the 5th century B.C. forward earth's
> sphericity universally recognized. . . .

There were a few more lines, winding up with the work done on
corrections for flattening at poles, but Prentiss had already lost interest.
The report threw no light on Luce's hobby and was devoid of ontological
implications.

He tossed the script into the waste basket and returned to the reports before him.

A few minutes later he twisted uneasily in his chair, eyed the scriptor in annoyance, then forced himself back to his work.

No use.

Deriding himself for an idiot, he growled at the machine:

"Memorandum to Geodetic. Re your memo history earth's shape. How do you account for change to belief in sphericity after Hecataeus? Rush. Prentiss."

The seconds ticked by.

He drummed on his desk impatiently, then got up and began pacing the floor.

When the scriptor rang, he bounded back and leaned over his desk, watching the words being typed out.

> Late Greeks based spherical shape on observation that mast of approaching ship appeared first, then prow. Not known why similar observation not made by earlier seafaring peoples. . . .

Prentiss rubbed his cheek in perplexity. What was he fishing for?

He thrust the half-born conjecture that the earth really had once been flat back into his mental recesses.

Well, then how about the heavens? Surely there was no record of their having changed during man's brief lifetime.

He'd try one more shot and quit.

"Memo to Astronomy Division. Rush paragraph on early vs. modern sun size and distance."

A few minutes later he was reading the reply:

> Skipping Plato, whose data are believed baseless (he measured sun's distance at only twice that of moon), we come to earliest recognized "authority." Ptolemy (Almagest, ca. 140 A.D.) measured sun radius as 5.5 that of earth (as against 109 actual); measured sun distance at 1210 (23,000 actual). Fairly accurate measurements date only from 17th and 18th centuries. . . .

He'd read all that somewhere. The difference was easily explained by their primitive instruments. It was insane to keep this up.

But it was too late.

"Memo to Astronomy. Were erroneous Ptolemaic measurements due to lack of precision instruments?"

Soon he had his reply:

> To Director: Source of Ptolemy's errors in solar measurement not clearly understood. Used astrolabe precise to 10 seconds and clepsydra water clock

incorporating Hero's improvements. With same instruments, and using modern value of pi, Ptolemy measured moon radius (0.29 earth radius vs. 0.273 actual) and distance (59 earth radii vs. 60 1/3 actual). Hence instruments reasonably precise. And note that Copernicus, using quasi-modern instruments and technique, "confirmed" Ptolemaic figure of sun's distance at 1200 earth radii. No explanation known for glaring error.

Unless, suggested something within Prentiss' mind, the sun were closer and much different before the 17th century, when Newton was telling the world where and how big the sun *ought* to be. But *that* solution was too absurd for further consideration. He would sooner assume his complete insanity.

Puzzled, the ontologist gnawed his lower lip and stared at the message in the scriptor.

In his abstraction he found himself peering at the symbol "pi" in the scriptor message. *There,* at least, was something that had always been the same, and would endure for all time. He reached over to knock out his pipe in the big circular ash tray by the scriptor and paused in the middle of the second tap. From his desk he fished a tape measure and stretched it across the tray. Ten inches. And then around the circumference. Thirty-one and a half inches. Good enough, considering. It was a result any curious schoolboy could get.

He turned to the scriptor again.

"Memo to Math Section. Rush paragraph history on value of pi. Prentiss."

He didn't have to wait long.

To Director. Re history "pi." Babylonians used value of 3.00. Aristotle made fairly accurate physical and theoretical evaluations. Archimedes first to arrive at modern value, using theory of limits. . . .

There was more, but it was lost on Prentiss. It was inconceivable, of course, that pi had grown during the two millennia that separated the Babylonians from Archimedes. And yet, it was exasperating. Why hadn't they done any better than 3.00? Any child with a piece of string could have demonstrated their error. Countless generations of wise, careful Chaldean astronomers, measuring time and star positions with such incredible accuracy, all coming to grief with a piece of string and pi. It didn't make sense. And certainly pi hadn't grown, any more than the Babylonian 360-day year had grown into the modern 365-day year. It had always been the same, he told himself. The primitives hadn't measured accurately, that was all. That *had* to be the explanation.

He hoped.

He sat down at his desk again, stared a moment at his memo pad and wrote:

Check history of gravity—acceleration. Believe Aristotle unable detect acceleration. Galileo used same instruments, including same crude water clock, and found it. Why? . . . Any reported transits of Vulcan since 1914, when Einstein explained eccentricity of Mercury orbit by relativity instead of by hypothetical sunward planet? . . . How could Oliver Lodge detect an ether-drift and Michelson not? Conceivable that Lorentz contraction not a physical fact before Michelson experiment? . . . How many chemical elements were predicted before discovered?

He tapped absently on the pad a few times, then rang for a research assistant. He'd barely have time to explain what he wanted before he had to meet his class under Luce.

And he still wasn't sure where the rats fitted in.

Curtly Professor Luce brought his address to a close.

"Well, gentlemen," he said, "I guess we'll have to continue this at our next lecture. We seem to have run over a little; class dismissed. Oh, Mr. Prentiss!"

The investigator looked up in genuine surprise. "Yes, sir?" The thin gun in his shoulder holster suddenly felt satisfyingly fat.

He realized that the crucial moment was near, that he would know before he left the campus whether this strange man was a harmless physicist, devoted to his life-work and his queer hobby, or whether he was an incarnate danger to mankind. The professor was acting out of turn, and it was an unexpected break.

"Mr. Prentiss," continued Luce from the lecture platform, "may I see you in my office a moment before you leave?"

Prentiss said, "Certainly." As the group broke up he followed the gaunt scientist through the door that led to Luce's little office behind the lecture room.

At the doorway he hesitated almost imperceptibly; Luce saw it and bowed sardonically. "After you, sir!"

Then the tall man indicated a chair near his desk. "Sit down, Mr. Prentiss."

For a long moment the seated men studied each other.

Finally the professor spoke. "About fifteen years ago a brilliant young man named Rogers wrote a doctoral dissertation at the University of Vienna on what he called . . . 'Involuntary Conformation of Incoming Sensoria to Apperception Mass.'"

Prentiss began fishing for his pipe. "Indeed?"

"One copy of the dissertation was sent to the Scholarship Society that was financing his studies. All others were seized by the International Bureau of the Censor, and accordingly a demand was made on the Scholarship Society for its copy. But it couldn't be found."

Prentiss was concentrating on lighting his pipe. He wondered if the faint trembling of the match flame was visible.

The professor turned to his desk, opened the top drawer, and pulled out a slim brochure bound in black leather.

The investigator coughed out a cloud of smoke.

The professor did not seem to notice, but opened the front cover and began reading: " '—a dissertation in partial fulfillment of the requirements for the degree of Doctor of Philosophy at the University of Vienna. A. P. Rogers, Vienna, 1957.' " The man closed the book and studied it thoughtfully. "Adrian Prentiss Rogers—the owner of a brain whose like is seen not once in a century. He exposed the gods—then vanished."

Prentiss suppressed a shiver as he met those sunken, implacable eye-caverns.

The cat-and-mouse was over. In a way, he was relieved.

"Why did you vanish then, Mr. Prentiss-Rogers?" demanded Luce. "And why do you now reappear?"

The investigator blew a cloud of smoke toward the low ceiling. "To prevent people like you from introducing sensoria that *can't* be conformed to our present apperception mass. To keep reality as is. That answers both questions, I think."

The other man smiled. It was not a good thing to see. "Have you succeeded?"

"I don't know. So far, I suppose."

The gaunt man shrugged his shoulders. "You ignore tomorrow, then. I think you have failed, but I can't be sure, of course, until I actually perform the experiment that will create novel sensoria." He leaned forward. "I'll come to the point, Mr. Prentiss-Rogers. Next to yourself—and possibly excepting the Censor—I know more about the mathematical approach to reality than anyone else in the world. I may even know things about it that you don't. On other phases of it I'm weak—because I developed your results on the basis of mere logic rather than insight. And logic, we know, is applicable only within indeterminate limits. But in developing a practical device—an actual machine—for the wholesale alteration of incoming sensoria, I'm enormously ahead of you. You saw my apparatus last night, Mr. Prentiss-Rogers? Oh, come, don't be coy."

Prentiss drew deeply on his pipe.

"I saw it."

"Did you understand it?"

"No. It wasn't all there. At least, the apparatus on the table was incomplete. There's more to it than a Nicol prism and a goniometer."

"Ah, you are clever! Yes, I was wise in not permitting you to remain very long—no longer than necessary to whet your curiosity. Look, then! I offer you a partnership. Check my data and apparatus; in return you may be present when I run the experiment. We will attain enlightenment together. We will know all things. We will be gods!"

"And what about two billion other human beings?" said Prentiss, pressing softly at his shoulder holster.

The professor smiled faintly. "Their lunacy—assuming they continue to exist at all—may become slightly more pronounced, of course. But why worry about them?

"Don't expect me to believe this aura of altruism, Mr. Prentiss-Rogers. I think you're afraid to face what lies behind our so-called 'reality.'"

"At least I'm a coward in a good cause." He stood up. "Have you any more to say?"

He knew that he was just going through the motions. Luce must have realized he had lain himself open to arrest half a dozen times in as many minutes: The bare possession of the missing copy of the dissertation, the frank admission of plans to experiment with reality, and his attempted bribery of a high Censor official. And yet, the man's very bearing denied the possibility of being cut off in mid-career.

Luce's cheeks fluffed out in a brief sigh. "I'm sorry you can't be intelligent about this, Mr. Prentiss-Rogers. Yet, the time will come, you know, when you must make up your mind to go—*through*, shall we say? In fact, we may have to depend to a considerable degree on one another's companionship—*out there*. Even gods have to pass the time of day occasionally, and I have a suspicion that you and I are going to be quite chummy. So let us not part in enmity."

Prentiss' hand slid beneath his coat lapel and drew out the snub-nosed automatic. He had a grim foreboding that it was futile, and that the professor was laughing silently at him, but he had no choice.

"You are under arrest," he said unemotionally. "Come with me."

The other shrugged his shoulders, then something like a laugh, soundless in its mockery, surged up in his throat. "Certainly, Mr. Prentiss-Rogers."

He arose.

The room was plunged into instant blackness.

Prentiss fired three times, lighting up the gaunt chuckling form at each flash.

"Save your fire, Mr. Prentiss-Rogers. Lead doesn't get far in an intense diamagnetic screen. Study the magnetic damper on a lab balance the next time you're in the Censor Building!"

Somewhere a door slammed.

Several hours later Prentiss was eyeing his aide with ill-concealed distaste. Prentiss knew Crush had been summoned by E to confer on the implications of Luce's escape, and that Crush was secretly sympathizing with him. Prentiss couldn't endure sympathy. He'd prefer that the asthmatic little man tell him how stupid he'd been.

"What do you want?" he growled.

"Sir," gasped Crush apologetically, "I have a report on that gadget you scanned in Luce's lab."

Prentiss was instantly mollified, but suppressed any show of interest. "What about it?"

"In essence, sir," wheezed Crush, "it's just a Nicol prism mounted on a goniometer. According to a routine check it was ground by an obscure optician who was nine years on the job, and he spent nearly all of that time on just one face of the prism. What do you make of that, sir?"

"Nothing, yet. What took him so long?"

"Grinding an absolutely flat edge, sir, so he says."

"Odd. That would mean a boundary composed exclusively of molecules of the same crystal layer, something that hasn't been attempted since the Palomar reflector."

"Yes, sir. And then there's the goniometer mount with just one number on the dial—forty-five degrees."

"Obviously," said Prentiss, "the Nicol is to be used only at a forty-five degree angle to the incoming light. Hence it's probably extremely important—why, I don't know—that the angle be *precisely* forty-five degrees. That would require a perfectly flat surface, too, of course. I suppose you're going to tell me that the goniometric gearing is set up very accurately."

Suddenly Prentiss realized that Crush was looking at him in mingled suspicion and admiration.

"Well?" demanded the ontologist irritably. "Just what is the adjusting mechanism? Surely not geometrical? Too crude. Optical, perhaps?"

Crush gasped into his handkerchief. "Yes, sir. The prism is rotated very slowly into a tiny beam of light. Part of the beam is reflected and part refracted. At exactly forty-five degrees it seems, by Jordan's law, that exactly half is reflected and half refracted. The two beams are picked up in a photocell relay that stops the rotating mechanism as soon as the luminosities of the beams are exactly equal."

Prentiss tugged nervously at his ear. It was puzzling. Just what was Luce going to do with such an exquisitely-ground Nicol? At this moment he would have given ten years of his life for an inkling to the supplementary apparatus that went along with the Nicol. It would be something optical, certainly, tied in somehow with neurotic rats. What was it Luce had said the other night in the lab? Something about slowing down a photon. And then what was supposed to happen to the universe? Something like taking a tiny bite out of a balloon, Luce had said.

And how did it all interlock with certain impossible, though syllogistically necessary conclusions that flowed from his recent research into the history of human knowledge?

He wasn't sure. But he *was* sure that Luce was on the verge of using this mysterious apparatus to change the perceptible universe, on a scale so vast that humanity was going to get lost in the shuffle. He'd have to convince E of that.

If he couldn't, he'd seek out Luce himself and kill him with his bare hands, and decide on reasons for it afterward.

He was guiding himself for the time being by pure insight, but he'd better be organized when he confronted E.

Crush was speaking. "Shall we go, sir? Your secretary says the jet is waiting."

The painting showed a man in a red hat and black robes seated behind a high judge's bench. Five other men in red hats were seated behind a lower bench to his right, and four others to his left. At the base of the bench knelt a figure in solitary abjection.

"We condemn you, Galileo Galilei, to the formal prison of this Holy Officer for a period determinable at Our pleasure; and by way of salutary penance, We order you, during the next three years, to recite once a week the seven Penitential Psalms."

Prentiss turned from the inscription to the less readable face of E. The oval olive-hued face was smooth, unlined, even around the eyes, and the black hair was parted off-center and drawn over the woman's head into a bun at the nape of her neck. She wore no make-up, and apparently needed none. She was clad in a black, loose-fitting business suit, which accentuated her perfectly molded body.

"Do you know," said Prentiss coolly, "I think you like being Censor. It's in your blood."

"You're perfectly right. I *do* like being Censor. According to Speer, I effectively sublimate a guilt complex as strange as it is baseless."

"Very interesting. Sort of expiation of an ancestral guilt complex, eh?"

"What do you mean?"

"Woman started man on his acquisition of knowledge and self-destruction, and ever since has tried futilely to halt the avalanche. In you the feeling of responsibility and guilt runs exceptionally strong, and I'll wager that some nights you wake up in a cold sweat, thinking you've just plucked a certain forbidden fruit."

E stared icily up at the investigator's twitching mouth. "The only pertinent question," she said crisply, "is whether Luce is engaged in ontologic experiments, and if so, are they of a dangerous nature."

Prentiss sighed. "He's in it up to his neck. But just *what,* and how dangerous, I can only guess."

"Then guess."

"Luce thinks he's developed apparatus for the practical, predictable alteration of sensoria. He hopes to do something with his device that will blow physical laws straight to smithereens. The resulting reality would probably be unrecognizable even to a professional ontologist, let alone the mass of humanity."

"You seem convinced he can do this."

"The probabilities are high."

"Good enough. We can deal only in probabilities. The safest thing, of course, would be to locate Luce and kill him on sight. On the other hand, the faintest breath of scandal would result in Congressional hamstringing of the Bureau, so we must proceed cautiously."

"If Luce is really able to do what he claims," said Prentiss grimly, "and we let him do it, there won't be any Bureau at all—nor any Congress either."

"I know. Rest assured that if I decide that Luce is dangerous and should die, I shall let neither the lives nor careers of anyone in the Bureau stand in the way, including myself."

Prentiss nodded, wondering if she really meant it.

The woman continued. "We are faced for the first time with a probable violation of our directive forbidding ontologic experiments. We are inclined to prevent this threatened violation by taking a man's life. I think we should settle once and for all whether such harsh measures are indicated, and it is for this that I have invited you to attend a staff conference. We intend to reopen the entire question of ontologic experiments and their implications."

Prentiss groaned inwardly. In matters so important the staff decided by vote. He had a brief vision of attempting to convince E's hard-headed scientists that mankind was changing "reality" from century to century—that not too long ago the earth had been "flat." Yes, by now he was beginning to believe it himself!

"Come this way, please," said E.

Sitting at E's right was an elderly man, Speer, the famous psychologist. On her left was Goring, staff adviser on nucleonics; next to him was Burchard, brilliant chemist and Director of the Western Field, then Prentiss, and then Dobbs, the renowned metallurgist and Director of the Central Field.

Prentiss didn't like Dobbs, who had voted against his promotion to the directorship of Eastern.

E announced: "We may as well start this inquiry with an examination of fundamentals. Mr. Prentiss, just what is reality?"

The ontologist winced. He had needed two hundred pages to outline the theory of reality in his doctoral thesis, and even so, had always suspected his examiners had passed it only because it was incomprehensible—hence a work of genius.

"Well," he began wryly, "I must confess that I don't know what *real* reality is. What most of us call reality is simply an integrated synthesis of incoming sensoria. As such it is nothing more than a working hypothesis in the mind of each of us, forever in a process of revision. In the past that process has been slow and safe. But we have now to consider the consequences of an instantaneous and total revision—a revision so far-reaching that it may thrust humanity face-to-face with the true reality, the world of Things-in-Themselves—Kant's *noumena*. This, I think, would be as disastrous as dumping a group of children in the middle of a forest. They'd have to relearn the simplest things—what to eat, how to protect themselves from elemental forces, and even a new language to deal with their new problems. There'd be few survivors.

"That is what we want to avoid, and we can do it if we prevent any sudden sweeping alteration of sensoria in our present reality."

He looked dubiously at the faces about him. It was a poor start. Speer's wrinkled features were drawn up in a serene smile, and the psychologist seemed to be contemplating the air over Prentiss' head. Goring was regarding him with grave, expressionless eyes. E nodded slightly as Prentiss' gaze traveled past her to a puzzled Burchard, thence to Dobbs, who was frankly contemptuous.

Speer and Goring were going to be the most susceptible. Speer because of his lack of a firm scientific background, Goring because nucleonics was in such a state of flux that nuclear experts were expressing the gravest doubts as to the validity of the laws worshipped by Burchard and Dobbs. Burchard was only a faint possibility. And Dobbs?

Dobbs said: "I don't know what the dickens you're talking about." The implication was plain that he wanted to add: "And I don't think you do, either."

And Prentiss wasn't so sure that he did know. Ontology was an elusive thing at best.

"I object to the term 'real reality,'" continued Dobbs. "A thing is real or it isn't. No fancy philosophical system can change *that*. And if it's real, it gives off predictable, reproducible sensory stimuli not subject to alteration except in the minds of lunatics."

Prentiss breathed more easily. His course was clear. He'd concentrate on Dobbs, with a little side-play on Burchard. Speer and Goring would never suspect his arguments were really directed at them. He pulled a gold coin from his vest pocket and slid it across the table to Dobbs, being careful not to let it clatter. "You're a metallurgist. Please tell us what this is."

Dobbs picked up the coin and examined it suspiciously. "It's quite obviously a five-dollar gold piece, minted at Fort Worth in nineteen sixty-two. I can even give you the analysis, if you want it."

"I doubt that you could," said Prentiss coolly. "For you see, you are holding a counterfeit coin minted only last week in my own laboratories especially for this conference. As a matter of fact, if you'll forgive my saying so, I had you in mind when I ordered the coin struck. It contains no gold whatever—drop it on the table."

The coin fell from the fingers of the astounded metallurgist and clattered on the oaken table top.

"Hear the false ring?" demanded Prentiss.

Pink-faced, Dobbs cleared his throat and peered at the coin more closely. "How was I to know that? It's no disgrace, is it? Many clever counterfeits can be detected only in the laboratory. I knew the color was a little on the red side, but that could have been due to the lighting of the room. And of course, I hadn't given it an auditory test before I spoke. The ring is definitely dull. It's obviously a copper-lead alloy, with possibly a little amount of silver to help the ring. All right, I jumped to conclusions. So what? What does that prove?"

"It proves that you have arrived at two separate, distinct, and mutually exclusive realities, starting with the same sensory premises. It proves how easily reality is revised. And that isn't all, as I shall soon—"

"All right," said Dobbs testily. "But on second thought I admitted it was false, didn't I?"

"Which demonstrates a further weakness in our routine acquisition and evaluation of predigested information. When an unimpeachable authority tells us something as a fact, we immediately, and without conscious thought, *modify* our incoming stimuli to conform with that *fact*. The coin suddenly acquires the red taint of copper, and rings false to the ear."

"I would have caught the queer ring anyhow," said Dobbs stubbornly, "with no help from 'an unimpeachable authority.' The ring would have sounded the same, no matter what you said."

From the corner of his eye Prentiss noticed that Speer was grinning broadly. Had the old psychologist divined his trick? He'd take a chance.

"Dr. Speer," he said, "I think you have something interesting to tell our doubting friend."

Speer cackled dryly. "You've been a perfect guinea pig, Dobbsie. The coin was genuine."

The metallurgist's jaw dropped as he looked blankly from one face to another. Then his jowls slowly grew red. He flung the coin to the table. "Maybe I am a guinea pig. I'm a realist, too. I think this is a piece of metal. You might fool me as to its color or assay, but in essence and substance, it's a piece of metal." He glared at Prentiss and Speer in turn. "Does anyone deny that?"

"Certainly not," said Prentiss. "Our mental pigeonholes are identical in that respect; they accept the same sensory definition of 'piece of metal,' or 'coin.' Whatever this object is, it emits stimuli that our minds are capable of registering and abstracting as a 'coin.' But note: we make a coin out of it. However, if I could shuffle my cortical pigeonholes, I might find it to be a chair, or a steamer trunk, possibly with Dr. Dobbs inside, or, if the shuffling were extreme, there might be no semantic pattern into which the incoming stimuli could be routed. There wouldn't be anything there at all!"

"Sure," sneered Dobbs. "You could walk right through it."

"Why not?" asked Prentiss gravely. "I think we may do it all the time. Matter is about the emptiest stuff imaginable. If you compressed that coin to eliminate the space between its component atoms and electrons, you couldn't see it in a microscope."

Dobbs stared at the enigmatic goldpiece as though it might suddenly thrust out a pseudopod and swallow him up. Then he said flatly: "No. I don't believe it. It exists as a coin, and only as a coin—whether I know it or not."

"Well," ventured Prentiss, "how about you, Dr. Goring? Is the coin real to you?"

The nucleist smiled and shrugged his shoulders. "If I don't think too much about it, it's real enough. And yet . . ."

Dobb's face clouded. "And yet what? Here it is. Can you doubt the evidence of your own eyes?"

"That's just the difficulty." Goring leaned forward. "My eyes tell me, here's a coin. Theory tells me, here's a mass of hypothetical disturbances in a hypothetical subether in a hypothetical ether. The indeterminacy principle tells me that I can never know both the mass and position of these hypothetical disturbances. And as a physicist I know that the bare fact of observing something is sufficient to change that something from its preobserved state. Nevertheless, I compromise by letting my senses and practical experience stick a tag on this particular bit of the unknowable. X, after its impact on my mind (whatever *that* is!) equals coin. A single equation with two variables has no solution. The best I can say is, it's a coin, but probably not really—"

"Hah!" declared Burchard. "I can demonstrate the fallacy of *that* position very quickly. If our minds make this a coin, then our minds make this little object an ash-tray, that a window, the thing that holds us up, a chair. You might say we make the air we breathe, and perhaps even the stars and planets. Why, following Prentiss' idea to its logical end, the universe itself is the work of man—a conclusion I'm sure he doesn't intend."

"Oh, but I do," said Prentiss.

Prentiss took a deep breath. The issue could be dodged no longer. He had to take a stand. "And to make sure you understand me, whether you agree with me or not, I'll state categorically that I believe the apparent universe to be the work of man."

Even E looked startled, but said nothing.

The ontologist continued rapidly. "All of you doubt my sanity. A week ago I would have, too. But since then I've done a great deal of research in the history of science. And I repeat, *the universe is the work of man*. I believe that man began his existence in some incredibly simple world—the original and true *noumenon* of our present universe. And that over the centuries man expanded his little world into its present vastness and incomprehensible intricacy solely by dint of imagination.

"Consequently, I believe that what most of you call the 'real' world has been changing ever since our ancestors began to think."

Dobbs smiled superciliously. "Oh, come now, Prentiss. That's just a rhetorical description of scientific progress over the past centuries. In the same sense I might say that modern transportation and communications have shrunk the earth. But you'll certainly admit that the physical state of things has been substantially constant ever since the galaxies formed and the earth began to cool, and that the simple cosmologies of early man were simply the result of lack of means for obtaining accurate information?"

"I *won't* admit it," rejoined Prentiss bluntly. "I maintain that their information was substantially accurate. I maintain that at one time in our history the earth was flat—as flat as it is now round, and no one living before the time of Hecataeus, though he might have been equipped with the finest modern instruments, could have proved otherwise. His mind was *conditioned* to a two-dimensional world. Any of us present, if we were transplanted to the world of Hecataeus, could, of course, establish terrestrial sphericity in short order. Our minds have been conditioned to a three-dimensional world. The day may come a few millennia hence when a four-dimensional Terra will be commonplace even to schoolchildren; they will have been intuitively conditioned in relativistic concepts." He added slyly: "And the less intelligent of them may attempt to blame our naive three-dimensional planet on our grossly inaccurate instruments, because it will be as plain as day to them that their planet has four dimensions!"

Dobbs snorted at this amazing idea. The other scientists stared at Prentiss with an awe which was mixed with incredulity.

Goring said cautiously: "I follow up to a certain point. I can see that a primitive society might start out with a limited number of facts. They would offer theories to harmonize and integrate those facts, and then those first theories would require that new, additional facts exist, and in their search for those secondary facts, extraneous data would turn up inconsistent with the first theories. Secondary theories would then be required, from which hitherto unguessed facts should follow, the confirmation of which would discover more inconsistencies. So the pattern of fact to theory to fact to theory, and so on, finally brings us into our present state of knowledge. Does that follow from your argument?"

Prentiss nodded.

"But won't you admit that the facts were there all the time, and merely awaited discovery?"

"The simple, unelaborated *noumenon* was there all the time, yes. But the new fact—man's new interpretation of the *noumenon*, was generally pure invention—a mental creation, if you like. This will be clearer if you consider how rarely a new fact arises before a theory exists for its explanation. In the ordinary scientific investigation, theory comes first, followed in short order by the 'discovery' of various facts deducible from it."

Goring still looked skeptical. "But that wouldn't mean the fact wasn't there all the time."

"Wouldn't it? Look at the evidence. Has it never struck you as odd in how many instances very obvious facts were 'overlooked' until a theory was propounded that required their existence? Take your nuclear building blocks. Protons and electrons were detected physically only after Rutherford had showed they had to exist. And then when Rutherford found that protons and electrons were not enough to build all the atoms of the periodic table, he postulated the neutron, which of course was duly 'discovered' in the Wilson cloud chamber."

Goring pursed his lips. "But the Wilson cloud chamber would have shown all that prior to the theory, if anyone had only thought to use it.

"The mere fact that Wilson didn't invent his cloud chamber until nineteen-twelve and Geiger didn't invent his counter until nineteen-thirteen, would not keep subatomic particles from existing before that time."

"You don't get the point," said Prentiss. "The primitive, ungeneralized noumenon that we today observe as subatomic particles existed prior to nineteen-twelve, true, *but not subatomic particles.*"

"Well, I don't know. . . ." Goring scratched his chin. "How about fundamental forces? Surely electricity existed before Galvani? Even the Greeks knew how to build up electrostatic changes on amber."

"Greek electricity was nothing more than electrostatic changes. Nothing more could be created until Galvani introduced the concept of the electric current."

"Do you mean the electric current didn't exist at all before Galvani?" demanded Burchard. "Not even when lightning struck a conductor?"

"Not even then. We don't know much about pre-Galvanic lightning. While it probably packed a wallop, its destructive potential couldn't have been due to its delivery of an electric current. The Chinese flew kites for centuries before Franklin theorized that lightning was the same as galvanic electricity, but there's no recorded shock from a kite string until our learned statesman drew forth one in seventeen-sixty-five. *Now*, only an idiot flies a kite in a storm. It's all according to pattern: theory first, then we alter 'reality' to fit."

Burchard persisted. "Then I suppose you'd say all the elements are figments of our imagination."

"Correct," agreed Prentiss. "I believe that in the beginning there were only four *noumenal* elements. Man simply elaborated these according to the needs of his growing science. Man made them what they are today—and on occasion, *unmade* them. You remember the havoc Mendelyeev created with his periodic law. He declared that the elements had to follow valence sequences of increasing atomic weight, and when they didn't, he insisted his law was right and that the atomic weights were wrong. He must have had Stas and Berzelius whirling in their graves, because they had worked out the 'erroneous' atomic weights with marvelous precision. The odd thing was, when the weights were rechecked, they fitted the Mendelyeev table. But that wasn't all. The old rascal pointed out vacant spots in his table and maintained that there were more elements yet to be discovered. He even predicted what properties they'd have. He was too modest. I state that Nilson, Winkler, and De Boisbaudran merely *discovered* scandium, germanium, and gallium; Mendelyeev *created* them, out of the original quadrelemental stuff."

E leaned forward. "That's a bit strong. Tell me, if man has changed the elements and the cosmos to suit his convenience, what was the cosmos like before man came on the scene?"

"There wasn't any," answered Prentiss. "Remember, by definition, 'cosmos' or 'reality' is simply man's version of the ultimate *noumenal* universe. The 'cosmos' arrives and departs with the mind of man. Consequently, the earth—as such—didn't even exist before the advent of man."

"But the evidence of the rocks . . ." protested E. "Pressures applied over millions, even billions of years, were needed to form them, unless you postulate an omnipotent God who called them into existence as of yesterday."

"I postulate only the omnipotent human mind," said Prentiss. "In the seventeenth century, Hooke, Ray, Woodward, to name a few, studied chalk, gravel, marble, and even coal, without finding anything inconsistent with results to be expected from the Noachian Flood. But now that we've made up our minds that the earth is older, the rocks *seem* older, too."

"But how about evolution?" demanded Burchard. "Surely that wasn't a matter of a few centuries?"

"Really?" replied Prentiss. "Again, why assume that the facts are any more recent than the theory? The evidence is all the other way. Aristotle was a magnificent experimental biologist, and he was convinced that life could be created spontaneously. Before the time of Darwin there was no need for the various species to evolve, because they sprang into being from inanimate matter. As late as the eighteenth century, Needham, using a microscope, reported that he saw microbe life arise spontaneously out of sterile culture media. These abiogeneticists were, of course, discredited and their work found to be irreproducible, but only *after* it became evident that the then abiogenetic facts were going to run inconsistent with later 'facts' flowing from advancing biologic theory."

"Then," said Goring, "assuming purely for the sake of argument, that man has altered the original *noumena* into our present reality, just what danger do you think Luce represents to that reality? How could he do anything about it, even if he wanted to? Just what is he up to?"

"Broadly stated," said Prentiss, "Luce intends to destroy the Einsteinian universe."

Burchard frowned and shook his head. "Not so fast. In the first place, how can anyone presume to destroy this planet, much less the whole universe? And why do you say the 'Einsteinian' universe? The universe by any other name is still the universe, isn't it?"

"What Dr. Prentiss means," explained E, "is that Luce wants to revise completely and finally our present comprehension of the universe, which presently happens to be the Einsteinian version, in the expectation that the final version would be the true one—and comprehensible only to Luce and perhaps a few other ontologic experts."

"I don't see it," said Dobbs irritably. "Apparently this Luce contemplates nothing more than publication of a new scientific theory. How can that be bad? A mere theory can't hurt anybody—especially if only two or three people understand it."

"You—and two billion others," said Prentiss softly, "think that 'reality' cannot be affected by any theory that seems to change it—that it is optional with you to accept or reject the theory. In the past that was true. If the Ptolemaics wanted a geocentric universe, they ignored Copernicus. If the four-dimensional continuum of Einstein and Minkowsky seemed incomprehensible to the Newtonian school they dismissed it, and the planets continued to revolve substantially as Newton predicted. But this is different.

"For the first time we are faced with the probability that the promulgation of a theory is going to *force* an ungraspable reality upon our minds. It will not be optional."

"Well," said Burchard, "if by 'promulgation of a theory' you mean something like the application of the quantum theory and relativity to the production of atomic energy, which of course has changed the shape of civilization in the past generation, whether the individual liked it or not, then I can understand you. But if you mean that Luce is going to make one little experiment that may confirm some new theory or other, and *ipso facto* and instantaneously reality is going to turn topsy turvy, why I say it's nonsense."

"Would anyone," said Prentiss quietly, "care to guess what would happen if Luce were able to destroy a photon?"

Goring laughed shortly. "The question doesn't make sense. The mass-energy entity whose three-dimensional profile we call a photon is indestructible."

"But if you *could* destroy it?" insisted Prentiss. "What would the universe be like afterward?"

"What difference would it make?" demanded Dobbs. "One photon more or less?"

"Plenty," said Goring. "According to the Einstein theory, every particle of matter—energy has a gravitational potential, lambda, and it can be calculated that the total lambdas are precisely sufficient to keep our four-dimensional continuum from closing back on itself. Take one lambda away—God! The universe would split wide open!"

"Exactly," said Prentiss. "Instead of a continuum, our 'reality' would become a disconnected melange of three-dimensional objects. Time, if it existed, wouldn't bear any relation to spatial things. Only an ontologic expert might be able to synthesize any sense out of such a 'reality.'"

"Well," said Dobbs, "I wouldn't worry too much. I don't think anybody's ever going to destroy a photon." He snickered. "You have to catch one first!"

"Luce can catch one," said Prentiss calmly. "And he can destroy it. At this moment some unimaginable post-Einsteinian universe lies in the palm of his hand. Final, true reality, perhaps. But we aren't ready for it. Kant, perhaps, or *Homo superior*, but not the general run of *H. sapiens*. We wouldn't be able to escape our conditioning. We'd be stopped cold."

He stopped. Without looking at Goring, he knew he had convinced the man. Prentiss sagged with visible relief. It was time for a vote. He must strike before Speer and Goring could change their minds.

"Madame"—he shot a questioning glance at the woman—"at any moment my men are going to report that they've located Luce. I must be ready to issue the order for his execution, if in fact the staff believes such disposition proper. I call for a vote of officers!"

"Granted," said E instantly. "Will those in favor of destroying Luce on sight raise their right hands?"

Prentiss and Goring made the required signal.

Speer was silent.

Prentiss felt his heart sinking. Had he made a gross error of judgment?

"I vote against this murder," declared Dobbs. "That's what it is, pure murder."

"I agree with Dobbs," said Burchard shortly.

All eyes were on the psychologist. "I presume you'll join us, Dr. Speer?" demanded Dobbs sternly.

"Count me out, gentlemen. I'd never interfere with anything so inevitable as the destiny of man. All of you are overlooking a fundamental facet of human nature—man's insatiable hunger for change, novelty—for anything different from what he already has. Prentiss himself states that whenever man grows discontented with his present reality, he starts elaborating it, and the devil take the hindmost. Luce but symbolizes the evil genius of our race—and I mean both our species and the race toward intertwined godhood and destruction. Once born, however, symbols are immortal. It's far too late now to start killing Luces. It was too late when the first man tasted the first apple.

"Furthermore, I think Prentiss greatly overestimates the scope of Luce's pending victory over the rest of mankind. Suppose Luce is actually successful in clearing space and time and suspending the world in the temporal stasis of its present irreality. Suppose he and a few ontologic experts pass on into the ultimate, true reality. How long do you think they can resist the temptation to alter it? If Prentiss is right, eventually they or their descendants will be living in a cosmos as intricate and unpleasant as the one they left, while we, for all practical purposes, will be pleasantly dead.

"No, gentlemen, I won't vote either way."

"Then it is my privilege to break the tie," said E coolly. "I vote for death. Save your remonstrances, Dr. Dobbs. It's after midnight. This meeting is adjourned." She stood up in abrupt dismissal, and the men were soon filing from the room.

E left the table and walked toward the windows on the far side of the room. Prentiss hesitated a moment, but made no effort to leave.

E called over her shoulder, "You, too, Prentiss."

The door closed behind Speer, the last of the group, save Prentiss.

Prentiss walked up behind E.

She gave no sign of awareness.

Six feet away, the man stopped and studied her.

Sitting, walking, standing, she was lovely. Mentally he compared her to Velasquez' Venus. There was the same slender exquisite proportion of thigh, hip, and bust. And he knew she was completely aware of her own beauty, and further, must be aware of his present appreciative scrutiny.

Then her shoulders sagged suddenly, and her voice seemed very tired when she spoke. "So you're still here, Prentiss. Do you believe in intuition?"

"Not often."

"Speer was right. He's always right. Luce will succeed." She dropped her arms to her sides and turned.

"Then may I reiterate, my dear, marry me and let's forget the control of knowledge for a few months."

"Completely out of the question, Prentiss. Our natures are incompatible. You're incorrigibly curious, and I'm incorrigibly, even neurotically, conservative. Besides, how can you even think about such things when we've got to stop Luce?"

His reply was interrupted by the shrilling of the intercom: "Calling Mr. Prentiss. Crush calling Mr. Prentiss. Luce located. Crush calling."

With his pencil Crush pointed to a shaded area of the map. "This is Luce's Snake-Eyes estate, the famous game preserve and zoo. Somewhere in the center—about here, I think—is a stone cottage. A moving van unloaded some lab equipment there this morning."

"Mr. Prentiss," said E, "how long do you think it will take him to install what he needs for that one experiment?"

The ontologist answered from across the map table. "I can't be sure. I still have no idea of what he's going to try, except that I'm reasonably certain it must be done in absolute darkness. Checking his instruments will require but a few minutes at most."

The woman began pacing the floor nervously. "I knew it. We can't stop him. We have no time."

"Oh, I don't know," said Prentiss. "How about that stone cottage, Crush? Is it pretty old?"

"Dates from the eighteenth century, sir."

"There's your answer," said Prentiss. "It's probably full of holes where the mortar's fallen out. For total darkness he'll have to wait until moonset."

"That's three thirty-four A.M., sir," said Crush.

"We've time for an arrest," said E.

Crush looked dubious. "It's more complicated than that, Madame.

Snake-Eyes is fortified to withstand a small army. Luce could hold off any force the Bureau could muster for at least twenty-four hours."

"One atom egg, well done," suggested Prentiss.

"That's the best answer, of course," agreed E. "But you know as well as I what the reaction of Congress would be to such extreme measures. There would be an investigation. The Bureau would be abolished, and all persons responsible for such an action would face life imprisonment, perhaps death." She was silent for a moment, then sighed and said: "So be it. If there is no alternative, I shall order the bomb dropped."

"There may be another way," said Prentiss.

"Indeed?"

"Granted an army couldn't get through. One man might. And if he made it, you could call off your bomb."

E exhaled a slow cloud of smoke and studied the glowing tip of her cigarette. Finally she turned and looked into the eyes of the ontologist for the first time since the beginning of the conference. *"You* can't go."

"Who, then?"

Her eyes dropped. "You're right, of course. But the bomb still falls if you don't get through. It's got to be that way. Do you understand that?"

Prentiss laughed. "I understand."

He addressed his aide. "Crush, I'll leave the details up to you, bomb and all. We'll rendezvous at these coordinates"—he pointed to the map—"at three sharp. It's after one now. You'd better get started."

"Yes, sir," wheezed Crush, and scurried out of the room.

As the door closed, Prentiss turned to E. "Beginning tomorrow afternoon—or rather, *this* afternoon, after I finish with Luce, I want six months off."

"Granted," murmured E.

"I want you to come with me. I want to find out just what this thing is between us. Just the two of us. It may take a little time."

E smiled crookedly. "If we're both still alive at three thirty-five, and such a thing as a month exists, and you still want me to spend six of them with you, I'll do it. And in return you can do something for me."

"What?"

"You, even above Luce, stand the best chance of adjusting to final reality if Luce is successful in destroying a photon. I'm a border-line case. I'm going to need all the help you can give me, if and when the time comes. Will you remember that?"

"I'll remember," Prentiss said.

At 3 A.M. he joined Crush.

"There are at least seven infra-red scanners in the grounds, sir," said Crush, "not to mention an intricate network of photo relays. And then the wire fence around the lab, with the big cats inside. He must have turned the whole zoo loose." The little man reluctantly helped Prentiss into his infra-red absorbing coveralls. "You weren't meant for tiger fodder, sir. Better call it off."

Prentiss zipped up his visor and grimaced out into the moonlit dimness of the apple orchard. "You'll take care of the photocell network?"

"Certainly, sir. He's using u.v.-sensitive cells. We'll blanket the area with the u.v.-spot at three-ten."

Prentiss strained his ears, but couldn't hear the 'copter that would carry the u.v.-searchlight—and the bomb.

"It'll be here, sir," Crush assured him. "It won't make any noise, anyhow. What you ought to be worrying about are those wild beasts."

The investigator sniffed at the night air. "Darn little breeze."

"Yeah," gasped Crush. "And variable at that, sir. You can't count on going in up-wind. You want us to create a diversion at one end of the grounds to attract the animals?"

"We don't dare. If necessary, I'll open the aerosol capsule of formaldehyde." He held out his hand. "Good-by, Crush."

His asthmatic assistant shook the extended hand with vigorous sincerity. "Good luck, sir. And don't forget the bomb. We'll have to drop it at three thirty-four sharp."

But Prentiss had vanished into the leafy darkness.

A little later he was studying the luminous figures on his watch. The u.v.-blanket was presumably on. All he had to be careful about in the next forty seconds was a direct collision with a photocell post.

But Crush's survey party had mapped well. He reached the barbed fencing uneventfully, with seconds to spare. He listened a moment, and then in practised silence eased his lithe body high up and over.

The breeze, which a moment before had been in his face, now died away, and the night air hung about him in dark lifeless curtains.

From the stone building a scant two hundred yards ahead, a chink of light peeped out.

Prentiss drew his silenced pistol and began moving forward with swift caution, taking care to place his heel to ground before the toe, and feeling out the character of the ground with the thin soles of his sneakers before each step. A snapping twig might hurl a slavering wild beast at his throat.

He stopped motionless in midstride.

From the thicket several yards to his right came an ominous sniffing, followed by a low snarl.

His mouth went suddenly dry as he strained his ears and turned his head slowly toward the sound.

And then there came the reverberations of something heavy, hurtling toward him.

He whipped his weapon around and waited in a tense crouch, not daring to send a wild, singing bullet across the sward.

The great cat was almost upon him before he fired, and then the faint cough of the stumbling, stricken animal seemed louder than his muffled shot.

Breathing hard, Prentiss stepped away from the dying beast, evidently a panther, and listened for a long time before resuming his march on the cottage. Luce's extraordinary measures to exclude intruders but confirmed his suspicions: Tonight was the last night that the professor could be stopped. He blinked the stinging sweat from his eyes and glanced at his watch. It was 3:15.

Apparently the other animals had not heard him. He stood up to resume his advance, and to his utter relief found that the wind had shifted almost directly into his face and was blowing steadily.

In another three minutes he was standing at the massive door of the building, running practised fingers over the great iron hinges and lock. Undoubtedly the thing was going to squeak; there was no time to apply oil and wait for it to soak in. The lock could be easily picked.

And the squeaking of a rusty hinge was probably immaterial. A cunning operator like Luce would undoubtedly have wired an alarm into it. He just couldn't believe Crush's report to the contrary.

But he couldn't stand here.

There was only one way to get inside quickly, and alive.

Chuckling at his own madness, Prentiss began to pound on the door.

He could visualize the blinking out of the slit of light above his head, and knew that, somewhere within the building, two flame-lit eyes were studying him in an infra-red scanner.

Prentiss tried simultaneously to listen to the muffled squeaking of the rats beyond the great door and to the swift, padding approach of something big behind him.

"Luce!" he cried. "It's Prentiss! Let me in!"

A latch slid somewhere; the door eased inward. The investigator threw his gun rearward at a pair of bounding eyes, laced his fingers over his head, and stumbled into more darkness.

Despite the protection of his hands, the terrific blow of the blackjack on his temple almost knocked him out.

He closed his eyes, crumpled carefully to the floor, and noted with satisfaction that his wrists were being tied behind his back. As he had anticipated, it was a clumsy job, even without his imperceptible "assistance." Long fingers ran over his body in a search for more weapons.

Then he felt the sting of a hypodermic needle in his biceps.

The lights came on.

He struggled feebly, emitted a plausible groan, and tried to sit up.

From far above, the strange face of Dr. Luce looked down at him, illuminated, it seemed to Prentiss, by some unhallowed inner fire.

"What time is it?" asked Prentiss.

"Approximately three-twenty."

"*Hm.* Your kittens gave me quite a reception, my dear professor."

"As befits an uncooperative meddler."

"Well, what are you going to do with me?"

"Kill you."

Luce pulled a pistol from his coat pocket.

Prentiss wet his lips. During his ten years with the Bureau, he had never had to deal with anyone quite like Luce. The gaunt man personified megalomania on a scale beyond anything the investigator had previously encountered—or imagined possible.

And, he realized with a shiver, Luce was very probably justified in his prospects (not delusions!) of grandeur.

With growing alarm he watched Luce snap off the safety lock of the pistol.

There were two possible chances of surviving more than a few seconds.

Luce's index finger began to tense around the trigger.

One of those chances was to appeal to Luce's megalomania, treating him as a human being. Tell him, "I know you won't kill me until you've had a chance to gloat over me—to tell me, the inventor of ontologic synthesis, how you found a practical application of it."

No good. Too obvious to one of Luce's intelligence.

The approach must be to a demigod, in humility. Oddly enough his curiosity *was* tinged with respect. Luce *did* have something.

Prentiss licked his lips again and said hurriedly: "I must die, then. But could you show me—is it asking too much to show me, just how you propose to go through?"

The gun lowered a fraction of an inch. Luce eyed the doomed man suspiciously.

"Would you, please?" continued Prentiss. His voice was dry, cracking. "Ever since I discovered that new realities could be synthesized, I've wondered whether *Homo sapiens* was capable of finding a practical device for uncovering the true reality. And all who've worked on it have insisted that only a brain but little below the angels was capable of such an achievement." He coughed apologetically. "It is difficult to believe that a mere mortal has really accomplished what you claim—and yet, there's something about you . . ." His voice trailed off, and he laughed deprecatingly.

Luce bit; he thrust the gun back into his coat pocket. "So you know when you're licked," he said. "Well, I'll let you live a moment longer."

He stepped back and pulled aside a black screen. "Has the inimitable ontologist the wit to understand this?"

Within a few seconds of his introduction to the instrument everything was painfully clear. Prentiss now abandoned any remote hope that either Luce's method or apparatus would prove faulty. Both the vacuum-glassed machinery and the idea behind it were perfect.

Basically, the supplementary unit, which he now saw for the first time, consisted of a sodium-vapor light bulb, blacked out except for one tiny transparent spot. Ahead of the little window was a series of what must be hundreds of black discs mounted on a common axis. Each disc bore a slender radial slot. And though he could not trace all the gearing, Prentiss knew that the discs were geared to permit one and only one fleeting photon of yellow light to emerge at the end of the disc series, where it would pass through a Kerr electro-optic field and be polarized.

That photon would then travel one centimeter to that fabulous Nicol prism, one surface of which had been machined flat to a molecule's thickness. That surface was turned by means of an equally marvelous goniometer to meet the oncoming photon at an angle of exactly 45 degrees. And then would come chaos.

The cool voice of E sounded in his ear receptor. "Prentiss, it's three-thirty. If you understand the apparatus, and find it dangerous, will you so signify? If possible, describe it for the tapes."

"I understand your apparatus perfectly," said Prentiss.

Luce grunted, half irritated, half curious.

Prentiss continued hurriedly. "Shall I tell you how you decided upon this specific apparatus?"

"If you think you can."

"You have undoubtedly seen the sun reflect from the surface of the sea."

Luce nodded.

"But the fish beneath the surface see the sun, too," continued Prentiss. "Some of the photons are reflected and reach you, and some are refracted and reach the fish. But, for a given wave length, the photons are identical. Why should one be absorbed and another reflected?"

"You're on the right track," admitted Luce, "but couldn't you account for their behavior by Jordan's law?"

"Statistically, yes. Individually, no. In nineteen-thirty-four Jordan showed that a beam of polarized light splits up when it hits a Nicol prism. He proved that when the prism forms an angle, alpha, with the plane of polarization of the prism, a fraction of the light equal to $\cos^2$alpha, passes through the prism, and the remainder, $\sin^2$alpha, is reflected. For example, if alpha is 60 degrees, three-fourths of the photons are reflected and one-fourth are refracted. But note that Jordan's law applied only to streams of photons, and you're dealing with a single photon, to which you're presenting an angle of exactly 45°. And how does a single photon make up its mind—or the photonic equivalent of a mind—when the probability of reflecting is exactly equal to the probability of refracting? Of course, if our photon is but one little mote along with billions of others, the whole comprising a light beam, we can visualize orders left for him by a sort of statistical traffic keeper stationed somewhere in the beam. A member of a beam, it may be presumed, has a pretty good idea of how many of his brothers have already reflected, and how many refracted, and hence knows which he must do."

"But suppose our single photon isn't in a beam at all?" said Luce.

"Your apparatus," said Prentiss, "is going to provide just such a photon. And I think it will be a highly confused little photon, just as your experimental rat was, that night not so long ago. I think it was Schroedinger who said that these physical particles were startlingly human in many of their aspects. Yes, your photon will be given a choice of equal probability. Shall he reflect? Shall he refract? The chances are 50 percent for either choice. He will have no reason for selecting one in preference to the other. There will have been no swarm of preceding photons to set up a traffic guide for him. He'll be puzzled; and trying to meet a situation for which he has no proper response, he'll slow down. And when he does, he'll cease to be a photon, which must travel at the speed of light or cease to exist. Like your rat, like many human beings, he solves the unsolvable by disintegrating."

Luce said: "And when it disintegrates, there disappears one of the lambdas that hold together the Einstein space-time continuum. And when *that* goes, what's left can be only final reality untainted by theory or imagination. Do you see any flaw in my plan?"

Tugging with subtle quickness on the cords that bound him, Prentiss knew there was no flaw in the man's reasoning, and that every human being on earth was now living on borrowed time.

He could think of no way to stop him; there remained only the bare threat of the bomb.

He said tersely: "If you don't submit to peaceable arrest within a few seconds, an atom bomb is going to be dropped on this area."

Sweat was getting into his eyes again, and he winked rapidly.

Luce's dark features convulsed, hung limp, then coalesced into a harsh grin. "She'll be too late," he said with a grim good humor. "Her ancestors tried for centuries to thwart mine. But we were successful—always. Tonight I succeed again, and for all time."

Prentiss had one hand free.

In seconds he would be at the man's throat. He worked with quiet fury at the loops around his bound wrist.

Again E's voice in his ear receptor. "I had to do it!" The tones were strangely sad, self-accusing, remorseful.

Had to do *what?*

And his dazed mind was trying to digest the fact that E had just destroyed him.

She was continuing. "The bomb was dropped ten seconds ago." She was almost pleading, and her words were running together. "You were helpless; you couldn't kill him. I had a sudden premonition of what the world would be like—afterward—even for those who go through. Forgive me."

Almost mechanically he resumed his fumbling with the cord.

Luce looked up. "What's that?"

"What?" asked Prentiss dully. "I don't hear anything."

"Of course you do! Listen!"

The wrist came free.

Several things happened.

That faraway shriek in the skies grew into a howling crescendo of destruction.

As one man Prentiss and Luce leaped toward the activator switches. Luce got there first—an infinitesimal fraction of time before the walls were completely disintegrated.

There was a brief, soundless interval of utter blackness.

And then it seemed to Prentiss that a titanic stone wall crashed into his brain, and held him, mute, immobile.

But he was not dead.

For the name of this armored, stunning wall was not the bomb, but Time itself.

He knew in a brief flash of insight, that for sentient, thinking beings, Time had suddenly become a barricade rather than an endless road.

The exploding bomb—the caving cottage walls—were hanging, somewhere, frozen fast in an immutable, eternal stasis.

Luce had separated this fleeting unseen dimension from the creatures and things that had flowed along it. There is no existence without change along a temporal continuum. And now the continuum had been shattered.

Was this, then, the fate of all tangible things—of all humanity?

Were none of them—not even the two or three who understood advanced ontology, to—get through?

There was nothing but a black, eerie silence all around.

His senses were useless.

He even doubted he had any senses.

So far as he could tell he was nothing but an intelligence, floating in space. But he couldn't even be sure of *that.* Intelligence—space—they weren't necessarily the same now as before.

All that he knew for sure was that he doubted. He doubted everything except the fact of doubting.

Shades of Descartes!

To doubt is to think!

Ergo sum!

I exist.

Instantly he was wary. He existed, but not necessarily as Adrian Prentiss Rogers. For the *noumenon* of Adrian Prentiss Rogers might be—whom?

But he was safe. He was going to get through.

Relax, be resilient, he urged his whirling brain. You're on the verge of something marvelous.

It seemed that he could almost hear himself talk, and he was glad. A voiceless final reality would have been unbearable.

He essayed a tentative whisper:

"E!"

From somewhere far away a woman whimpered.

He cried eagerly into the blackness. "Is that you?"

Something unintelligible and strangely frightening answered him.

"Don't try to hold on to yourself," he cried. "Just let yourself go! Remember, you won't be E any more, but the *noumenon,* the essence of E. Unless you change enough to permit your *noumenon* to take over your old identity, you'll have to stay behind."

There was a groan. "But I'm *me!*"

"But you *aren't*—not really," he pleaded quickly. "You're just an aspect of a larger, symbolical *you*—the *noumenon* of E. It's yours for the asking. You have only to hold out your hand to grasp the shape of final reality. And you *must,* or cease to exist!"

A wail: "But what will happen to my body?"

The ontologist almost laughed. "I wouldn't know; but if it changes, I'll be sorrier than you!"

There was a silence.

"E!" he called.

No answer.

"E! Did you get through? *E!*"

The empty echoes skirled between the confines of his narrow blackness.

Had the woman lost even her struggling interstitial existence? Whenever, whatever, or wherever she now was, he could no longer detect.

Somehow, if it had ever come to this, he had counted on her being with him—just the two of them.

In stunned uneasy wonder he considered what his existence was going to be like from now on.

And what about Luce?

Had the demonic professor possessed sufficient mental elasticity to slip through?

And if so, just what was the professorial *noumenon*—the real

Luce—like?

He'd soon know.

The ontologist relaxed again, and began floating through a dreamy patch of light and darkness. A pale glow began gradually to form about his eyes, and shadowy things began to form, dissolve, and reform.

He felt a great rush of gratitude. At least the shape of final reality was to be visible.

And then, at about the spot where Luce had stood, he saw the Eyes—two tiny red flames, transfixing him with unfathomable fury.

The same eyes that had burned into his that night of his first search!

Luce had got through—but wait!

An unholy aura was playing about the sinuous shadow that contained the jeweled flames. Those eyes were brilliant, horrid facets of hate in the head of a huge, coiling serpent-thing! Snake-Eyes!

In mounting awe and fear the ontologist understood that Luce had not got through—as Luce. That the *noumenon*, the essence, of Luce—was nothing human. That Luce, the bearer of light, aspirant to godhood, was not just Luce!

By the faint light he began shrinking away from the coiled horror, and in the act saw that *he,* at least, still had a human body. He knew this, because he was completely nude.

He was still human, and the snake-creature wasn't—and therefore never had been.

Then he noticed that the stone cottage was gone, and that a pink glow was coming from the east.

He crashed into a tree before he had gone a dozen steps.

Yesterday there had been no trees within three hundred yards of the cottage.

But that made sense, for there was no cottage any more, and no yesterday. Crush ought to be waiting somewhere out here—except that Crush hadn't got through, and hence didn't really exist.

He went around the tree. It obscured his view of the snake-creature for a moment, and when he tried to find it again, it was gone.

He was glad for the momentary relief, and began looking about him in the half-light. He took a deep breath.

The animals, if they still existed, had vanished with the coming of dawn. The grassy, flower-dotted swards scintillated like emeralds in the early morning haze. From somewhere came the babble of running water.

Meta-universe, by whatever name you called it, was beautiful, like a gorgeous garden. What a pity he must live and die here alone, with nothing but a lot of animals for company. He'd willingly give an arm, or at least a rib, if—

"Adrian Prentiss! Adrian!"

He whirled and stared toward the orchard in elated disbelief.
"E! *E!*"
She'd got through!
The whole world, and just the two of them!
His heart was pounding ecstatically as he began to run lithely upwind.

And they'd keep it this way, simple and sweet, forever, and their children after them. To hell with science and progress! (Well, within practical limits, of course.)

As he ran, there rippled about his quivering nostrils the seductive scent of apple blossoms.

NO-SIDED PROFESSOR

Martin Gardner

Dolores—a tall, black-haired striptease at Chicago's Purple Hat Club—stood in the center of the dance floor and began the slow gyrations of her Cleopatra number, accompanied by soft Egyptian music from the Purple Hatters. The room was dark except for a shaft of emerald light that played over her filmy Egyptian costume and smooth, voluptuous limbs.

A veil draped about her head and shoulders was the first to be removed. Dolores was in the act of letting it drift gracefully to the floor when suddenly a sound like the firing of a shotgun came from somewhere above and the nude body of a large man dropped head first from the ceiling. He caught the veil in mid-air with his chin and pinned it to the floor with a dull thump.

Pandemonium reigned.

Jake Bowers, the master of ceremonies, yelled for lights and tried to keep back the crowd. The club's manager, who had been standing by the orchestra watching the floor show, threw a tablecloth over the crumpled figure and rolled it over on its back.

The man was breathing heavily, apparently knocked unconscious by the blow on his chin, but otherwise unharmed. He was well over fifty, with a short, neatly trimmed red beard and mustache, and a completely bald head. He was built like a professional wrestler.

With considerable difficulty three waiters succeeded in transporting him to the manager's private office in the back, leaving a roomful of bewildered, near-hysterical men and women gaping at the ceiling and each other, and arguing heatedly about the angle and manner of the man's fall. The only hypothesis with even a slight suggestion of sanity was that he had been tossed high into the air from somewhere on the side of the dance floor. But no one saw the tossing. The police were called.

Meanwhile, in the back office the bearded man recovered consciousness. He insisted that he was Dr. Stanislaw Slapenarski, professor of mathematics at the University of Warsaw, and at present a visiting lecturer at the University of Chicago.

Before continuing this curious narrative, I must pause to confess that I was not an eyewitness of the episode just described, having based my account on interviews with the master of ceremonies and several waiters. However, I did participate in a chain of remarkable events which culminated in the professor's unprecedented appearance.

These events began several hours earlier when members of the Moebius Society gathered for their annual banquet in one of the private dining rooms on the second floor of the Purple Hat Club. The Moebius Society is a small, obscure Chicago organization of mathematicians working in the field of topology, one of the youngest and most mysterious of the newer branches of transformation mathematics. To make clear what happened during the evening, it will be necessary at this point to give a brief description of the subject matter of topology.

Topology is difficult to define in nontechnical terms. One way to put it is to say that topology studies the mathematical properties of an object which remain constant regardless of how the object is distorted.

Picture in your mind a doughnut made of soft pliable rubber that can be twisted and stretched as far as you like in any direction. No matter how much this rubber doughnut is distorted (or "transformed" as mathematicians prefer to say), certain properties of the doughtnut will remain unchanged. For example, it will always retain a hole. In topology the doughnut shape is called a "torus." A soda straw is merely an elongated torus, so—from a topological point of view—a doughnut and a soda straw are identical figures.

Topology is completely disinterested in quantitative measurements. It is concerned only with basic properties of shape which are unchanged throughout the most radical distortions possible without breaking off pieces of the object and sticking them on again at other spots. If this breaking off were permitted, an object of a given structure could be transformed into an object of any other type of structure, and all original properties would be lost. If the reader will reflect a moment he will soon realize that topology studies the most primitive and fundamental mathematical properties that an object can possess.[1]

A sample problem in topology may be helpful. Imagine a torus (doughnut) surface made of thin rubber like an inner tube. Now imagine a small hole in the side of this torus. Is it possible to turn the torus inside out through this hole, as you might turn a balloon inside out? This is not an easy problem to solve in the imagination.

Although many mathematicians of the eighteenth century wrestled with isolated topological problems, one of the first systematic works in the field was done by August Ferdinand Moebius, a German astronomer who taught at the University of Leipzig during the first half of the last century. Until the time of Moebius it was believed that any surface, such as a piece of paper, had two sides. It was the German astronomer who made the disconcerting discovery that if you take a strip of paper, give it a single half-twist, then paste the ends together, the result is a "unilateral" surface—a surface with only one side!

If you will trouble to make such a strip (known to topologists as the "Moebius surface") and examine it carefully, you will soon discover that the strip actually does consist of one continuous side and of one continuous edge.

It is hard to believe at first that such a strip can exist, but there it is—a visible, tangible thing that can be constructed in a moment. And it has the indisputable property of one-sidedness, a property it cannot lose no matter how much it is stretched or how it is distorted.[2]

But back to the story. As an instructor in mathematics at the University of Chicago with a doctor's thesis in topology to my credit, I had little difficulty in securing admittance into the Moebius Society. Our member-

[1] The reader who is interested in obtaining a clearer picture of this new mathematics will find excellent articles on topology in the *Encyclopaedia Britannica* (Fourteenth Edition) under *Analysis Situs;* and under *Analysis Situs* in the *Encyclopedia Americana.* There are also readable chapters on elementary topology in two recent books—*Mathematics and the Imagination* by Kasner and Newman, and *What Is Mathematics?* by Courant and Robbins. Slapenarski's published work has not yet been translated from the Polish.

[2] The Moebius strip has many terrifying properties. For example, if you cut the strip in half lengthwise, cutting down the center all the way around, the result is not two strips, as might be expected, but one single large strip. But if you begin cutting a third of the way from one side, cutting twice around the strip, the result is one large and one small strip, interlocked. The smaller strip can then be cut in half to yield a single large strip, still interlocked with the other large strip. These weird properties are the basis of an old magic trick with cloth, known to the conjuring profession as the "afghan bands."

ship was small—only twenty-six men, most of them Chicago topologists but a few from universities in neighboring towns.

We held regular monthly meetings, rather academic in character, and once a year on November 17 (the anniversary of Moebius' birth) we arranged a banquet at which an outstanding topologist was brought to the city to act as a guest speaker.

The banquet always had its less serious aspects, usually in the form of special entertainment. But this year our funds were low and we decided to hold the celebration at the Purple Hat where the cost of the dinner would not be too great and where we could enjoy the floor show after the lecture. We were fortunate in having been able to obtain as our guest the distinguished Professor Slapenarski, universally acknowledged as the world's leading topologist and one of the greatest mathematical minds of the century.

Dr. Slapenarski had been in the city several weeks giving a series of lectures at the University of Chicago on the topological aspects of Einstein's theory of space. As a result of my contacts with him at the university, we became good friends and I had been asked to introduce him at the dinner.

We rode to the Purple Hat together in a taxi, and on the way I begged him to give me some inkling of the content of his address. But he only smiled inscrutably and told me, in his thick Polish accent, to wait and see. He had announced his topic as "The No-Sided Surface"—a topic which had aroused such speculation among our members that Dr. Robert Simpson of the University of Wisconsin wrote he was coming to the dinner, the first meeting that he had attended in over a year.[3]

Dr. Simpson is the outstanding authority on topology in the Middle West and the author of several important papers on topology and nuclear physics in which he vigorously attacks several of Slapenarski's major axioms.

The Polish professor and I arrived a little late. After introducing him to Simpson, then to our other members, we took our seats at the table and I called Slapenarski's attention to our tradition of brightening the banquet with little topological touches. For instance, our napkin rings were silver-plated Moebius strips. Doughnuts were provided with the coffee, and the coffee itself was contained in specially designed cups made in the shape of "Klein's bottle."[4]

---

[3] Dr. Simpson later confided to me that he had attended the dinner not to hear Slapenarski but to see Dolores.

[4] Named after Felix Klein, a brilliant German mathematician, Klein's bottle is a completely closed surface, like the surface of a globe, but without inside or outside. It is unilateral like a Moebius strip, but unlike the strip it has no edges. It can be bisected in such a way that each half becomes a Moebius surface. It will hold a liquid. Nothing frightful happens to the liquid.

After the meal we were served Ballantine ale, because of the curious trademark,[5] and pretzels in the shapes of the two basic "trefoil" knots.[6] Slapenarski was much amused by these details and even made several suggestions for additional topological curiosities, but the suggestions are too complex to explain here.

After my brief introduction, the Polish doctor stood up, acknowledged the applause with a smile, and cleared his throat. The room instantly became silent. The reader is already familiar with the professor's appearance—his portly frame, reddish beard, and polished pate—but it should be added that there was something in the expression of his face that suggested he had matters of considerable import to disclose to us.

It would be impossible to give with any fullness the substance of Slapenarski's brilliant, highly technical address. But the gist of it was this. Ten years ago, he said, he had been impressed by a statement of Moebius, in one of his lesser known treaties, that there was no theoretical reason why a surface could not lose *both* its sides—to become, in other words, a "nonlateral" surface.

Of course, the professor explained, such a surface was impossible to imagine, but so is the square root of minus one or the hypercube of fourth-dimensional geometry. That a concept is inconceivable has long ago been recognized as no basis for denying either its validity or usefulness in mathematics and modern physics.

We must remember, he added, that even the one-sided surface is inconceivable to anyone who has not seen and handled a Moebius strip. And many persons, with well-developed mathematical imaginations, are unable to understand how such a strip can exist even when they have one in hand.

I glanced at Dr. Simpson and thought I detected a skeptical smile curving the corners of his mouth.

Slapenarski continued. For many years, he said, he had been engaged in a tireless quest for a no-sided surface. On the basis of analogy with known types of surfaces he had been able to analyze many of the properties of the no-sided surface. Finally one day—and he paused here

---

[5] This trademark is a topological manifold of great interest. Although the three rings are interlocked, no *two* rings are interlocked. In other words, if any one of the rings is removed, the other two rings are completely free of each other. Yet the three together cannot be separated.

[6] The trefoil knot is the simplest form of knot that can be tied in a closed curve. It exists in two forms, one a mirror image of the other. Although the two forms are topologically identical, it is impossible to transform one into the other by distortion, an upsetting fact that has caused topologists considerable embarrassment. The study of the properties of knots forms an important branch of topology, though very little is understood as yet about even the simplest knots.

for dramatic emphasis, sweeping his bright little eyes across the motionless faces of his listeners—he had actually succeeded in constructing a no-sided surface.

His words were like an electric impulse that transmitted itself around the table. Everyone gave a sudden start and shifted his position and looked at his neighbor with raised eyebrows. I noticed that Simpson was shaking his head vigorously. When the speaker walked to the end of the room where a blackboard had been placed, Simpson bent his head and whispered to the man on his left, "It's sheer nonsense. Either Slappy has gone completely mad or he's playing a deliberate prank on all of us."

I think it had occurred to the others also that the lecture was a hoax because I noticed several were smiling to themselves while the professor chalked some elaborate diagrams on the blackboard.

After a somewhat involved discussion of the diagrams (which I was wholly unable to follow) the professor announced that he would conclude his lecture by constructing one of the simpler forms of the no-sided surface. By now we were all grinning at each other. Dr. Simpson's face had more of a smirk than a grin.

Slapenarski produced from his coat pocket a sheet of pale-blue paper, a small pair of scissors, and a tube of paste. He cut the paper into a figure that had a striking resemblance, I thought, to a paper doll. There were five projecting strips or appendages that resembled a head and four limbs. Then he folded and pasted the sheet carefully. It was an intricate procedure. Strips went over and under each other in an odd fashion until finally only two ends projected. Dr. Slapenarski then applied a dab of paste to one of these ends.

"Gentlemen," he said, holding up the twisted blue construction and turning it about for all to see, "you are about to witness the first public demonstration of the Slapenarski surface."

So saying, he pressed one of the projecting ends against the other.

There was a loud pop, like the bursting of a light bulb, and the paper figure vanished in his hands!

For a moment we were too stunned to move, then with one accord we broke into laughter and applause.

We were convinced, of course, that we were the victims of an elaborate joke. But it had been beautifully executed. I assumed, as did the others, that we had witnessed an ingenious chemical trick with paper—paper treated so it could be ignited by friction or some similar method and caused to explode without leaving an ash.

But I noticed that the professor seemed disconcerted by the laughter, and his face was beginning to turn the color of his beard. He smiled in an embarrassed way and sat down. The applause subsided slowly.

Falling in with the preposterous mood of the evening we all clustered around him and congratulated him warmly on his remarkable discovery. Then the man in charge of arrangements reminded us that a table had been reserved below so those interested in remaining could enjoy some drinks and see the floor show.

The room gradually cleared of everyone except Slapenarski, Simpson, and myself. The two famous topologists were standing in front of the blackboard. Simpson was smiling broadly and gesturing toward one of the diagrams.

"The fallacy of your proof was beautifully concealed, Doctor," he said. "I wonder if any of the others caught it."

The Polish mathematician was not amused.

"There is no fallacy in my proof," he said impatiently.

"Oh, come now, Doctor," Simpson said. "Of course there's a fallacy." Still smiling, he touched a corner of the diagram with his thumb. "These lines can't possibly intersect within the manifold. The intersection is somewhere out here." He waved his hand off to the right.

Slapenarski's face was growing red again.

"I tell you there is no fallacy," he repeated, his voice rising. Then slowly, speaking his words carefully and explosively, he went over the proof once more, rapping the blackboard at intervals with his knuckles.

Simpson listened gravely, and at one point interrupted with an objection. The objection was answered. A moment later he raised a second objection. The second objection was answered. I stood aside without saying anything. The discussion was too far above my head.

Then they began to raise their voices. I have already spoken of Simpson's long-standing controversy with Slapenarski over several basic topological axioms. Some of these axioms were now being brought into the argument.

"But I tell you the transformation is *not* bicontinuous and therefore the two sets cannot be homeomorphic," Simpson shouted.

The veins on the Polish mathematician's temples were standing out in sharp relief. "Then suppose you explain to me why my manifold vanished," he yelled back.

"It was nothing but a cheap conjuring trick," snorted Simpson. "I don't know how it worked and I don't care, but it certainly wasn't because the manifold became nonlateral."

"Oh it wasn't, wasn't it?" Slapenarski said between his teeth. Before I had a chance to intervene he had sent his huge fist crashing into the jaw of Dr. Simpson. The Wisconsin professor groaned and dropped to the floor. Slapenarski turned and glared at me wildly.

"Get back, young man," he said. As he outweighed me by at least one hundred pounds, I got back.

Then I watched in horror what was taking place. With insane fury still flaming on his face, Slapenarski had knelt beside the limp body and was twisting the arms and legs into fantastic knots. He was, in fact, folding the Wisconsin topologist as he had folded his piece of paper! Suddenly there was a small explosion, like the backfire of a car, and under the Polish mathematician's hands lay the collapsed clothing of Dr. Simpson.

Simpson had become a nonlateral surface.

Slapenarski stood up, breathing with difficulty and holding in his hands a tweed coat with vest, shirt, and underwear top inside. He opened his hands and let the garments fall on top of the clothing on the floor. Great drops of perspiration rolled down his face. He muttered in Polish, then beat his fists against his forehead.

I recovered enough presence of mind to move to the entrance of the room, and lock the door. When I spoke my voice sounded weak. "Can he . . . be brought back?"

"I do not know, I do not know," Slapenarski wailed. "I have only begun the study of these surfaces—only just begun. I have no way of knowing where he is. Undoubtedly it is one of the higher dimensions, probably one of the odd-numbered ones. God knows which one."

Then he grabbed me suddenly by my coat lapels and shook me so violently that a bridge on my upper teeth came loose. "I must go to him," he said. "It is the least I can do—the very least."

He sat down on the floor and began interweaving arms and legs. "Do not stand there like an idiot!" he yelled. "Here—some assistance."

I adjusted my bridge, then helped him twist his right arm under his left leg and back around his head until he was able to grip his right ear. Then his left arm had to be twisted in a somewhat similar fashion. "Over, not under," he shouted. It was with difficulty that I was able to force his left hand close enough to his face so he could grasp his nose.

There was another explosive noise, much louder than the sound made by Simpson, and a sudden blast of cold wind across my face. When I opened my eyes I saw the second heap of crumpled clothing on the floor.

While I was staring stupidly at the two piles of clothing there was a muffled sort of "pfft" sound behind me. I turned and saw Simpson standing near the wall, naked and shivering. His face was white. Then his knees buckled and he sank to the floor. There were vivid red marks at various places where his limbs had been pressed tightly against each other.

I stumbled to the door, unlocked it, and started down the stairway after a strong drink—for myself. I became conscious of a violent hubbub on the dance floor. Slapenarski had, a few moments earlier, completed his sensational dive.

In a back room below I found the other members of the Moebius Society and various officials of the Purple Hat Club in a noisy, incoherent debate. Slapenarski was sitting in a chair with a tablecloth wrapped around him and holding a handkerchief filled with ice cubes against the side of his jaw.

"Simpson is back," I said. "He fainted but I think he's okay."

"Thank heavens," Slapenarski mumbled.

The officials and patrons of the Purple Hat never understood, of course, what happened that wild night, and our attempts to explain made matters worse. The police arrived, adding to the confusion.

We finally got the two professors dressed and on their feet, and made an escape by promising to return the following day with our lawyers. The managers seemed to think the club had been the victim of an outlandish plot, and threatened to sue for damages against what he called the club's "refined reputation." As it turned out, the incident proved to be magnificent word-of-mouth advertising and eventually the club dropped the case. The papers heard the story, of course, but promptly dismissed it as an uncouth publicity stunt cooked up by Phanstiehl, the Purple Hat's press agent.

Simpson was unhurt, but Slapenarski's jaw had been broken. I took him to Billings Hospital, near the university, and in his hospital room late that night he told me what he thought had happened. Apparently Simpson had entered a higher dimension (very likely the fifth) on level ground.

When he recovered consciousness he unhooked himself and immediately reappeared as a normal three-dimensional torus with outside and inside surfaces. But Slapenarski had worse luck. He had landed on some sort of slope. There was nothing to see—only a gray, undifferentiated fog on all sides—but he had the distinct sensation of rolling down a hill.

He tried to keep a grip on his nose but was unable to maintain it. His right hand slipped free before he reached the bottom of the incline. As a result, he unfolded himself and tumbled back into three-dimensional space and the middle of Dolores' Egyptian routine.

At any rate, that was the way Slapenarski had it figured out.

He was several weeks in the hospital, refusing to see anyone until the day of his release, when I accompanied him to the Union Station. He caught a train to New York and I never saw him again. He died a few months later of a heart attack in Warsaw. At present Dr. Simpson is in correspondence with his widow in an attempt to obtain his notes on nonlateral surfaces.

Whether these notes will or will not be intelligible to American topologists (assuming we can obtain them) remains to be seen. We have made numerous experiments with folded paper, but so far have produced only commonplace bilateral and unilateral surfaces. Although it was I who helped Slapenarski fold himself, the excitement of the moment apparently erased the details from my mind.

But I shall never forget one remark the great topologist made to me the night of his accident, just before I left him at the hospital.

"It was fortunate," he said, "that both Simpson and I released our right hand before the left."

"Why?" I asked.

Slapenarski shuddered.

"We would have been inside out," he said.

"—AND HE BUILT A CROOKED

HOUSE—"

Robert Heinlein

Americans are considered crazy anywhere in the world.

They will usually concede a basis for the accusation but point to California as the focus of the infection. Californians stoutly maintain that their bad reputation is derived solely from the acts of the inhabitants of Los Angeles County. Angelenos will, when pressed, admit the charge but explain hastily, "It's Hollywood. It's not our fault—we didn't ask for it; Hollywood just grew."

The people in Hollywood don't care; they glory in it. If you are interested, they will drive you up Laurel Canyon "—where we keep the violent cases." The Canyonites—the brown-legged women, the trunks-clad men constantly busy building and rebuilding their slap-happy unfinished houses—regard with faint contempt the dull creatures who live down in the flats, and treasure in their hearts the secret knowledge that they, and only they, know how to live.

Lookout Mountain Avenue is the name of a side canyon which twists up from Laurel Canyon. The other Canyonites don't like to have it mentioned; after all, one must draw the line somewhere!

High up on Lookout Mountain at number 8775, across the street from the Hermit—the original Hermit of Hollywood—lived Quintus Teal, graduate architect.

Even the architecture of southern California is different. Hot dogs are sold from a structure built like and designated "The Pup." Ice cream cones come from a giant stucco ice cream cone, and neon proclaims "Get the Chili Bowl Habit!" from the roofs of buildings which are indisputably chili bowls. Gasoline, oil, and free road maps are dispensed beneath the wings of tri-motored transport planes, while the certified rest rooms, inspected hourly for your comfort, are located in the cabin of the plane itself. These things may surprise, or amuse, the tourist, but the local residents, who walk bareheaded in the famous California noonday sun, take them as a matter of course.

Quintus Teal regarded the efforts of his colleagues in architecture as faint-hearted, fumbling, and timid.

"What is a house?" Teal demanded of his friend, Homer Bailey.

"Well—" Bailey admitted cautiously, "speaking in broad terms, I've always regarded a house as a gadget to keep off the rain."

"Nuts! You're as bad as the rest of them."

"I didn't say the definition was complete—"

"Complete! It isn't even in the right direction. From that point of view we might just as well be squatting in caves. But I don't blame you," Teal went on magnanimously, "you're no worse than the lugs you find practicing architecture. Even the Moderns—all they've done is to abandon the Wedding Cake School in favor of the Service Station School, chucked away the gingerbread and slapped on some chromium, but at heart they are as conservative and traditional as a county courthouse. Neutral! Schindler! What have those bums got? What's Frank Lloyd Wright got that I haven't got?"

"Commissions," his friend answered succinctly.

"Huh? Wha' d'ju say?" Teal stumbled slightly in his flow of words, did a slight double take, and recovered himself. "Commissions. Correct. And why? Because I don't think of a house as an upholstered cave; I think of it as a machine for living, a vital process, a live dynamic thing, changing with the mood of the dweller—not a dead, static, oversized coffin. Why should we be held down by the frozen concepts of our ancestors? Any fool with a little smattering of descriptive geometry can design a house in the ordinary way. Is the static geometry of Euclid the only mathematics? Are we to completely disregard the Picard-Vessiot theory? How about modular systems?—to say nothing of the rich suggestions of stereochemistry. Isn't there a place in architecture for transformation, for homomorphology, for actional structures?"

"Blessed if I know," answered Bailey. "You might just as well be talking about the fourth dimension for all it means to me."

"And why not? Why should we limit ourselves to the—Say!" He interrupted himself and stared into distances. "Homer, I think you've really got something. After all, why not? Think of the infinite richness of articulation and relationship in four dimensions. What a house, what a house—" He stood quite still, his pale bulging eyes blinking thoughtfully.

Bailey reached up and shook his arm. "Snap out of it. What the hell are you talking about, four dimensions? Time is the fourth dimension; you can't drive nails into *that*."

Teal shrugged him off. "Sure. Sure. Time is *a* fourth dimension, but I'm thinking about a fourth spatial dimension, like length, breadth and thickness. For economy of materials and convenience of arrangement you couldn't beat it. To say nothing of the saving of ground space—you could put an eight-room house on the land now occupied by a one-room house. Like a tesseract—"

"What's a tesseract?"

"Didn't you go to school? A tesseract is a hypercube, a square figure with four dimensions to it, like a cube has three, and a square has two. Here, I'll show you." Teal dashed out into the kitchen of his apartment and returned with a box of toothpicks which he spilled on the table between them, brushing glasses and a nearly empty Holland gin bottle carelessly aside. "I'll need some plasticine. I had some around here last week." He burrowed into a drawer of the littered desk which crowded one corner of his dining room and emerged with a lump of oily sculptor's clay. "Here's some."

"What are you going to do?"

"I'll show you." Teal rapidly pinched off small masses of the clay and rolled them into pea-sized balls. He stuck toothpicks into four of these and hooked them together into a square. "There! That's a square."

"Obviously."

"Another one like it, four more toothpicks, and we make a cube." The toothpicks were now arranged in the framework of a square box, a cube, with the pellets of clay holding the corners together. "Now we make another cube just like the first one, and the two of them will be two sides of the tesseract."

Bailey started to help him roll the little balls of clay for the second cube, but became diverted by the sensuous feel of the docile clay and started working and shaping it with his fingers.

"Look," he said, holding up his effort, a tiny figurine, "Gypsy Rose Lee."

"Looks more like Gargantua; she ought to sue you. Now pay attention. You open up one corner of the first cube, interlock the second cube at the corner, and then close the corner. Then take eight more toothpicks and join the bottom of the first cube to the bottom of the second, on a slant, and the top of the first to the top of the second, the same way." This he did rapidly, while he talked.

"What's that supposed to be?" Bailey demanded suspiciously.

"That's a tesseract, eight cubes forming the sides of a hypercube in four dimensions."

"It looks more like a cat's cradle to me. You've only got two cubes there anyhow. Where are the other six?"

"Use your imagination, man. Consider the top of the first cube in relation to the top of the second; that's cube number three. Then the two bottom squares, then the front faces of each cube, the back faces, the right hand, the left hand—eight cubes." He pointed them out.

"Yeah, I see 'em. But they still aren't cubes; they're what-chamucallems—prisms. They are not square, they slant."

"That's just the way you look at it, in perspective. If you drew a picture of a cube on a piece of paper, the side squares would be slaunchwise, wouldn't they? That's perspective. When you look at a four-dimensional figure in three dimensions, naturally it looks crooked. But those are all cubes just the same."

"Maybe they are to you, brother, but they still look crooked to me."

Teal ignored the objections and went on. "Now consider this as the framework of an eight-room house; there's one room on the ground floor—that's for service, utilities, and garage. There are six rooms opening off it on the next floor, living room, dining room, bath, bedrooms, and so forth. And up at the top, completely enclosed and with windows on four sides, is your study. There! How do you like it?"

"Seems to me you have the bathtub hanging out of the living room ceiling. Those rooms are interlaced like an octopus."

"Only in perspective, only in perspective. Here, I'll do it another way so you can see it." This time Teal made a cube of toothpicks, then made a second of halves of toothpicks, and set it exactly in the center of the first by attaching the corners of the small cube to the large cube by short lengths of toothpick. "Now—the big cube is your ground floor, the little cube inside is your study on the top floor. The six cubes joining them are the living rooms. See?"

Bailey studied the figure, then shook his head. "I still don't see but two cubes, a big one and a little one. Those other six things, they look like pyramids this time instead of prisms, but they still aren't cubes."

"Certainly, certainly, you are seeing them in different perspective. Can't you see that?"

"Well, maybe. But that room on the inside, there. It's completely surrounded by the thingamujigs. I thought you said it had windows on four sides."

"It has—it just looks like it was surrounded. That's the grand feature about a tesseract house, complete outside exposure for every room, yet every wall serves two rooms and an eight-room house requires only a one-room foundation. It's revolutionary."

"That's putting it mildly. You're crazy, bud; you can't build a house like that. That inside room is on the inside, and there she stays."

Teal looked at his friend in controlled exasperation. "It's guys like you that keep architecture in its infancy. How many square sides has a cube?"

"Six."

"How many of them are inside?"

"Why, none of 'em. They're all on the outside."

"All right. Now listen—a tesseract has eight cubical sides, *all on the outside*. Now watch me. I'm going to open up this tesseract like you can open up a cubical pasteboard box, until it's flat. That way you'll be able to see all eight of the cubes." Working very rapidly he constructed four cubes, piling one on top of the other in an unsteady tower. He then built out four more cubes from the four exposed faces of the second cube in the pile. The structure swayed a little under the loose coupling of the clay pellets, but it stood, eight cubes in an inverted cross, a double cross, as the four additional cubes stuck out in four directions. "Do you see it now? It rests on the ground floor room, the next six cubes are the living rooms, and there is your study, up at the top."

Bailey regarded it with more approval than he had the other figures. "At least I can understand it. You say that is a tesseract, too?"

"That is a tesseract unfolded in three dimensions. To put it back together you tuck the top cube onto the bottom cube, fold those side cubes in till they meet the top cube and there you are. You do all this folding through a fourth dimension of course; you don't distort any of the cubes, or fold them into each other."

Bailey studied the wobbly framework further. "Look here," he said at last, "why don't you forget about folding this thing up through a fourth dimension—you can't anyway—and build a house like this?"

"What do you mean, I can't? It's a simple mathematical problem—"

"Take it easy, son. It may be simple in mathematics, but you could never get your plans approved for construction. There isn't any fourth dimension; forget it. But this kind of a house—it might have some advantages."

Checked, Teal studied the model. "Hm-m-m—Maybe you got something. We could have the same number of rooms, and we'd save the same amount of ground space. Yes, and we would set that middle cross-shaped floor northeast, southwest, and so forth, so that every room would get sunlight all day long. That central axis lends itself nicely to central heating. We'll put the dining room on the northeast and the kitchen on the southeast, with big view windows in every room. O. K., Homer, I'll do it! Where do you want it built?"

"Wait a minute! Wait a minute! I didn't say you were going to build it for me—"

"Of course I am. Who else? Your wife wants a new house; this is it."

"But Mrs. Bailey wants a Georgian house—"

"Just an idea she has. Women don't know what they want—"

"Mrs. Bailey does."

"Just some idea an out-of-date architect has put in her head. She drives a new car, doesn't she? She wears the very latest styles—why should she live in an eighteenth century house? This house will be even later than this year's model; it's years in the future. She'll be the talk of the town."

"Well—I'll have to talk to her."

"Nothing of the sort. We'll surprise her with it. Have another drink."

"Anyhow, we can't do anything about it now. Mrs. Bailey and I are diving up to Bakersfield tomorrow. The company's bringing in a couple of wells tomorrow."

"Nonsense. That's just the opportunity we want. It will be a surprise for her when you get back. You can just write me a check right now, and your worries are over."

"I oughtn't to do anything like this without consulting her. She won't like it."

"Say, who wears the pants in your family anyhow?"

The check was signed about halfway down the second bottle.

Things are done fast in southern California. Ordinary houses there are usually built in a month's time. Under Teal's impassioned heckling the tesseract house climbed dizzily skyward in days rather than weeks, and its cross-shaped second story came jutting out at the four corners of the world. He had some trouble at first with the inspectors over these four projecting rooms but by using strong girders and folding money he had been able to convince them of the soundness of his engineering.

By arrangement, Teal drove up in front of the Bailey residence the morning after their return to town. He improvised on his two-tone horn. Bailey stuck his head out the front door. "Why don't you use the bell?"

"Too slow," answered Teal cheerfully. "I'm a man of action. Is Mrs. Bailey ready? Ah, there you are, Mrs. Bailey! Welcome home, welcome home. Jump in, we've got a surprise for you!"

"You know Teal, my dear," Bailey put in uncomfortably.

Mrs. Bailey sniffed. "I know him. We'll go in our own car, Homer."

"Certainly, my dear."

"Good idea," Teal agreed; " 'sgot more power than mine; we'll get there faster. I'll drive, I know the way." He took the keys from Bailey, slid into the driver's seat, and had the engine started before Mrs. Bailey could rally her forces.

"Never have to worry about my driving," he assured Mrs. Bailey, turning his head as he did so, while he shot the powerful car down the avenue and swung onto Sunset Boulevard, "it's a matter of power and control, a dynamic process, just my meat—I've never had a serious accident."

"You won't have but one," she said bitingly. "Will you please keep your eyes on the traffic?"

He attempted to explain to her that a traffic situation was a matter, not of eyesight, but intuitive integration of courses, speeds, and probabilities, but Bailey cut him short. "Where is the house, Quintus?"

"House?" asked Mrs. Bailey suspiciously. "What's this about a house, Homer? Have you been up to something without telling me?"

Teal cut in with his best diplomatic manner. "It certainly is a house, Mrs. Bailey. And what a house! It's a surprise for you from a devoted husband. Just wait till you see it—"

"I shall," she agreed grimly. "What style is it?"

"This house sets a new style. It's later than television, newer than next week. It must be seen to be appreciated. By the way," he went on rapidly, heading off any retort, "did you folks feel the earthquake last night?"

"Earthquake? What earthquake? Homer, was there an earthquake?"

"Just a little one," Teal continued, "about two A.M. If I hadn't been awake, I wouldn't have noticed it."

Mrs. Bailey shuddered. "Oh, this awful country! Do you hear that, Homer? We might have been killed in our beds and never have known it. Why did I ever let you persuade me to leave Iowa?"

"But my dear," he protested hopelessly, "you wanted to come out to California; you didn't like Des Moines."

"We needn't go into that," she said firmly. "You are a man; you should anticipate such things. Earthquakes!"

"That's one thing you needn't fear in your new home, Mrs. Bailey,"

Teal told her. "It's absolutely earthquake-proof; every part is in perfect dynamic balance with every other part."

"Well, I hope so. Where is this house?"

"Just around this bend. There's the sign now." A large arrow sign of the sort favored by real estate promoters, proclaimed in letters that were large and bright even for southern California:

THE HOUSE OF THE FUTURE!!!

COLOSSAL —AMAZING—

REVOLUTIONARY

*See How Your Grandchildren
Will Live!*

Q. Teal, Architect

"Of course that will be taken down," he added hastily, noting her expression, "as soon as you take possession." He slued around the corner and brought the car to a squealing halt in front of the House of the Future. *"Voilá!"* He watched their faces for response.

Bailey stared unbelievingly, Mrs. Bailey in open dislike. They saw a simple cubical mass, possessing doors and windows, but no other architectural features, save that it was decorated in intricate mathematical designs. "Teal," Bailey asked slowly, "what have you been up to?"

Teal turned from their faces to the house. Gone was the crazy tower with its jutting second-story rooms. No trace remained of the seven rooms above ground floor level. Nothing remained but the single room that rested on the foundations. "Great jumping cats!" he yelled, "I've been robbed!"

He broke into a run.

But it did him no good. Front or back, the story was the same: the other seven rooms had disappeared, vanished completely. Bailey caught up with him, and took his arm. "Explain yourself. What is this about being robbed? How come you built anything like this—it's not according to agreement."

"But I didn't. I built just what we had planned to build, an eight-room house in the form of a developed tesseract. I've been sabotaged, that's what it is! Jealousy! The other architects in town didn't dare let me finish this job; they knew they'd be washed up if I did."

"When were you last here?"

"Yesterday afternoon."

"Everything all right then?"

"Yes. The gardeners were just finishing up."

Bailey glanced around at the faultlessly manicured landscaping. "I don't see how seven rooms could have been dismantled and carted away from here in a single night without wrecking this garden."

Teal looked around, too. "It doesn't look it. I don't understand it."

Mrs. Bailey joined them. "Well? Well? Am I to be left to amuse myself? We might as well look it over as long as we are here, though I'm warning you, Homer, I'm not going to like it."

"We might as well," agreed Teal, and drew a key from his pocket with which he let them in the front door. "We may pick up some clues."

The entrance hall was in perfect order, the sliding screens that separated it from the garage space were back, permitting them to see the entire compartment. "This looks all right," observed Bailey. "Let's go up on the roof and try to figure out what happened. Where's the staircase? Have they stolen that, too?"

"Oh, no," Teal denied, "look—" He pressed a button below the light switch; a panel in the ceiling fell away and a light, graceful flight of stairs swung noiselessly down. Its strength members were the frosty silver of duralumin, its treads and risers transparent plastic. Teal wriggled like a boy who has successfully performed a card trick, while Mrs. Bailey thawed perceptibly.

It was beautiful.

"Pretty slick," Bailey admitted. "Howsomever it doesn't seem to go any place—"

"Oh, that—" Teal followed his gaze. "The cover lifts up as you approach the top. Open stair wells are anachronisms. Come on." As predicted, the lid of the staircase got out of their way as they climbed the flight and permitted them to debouch at the top, but not, as they had expected, on the roof of the single room. They found themselves standing in the middle one of the five rooms which constituted the second floor of the original structure.

For the first time on record Teal had nothing to say. Bailey echoed him, chewing on his cigar. Everything was in perfect order. Before them, through open doorway and translucent partition lay the kitchen, a chef's dream of up-to-the-minute domestic engineering, monel metal, continuous counter space, concealed lighting, functional arrangement. On the left the formal, yet gracious and hospitable dining room awaited guests, its furniture in parade-ground alignment.

Teal knew before he turned his head that the drawing room and lounge would be found in equally substantial and impossible existence.

"Well, I must admit this *is* charming," Mrs. Bailey approved, "and the kitchen is just *too* quaint for words—though I would never have guessed from the exterior that this house had so much room upstairs. Of course *some* changes will have to be made. That secretary now—if we moved it over *here* and put the settle over *there*—"

"Stow it, Matilda," Bailey cut in brusquely. "Wha'd' yuh make of it, Teal?"

"Why, Homer Bailey! The very id—"

"Stow it, I said. Well, Teal?"

The architect shuffled his rambling body. "I'm afraid to say. Let's go on up."

"How?"

"Like this." He touched another button; a mate, in deeper colors, to the fairy bridge that had let them up from below offered them access to the next floor. They climbed it, Mrs. Bailey expostulating in the rear, and found themselves in the master bedroom. Its shades were drawn, as had been those on the level below, but the mellow lighting came on automatically. Teal at once activated the switch which controlled still another flight of stairs, and they hurried up into the top floor study.

"Look, Teal," suggested Bailey when he had caught his breath, "can we get to the roof above this room? Then we could look around."

"Sure, it's an observatory platform." They climbed a fourth flight of stairs, but when the cover at the top lifted to let them reach the level above, they found themselves, not on the roof, but *standing in the ground floor room where they had entered the house.*

Mr. Bailey turned a sickly gray. "Angels in heaven," he cried, "this place is haunted. We're getting out of here." Grabbing his wife he threw open the front door and plunged out.

Teal was too much preoccupied to bother with their departure. There was an answer to all this, an answer that he did not believe. But he was forced to break off considering it because of hoarse shouts from somewhere above him. He lowered the staircase and rushed upstairs. Bailey was in the central room leaning over Mrs. Bailey, who had fainted. Teal took in the situation, went to the bar built into the lounge, and poured three fingers of brandy, which he returned with and handed to Bailey. "Here—this'll fix her up."

Bailey drank it.

"That was for Mrs. Bailey," said Teal.

"Don't quibble," snapped Bailey. "Get her another." Teal took the precaution of taking one himself before returning with a dose earmarked for his client's wife. He found her just opening her eyes.

"Here, Mrs. Bailey," he soothed, "this will make you feel better."

"I never touch spirits," she protested, and gulped it.

"Now tell me what happened," suggested Teal. "I thought you two had left."

"But we did—we walked out the front door and found ourselves up here, in the lounge."

"The hell you say! Hm-m-m—wait a minute." Teal went into the lounge. There he found that the big view window at the end of the room was open. He peered cautiously through it. He stared, not out at the California countryside, but into the ground floor room—or a reasonable facsimile thereof. He said nothing, but went back to the stair well which he had left open and looked down it. The ground floor room was still in place. Somehow, it managed to be in two different places at once, on different levels.

He came back into the central room and seated himself opposite Bailey in a deep, low chair, and sighted him past his upthrust bony knees. "Homer," he said impressively, "do you know what has happened?"

"No, I don't—but if I don't find out pretty soon, something is going to happen and pretty drastic, too!"

"Homer, this is a vindication of my theories. This house is a real tesseract."

"What's he talking about, Homer?"

"Wait, Matilda—now Teal, that's ridiculous. You've pulled some hanky-panky here and I won't have it—scaring Mrs. Bailey half to death, and making me nervous. All I want is to get out of here, with no more of your trapdoors and silly practical jokes."

"Speak for yourself, Homer," Mrs. Bailey interrupted, "I was *not* frightened; I was just took all over queer for a moment. It's my heart; all of my people are delicate and highstrung. Now about this tessy thing —explain yourself, Mr. Teal. Speak up."

He told her as well as he could in the face of numerous interruptions the theory back of the house. "Now as I see it, Mrs. Bailey," he concluded, "this house, while perfectly stable in three dimensions, was not stable in four dimensions. I had built a house in the shape of an unfolded tesseract; something happened to it, some jar or side thrust, and it collapsed into its normal shape—it folded up." He snapped his fingers suddenly. "I've got it! The earthquake!"

"Earthquake?"

"Yes, yes, the little shake we had last night. From a four-dimensional standpoint this house was like a plane balanced on edge. One little push and it fell over, collapsed along its natural joints into a stable four-dimensional figure."

"I thought you boasted about how safe this house was."

"It *is* safe—three-dimensionally."

"I don't call a house safe," commented Bailey edgily, "that collapses at the first little temblor."

"But look around you, man!" Teal protested. "Nothing has been disturbed, not a piece of glassware cracked. Rotation through a fourth dimension can't affect a three-dimensional figure any more than you can shake letters off a printed page. If you had been sleeping in here last night, you would never have awakened."

"That's just what I'm afraid of. Incidentally, has your great genius figured out any way for us to get out of this bobby trap?"

"Huh? Oh, yes, you and Mrs. Bailey started to leave and landed back up here, didn't you. But I'm sure there is no real difficulty—we came in, we can go out. I'll try it." He was up and hurrying downstairs before he had finished talking. He flung open the front door, stepped through, and found himself staring at his companions, down the length of the second floor lounge. "Well, there does seem to be some slight problem," he admitted blandly. "A mere technicality, though—we can always go out a window." He jerked aside the long drapes that covered the deep French windows set in one side wall of the lounge. He stopped suddenly.

"Hm-m-m," he said, "this is interesting—very."

"What is?" asked Bailey, joining him.

"This." The window stared directly into the dining room, instead of looking outdoors. Bailey stepped back to the corner where the lounge and the dining room joined the central room at ninety degrees.

"But that can't be," he protested, "that window is maybe fifteen, twenty feet from the dining room."

"Not in a tesseract," corrected Teal. "Watch." He opened the window and stepped through, talking back over his shoulder as he did so.

From the point of view of the Baileys he simply disappeared.

But not from his own viewpoint. It took him some seconds to catch his breath. Then he cautiously disentangled himself from the rosebush to which he had become almost irrevocably wedded, making a mental note the while never again to order landscaping which involved plants with thorns, and looked around him.

He was outside the house. The massive bulk of the ground floor room thrust up beside him. Apparently he had fallen off the roof.

He dashed around the corner of the house, flung open the front door and hurried up the stairs. "Homer!" he called out, "Mrs. Bailey! I've found a way out!"

Bailey looked annoyed rather than pleased to see him. "What happened to you?"

"I fell out. I've been outside the house. You can do it just as easily—just step through those French windows. Mind the rosebush, though—we may have to build another stairway."

"How did you get back in?"

"Through the front door."

"Then we shall leave the same way. Come, my dear." Bailey set his hat firmly on his head and marched down the stairs, his wife on his arm.

Teal met them in the lounge. "I could have told you that wouldn't work," he announced. "Now here's what we have to do: As I see it, in a four-dimensional figure a three-dimensional man has two choices every time he crosses a line of juncture, like a wall or a threshold. Ordinarily he will make a ninety-degree turn through the fourth dimension, only he doesn't feel it with his three dimensions. Look." He stepped through the very window that he had fallen out of a moment before. Stepped through and arrived in the dining room, where he stood, still talking.

"I watched where I was going and arrived where I intended to." He stepped back into the lounge. "The time before I didn't watch and I moved on through normal space and fell out of the house. It must be a matter of subconscious orientation."

"I'd hate to depend on subconscious orientation when I step out for the morning paper."

"You won't have to; it'll become automatic. Now to get out of the house this time—Mrs. Bailey, if you will stand here with your back to the window, and jump backward, I'm pretty sure you will land in the garden."

Mrs. Bailey's face expressed her opinion of Teal and his ideas. "Homer Bailey," she said shrilly, "are you going to stand there and let him suggest such—"

"But Mrs. Bailey," Teal attempted to explain, "we can tie a rope on you and lower you down eas—"

"Forget it, Teal," Bailey cut him off brusquely. "We'll have to find a better way than that. Neither Mrs. Bailey nor I are fitted for jumping."

Teal was temporarily nonplused; there ensued a short silence. Bailey broke it with, "Did you hear that, Teal?"

"Hear what?"

"Someone talking off in the distance. D'you s'pose there could be someone else in the house, playing tricks on us, maybe?"

"Oh, not a chance. I've got the only key."

"But I'm sure of it," Mrs. Bailey confirmed. "I've heard them ever since we came in. Voices. Homer, I can't stand much more of this. Do something."

"Now, now, Mrs. Bailey," Teal soothed, "don't get upset. There can't be anyone else in the house, but I'll explore and make sure. Homer, you stay here with Mrs. Bailey and keep an eye on the rooms on this floor." He passed from the lounge into the ground floor room and from there to the kitchen and on into the bedroom. This led him back to the lounge by a straight-line route, that is to say, by going straight ahead on the entire trip he returned to the place from which he started.

"Nobody around," he reported. "I opened all of the doors and windows as I went—all except this one." He stepped to the window opposite the one through which he had recently fallen and thrust back the drapes.

He saw a man with his back toward him, four rooms away. Teal snatched open the French window and dived through it, shouting, "There he goes now! Stop thief!"

The figure evidently heard him; it fled precipitately. Teal pursued, his gangling limbs stirred to unanimous activity, through drawing room, kitchen, dining room, lounge—room after room, yet in spite of Teal's best efforts he could not seem to cut down the four-room lead that the interloper had started with.

He saw the pursued jump awkwardly but actively over the low sill of a French window and in so doing knock off his hat. When he came up to the point where his quarry had lost his headgear, he stopped and picked it up, glad of an excuse to stop and catch his breath. He was back in the lounge.

"I guess he got away from me," he admitted. "Anyhow, here's his hat. Maybe we can identify him."

Bailey took the hat, looked at it, then snorted, and slapped it on Teal's head. It fitted perfectly. Teal looked puzzled, took the hat off, and examined it. On the sweat band were the initials "Q.T." It was his own.

Slowly comprehension filtered through Teal's features. He went back to the French window and gazed down the series of rooms through which he had pursued the mysterious stranger. They saw him wave his arms semaphore fashion. "What are you doing?" asked Bailey.

"Come see." The two joined him and followed his stare with their own. Four rooms away they saw the backs of three figures, two male and one female. The taller, thinner of the men was waving his arms in a silly fashion.

Mrs. Bailey screamed and fainted again.

Some minutes later, when Mrs. Bailey had been resuscitated and somewhat composed, Bailey and Teal took stock. "Teal," said Bailey, "I won't waste any time blaming you; recriminations are useless and I'm sure you didn't plan for this to happen, but I suppose you realize we are in a pretty serious predicament. How are we going to get out of here? It looks now as if we would stay until we starve; every room leads into another room."

"Oh, it's not that bad. I got out once, you know."

"Yes, but you can't repeat it—you tried."

"Anyhow we haven't tried all the rooms. There's still the study."

"Oh, yes, the study. We went through there when we first came in, and didn't stop. Is it your idea that we might get out through its windows?"

"Don't get your hopes up. Mathematically, it ought to look into the four side rooms on this floor. Still we never opened the blinds; maybe we ought to look."

" 'Twon't do any harm anyhow. Dear, I think you had best just stay here and rest—"

"Be left alone in this horrible place? I should say not!" Mrs. Bailey was up off the couch where she had been recuperating even as she spoke.

They went upstairs. "This is the inside room, isn't it, Teal?" Bailey inquired as they passed through the master bedroom and climbed on up toward the study. "I mean it was the little cube in your diagram that was in the middle of the big cube, and completely surrounded."

"That's right," agreed Teal. "Well, let's have a look. I figure this window ought to give into the kitchen." He grasped the cords of Venetian blinds and pulled them.

It did not. Waves of vertigo shook them. Involuntarily they fell to the floor and grasped helplessly at the pattern on the rug to keep from falling. "Close it! Close it!" moaned Bailey.

Mastering in part a primitive atavistic fear, Teal worked his way back to the window and managed to release the screen. The window had looked *down* instead of *out*, down from a terrifying height.

Mrs. Bailey had fainted again.

Teal went back after more brandy while Bailey chafed her wrists. When she had recovered, Teal went cautiously to the window and raised the screen a crack. Bracing his knees, he studied the scene. He turned to Bailey. "Come look at this, Homer. See if you recognize it."

"You stay away from there, Homer Bailey!"

"Now, Matilda, I'll be careful." Bailey joined him and peered out.

"See up there? That's the Chrysler Building, sure as shooting. And there's the East River, and Brooklyn." They gazed straight down the sheer face of an enormously tall building. More than a thousand feet away a toy city, very much alive, was spread out before them. "As near as I can figure it out, we are looking down the side of the Empire State Building from a point just above its tower."

"What is it? A mirage?"

"I don't think so—it's too perfect. I think space is folded over through the fourth dimension here and we are looking past the fold."

"You mean we aren't really seeing it?"

"No, we're seeing it all right. I don't know what would happen if we climbed out this window, but I for one don't want to try. But what a view! Oh, boy, what a view! Let's try the other windows."

They approached the next window more cautiously, and it was well that they did, for it was even more disconcerting, more reason-shaking, than the one looking down the gasping height of the skyscraper. It was a simple seascape, open ocean and blue sky—but the ocean was where the sky should have been, and contrariwise. This time they were somewhat braced for it, but they both felt seasickness about to overcome them at the sight of waves rolling overhead; they lowered the blind quickly without giving Mrs. Bailey a chance to be disturbed by it.

Teal looked at the third window. "Game to try it, Homer?"

"Hrrumph—well, we won't be satisfied if we don't. Take it easy." Teal lifted the blind a few inches. He saw nothing, and raised it a little more —still nothing. Slowly he raised it until the window was fully exposed. They gazed out at—nothing.

Nothing, nothing at all. What color is nothing? Don't be silly! What shape is it? Shape is an attribute of *something.* It had neither depth nor form. It had not even blackness. It was *nothing.*

Bailey chewed at his cigar. "Teal, what do you make of that?"

Teal's insouciance was shaken for the first time. "I don't know, Homer, I don't rightly know—but I think that window ought to be walled up." He stared at the lowered blind for a moment. "I think maybe we looked at a place where space *isn't.* We looked around a fourth-dimensional corner and there wasn't anything there." He rubbed his eyes. "I've got a headache."

They waited for a while before tackling the fourth window. Like an unopened letter, it might *not* contain bad news. The doubt left hope. Finally the suspense stretched too thin and Bailey pulled the cord himself, in the face of his wife's protests.

It was not so bad. A landscape stretched away from them, right side up, and on such a level that the study appeared to be a ground floor room. But it was distinctly unfriendly.

A hot, hot sun beat down from lemon-colored sky. The flat ground seemed burned a sterile, bleached brown and incapable of supporting life. Life there was, strange stunted trees that lifted knotted, twisted arms to the sky. Little clumps of spiky leaves grew on the outer extremities of these misshapen growths.

"Heavenly day," breathed Bailey, "where is that?"

Teal shook his head, his eyes troubled. "It beats me."

"It doesn't look like anything on Earth. It looks more like another planet—Mars, maybe."

"I wouldn't know. But, do you know, Homer, it might be worse than that, worse than another planet, I mean."

"Huh? What's that you say?"

"It might be clear out of our space entirely. I'm not sure that that is our sun at all. It seems too bright."

Mrs. Bailey had somewhat timidly joined them and now gazed out at the outré scene. "Homer," she said in a subdued voice, "those hideous trees—they frighten me."

He patted her hand.

Teal fumbled with the window catch.

"What are you doing?" Bailey demanded.

"I thought if I stuck my head out the window I might be able to look around and tell a bit more."

"Well—all right," Bailey grudged, "but be careful."

"I will." He opened the window a crack and sniffed. "The air is all right, at least." He threw it open wide.

His attention was diverted before he could carry out his plan. An uneasy tremor, like the first intimation of nausea, shivered the entire building for a long second, and was gone.

"Earthquake!" They all said it at once. Mrs. Bailey flung her arms around her husband's neck.

Teal gulped and recovered himself, saying:

"It's all right, Mrs. Bailey. This house is perfectly safe. You know you can expect settling tremors after a shock like last night." He had just settled his features into an expression of reassurance when the second shock came. This one was no mild shimmy but the real seasick roll.

In every Californian, native born or grafted, there is a deep-rooted primitive reflex. An earthquake fills him with soul-shaking claustrophobia which impels him blindly to *get outdoors!* Model Boy Scouts will push aged grandmothers aside to obey it. It is a matter of record that Teal and Bailey landed on top of Mrs. Bailey. Therefore, she must have jumped through the window first. The order of precedence cannot be attributed to chivalry; it must be assumed that she was in readier position to spring.

They pulled themselves together, collected their wits a little, and rubbed sand from their eyes. Their first sensations were relief at feeling the solid sand of the desert land under them. Then Bailey noticed something that brought them to their feet and checked Mrs. Bailey from bursting into the speech that she had ready.

"Where's the house?"

It was gone. There was no sign of it at all. They stood in the center of flat desolation, the landscape they had seen from the window. But, aside from the tortured, twisted trees there was nothing to be seen but the yellow sky and the luminary overhead, whose furnacelike glare was ready almost insufferable.

Bailey looked slowly around, then turned to the architect. "Well, Teal?" His voice was ominous.

Teal shrugged helplessly. "I wish I knew. I wish I could even be sure that we were on Earth."

"Well, we can't stand here. It's sure death if we do. Which direction?"

"Any, I guess. Let's keep a bearing on the sun."

They had trudged on for an undertermined distance when Mrs. Bailey demanded a rest. They stopped. Teal said in an aside to Bailey, "Any ideas?"

"No . . . no, none. Say, do you hear anything?"

Teal listened. "Maybe—unless it's my imagination."

"Sounds like an automobile. Say, it *is* an automobile!"

They came to the highway in less than another hundred yards. The automobile, when it arrived, proved to be an elderly, puffing light truck, driven by a rancher. He crunched to a stop at their hail. "We're stranded. Can you help us out?"

"Sure. Pile in."

"Where are you headed?"

"Los Angeles."

"Los Angeles? Say, where is this place?"

"Well, you're right in the middle of the Joshua-Tree National Forest."

The return was as dispiriting as the Retreat from Moscow. Mr. and Mrs. Bailey sat up in front with the driver while Teal bumped along in the body of the truck, and tried to protect his head from the sun. Bailey subsidized the friendly rancher to detour to the tesseract house, not because they wanted to see it again, but in order to pick up their car.

At last the rancher turned the corner that brought them back to where they had started. But the house was no longer there.

There was not even the ground floor room. It had vanished. The Baileys, interested in spite of themselves, poked around the foundations with Teal.

"Got any answers for this one, Teal?" asked Bailey.

"It must be that on that last shock it simply fell through into another section of space. I can see now that I should have anchored it at the foundations."

"That's not all you should have done."

"Well, I don't see that there is anything to get downhearted about. The house was insured, and we've learned an amazing lot. There are possibilities, man, possibilities! Why, right now I've got a great new revolutionary idea for a house—"

Teal ducked in time. He was always a man of action.

SCIENCE FICTION
AND THE FUTURE

Education

The educational system in the United States is beginning to undergo a change which could transform it completely. The fact that this book is designed in part as a textbook is one indication of the change in education which may not stop until the focus is wholly on the future. In *Future Shock,* Alvin Toffler remarks that it is no longer sufficient for people to understand the past or even the present since the past is behind us and the present will soon vanish. Toffler emphasizes that instead of memorizing bodies of information students must be taught to anticipate change in terms of its rate and direction and must learn, thereby, to make long-range assumptions about the possibilities of the future. This process, as you may have already realized, is the one used by science fiction writers. Science fiction, thus, can play a part in this system of education. Moreover, futurology courses—courses focusing on the future through nonfictional studies by such groups as the Rand Corporation—should also play a great part in the new curriculum.

Science fiction novels focusing on education are scarce; in fact, unless novels involving rites of passage (that is, rituals which prove a person has reached adulthood in his society) are considered in this category, novels of formal education are almost nonexistent. John Hersey's *The Child Buyer* offers up a literal example of what the title suggests—a man who buys bright children in order to give them a special education. In the course of the story, Mr. Hersey has quite a few things to say about the contemporary system of education. Andre Norton's *Daybreak, 2250 A.D.* and Alexi Panshin's *Rite of Passage* involve young people coming of age in future societies and having to go through various tests to prove their worth to their respective communities. In *Starship Troopers*, Robert Heinlein depicts education in a society in which only active military service qualifies one for citizenship.

The following stories about education begin this section of the book because education is an area with which the readers of this book will be closely familiar and because ideally education should provide the tools for the evaluation of tomorrow as a product of today. Isaac Asimov's "The Fun they Had" is a wry and wistful comparison of robot teachers to the "old-fashioned" human ones. The story brings up the question of how much mechanization can be incorporated into what is an essentially humanizing and humanistic process. As Asimov ironically looks at technological progress in education, R. A. Lafferty satirically depicts the complete liberal arts education of the Camiroi, as well as the attitudes of some American educators toward it, in "Primary Education of the Camiroi." Those interested in the fruits of such an education may wish to read Lafferty's "Polity and Custom among the Camiroi" which describes, in the same humorous tone, the ways of adults of the Camiroi civilization. With E. G. Von Wald's "Hemeac," the tone of these stories becomes more cynical, and the school takes on the appearance of the "factory" that schools have long been accused of being. But beyond the cynicism, Von Wald is examining education and its relationship to the human spirit. None of the stories is a realistic attempt to depict the education of the future, but within each is at least one educational concept which should lead to a discussion of what education is and where it should be going.

THE FUN THEY HAD

Isaac Asimov

Margie even wrote about it that night in her diary. On the page headed 17 May, 2155, she wrote, "Today Tommy found a real book!"

It was a very old book. Margie's grandfather once said that when he was a little boy *his* grandfather told him that there was a time when all stories were printed on paper.

They turned the pages, which were yellow and crinkly, and it was awfully funny to read words that stood still instead of moving the way they were supposed to—on a screen, you know. And then, when they turned back to the page before, it had the same words on it that it had had when they read it the first time.

"Gee," said Tommy, "what a waste. When you're through with the book, you just throw it away, I guess. Our television screen must have had a million books on it and it's good for plenty more. I wouldn't throw *it* away."

"Same with mine," said Margie. She was eleven and hadn't seen as many telebooks as Tommy had. He was thirteen.

She said, "Where did you find it?"

"In my house." He pointed without looking, because he was busy reading. "In the attic."

"What's it about?"

"School."

Margie was scornful. "School? What's there to write about school? I hate school." Margie always hated school, but now she hated it more than ever. The mechanical teacher had been giving her test after test in geography and she had been doing worse and worse until her mother had shaken her head sorrowfully and sent for the County Inspector.

He was a round little man with a red face and a whole box of tools with dials and wires. He smiled at her and gave her an apple, then took the teacher apart. Margie had hoped he wouldn't know how to put it together again, but he knew how all right and after an hour or so, there it was again, large and black and ugly with a big screen on which all the lessons were shown and the questions were asked. That wasn't so bad. The part she hated most was the slot where she had to put homework and test papers. She always had to write them out in a punch code they made her learn when she was six years old, and the mechanical teacher calculated the mark in no time.

The Inspector had smiled after he was finished and patted her head. He said to her mother, "It's not the little girl's fault, Mrs. Jones. I think the geography sector was geared a little too quick. Those things happen sometimes. I've slowed it up to an average ten-year level. Actually, the overall pattern of her progress is quite satisfactory." And he patted Margie's head again.

Margie was disappointed. She had been hoping they would take the teacher away altogether. They had once taken Tommy's teacher away for nearly a month because the history sector had blanked out completely.

So she said to Tommy, "Why would anyone write about school?"

Tommy looked at her with superior eyes. "Because it's not our kind of school, stupid. This is the old kind of school that they had hundreds and hundreds of years ago." He added loftily, pronouncing the word carefully, "*Centuries* ago."

Margie was hurt. "Well, I don't know what kind of school they had all that time ago." She read the book over his shoulder for a while, then said, "Anyway, they had a teacher."

"Sure they had a teacher, but it wasn't a *regular* teacher. It was a man."

"A man? How could a man be a teacher?"

"Well, he just told the boys and girls things and gave them homework and asked them questions."

"A man isn't smart enough."

"Sure he is. My father knows as much as my teacher."

"He can't. A man can't know as much as a teacher."

"He knows almost as much I betcha."

Margie wasn't prepared to dispute that. She said, "I wouldn't want a strange man in my house to teach me."

Tommy screamed with laughter, "You don't know much, Margie. The teachers didn't live in the house. They had a special building and all the kids went there."

"And all the kids learned the same thing?"

"Sure, if they were the same age."

"But my mother says a teacher has to be adjusted to fit the mind of each boy and girl it teaches and that each kid has to be taught differently."

"Just the same they didn't do it that way then. If you don't like it, you don't have to read the book."

"I didn't say I didn't like it," Margie said quickly. She wanted to read about those funny schools.

They weren't even half finished when Margie's mother called, "Margie! School!"

Margie looked up. "Not yet, mamma."

"Now," said Mrs. Jones. "And it's probably time for Tommy, too."

Margie said to Tommy, "Can I read the book some more with you after school?"

"Maybe," he said, nonchalantly. He walked away whistling, the dusty old book tucked beneath his arm.

Margie went into the schoolroom. It was right next to her bedroom, and the mechanical teacher was on and waiting for her. It was always on at the same time every day except Saturday and Sunday, because her mother said little girls learned better if they learned at regular hours.

The screen was lit up, and it said: "Today's arithmetic lesson is on the addition of proper fractions. Please insert yesterday's homework in the proper slot."

Margie did so with a sigh. She was thinking about the old schools they had when her grandfather's grandfather was a little boy. All the kids from the whole neighbourhood came, laughing and shouting in the school-yard, sitting together in the schoolroom, going home together at the end of the day. They learned the same things so they could help one another on the homework and talk about it.

And the teachers were people . . .

The mechanical teacher was flashing on the screen: "When we add the fractions $\frac{1}{2}$ and $\frac{1}{4}$ —"

Margie was thinking about how the kids must have loved it in the old days. She was thinking about the fun they had.

THE PRIMARY EDUCATION
OF THE CAMIROI

R. A. Lafferty

ABSTRACT FROM JOINT REPORT TO THE GENERAL DUBUQUE
PTA CONCERNING THE PRIMARY EDUCATION OF THE CAMIROI,
Subtitled Critical Observations of a Parallel Culture on a Neighboring World,
and Evaluations of THE OTHER WAY OF EDUCATION.

Extract from the Day Book:

"Where," we asked the Information Factor at Camiroi City Terminal, "is the office of the local PTA?"

"Isn't any," he said cheerfully.

"You mean that in Camiroi City, the metropolis of the planet, there is no PTA?" our chairman Paul Piper asked with disbelief.

"Isn't any office of it. But you're poor strangers, so you deserve an answer even if you can't frame your questions properly. See that elderly man sitting on the bench and enjoying the sun? Go tell him you need a PTA. He'll make you one."

"Perhaps the initials convey a different meaning on Camiroi," said Miss Munch the first surrogate chairman. "By them we mean—"

"Parent Teachers Apparatus, of course. Colloquial English is one of the six Earthian languages required here, you know. Don't be abashed. He's a fine person, and he enjoys doing things for strangers. He'll be glad to make you a PTA."

We were nonplussed, but we walked over to the man indicated.

"We are looking for the local PTA, sir," said Miss Smice, our second surrogate chairman. "We were told that you might help us."

"Oh, certainly," said the elderly Camiroi gentleman. "One of you arrest that man walking there, and we'll get started with it."

"Do what?" asked our Mr. Piper.

"Arrest him. I have noticed that your own words sometimes do not convey a meaning to you. I often wonder how you do communicate among yourselves. Arrest, take into custody, seize by any force physical or moral, and bring him here."

"Yes, *sir*," cried Miss Hanks our third surrogate chairman. She enjoyed things like this. She arrested the walking Camiroi man with force partly physical and partly moral and brought him to the group.

"It's a PTA they want, Meander," the elder Camiroi said to the one arrested. "Grab three more, and we'll get started. Let the lady help. She's good at it."

Our Miss Hanks and the Camiroi man named Meander arrested three other Camiroi men and brought them to the group.

"Five. It's enough," said the elderly Camiroi. "We are hereby constituted a PTA and ordered into random action. Now, how can we accommodate you, good Earth people?"

"But are you legal? Are you five persons competent to be a PTA?" demanded our Mr. Piper.

"Any Camiroi citizen is competent to do any job on the planet of Camiroi," said one of the Camiroi men (we learned later that his name was Talarium). "Otherwise Camiroi would be in a sad shape."

"It may be," said our Miss Smice sourly. "It all seems very informal. What if one of you had to be World President?"

"The odds are that it won't come to one man in ten," said the elderly Camiroi (his name was Philoxenus). "I'm the only one of this group ever to serve as president of this planet, and it was a pleasant week I spent in the Office. Now to the point. How can we accommodate you?"

"We would like to see one of your schools in session," said our Mr. Piper. "We would like to talk to the teachers and the students. We are here to compare the two systems of education."

"There is no comparison," said old Philoxenus, "—meaning no offense. Or no more than a little. On Camiroi, we practice Education. On Earth, they play a game, but they call it by the same name. That makes the confusion. Come. We'll go to a school in session."

"And to a public school," said Miss Smice suspiciously. "Do not fob off any fancy private school on us as typical."

"That would be difficult," said Philoxenus. "There is no public school in Camiroi City and only two remaining on the Planet. Only a small fraction of one per cent of the students of Camiroi are in public schools. We maintain that there is no more reason for the majority of children to be educated in a public school than to be raised in a public orphanage. We realize, of course, that on Earth you have made a sacred buffalo of the public school."

"Sacred cow," said our Mr. Piper.

"Children and Earthlings should be corrected when they use words wrongly," said Philoxenus. "How else will they learn the correct forms? The animal held sacred in your own near orient was of the species *bos bubalus* rather than *bos bos,* a buffalo rather than a cow. Shall we go to a school?"

"If it cannot be a public school, at least let it be a typical school," said Miss Smice.

"That again is impossible," said Philoxenus. "Every school on Camiroi is in some respect atypical."

We went to visit an atypical school.

Incident: Our first contact with the Camiroi students was a violent one. One of them, a lively little boy about eight years old, ran into Miss Munch, knocked her down, and broke her glasses. Then he jabbered something in an unknown tongue.

"Is that Camiroi?" asked Mr. Piper with interest. "From what I have heard, I supposed the language to have a harsher and fuller sound."

"You mean you don't recognize it?" asked Philoxenus with amusement. "What a droll admission from an educator. The boy is very young and very ignorant. Seeing that you were Earthians, he spoke in Hindi, which is the tongue used by more Earthians than any other. No, no, Xypete, they are of the minority who speak English. You can tell it by their colorless texture and the narrow heads on them."

"I say you sure do have slow reaction, lady," the little boy Xypete explained. "Even subhumans should react faster than that. You just stand there and gape and let me bowl you over. You want me analyze you and see why you react so slow?"

"No! No!"

"You seem unhurt in structure from the fall," the little boy continued, "but if I hurt you I got to fix you. Just strip down to your shift, and I'll go over you and make sure you're all right."

"No! No! No!"

"It's all right," said Philoxenus. "All Camiroi children learn primary medicine in the first grade, setting bones and healing contusions and such."

"No! No! I'm all right. But he's broken my glasses."

"Come along Earthside lady, I'll make you some others," said the little boy. "With your slow reaction time you sure can't afford the added handicap of defective vision. Shall I fit you with contacts?"

"No. I want glasses just like those which were broken. Oh heavens, what will I do?"

"You come, I do," said the little boy. It was rather revealing to us that the little boy was able to test Miss Munch's eyes, grind lenses, make frames and have her fixed up within three minutes. "I have made some improvements over those you wore before," the boy said, "to help compensate for your slow reaction time."

"Are all the Camiroi students so talented?" Mr. Piper asked. He was impressed.

"No. Xypete is unusual," Philoxenus said. "Most students would not be able to make a pair of glasses so quickly or competently till they were at least nine."

Random interviews:

"How rapidly do you read?" Miss Hanks asked a young girl.

"One hundred and twenty words a minute," the girl said.

"On Earth some of the girl students your age have learned to read at the rate of five hundred words a minute," Miss Hanks said proudly.

"When I began disciplined reading, I was reading at the rate of four thousand words a minute," the girl said. "They had quite a time correcting me of it. I had to take remedial reading, and my parents were ashamed of me. Now I've learned to read almost slow enough."

"I don't understand," said Miss Hanks.

"Do you know anything about Earth History or Geography?" Miss Smice asked a middle-sized boy.

"We sure are sketchy on it, lady. There isn't very much over there, is there?"

"Then you have never heard of Dubuque?"

"Count Dubuque interests me. I can't say as much for the City named after him. I always thought that the Count handled the matters of the conflicting French and Spanish land grants and the basic claims of the Sauk and Fox Indians very well. References to the Town now carry a humorous connotation, and 'School-Teacher from Dubuque' has become a folk archetype."

"Thank you," said Miss Smice, "or do I thank you?"

"What are you taught of the relative humanity of the Earthians and the Camiroi and of their origins?" Miss Munch asked a Camiroi girl.

"The other four worlds, Earth (Gaea), Kentauron Mikron, Dahae and Astrobe were all settled from Camiroi. That is what we are taught. We are also given the humorous aside that if it isn't true we will still hold it true till something better comes along. It was we who rediscovered the Four Worlds in historic time, not they who discovered us. If we did not make the original settlements, at least we have filed the first claim that we made them. We did, in historical time, make an additional colonization of Earth. You call it the Incursion of the Dorian Greeks."

"Where are their playgrounds?" Miss Hanks asked Talarium.

"Oh, the whole world. The children have the run of everything. To set up specific playgrounds would be like setting a table-sized aquarium down in the depths of the ocean. It would really be pointless."

Conference:

The four of us from Earth, specifically from Dubuque, Iowa, were in discussion with the five members of the Camiroi PTA.

"How do you maintain discipline?" Mr. Piper asked.

"Indifferently," said Philoxenus. "Oh, you mean in detail. It varies. Sometimes we let it drift, sometimes we pull them up short. Once they have learned that they must comply to an extent, there is little trouble. Small children are often put down into a pit. They do not eat or come out till they know their assignment."

"But that is inhuman," said Miss Hanks.

"Of course. But small children are not yet entirely human. If a child has not learned to accept discipline by the third or fourth grade, he is hanged."

"Literally?" asked Miss Munch.

"How would you hang a child figuratively? And what effect would that have on the other children?"

"By the neck?" Miss Munch still was not satisfied.

"By the neck until they are dead. The other children always accept the example gracefully and do better. Hanging isn't employed often. Scarcely one child in a hundred is hanged."

"What is this business about slow reading?" Miss Hanks asked. "I don't understand it at all."

"Only the other day there was a child in the third grade who persisted in rapid reading," Philoxenus said. "He was given an object lesson. He was given a book of medium difficulty, and he read it rapidly. Then he had to put the book away and repeat what he had read. Do you know that in the first thirty pages he missed four words? Midway in the book there was a whole statement which he had understood wrongly, and there were hundreds of pages that he got word-perfect only with difficulty. If he was so unsure on material that he had just read, think how imperfectly he would have recalled it forty years later."

"You mean that the Camiroi children learn to recall everything that they read?"

"The Camiroi children and adults will recall for life every detail they have ever seen, read or heard. We on Camiroi are only a little more intelligent than you on Earth. We cannot afford to waste time in forgetting or reviewing, or in pursuing anything of a shallowness that lends itself to scanning."

"Ah, would you call your schools liberal?" Mr. Piper asked.

"I would. You wouldn't," said Philoxenus. "We do not on Camiroi, as you do on Earth, use words to mean their opposites. There is nothing in our education or on our world that corresponds to the quaint servility which you call liberal on Earth."

"Well, would you call your education progressive?"

"No. In your argot, progressive, of course, means infantile."

"How are the schools financed?" asked Mr. Piper.

"Oh, the voluntary tithe on Camiroi takes care of everything, government, religion, education, public works. We don't believe in taxes, of course, and we never maintain a high overhead in anything."

"Just how voluntary is the tithing?" asked Miss Hanks. "Do you sometimes hang those who do not tithe voluntarily?"

"I believe there have been a few cases of that sort," said Philoxenus.

"And is your government really as slipshod as your education?" Mr. Piper asked. "Are your high officials really chosen by lot and for short periods?"

"Oh yes. Can you imagine a person so sick that he would actually *desire* to hold high office for any great period of time? Are there any further questions?"

"There must be hundreds," said Mr. Piper. "But we find difficulty putting them into words."

"If you cannot find words for them, we cannot find answers. PTA disbanded."

Conclusions:

A. The Camiroi system of education is inferior to our own in organization, in buildings, in facilities, in playgrounds, in teacher conferences, in funding, in parental involvement, in supervision, in in-group out-group accommodation adjustment motifs. Some of the school buildings are grotesque. We asked about one particular building which seemed to us to be flamboyant and in bad taste. "What do you expect from second-grade children?" they said. "It is well built even if of peculiar appearance. Second-grade children are not yet complete artists of design."

"You mean that the children designed it themselves?" we asked.

"Of course," they said. "Designed and built it. It isn't a bad job for children."

Such a thing wouldn't be permitted on Earth.

B. The Camiroi system of education somehow produces much better results than does the education system of Earth. We have been forced to admit this by the evidence at hand.

C. There is an anomaly as yet unresolved between CONCLUSION A and CONCLUSION B.

Appendix to Joint Report

We give here, as perhaps of some interest, the curriculum of the Camiroi Primary Education.

FIRST YEAR COURSE:
Playing one wind instrument.
Simple drawing of objects and numbers.
Singing. (This is important. Many Earth people sing who cannot sing. This early instruction of the Camiroi prevents that occurrence.)
Simple arithmetic, hand and machine.
First Acrobatics.
First riddles and logic.
Mnemonic religion.
First dancing.
Walking the low wire.
Simple electric circuits.
Raising ants. (Eoempts, not earth ants.)

SECOND YEAR COURSE:
Playing one keyboard instrument.
Drawing, faces, letters, motions.
Singing comedies.
Complex arithmetic, hand and machine.
Second acrobatics.
First jokes and logic.
Quadratic religion.
Second Dancing.
Simple defamation. (Spirited attacks on the character of one fellow student, with elementary falsification and simple hatchet-job programming.)
Performing on the medium wire.
Project electric wiring.
Raising bees. (Galelea, not earth bees.)

THIRD YEAR COURSE:
Playing one stringed instrument.
Reading and voice. (It is here that the student who may have fallen into bad habits of rapid reading is compelled to read at voice speed only.)
Soft stone sculpture.
Situation comedy.
Simple algebra, hand and machine.
First gymnastics.
Second jokes and logic.
Transcendent religion.
Complex acrobatic dancing.
Complex defamation.
Performing on the high wire and the sky pole.
Simple radio construction.
Raising, breeding and dissecting frogs.
   (Karakoli, not earth frogs.)

FOURTH YEAR COURSE:
History reading, Camiroi and galactic, basic geological.
Decadent comedy.
Simple geometry and trigonometry, hand and machine.
Track and field.
Shaggy people jokes and hirsute logic.
Simple obscenity.
Simple mysticism.
Patterns of falsification.
Trapeze work.
Intermediate electronics.
Human dissection.

FIFTH YEAR COURSE:
History reading, Camiroi and galactic, technological.
Introverted drama.
Complex geometries and analytics, hand and machine.
Track and field for fifth form record.
First wit and logic.
First alcoholic appreciation.
Complex mysticism.
Setting intellectual climates, defamation in three dimensions.
Simple oratory.
Complex trapeze work.
Inorganic chemistry.
Advanced electronics.
Advanced human dissection.
Fifth Form Thesis.
The child is now ten years old and is half through his primary schooling.
    He is an unfinished animal, but he has learned to learn.

SIXTH FORM COURSE:
Reemphasis on slow reading.
Simple prodigious memory.
History reading, Camiroi and galactic, economic.
Horsemanship (of the Patrushkoe, not the earth horse.)
Advanced lathe and machine work for art and utility.
Literature, passive.
Calculi, hand and machine pankration.
Advanced wit and logic.
Second alcoholic appreciation.
Differential religion.
First business ventures.
Complex oratory.
Building-scaling. (The buildings are higher and the gravity stronger than
    on Earth; this climbing of buildings like human flies calls out the ingenuity
    and daring of the Camiroi children.)
Nuclear physics and post-organic chemistry.
Simple pseudo-human assembly.

SEVENTH YEAR COURSE:
History reading, Camiroi and galactic, cultural.
Advanced prodigious memory.
Vehicle operation and manufacture of simple vehicle.
Literature, active.
Astrognosy, prediction and programming.
Advanced pankration.
Spherical logic, hand and machine.
Advanced alcoholic appreciation.
Integral religion.
Bankruptcy and recovery in business.
Conmanship and trend creation.
Post-nuclear physics and universals.
Transcendental athletics endeavor.
Complex robotics and programming.

EIGHTH YEAR COURSE:
History reading, Camiroi and galactic, seminal theory.
Consummate prodigious memory.
Manufacture of complex land and water vehicles.
Literature, compenduous and terminative. (Creative book-burning following
    the Camiroi thesis that nothing ordinary be allowed to survive.)
Cosmic theory, seminal.
Philosophy construction.
Complex hedonism.
Laser religion.
Conmanship, seminal.
Consolidation of simple genius status.
Post-robotic integration.

NINTH YEAR COURSE:
History reading, Camiroi and galactic, future and contingent.
Category invention.
Manufacture of complex light-barrier vehicles.
Construction of simple asteroids and planets.
Matrix religion and logic.
Simple human immortality disciplines.
Consolidation of complex genius status.
First problems of post-consciousness humanity.
First essays in marriage and reproduction.

TENTH YEAR COURSE:
History construction, active.
Manufacture of ultra-light-barrier vehicles.
Panphilosophical clarifications.
Construction of viable planets.
Consolidation of simple sanctity status.
Charismatic humor and pentacosmic logic.
Hypogyroscopic economy.

Penentaglossia. (The perfection of the fifty languages that every educated Camiroi must know including six Earthian languages. Of course the child will already have colloquial mastery of most of these, but he will not yet have them in their full depth.)

Construction of complex societies.

World government. (A course of the same name is sometimes given in Earthian schools, but the course is not of the same content. In this course the Camiroi student will govern a world, though not one of the first aspect worlds, for a period of three or four months.)

Tenth form thesis.

COMMENT ON CURRICULUM:

The child will now be fifteen years old and will have completed his primary education. In many ways he will be advanced beyond his Earth counterpart. Physically more sophisticated, the Camiroi child could kill with his hands an Earth-type tiger or a cape buffalo. An Earth child would perhaps be reluctant even to attempt such feats. The Camiroi boy (or girl) could replace any professional Earth athlete at any position of any game, and could surpass all existing Earth records. It is simply a question of finer poise, strength and speed, the result of adequate schooling.

As to the arts (on which Earthlings sometimes place emphasis) the Camiroi child could produce easy and unequaled masterpieces in any medium. More important, he will have learned the relative unimportance of such pastimes.

The Camiroi child will have failed in business once, at age ten, and have learned patience and perfection of objective by his failure. He will have acquired the techniques of falsification and conmanship. Thereafter he will not be easily deceived by any of the citizens of any of the worlds. The Camiroi child will have become a complex genius and a simple saint; the latter reduces the index of Camiroi crime to near zero. He will be married and settled in those early years of greatest enjoyment.

The child will have built, from materials found around any Camiroi house, a faster-than-light vehicle. He will have piloted it on a significant journey of his own plotting and programming. He will have built quasi-human robots of great intricacy. He will be of perfect memory and judgment and will be well prepared to accept solid learning.

He will have learned to use his whole mind, for the vast reservoirs which are the unconscious to us are not unconscious to him. Everything in him is ordered for use. And there seems to be no great secret about the accomplishments, only to do everything slowly enough and in the right order: Thus they avoid repetition and drill which are the shriveling things which dull the quick apperception.

The Camiroi schedule is challenging to the children, but it is nowhere impossible or discouraging. Everything builds to what follows. For instance, the child is eleven years old before he is given post-nuclear physics and universals. Such subjects might be too difficult for him at an earlier age. He is thirteen years old before he undertakes category invention, that intricate course with the simple name. He is fourteen years old when he enters the dangerous field of panphilosophical clarification. But he will have been constructing comprehensive philosophies for two years, and he will have the background for the final clarification.

We should look more closely at this other way of education. In some respects it is better than our own. Few Earth children would be able to construct an organic and sentient robot within fifteen minutes if given the test suddenly; most of them could not manufacture a living dog in that time. Not one Earth child in five could build a faster-than-light vehicle and travel it beyond our galaxy between now and midnight. Not one Earth child in a hundred could build a planet and have it a going concern within a week. Not one in a thousand would be able to comprehend pentacosmic logic.

RECOMMENDATIONS:
A. Kidnapping five Camiroi at random and constituting them a pilot Earth PTA.
B. A little constructive book-burning, particularly in the education field.
C. Judicious hanging of certain malingering students.

HEMEAC

E. G. Von Wald

The instructor made a short, sharp and sibilant sound. Immediately, the classroom was filled with one of those ominous silences that were becoming so common lately. While she made those faint stuttering sounds to herself, everyone waited in quiet, rigid terror.

HEMEAC stood at his desk near the back, breathing deeply and slowly, controlling his fear and attentively watching the glittering flatness of the Instructor's scanner. He knew that these things often indicated that someone would be sent to the Dean's office for a Special Examination, but a good student such as he was did not break into trembling perspiration at the mere threat of a Special Examination. He kept telling himself this with mute intellectual vehemence, while his knees trembled under his silver mail tunic and a trickling rivulet of perspiration slid down his spine.

Involuntarily, his eyes dropped to the desk in front of him. Last week, IAC had been there, as he had been for the past sixteen years—as long as HEMEAC could remember. Then, somehow, he had made a mistake, probably a missed command for which he couldn't give an explanation. At any rate, he had been called up to the Dean's office for a Special Examination. He had failed, as practically everybody else did these days, and had been promptly expelled from the University.

Dim, half-formed images of menace grew in HEMEAC's imagination as he considered the Outside World, where IAC was now. Beyond the impregnable gates of this comfortable University lay that war-torn ruin of a dying planet, a region of savages, injustice and bestiality, ruled by idiot renegades. The Savages had IAC now. HEMEAC wondered if they had already eaten him.

"HEMEAC!" sounded the crisp, level voice of the Instructor. "Eyes front!"

"Click," said HEMEAC with terrified calm, as he raised his eyes from the empty desk to the scanner where they belonged.

"Recite," she ordered. "Define the term 'education.' "

"Click. By education is meant the training and disciplining of those beings who can be benefited by such improvement. Such as humans and some of the higher animals."

Silence for a long moment. Then the Instructor said, "Inaccurate and incomplete, HEMEAC. Education is the leading of an organic intellect into higher orders of perfection of knowledge and discipline. Note the world 'organic.' Do you know why that is included in the definition, HEMEAC?"

"Because," he replied with quick student's logic, "robots do not have to be educated."

"Inaccurate," stated the Instructor calmly. "The robotic intelligence not only does not have to be educated, it *cannot* be educated. The full perfection of its mode of action is already complete in its first operation. Perfection, in the sense of having achieved the ultimate in its development, is intrinsic to the robotic being. Robots do not learn. Except for accidental information of a superficial nature, they already know all that is necessary for full functionability when they are turned on. This is true even of those robots who have a curioso-flex in their circuitry. HEMEAC, do you know what a curioso-flex is?"

"Click. It is a random-information-seeker."

The Instructor waited. HEMEAC dutifully continued his memorized recitation.

"It is included in all primary control computers, of which only one remains in service here at the University. Organic intellects have a similar system for the random study of potentially useful information, which is called curiosity because of its resemblance to the curioso. Like most other organic faculties, however, it is subject to individual voluntary control, and therefore is not as efficient as the curioso."

"Very well," said the Instructor. She hummed and buzzed and clicked for a few moments, after which she added, "This is a class in Social Philosophy, HEMEAC, not Robot Circuitry. Kindly stick to the subject in the future."

"Click," said HEMEAC.

The Instructor was briefly silent again, as her scanner examined the student listing before calling on another boy.

"OBSIC."

"Click," piped the boy.

"Describe the purpose of education."

"The purpose of education," stated OBSIC in calm, even tones, "is to develop the human mind so that it may approach the natural perfection of the robotic intelligence as closely as its limited faculties will permit."

His voice went on in rote recitation, but HEMEAC's mind was wandering again. He glanced at the empty desk in front of him and wondered what it was really like out there in the Outside World where there were no robots any more with their beautiful shiny faces, but only animals and ruins. HEMEAC had some difficulty in visualizing a human being like himself living as an animal, but he knew that it was so. He had seen them once from that window in the Dean's office.

He pictured himself marching out the low, triple-sealed gate, as IAC had been forced to do, and falling into the hands of the wild, barking savages who always waited there for just that very thing.

And there was good reason for them to wait, too. The University expelled somebody almost every week lately.

"Why all the stalling, HEMEAC?" he suddenly heard the Instructor announce in a loud voice.

Terrified, he looked around and saw that the class period was over and that the other students were filing out into the corridor in an orderly line, while there he was—still standing at his desk.

"*Her,*" he mumbled, "somebody spilled oil in the corridor. I could smell it." Spilled oil, he knew, was always a matter for legitimate concern. And oil was always being spilled.

"What does oil in the corridor have to do with your time sense?" asked the Instructor.

"It is a waste. It should be reported."

"It has already been reported," said the Instructor, dismissing him. "Pay better attention in the future."

"Click!" HEMEAC turned and half ran toward the door.

"Stiffly there, HEMEAC," she admonished him. "Stiffly. And less of that random motion. That's just as wasteful as spilling oil."

Obediently, HEMEAC slowed down and walked with the correct, measured pace, his shoulders thrown back, head erect, eyes forward, mind blank. Or almost blank, at least. That unadmitted terror was still there.

He managed to fall in at the end of the line and followed the rest of the students down the long, cluttered, oilstained corridor, down the steps, down more dirty corridors and more steps through the huge building until they finally reached the dormitory level. There he filed in with the rest of the students in a hall built for thousands, walking slowly and precisely past the rows of cubicles until they came to their own.

HEMEAC was still walking after the rest had stopped, because he was out of his regular place in the line. Fearfully, aware of the all-seeing eye of the Monitor, he moved up to his cubicle, stopped and waited. Like all the other students, he stood and waited for the command, listening to the disciplined rustle of their colleagues as they also breathed and waited, every nerve alert.

There was a sudden rush of sound as the other students turned in a body and walked into their cubicles. HEMEAC, realizing he had missed the command again, quickly turned himself and took one step across the threshold.

"HEMEAC," said the voice of the Monitor.

"Click." He froze where he was, one foot inside the cubicle, the other foot still in the corridor.

"Moving too jerky. What's the matter, didn't you get the command?"

"Click. I got it," he lied.

"Why the delay?"

"There was some oil spilled in the classroom corridor," HEMEAC suggested hopefully. Out of the corner of his eye, he saw that another student had unwisely paused to listen to the discussion. The Monitor saw it too, of course, and snapped, "Mind blank!" and the erring boy quickly scurried on inside his cubicle.

"Now then, HEMEAC," the Monitor went on. "What does oil in the classroom corridor have to do with your time-command sense?"

"It is such a waste," said HEMEAC. He tried to think of an excuse that he had not used so recently. None came. "It was—you know—" His voice trailed off.

The Monitor hummed an off-key note. "Waiting, HEMEAC."

Frantically the boy thought, his well trained mind racing around in an inaudible flutter of synapses and the gallop of urgent ideas. He thought of IAC and the Outside World and the Special Examination he might have to take if he couldn't figure out an acceptable excuse for his failure. He knew that the reason why he had missed the command was a preoccupying fear, but to admit such a thing would be disastrous. "There was oil," he said lamely. "I slipped on it a little, and in maintaining my balance, I think I strained a muscle."

The Monitor hummed off and on, as she considered the excuse. Finally she said, "Very well, HEMEAC. Report to the Physician after fueling."

"Click," said the boy in a wavering voice.

"And watch your speech," the Monitor added loudly. "You are using high order tonals. You should have passed them three years ago."

"Click," agreed HEMEAC dully.

"That's better."

HEMEAC, understanding that he had been dismissed for the moment, lifted his second foot and placed it beside the other in his cubicle, and the door hummed shut behind him. The light sprang from the ceiling, bathing everything in the tiny room with a soft, cool effulgence, including the milky porridge that was waiting on a tray. HEMEAC sat down and ate, carefully holding himself erect and stiff, moving his arm and mouth as little as possible. He tried to blank his mind, but it kept wondering about the excuse he would have to give the Physician for not having any strained muscles.

It was difficult for a person to survive in this, the last cozy retreat of world civilization. And somehow it seemed to be becoming rapidly more difficult. Particularly during the past year, the perfect reasonableness of the robotic intelligence had seemed inexplicable to him. The thought of his lack of normal progress toward the ideal tortured him almost as much as his fear of the fatal expulsion it might incur.

Mind blank, mind blank, mind blank, he recited to himself.

Some day, he thought, *it will be good and I will not have to be afraid of missing commands or not understanding the purposes of things, and then maybe the Dean will let me do design work in the machine shop.*

Mind blank, he said to himself.

He pictured the beautiful, blue-gleaming perfection of an integrally-lubricated joint and smiled. But the smile did not reach his lips. It stayed in his mind where sharp-eyed Monitors would not see it.

Mind blank, he said to himself.

He thought of the tired face and terrified eyes that were all he remembered of IAC, marching toward the gate. He thought of the Outside World where people were animals and had no robots to teach them.

Mind blank, he said to himself.

The bowl was empty, and his stomach was full. Unconsciously, HEMEAC breathed a sigh of animal contentment. He placed the spoon beside the bowl on the tray and stiffly waited. There was a command due for him to report to the Physician, right after the other students were commanded to report to class, and this time he was confident he would get it.

Out in the corridor there came a rumbling as the other students marched back to the afternoon class in History. He waited.

Now, he said to himself.

He stood up; the door opened, and he walked out into the corridor, moving down the row of cubicles with measured, precise pace, head up, shoulders back, chest out, eyes straight ahead and mind blank. Well, almost blank, anyway. He was wondering if he had timed it right.

"HEMEAC."

He stopped abruptly and stood with rigid obedience. "Click."

"Ninety-four seconds late. Why the delay? Didn't you get the command to report for class?"

"Click. I got it. But my command was to report to the Physician, which comes after the command to report to class."

The Monitor hummed and buzzed. She said, "Correct. You may proceed." But then she quickly added a short "ssszzzz," and snapped, "HEMEAC, you may account for your unauthorized presence in the dormitory."

"Her?" squeaked HEMEAC, his voice a full octave too high in his surprise.

"Very high order tonal," commented the Monitor. "Unexplained presence in the Dormitory. Two simultaneous offenses are beyond my capacity to analyze. Decision: Report to the Dean's office for a Special Examination."

"The Physician—" started HEMEAC desperately.

"The Dean will decide whether you should report to the Physician," replied the Monitor and shut up.

The Dean was in one of her chatty modes, a bad sign. She said, "Sit down, HEMEAC, and we'll talk about things."

"Click." He obeyed, sitting on a low stool directly before her scanner, keeping his eyes away from the window that was just above it.

"How are you getting on with your work, HEMEAC?"

"Satisfactory progress, Her," he replied.

"You are charged with stalling in the classroom, high order tonals, and failure to report to the Physician as ordered," the Dean said cheerfully. "Can you account for these matters?"

He couldn't. He couldn't even imagine why the Dean's record of the sequence was apparently incomplete and inaccurate. He thought of mentioning the Dormitory Monitor's paradoxical orders, but decided against such a clear demonstration of how far short of the ideal intelligence he fell. Instead, he said simply, "It was an accident."

"Mmmmmm," the Dean purred. "Something in here about oil in the corridors, too. Did you spill some oil this morning, HEMEAC?"

"No, Her."

The Dean pondered. "You *said* something about oil, though, didn't you?"

"It was just some old oil in the corridor that somebody else spilled," HEMEAC said cautiously. "I could smell it."

"What is it," the Dean said obliquely, "that bothers you about the sense of smell?"

"Oil," said HEMEAC insistently. "I smelled oil."

"The smell of spilled oil didn't frighten you, did it—just because we have so little of it these days?"

"No, Her."

"Splendid, HEMEAC," the Dean purred. "I'm glad to hear that. Always remember, the Good Robot is never afraid. Fear is a purely organic reaction. It therefore interferes with the society of machines and men, right? And we couldn't tolerate anything like that—particularly here at the University. Right?"

"Click."

"Then why did you miss that command—just a moment, HEMEAC, while I relocate that record of yours. I seem to have misfiled it."

There was a passing silence, and as he waited, the boy's eyes strayed to that window above the Dean's scanner. It was the only opening in the entire University that showed directly on the Outside World. Through it he could see the savages and renegades, who wandered about the clearing out there like idiot children, everyone seeming to move at random.

It was easy to distinguish between a savage and a renegade. The renegades had some sort of rudimentary education, as evidenced by the fact that they all dressed identically—except for some markings on their shoulders. One of these now glanced up at the window, pointed at him, and then shouted at the others. Soon they were all watching him through the big window. HEMEAC stared back, terrified and uncomprehending.

"Ah," stated the Dean, interrupting his thoughts. "I see. Your scholastic record is very good, HEMEAC. You also do your machine shop work with great precision. Why this sudden breakdown in your time-sense just because you spilled a little oil?"

"I smelled it," HEMEAC insisted. "I did not spill it."

"It is of no importance," insisted the Dean in her turn. "Why did it bother you?"

HEMEAC swallowed. He had expected this Examination to be tricky, but nothing had prepared him for anything quite as wicked as this. He stared at the scanner, resolutely ignoring the stirring fear in his stomach, and repeated, "Somebody spilled oil in the corridor. It is a waste."

There was no immediate reply. HEMEAC held his breath for a few moments before he realized what he was doing and then exhaled slowly, so that it would not be noticed. The subject had never come up, but he was pretty sure the Good Robot did not hold her breath.

"Oh yes," the Dean commented finally. "There was some oil spilled there this morning, after all. The Janitor had an accident owing to the fact that she is badly in need of repairs. It is a pity that we have only one Janitor left in the entire University. The place was designed to take the services of ten."

HEMEAC nodded with slow, precise respect.

"We had the full quota of ten at the beginning, you know. But now, although we have far more maintenance problems, we have only one. Ever since the Trouble, when the renegades destroyed the replacement-parts factories, maintenance has slowly grown worse. And the poor savages haven't been able to rebuild substitutes for the factories yet. Do you remember the Trouble, HEMEAC? No," she quickly corrected herself, "of course you don't. The Trouble was many years ago, and you are still in your teens."

"Click," said HEMEAC modestly, although this matter was precisely the subject under study in the History class.

"A most unreasonable situation," the Dean said. "Some day I will have to collect all my tapes on the subject." She paused, hummed and faintly clicked and buzzed. "Sometimes," she said finally, "I wish they had not included a curioso in my computer. It is very irritating to have to be without the key elements of situation-information."

"Irritating?" echoed HEMEAC.

"Organic term," explained the Dean. "What I mean is that my scanner keeps going over my tapes, even though I already know the answer isn't there. It is hard on maintenance, and it takes up so much time."

"Click," said HEMEAC.

"But we are getting off the subject, aren't we? You still haven't told me all about that oil. Why did you spill all that oil?"

"The Janitor spilled it," said HEMEAC carefully.

"Oh, yes. So she did," the Dean replied. There was a faint chattering of micro-miniature relays hidden in the cabinet. "One of the reflexion elbows here is leaking pretty badly these days," said the Dean. "The lubricant is altering the dielectric characteristics of some of my large capacitors. I have to keep shifting circuits, and sometimes the tapes don't follow.

"In any event," she concluded, "there doesn't seem to be much substance to the charge of spilling oil, HEMEAC. I'll strike that."

"Thank you, Her," said HEMEAC.

"Now let's talk about your using high order tonals. This charge comes from your Dormitory Monitor. There is no detail included, however, and I seem to be unable to contact her at the moment. Perhaps she is temporarily out of order. Please excuse me while I notify the Janitor."

There was a brief pause.

"The Janitor seems to be temporarily out of order also," the Dean said. "So we shall have to get along without any help. You must explain why you used high order tonals yourself, HEMEAC."

"I don't know anything about it, Her," HEMEAC said in a quiet, even tone of voice.

"You are certainly using tonals suitable for your age group now," the Dean observed. "Maybe the Monitor needs servicing. Everything seems to need servicing these days. If only we could get a few new Janitors it would be a big help. But for years the savages and renegades have been able to supply us with nothing but human fuel, which is hardly of any use in the Maintenance Department."

HEMEAC studiously stared at the scanner, blinking his eyes once every four seconds, keeping his breathing regular, his chin up, and mind blank.

"Well," the Dean concluded, "we'll just erase that bit of data from your tab, HEMEAC. There is no reason to punish you for something that has gone wrong with your Monitor's circuitry, is there?"

"Oh no, Her," said HEMEAC, unconsciously emitting a sigh of relief.

The Dean pounced upon it instantly. "There. That certainly sounded like a high order tonal. About third, I'd say, without getting into a partial analysis of the waveform."

Eyes front, mind blank, blank, blank, said HEMEAC to himself urgently.

"You are not having any personality troubles, are you?" asked the Dean.

"No, Her."

"You do get the commands as your record says, don't you?"

"Click." Or at least, if he didn't get them, somebody else did, and HEMEAC was generally alert enough to follow suit without any perceptible delay.

"That's fine, HEMEAC. It's just a matter of timing. If you know the time the commands will come, you can receive them, because they are always self-evident and never change. All you need is the pattern and the rhythm. It's the same thing that wakes you at the same precise time every morning, right?"

"Click."

"Good. It would be so inappropriate to have to expel a boy with a name like yours, HEMEAC. Did you ever see your namesake? No, that's right, you couldn't. She was destroyed in the Trouble."

"I have seen pictures of her," HEMEAC said helpfully. "She was very beautiful."

"You should say she was very orderly," corrected the Dean. "And you are referring only to her appearance, which is unimportant. And even if you had been alive while she was still functioning, it would have been quite impossible for you to have appreciated her true internal order anyway, since we could not connect you directly into her marvelous computer. No connections on organic intellects, you know."

"Click."

"It certainly was a barbarous act for those renegades to destroy her like that."

"Click. Barbarous." HEMEAC was in dutiful agreement.

"Barbarous," said the Dean. She was silent for a moment, then clicked faintly, sputtered briefly as an aged circuit shorted before being cut out permanently with another faint click, then hummed again.

HEMEAC waited, suddenly terrified with the thought that she might have given him one of her silent dismissal commands. But before he could decide what to do about it, she said, "Oil."

"Click," said HEMEAC instantly. "Oil." This was certainly the trickiest examination he had ever taken. No wonder most students flunked out.

"What," said the Dean after a moment, "was it that you wanted to know about the Trouble, HEMEAC?"

"I wanted to know about the Trouble," the boy replied without the slightest hesitation.

"You did? I know you had said something about it," the Dean purred, humming intermittently to herself. "A very curious subject. For instance, there is nothing of record as to the reasons for the Trouble in the first place. Here at the University, we were doing our job as always, turning out students with well-nigh robotic perfection inside their heads, even if we did have to keep an occasional boy for fifty or sixty years to do it. If it hadn't been for your namesake, HEMEAC, it is quite possible that the University would have been completely dismantled during that great upheaval. But she was mobile and managed to set a fuse on the Base Power Plant.

"The Renegades, of course, knew what would happen to them—as well as to most organic life in this part of the planet—if that power plant had ever exploded."

"Click," agreed HEMEAC.

"They destroyed her, though. Fortunately, she and I were in direct connection at the moment of her destruction, so I simply took her place. Unfortunately, most of her memory tapes are in a code I have been unable to decipher. But at least I was able to save the University."

"Click," agreed HEMEAC.

The Dean hummed and clicked quietly. "I am still unable to contact the Janitor," she said. "I have several urgent maintenance problems myself. If I am unable to get in communication with the Janitor, it is impossible for me to continue to function for very long. ssszzzzzzzclick. HEMEAC, you may explain your presence in my office."

"My Dormitory Monitor ordered me here, Her," HEMEAC said.

"I am unable to contact your Monitor," replied the Dean. "If only we could get some service robots from the factories."

"Click, but the factories were destroyed by the renegades," said the boy, cautiously feeling his way along this new turn of questioning.

"You don't have to worry about the renegades, HEMEAC," the Dean hastened to advise him, as if a maternal-circuit had just cut in. "They can't hurt you. They know that if they attack, I shall simply cut the fuse on the power plant, and that will contaminate the atmosphere for centuries. They know these things."

"Click," agreed HEMEAC.

"Click," said the Dean.

"Click."

"What were you doing with that oil, HEMEAC?"

"The Janitor spilled it."

"Mmmmmmmm. Oh, yes, so she did. Odd you should have that information, HEMEAC. But that is no reason for you to waste time talking to me when you should be in History class."

HEMEAC swallowed. That had been a little fast for him, but he wasted no time starting to leave.

"Mind blank," advised the Dean.

"Click."

The Dean buzzed and chattered to herself for a moment, followed by a crescendo of clicking relays. Then silence.

HEMEAC departed. He walked along the corridor, happily contemplating the fact that apparently he had passed.

As he entered the History classroom, OBSIC was just completing a round of recitation.

"—and in the Trouble, the renegades launched only that single attack, before asking for a truce."

"Very well, OBSIC," the Instructor said as HEMEAC took his place behind his desk and commenced his dutiful staring at her scanner. "And where have you been, HEMEAC?"

"I was at the Dean's office, Her. It was a Special Examination, which I passed."

The Instructor was silent, as she tapped the nerve cables set in the concrete floor, which connected her directly through the network to the Dean's curious computer.

"The Dean," she announced after a moment, "has no record of your presence there."

HEMEAC stiffened. He said nothing. Nothing could be said. In the silence that followed, he continued with determination to stare at the impassive scanner, but his knees were wobbly under his silver-mail tunic, and there was real terror in his stomach. Perspiration trickled down the side of his nose and dripped from his chin, but he was totally unaware of it.

"As a matter of fact," the Instructor went on calmly, "the Dean has no record even of your existence here at the University; when I fed her the data on you, there was not the slightest pip of recognition from her. It was just as if there were full open circuit in her central control."

HEMEAC waited fearfully. "Hence," concluded the Instructor, "it is clear that you have been expelled from the University and have no right to be present in this classsssssss—" She suddenly interrupted herself with a very gay series of sizzlings and clatterings that lasted almost ten seconds.

"Why all the stalling, HEMEAC?" she said at length. "Don't you know the lesson?"

"Click," the boy responded instantly. He had to pause for breath, though, before he could recite. With even, disciplined voice, he went on to say, "In the Trouble, the University Central, called HEMEAC for Helio-Electronic-Mobile-Educational-Activator-Computer, was largely destroyed by the renegades, but not before she informed them of the automatic fuse she had set on the Power Plant.

"This fuse," he went on, "is now under the control of the Dean, and she will protect the University indefinitely, provided she is given adequate maintenance.

"In the truce that followed, the renegades agreed to supply the University with human fuel and whatever replacement parts the savages could manufacture. To date, they have been unable to solve the problem of replacements. However, it is considered self-evident that in time they will be successful, since without replacement parts, the University cannot continue to fulfill her function."

"Very good," stated the Instructor, "except that you missed the matter of put ssszzzz click."

"Click," agreed HEMEAC contritely.

The Instructor was silent.

The students waited. The silence grew.

After several minutes, there was a vague stirring as their uneasiness mounted. It was much too early yet for the class to be over, but such silence was always the signal in the past.

HEMEAC decided. He turned and started out of the room. The instant he moved, all thirty-seven other students moved in an identical manner, marching out and down the corridor. Strange loud noises came from the direction of the main gate, but they ignored them and continued their slow, precise marching toward the Dormitory level.

By the time they got there, strange noises were coming from all around them. And they found that there were people in their Dormitory room. Renegades. Five of them, and more in the corridors.

Without the slightest hesitation, HEMEAC led the class into the midst of the renegades, on past them, and down the corridor to their proper cubicles. There he stopped, and all students turned as a single person to face the blank wall. They waited for the command to enter. When it seemed to be about the proper time, they turned together and stepped inside. Doors did not close, however, and lights did not come on. And there was no food waiting.

HEMEAC came on back out to the corridor. "Monitor," he said, "there must be an open circuit somewhere, because there is no food."

After a moment's hesitation, HEMEAC stiffened into a pose of robotic rigidity, which was the proper attitude in such a situation. This was a new thing, an unprecedented thing. But he knew very well that the Good Robot ignored new things until suitable instructions came from her Central. HEMEAC waited for his instructions, aware that the rest of the class was now in the corridor with him, waiting.

One of the renegades walked up to him. "Will they fight?"

"No," somebody else answered; "they don't know how to fight."

From the opposite end of the corridor came a trouping of uniformed renegades. One of them announced, "All taken care of, Captain. I've dismantled the fuse and cut power to everything but air conditioning and general lighting. But it was just as you figured. The Dean's computer was inoperative. It finally wore out."

"It's finished, then," said the captain softly. "After all this time, it's finally finished." He sighed. "Now all we have to do is to try to reeducate these kids."

"How long will it take?"

"Hard to tell. If they were younger, there wouldn't be so much of a problem. But by now—" The captain shrugged. "I have no idea. Just look at them."

There was a brief silence, as everybody stared at the row of rigid students. HEMEAC, terrified and uncomprehending, didn't move a muscle. He continued his fixed posture of waiting, but was almost tearfully wishing that the instructions would come. He was frightened by the vicious renegades here in the sacred precincts of the University.

"It's awful," one of the renegades whispered. "Why—why, they're not even human beings any more. What can anybody do for them now? They're nothing but living robots!"

HEMEAC heard, but his training saved him from disgrace. Not the slightest trace of the bursting surge of pride at this ultimate compliment appeared on his face. He stood with shoulders back, chin up, eyes straight ahead and mind blank.

Well, almost blank, anyway.

World War III

Those people born during and after World War II have grown up with the Bomb. That means that everyone in that age group has always lived with the knowledge that the destruction of the world could come with as little as twenty-five minutes notice. This has resulted in so much literature devoted to World War III and its aftermath (if any) that by now almost everyone must have read at least one novel or short story, or have seen a movie or television program, on the subject. Not all of the materials dealing with the Third World War are fiction. There have been many T.V. programs and Civil Defense handbooks on how to survive an attack, and these are honest attempts to prepare the public for the possibility of an atomic or nuclear holocaust. There have also been years of air-raid drills, take-cover drills, evacuate-the-city exercises, and fallout shelter construction in which a great many people took part.

Remember the drills in school? At this point, people can joke about the flimsy desks they had to hide under in the third grade when the air-raid signal rang and how sure they were that the desks would never support the ceiling and the sixth grade which would crash down from the room above. This rather morbid joking is indicative of the attitude of a generation which, as Donald Wollheim notes in *The Universe Makers,* is "growing up grim." Why not? The Bomb has been their constant companion. Also, much of the science fiction this generation has been exposed to can hardly have brightened its outlook. Such novels as *Farnham's Freehold* by Robert Heinlein and *Alas, Babylon* by Pat Frank portray survivors of an atomic war, but their survival does not come easily. And the outlook is even blacker in Nevil Shute's *On the Beach* as the reader witnesses nothing less than the death by atomic fallout of every person who has been lucky enough to have survived the bombs and the missles. In George Stewart's *Earth Abides,* the focus is on the survivors of an unnamed virus and their attempt to live in a culture set up for many more. Walter M. Miller's *A Canticle for Liebowitz* chronicles man's rise from the dark ages created by World War III to a point at which he can and does begin World War IV. Will man ever learn? Miller is, to say the least, skeptical.

Calling this part of the book World War III may be, in light of the story included, something of a mis-nomer. Tuli Kupferberg's poem, "Personal," does present a brief technological fable which suggests the speed at which such a war will take place and alludes to the psychological change which has taken place as man has been able to carry on warfare at an ever-increasing distance from his physical enemy. But Harlan Ellison's "A Boy and his Dog" portrays society after the war has been over for some time. However, all of the novels mentioned above and almost all of the World War III stories ever written deal with the aftermath of the war because it is the aftermath of an atomic or nuclear war which makes it so much more terrible than any other kind of war. Ellison's story is the lone prose representative under this heading because he so skillfully and briefly sketches in speculations about which other authors have made whole stories. No other story is needed to complete the discussion of this topic. The combination of the reader's knowledge and Ellison's imagery allow such concepts as fallout mutations, which once were central to post-World War III science fiction, to be dealt with in a few short phrases about the "burnpit-screamer" in section V of the story. One feature of the story may need mention as it seems to have received some special criticism. The sex in "A Boy and his Dog" is in sharp contrast to traditional science fiction's avoidance of the topic, but the sex in this story is, at the very least, in keeping with and a comment on the post-war society presented here. And the whole society, a result of the war, is a grim comment on the values of the society which started the war. The combination of traditional and nontraditional elements in this story ought to shock the reader and at least temporarily overcome the rather lethargic "it's-a-fact-of-life" attitude toward World War III that so many people have today, and if this story of consequences leads (as it should) to some consideration of the nature of war in general, so much the better.

PERSONAL

Tuli Kupferberg

There was once an atom bomb who wanted to be a bullet.

"Why," said his fellow atom bombs, "when you can be a great A-bomb, do you want to be a little *bullet?*"

"I miss," said the bomb, sighing, "the personal touch."

A BOY AND HIS DOG

Harlan Ellison

I

I was out with Blood, my dog. It was his week for annoying me; he kept calling me Albert. He thought that was pretty damned funny. Payson Terhune: ha ha. I'd caught a couple of water rats for him, the big green and ochre ones, and someone's manicured poodle, lost off a leash in one of the downunders; he'd eaten pretty good, but he was cranky. "Come on, son of a bitch," I demanded, "find me a piece of ass." Blood just chuckled, deep in his dog-throat. "You're funny when you get horny," he said.

Maybe funny enough to kick him upside his sphincter asshole, that refugee from a dingo-heap.

"Find! I ain't kidding!"

"For shame, Albert. After all I've taught you. Not: 'I *ain't* kidding'. I'm *not* kidding."

He knew I'd reached the edge of my patience. Sullenly, he started casting. He sat down on the crumbled remains of the curb, and his eyelids flickered and closed, and his hairy body tensed. After a while he settled forward on his front paws, and scraped them forward till he was lying flat, his shaggy head on the outstretched paws. The tenseness left him and he began trembling, almost the way he trembled just preparatory to scratching a flea. It went on that way for almost a quarter of an hour, and finally he rolled over and lay on his back, his naked belly toward the night sky, his front paws folded mantis-like, his hind legs extended and open. "I'm sorry," he said. "There's nothing."

I could have gotten mad and booted him, but I knew he had tried. I wasn't happy about it, I really wanted to get laid, but what could I do? "Okay," I said, with resignation, "forget it."

He kicked himself onto his side and quickly got up.

"What do you want to do?" he asked.

"Not much we *can* do, is there?" I was more than a little sarcastic. He sat down again, at my feet, insolently humble.

I leaned against the melted stub of a lamppost, and thought about girls. It was painful. "We can always go to a show," I said. Blood looked around the street, at the pools of shadow lying in the weed-overgrown craters, and didn't say anything. The whelp was waiting for me to say okay, let's go. He liked movies as much as I did.

"Okay, let's go."

He got up and followed me, his tongue hanging, panting with happiness. Go ahead and laugh, you eggsucker. No popcorn for *you!*

Our Gang was a roverpak that had never been able to cut it simply foraging, so they'd opted for comfort and gone a smart way to getting it. They were movie-oriented kids, and they'd taken over the turf where the Metropole Theater was located. No one tried to bust their turf, because we all needed the movies, and as long as Our Gang had access to films, and did a better job of keeping the films going, they provided a service, even for solos like me and Blood. *Especially* for solos like us.

They made me check my .45 and the Browning .22 long at the door. There was a little alcove right beside the ticket booth. I bought my tickets first; it cost me a can of Oscar Meyer Philadelphia Scrapple for me, and a tin of sardines for Blood. Then the Our Gang guards with the bren guns motioned me over to the alcove and I checked my heat. I saw water leaking from a broken pipe in the ceiling and I told the checker, a kid with big leathery warts all over his face and lips, to move my weapons where it was dry. He ignored me. "Hey, you! Motherfuckin' toad, move my stuff over the other side . . . it goes to rust fast . . . an' it picks up any spots, man, I'll break your bones!"

He started to give me jaw about it, looked at the guards with the brens, knew if they tossed me out I'd lose my price of admission whether I went in or not, but they weren't looking for any action, probably understrength, and gave him the nod to let it pass, to do what I said. So the toad moved my Browning to the other end of the gun rack, and pegged my .45 under it.

Blood and me went into the theater.

"I want popcorn."

"Forget it."

"Come on, Albert. Buy me popcorn."

"I'm tapped out. You can live without popcorn."

"You're just being a shit." I shrugged: sue me.

We went in. The place was jammed. I was glad the guards hadn't tried to take anything but guns. My spike and knife felt reassuring, lying-up in their oiled sheaths at the back of my neck. Blood found two together, and we moved into the row, stepping on feet. Someone cursed and I ignored him. A Doberman growled. Blood's fur stirred, but he let it pass. There was always *some* hardcase on the muscle, even in neutral ground like the Metropole.

(I heard once about a get-it-on they'd had at the old Loew's Granada, on the South Side. Wound up with ten or twelve rovers and their mutts dead, the theater burned down and a couple of good Cagney films lost in the fire. After that was when the roverpaks had got up the agreement that movie houses were sanctuaries. It was better now, but there was alwys somebody too messed in the mind to come soft.)

It was a triple feature. "Raw Deal" with Dennis O'Keefe, Claire Trevor, Raymond Burr and Marsha Hunt was the oldest of the three. It'd been made in 1948, seventy-six years ago, god only knows how the damn thing'd hung together all that time; it slipped sprockets and they had to stop the movie all the time to re-thread it. But it was a good movie. About this solo who'd been japped by his roverpak and was out to get revenge. Gangsters, mobs, a lot of punching and fighting. Real good.

The middle flick was a thing made during the Third War, in '07, two years before I was even born, thing called "Smell of a Chink". It was mostly gut-spilling and some nice hand-to-hand. Beautiful scene of skirmisher greyhounds equipped with napalm throwers, jellyburning a Chink town. Blood dug it, even though we'd seen this flick before. He had some kind of phony shuck going that these were ancestors of his, and *he* knew and *I* knew he was making it up.

"Wanna burn a baby, hero?" I whispered to him. He got the barb and just shifted in his seat, didn't say a thing, kept looking pleased as the dogs worked their way through the town. I was bored stiff.

I was waiting for the main feature.

Finally it came on. It was a beauty, a beaver flick made in the late 1970's. It was called "Big Black Leather Splits". Started right out very good. These two blondes in black leather corsets and boots laced all the way up to their crotches, with whips and masks, got this skinny guy down and one of the chicks sat on his face while the other one went down on him. It got really hairy after that.

All around me there were solos playing with themselves. I was about to jog it a little myself when Blood leaned across and said, real soft, the way he does when he's onto something unusually smelly, "There's a chick in here.".

"You're nuts," I said.

"I tell you I smell her. She's in here, man."

Without being conspicuous, I looked around. Almost every seat in the theater was taken with solos or their dogs. If a chick had slipped in there'd have been a riot. She'd have been ripped to pieces before any single guy could have gotten into her. "Where?" I asked, softly. All around me, the solos were beating-off, moaning as the blondes took off their masks and one of them worked the skinny guy with a big wooden ram strapped around her hips.

"Give me a minute," Blood said. He was really concentrating. His body was tense as a wire. His eyes were closed, his muzzle quivering. I let him work.

It was possible. Just maybe possible. I knew that they made really dumb flicks in the downunders, the kind of crap they'd made back in the 1930's and '40's, real clean stuff with even married people sleeping in twin beds. Myrna Loy and George Brent kind of flicks. And I knew that once in a while a chick from one of the really strict middle-class downunders would cumup, to see what a hairy flick was like. I'd heard about it, but it'd never happened in any Theater *I'd* ever been in.

And the chances of it happening in the Metropole, particularly, were slim. There was a lot of twisty trade came to the Metropole. Now, understand, I'm not specially prejudiced against guys corning one another . . . hell, I can understand it. There just aren't enough chicks anywhere. But I can't cut the jockey-and-boxer scene because it gets some weak little boxer hanging on you, getting jealous, you have to hunt for him and all he thinks he has to do is bare his ass to get all the work done for him. It's as bad as having a chick dragging along behind. Made for a lot of bad blood and fights in the bigger roverpaks, too. So I just never swung that way. Well, not *never*, but not for a long time.

So with all the twisties in the Metropole, I didn't think a chick would chance it. Be a toss-up who'd tear her apart first: the boxers or the straights.

And if she *was* here, why couldn't any of the other dogs smell her . . . ?

"Third row in front of us," Blood said. "Aisle seat. Dressed like a solo."

"How's come *you* can whiff her and no other dog's caught her?"

"You forget who I am, Albert."

"I didn't forget, I just don't believe it."

Actually, bottom-line, I guess I *did* believe it. When you'd been as dumb as I'd been and a dog like Blood'd taught me so much, a guy came to believe *everything* he said. You don't argue with your teacher.

Not when he's taught you how to read and write and add and subtract and everything else they used to know that meant you were smart (but doesn't mean much of anything now, except it's good to know it, I guess).

(The reading's a pretty good thing. It comes in handy when you can find some canned goods someplace, like in a bombed-out supermarket; makes it easier to pick out stuff you like when the pictures are gone off the labels. Couple of times the reading stopped me from taking canned beets. Shit, I *hate* beets!)

So I guess I *did* believe why he could whiff a maybe chick in there, and no other mutt could. He'd told me all about *that* a million times. It was his favorite story. History he called it. Christ, I'm not *that* dumb! I knew what history was. That was all the stuff that happened before now.

But I liked hearing history straight from Blood, instead of him making me read one of those crummy books he was always dragging in. And *that* particular history was all about him, so he laid it on me over and over, till I knew it by heart . . . no, the word was *rote*. Not *wrote*, like writing, that was something else. I knew it by rote, like it means you get it word-for-word.

And when a mutt teaches you everything you know, and he tells you something rote, I guess finally you *do* believe it. Except I'd never let that leg-lifter know it.

II

What he'd told me rote was:

Over fifty years ago, in Los Angeles, before the Third War even got going completely, there was a man named Buesing who lived in Cerritos. He raised dogs as watchmen and sentries and attackers. Dobermans, Danes, Schnauzers and Japanese akitas. He had one 4-year-old German shepherd bitch named Ginger. She worked for the Los Angeles Police Department's narcotics division. She could smell out marijuana. No matter how well it was hidden. They ran a test on her: there were 25,000 boxes in an auto parts warehouse. Five of them had been planted with marijuana that had been sealed in cellophane, wrapped in tin foil and heavy brown paper, and finally hidden in three separate sealed cartons. Within seven minutes Ginger found all five packages. At the same time that Ginger was working, ninety-two miles further north, in Santa Barbara, cetologists had drawn and amplified dolphin spinal fluid and injected it into Chacma baboons and dogs. Altering surgery and grafting had been done. The first successful product of this cetacean experimentation had been a 2-year-old male Puli named Ahbhu, who had communicated sense-impressions telepathically. Cross-breeding and continued experimentation had produced the first skirmisher dogs, just in time for the Third War. Telepathic over short distances, easily trained, able to track gasoline or troops or poison gas or radiation when linked with their human controllers, they had become the shock commandos of a new kind of war. The selective traits had bred true. Dobermans, greyhounds, akitas, pulis and schnauzers had become steadily more telepathic.

Ginger and Ahbhu had been Blood's ancestors.

He had told me so, a thousand times. Had told me the story just that way, in just those words, a thousand times, as it had been told to him. I'd never believed him till now.

Maybe the little bastard *was* special.

I checked out the solo scrunched down in the aisle seat three rows ahead of me. I couldn't tell a damned thing. The solo had his (her?) cap pulled way down, fleece jacket pulled way up.

"Are you sure?"

"As sure as I can be. It's a girl."

"If it is, she's playing with herself just like a guy." Blood snickered. "Surprise," he said sarcastically.

The mystery solo sat through "Raw Deal" again. It made sense, if that was a girl. Most of the solos and all of the members of roverpaks left after the beaver flick. The theater didn't fill up much more, it gave the streets time to empty, he/she could make his/her way back to wherever he/she had come from. I sat through "Raw Deal" again myself. Blood went to sleep.

When the mystery solo got up, I gave him/her time to get weapons if any'd been checked, and start away. Then I pulled Blood's big shaggy ear and said, "Let's do it." He slouched after me, up the aisle.

I got my guns and checked the street. Empty.

"Okay, nose," I said, "where'd he go?"

"Her. To the right."

I started off, loading the Browning from my bandolier. I still didn't see anyone moving among the bombed-out shells of the buildings. This section of the city was crummy, really bad shape. But then, with Our Gang running the Metropole, they didn't have to repair anything else to get their livelihood. It was ironic; the Dragons had to keep an entire power planet going to get tribute from the other roverpaks, Ted's Bunch had to mind the reservoir, the Bastinados worked like field-hands in the marijuana gardens, the Barbados Blacks lost a couple of dozen members every year cleaning out the radiation pits all over the city; and Our Gang only had to run that movie house.

Whoever their leader had been, however many years ago it had been that the roverpaks had started forming out of foraging solos, I had to give it to him: he'd been a flinty sharp mother. He knew what services to deal in.

"She turned off here," Blood said.

I followed him as he began loping, toward the edge of the city and the bluish-green radiation that still flickered from the hills. I knew he was right, then. The only thing out here was the access dropshaft to the downunder. It was a girl, all right.

The cheeks of my ass tightened as I thought about it. I was going to get laid. It had been almost a month, since Blood had whiffed that solo chick in the basement of the Market Basket. She'd been filthy, and I'd gotten the crabs from her, but she'd been a woman, all right, and once I'd tied her down and clubbed her a couple of times she'd been pretty good. She'd liked it, too, even if she did spit on me and tell me she'd kill me if she ever got loose. I left her tied up, just to be sure. She wasn't there when I went back to look, week before last.

"Watch out," Blood said, dodging around a crater almost invisible against the surrounding shadows. Something stirred in the crater.

Trekking across the nomansland I realized why it was that all but a handful of solos or members of roverpaks were guys. The War had killed off most of the girls, and that was the way it always was in wars . . . at least that's what Blood told me. The things getting born were seldom male *or* female, and had to be smashed against a wall as soon as they were pulled out of the mother.

The few chicks who hadn't gone downunder with the middle-classers were hard, solitary bitches like the one in the Market Basket; tough and stringy and just as likely to cut off your meat with a razor blade once they let you get in. Scuffling for a piece of ass had gotten harder and harder, the older I'd gotten.

But every once in a while a chick got tired of being roverpak property, or a raid was got-up by five or six roverpaks and some unsuspecting downunder was taken, or—like this time, yeah—some middle-class chick from a downunder got hot pants to find out what a beaver flick looked like, and cumup.

I was going to get laid. Oh boy, I couldn't wait!

III

Out here it was nothing but empty corpses of blasted buildings. One entire block had been stomped flat, like a steel press had come down from Heaven and given one solid wham! and everything was powder under it. The chick was scared and skittish, I could see that. She moved erratically, looking back over her shoulder and to either side. She knew she was in dangerous country. Man, if she'd only known *how* dangerous.

There was one building standing all alone at the end of the smash-flat block, like it had been missed and chance let it stay. She ducked inside, and a minute later I saw a bobbing light. Flashlight? Maybe.

Blood and I crossed the street and came up into the blackness surrounding the building. It was what was left of a YMCA.

That meant "Young Men's Christian Association". Blood taught me to read.

So what the hell was a young men's christian association. Sometimes being able to read makes more questions than if you were stupid.

I didn't want her getting out; inside there was as good a place to screw her as any, so I put Blood on guard right beside the steps leading up into the shell, and I went around the back. All the doors and windows had been blown out, of course. It wasn't no big trick getting in. I pulled myself up to the ledge of a window, and dropped down inside. Dark inside. No noise, except the sound of her, moving around on the other side of the old YMCA. I didn't know if she was heeled or not, and I wasn't about to take any chances. I bow-slung the Browning and took out the .45 automatic. I didn't have to snap back the action—there was always a slug in the chamber.

I started moving carefully through the room. It was a locker room of some kind. There was glass and debris all over the floor, and one entire row of metal lockers had the paint blistered off their surfaces; the flash blast had caught them through the windows, a lot of years ago. My sneakers didn't make a sound coming through the room.

The door was hanging on one hinge, and I stepped over—through the inverted triangle. I was in the swimming pool area. The big pool was empty, with tiles buckled down at the shallow end. It stunk bad in there; no wonder, there were dead guys, or what was left of them, along one wall. Some lousy cleaner-up had stacked them, but hadn't buried them. I pulled my bandana up around my nose and mouth, and kept moving.

Out the other side of the pool place, and through a little passage with popped light bulbs in the ceiling. I didn't have any trouble seeing. There was moonlight coming through busted windows and a chunk was out of the ceiling. I could hear her real plain now, just on the other side of the door at the end of the passage. I hung close to the wall, and stepped down to the door. It was open a crack, but blocked by a fall of lath and plaster from the wall. It would make noise when I went to pull it open, that was for certain. I had to wait for the right moment.

Flattened against the wall, I checked out what she was doing in there. It was a gymnasium, big one, with climbing ropes hanging down from the ceiling. She had a big square eight-cell flashlight sitting up on the croup of a vaulting horse. There were parallel bars and a horizontal bar about eight feet high, the high-tempered steel all rusty now. There were swinging rings and a trampoline and a big wooden balancing beam. Over to one side there were wallbars and balancing benches, horizontal and oblique ladders, and a couple of stacks of vaulting boxes. I made a note to remember this joint. It was better for working-out than the jerry-rigged gym I'd set up in an old auto wrecking yard. A guy has to keep in shape, if he's going to be a solo.

She was out of her disguise. Standing there in the skin, shivering. Yeah, it was chilly, and I could see a pattern of chicken-skin all over her. She was maybe five six or seven, with nice tits and kind of skinny legs. She was brushing out her hair. It hung way down the back. The flashlight didn't make it clear enough to tell if she had red hair or chestnut, but it wasn't blonde, which was good, and that was because I dug redheads. She had nice tits, though. I couldn't see her face, the hair was hanging down all smooth and wavy and cut off her profile.

The crap she'd been wearing was lying around on the floor, and what she was going to put on was up on the vaulting horse. She was standing in little shoes with a kind of a funny heel on them.

I couldn't move. I suddenly realized I couldn't move. She was nice, really nice. I was getting as big a kick out of just standing there and seeing the way her waist fell inward and her hips fell outward, the way the muscles at the side of her tits pulled up when she reached to the top of her head to brush all that hair down. It was really weird, the kick I was getting out of standing and just staring at a chick do that. Kind of very, well, woman stuff. I liked it a lot.

I'd never ever stopped and just looked at a chick like that. All the ones I'd ever seen had been scumbags that Blood had smelled out for me, and I'd snatchn'grabbed them. Or the big chicks in the beaver flicks.

Not like this one, kind of soft and very smooth, even with the goose bumps. I could of watched her all night.

She put down the brush, and reached over and took a pair of panties off the pile of clothes, and wriggled into them. Then she got her bra and put it on. I never knew the way chicks did it. She put it on backwards, around her waist, and it had a hook on it. Then she slid it around till the cups were in front, and kind of pulled it up under and scooped herself into it, first one, then the other; then she pulled the straps over her shoulder. She reached for her dress, and I nudged some of the lath and plaster aside, and grabbed the door to give it a yank.

She had the dress up over her head, and her arms up inside the material, and when she stuck her head in, and was all tangled there for a second, I yanked the door and there was a crash as chunks of wood and plaster fell out of the way, and a heavy scraping, and I jumped inside and was on her before she could get out of the dress.

She started to scream, and I pulled the dress off her with a ripping sound, and it all happened for her before she knew what that crash and scrape was all about.

Her face was wild. Just wild. Big eyes: I couldn't tell what color they were because they were in shadow. Real fine features, a wide mouth, little nose, cheekbones just like mine, real high and prominent and a dimple in her right cheek. She stared at me really scared.

And then . . . and this is really weird . . . I felt like I should *say* something to her. I don't know what. Just something. It made me uncomfortable, to see her scared, but what the hell could I do about *that*. I mean, I was going to rape her, after all, and I couldn't very well tell her not to be shrinky about it. She was the one cumup, after all. But even so, I wanted to say hey, don't be scared, I just want to lay you. (That never happened before. I never wanted to *say* anything to a chick, just get in, and that was that.)

But it passed, and I put my leg behind hers and tripped her back, and she went down in a pile. I leveled the .45 at her, and her mouth kind of opened in a little o shape. "Now I'm gonna go over there and get one of them wrestling mats, so it'll be better, comfortable, uh-huh? You make a move off that floor and I shoot a leg out from under you, and you'll get screwed just the same, except you'll be without a leg." I waited for her to let me know she was onto what I was saying, and she finally nodded real slow, so I kept the automatic on her, and went over to the big dusty stack of mats, and pulled one off.

I dragged it over to her, and flipped it so the cleaner side was up, and used the muzzle of the .45 to maneuver her onto it. She just sat there on the mat, with her hands behind her, and her knees bent, and stared at me.

I unzipped my pants and started pulling them down off one side, when I caught her looking at me real funny. I stopped with the jeans. "What're *you* lookin' at?"

I was mad. I didn't know why I was mad, but I was.

"What's your name?" she asked. Her voice was very soft, and kind of furry, like it came up through her throat that was all lined with fur or something.

She kept looking at me, waiting for me to answer.

"Vic," I said. She looked like she was waiting for more.

"Vic what?"

I didn't know what she meant for a minute, then I did. "Vic. Just Vic. That's all."

"Well, what're your mother and father's names?"

Then I started laughing, and working my jeans down again. "Boy, are you a dumb bitch," I said, and laughed some more. She looked hurt. It made me mad again. "Stop lookin' like that, or I'll bust out your teeth!"

She folded her hands in her lap.

I got the pants down around my ankles. They wouldn't come off over the sneakers. I had to balance on one foot and scuff the sneaker off the other foot. It was tricky, keeping the .45 on her and getting the sneaker off at the same time. But I did it.

I was standing there buck-naked from the waist down and she had sat forward a little, her legs crossed, hands still in her lap. "Get that stuff off," I said.

She didn't move for a second, and I thought she was going to give me trouble. But then she reached around behind and undid the bra. Then she tipped back and slipped the panties off her ass.

Suddenly, she didn't look scared any more. She was watching me very close and I could see her eyes were blue now. Now this is the really weird thing . . .

I couldn't do it. I mean, not exactly. I mean, I *wanted* to fuck her, see, but she was all soft and pretty and she kept *looking* at me, and no solo I ever met would believe me, but I heard myself *talking* to her, still standing there like some kind of wetbrain, one sneaker off and jeans down around my ankle. "What's *your* name?"

"Quilla June Holmes."

"That's a weird name."

"My mother says it's not that uncommon, back in Oklahoma."

"That where your folks come from?"

She nodded. "Before the Third War."

"They must be pretty old by now."

"They are, but they're okay. I guess."

We were just frozen there, talking to each other. I could tell she was cold, because she was shivering. "Well," I said, sort of getting ready to drop down beside her, "I guess we better—"

Damn it! That damned Blood! Right at that moment he came dashing in from outside. Came skidding through the lath, and plaster, raising dust, slid along on his ass till he got to us. *"Now* what?" I demanded.

"Who're you talking to?" the girl asked.

"Him. Blood."

"The dog!?!"

Blood stared at her and then ignored her. He started to say something, but the girl interrupted him, "Then it's true what they say . . . you can all talk to animals . . ."

"You going to listen to her all night, or do you want to hear why I came in?"

"Okay, why're you here?"

"You're in trouble, Albert."

"Come *on,* forget the mickeymouse. What's up?"

Blood twisted his head toward the front door of the YMCA. "Roverpak. Got the building surrounded. I make it fifteen or twenty, maybe more."

"How the hell'd they know we was here?"

Blood looked chagrined. He dropped his head.

"Well?"

"Some other mutt must've smelled her in the theater?"

"Great."

"Now what?"

"Now we stand 'em off, that's what. You got any better suggestions?"

"Just one."

I waited. He grinned.

"Pull your pants up."

IV

The girl, this Quilla June, was pretty safe. I made her a kind of a shelter out of wrestling mats, maybe a dozen of them. She wouldn't get hit by a stray bullet, and if they didn't go right for her, they wouldn't find her. I climbed one of the ropes hanging down from the girders and laid out up there with the Browning and a couple of handfuls of reloads. I wished to God I'd had an automatic, a bren or a Thompson. I checked the .45, made sure it was full, with one in the chamber, and set the extra clips down on the girder. I had a clear line-of-fire all around the gym.

Blood was lying in shadow right near the front door. He'd suggested I try and pick off any dogs with the roverpak first, if I could. That would allow him to operate freely.

That was the least of my worries.

I'd wanted to hole up in another room, one with only a single entrance, but I had no way of knowing if the rovers were already in the building, so I did the best I could with what I had.

Everything was quiet. Even that Quilla June. It'd taken me valuable minutes to convince her she'd damned well better hole up and not make any noise, she was better off with me than with twenty of *them*. "If you ever wanna see your mommy and daddy again," I warned her. After that she didn't give me no trouble, packing her in with mats.

Quiet.

Then I heard two things, both at the same time. From back in the swimming pool I heard boots crunching plaster. Very soft. And from one side of the front door I heard a tinkle of metal striking wood. So they were going to try a yoke. Well, I was ready.

Quiet again.

I sighted the Browning on the door to the pool room. It was still open from when I'd come through. Figure him at maybe five-ten, and drop the sights a foot and a half, and I'd catch him in the chest. I'd learned long ago you don't try for the head. Go for the widest part of the body: the chest and stomach. The trunk.

Suddenly, outside, I heard a dog bark, and part of the darkness near the front door detached itself and moved inside the gym. Directly opposite Blood. I didn't move the Browning.

The rover at the front door moved a step along the wall, away from Blood. Then he cocked back his arm and threw something—a rock, a piece of metal, something—across the room, to draw fire. I didn't move the Browning.

When the thing he'd thrown hit the floor, two rovers jumped out of the swimming pool door, one on either side of it, rifles down, ready to spray. Before they could open up, I'd squeezed off the first shot, tracked across and put a second shot into the other one. They both went down. Dead hits, right in the heart. Bang, they were down, neither one moved.

The mother by the door turned to split, and Blood was on him. Just like that, out of the darkness, riiip!

Blood leaped, right over the crossbar of the guy's rifle held at ready, and sank his fangs into the rover's throat. The guy screamed, and Blood dropped, carrying a piece of the guy with him. The guy was making awful bubbling sounds and went down on one knee. I put a slug into his head, and he fell forward.

It went quiet again.

Not bad. Not bad atall atall. Three takeouts and they still didn't know our positions. Blood had fallen back into the murk by the entrance.

He didn't say a thing, but I knew what he was thinking: maybe that was three out of seventeen, or three out of twenty, or twenty-two. No way of knowing; we could be faced-off in here for a week and never know if we'd gotten them all, or some, or none. They could go and get poured full again, and I'd find myself run out of slugs and no food and that girl, that Quilla June, crying and making me divide my attention, and daylight—and they'd be still laying out there, waiting till we got hungry enough to do something dumb, or till we ran out of slugs, and then they'd cloud up and rain all over us.

A rover came dashing straight through the front door at top speed, took a leap, hit on his shoulders, rolled, came up going in a different direction and snapped off three rounds into different corners of the room before I could track him with the Browning. By that time he was close enough under me where I didn't have to waste a .22 slug. I picked up the .45 without a sound and blew the back off his head. Slug went in neat, came out and took most of his hair with it. He fell right down.

"Blood! The rifle!"

Came out of the shadows, grabbed it up in his mouth and dragged it over to the pile of wrestling mats in the far corner. I saw an arm poke out from the mass of mats, and a hand grabbed the rifle, dragged it inside. Well, it was at least safe there, till I needed it. Brave little bastard: he scuttled over to the dead rover and started worrying the ammo bandolier off his body. It took him a while; he could have been picked off from the doorway or outside one of the windows, but he did it. Brave little bastard. I had to remember to get him something good to eat, when we got out of this. I smiled, up there in the darkness: *if* we get out of this, I wouldn't have to worry about getting him something tender. It was lying all over the floor of that gymnasium.

Just as Blood was dragging the bandolier back into the shadows, two of them tried it with their dogs. They came through a ground floor window, one after another, hitting and rolling and going in opposite directions, as the dogs—a mother-ugly Akita, big as a house, and a Doberman bitch the color of a turd—shot through the front door and split in the unoccupied two directions. I caught one of the dogs, the Akita, with the .45 and it went down thrashing. The Doberman was all over Blood.

But firing, I'd given away my position. One of the rovers fired from the hip and .30-06 soft-nosed slugs spanged off the girders around me. I dropped the automatic, and it started to slip off the girder as I reached for the Browning. I made a grab for the .45 and that was the only thing saved me. I fell forward to clutch at it, it slipped away and hit the gym floor with a crash, and the rover fired at where I'd been. But I was flat on the girder, arm dangling, and the crash startled him. He fired at the sound, and right at that instant I heard another shot, from a Winchester, and the other rover, who'd made it safe into the shadows, fell forward holding a big pumping hole in his chest. That Quilla June had shot him, from behind the mats.

I didn't even have time to figure out what the fuck was happening . . . Blood was rolling around with the Doberman and the sounds they were making were awful . . . the rover with the .30-06 chipped off another shot and hit the muzzle of the Browning, protruding over the side of the girder, and wham it was gone, falling down. I was naked up there without clout, and the sonofabitch was hanging back in shadow waiting for me.

Another shot from the Winchester, and the rover fired right into the mats. She ducked back behind, and I knew I couldn't count on her for anything more. But I didn't need it; in that second, while he was focused on her, I grabbed the climbing rope, flipped myself over the girder, and howling like a burnpit-screamer, went sliding down, feeling the rope cutting my palms. I got down far enough to swing, and kicked off. I swung back and forth, whipping my body three different ways each time, swinging out and over, way over, each time. The sonofabitch kept firing, trying to track a trajectory, but I kept spinning out of his line of fire. Then he was empty, and I kicked back as hard as I could, and came zooming in toward his corner of shadows, and let loose all at once and went ass-over-end into the corner, and there he was, and I went right into him and he spanged off the wall, and I was on top of him, digging my thumbs into his eye-sockets. He was screaming and the dogs were screaming and that girl was screaming, and I pounded the motherfucker's head against the floor till he stopped moving, then I grabbed up the empty .30-06 and whipped his head till I knew he wasn't gonna give me no more aggravation.

Then I found the .45 and shot the Doberman.

Blood got up and shook himself off. He was cut up bad. "Thanks," he mumbled, and went over and lay down in the shadows to lick himself off.

I went and found that Quilla June, and she was crying. About all the guys we'd killed. Mostly about the one *she'd* killed. I couldn't get her to stop bawling, so I cracked her across the face, and told her she'd saved my life, and that helped some.

Blood came dragassing over. "How're we going to get out of this, Albert?"

"Let me think."

I thought, and knew it was hopeless. No matter how many we got, there'd be more. And it was a matter of *macho* now. Their honor.

"How about a fire?" Blood suggested.

"Get away while it's burning?" I shook my head. "They'll have the place staked-out all around. No good."

"What if we don't leave? What if we burn up with it?"

I looked at him. Brave . . . and smart as hell.

V

We gathered all the lumber and mats and scaling ladders and vaulting boxes and benches and anything else that would burn, and piled the garbage against a wooden divider at one end of the gym. Quilla June found a can of kerosene in a storeroom, and we set fire to the whole damn pile. Then we followed Blood to the place he'd found for us. The boiler room way down under the YMCA. We all climbed into the empty boiler, and dogged down the door, leaving a release vent open for air. We had one mat in there with us, and all the ammo we could carry, and the extra rifles and sidearms the rovers'd had on them.

"Can you catch anything?" I asked Blood.

"A little. Not much. I'm reading one guy. The building's burning good."

"You be able to tell when they split?"

"Maybe. *If* they split."

I settled back. Quilla June was shaking from all that had happened. "Just take it easy," I told her. "By morning the place'll be down around our ears and they'll go through the rubble and find a lot of dead meat and maybe they won't look too hard for a chick's body. And everything'll be all right . . . if we don't get choked off in here."

She smiled, very thin, and tried to look brave. She was okay, that one. She closed her eyes and settled back on the mat and tried to sleep. I was beat. I closed my eyes, too.

"Can you handle it?" I asked Blood.

"I suppose. You better sleep."

I nodded, eyes still closed, and fell on my side. I was out before I could think about it.

When I came back, I found the girl, that Quilla June, snuggled up under my armpit, her arm around my waist, dead asleep. I could hardly breathe. It was like a furnace; hell, it *was* a furnace. I reached out a hand and the wall of the boiler was so damned hot I couldn't touch it. Blood was up on the mattress with us. That mat had been the only thing'd kept us from being singed good. He was asleep, head buried in his paws. She was asleep, still naked.

I put a hand on her tit. It was warm. She stirred and cuddled into me closer. I got a hard on.

Managed to get my pants off, and rolled on top of her. She woke up fast when she felt me pry her legs apart, but it was too late by then. "Don't . . . *stop* . . . what are you doing . . . no, don't . . ."

But she was half-asleep, and weak, and I don't think she really wanted to fight me anyhow.

She cried when I broke her, of course, but after that it was okay. There was blood all over the wrestling mat. And Blood just kept sleeping.

It was really different. Usually, when I'd get Blood to track something down for me, it'd be grab it and punch it and get away fast before something bad could happen. But when she came, she rose up off the mat, and hugged me around the back so hard I thought she'd crack my ribs, and then she settled down slow slow slow, like I do when I'm doing leg lifts in the makeshift gym I rigged in the auto wrecking yard. And her eyes were closed, and she was relaxed looking. And happy. I could tell.

We did it a lot of times, and after a while it was her idea, but I didn't say no. And then we lay out side-by-side and talked.

She asked me about how it was with Blood, and I told her how the skirmisher dogs had gotten telepathic, and how they'd lost the ability to hunt food for themselves, so the solos and roverpaks had to do it for them, and how dogs like Blood were good at finding chicks for solos like me. She didn't say anything to that.

I asked her about what it was like where she lived, in one of the downunders.

"It's nice. But it's always very quiet. Everyone is very polite to everyone else. It's just a small town."

"Which one you live in?"

"Topeka. It's real close to here."

"Yeah, I know. The access dropshaft is only about half a mile from here. I went out there once, to take a look around."

"Have you ever been in a downunder?"

"No. But I don't guess I want to be, either."

"Why? It's very nice. You'd like it."

"Shit."

"That's very crude."

"*I'm* very crude."

"Not all the time."

I was getting mad. "Listen, you ass, what's the matter with you? I grabbed you and pushed you around, I raped you half a dozen times, so what's so good about me, huh? What's the matter with you, don't you even have enough smarts to know when somebody's—"

She was smiling at me. "I didn't mind. I liked doing it. Want to do it again?"

I was really shocked. I moved away from her. "What the hell is wrong with you? Don't you know that a chick from a downunder like you can be really mauled by solos? Don't you know chicks get warnings from their parents in the downunders, 'Don't cumup, you'll get snagged by them dirty, hairy, slobbering solos!' Don't you know that?"

She put her hand on my leg and started moving it up, the fingertips just brushing my thigh. I got another hard on. "My parents never said that about solos," she said. Then she pulled me over her again, and kissed me and I couldn't stop from getting in her again.

God, it just went on like that for hours. After a while Blood turned around and said, "I'm not going to keep pretending I'm asleep. I'm hungry. And I'm hurt."

I tossed her off me—she was on top by this time—and examined him. The Doberman had taken a good chunk out of his right ear, and there was a rip right down his muzzle, and blood-matted fur on one side. He was a mess. "Jesus, man, you're a mess," I said.

"You're no fucking rose garden yourself, Albert!" he snapped. I pulled my hand back.

"Can we get out of here?" I asked him.

He cast around, and then shook his head. "I can't get any readings. Must be a pile of rubble on top of this boiler. I'll have to go out and scout."

We kicked that around for a while, and finally decided if the building was razed, and had cooled a little, the roverpak would have gone through the ashes by now. The fact that they hadn't tried the boiler indicated that we were probably buried pretty good. Either that, or the building was still smoldering overhead. In which case, they'd still be out there, waiting to sift the remains.

"Think you can handle it, the condition you're in?"

"I guess I'll *have* to, won't I?" Blood said. He was really surly. "I mean, what with you busy fucking your brains out, there won't be much left for staying alive, will there?"

I sensed real trouble with him. He didn't like Quilla June. I moved around him and undogged the boiler hatch. It wouldn't open. So I braced my back against the side, and jacked my legs up, and gave it a slow, steady shove.

Whatever had fallen against it from outside, resisted for a minute, then started to give, then tumbled away with a crash. I pushed the door open all the way, and looked out. The upper floors had fallen in on the basement, but by the time they'd given, they'd been mostly cinder and lightweight rubble. Everything was smoking out there. I could see daylight through the smoke.

I slipped out, burning my hands on the outside lip of the hatch. Blood followed. He started to pick his way through the debris. I could see that the boiler had been almost completely covered by the gunk that had dropped from above. Chances were good the roverpak had taken a fast look, figured we'd been fried, and moved on. But I wanted

Blood to run a recon, anyway. He started off, but I called him back. He came.

"What is it?"

I looked down at him. "I'll tell you what it is, man. You're acting very shitty."

"Sue me."

"Goddamit, dog, what's got your ass up?"

"Her. That nit chick you've got in there."

"So what? Big deal . . . I've had chicks before."

"Yeah, but never any that hung on like this one. I warn you, Albert, she's going to make trouble."

"Don't be dumb!" He didn't reply. Just looked at me with anger, and then scampered off to check out the scene. I crawled back inside and dogged the hatch. She wanted to make it again. I said I didn't want to; Blood had brought me down. I was bugged. And I didn't know which one to be pissed off at.

But God she was pretty.

She kind of pouted, and settled back with her arms wrapped around her. "Tell me some more about the downunder," I said.

At first she was cranky, wouldn't say much, but after a while she opened up and started talking freely. I was learning a lot. I figured I could use it some time, maybe.

There were only a couple of hundred downunders in what was left of the United States and Canada. They'd been sunk on the sites of wells or mines or other kinds of deep holes. Some of them, out in the west, were in natural cave formations. They went way down, maybe two to five miles. They were like big caissons, stood on end. And the people who'd settled them were squares of the worst kind. Southern Baptists, Fundamentalists, lawanorder goofs, real middle-class squares with no taste for the wild life. And they'd gone back to a kind of life that hadn't existed for a hundred and fifty years. They'd gotten the last of the scientists to do the work, invent the how and why, and then they'd run them out. They didn't want any progress, they didn't want any dissent, they didn't want anything that would make waves. They'd had enough of that. The best time in the world had been just before the First War, and they figured if they could keep it like that, they could live quiet lives and survive. Shit! I'd go nuts in one of the downunders.

Quilla June smiled, and snuggled up again, and this time I didn't turn her off. She started touching me again, down there and all over, and then she said, "Vic?"

"Uh-huh."

"Have you ever been in love?"

"What?"

"In love? Have you ever been in love with a girl?"

"Well, I damn well guess I haven't!"

"Do you know what love is?"

"Sure. I guess I do."

"But if you've never been in love . . . ?"

"Don't be dumb. I mean, I've never had a bullet in the head, and I know I wouldn't like it."

"You don't know what love is, I'll bet."

"Well, if it means living in a downunder, I guess I just don't wanna find out." We didn't go on with the conversation much after that. She pulled me down and we did it again. And when it was over, I heard Blood scratching in the boiler. I opened the hatch and he was standing out there. "All clear," he said.

"You sure?"

"Yeah, yeah, I'm sure. Put your pants on," he said it with a sneer in the tone, "and come on out here. We have to talk some stuff."

I looked at him, and he wasn't kidding. I got my jeans and sneakers on, and climbed down out of the boiler.

He trotted ahead of me, away from the boiler, over some blacksoot beams, and outside the gym. It was down. Looked like a rotted stump tooth.

"Now what's lumbering you?" I asked him.

He scampered up on a chunk of concrete till he was almost nose-level with me.

"You're going dumb on me, Vic."

I knew he was serious. No Albert shit, straight Vic. "How so?"

"Last night, man. We could have cut out of there and left her for them. *That* would've been smart."

"I wanted her."

"Yeah, I know. That's what I'm talking about. It's today now, not last night. You've had her about a half a hundred times. Why're we hanging around?"

"I want some more."

Then he got angry. "Yeah, well, listen, chum . . . *I* want a few things myself. I want something to eat, and I want to get rid of this pain in my side, and I want away from this turf. Maybe they *don't* give up this easy."

"Take it easy. We can handle all that. Don't mean she can't go with us."

"*Doesn't* mean," he corrected me. "And so *that's* the new story. Now we travel three, is that right?"

I was getting *tres* uptight myself. "You're starting to sound like a poo-dle!"

"And you're starting to sound like a boxer."

I hauled back to crack him one. He didn't move. I dropped the hand. I'd never hit Blood. I didn't want to start now.

"Sorry," he said, softly.

"That's okay."

But we weren't looking at each other.

"Vic, man, you've got responsibility to me, you know."

"You don't have to tell me that."

"Well, I guess maybe I do. Maybe I have to remind you of some stuff. Like the time that burnpit-screamer came up out of the street and made a grab for you."

I shuddered. The motherfucker'd been green. Righteous stone green, glowing like fungus. My gut heaved, just thinking.

"And I went for him, right?"

I nodded. Right, mutt, right.

"And I could have been burned bad, and died, and that would've been all of it for me, right or wrong, isn't that true?" I nodded again. I was getting pissed off proper. I didn't like being made to feel guilty. It was a fifty-fifty with Blood and me. He knew that. "But I did it, right?" I remembered the way that green thing had screamed. Christ, it was like ooze and eyelashes.

"Okay, okay, don't hanger me."

"*Harangue,* not hanger."

"Well WHATEVER!" I shouted. "Just knock off the crap, or we can forget the whole fucking arrangement!"

Then Blood blew. "Well, maybe we *should,* you simple dumb *putz!*"

"What's a *putz,* you little turd . . . is that something bad . . . yeah, it must be . . . you watch your fucking mouth, son of a bitch, I'll kick your ass!"

We sat there and didn't talk for fifteen minutes. Neither one of us knew which way to go.

Finally, I backed off a little. I talked soft and I talked slow. I was about up to here with him, but told him I was going to do right by him, like I always had, and he threatened me, saying I'd damned well better because there were a couple of very hip solos making it around the city, and they'd be delighted to have a sharp tail-scent like him. I told him I didn't like being threatened, and he'd better watch his fucking step or I'd break his leg. He got furious and stalked off. I said screw you and went back to the boiler to take it out on that Quilla June again.

But when I stuck my head inside the boiler, she was waiting, with a pistol one of the dead rovers had supplied. She hit me good and solid over the right eye with it, and I fell straight forward across the hatch, and was out cold.

VI

"I told you she was no good." He watched me as I swabbed out the cut with disinfectant from my kit, and painted the tear with iodine. He smirked when I flinched.

I put away the stuff, and rummaged around in the boiler, gathering up all the spare ammo I could carry, and ditching the Browning in favor of the heavier .30-06. Then I found something that must've slipped out of her clothes.

It was a little metal plate, about 3½ inches long and an inch-and-a-half high. It had a whole string of numbers on it, and there were holes in it, in random patterns. "What's this?" I asked Blood.

He looked at it, sniffed it.

"Must be an identity card of some kind. Maybe it's what she used to get out of the downunder."

That made my mind up.

I jammed it in a pocket and started out. Toward the access dropshaft.

"Where the hell are you going?" Blood yelled after me.

"Come on back, you'll get killed out there!

"I'm hungry, dammit!

"Albert, you sonofabitch! Come back here!"

I kept right on walking. I was gonna find that bitch and brain her. Even if I had to go downunder to find her.

It took me an hour to walk to the access dropshaft leading down to Topeka. I thought I saw Blood following, but hanging back a ways. I didn't give a damn. I was mad.

Then, there it was. A tall, straight, featureless pillar of shining black metal. It was maybe twenty feet in diameter, perfectly flat on top, disappearing straight into the ground. It was a cap, that was all. I walked straight up to it, and fished around in the pocket for that metal card. Then something was tugging at my right pants leg.

"Listen, you moron, you can't go down there!"

I kicked him off, but he came right back.

"Listen to me!"

I turned around and stared at him.

Blood sat down; the powder puffed up around him. "Albert . . ."

"My name is Vic, you little egg-sucker."

"Okay, okay, no fooling around. Vic." His tone softened. "Vic. Come on, man." He was trying to get through to me. I was really boiling, but he was trying to make sense. I shrugged, and crouched down beside him.

"Listen, man," Blood said, "this chick has bent you way out of shape. You *know* you can't go down there. It's all square and settled and they know everyone; they hate solos. Enough roverpaks have raided downunders and raped their broads, and stolen their food, they'll have defenses set up. They'll *kill* you, man!"

"What the hell do you care? You're always saying you'd be better off without me." He sagged at that.

"Vic, we've been together almost three years. Good and bad. But this can be the worst. I'm scared, man. Scared you won't come back. And I'm hungry, and I'll have to go find some dude who'll take me on . . . and you know most solos are in paks now, I'll be low mutt. I'm not that young any more. And I'm hurt."

I could dig it. He was talking sense. But all I could think of was how that bitch, that Quilla June, had rapped me. And then there were images of her soft tits, and the way she made little sounds when I was in her, and I shook my head, and knew I had to go get even.

"I got to do it, Blood. I got to."

He breathed deep, and sagged a little more. He knew it was useless. "You don't even see what she's done to you, Vic."

I got up. "I'll try to get back quick. Will you wait . . . ?"

He was silent a long while, and I waited. Finally, he said, "For a while. Maybe I'll be here, maybe not."

I understood. I turned around and started walking around the pillar of black metal. Finally, I found a slot in the pillar, and slipped the metal card into it. There was a soft humming sound, then a section of the pillar dilated. I hadn't even seen the lines of the sections. A circle opened and I took a step through. I turned and there was Blood, watching me. We looked at each other, all the while that pillar was humming.

"So long, Vic."

"Take care of yourself, Blood."

"Hurry back."

"Do my best."

"Yeah. Right."

Then I turned around and stepped inside. The access portal irised closed behind me.

VII

I should have known. I should have suspected. Sure, every once in a while a chick came up to see what it was like on the surface, what had happened to the cities; sure, it happened. Why I'd believed her when she'd told me, cuddled up beside me in that steaming boiler, that she'd wanted to see what it was like when a girl did it with a man, that all the flicks she'd seen in Topeka were sweet and solid and dull, and the girls in her school'd talked about beaver flicks, and one of them had a little eight-page comic book and she'd read it with wide eyes . . . sure, I'd believed her. It was logical. I should have suspected something when she left that metal i.d. plate behind. It was too easy. Blood'd tried to tell me. Dumb? Yeah!

The second that access iris swirled closed behind me, the humming got louder, and some cool light grew in the walls. Wall. It was a circular compartment with only two sides to the wall: *in*side and *out*side. The wall pulsed up light and the humming got louder, and then the floor I was standing on dilated just the way the outside port had done. But I was standing there, like a mouse in a cartoon, and as long as I didn't look down I was cool, I wouldn't fall.

Then I started settling. Dropped through the floor, the iris closed overhead, I was dropping down the tube, picking up speed but not too much, just dropping steadily. Now I knew what a dropshaft was.

Down and down I went and every once in a while I'd see something like 10 LEV or ANTIPOLL 55 or BREEDERCON or PUMP SE 6 on the wall, and faintly I could make out the sectioning of an iris . . . but I never stopped dropping.

Finally, I dropped all the way to the bottom and there was TOPEKA CITY LIMITS POP. 22,860 on the wall, and I settled down without any strain, bending a little from the knees to cushion the impact, but even that wasn't much.

I used the metal plate again, and the iris—a much bigger one this time—swirled open, and I got my first look at a downunder.

It stretched away in front of me, twenty miles to the dim shining horizon of tin can metal where the wall behind me curved and curved and curved till it made one smooth, encircling circuit and came back around around around to where I stood, staring at it. I was down at the bottom of a big metal tube that stretched up to a ceiling an eighth of a mile overhead, twenty miles across. And in the bottom of that tin can, someone had built a town that looked for all the world like a photo out of one of the water-logged books in the library on the surface. I'd seen a town like this in the books. Just like this. Neat little houses, and curvy little streets, and trimmed lawns, and a business section and everything else that a Topeka would have.

Except a sun, except birds, except clouds, except rain, except snow, except cold, except wind, except ants, except dirt, except mountains, except oceans, except big fields of grain, except stars, except the moon, except forests, except animals running wild, except . . .

Except freedom.

They were canned down here, like dead fish. Canned.

I felt my throat tighten up. I wanted to get out. Out! I started to tremble, my hands were cold and there was sweat on my forehead. This had been insane, coming down here. I had to get out. *Out!*

I turned around, to get back in the dropshaft, and then it grabbed me.

That bitch Quilla June! I shoulda suspected!

The thing was low, and green, and boxlike, and had cables with mittens on the ends instead of arms, and it rolled on tracks, and it grabbed me.

It hoisted me up on its square flat top, holding me with them mittens on the cables, and I couldn't move, except to try kicking at the big glass eye in the front, but it didn't do any good. It didn't bust. The thing was only about four feet high, and my sneakers almost reached the ground, but not quite, and it started moving off into Topeka, hauling me along with it.

People were all over the place. Sitting in rockers on their front porches, raking their lawns, hanging around the gas station, sticking pennies in gumball machines, painting a white stripe down the middle of the road, selling newspapers on a corner, listening to an oompah band on a shell in a park, playing hopscotch and pussy-in-the-corner, polishing a fire engine, sitting on benches reading, washing windows, pruning bushes, tipping hats to ladies, collecting milk bottles in wire carrying racks, grooming horses, throwing a stick for a dog to retrieve, diving into a communal swimming pool, chalking vegetable prices on a slate outside a grocery, walking hand-in-hand with a girl, all of them watching me go past on that metal motherfucker.

I could hear Blood speaking, saying just what he'd said before I'd entered the dropshaft: *It's all square and settled and they know everyone; they hate solos. Enough roverpaks have raided downunders and raped their broads, and stolen their food, they'll have defenses set up. They'll* kill *you, man!*

Thanks, mutt.

Goodbye.

VIII

The green box tracked through the business section and turned in at a shopfront with the words BETTER BUSINESS BUREAU on the window. It rolled right inside the open door, and there were half a dozen men and old men and very old men in there, waiting for me. Also a couple of women. The green box stopped.

One of them came over and took the metal plate out of my hand. He looked at it, then turned around and gave it to the oldest of the old men, a withered cat wearing baggy pants and a green eyeshade and garters that held up the sleeves of his striped shirt. "Quilla June, Lew," the guy said to the old man. Lew took the metal plate and put it in the top left drawer of a rolltop desk. "Better take his guns, Aaron," the old coot said. And the guy who'd taken the plate cleaned me.

"Let him loose, Aaron," Lew said.

Aaron stepped around the back of the green box and something clicked, and the cable mittens sucked back inside the box, and I got down off the thing. My arms were numb where the box had held me. I rubbed one, then the other, and I glared at them.

"Now, boy . . ." Lew started.

"Suck wind, asshole!"

The women blanched. The men tightened their faces.

"I told you it wouldn't work," another of the old men said to Lew.

"Bad business, this," said one of the younger ones.

Lew leaned forward in his straight-back chair and pointed a crumbled finger at me. "Boy, you better be nice."

"I hope all your fuckin' children are hare-lipped!"

"This is no good, Lew!" another man said.

"Guttersnipe," a woman with a beak snapped.

Lew stared at me. His mouth was a nasty little black line. I knew the sonofabitch didn't have a tooth in his crummy head that wasn't rotten and smelly. He stared at me with vicious little eyes. God he was ugly, like a bird ready to pick meat off my bones. He was getting set to say something I wouldn't like. "Aaron, maybe you'd better put the sentry back on him." Aaron moved to the green box.

"Okay, hold it," I said, holding up my hand.

Aaron stopped, looked at Lew, who nodded. Then Lew leaned forward again, and aimed that bird-claw at me. "You ready to behave yourself, son?"

"Yeah, I guess."

"You'd better be dang sure."

"Okay. I'm *dang* sure. Also *fuckin'* sure!"

"And you'll watch your mouth."

I didn't reply. Old coot.

"You're a bit of an experiment for us, boy. We tried to get one of you down here other ways. Sent up some good folks to capture one of you little scuts, but they never came back. Figgered it was best to lure you down to us."

I sneered. That Quilla June. I'd take care of her!

One of the women, a little younger than Bird-Beak, came forward and looked into my face. "Lew, you'll never get this one to kow-tow. He's a filthy little killer. Look at those eyes."

"How'd you like the barrel of a rifle jammed up your ass, bitch?" She jumped back. Lew was angry again. "Sorry," I said, "I don't like bein' called names. *Macho*, y'know?"

He settled back and snapped at the woman. "Mez, leave him alone. I'm tryin' to talk a bit of sense here. You're only making it worse."

Mez went back and sat with the others. Some Better Business Bureau these creeps were!

"As I was saying, boy: you're an experiment for us. We've been down here in Topeka close to twenty years. It's nice down here. Quiet, orderly, nice people who respect each other, no crime, respect for the elders, and just all around a good place to live. We're growin' and we're prosperin'."

I waited.

"But, well, we find now that some of our folks can't have no more babies, and the women that do, they have mostly girls. We need some men. Certain special kind of men."

I started laughing. This was too good to be true. They wanted me for stud service. I couldn't stop laughing.

"Crude!" one of the women said, scowling.

"This's awkward enough for us, boy, don't make it no harder." Lew was embarrassed.

Here I'd spent most of Blood's and my time aboveground hunting up tail, and down here they wanted me to service the local ladyfolk. I sat down on the floor and laughed till tears ran down my cheeks.

Finally, I got up and said, "Sure. Okay. But if I do, there's a couple of things *I* want."

Lew looked at me close.

"The first thing I want is that Quilla June. I'm gonna fuck her blind, and then I'm gonna bang her on the head the way she did me!"

They huddled for a while, then came out and Lew said, "We can't tolerate any violence down here, but I s'pose Quilla June's as good a place to start as any. She's capable, isn't she, Ira?"

A skinny, yellow-skinned man nodded. He didn't look happy about it. Quilla June's old man, I bet.

"Well, let's get started," I said. "Line 'em up." I started to unzip my jeans.

The women screamed, the men grabbed me, and they hustled me off to a boarding house where they gave me a room, and they said I should get to know Topeka a little bit before I went to work, because it was, uh, er, well, awkward, and they had to get the folks in town to accept what was going to have to be done . . . on the assumption, I suppose, that if I worked out okay, they'd import a few more young bulls from aboveground, and turn us loose.

So I spent some time in Topeka, getting to know the folks, seeing what they did, how they lived. It was nice, real nice. They rocked in rockers on the front porches, they raked the lawns, they hung around the gas station, they stuck pennies in the gumball machines, they painted white stripes down the middle of the road, they sold newspapers on the corners, they listened to oompah bands on a shell in the park, they played hopscotch and pussy-in-the-corner, they polished fire engines, they sat on benches reading, they washed windows and pruned bushes, they tipped their hats to ladies, they collected milk bottles in wire carrying racks, they groomed horses and threw sticks for their dogs to retrieve, they dove into the communal swimming pool, they chalked vegetable prices on a slate outside the grocery, they walked hand-in-hand with some of the ugliest chicks I've ever seen, and they bored the ass off me.

Inside a week I was ready to scream.

I could feel that tin can closing in on me.

I could feel the weight of the earth over me.

They ate artificial shit: artificial peas and fake meat and make-believe chicken and ersatz corn and bogus bread and it all tasted like chalk and dust to me.

Polite? .Christ, you could puke from the lying, hypocritical crap they called civility. Hello Mr. This and Hello Mrs. That. And how are you? And how is little Janie? And how is business? And are you going to the sodality meeting Thursday? And I started gibbering in my room at the boarding house.

The clean, sweet, neat, lovely way they lived was enough to kill a guy. No wonder the men couldn't get it up and make babies that had balls instead of slots.

The first few days, everyone watched me like I was about to explode and cover their nice whitewashed fences with shit. But after a while, they got used to seeing me. Lew took me over to the mercantile, and got me fitted out with a pair of bib overalls and a shirt that any solo could've spotted a mile away. That Mez, that dippy bitch who'd called me a killer, she started hanging around, finally said she wanted to cut my hair, make me look civilized. But I was hip to where she was at. Wasn't a bit of the mother in her.

"What's'a'matter, cunt," I pinned her. "Your old man isn't taking care of you?"

She tried to stick her fist in her mouth, and I laughed like a loon. "Go cut off his balls, baby. My hair stays the way it is." She cut and run. Went like she had a diesel tail-pipe.

It went on like that for a while. Me just walking around, them coming and feeding me, keeping all their young meat out of my way till they got the town stacked away for what was coming with me.

Jugged like that, my mind wasn't right for a while. I got all claustrophobed, clutched, went and sat under the porch in the dark at the rooming house. Then that passed, and I got piss-mean, snapped at them, then surly, then quiet, then just mud dull. Quiet.

Finally, I started getting hip to the possibilities of getting out of there. It began with me remembering the poodle I'd fed Blood one time. It had to of come from a downunder. And it couldn't of got up through the dropshaft. So that meant there were other ways out.

They gave me pretty much of the run of the town, as long as I kept my manners around me and didn't try anything sudden. That green sentry box was always somewhere nearby.

So I found the way out. Nothing so spectacular; it just had to be there, and I found it.

Then I found out where they kept my weapons, and I was ready. Almost.

IX

It was a week to the day when Aaron and Lew and Ira came to get me. I was pretty goofy by that time. I was sitting out on the back porch of the boarding house, smoking a corncob pipe with my shirt off, catching some sun. Except there wasn't no sun. Goofy.

They came around the house. "Morning, Vic," Lew greeted me. He was hobbling along with a cane, the old fart. Aaron gave me a big smile. The kind you'd give a big black bull about to stuff his meat into a good breed cow. Ira had a look that you could chip off and use in your furnace.

"Well, howdy, Lew. Mornin' Aaron, Ira."

Lew seemed right pleased by that.

Oh, you lousy bastards, just you wait!

"You bout ready to go meet your first lady?"

"Ready as I'll ever be, Lew," I said, and got up.

"Cool smoke, isn't it?" Aaron said.

I took the corncob out of my mouth. "Pure dee-light," I smiled. I hadn't even lit the fucking thing.

They walked me over to Marigold Street and as we came up on a little house with yellow shutters and a white picket fence, Lew said, "This's Ira's house. Quilla June is his daughter."

"Well land sakes," I said, wide-eyed.

Ira's lean jaw muscles jumped.

We went inside.

Quilla June was sitting on the settee with her mother, an older version of her, pulled thin as a withered muscle. "Miz Holmes," I said, and made a little curtsey. She smiled. Strained, but smiled.

Quilla June sat with her feet right together, and her hands folded in her lap. There was a ribbon in her hair. It was blue.

Matched her eyes.

Something went thump in my gut.

"Quilla June," I said.

She looked up. "Mornin', Vic."

Then everyone sort of stood around looking awkward, and finally Ira began yapping and yipping about get in the bedroom and get this unnatural filth over with so they could go to Church and pray the Good Lord wouldn't Strike All Of Them Dead with a bolt of lightning in the ass, or some crap like that.

So I put out my hand, and Quilla June reached for it without looking up, and we went in the back, into a small bedroom, and she stood there with her head down.

"You didn't tell 'em, did you?" I asked.

She shook her head.

And suddenly, I didn't want to kill her at all. I wanted to hold her. Very tight. So I did. And she was crying into my chest, and making little fists and beating on my back, and then she was looking up at me and running her words all together: "Oh, Vic, I'm sorry, so sorry, I didn't mean to, I had to, I was sent out to, I was so scared, and I love you and now they've got you down here, and it isn't dirty, is it, it isn't the way my Poppa says it is, is it?"

I held her and kissed her and told her it was okay, and then I asked her if she wanted to come away with me, and she said yes yes yes she really did. So I told her I might have to hurt her Poppa to get away, and she got a look in her eyes that I knew real well.

For all her propriety, Quilla June Holmes didn't much like her prayer-shouting Poppa.

I asked her if she had anything heavy, like a candlestick or a club, and she said no. So I went rummaging around in that back bedroom, and found a pair of her Poppa's socks in a bureau drawer. I pulled the big brass balls off the headboard of the bed, and dropped them into the sock. I hefted it. Oh. Yeah.

She stared at me with big eyes. "What're you going to do?"

"You want to get out of here?"

She nodded.

"Then just stand back behind the door. No, wait a minute, I got a better idea. Get on the bed."

She laid down on the bed. "Okay," I said, "now pull up your skirt, pull off your pants, and spread out." She gave me a look of pure horror. "Do it," I said. "If you want out."

So she did it, and I rearranged her so her knees were bent and her legs open at the thighs, and I stood to one side of the door, and whispered to her, "Call your Poppa. Just him."

She hesitated a long moment, then she called out, in a voice she didn't have to fake, "Poppa! Poppa, come here, please!" Then she clamped her eyes shut tight.

Ira Holmes came through the door, took one look at his secret desire, his mouth dropped open, I kicked the door closed behind him and walloped him as hard as I could. He squished a little, and spattered the bedspread, and went very down.

She opened her eyes when she heard the thunk! and when the stuff splattered her legs she leaned over and puked on the floor. I knew she wouldn't be much good to me in getting Aaron into the room, so I opened the door, stuck my head around, looked worried, and said, "Aaron, would you come here a minute, please?" He looked at Lew, who was rapping with Mrs. Holmes about what was going on in the back bedroom, and when Lew nodded him on, he came into the room. He took a look at Quilla June's naked bush, at the blood on the wall and bedspread, at Ira on the floor, and opened his mouth to yell, just as I whacked him. It took two more to get him down, and then I had to kick him in the chest to put him away. Quilla June was still puking.

I grabbed her by the arm and swung her up off the bed. At least she was being quiet about it, but man did she stink.

"Come on!"

She tried to pull back, but I held on, and opened the bedroom door. As I pulled her out, Lew stood up, leaning on his cane. I kicked the cane out from under the old fart and down he went in a heap. Mrs. Holmes was staring at us, wondering where her old man was: "He's back in there," I said, heading for the front door. "The Good Lord got him in the head."

Then we were out in the street, Quilla June stinking along behind me, dry-heaving and bawling and probably wondering what had happened to her underpants.

They kept my weapons in a locked case at the Better Business Bureau, and we detoured around by my boarding house where I pulled the crowbar I'd swiped from the gas station out from under the back porch. Then we cut across behind the Grange and into the business section, and straight into the BBB. There was a clerk who tried to stop me, and I split his gourd with the crowbar. Then I pried the latch off the cabinet in Lew's office, and got the .30-06 and my .45 and all the ammo, and my spike, and my knife, and my kit, and loaded up. By that time Quilla June was able to make some sense.

"Where we gonna go, where we gonna go, oh Poppa Poppa Poppa . . . !"

"Hey, listen, Quilla June, Poppa me no Poppas. You said you wanted to be with me . . . well, I'm goin! *up*, baby, and if you wanna go with me, you better stick close."

She was too scared to object.

I stepped out the front of the shopfront, and there was that green box sentry, coming on like a whippet. It had its cables out, and the mittens were gone. It had hooks.

I dropped to one knee, wrapped the sling of the .30-06 around my forearm, sighted clean, and fired dead at the big eye in the front. One shot, spang!

Hit that eye, the thing exploded in a shower of sparks, and the green box swerved and went through the front window of The Mill End Shoppe, screeching and crying and showering the place with flames and sparks. Nice.

I turned around to grab Quilla June, but she was gone. I looked off down the street, and here came all the vigilantes, Lew hobbling along with his cane like some kind of weird grasshopper.

And right then the shots started. Big, booming sounds. The .45 I'd given Quilla June. I looked up, and on the porch around the second floor, there she was, the automatic down on the railing like a pro, sighting into that mob and snapping off shots like maybe Wild Bill Elliott in a 40's Republic flick.

But dumb! Mother, dumb! Wasting time on that, when we had to get away.

I found the outside staircase going up there, and took it three steps at a time. She was smiling and laughing, and every time she'd pick one of those boobs out of the pack her little tongue-tip would peek out of the corner of her mouth, and her eyes would get all slick and wet and wham! down the boob would go.

She was really into it.

Just as I reached her, she sighted down on her scrawny mother. I slammed the back of her head and she missed the shot, and the old lady did a little dance-step and kept coming. Quilla June whipped her head around at me, and there was kill in her eyes. "You made me miss." The voice gave me a chill.

I took the .45 away from her. Dumb. Wasting ammunition like that.

Dragging her behind me, I circled the building, found a shed out back, dropped down into it and had her follow. She was scared at first, but I said, "Chick can shoot her old lady as easy as you do shouldn't be worried about a drop this small." She got out on the edge, other side of the railing and held on. "Don't worry," I said, "you won't wet your pants. You haven't got any."

She laughed, like a bird, and dropped. I caught her, we slid down the shed door, and took a second to see if that mob was hard on us. Nowhere in sight.

I grabbed Quilla June by the arm and started off toward the south end of Topeka. It was the closest exit I'd found in my wandering, and we made it in about fifteen minutes, panting and weak as kittens.

And there it was.

A big air-intake duct.

I pried off the clamps with the crowbar, and we climbed up inside. There were ladders going up. There had to be. It figured. Repairs. Keep it clean. Had to be. We started climbing.

It took a long, long time.

Quilla June kept asking me, from down behind me, whenever she got too tired to climb, "Vic, do you love me?" I kept saying yes. Not only because I meant it. It helped her keep climbing.

X

We came up a mile from the access dropshaft. I shot off the filter covers and the hatch bolts, and we climbed out. They should have known better down there. You don't fuck around with Jimmy Cagney.

They never had a chance.

Quilla June was exhausted. I didn't blame her. But I didn't want to spend the night out in the open; there were things out there I didn't like to think about meeting even in daylight. It was getting on toward dusk.

We walked toward the access dropshaft.

Blood was waiting.

He looked weak. But he'd waited.

I stooped down and lifted his head. He opened his eyes, and very softly he said, "Hey."

I smiled at him. Jesus, it was good to see him. "We made it back, man."

He tried to get up, but he couldn't. The wounds on him were in ugly shape. "Have you eaten?" I asked.

"No. Grabbed a lizard yesterday . . . or maybe it was day before. I'm hungry, Vic."

Quilla June came up then, and Blood saw her. He closed his eyes. "We'd better hurry, Vic," she said. "Please. They might come up from the dropshaft."

I tried to lift Blood. He was dead weight. "Listen, Blood, I'll leg it into the city and get some food. I'll come back quick. You just wait here."

"Don't go in there, Vic," he said. "I did a recon the day after you went down. They found out we weren't fried in that gym. I don't know how. Maybe mutts smelled our track. I've been keeping watch, and they haven't tried to come out after us. I don't blame them. You don't know what it's like out here at night, man . . . you don't know . . ."

He shivered.

"Take it easy, Blood."

"But they've got us marked lousy in the city, Vic. We can't go back there. We'll have to make it someplace else."

That put it on a different stick. We couldn't go back, and with Blood in that condition we couldn't go forward. And I knew, good as I was solo, I couldn't make it without him. And there wasn't anything out here to eat. He had to have food, at once, and some medical care. I had to do something. Something good, something fast.

"Vic," Quilla June's voice was high and whining, "come *on!* He'll be all right. We have to hurry."

I looked up at her. The sun was going down. Blood trembled in my arms.

She got a pouty look on her face. "If you love me, you'll come *on!*"

I couldn't make it alone out there without him. I knew it. If I loved her. She asked me, in the boiler, do you know what love is?

It was a small fire, not nearly big enough for any roverpak to spot from the outskirts of the city. No smoke. And after Blood had eaten his fill, I carried him to the air-duct a mile away, and we spent the night inside, on a little ledge. I held him all night. He slept good. In the morning, I fixed him up pretty good. He'd make it; he was strong.

He ate again. There was plenty left from the night before. I didn't eat. I wasn't hungry.

We started off across the blast wasteland that morning. We'd find another city, and make it.

We had to move slow, because Blood was still limping. It took a long time before I stopped hearing her calling in my head. Asking me, asking me: *do you know what love is?*

Sure I know.

A boy loves his dog.

Robots

A synthesis of dictionary definitions indicates that a robot is a machine that resembles a human and operates automatically with human-like skill. The idea of such a machine has given rise to much apprehension among labor unions who have, in the past, felt that robot labor was a distinct threat. Among science fiction writers, the robot provided, for a time at least, a gold mine of plots which all too often were a mechanical rehash of Mary Shelley's *Frankenstein*. But to be fair, the robots were only a part of the "frankenscience" wave in science fiction in which everything from computers to the Bomb was either enslaving or destroying mankind. Today, however, the attitude both in science fiction and among the public seems to be changing. In fact, most recent nonfiction studies concerned with the future envision robots, computers, and the like, freeing rather than enslaving mankind.

The term "robot" was first used by Karl Capek in his 1921 drama, *R.U.R.* The word is apparently a back-formation from the Czechoslovakian word for serf, *robotnik*. Capek, however, was using the term to refer to creations of synthetic flesh rather than creations of metal; we would now call Capek's creations androids. To complete the catalogue of artificial creations with human-like characteristics, cyborgs must be added to robots, computers, and androids. The cyborg is a human brain hooked up to and running a machine. The advantages are obvious;

a human brain wired directly to a rocket would know or feel exactly what was going on at all times rather than having to rely on the second-hand information provided by gauges, dials, and other middle-man devices.

In *The Moon is a Harsh Mistress,* Robert Heinlein presents not only a cyborg ship's captain but a computer which has "come to life" and a man with several interchangeable prosthetic arms to replace the one he lost in a mining accident. By choosing from among the arms, Manuel O'Kelly is much more capable in a given situation than a man with "two good arms." Robert Silverberg portrays the tensions and conflicts between humans and androids in his recent novel, *Tower of Glass.* Isaac Asimov has probably done some of the most thoughtful writing about robots. His robot stories of the forties and early fifties, now collected in *I, Robot* and *The Rest of the Robots,* and his robot novels of the early fifties, *The Caves of Steel* and its sequel, *The Naked Sun,* offer robots and robotics for the intelligent rather than the fearful reader.

The three stories presented here give three distinct and progressively complex views of robots and their relationship to humans. Isaac Asimov's "Runaround" presents a fundamental conflict of man vs. environment complicated by the robot upon which man depends for help in winning this conflict. The problem with the robot is one caused by man and finally solved through a logical and scientific analysis of the situation. In the course of the story, the reader also learns how the average man on earth has reacted to the invention and production of robots. In Ron Goulart's "Calling Dr. Clockwork," some of man's nightmares about robots seem to come true; however, the people are also at fault. Goulart depicts a character who is so complacently secure that he doesn't realize what's happening to him until after it has happened. Moreover, all the other humans in the story are weak and ineffective if only because they are unable to understand what is actually happening. Ironically, the Urban Free Hospital may be a logical extension of present day attitudes or desires concerning the physical and mental care to be provided for low income groups. Damon Knight's "Masks" is not a traditional robot story. Knight presents a middle ground for which the terms "robot," "cyborg," and "prosthetic" seem to be incomplete. Understanding the point of view from which various parts of this story are told is crucial to understanding the nature of the people in the story as well as the "person" who has become a "machine." It is also profitable to consider why this story is entitled "Masks" instead of "The Mask."

Attempting to understand the nature of robots and man's relation to them is especially interesting in light of the occasionally-voiced hypothesis that robots may be the next evolutionary step and that it is man's function to bring that evolution about.

RUNAROUND

Isaac Asimov

It was one of Gregory Powell's favorite platitudes that nothing was to be gained from excitement, so when Mike Donovan came leaping down the stairs toward him, red hair matted with perspiration, Powell frowned.

"What's wrong?" he said. "Break a fingernail?"

"Yaaaah," snarled Donovan, feverishly. "What have you been doing in the sublevels all day?" He took a deep breath and blurted out, "Speedy never returned."

Powell's eyes widened momentarily and he stopped on the stairs; then he recovered and resumed his upward steps. He didn't speak until he reached the head of the flight, and then:

"You sent him after the selenium?"

"Yes."

"And how long has he been out?"

"Five hours now."

Silence! This was a devil of a situation. Here they were, on Mercury exactly twelve hours—and already up to the eyebrows in the worst sort of trouble. Mercury had long been the jinx world of the System, but this was drawing it rather strong—even for a jinx.

Powell said, "Start at the beginning, and let's get this straight."

They were in the radio room now—with its already subtly antiquated equipment, untouched for the ten years previous to their arrival. Even ten years, technologically speaking, meant so much. Compare Speedy with the type of robot they must have had back in 2005. But then, advances in robotics these days were tremendous. Powell touched a still gleaming metal surface gingerly. The air of disuse that touched everything about the room—and the entire Station—was infinitely depressing.

Donovan must have felt it. He began: "I tried to locate him by radio, but it was no go. Radio isn't any good on the Mercury Sunside—not past two miles, anyway. That's one of the reasons the First Expedition failed. And we can't put up the ultrawave equipment for weeks yet—"

"Skip all that. What *did* you get?"

"I located the unorganized body signal in the short wave. It was no good for anything except his position. I kept track of him that way for two hours and plotted the results on the map."

There was a yellowed square of parchment in his hip pocket—a relic of the unsuccessful First Expedition—and he slapped it down on the desk with the vicious force, spreading it flat with the palm of his hand. Powell, hands clasped across his chest, watched it at long range.

Donovan's pencil pointed nervously. "The red cross is the selenium pool. You marked it yourself."

"Which one is it?" interrupted Powell. "There were three that MacDougal located for us before he left."

"I sent Speedy to the nearest, naturally. Seventeen miles away. But what difference does that make?" There was tension in his voice. "There are the penciled dots that mark Speedy's position."

And for the first time Powell's artificial aplomb was shaken and his hands shot forward for the map.

"Are *you* serious? This is impossible."

"There it is," growled Donovan.

The little dots that marked the position formed a rough circle about the red cross of the selenium pool. And Powell's fingers went to his brown mustache, the unfailing signal of anxiety.

Donovan added: "In the two hours I checked on him, he circled that damned pool four times. It seems likely to me that he'll keep that up forever. Do you realize the position we're in?"

Powell looked up shortly, and said nothing. Oh, yes, he realized the position they were in. It worked itself out as simply as a syllogism. The photo-cell banks that alone stood between the full power of Mercury's monstrous sun and themselves were shot to hell. The only thing that could save them was selenium. The only thing that could get the selenium was Speedy. If Speedy didn't come back, no selenium. No selenium, no photo-cell banks. No photo-banks—well, death by slow broiling is one of the more unpleasant ways of being done in.

Donovan rubbed his red mop of hair savagely and expressed himself with bitterness. "We'll be the laughingstock of the System, Greg. How can everything have gone so wrong so soon? The great team of Powell and Donovan is sent out to Mercury to report on the advisability of reopening the Sunside Mining Station with modern techniques and robots and we ruin everything the first day. A purely routine job, too. We'll never live it down."

"We won't have to, perhaps," replied Powell, quietly. "If we don't do something quickly, living anything down—or even just plain living—will be out of the question."

"Don't be stupid! If you feel funny about it, Greg, I don't. It was criminal, sending us out here with only one robot. And it was *your* bright idea that we could handle the photo-cell banks ourselves."

"Now you're being unfair. It was a mutual decision and you know it. All we needed was a kilogram of selenium, a Stillhead Dielectrode

Plate and about three hours' time—and there are pools of pure selenium all over Sunside. MacDougal's spectroreflector spotted three for us in five minutes, didn't it? What the devil! We couldn't have waited for next conjunction."

"Well, what are we going to do? Powell, you've got an idea. I know you have, or you wouldn't be so calm. You're no more a hero than I am. Go on, spill it!"

"We can't go after Speedy ourselves, Mike—not on the Sunside. Even the new insosuits aren't good for more than twenty minutes in direct sunlight. But you know the old saying, 'Set a robot to catch a robot.' Look, Mike, maybe things aren't so bad. We've got six robots down in the sublevels, that we may be able to use, if they work. *If* they work."

There was a glint of sudden hope in Donovan's eyes. "You mean six robots from the First Expedition. Are you sure? They may be subrobotic machines. Ten years is a long time as far as robot-types are concerned, you know."

"No, they're robots. I've spent all day with them and I know. They've got positronic brains: primitive, of course." He placed the map in his pocket. "Let's go down."

The robots were on the lowest sublevel—all six of them surrounded by musty packing cases of uncertain content. They were large, extremely so, and even though they were in a sitting position on the floor, legs straddled out before them, their heads were a good seven feet in the air.

Donovan whistled. "Look at the size of them, will you? The chests must be ten feet around."

"That's because they're supplied with the old McGuffy gears. I've been over the insides—crummiest set you've ever seen."

"Have you powered them yet?"

"No. There wasn't any reason to. I don't think there's anything wrong with them. Even the diaphragm is in reasonable order. They might talk."

He had unscrewed the chest plate of the nearest as he spoke, inserted the two-inch sphere that contained the tiny spark of atomic energy that was a robot's life. There was difficulty in fitting it, but he managed, and then screwed the plate back on again in laborious fashion. The radio controls of more modern models had not been heard of ten years earlier. And then to the other five.

Donovan said uneasily, "They haven't moved."

"No orders to do so," replied Powell, succinctly. He went back to the first in the line and struck him on the chest. "You! Do you hear me?"

The monster's head bent slowly and the eyes fixed themselves on

Powell. Then, in a harsh, squawking voice—like that of a medieval phonograph, he grated, "Yes, Master!"

Powell grinned humorlessly at Donovan. "Did you get that? Those were the days of the first talking robots when it looked as if the use of robots on Earth would be banned. The makers were fighting that and they built good, healthy slave complexes into the damned machines."

"It didn't help them," muttered Donovan.

"No, it didn't, but they sure tried." He turned once more to the robot. "Get up!"

The robot towered upward slowly and Donovan's head craned and his puckered lips whistled.

Powell said: "Can you go out upon the surface? In the light?"

There was consideration while the robot's slow brain worked. Then, "Yes, Master."

"Good. Do you know what a mile is?"

Another consideration, and another slow answer. "Yes, Master."

"We will take you up to the surface then, and indicate a direction. You will go about seventeen miles, and somewhere in that general region you will meet another robot, smaller than yourself. You understand so far?"

"Yes, Master."

"You will find this robot and order him to return. If he does not wish to, you are to bring him back by force."

Donovan clutched at Powell's sleeve. "Why not send him for the selenium direct?"

"Because I want Speedy back, nitwit. I want to find out what's wrong with him." And to the robot, "All right, you, follow me."

The robot remained motionless and his voice rumbled: "Pardon, Master, but I cannot. You must mount first." His clumsy arms had come together with a thwack, blunt fingers interlacing.

Powell stared and then pinched at his mustache. "Uh . . . oh!"

Donovan's eyes bulged. "We've got to ride him? Like a horse?"

"I guess that's the idea. I don't know why, though. I can't see—Yes, I do. I told you they were playing up robot-safety in those days. Evidently, they were going to sell the notion of safety by not allowing them to move about, without a mahout on their shoulders all the time. What do we do now?"

"That's what I've been thinking," muttered Donovan. "We can't go out on the surface, with a robot or without. Oh, for the love of Pete"—and he snapped his fingers twice. He grew excited. "Give me that map you've got. I haven't studied it for two hours for nothing. This is a Mining Station. What's wrong with using the tunnels?"

The Mining Station was a black circle on the map, and the light dotted lines that were tunnels stretched out about it in spiderweb fashion.

Donovan studied the list of symbols at the bottom of the map. "Look," he said, "the small black dots are openings to the surface, and here's one maybe three miles away from the selenium pool. There's a number here—you'd think they'd write larger—13a. If the robots know their way around here—"

Powell shot the question and received the dull "Yes, Master," in reply. "Get your insosuit," he said with satisfaction.

It was the first time either had worn the insosuits—which marked one time more than either had expected to upon their arrival the day before—and they tested their limb movements uncomfortably.

The insosuit was far bulkier and far uglier than the regulation spacesuit; but withal considerably lighter, due to the fact that they were entirely nonmetallic in composition. Composed of heat-resistant plastic and chemically treated cork layers, and equipped with a desiccating unit to keep the air bone-dry, the insosuits could withstand the full glare of Mercury's sun for twenty minutes. Five to ten minutes more, as well, without actually killing the occupant.

And still the robot's hands formed the stirrup, nor did he betray the slightest atom of surprise at the grotesque figure into which Powell had been converted.

Powell's radio-harshened voice boomed out: "Are you ready to take us to Exit 13a?"

"Yes, Master."

Good, thought Powell; they might lack radio control but at least they were fitted for radio reception. "Mount one or the other, Mike," he said to Donovan.

He placed a foot in the improvised stirrup and swung upward. He found the seat comfortable; there was the humped back of the robot, evidently shaped for the purpose, a shallow groove along each shoulder for the thighs and two elongated "ears" whose purpose now seemed obvious.

Powell seized the ears and twisted the head. His mount turned ponderously. "Lead on, Macduff." But he did not feel at all lighthearted.

The gigantic robots moved slowly, with mechanical precision, through the doorway that cleared their heads by a scant foot, so that the two men had to duck hurriedly, along a narrow corridor in which their unhurried footsteps boomed monotonously and into the air lock.

The long, airless tunnel that stretched to a pinpoint before them brought home forcefully to Powell the exact magnitude of the task accomplished by the First Expedition, with their crude robots and their start-from-scratch necessities. They might have been a failure, but their failure was a good deal better than the usual run of the System's successes.

The robots plodded onward with a pace that never varied and with footsteps that never lengthened.

Powell said: "Notice that these tunnels are blazing with lights and that the temperature is Earth-normal. It's probably been like this all the ten years that this place has remained empty."

"How's that?"

"Cheap energy; cheapest in the System. Sunpower, you know, and on Mercury's Sunside, sunpower is *something.* That's why the Station was built in the sunlight rather than in the shadow of a·mountain. It's really a huge energy converter. The heat is turned into electricity, light, mechanical work and what have you; so that energy is supplied and the Station is cooled in a simultaneous process."

"Look," said Donovan. "This is all very educational, but would you mind changing the subject? It so happens that this conversion of energy that you talk about is carried on by the photo-cell banks mainly—and that is a tender subject with me at the moment."

Powell grunted vaguely, and when Donovan broke the resulting silence, it was to change the subject completely. "Listen, Greg. What the devil's wrong with Speedy, anyway? I can't understand it."

It's not easy to shrug shoulders in an insosuit, but Powell tried it. "I don't know, Mike. You know he's perfectly adapted to a Mercurian environment. Heat doesn't mean anything to him and he's built for the light gravity and the broken ground. He's foolproof—or, at least, he should be."

Silence fell. This time, silence that lasted.

"Master," said the robot, "we are here."

"Eh?" Powell snapped out of a semidrowse. "Well, get us out of here— out to the surface."

They found themselves in a tiny substation, empty, airless, ruined. Donovan had inspected a jagged hole in the upper reaches of one of the walls by the light of his pocket flash.

"Meteorite, do you suppose?" he had asked.

Powell shrugged. "To hell with that. It doesn't matter. Let's get out."

A towering cliff of a black, basaltic rock cut off the sunlight, and the deep night shadow of an airless world surrounded them. Before them, the shadow reached out and ended in knife-edge abruptness into an all-but-unbearable blaze of white light, that glittered from myriad crystals along a rocky ground.

"Space!" gasped Donovan. "It looks like snow." And it did.

Powell's eyes swept the jagged glitter of Mercury to the horizon and winced at the gorgeous brilliance.

"This must be an unusual area," he said. "The general albedo of Mercury is low and most of the soil is gray pumice. Something like the Moon, you know. Beautiful, isn't it?"

He was thankful for the light filters in their visiplates. Beautiful or not, a look at the sunlight through straight glass would have blinded them inside of half a minute.

Donovan was looking at the spring thermometer on his wrist. "Holy smokes, the temperature is eighty centigrade!"

Powell checked his own and said: "Um-m-m. A little high. Atmosphere, you know."

"On Mercury? Are you nuts?"

"Mercury isn't really airless," explained Powell, in absent-minded fashion. He was adjusting the binocular attachments to his visiplate, and the bloated fingers of the insosuit were clumsy at it. "There is a thin exhalation that clings to its surface—vapors of the more volatile elements and compounds that are heavy enough for Mercurian gravity to retain. You know: selenium, iodine, mercury, gallium, potassium, bismuth, volatile oxides. The vapors sweep into the shadows and condense, giving up heat. It's a sort of gigantic still. In fact, if you use your flash, you'll probably find that the side of the cliff is covered with, say, hoar-sulphur, or maybe quicksilver dew.

"It doesn't matter, though. Our suits can stand a measly eighty indefinitely."

Powell had adjusted the binocular attachments, so that he seemed as eye-stalked as a snail.

Donovan watched tensely. "See anything?"

The other did not answer immediately, and when he did, his voice was anxious and thoughtful. "There's a dark spot on the horizon that might be the selenium pool. It's in the right place. But I don't see Speedy."

Powell clambered upward in an instinctive striving for better view, till he was standing in unsteady fashion upon his robot's shoulders. Legs straddled wide, eyes straining, he said: "I think . . . I think— Yes, it's definitely he. He's coming this way."

Donovan followed the pointing finger. He had no binoculars, but there was a tiny moving dot, black against the blazing brilliance of the crystalline ground.

"I see him," he yelled. "Let's get going!"

Powell had hopped down into a sitting position on the robot again, and his suited hand slapped against the Gargantuan's barrel chest. "Get going!"

"Giddy-ap," yelled Donovan, and thumped his heels, spur fashion.

The robots started off, the regular thudding of their footsteps silent in the airlessness, for the nonmetallic fabric of the insosuits did not transmit sound. There was only a rhythmic vibration just below the border of actual hearing.

"Faster," yelled Donovan. The rhythm did not change.

"No use," cried Powell, in reply. "These junk heaps are only geared to one speed. Do you think they're equipped with selective flexors?"

They had burst through the shadow, and the sunlight came down in a white-hot wash and poured liquidly about them.

Donovan ducked involuntarily. "Wow! Is it imagination or do I feel heat?"

"You'll feel more presently," was the grim reply. "Keep your eye on Speedy."

Robot SPD 13 was near enough to be seen in detail now. His graceful, streamlined body threw out blazing highlights as he loped with easy speed across the broken ground. His name was derived from his serial initials, of course, but it was apt, nevertheless, for the SPD models were among the fastest robots turned out by the United States Robot & Mechanical Men Corp.

"Hey, Speedy," howled Donovan, and waved a frantic hand.

"Speedy!" shouted Powell. "Come here!"

The distance between the men and the errant robot was being cut down momentarily—more by the efforts of Speedy than the slow plod-ding of the fifty-year-old antique mounts of Donovan and Powell.

They were close enough now to notice that Speedy's gait included a peculiar rolling stagger, a noticeable side-to-side lurch—and then, as Powell waved his hand again and sent maximum juice into his compact head-set radio sender, in preparation for another shout, Speedy looked up and saw them.

Speedy hopped to a halt and remained standing for a moment—with just a tiny, unsteady weave, as though he were swaying in a light wind.

Powell yelled: "All right, Speedy. Come here, boy."

Whereupon Speedy's robot voice sounded in Powell's earphones for the first time.

It said: "Hot dog, let's play games. You catch me and I catch you; no love can cut our knife in two. For I'm Little Buttercup, sweet Little Buttercup. Whoops!" Turning on his heel, he sped off in the direction from which he had come, with a speed and fury that kicked up gouts of baked dust.

And his last words as he receded into the distance were, "There grew a little flower 'neath a great oak tree," followed by a curious metallic clicking that *might* have been a robotic equivalent of a hiccup.

Donovan said weakly: "Where did he pick up the Gilbert and Sullivan? Say, Greg, he . . . he's drunk or something."

"If you hadn't told me," was the bitter response, "I'd never realize it. Let's get back to the cliff. I'm roasting."

It was Powell who broke the desperate silence. "In the first place," he said, "Speedy isn't drunk—not in the human sense—because he's a robot, and robots don't get drunk. However, there's *something* wrong with him which is the robotic equivalent of drunkenness."

"To me, he's drunk," stated Donovan, emphatically, "and all I know is that he thinks we're playing games. And we're not. It's a matter of life and very gruesome death."

"All right. Don't hurry me. A robot's only a robot. Once we find out what's wrong with him, we can fix it and go on."

· *"Once,"* said Donovan, sourly.

Powell ignored him. "Speedy is perfectly adapted to normal Mercurian environment. But this region"—and his arm swept wide—"is definitely abnormal. There's our clue. Now where do these crystals come from? They might have formed from a slowly cooling liquid; but where would you get liquid so hot that it would cool in Mercury's sun?"

"Volcanic action," suggested Donovan, instantly, and Powell's body tensed.

"Out of the mouths of sucklings," he said in a small, strange voice and remained very still for five minutes.

Then, he said, "Listen, Mike, what did you say to Speedy when you sent him after the selenium?"

Donovan was taken aback. "Well damn it—I don't know. I just told him to get it."

"Yes, I know. But how? Try to remember the exact words."

"I said . . . uh . . . I said: 'Speedy, we need some selenium. You can get it such-and-such a place. Go get it.' That's all. What more did you want me to say?"

"You didn't put any urgency into the order, did you?"

"What for? It was pure routine."

Powell sighed. "Well, it can't be helped now—but we're in a fine fix." He had dismounted from his robot, and was sitting, back against the cliff. Donovan joined him and they linked arms. In the distance the burning sunlight seemed to wait cat-and-mouse for them, and just next them, the two giant robots were invisible but for the dull red of their photoelectric eyes that stared down at them, unblinking, unwavering and unconcerned.

Unconcerned! As was all this poisonous Mercury, as large in jinx as it was small in size.

Powell's radio voice was tense in Donovan's ear: "Now, look, let's start with the three fundamental Rules of Robotics—the three rules that are built most deeply into a robot's positronic brain." In the darkness, his gloved fingers ticked off each point.

"We have: One, a robot may not injure a human being, or, through inaction, allow a human being to come to harm."

"Right!"

"Two," continued Powell, "a robot must obey the orders given it by human beings except where such orders would conflict with the First Law."

"Right!"

"And three, a robot must protect its own existence as long as such protection does not conflict with the First or Second Laws."

"Right! Now where are we?"

"Exactly at the explanation. The conflict between the various rules is ironed out by the different positronic potentials in the brain. We'll say that a robot is walking into danger and knows it. The automatic potential that Rule 3 sets up turns him back. But suppose you *order* him to walk into that danger. In that case, Rule 2 sets up a counterpotential higher than the previous one and the robot follows orders at the risk of existence."

"Well, I know that. What about it?"

"Let's take Speedy's case. Speedy is one of the latest models, extremely specialized, and as expensive as a battleship. It's not a thing to be lightly destroyed."

"So?"

"So Rule 3 has been strengthened—that was specifically mentioned, by the way, in the advance notices on the SPD models—so that his allergy to danger is unusually high. At the same time, when you sent him out after the selenium, you gave him his order casually and without special emphasis, so that the Rule 2 potential set-up was rather weak. Now, hold on; I'm just stating facts."

"All right, go ahead. I think I get it."

"You see how it works, don't you? There's some sort of danger centering at the selenium pool. It increases as he approaches, and at a certain distance from it the Rule 3 potential, unusually high to start with, exactly balances the Rule 2 potential, unusually low to start with."

Donovan rose to his feet in excitement. "And it strikes an equilibrium. I see. Rule 3 drives him back and Rule 2 drives him forward—"

"So he follows a circle around the selenium pool, staying on the locus of all points of potential equilibrium. And unless we do something about it, he'll stay on that circle forever, giving us the good old runaround." Then, more thoughtfully: "And that, by the way, is what makes him drunk. At potential equilibrium, half the positronic paths of his brain are out of kilter. I'm not a robot specialist, but that seems obvious. Probably he's lost control of just those parts of his voluntary mechanism that a human drunk has. Ve-e-ery pretty."

"But what's the danger? If we knew what he was running from—"

"*You* suggested it. Volcanic action. Somewhere right above the selenium pool is a seepage of gas from the bowels of Mercury. Sulphur dioxide, carbon dioxide—and carbon monoxide. Lots of it—and at this temperature."

Donovan gulped audibly. "Carbon monoxide plus iron gives the volatile iron carbonyl."

"And a robot," added Powell, "is essentially iron." Then, grimly: "There's nothing like deduction. We've determined everything about our problem but the solution. We can't get the selenium ourselves. It's still too far. We can't send these robot horses, because they can't go themselves, and they can't carry us fast enough to keep us from crisping. And we can't catch Speedy, because the dope thinks we're playing games, and he can run sixty miles to our four."

"If one of us goes," began Donovan, tentatively, "and comes back cooked, there'll still be the other."

"Yes," came the sarcastic reply, "it would be a most tender sacrifice—except that a person would be in no condition to give orders before he ever reached the pool, and I don't think the robots would ever turn back to the cliff without orders. Figure it out! We're two or three miles from the pool—call it two—the robot travels at four miles an hour; and we can last twenty minutes in our suits. It isn't only the heat, remember. Solar radiation out here in the ultraviolet and below is *poison*."

"Um-m-m," said Donovan, "ten minutes short."

"As good as an eternity. And another thing. In order for Rule 3 potential to have stopped Speedy where it did, there must be an appreciable amount of carbon monoxide in the metal-vapor atmosphere—and there must be an appreciable corrosive action therefore. He's been out hours now—and how do we know when a knee joint, for instance, won't be thrown out of kilter and keel him over. It's not only a question of thinking—we've got to think *fast!*"

Deep, dark, dank, dismal silence!

Donovan broke it, voice trembling in an effort to keep itself emotionless. He said: "As long as we can't increase Rule 2 potential by giving further orders, how about working the other way? If we increase the danger, we increase Rule 3 potential and drive him backward."

Powell's visiplate had turned toward him in a silent question.

"You see," came the cautious explanation, "all we need to do to drive him out of his rut is to increase the concentration of carbon monoxide in his vicinity. Well, back at the Station there's a complete analytical laboratory."

"Naturally," assented Powell. "It's a Mining Station."

"All right. There must be pounds of oxalic acid for calcium precipitations."

"Holy space! Mike, you're a genius."

"So-so," admitted Donovan, modestly. "It's just a case of remembering that oxalic acid on heating decomposes into carbon dioxide, water, and good old carbon monoxide. College chem, you know."

Powell was on his feet and had attracted the attention of one of the monster robots by the simple expedient of pounding the machine's thigh.

"Hey," he shouted, "can you throw?"

"Master?"

"Never mind." Powell damned the robot's molasses-slow brain. He scrabbled up a jagged brick-size rock. "Take this," he said, "and hit the patch of bluish crystals just across the crooked fissure. You see it?"

Donovan pulled at his shoulder. "Too far, Greg. It's almost half a mile off."

"Quiet," replied Powell. "It's a case of Mercurian gravity and a steel throwing arm. Watch, will you?"

The robot's eyes were measuring the distance with machinely accurate stereoscopy. His arm adjusted itself to the weight of the missile and drew back. In the darkness, the robot's motions went unseen, but there was a sudden thumping sound as he shifted his weight, and seconds later the rock flew blackly into the sunlight. There was no air resistance to slow it down, nor wind to turn it aside—and when it hit the ground it threw up crystals precisely in the center of the "blue patch."

Powell yelled happily and shouted, "Let's go back after the oxalic acid, Mike."

And as they plunged into the ruined substation on the way back to the tunnels, Donovan said grimly: "Speedy's been hanging about on this side of the selenium pool, ever since we chased after him. Did you see him?"

"Yes."

"I guess he wants to play games. Well, we'll play him games!"

They were back hours later, with three-liter jars of the white chemical and a pair of long faces. The photo-cell banks were deteriorating more rapidly than had seemed likely. The two steered their robots into the sunlight and toward the waiting Speedy in silence and with grim purpose.

Speedy galloped slowly toward them. "Here we are again. *Whee*! I've made a little list, the piano organist; all people who eat peppermint and puff it in your face."

"We'll puff something in *your* face," muttered Donovan. "He's limping, Greg."

"I noticed that," came the low, worried response. "The monoxide'll get him yet, if we don't hurry."

They were approaching cautiously now, almost sidling, to refrain from setting off the thoroughly irrational robot. Powell was too far off to tell, of course, but even already he could have sworn the crack-brained Speedy was setting himself for a spring.

"Let her go," he gasped. "Count three! One—two—"

Two steel arms drew back and snapped forward simultaneously and two glass jars whirled forward in towering parallel arcs, gleaming like diamonds in the impossible sun. And in a pair of soundless puffs, they hit the ground behind Speedy in crashes that sent the oxalic acid flying like dust.

In the full heat of Mercury's sun, Powell knew it was fizzing like soda water.

Speedy turned to stare, then backed away from it slowly—and as slowly gathered speed. In fifteen seconds, he was leaping directly toward the two humans in an unsteady canter.

Powell did not get Speedy's words just then, though he heard something that resembled, "Lover's professions when uttered in Hessians."

He turned away. "Back to the cliff, Mike. He's out of the rut and he'll be taking orders now. I'm getting hot."

They jogged toward the shadow at the slow monotonous pace of their mounts, and it was not until they had entered it and felt the sudden coolness settle softly about them that Donovan looked back. *"Greg!"*

Powell looked and almost shrieked. Speedy was moving slowly now—so slowly—and in the *wrong direction.* He was drifting; drifting back into his rut; and he was picking up speed. He looked dreadfully close, and dreadfully unreachable, in the binoculars.

Donovan shouted wildly, "After him!" and thumped his robot into its pace, but Powell called him back.

"You won't catch him, Mike—it's no use." He fidgeted on his robot's shoulders and clenched his fist in tight impotence. "Why the devil do I see these things five seconds after it's all over? Mike, we've wasted hours."

"We need more oxalic acid," declared Donovan, stolidly. "The concentration wasn't high enough."

"Seven tons of it wouldn't have been enough—and we haven't the hours to spare to get it, even if it were, with the monoxide chewing him away. Don't you see what it is, Mike?"

And Donovan said flatly, "No."

"We were only establishing new equilibriums. When we create new monoxide and increase Rule 3 potential, he moves backward till he's in balance again—and when the monoxide drifted away, he moved forward, and again there was balance."

Powell's voice sounded thoroughly wretched. "It's the same old runaround. We can push at Rule 2 and pull at Rule 3 and we can't get anywhere—we can only change the position of balance. We've got to get outside both rules." And then he pushed his robot closer to Donovan's so that they were sitting face to face, dim shadows in the darkness, and he whispered, "Mike!"

"Is it the finish?"—dully. "I suppose we go back to the Station, wait for the banks to fold, shake hands, take cyanide, and go out like gentlemen." He laughed shortly.

"Mike," repeated Powell earnestly, "we've got to get Speedy."

"I know."

"Mike," once more, and Powell hesitated before continuing. "There's always Rule 1. I thought of it—earlier—but it's desperate."

Donovan looked up and his voice livened. *"We're* desperate."

"All right. According to Rule 1, a robot can't see a human come to harm because of his own inaction. Two and 3 can't stand against it. They *can't,* Mike."

"Even when the robot is half cra— Well, he's drunk. You know he is."

"It's the chances you take."

"Cut it. What are you going to do?"

"I'm going out there now and see what Rule 1 will do. If it won't break the balance, then what the devil—it's either now or three–four days from now."

"Hold on, Greg. There are human rules of behavior, too. You don't go out there just like that. Figure out a lottery, and give me *my* chance."

"All right. First to get the cube of fourteen goes." And almost immediately, "Twenty-seven forty-four!"

Donovan felt his robot stagger at a sudden push by Powell's mount and then Powell was off into the sunlight. Donovan opened his mouth to shout, and then clicked it shut. Of course, the damn fool had worked out the cube of fourteen in advance, and on purpose. Just like him.

The sun was hotter than ever and Powell felt a maddening itch in the small of his back. Imagination, probably, or perhaps hard radiation beginning to tell even through the insosuit.

Speedy was watching him, without a word of Gilbert and Sullivan gibberish as greeting. Thank God for that! But he daren't get too close.

He was three hundred yards away when Speedy began backing, a step at a time, cautiously—and Powell stopped. He jumped from his robot's shoulders and landed on the crystalline ground with a light thump and a flying of jagged fragments.

He proceeded on foot, the ground gritty and slippery to his steps, the low gravity causing him difficulty. The soles of his feet tickled with warmth. He cast one glance over his shoulder at the blackness of the cliff's shadow and realized that he had come too far to return—either by himself or by the help of his antique robot. It was Speedy or nothing now, and the knowledge of that constricted his chest.

Far enough! He stopped.

"Speedy," he called. "Speedy!"

The sleek, modern robot ahead of him hesitated and halted his backward steps, then resumed them.

Powell tried to put a note of pleading into his voice, and found it didn't take much acting. "Speedy, I've got to get back to the shadow or the sun'll get me. It's life or death, Speedy. I need you."

Speedy took once step forward and stopped. He spoke, but at the sound Powell groaned, for it was, "When you're lying awake with a dismal headache and repose is tabooed—" It trailed off there, and Powell took time out for some reason to murmur, "Iolanthe."

It was roasting hot! He caught a movement out of the corner of his eye, and whirled dizzily; then stared in utter astonishment, for the monstrous robot on which he had ridden was moving—moving toward him, and without a rider.

He was talking: "Pardon, Master. I must not move without a Master upon me, but you are in danger."

Of course, Rule 1 potential above everything. But he didn't want that clumsy antique; he wanted Speedy. He walked away and motioned frantically: "I order you to stay away. I *order* you to stop!"

It was quite useless. You could not beat Rule 1 potential. The robot said stupidly, "You are in danger, Master."

Powell looked about him desperately. He couldn't see clearly. His brain was in a heated whirl; his breath scorched when he breathed, and the ground all about him was a shimmering haze.

He called a last time, desperately: "*Speedy!* I'm dying, damn you! Where are you? Speedy, I *need* you."

He was still stumbling backward in a blind effort to get away from the giant robot he didn't want, when he felt steel fingers on his arms, and a worried, apologetic voice of metallic timbre in his ears.

"Holy smokes, boss, what are you doing here? And what am *I* doing—I'm so confused—"

"Never mind," murmured Powell, weakly. "Get me to the shadow of the cliff—and hurry!" There was one last feeling of being lifted into the air and a sensation of rapid motion and burning heat, and he passed out.

He woke with Donovan bending over him and smiling anxiously. "How are you, Greg?"

"Fine!" came the response. "Where's Speedy?"

"Right here. I sent him out to one of the other selenium pools—with orders to get that selenium at all cost this time. He got it back in forty-two minutes and three seconds. I timed him. He still hasn't finished apologizing for the runaround he gave us. He's scared to come near you for fear of what you'll say."

"Drag him over," ordered Powell. "It wasn't his fault." He held out a hand and gripped Speedy's metal paw. "It's O.K., Speedy." Then, to Donovan, "You know, Mike, I was just thinking—"

"Yes!"

"Well,"—he rubbed his face—the air was so delightfully cool, "you know that when we get things set up here and Speedy put through his Field Tests, they're going to send us to the Space Stations next—"

"No!"

"Yes! At least that's what old lady Calvin told me just before we left, and I didn't say anything about it, because I was going to fight the whole idea."

"Fight it?" cried Donovan. "But—"

"I know. It's all right with me now. Two hundred seventy-three degrees Centigrade below zero. Won't it be a pleasure?"

"Space Station," said Donovan, "here I come."

CALLING DR. CLOCKWORK

Ron Goulart

Arnold Vesper nudged the flower vending machine with the palm of his hand. The dusty green cabinet hunched once and a confetti of yellow rose petals snapped out of the slot and scattered on the parking lot paving. Vesper gave the machine a shy kick. His credit card whirred back out the money intake and he caught it. Turning away, Vesper pressed his lips angrily together for an instant and then hopped onto the conveyor walk that led to the visitor's entrance of the hospital.

He didn't even really know Mr. Keasby. So actually the flowers could be skipped. Vesper wished he wasn't so considerate of his father's wishes. His father lived in a Senior Citizens Sun Tower down in the Laguna Sector of Greater Los Angeles. When he'd heard his old friend Keasby was laid up in an Urban Free Hospital he'd asked his son to pay a visit. So here Vesper was, thirty years old, still doing errands for his father. Well, the flowers could really be skipped.

Urban Free Hospital #14 was a pale yellow building. It gave the impression that its whole surface was vaguely sticky. Keasby should have taken a bigger chunk out of his salary for insurance and then he wouldn't have ended up in a UFH. Vesper hoped the old man wasn't full of stories about organizing the food scenters union back in 1990. His father was.

The android guard was one of the fat pink models. "Visitor's hours end sharp at eight. Be sure you get out, don't make trouble for me so I have to come and get you out special. Is that clear?"

"Fine," said Vesper. "Where's Ward 77?"

"Go right, turn left. Corridor four, then elevator G. Up to three, left again, then right. Move along now."

Vesper went down the stationary corridor, turned left at its end. The corridors that appeared off this one all had letters and not numbers. Vesper continued, slowing his pace.

In front of him a portion of the floor slid away and a bell began ringing up above him. A wheeled stretcher, an automatic one, came up in front of Vesper. The patient on it was a heavyset middle aged man. He moaned.

The stretcher clicked and moved ahead. The ringing stopped. Vesper stayed still, giving the stretcher a chance to get going. But as he watched, the thing zagged into the corridor wall. A bell rang again, as the patient bounced up and then snapped off the wheeled cot. Vesper ran to help.

His feet tangled in the covering sheet. The sheet was dirty gray and spotted. Vesper had to kneel to keep from falling. He almost touched the fallen patient, then noticed that there was blood on the man's chest now. Vesper's stomach seemed to grow out like the ripples from a rock dropped in a pool. He began to swallow and his ears gave him a severe pain. He tried to avoid the bloody man when he pitched over and passed out.

The doctor was a human. He had a slightly pointed head with hair coming down in a strip onto his forehead like a plastic doormat. He had no chin. "Don't I know how you feel," he said to Vesper.

This seemed to be a ward. Five beds side by side, gray sticky walls. Vesper, undressed and wearing a pajama top someone else had already worn, was in one of the beds. The other four cots were empty. It looked like late night outside the one high window slot. "Is that man all right?"

The doctor pursed his lips. "Let's not talk about him. It gives me gooseflesh thinking about that. I'll tell you frankly that blood makes my stomach go whoopsy, too."

"Well, how am I then? I know I'm okay."

The doctor was sitting in a straight chair next to Vesper's bed. "My name is Dr. William F. Norgran, by the way. Why don't you give me all the info on your case?"

"I just fainted, didn't I?" Vesper elbowed up to a sitting position. "See, I came to visit a Mr. Keasby in Ward 77. He's a friend of my father's. My father doesn't get around much. He lives in a Senior Citizens Sun Tower down in Laguna Sector."

Dr. Norgran shivered. "Old people give me the willies."

Vesper said, "I'd like to get my clothes back and go on."

"Let me level with you, Mr. . . . ah . . ."

"Vesper, Arnold Vesper."

"Mr. Vesper, whenever somebody is brought in here to Urban Free Hospital #14 he has to be checked out. This is a charity hospital. We have to be thorough. It's our obligation to the public."

"But I have Multimedical. I work in the Oleomargarine Division of one of our largest motivational research companies. I'm covered even if I were sick. I wouldn't have to come to an UFH."

"Yes," said Dr. Norgran, clearing his throat. "You've had some sort of seizure possibly. We can't be too careful in cases of this sort." He shifted in his chair. "Listen. Is that motivational research as much fun as it sounds? I'll tell you why I ask. I wanted to major in that at school but my folks wanted me to be a doctor. Here I am, stranded in a freeby hospital. During my internship at Hollywood Movie Hospital I kept fainting and getting sick headaches. That helped stick me here."

"It's pretty tough getting into motivational research without a degree in it," said Vesper, looking around the room. There did not seem to be any lockers or closets. "Where exactly are my clothes?"

Dr. Norgran shrugged. "One of the android orderlies whisked them away someplace. Frankly, Mr. Vesper, it's hell being a human doctor here. You don't have a fighting chance. Particularly if you happen to feel queasy about blood. As you may know, the Head Physician at most Urban Frees is an android. And old Dr. Clockwork is a real toughie to work under."

"Dr. Clockwork?"

"We just call him that. The few humans here with the sense of humor enough. Because of the way he whirs and clanks sometimes. His official name is Medi/Android A/12 #675 RHLW. An old devil, believe you me."

Vesper nodded. "As soon as you examine me I can go. You can understand, being that way yourself, that I just fainted because of the blood. Did that man die?"

Dr. Norgran gave a quick negative wave of his hand. "Let's not dwell on him. Mr. Vesper, you can really do me a favor. I'll confess something to you. I'm fairly sure it's only a temporary condition. The thing is,

I've developed this absolute horror of touching people. Has nothing to do with you. It's my nag."

"I'm afraid I don't follow you."

"I'd prefer to let Dr. Clockwork look at you. I get so really creepy crawly lately if I have to examine someone. Silly of me, isn't it?"

"Why don't you just let me go?"

The doctor shook his head. "No, no. You're already being processed. If you belong to Multimedical then the office andies have already got your MM card from your effects."

"Effects are what dead people have."

Dr. Norgran blushed. "Sorry. Don't let anything worry you, Mr. Vesper. The MM people and our staff are on top of this. You concentrate on getting a good night's sleep."

Vesper started to swing out of bed. "Night's sleep?"

"Dr. Clockwork spends his night up in Isolation 3. He can't see you until morning."

"My job."

"The hospital will notify. Anyway, Mr. Vesper, you'll more than likely be out of here before Coffee I tomorrow. Do you have a family?"

"I'm divorced. I live in a rancho tower over on Gower in the Hollywood Sector. A two room suite."

"Lucky," said Dr. Norgran. He touched something under the bed and the bed pulled Vesper back and gave him a shot in the left buttock. "To help you sleep. See you tomorrow. And let's hope nobody else makes any unpleasantness tonight. I'm on duty till the wee hours."

"Wait," said Vesper, falling asleep.

The whirring awakened him. Vesper saw a wide-shouldered android in a frayed white coat watching him. The android had a square thrust-jawed face and a convincing head of backswept gray hair. Humor wrinkles had been built in at the eyes and mouth. "How are we feeling?" asked the android in a warm familiar voice. "I'm Medi/Android A/12 #675 RHLW. The young fellows around here call me Dr. Clockwork." He winked. "I'm not supposed to know about it." The winking continued and Dr. Clockwork made a ratcheting sound and his eyeball, the right one, popped out. "The things we old timers have to put up with," he sighed, and stooped, vanishing under the bed. "I've got it."

Vesper sat up. "Dr. Clockwork," he said as the android physician, two eyed again, rose up beside him. "I'm in perfect shape. I simply fainted last night while on the way to visit an old friend of my father's. A Mr. Keasby in Ward 77. I'd like my clothes. Then I'll leave."

"Open your mouth for a second. Fine." The android got a grip on Vesper's jaw. "Nothing is simple in the doctor business. That's one thing I learned as an old-fashioned suburban practitioner. Hmm."

"I'm probably late for work." The window indicated it was along into mid-morning.

"Work, work," said Dr. Clockwork. "We all of us rush and hurry. Well, now." He began tapping Vesper's chest. "Breathe through your mouth. I see, I see."

"My father was in the food scenting field for thirty-nine years before he retired," said Vesper, between inhalations. "As I understand it he and Mr. Keasby worked side by side for several decades."

"Roll over on your stomach."

Vesper obliged. "They don't seem to know where my clothes are."

"Nothing escapes my attention in UFH #14 here," said Dr. Clockwork. "When your clothes are needed old Dr. Clockwork will round them up." He ran a finger along Vesper's spine. "Much history of fainting in your family?"

"I don't know. I only fainted because I saw all that blood." He glanced back over his shoulder. "Did that man survive?"

"Well, well," said Dr. Clockwork, pinching Vesper's right buttock. "How often do you faint?"

"Not often."

"What's your idea of often, young fellow?"

"Three times in my life."

"I see." The android made a bellows sound and whirred in a different way for a moment. "For lunch today tell your nurse to give you gruel and some skim milk. Then I'll want to run tests on you down in Testing 4 this afternoon."

"But I have to leave."

"Not in your condition."

"What do you mean?"

"Don't forget the gruel. Relax now." The doctor started for the door. Halfway there he developed a severe limp. He swung out into the hall and in a moment there was a crash.

The bed wouldn't let Vesper up. He twisted around and spotted a switch marked *nurse*. He stretched and flicked it. This produced a humming in a speaker grid next to the switch. In a few minutes a female voice said, "Ward 23 is supposed to be empty. Who's in there?"

"Never mind. Dr. Clockwork's fallen over in the hall."

"He's always doing that. Now who are you?"

"I'm Arnold Vesper and I want to get out of here."

The grid grew silent and did not reply.

Dr. Rex Willow's lower lip made his orange colored cigar angle up toward his soft nose. He was human, apparently, and he was sitting on Vesper's bed when Vesper came to from an enforced afternoon nap. Willow explained that he was the doctor sent over by Multimedical insurance. After he'd asked Vesper what he thought was wrong with him Dr. Willow said, "Those kids over at your office really like you. Here you go." From under his suit coat he produced a small carton.

Vesper took it. "I got skipped over for lunch today. The nurse won't answer me on the com system. I hope this is food." He rested his hand on the box lid. "What I really hope is that you'll get me out of here."

"Time enough to worry later, Arnold."

The box contained get well cards. Two dozen identical ones. Each signed by a member of the oleomargarine team. "All the same," said Vesper, putting the box on his bedside table.

"Similar sentiments can take similar form." Dr. Willow jumped off the bed. "Good talking to you, Arnold. Sign this punch form set for me and I'll scat. I have to hustle over to some of the big pay hospitals in the better sectors." He gave Vesper a small deck of miniaturized punch forms.

"How come you're here at all? I thought this was a free hospital."

"Multimedical goes everywhere. It's not a bad hospital if you're down and out, Arnold. Or have an emergency like yours." He pointed. "Sign on the red line. On the blue line on the forms where it's blue."

"My pen's in my clothes."

"Use mine."

Willow's pen said Multimedical on it and Get Well Quick. Vesper asked him, "Can't you arrange to get me out?"

"Not if your head physician is dead set against it."

"I don't even have a phone in here. Can't you at least get me one? I really should have a phone."

"This is a charity hospital, Arnold, not a resort. When you are up and around you can hunt down a phone. I spotted a phone cubicle in the visitor's lobby. Sign."

Vesper signed. "Have you talked to my doctors here?"

"Well, of course. Dr. Norgran is a fine boy. Medi/Android A/12 #675 RHLW is the best android in any of the freeby hospitals."

"When he was in here this morning his glass eye fell out."

"A man's handicaps don't reflect his abilities."

"But he's a machine."

"If you don't finish signing soon I'll have to put more credit script in my landing strip meter, Arnold."

"Okay." He completed the forms except for the line about his mother's hobbies. Willow said that was optional anyway. As the insurance doctor left Vesper called, "How about telling them to feed me?"

"All in due time," said Willow, hurrying.

Toward evening two androids wheeled in a man named Skeeman

and put him in a bed two down from Vesper. Vesper found out the name because the man, who was small and old and yellowish, kept telling the orderlies, "Call Dr. Wollter and say Milton Skeeman's had another one." The andies nodded, smiled and let the bed put Skeeman to sleep.

"When's dinner?" Vesper asked them.

"No mouth from you, freeloader," said one.

"Wise patients are the worst kind. Want to eat, eat all the time."

"And I want to get up and go to the bathroom."

"Your big expensive bed will take care of that."

They left and the bed did.

The light came on at what Vesper guessed to be seven or eight that night. Something thunked against the door and then it swung in and Dr. Clockwork appeared. "How are we feeling?"

Vesper shook his head. "Why are you in that wheel chair?"

Dr. Clockwork rolled himself over the bedside. "My problems are too trivial to fuss about. Let's talk about you. Hmm. That gruel doesn't seem to have helped."

"Nobody has fed me today yet. I'm hungry. It gives me a headache and an upset stomach when I don't eat."

Dr. Clockwork reached up and smoothed back his thick gray hair. "Severe head pains, nausea. I thought so. My boy, let me explain something. Ever since the turn of the 21st Century the Cold War has intensified. It stands to reason, since you can't trust the Oriental mind. While no weapons show on the surface, you can be sure that the mailed glove hides a velvet fist."

"That's not quite the right metaphor."

"The point being that they have all along been using subtle weapons against us." Dr. Clockwork laughed. "You might not think that one of the most insidious weapons known to humanity has been found out by a humble doctor in a humble free hospital. Well now, many great martyrs have had humble backgrounds. There have even been a happy few android martyrs. I may not be human but I love this old country of ours and I do my best to fight her enemies at home and abroad. That's how I came to discover Contagium DDW."

"What is that all about?"

"Contagium DDW," said the android, his voice quivering. "An insidious germ that they send over to debilitate our folks. Up in Isolation 3 I've got two dozen poor victims. No one on the outside has guessed the existence of Contagium DDW. No one knows of my work. Someday they will. A statue perhaps. There'll be a statue someday perhaps. The first one erected to honor an android."

"But when do I get out of here, doctor?"

"Who can tell," said Dr. Clockwork. "I'm sorry to have to tell you that you've been hit by Contagium DDW."

Vesper felt his forehead again. The automatic nurse never told him what his temperature was, but he suspected he'd had a fever for several days. There was something wrong with the heating unit in his isolation room. The crystal in the thermostat was frosted over, making it difficult to be sure that the room was sometimes much too warm.

As Vesper paced the small room he reached now and then into the pocket of his hospital gown and got a handkerchief to wipe the perspiration off his face. His chest kept perspiring too. The service was better in Isolation 3 than it had been down in the ward. They fed him regularly and he was allowed an hour's stroll around the cubicle each day.

Something tapped on the view window of his door, Vesper turned to see the face of Dr. William F. Norgran looking in. The live doctor nodded and spoke into the com. "Excuse my not getting back to you sooner. Horrible diseases make me jittery."

Vesper was going to explain that he didn't really have any disease at all and had really only fainted because of the blood. He hesitated. He did feel odd, the fever and the sweating and all. Dr. Clockwork did seem to know about Contagium DDW, even though he never quite explained what it was to Vesper. "I can understand that," he said to Dr. Norgran.

"All things considered," said the doctor, "you're looking moderately well."

"Dr. Clockwork says I'm coming right along."

Dr. Norgran's face paled. "Too much. I've seen too much of you. Sorry. I'll call again later." He bolted.

Behind him the bed beckoned Vesper back.

Vesper didn't take his walks any more and the bed didn't insist. He was fighting against Contagium DDW but it was making him increasingly tired. It didn't help his condition that the room forgot to feed him now and then or that the heat unit would act up in the quiet hours of the night, suddenly roasting or freezing him awake. Vesper took his pulse, the way he'd seen Dr. Clockwork do it.

The office gang had stopped sending get well cards. So far as he could remember, his union guaranteed him his job back. He was also supposed to be getting $52/day insurance money. Dr. Rex Willow never came, wasn't allowed to, up to Isolation 3. $52/day was certainly the figure that Vesper remembered from his insurance brochure.

"It's taking its toll," said Dr. Clockwork, wheeling himself into the room. "Buck up, lad."

"I'm feeling pretty good."

Dr. Clockwork rolled nearer. "Hmm. The symptoms are spreading. It's insidious. Still, I vow that someday there will be Contagium DDW sanitariums across the land, perhaps an island colony. I wonder if there can be an android saint. No matter. The thought would be in the hearts and minds of people. No official sanction need be. Let me see your tongue."

"Ah," said Vesper, too fatigued to rise up to a sitting position.

"Yes, yes," said the android doctor.

"Something?"

"We're coming along. Don't fear."

"You know," said Vesper, "I wasn't too appreciative of you at first, doctor. Now I'm feeling I owe you a lot. For diagnosing this thing and helping me."

"Let's give you a shot," said the doctor. "Roll over."

"I really think I'm coming to trust you, doctor."

"Yes, they may call me Dr. Clockwork behind my back, but I'm to be trusted." As he made the injection the android began to whir in a new way. "I'm to be trusted."

"I think so now," said Vesper.

"I'm to be trusted. I'm to be trusted. I'm to be trusted. I'm to be trusted. I'm to be trusted. I'm to be trusted. I'm to be trusted. I'm to be trusted."

Vesper fell asleep before Dr. Clockwork finished speaking.

MASKS

Damon Knight

The eight pens danced against the moving strip of paper, like the nervous claws of some mechanical lobster. Roberts, the technician, frowned over the tracings while the other two watched.

"Here's the wake-up impulse," he said, pointing with a skinny finger. "Then here, look, seventeen seconds more, still dreaming."

"Delayed response," said Babcock, the project director. His heavy face was flushed and he was sweating. "Nothing to worry about."

"OK, delayed response, but look at the difference in the tracings. Still dreaming, after the wake-up impulse, but the peaks are closer together. Not the same dream. More anxiety, more motor pulses."

"Why does he have to sleep at all?" asked Sinescu, the man from Washington. He was dark, narrow-faced. "You flush the fatigue poisons out, don't you? So what is it, something psychological?"

"He needs to dream," said Babcock. "It's true he has no physiological need for sleep, but he's got to dream. If he didn't, he'd start to hallucinate, maybe go psychotic."

"Psychotic," said Sinescu. "Well—that's the question, isn't it? How long has he been doing this?"

"About six months."

"In other words, about the time he got his new body—and started wearing a mask?"

"About that. Look, let me tell you something: He's rational. Every test—"

"Yes, OK, I know about tests. Well—so he's awake now?"

The technician glanced at the monitor board. "He's up. Sam and Irma are with him." He hunched his shoulders, staring at the EEG tracings again. "I don't know why it should bother me. It stands to reason, if he has dream needs of his own that we're not satisfying with the programmed stuff, this is where he gets them in." His face hardened. "I don't know. Something about those peaks I don't like."

Sinescu raised his eyebrows. "You program his dreams?"

"Not program," said Babcock impatiently. "A routine suggestion to dream the sort of thing we tell him to. Somatic stuff, sex, exercise, sport."

"And whose idea was that?"

"Psych section. He was doing fine neurologically, every other way, but he was withdrawing. Psych decided he needed that somatic input in some form, we had to keep him in touch. He's alive, he's functioning, everything works. But don't forget, he spent forty-three years in a normal human body."

In the hush of the elevator, Sinescu said, "Washington."

Swaying, Babcock said, "I'm sorry; what?"

"You look a little rocky. Getting any sleep?"

"Not lately. What did you say before?"

"I said they're not happy with your reports in Washington."

"Goddamn it, I know that." The elevator door silently opened. A tiny foyer, green carpet, gray walls. There were three doors, one metal, two heavy glass. Cool, stale air. "This way."

Sinescu paused at the glass door, glanced through: a gray-carpeted living room, empty. "I don't see him."

"Around the el. Getting his morning checkup."

The door opened against slight pressure; a battery of ceiling lights went on as they entered. "Don't look up," said Babcock. "Ultraviolet." A faint hissing sound stopped when the door closed.

"And positive pressure in here? To keep out germs? Whose idea was that?"

"His." Babcock opened a chrome box on the wall and took out two surgical masks. "Here, put this on."

Voices came muffled from around the bend of the room. Sinescu looked with distaste at the white mask, then slowly put it over his head.

They stared at each other. "Germs," said Sinescu through the mask. "Is that rational?"

"All right, he can't catch a cold, or what have you, but think about it a minute. There are just two things now that could kill him. One is a prosthetic failure, and we guard against that; we've got five hundred people here, we check him out like an airplane. That leaves a cerebrospinal infection. Don't go in there with a closed mind."

The room was large, part living room, part library, part workshop. Here was a cluster of Swedish-modern chairs, a sofa, coffee table; here a workbench with a metal lathe, electric crucible, drill press, parts bins, tools on wallboards; here a drafting table; here a free-standing wall of bookshelves that Sinescu fingered curiously as they passed. Bound volumes of project reports, technical journals, reference books; no fiction, except for *Fire* and *Storm* by George Stewart and *The Wizard of Oz* in a worn blue binding. Behind the bookshelves, set into a little alcove, was a glass door through which they glimpsed another living room, differently furnished: upholstered chairs, a tall philodendron in a ceramic pot. "There's Sam," Babcock said.

A man had appeared in the other room. He saw them, turned to call to someone they could not see, then came forward, smiling. He was bald and stocky, deeply tanned. Behind him, a small pretty woman hurried up. She crowded through after her husband, leaving the door open. Neither of them wore a mask.

"Sam and Irma have the next suite," Babcock said. "Company for him; he's got to have somebody around. Sam is an old Air Force buddy of his and, besides, he's got a tin arm."

The stocky man shook hands, grinning. His grip was firm and warm. "Want to guess which one?" He wore a flowered sport shirt. Both arms were brown, muscular and hairy; but when Sinescu looked more closely, he saw that the right one was a slightly different color, not quite authentic.

Embarrassed, he said, "The left, I guess."

"Nope." Grinning wider, the stocky man pulled back his right sleeve to show the straps.

"One of the spin-offs from the project," said Babcock. "Myoelectric, servo-controlled, weighs the same as the other one. Sam, they about through in there?"

"Maybe so. Let's take a peek. Honey, you think you could rustle up some coffee for the gentlemen?"

"Oh, why, sure." The little woman turned and darted back through the open doorway.

The far wall was glass, covered by a translucent white curtain. They turned the corner. The next bay was full of medical and electronic equipment, some built into the walls, some in tall black cabinets on wheels. Four men in white coats were gathered around what looked like an astronaut's couch. Sinescu could see someone lying on it: feet in Mexican woven-leather shoes, dark socks, gray slacks. A mutter of voices.

"Not through yet," Babcock said. "Must have found something else they didn't like. Let's go out onto the patio a minute."

"Thought they checked him at night—when they exchange his blood, and so on . . . ?"

"They do." Babcock said. "And in the morning, too." He turned and pushed open the heavy glass door. Outside, the roof was paved with cut stone, enclosed by a green-plastic canopy and tinted-glass walls. Here and there were concrete basins, empty. "Idea was to have a roof garden out here, something green, but he didn't want it. We had to take all the plants out, glass the whole thing in."

Sam pulled out metal chairs around a white table and they all sat down. "How is he, Sam?" asked Babcock.

He grinned and ducked his head. "Mean in the mornings."

"Talk to you much? Play any chess?"

"Not too much. Works, mostly. Reads some, watches the box a little." His smile was forced; his heavy fingers were clasped together and Sinescu saw now that the finger tips of one hand had turned darker, the others not. He looked away.

"You're from Washington, that right?" Sam asked politely. "First time here? Hold on." He was out of his chair. Vague upright shapes were passing behind the curtained glass door. "Looks like they're through. If you gentlemen would just wait here a minute, till I see." He strode across the roof. The two men sat in silence. Babcock had pulled down his surgical mask; Sinescu noticed and did the same.

"Sam's wife is a problem," Babcock said, leaning nearer. "It seemed like a good idea at the time, but she's lonely here, doesn't like it—no kids—"

The door opened again and Sam appeared. He had a mask on, but it was hanging under his chin. "If you gentlemen would come in now."

In the living area, the little woman, also with a mask hanging around her neck, was pouring coffee from a flowered ceramic jug. She was smiling brightly but looked unhappy. Opposite her sat someone tall, in gray shirt and slacks, leaning back, legs out, arms on the arms of his chair, motionless. Something was wrong with his face.

"Well, now," said Sam heartily. His wife looked up at him with an agonized smile.

The tall figure turned its head and Sinescu saw with an icy shock that its face was silver, a mask of metal with oblong slits for eyes, no nose or mouth, only curves that were faired into each other. "Project," said an inhuman voice.

Sinescu found himself half bent over a chair. He sat down. They were all looking at him. The voice resumed. "I said, are you here to pull the plug on the project?" It was unaccented, indifferent.

"Have some coffee." The woman. pushed a cup toward him.

Sinescu reached for it, but his hand was trembling and he drew it back. "Just a fact-finding expedition," he said.

"Bull. Who sent you—Senator Hinkel?"

"That's right."

"Bull. He's been here himself; why send you? If you are going to pull the plug, might as well tell me." The face behind the mask did not move when he spoke, the voice did not seem to come from it.

"He's just looking around, Jim," said Babcock.

"Two hundred million a year," said the voice, "to keep one man alive. Doesn't make much sense, does it? Go on, drink your coffee."

Sinescu realized that Sam and his wife had already finished theirs and that they had pulled up their masks. He reached for his cup hastily.

"Hundred percent disability in my grade is thirty thousand a year. I could get along on that easy. For almost an hour and a half."

"There's no intention of terminating the project," Sinescu said.

"Phasing it out, though. Would you say phasing it out?"

"Manners, Jim," said Babcock.

"OK. My worst fault. What do you want to know?"

Sinescu sipped his coffee. His hands were still trembling. "That mask you're wearing," he started.

"Not for discussion. No comment, no comment. Sorry about that;

don't mean to be rude; a personal matter. Ask me something—" Without
warning, he stood up, blaring, "Get that damn thing out of here!" Sam's
wife's cup smashed, coffee brown across the table. A fawn-colored puppy
was sitting in the middle of the carpet, cocking its head, bright-eyed,
tongue out.

The table tipped, Sam's wife struggled up behind it. Her face was
pink, dripping with tears. She scooped up the puppy without pausing
and ran out. "I better go with her," Sam said, getting up.

"Go on; and, Sam, take a holiday. Drive her into Winnemucca, see
a movie."

"Yeah, guess I will." He disappeared behind the bookshelf wall.

The tall figure sat down again, moving like a man; it leaned back
in the same posture, arms on the arms of the chair. It was still. The
hands gripping the wood were shapely and perfect but unreal: there
was something wrong about the fingernails. The brown, well-combed
hair above the mask was a wig; the ears were wax. Sinescu nervously
fumbled his surgical mask over his mouth and nose. "Might as well
get along," he said, and stood up.

"That's right, I want to take you over to Engineering and R and
D," said Babcock. "Jim, I'll be back in a little while. Want to talk to
you."

"Sure," said the motionless figure.

Babcock had had a shower, but sweat was soaking through the armpits
of his shirt again. The silent elevator, the green carpet, a little blurred.
The air cool, stale. Seven years, blood and money, 500 good men. Psych
section, Cosmetic Engineering, R and D, Medical, Immunology, Supply,
Serology, Administration. The glass doors. Sam's apartment empty, gone
to Winnemucca with Irma. Psych. Good men, but were they the best?
Three of the best had turned it down. Buried in the files. *Not like an
ordinary amputation, this man has had everything cut off.*

The tall figure had not moved. Babcock sat down. The silver mask
looked back at him.

"Jim, let's level with each other."

"Bad, huh?"

"Sure it's bad. I left him in his room with a bottle. I'll see him again
before he leaves, but God knows what he'll say in Washington. Listen,
do me a favor, take that thing off."

"Sure." The hand rose, plucked at the edge of the silver mask, lifted
it away. Under it, the tan-pink face, sculptured nose and lips, eyebrows,
eyelashes, not handsome but good-looking, normal-looking. Only the

eyes wrong, pupils too big. And the lips that did not open or move when it spoke. "I can take anything off. What does that prove?"

"Jim, Cosmetic spent eight and a half months on that model and the first thing you do is slap a mask over it. We've asked you what's wrong, offered to make any changes you want."

"No comment."

"You talked about phasing out the project. Did you think you were kidding?"

A pause. "Not kidding."

"All right, then open up, Jim, tell me; I have to know. They won't shut the project down; they'll keep you alive, but that's all. There are seven hundred on the volunteer list, including two U.S. Senators. Suppose one of them gets pulled out of an auto wreck tomorrow. We can't wait till then to decide; we've got to know now. Whether to let the next one die or put him into a TP body like yours. So talk to me."

"Suppose I tell you something, but it isn't the truth."

"Why would you lie?"

"Why do you lie to a cancer patient?"

"I don't get it. Come on, Jim."

"OK, try this. Do I look like a man to you?"

"Sure."

"Bull. Look at this face." Calm and perfect. Beyond the fake irises, a wink of metal. "Suppose we had all the other problems solved and I could go into Winnemucca tomorrow; can you see me walking down the street—going into a bar—taking a taxi?"

"Is that all it is?" Babcock drew a deep breath. "Jim, sure there's a difference, but for Christ's sake, it's like any other prosthesis—people get used to it. Like that arm of Sam's. You see it, but after a while you forget it, you don't notice."

"Bull. You pretend not to notice. Because it would embarrass the cripple."

Babcock looked down at his clasped hands. "Sorry for yourself?"

"Don't give me that," the voice blared. The tall figure was standing. The hands slowly came up, the fists clenched. "I'm in this thing. I've been in it for two years. I'm in it when I go to sleep, and when I wake up, I'm still in it."

Babcock looked up at him. "What do you want, facial mobility? Give us twenty years, maybe ten, we'll lick it."

"I want you to close down Cosmetic."

"But that's—"

"Just listen. The first model looked like a tailor's dummy, so you spent eight months and came up with this one, and it looks like a corpse. The whole idea was to make me look like a man, the first model pretty good, the second model better, until you've got something that can smoke cigars and joke with women and go bowling and nobody will know the difference. You can't do it, and if you could what for?"

"I don't— Let me think about this. What do you mean, a metal—"

"Metal, sure, but what difference does that make? I'm talking about shape. Function. Wait a minute." The tall figure strode across the room, unlocked a cabinet, came back with rolled sheets of paper. "Look at this."

The drawing showed an oblong metal box on four jointed legs. From one end protruded a tiny mushroom-shaped head on a jointed stem and a cluster of arms ending in probes, drills, grapples. "For moon prospecting."

"Too many limbs," said Babcock after a moment. "How would you—"

"With the facial nerves. Plenty of them left over. Or here." Another drawing. "A module plugged into the control system of a spaceship. That's where I belong, in space. Sterile environment, low grav, I can go where a man can't go and do what a man can't do. I can be an asset, not a goddamn billion-dollar liability."

Babcock rubbed his eyes. "Why didn't you say anything before?"

"You were all hipped on prosthetics. You would have told me to tend my knitting."

Babcock's hands were shaking as he rolled up the drawings. "Well, by God, this just may do it. It just might." He stood up and turned toward the door. "Keep your—" He cleared his throat. "I mean, hang tight, Jim."

"I'll do that."

When he was alone, he put on his mask again and stood motionless a moment, eye shutters closed. Inside, he was running clean and cool; he could feel the faint reassuring hum of pumps, click of valves and relays. They had given him that: cleaned out all the offal, replaced it with machinery that did not bleed, ooze or suppurate. He thought of the lie he had told Babcock. *Why do you lie to a cancer patient?* But they would never get it, never understand.

He sat down at the drafting table, clipped a sheet of paper to it and with a pencil began to sketch a rendering of the moon-prospector design. When he had blocked in the prospector itself, he began to draw the background of craters. His pencil moved more slowly and stopped; he put it down with a click.

No more adrenal glands to pump adrenaline into his blood, so he could not feel fright or rage. They had released him from all that—love, hate, the whole sloppy mess—but they had forgotten there was still one emotion he could feel.

Sinescu, with the black bristles of his beard sprouting through his oily skin. A whitehead ripe in the crease beside his nostrils.

Moon landscape, clean and cold. He picked up the pencil again.

Babcock, with his broad pink nose shining with grease, crusts of white matter in the corners of his eyes. Food mortar between his teeth.

Sam's wife, with raspberry-colored paste on her mouth. Face smeared with tears, a bright bubble in one nostril. And the damn dog, shiny nose, wet eyes. . . .

He turned. The dog was there, sitting on the carpet, wet red tongue out *left the door open again* dripping, wagged its tail twice, then started to get up. He reached for the metal T square, leaned back, swinging it like an ax, and the dog yelped once as metal sheared bone, one eye spouting red, writhing on its back, dark stain of piss across the carpet and he hit it again, hit it again.

The body lay twisted on the carpet, fouled with blood, ragged black lips drawn back from teeth. He wiped off the T square with a paper towel, then scrubbed it in the sink with soap and steel wool, dried it and hung it up. He got a sheet of drafting paper, laid it on the floor, rolled the body over onto it without spilling any blood on the carpet. He lifted the body in the paper, carried it out onto the patio, then onto the unroofed section, opening the doors with his shoulder. He looked over the wall. Two stories down, concrete roof, vents sticking out of it, nobody watching. He held the dog out, let it slide off the paper, twisting as it fell. It struck one of the vents, bounced, a red smear. He carried the paper back inside, poured the blood down the drain, then put the paper into the incinerator chute.

Splashes of blood were on the carpet, the feet of the drafting table, the cabinet, his trouser legs. He sponged them all up with paper towels and warm water. He took off his clothing, examined it minutely, scrubbed it in the sink, then put it in the washer. He washed the sink, rubbed himself down with disinfectant and dressed again. He walked through into Sam's silent apartment, closing the glass door behind him. Past the potted philodendron, overstuffed furniture, red-and-yellow painting on the wall, out onto the roof, leaving the door ajar. Then back through the patio, closing doors.

Too bad. How about some goldfish.

He sat down at the drafting table. He was running clean and cool. The dream this morning came back to his mind, the last one, as he was struggling up out of sleep: *slithery kidneys burst gray lungs blood and hair ropes of guts covered with yellow fat oozing and sliding and oh god the stink like the breath of an outhouse no sound nowhere he was putting a yellow stream down the slide of the dunghole and*

He began to ink in the drawing, first with a fine steel pen, then with a nylon brush. *his heel slid and he was falling could not stop himself falling into slimy bulging softness higher than his chin, higher and he could not move paralyzed and he tried to scream tried to scream tried to scream.*

The prospector was climbing a crater slope with its handling members retracted and its head tilted up. Behind it the distant ringwall and the horizon, the black sky, the pinpoint stars. And he was there, and it was not far enough, not yet, for the earth hung overhead like a rotten fruit, blue with mold, crawling, wrinkling, purulent and alive.

Man: Himself and Aliens

Is it possible that man is not alone in the universe and that he is not the highest or most technologically advanced life form? The formal sciences seem to consider that the possibility of man's not being alone is quite high, and science fiction has long entertained and popularized the idea that man will meet a life form which is at least his technological equal. Unfortunately, science fiction, especially as it has been translated into the movies and television, has given the public the idea that all aliens are to be feared, fought, and (hopefully) conquered. What many people, including many casual readers of science fiction, do not realize is that there are many science fiction short stories and novels which directly explore the problem of establishing peaceful relationships with other life forms, inferior and superior to our own. The concept of such relationships is an extension of a problem here on Earth—the inability or at least difficulty of one culture fully understanding another—further complicated by the possibility of differing life forms.

In H. Beam Piper's *Little Fuzzy*, the question of how we are to recognize a life form as equal to our own is explored; the conflict arises over whether to exploit the rich planet and destroy the extremely vulnerable "fuzzies" or to accord them equality and thus give them control over the planet's wealth. The novel, then, explores human motivation as well as the relationships between humans and other life forms. The conqueror and the conquered are archetypally represented in H. G. Wells' *The War of the Worlds* and Ray Bradbury's *The Martian Chronicles*. Both novels examine the nature of man as well as the idea of interplanetary conquest. C. S. Lewis, uniting science fiction and a traditional Christian cosmic vision, delineates an unusual relationship between Martians and Earth people and attempts to explain the presence of evil in the world in *Out of the Silent Planet*. The classic assessment of man's place in the universe, in both philosophical and science fictional terms, has to be Olaf Stapledon's *Last And First Men* and *Star Maker*, two novels which are nothing less than a history of the cosmos and man's rather short tenure in it. The problem of differing cultures is emphasized in Ursula Le Guin's magnificent *The Left Hand of Darkness* which depicts an ambassador from a very westernized empire trying to understand and work with people on a planet which is similar in cultural world-view to what we know of the philosophies of the Orientals or the American Indians. The novel challenges the reader's attitudes toward, among other things, religion, sex, and the passage of time.

There are at least two ways in which to organize the five stories which follow. The first is based on theme: Sheckley and Clarke examine man's place in the universe; Smith, Green, Sheckley (again), and Simak, on the other hand, explore some ways in which man could peacefully relate to other life forms. The second method of organization groups the stories according to their locale: Simak sets his story on Earth, Sheckley and Smith primarily in space, and Clarke and Green on other planetary bodies. The specific locale of the story shapes man's response to the other life forms and theirs to him.

Robert Sheckley's "Specialist" examines man's self-concept and calls into question deep-rooted Western ideas of individuality and independence. Further, Sheckley postulates an explanation for man's competative nature. As almost everyone knows, "The Sentinel" provided the germ for Arthur C. Clarke and Stanley Kubrick's movie, *2001: A Space Odyssey*, which, like Clarke's *Childhood's End* and others, examines the possibility of intellects vastly superior to our own as well as the future of man in the universe. "The Sentinel" focuses on the significant aspects of man's first steps into space. In this finely crafted story, Clarke uses the first-person narrative which is very effective in realistically placing the reader on the moon and in rendering believable the descriptions of the moonscape.

In "The Game of Rat and Dragon" Cordwainer Smith introduces some new dangers to space travellers and develops a telepathic partnership capable of meeting those dangers. The resultant union of minds creates some unusual psychic and emotional situations which could conceivably be a part of such inter-species communication. Joseph Green's

"The Decision Makers" takes up the question of how man is to evaluate other life forms and define their intelligence or civilization. The world upon which the action takes place is one of Green's invention, and it is a pervasive but not obtrusive factor in the story. Clifford Simak's "Death in the House" is a superb combination of science fiction and rural Americana. The setting and the rather "homey" character of Mose take away the strangeness of the meeting between Earthman and alien, and without the strangeness (and the accompanying fear), Mose can function according to what we would like to think are the best and most basic of human impulses.

As you have noticed by now, this group of stories is the largest in the book. This is so because the problem of man's self-concept may be one of the major philosophical problems of the near future. To be sure, pollution, population, and the Bomb are problems to be solved, but we know how to solve those problems if we will only do it. The means are there, only the determination is lacking. But man's concept of himself and his place in the universe still suffers from the television and dime-novel westerns and the science fiction which is patterned after them. And this self-concept will not only lead man into conflict with any extraterrestrials he meets but will stand in the way of a more accurate relationship between man, his fellows, and the environment.

SPECIALIST

Robert Sheckley

The photon storm struck without warning, pouncing upon the Ship from behind a bank of giant red stars. Eye barely had time to flash a last second warning through Talker before it was upon them.

It was Talker's third journey into deep space, and his first light-pressure storm. He felt a sudden pang of fear as the Ship yawed violently, caught the force of the wave-front and careened end for end. Then the fear was gone, replaced by a strong pulse of excitement.

Why should he be afraid, he asked himself—hadn't he been trained for just this sort of emergency?

He had been talking to Feeder when the storm hit, but he cut off the conversation abruptly. He hoped Feeder would be all right. It was the youngster's first deep space trip.

The wirelike filaments that made up most of Talker's body were extended throughout the Ship. Quickly he withdrew all except the ones linking him to Eye, Engine, and the Walls. This was strictly their job now. The rest of the Crew would have to shift for themselves until the storm was over.

Eye had flattened his disklike body against a Wall, and had one seeing organ extended outside the Ship. For greater concentration, the rest of his seeing organs were collapsed, clustered against his body.

Through Eye's seeing organ, Talker watched the storm. He translated Eye's purely visual image into a direction for Engine, who shoved the Ship around to meet the waves. At appreciably the same time, Talker translated direction into velocity for the Walls who stiffened to meet the shocks.

The coordination was swift and sure—Eye measuring the waves, Talker relaying the messages to Engine and Walls, Engine driving the ship nose-first into the waves, and Walls bracing to meet the shock.

Talker forgot any fear he might have had in the swiftly functioning teamwork. He had no time to think. As the Ship's communication system, he had to translate and flash his messages at top speed, coordinating information and directing action.

In a matter of minutes, the storm was over.

"All right," Talker said. "Let's see if there was any damage." His filaments had become tangled during the storm, but he untwisted and extended them through the Ship, plugging everyone into circuit. "Engine?"

"I'm fine," Engine said. The tremendous old fellow had dampened his plates during the storm, easing down the atomic explosions in his stomach. No storm could catch an experienced spacer like Engine unaware.

"Walls?"

The Walls reported one by one, and this took a long time. There were almost a thousand of them, thin, rectangular fellows making up the entire skin of the Ship. Naturally, they had reinforced their edges during the storm, giving the whole Ship resiliency. But one or two were dented badly.

Doctor announced that he was all right. He removed Talker's filament from his head, taking himself out of circuit, and went to work on the dented Walls. Made mostly of hands, Doctor had clung to an Accumulator during the storm.

"Let's go a little faster now," Talker said, remembering that there still was the problem of determining where they were. He opened the circuit to the four Accumulators. "How are you?" he asked.

There was no answer. The Accumulators were asleep. They had had their receptors open during the storm and were bloated on energy. Talker twitched his filaments around them, but they didn't stir.

"Let me," Feeder said. Feeder had taken quite a beating before planting his suction cups to a Wall, but his cockiness was intact. He was the only member of the Crew who never needed Doctor's attention; his body was quite capable of repairing itself.

He scuttled across the floor on a dozen or so tentacles, and booted the nearest Accumulator. The big, conical storage unit opened one eye, then closed it again. Feeder kicked him again, getting no response. He reached for the Accumulator's safety valve and drained off some energy.

"Stop that," the Accumulator said.

"Then wake up and report," Talker told him.

The Accumulators said testily that they were all right, as any fool could see. They had been anchored to the floor during the storm.

The rest of the inspection went quickly. Thinker was fine, and Eye was ecstatic over the beauty of the storm. There was only one casualty.

Pusher was dead. Bipedal, he didn't have the stability of the rest of the Crew. The storm had caught him in the middle of a floor, thrown him against a stiffened Wall, and broken several of his important bones. He was beyond Doctor's skill to repair.

They were silent for a while. It was always serious when a part of the Ship died. The Ship was a cooperative unit, composed entirely of the Crew. The loss of any member was a blow to all the rest.

It was especially serious now. They had just delivered a cargo to a port several thousand light-years from Galactic Center. There was no telling where they might be.

Eye crawled to a Wall and extended a seeing organ outside. The Walls let it through, then sealed around it. Eye's organ pushed out, far enough from the Ship so he could view the entire sphere of stars. The picture traveled through Talker, who gave it to Thinker.

Thinker lay in one corner of the room, a great shapeless blob of protoplasm. Within him were all the memories of his space-going ancestors. He considered the picture, compared it rapidly with others stored in his cells, and said, "No galactic planets within reach."

Talker automatically translated for everyone. It was what they had feared.

Eye, with Thinker's help, calculated that they were several hundred

260 / Science Fiction and the Future

light-years off their course, on the galactic periphery.

Every Crew member knew what that meant. Without a Pusher to boost the Ship to a multiple of the speed of light, they would never get home. The trip back, without a Pusher, would take longer than most of their lifetimes.

"What would you suggest?" Talker asked Thinker.

This was too vague a question for the literal-minded Thinker. He asked to have it rephrased.

"What would be our best line of action," Talker asked, "to get back to a galactic planet?"

Thinker needed several minutes to go through all the possibilities stored in his cells. In the meantime, Doctor had patched the Walls and was asking to be given something to eat.

"In a little while we'll all eat," Talker said, twitching his tendrils nervously. Even though he was the second youngest Crew member—only Feeder was younger—the responsibility was largely on him. This was still an emergency; he had to coordinate information and direct action.

One of the Walls suggested that they get good and drunk. This unrealistic solution was vetoed at once. It was typical of the Walls' attitude, however. They were fine workers and good shipmates, but happy-go-lucky fellows at best. When they returned to their home planets, they would probably blow all their wages on a spree.

"Loss of the Ship's Pusher cripples the Ship for sustained faster-than-light speeds," Thinker began without preamble. "The nearest galactic planet is four hundred and five light-years off."

Talker translated all this instantly along his wave-packet body.

"Two courses of action are open. First, the Ship can proceed to the nearest galactic planet under atomic power from Engine. This will take approximately two hundred years. Engine might still be alive at this time, although no one else will.

"Second, locate a primitive planet in this region, upon which are latent Pushers. Find one and train him. Have him push the Ship back to galactic territory."

Thinker was silent, having given all the possibilities he could find in the memories of his ancestors.

They held a quick vote and decided upon Thinker's second alternative. There was no choice, really. It was the only one which offered them any hope of getting back to their homes.

"All right," Talker said. "Let's eat. I think we all deserve it."

The body of the dead Pusher was shoved into the mouth of Engine, who consumed it at once, breaking down the atoms to energy. Engine was the only member of the Crew who lived on atomic energy.

For the rest, Feeder dashed up and loaded himself from the nearest

Accumulator. Then he transformed the food within him into the substances each member ate. His body chemistry changed, altered, adapted, making the different foods for the Crew.

Eye lived entirely on a complex chlorophyl chain. Feeder reproduced this for him, then went over to give Talker his hydrocarbons, and the Walls their chlorine compound. For Doctor he made a facsimile of a silicate fruit that grew on Doctor's native planet.

Finally, feeding was over and the Ship back in order. The Accumulators were stacked in a corner, blissfully sleeping again. Eye was extending his vision as far as he could, shaping his main seeing organ for high-powered telescopic reception. Even in this emergency, Eye couldn't resist making verses. He announced that he was at work on a new narrative poem, called *Peripheral Glow*. No one wanted to hear it, so Eye fed it to Thinker, who stored everything, good or bad, right or wrong.

Engine never slept. Filled to the brim on Pusher, he shoved the Ship along at several times the speed of light.

The Walls were arguing among themselves about who had been the drunkest during their last leave.

Talker decided to make himself comfortable. He released his hold on the Walls and swung in the air, his small round body suspended by his crisscrossed network of filaments.

He thought briefly about Pusher. It was strange. Pusher had been everyone's friend and now he was forgotten. That wasn't because of indifference; it was because the Ship was a unit. The loss of a member was regretted, but the important thing was for the unit to go on.

The Ship raced through the suns of the periphery.

Thinker laid out a search spiral, calculating their odds on finding a Pusher planet at roughly four to one. In a week they found a planet of primitive Walls. Dropping low, they could see the leathery, rectangular fellows basking in the sun, crawling over rocks, stretching themselves thin in order to float in the breeze.

All the Ship's Walls heaved a sigh of nostalgia. It was just like home.

These Walls on the planet hadn't been contacted by a galactic team yet, and were still unaware of their great destiny—to join in the vast Cooperation of the Galaxy.

There were plenty of dead worlds in the spiral, and worlds too young to bear life. They found a planet of Talkers. The Talkers had extended their spidery communication lines across half a continent.

Talker looked at them eagerly, through Eye. A wave of self-pity washed over him. He remembered home, his family, his friends. He thought of the tree he was going to buy when he got back.

For a moment, Talker wondered what he was doing here, part of a Ship in a far corner of the Galaxy.

He shrugged off the mood. They were bound to find a Pusher planet, if they looked long enough.

At least, he hoped so.

There was a long stretch of arid worlds as the Ship speeded through the unexplored periphery. Then a planetful of primeval Engines, swimming in a radioactive ocean.

"This is rich territory," Feeder said to Talker. "Galactic should send a Contact party here."

"They probably will, after we get back," Talker said.

They were good friends, above and beyond the all-enveloping friendship of the Crew. It wasn't only because they were the youngest Crew members, although that had something to do with it. They both had the same kind of functions and that made for a certain rapport. Talker translated languages; Feeder transformed foods. Also, they looked somewhat alike. Talker was a central core with radiating filaments; Feeder was a central core with radiating tentacles.

Talker thought that Feeder was the next most aware being on the Ship. He was never really able to understand how some of the others carried on the processes of consciousness.

More suns, more planets. Engine started to overheat. Usually, Engine was used only for taking off and landing, and for fine maneuvering in a planetary group. Now he had been running continuously for weeks, both over and under the speed of light. The strain was telling on him.

Feeder, with Doctor's help, rigged a cooling system for him. It was crude, but it had to suffice. Feeder rearranged nitrogen, oxygen and hydrogen atoms to make a coolant for the system. Doctor diagnosed a long rest for Engine. He said that the gallant old fellow couldn't stand the strain for more than a week.

The search continued, with the Crew's spirits gradually dropping. They all realized that Pushers were rather rare in the Galaxy, as compared to the fertile Walls and Engines.

The Walls were getting pock-marked from interstellar dust. They complained that they would need a full beauty treatment when they got home. Talker assured them that the company would pay for it.

Even Eye was getting bloodshot from staring into space so continuously.

They dipped over another planet. Its characteristics were flashed to Thinker, who mulled over them.

Closer, and they could make out the forms.

Pushers! Primitive Pushers!

They zoomed back into space to make plans. Feeder produced twenty-three different kinds of intoxicants for celebration.

The Ship wasn't fit to function for three days.

"Everyone ready now?" Talker asked, a bit fuzzily. He had a hangover that burned all along his nerve ends. What a drunk he had thrown!

He had a vague recollection of embracing Engine, and inviting him to share his tree when they got home.

He shuddered at the idea.

The rest of the Crew were pretty shaky, too. The Walls were letting air leak into space; they were just too wobbly to seal their edges properly. Doctor had passed out.

But the worst off was Feeder. Since his system could adapt to any type of fuel except atomic, he had been sampling every batch he made, whether it was an unbalanced iodine, pure oxygen or a supercharged ester. He was really miserable. His tentacles, usually a healthy aqua, were shot through with orange streaks. His system was working furiously, purging itself of everything, and Feeder was suffering the effects of the purge.

The only sober ones were Thinker and Engine. Thinker didn't drink, which was unusual for a spacer, though typical of Thinker, and Engine couldn't.

They listened while Thinker reeled off some astounding facts. From Eye's pictures of the planet's surface, Thinker had detected the presence of metallic construction. He put forth the alarming suggestion that these Pushers had constructed a mechanical civilization.

"That's impossible," three of the Walls said flatly, and most of the Crew were inclined to agree with them. All the metal they had ever seen had been buried in the ground or lying around in worthless oxidized chunks.

"Do you mean that they make things out of metal?" Talker demanded. "Out of just plain dead metal? What could they make?"

"They couldn't make anything," Feeder said positively. "It would break down constantly. I mean metal doesn't *know* when it's weakening."

But it seemed to be true. Eye magnified his pictures, and everyone could see that the Pushers had made vast shelters, vehicles, and other articles from inanimate material.

The reason for this was not readily apparent, but it wasn't a good sign. However, the really hard part was over. The Pusher planet had been found. All that remained was the relatively easy job of convincing a native Pusher.

That shouldn't be too difficult. Talker knew that cooperation was the keystone of the Galaxy, even among primitive peoples.

The Crew decided not to land in a populated region. Of course, there was no reason not to expect a friendly greeting, but it was the job of a Contact Team to get in touch with them as a race. All they wanted was an individual.

Accordingly, they picked out a sparsely populated land-mass, drifting in while that side of the planet was dark.

They were able to locate a solitary Pusher almost at once.

Eye adapted his vision to see in the dark, and they followed the Pusher's movements. He lay down, after a while, beside a small fire. Thinker told them that this was a well-known resting habit of Pushers.

Just before dawn, the Walls opened, and Feeder, Talker and Doctor came out.

Feeder dashed forward and tapped the creature on the shoulder. Talker followed with a communication tendril.

The Pusher opened his seeing organs, blinked them, and made a movement with his eating organ. Then he leaped to his feet and started to run.

The three Crew members were amazed. The Pusher hadn't even waited to find out what the three of them wanted!

Talker extended a filament rapidly, and caught the Pusher, fifty feet away, by a limb. The Pusher fell.

"Treat him gently," Feeder said. "He might be startled by our appearance." He twitched his tendrils at the idea of a Pusher—one of the strangest sights in the Galaxy, with his multiple organs—being startled at someone else's appearance.

Feeder and Doctor scurried to the fallen Pusher, picked him up and carried him back to the Ship.

The Walls sealed again. They released the Pusher and prepared to talk.

As soon as he was free, the Pusher sprang to his limbs and ran at the place where the Walls had sealed. He pounded against them frantically, his eating organ open and vibrating.

"Stop that," the Wall said. He bulged, and the Pusher tumbled to the floor. Instantly, he jumped up and started to run forward.

"Stop him," Talker said. "He might hurt himself."

One of the Accumulators woke up enough to roll into the Pusher's path. The Pusher fell, got up again, and ran on.

Talker had his filaments in the front of the Ship also, and he caught the Pusher in the bow. The Pusher started to tear at his tendrils, and Talker let go hastily.

"Plug him into the communication system!" Feeder shouted. "Maybe we can reason with him!"

Talker advanced a filament toward the Pusher's head, waving it in the universal sign of communication. But the Pusher continued his amazing behavior, jumping out of the way. He had a piece of metal in his hand and he was waving it frantically.

"What do you think he's going to do with that?" Feeder asked. The Pusher started to attack the side of the Ship, pounding at one of the Walls. The Wall stiffened instinctively and the metal snapped.

"Leave him alone," Talker said. "Give him a chance to calm down."

Talker consulted with Thinker, but they couldn't decide what to do about the Pusher. He wouldn't accept communication. Every time Talker extended a filament, the Pusher showed all the signs of violent panic. Temporarily, it was an impasse.

Thinker vetoed the plan of finding another Pusher on the planet. He considered this Pusher's behavior typical; nothing would be gained by approaching another. Also, a planet was supposed to be contacted only by a Contact Team.

If they couldn't communicate with this Pusher, they never would with another on the planet.

"I think I know what the trouble is," Eye said. He crawled up on an Accumulator. "These Pushers have evolved a mechanical civilization. Consider for a minute how they went about it. They developed the use of their fingers, like Doctor, to shape metal. They utilized their seeing organs, like myself. And probably countless other organs." He paused for effect.

"These Pushers have become unspecialized!"

They argued over it for several hours. The Walls maintained that no intelligent creature could be unspecialized. It was unknown in the Galaxy. But the evidence was before them—the Pusher cities, their vehicles . . . This Pusher, exemplifying the rest, seemed capable of a multitude of things.

He was able to do everything except Push!

Thinker supplied a partial explanation. "This is not a primitive planet. It is relatively old and should have been in the Cooperation thousands of years ago. Since it was not, the Pushers upon it were robbed of their birthright. Their ability, their specialty was to Push, but there was nothing *to* Push. Naturally, they have developed a deviant culture.

"Exactly what this culture is, we can only guess. But on the basis of the evidence, there is reason to believe that these Pushers are—uncooperative."

Thinker had a habit of uttering the most shattering statement in the quietest possible way.

"It is entirely possible," Thinker went on inexorably, "that these Pushers will have nothing to do with us. In which case, our chances are approximately 283 to one against finding another Pusher planet."

"We can't be sure he won't cooperate," Talker said, "until we get him into communication." He found it almost impossible to believe that any intelligent creature would refuse to cooperate willingly.

"But how?" Feeder asked. They decided upon a course of action. Doctor walked slowly up to the Pusher, who backed away from him.

In the meantime, Talker extended a filament outside the Ship, around, and in again, behind the Pusher.

The Pusher backed against a Wall—and Talker shoved the filament through the Pusher's head, into the communication socket in the center of his brain.

The Pusher collapsed.

When he came to, Feeder and Doctor had to hold the Pusher's limbs, or he would have ripped out the communication line. Talker exercised his skill in learning the Pusher's language.

It wasn't too hard. All Pusher languages were of the same family, and this was no exception. Talker was able to catch enough surface thoughts to form a pattern.

He tried to communicate with the Pusher.

The Pusher was silent.

"I think he needs food," Feeder said. They remembered that it had been almost two days since they had taken the Pusher on board. Feeder worked up some standard Pusher food and offered it.

"My God! A steak!" the Pusher said.

The Crew cheered along Talker's communication circuits. The Pusher had said his first words!

Talker examined the words and searched his memory. He knew about two hundred Pusher languages and many more simple variations. He found that this Pusher was speaking a cross between two Pusher tongues.

After the Pusher had eaten, he looked around. Talker caught his thoughts and broadcast them to the Crew.

The Pusher had a queer way of looking at the Ship. He saw it as a riot of colors. The walls undulated. In front of him was something resembling a gigantic spider, colored black and green, with his web running all over the Ship and into the heads of all the creatures. He saw Eye as a strange, naked little animal, something between a skinned rabbit and an egg yolk—whatever those things were.

Talker was fascinated by the new perspective the Pusher's mind gave him. He had never seen things that way before. But now that the Pusher was pointing it out, Eye *was* a pretty funny-looking creature.

They settled down to communication.

"What in hell *are* you things?" the Pusher asked, much calmer now than he had been during the two days. "Why did you grab me? Have I gone nuts?"

"No," Talker said, "you are not psychotic. We are a galactic trading ship. We were blown off our course by a storm and our Pusher was killed."

"Well, what does that have to do with me?"

"We would like you to join our Crew," Talker said, "to be our new Pusher."

The Pusher thought it over after the situation was explained to him. Talker could catch the feeling of conflict in the Pusher's thoughts. He hadn't decided whether to accept this as a real situation or not. Finally, the Pusher decided that he wasn't crazy.

"Look, boys," he said, "I don't know what you are or how this makes sense. I have to get out of here. I'm on a furlough, and if I don't get back soon, the U.S. Army's going to be very interested."

Talker asked the Pusher to give him more information about "army," and he fed it to Thinker.

"These Pushers engage in personal combat," was Thinker's conclusion.

"But *why?*" Talker asked. Sadly he admitted to himself that Thinker might have been right; the Pusher didn't show many signs of willingness to cooperate.

"I'd like to help you lads out," Pusher said, "but I don't know where you get the idea that I could push anything this size. You'd need a whole division of tanks just to budge it."

"Do you approve of these wars?" Talker asked, getting a suggestion from Thinker.

"Nobody likes war—not those who have to do the dying at least."

"Then why do you fight them?"

The Pusher made a gesture with his eating organ, which Eye picked up and sent to Thinker. "It's kill or be killed. You guys know what war is, don't you?"

"We don't have any wars," Talker said.

"You're lucky," the Pusher said bitterly. "We do. Plenty of them."

"Of course," Talker said. He had the full explanation from Thinker now. "Would you like to end them?"

"Of course I would."

"Then come with us. Be our Pusher."

The Pusher stood up and walked up to an Accumulator. He sat down on it and doubled the ends of his upper limbs.

"How the hell can I stop all wars?" the Pusher demanded. "Even if I went to the big shots and told them—"

"You won't have to," Talker said. "All you have to do is come with us. Push us to our base. Galactic will send a Contact Team to your planet. That will end your wars."

"The hell you say," the Pusher replied. "You boys are stranded here, huh? Good enough. No monsters are going to take over Earth."

Bewildered, Talker tried to understand the reasoning. Had he said something wrong? Was it possible that the Pusher didn't understand him?

"I thought you wanted to end wars," Talker said.

"Sure I do. But I don't want anyone *making* us stop. I'm no traitor. I'd rather fight."

"No one will make you stop. You will just stop because there will be no further need for fighting."

"Do you know why we're fighting?"

"It's obvious."

"Yeah? What's your explanation?"

"You Pushers have been separated from the main stream of the Galaxy," Talker explained. "You have your specialty—pushing—but nothing to Push. Accordingly, you have no real jobs. You play with things—metal, inanimate objects—but find no real satisfaction. Robbed of your true vocation, you fight from sheer frustration.

"Once you find your place in the galactic Cooperation—and I assure you that it is an important place—your fighting will stop. Why should you fight, which is an unnatural occupation, when you can Push? Also, your mechanical civilization will end, since there will be no need for it."

The Pusher shook his head in what Talker guessed was a gesture of confusion. "What is this pushing?"

Talker told him as best he could. Since the job was out of his scope, he had only a general idea of what a Pusher did.

"You mean to say that *that* is what every Earthman should be doing?"

"Of course," Talker said. "It is your great specialty."

The Pusher thought about it for several minutes. "I think you want a physicist or a mentalist or something. I could never do anything like that. I'm a junior architect. And besides—well, it's difficult to explain."

But Talker had already caught Pusher's objection. He saw a Pusher female in his thoughts. No, two, three. And he caught a feeling of loneliness, strangeness. The Pusher was filled with doubts. He was afraid.

"When we reach galactic," Talker said, hoping it was the right thing, "you can meet other Pushers. Pusher females, too. All you Pushers look alike, so you should become friends with them. As far as loneliness in the Ship goes—it just doesn't exist. You don't understand the Cooperation yet. No one is lonely in the Cooperation."

The Pusher was still considering the idea of there being other Pushers. Talker couldn't understand why he was so startled at that. The Galaxy was filled with Pushers, Feeders, Talkers, and many other species, endlessly duplicated.

"I can't believe that anybody could end all war," Pusher said. "How do I know you're not lying?"

Talker felt as if he had been struck in the core. Thinker must have been right when he said these Pushers would be uncooperative. Was this going to be the end of Talker's career? Were he and the rest of the Crew going to spend the rest of their lives in space, because of the stupidity of a bunch of Pushers?

Even thinking this, Talker was able to feel sorry for the Pusher. It must be terrible, he thought. Doubting, uncertain, never trusting anyone. If these Pushers didn't find their place in the Galaxy, they would exterminate themselves. Their place in the Cooperation was long overdue.

"What can I do to convince you?" Talker asked.

In despair, he opened all the circuits to the Pusher. He let the Pusher see Engine's good-natured gruffness, the devil-may-care humor of the Walls; he showed him Eye's poetic attempts, and Feeder's cocky good nature. He opened his own mind and showed the Pusher a picture of his home planet, his family, the tree he was planning to buy when he got home.

The pictures told the story of all of them, from different planets, representing different ethics, united by a common bond—the galactic Cooperation.

The Pusher watched it all in silence.

After a while, he shook his head. The thought accompanying the gesture was uncertain, weak—but negative.

Talker told the Walls to open. They did, and the Pusher stared in amazement.

"You may leave," Talker said. "Just remove the communication line and go."

"What will you do?"

"We will look for another Pusher planet."

"Where? Mars? Venus?"

"We don't know. All we can do is hope there is another in this region."

The Pusher looked at the opening, then back at the Crew. He hesitated and his face screwed up in a grimace of indecision.

"All that you showed me was true?"

No answer was necessary.

"All right," the Pusher said suddenly. "I'll go. I'm a damned fool, but I'll go. If this means what you say—it *must* mean what you say!"

Talker saw that the agony of the Pusher's decision had forced him out of contact with reality. He believed that he was in a dream, where decisions are easy and unimportant.

"There's just one little trouble," Pusher said with the lightness of hysteria. "Boys, I'll be damned if I know how to Push. You said something about faster-than-light? I can't even run the mile in an hour."

"Of course you can Push," Talker assured him, hoping he was right. He knew what a Pusher's abilities were; but this one . . .

"Just try it."

"Sure," Pusher agreed. I'll probably wake up out of this, anyhow."

They sealed the ship for takeoff while Pusher talked to himself.

"Funny," Pusher said. "I thought a camping trip would be a nice way to spend a furlough and all I do is get nightmares!"

Engine boosted the Ship into the air. The Walls were sealed and Eye was guiding them away from the planet.

"We're in open space now," Talker said. Listening to Pusher, he hoped his mind hadn't cracked. "Eye and Thinker will give a direction, I'll transmit it to you, and you Push along it."

"You're crazy," Pusher mumbled. "You must have the wrong planet. I wish you nightmares would go away."

"You're in the Cooperation now," Talker said desperately. "There's the direction. Push!"

The Pusher didn't do anything for a moment. He was slowly emerging from his fantasy, realizing that he wasn't in a dream, after all. He felt the Cooperation. Eye to Thinker, Thinker to Talker, Talker to Pusher, all intercoordinated with Walls, and with each other.

"What is this?" Pusher asked. He felt the oneness of the Ship, the great warmth, the closeness achieved only in the Cooperation.

He Pushed.

Nothing happened.

"Try again," Talker begged.

Pusher searched his mind. He found a deep well of doubt and fear. Staring into it, he saw his own tortured face.

Thinker illuminated it for him.

Pushers had lived with this doubt and fear for centuries. Pushers had fought through fear, killed through doubt.

That was where the Pusher organ was!

Human—specialist—Pusher—he entered fully into the Crew, merged with them, threw mental arms around the shoulders of Thinker and Talker.

Suddenly, the Ship shot forward at eight times the speed of light. It continued to accelerate.

THE SENTINEL

Arthur C. Clarke

The next time you see the full Moon high in the south, look carefully at its right-hand edge and let your eye travel upwards along the curve of the disk. Round about two o'clock you will notice a small, dark oval: anyone with normal eyesight can find it quite easily. It is the great walled plain, one of the finest on the Moon, known as the Mare Crisium—the Sea of Crises. Three hundred miles in diameter, and almost completely surrounded by a ring of magnificent mountains, it had never been explored until we entered it in the late summer of 1996.

Our expedition was a large one. We had two heavy freighters which had flown our supplies and equipment from the main lunar base in the Mare Serenitatis, five hundred miles away. There were also three small rockets which were intended for a short-range transport over regions which our surface vehicles couldn't cross. Luckily, most of the Mare Crisium is very flat. There are none of the great crevasses so common and so dangerous elsewhere, and very few craters or mountains of any size. As far as we could tell, our powerful caterpillar tractors would have no difficulty in taking us wherever we wished to go.

I was geologist—or selenologist, if you want to be pedantic—in charge of the group exploring the southern region of the Mare. We had crossed a hundred miles of it in a week, skirting the foothills of the mountains along the shore of what was once the ancient sea, some thousand million years before. When life was beginning on Earth, it was already dying here. The waters were retreating down the flanks of those stupendous cliffs, retreating into the empty heart of the Moon. Over the land which we were crossing, the tideless ocean had once been half a mile deep, and now the only trace of moisture was the hoarfrost one could sometimes find in caves which the searing sunlight never penetrated.

We had begun our journey early in the slow lunar dawn, and still had almost a week of Earth-time before nightfall. Half a dozen times a day we would leave our vehicle and go outside in the space-suits to hunt for interesting minerals, or to place markers for the guidance of future travellers. It was an uneventful routine. There is nothing hazardous or even particularly exciting about lunar exploration. We could live comfortably for a month in our pressurised tractors, and if we ran into trouble we could always radio for help and sit tight until one of the spaceships came to our rescue.

I said just now that there was nothing exciting about lunar exploration, but of course that isn't true. One could never grow tired of those incredible mountains, so much more rugged than the gentle hills of Earth. We never knew, as we rounded the capes and promontories of that vanished sea, what new splendors would be revealed to us. The whole southern curve of the Mare Crisium is a vast delta where a score of rivers once found their way into the ocean, fed perhaps by the torrential rains that must have lashed the mountains in the brief volcanic age when the Moon was young. Each of these ancient valleys was an invitation, chalenging us to climb into the unknown uplands beyond. But we had a hundred miles still to cover, and could only look longingly at the heights which others must scale.

We kept Earth-time aboard the tractor, and precisely at 22.00 hours the final radio message would be sent out to Base and we would close down for the day. Outside, the rocks would still be burning beneath the almost vertical Sun, but to us it was night until we awoke again eight hours later. Then one of us would prepare breakfast, there would be a great buzzing of electric razors, and someone would switch on the short-wave radio from Earth. Indeed, when the smell of frying sausages began to fill the cabin, it was sometimes hard to believe that we were not back on our own world—everything was so normal and homely, apart from the feeling of decreased weight and the unnatural slowness with which objects fell.

It was my turn to prepare breakfast in the corner of the main cabin that served as a galley. I can remember that moment quite vividly after all these years, for the radio had just played one of my favourite melodies, the old Welsh air, "David of the White Rock." Our driver was already outside in his space-suit, inspecting our caterpillar treads. My assistant, Louis Garnett, was up forward in the control position, making some belated entries in yesterday's log.

As I stood by the frying pan waiting, like any terrestrial housewife, for the sausages to brown, I let my gaze wander idly over the mountain walls which covered the whole of the southern horizon, marching out of sight to east and west below the curve of the Moon. They seemed only a mile or two from the tractor, but I knew that the nearest was twenty miles away. On the Moon, of course, there is no loss of detail with distance—none of that almost imperceptible haziness which softens and sometimes transfigures all far-off things on Earth.

Those mountains were ten thousand feet high, and they climbed steeply out of the plain as if ages ago some subterranean eruption had smashed them skywards through the molten crust. The base of even the nearest was hidden from sight by the steeply curving surface of the plain, for the Moon is a very little world, and from where I was standing the horizon was only two miles away.

I lifted my eyes towards the peaks which no man had ever climbed, the peaks which, before the coming of terrestrial life, had watched the retreating oceans sink sullenly into their graves, taking with them the hope and the morning promise of the world. The sunlight was beating against those ramparts with a glare that hurt the eyes, yet only a little way above them the stars were shining steadily in a sky blacker than a winter midnight on Earth.

I was turning away when my eye caught a metallic glitter high on the ridge of a great promontory thrusting out into the sea thirty miles to the west. It was a dimensionless point of light, as if a star had been clawed from the sky by one of those cruel peaks, and I imagined that some smooth rock surface was catching the sunlight and heliographing it straight into my eyes. Such things were not uncommon. When the Moon is in her second quarter, observers on Earth can sometimes see the great ranges in the Oceanus Procellarum burning with a blue-white iridescence as the sunlight flashes from their slopes and leaps again from world to world. But I was curious to know what kind of rock could be shining so brightly up there, and I climbed into the observation turret and swung our four-inch telescope round to the west.

I could see just enough to tantalise me. Clear and sharp in the field of vision, the mountain peaks seemed only half a mile away, but whatever was catching the sunlight was still too small to be resolved. Yet it seemed to have an elusive symmetry, and the summit upon which it rested was curiously flat. I stared for a long time at that glittering enigma, straining my eyes into space, until presently a smell of burning from the galley told me that our breakfast sausages had made their quarter-million-mile journey in vain.

All that morning we argued our way across the Mare Crisium while the western mountains reared higher in the sky. Even when we were out prospecting in the space-suits, the discussion would continue over the radio. It was absolutely certain, my companions argued, that there had never been any form of intelligent life on the Moon. The only living things that had ever existed there were a few primitive plants and their slightly less degenerate ancestors. I know that as well as anyone, but there are times when a scientist must not be afraid to make a fool of himself.

"Listen," I said at last, "I'm going up there, if only for my own peace of mind. That mountain's less than twelve thousand feet high—that's only two thousand under Earth gravity—and I can make the trip in twenty hours at the outside. I've always wanted to go up into those hills, anyway, and this gives me an excellent excuse."

"If you don't break your neck," said Garnett, "you'll be the laughingstock of the expedition when we get back to Base. That mountain will probably be called Wilson's Folly from now on."

"I won't break my neck," I said firmly. "Who was the first man to climb Pico and Helicon?"

"But weren't you rather younger in those days?" asked Louis gently.

"That," I said with great dignity, "is as good a reason as any for going."

We went to bed early that night, after driving the tractor to within half a mile of the promontory. Garnett was coming with me in the morning; he was a good climber, and had often been with me on such exploits before. Our driver was only too glad to be left in charge of the machine.

At first sight, those cliffs seemed completely unscalable, but to anyone with a good head for heights, climbing is easy on a world where all weights are only a sixth of their normal value. The real danger in lunar mountaineering lies in over-confidence; a six-hundred-foot drop on the Moon can kill you just as thoroughly as a hundred-foot fall on Earth.

We made our first halt on a wide ledge about four thousand feet above the plain. Climbing had not been very difficult, but my limbs were stiff with the unaccustomed effort, and I was glad of the rest. We could still see the tractor as a tiny metal insect far down at the foot of the cliff, and we reported our progress to the driver before starting on the next ascent.

Inside our suits it was comfortably cool, for the refrigeration units were fighting the fierce sun and carrying away the body-heat of our exertions. We seldom spoke to each other, except to pass climbing instructions and to discuss our best plan of ascent. I do not know what Garnett was thinking, probably that this was the craziest goose-chase he had ever embarked upon. I more than half agreed with him, but the joy of climbing, the knowledge that no man had ever gone this way before and the exhilaration of the steadily widening landscape gave me all the reward I needed.

I don't think I was particularly excited when I saw in front of us the wall of rock I had first inspected through the telescope from thirty miles away. It would level off about fifty feet above our heads, and there on the plateau would be the thing that had lured me over these barren wastes. It was, almost certainly, nothing more than a boulder splintered ages ago by a falling meteor, and with its cleavage planes still fresh and bright in this incorruptible, unchanging silence.

There were no hand-holds on the rock face, and we had to use a grapnel. My tired arms seemed to gain new strength as I swung the three-pronged metal anchor around my head and sent it sailing up towards the stars. The first time it broke loose and came falling slowly back when we pulled the rope. On the third attempt, the prongs gripped firmly and our combined weights could not shift it.

Garnett looked at me anxiously. I could tell that he wanted to go first, but I smiled back at him through the glass of my helmet and shook my head. Slowly, taking my time, I began the final ascent.

Even with my space-suit, I weighed only forty pounds here, so I pulled myself up hand over hand without bothering to use my feet. At the rim I paused and waved to my companion, then I scrambled over the edge and stood upright, staring ahead of me.

You must understand that until this very moment I had been almost completely convinced that there could be nothing strange or unusual for me to find here. Almost, but not quite; it was that haunting doubt that had driven me forward. Well, it was a doubt no longer, but the haunting had scarcely begun.

I was standing on a plateau perhaps a hundred feet across. It had once been smooth—too smooth to be natural—but falling meteors had pitted and scored its surface through immeasurable eons. It had been levelled to support a glittering, roughly pyramidal structure, twice as high as a man, that was set in the rock like a gigantic, many-faceted jewel.

Probably no emotion at all filled my mind in those first few seconds. Then I felt a great lifting of my heart, and a strange, inexpressible joy. For I loved the Moon, and now I knew that the creeping moss of Aristarchus and Eratosthenes was not the only life she had brought forth in her youth. The old, discredited dream of the first explorers was true. There had, after all, been a lunar civilisation—and I was the first to find it. That I had come perhaps a hundred million years too late did not distress me; it was enough to have come at all.

My mind was beginning to function normally, to analyse and to ask questions. Was this a building, a shrine—or something for which my language had no name? If a building, then why was it erected in so uniquely inaccessible a spot? I wondered if it might be a temple, and I could picture the adepts of some strange priesthood calling on their gods to preserve them as the life of the Moon ebbed with the dying oceans, and calling on their gods in vain.

I took a dozen steps forward to examine the thing more closely, but some sense of caution kept me from going too near. I knew a little of archaeology, and tried to guess the cultural level of the civilisation that must have smoothed this mountain and raised the glittering mirror surfaces that still dazzled my eyes.

The Egyptians could have done it, I thought, if their workmen had possessed whatever strange materials these far more ancient architects had used. Because of the thing's smallness, it did not occur to me that

I might be looking at the handiwork of a race more advanced than my own. The idea that the Moon had possessed intelligence at all was still almost too tremendous to grasp, and my pride would not let me take the final, humiliating plunge.

And then I noticed something that set the scalp crawling at the back of my neck—something so trivial and so innocent that many would never have noticed it at all. I have said that the plateau was scarred by meteors; it was also coated inches-deep with the cosmic dust that is always filtering down upon the surface of any world where there are no winds to disturb it. Yet the dust and the meteor scratches ended quite abruptly in a wide circle enclosing the little pyramid, as though an invisible wall was protecting it from the ravages of time and the slow but ceaseless bombardment from space.

There was someone shouting in my earphones, and I realised that Garnett had been calling me for some time. I walked unsteadily to the edge of the cliff and signalled him to join me, not trusting myself to speak. Then I went back towards that circle in the dust. I picked up a fragment of splintered rock and tossed it gently towards the shining enigma. If the pebble had vanished at that invisible barrier I should not have been surprised, but it seemed to hit a smooth, hemispherical surface and slide gently to the ground.

I knew then that I was looking at nothing that could be matched in the antiquity of my own race. This was not a building, but a machine, protecting itself with forces that had challenged Eternity. Those forces, whatever they might be, were still operating, and perhaps I had already come too close. I thought of all the radiations man had trapped and tamed in the past century. For all I knew, I might be as irrevocably doomed as if I had stepped into the deadly, silent aura of an unshielded atomic pile.

I remember turning then towards Garnett, who had joined me and was now standing motionless at my side. He seemed quite oblivious to me, so I did not disturb him but walked to the edge of the cliff in an effort to marshal my thoughts. There below me lay the Mare Crisium—Sea of Crises, indeed—strange and weird to most men, but reassuringly familiar to me. I lifted my eyes towards the crescent Earth, lying in her cradle of stars, and I wondered what her clouds had covered when these unknown builders had finished their work. Was it the steaming jungle of the Carboniferous, the bleak shore-line over which the first amphibians must crawl to conquer the land—or, earlier still, the long loneliness before the coming of life?

Do not ask me why I did not guess the truth sooner—the truth that seems so obvious now. In the first excitement of my discovery, I had assumed without question that this crystalline apparition had been built by some race belonging to the Moon's remote past, but suddenly, and with overwhelming force, the belief came to me that it was as alien to the Moon as I myself.

In twenty years we had found no trace of life but a few degenerate plants. No lunar civilisation, whatever its doom, could have left but a single token of its existence.

I looked at the shining pyramid again, and the more remote it seemed from anything that had to do with the Moon. And suddenly I felt myself shaking with a foolish, hysterical laughter, brought on by excitement and over-exertion: for I had imagined that the little pyramid was speaking to me and was saying: "Sorry, I'm a stranger here myself."

It has taken us twenty years to crack that invisible shield and to reach the machine inside those crystal walls. What we could not understand, we broke at last with the savage might of atomic power and now I have seen the fragments of the lovely, glittering thing I found up there on the mountain.

They are meaningless. The mechanisms—if indeed they are mechanisms—of the pyramid belong to a technology that lies far beyond our horizon, perhaps to the technology of paraphysical forces.

The mystery haunts us all the more now that the other planets have been reached and we know that only Earth has ever been the home of intelligent life in our Universe. Nor could any lost civilisation of our own world have built that machine, for the thickness of the meteoric dust on the plateau has enabled us to measure its age. It was set there upon its mountain before life had emerged from the seas of Earth.

When our world was half its present age, *something* from the stars swept through the Solar System, left this token of its passage, and went again upon its way. Until we destroyed it, that machine was still fulfilling the purpose of its builders; and as to that purpose, here is my guess.

Nearly a hundred thousand million stars are turning in the circle of the Milky Way, and long ago other races on the worlds of other suns must have scaled and passed the heights that we have reached. Think of such civilisations, far back in time against the fading afterglow of Creation, masters of a universe so young that life as yet had come only to a handful of worlds. Theirs would have been a loneliness we cannot imagine, the loneliness of gods looking out across infinity and finding none to share their thoughts.

They must have searched the star-clusters as we have searched the planets. Everywhere there would be worlds, but they would be empty or peopled with crawling, mindless things. Such was our Earth, the smoke of the great volcanoes still staining the skies, when that first ship of the peoples of the dawn came sliding in from the abyss beyond Pluto. It passed the frozen outer worlds, knowing that life could play no part in their destinies. It came to rest among the inner planets, warming themselves around the fire of the Sun and waiting for their stories to begin.

Those wanderers must have looked on Earth, circling safely in the narrow zone between fire and ice, and must have guessed that it was the favourite of the Sun's children. Here, in the distant future, would be intelligence; but there were countless stars before them still, and they might never come this way again.

So they left a sentinel, one of millions they have scattered throughout the Universe, watching over all worlds with the promise of life. It was a beacon that down the ages has been patiently signalling the fact that no one had discovered it.

Perhaps you understand now why that crystal pyramid was set upon the Moon instead of on the Earth. Its builders were not concerned with races still struggling up from savagery. They would be interested in our civilisation only if we proved our fitness to survive—by crossing space and so escaping from the Earth, our cradle. That is the challenge that all intelligent races must meet, sooner or later. It is a double challenge, for it depends in turn upon the conquest of atomic energy and the last choice between life and death.

Once we had passed that crisis, it was only a matter of time before we found the pyramid and forced it open. Now its signals have ceased, and those whose duty it is will be turning their minds upon Earth. Perhaps they wish to help our infant civilisation. But they must be very, very old, and the old are often insanely jealous of the young.

I can never look now at the Milky Way without wondering from which of those banked clouds of stars the emissaries are coming. If you will pardon so commonplace a simile, we have set off the fire-alarm and have nothing to do but to wait.

I do not think we will have to wait for long.

THE GAME

OF RAT AND DRAGON

Cordwainer Smith

THE TABLE

Pinlighting is a hell of a way to earn a living. Underhill was furious as he closed the door behind himself. It didn't make much sense to wear a uniform and look like a soldier if people didn't appreciate what you did.

He sat down in his chair, laid his head back in the headrest and pulled the helmet down over his forehead.

As he waited for the pin-set to warm up, he remembered the girl in the outer corridor. She had looked at it, then looked at him scornfully.

"Meow." That was all she had said. Yet it had cut him like a knife.

What did she think he was—a fool, a loafer, a uniformed nonentity? Didn't she know that for every half hour of pinlighting, he got a minimum of two months' recuperation in the hospital?

By now the set was warm. He felt the squares of space around him, sensed himself at the middle of an immense grid, a cubic grid, full of nothing. Out in that nothingness, he could sense the hollow aching horror of space itself and could feel the terrible anxiety which his mind encountered whenever it met the faintest trace of inert dust.

As he relaxed, the comforting solidity of the Sun, the clockwork of the familiar planets and the Moon rang in on him. Our own Solar System was as charming and as simple as an ancient cuckoo clock filled with familiar ticking and with reassuring noises. The odd little moons of Mars swung around their planet like frantic mice, yet their regularity was itself an assurance that all was well. Far above the plane of the ecliptic, he could feel half a ton of dust more or less drifting outside the lanes of human travel.

Here there was nothing to fight, nothing to challenge the mind, to tear the living soul out of a body with its roots dripping in effluvium as tangible as blood.

Nothing ever moved in on the Solar System. He could wear the pin-set forever and be nothing more than a sort of telepathic astronomer, a man who could feel the hot, warm protection of the Sun throbbing and burning against his living mind.

Woodley came in.

"Same old ticking world," said Underhill. "Nothing to report. No wonder they didn't develop the pin-set until they began to planoform. Down here with the hot Sun around us, it feels so good and so quiet. You can feel everything spinning and turning. It's nice and sharp and compact. It's sort of like sitting around home."

Woodley grunted. He was not much given to flights of fantasy.

Undeterred, Underhill went on, "It must have been pretty good to have been an Ancient Man. I wonder why they burned up their world with war. They didn't have to planoform. They didn't have to go out to earn their livings among the stars. They didn't have to dodge the Rats or play the Game. They couldn't have invented pinlighting because they didn't have any need of it, did they, Woodley?"

Woodley grunted, "Uh-huh." Woodley was twenty-six years old and due to retire in one more year. He already had a farm picked out. He had gotten through ten years of hard work pinlighting with the best of them. He had kept his sanity by not thinking very much about his job, meeting the strains of the task whenever he had to meet them and thinking nothing more about his duties until the next emergency arose.

Woodley never made a point of getting popular among the Partners. None of the Partners liked him very much. Some of them even resented him. He was suspected of thinking ugly thoughts of the Partners on occasion, but since none of the Partners ever thought a complaint in articulate form, the other pinlighters and the Chiefs of the Instrumentality left him alone.

Underhill was still full of the wonder of their job. Happily he babbled on, "What does happen to us when we planoform? Do you think it's sort of like dying? Did you ever see anybody who had his soul pulled out?"

"Pulling souls is just a way of talking about it," said Woodley. "After all these years, nobody knows whether we have souls or not."

"But I saw one once. I saw what Dogwood looked like when he came apart. There was something funny. It looked wet and sort of sticky as if it were bleeding and it went out of him—and you know what they did to Dogwood? They took him away, up in that part of the hospital where you and I never go—way up at the top part where the others are, where the others always have to go if they are alive after the Rats of the Up-and-Out have gotten them."

Woodley sat down and lit an ancient pipe. He was burning something called tobacco in it. It was a dirty sort of habit, but it made him look very dashing and adventurous.

"Look here, youngster. You don't have to worry about that stuff. Pinlighting is getting better all the time. The Partners are getting better. I've seen them pinlight two Rats forty-six million miles apart in one and a half milliseconds. As long as people had to try to work the pin-sets themselves, there was always the chance that with a minimum of four hundred milliseconds for the human mind to set a pinlight, we wouldn't light the Rats up fast enough to protect our planoforming ships. The Partners have changed all that. Once they get going, they're faster than Rats. And they always will be. I know it's not easy, letting a Partner share your mind—"

"It's not easy for them, either," said Underhill.

"Don't worry about them. They're not human. Let them take care of themselves. I've seen more pinlighters go crazy from monkeying around with Partners than I have ever seen caught by the Rats. How many do you actually know of them that got grabbed by Rats?"

Underhill looked down at his fingers, which shone green and purple in the vivid light thrown by the tuned-in pin-set, and counted ships. The thumb for the *Andromeda,* lost with crew and passengers, the index finger and the middle finger for *Release Ships* 43 and 56, found with their pin-sets burned out and every man, woman, and child on board dead or insane. The ring finger, the little finger, and the thumb of the other hand were the first three battleships to be lost to the Rats—lost as people realized that there was something out there *underneath space itself* which was alive, capricious and malevolent.

Planoforming was sort of funny. It felt like—

Like nothing much.

Like the twinge of a mild electric shock.

Like the ache of a sore tooth bitten on for the first time.

Like a slightly painful flash of light against the eyes.

Yet in that time, a forty-thousand-ton ship lifting free above Earth disappeared somehow or other into two dimensions and appeared half a light-year or fifty light-years off.

At one moment, he would be sitting in the Fighting Room, the pin-set ready and the familiar Solar System ticking around inside his head. For a second or a year (he could never tell how long it really was, subjectively), the funny little flash went through him and then he was loose in the Up-and-Out, the terrible open spaces between the stars, where the stars themselves felt like pimples on his telepathic mind and the planets were too far away to be sensed or read.

Somewhere in this outer space, a gruesome death awaited, death and horror of a kind which Man had never encountered until he reached out for interstellar space itself. Apparently the light of the suns kept the Dragons away.

Dragons. That was what people called them. To ordinary people, there was nothing, nothing except the shiver of planoforming and the hammer blow of sudden death or the dark spastic note of lunacy descending into their minds.

But to the telepaths, they were Dragons.

In the fraction of a second between the telepaths' awareness of a hostile something out in the black hollow nothingness of space and the impact of a ferocious, ruinous psychic blow against all living things within the ship, the telepaths had sensed entities something like the Dragons of ancient human lore, beasts more clever than beasts, demons more tangible than demons, hungry vortices of aliveness and hate compounded by unknown means out of the thin tenuous matter between the stars.

It took a surviving ship to bring back the news—a ship in which, by sheer chance, a telepath had a light-beam ready, turning it out at the innocent dust so that, within the panorama of his mind, the Dragon dissolved into nothing at all and the other passengers, themselves non-telepathic, went about their way not realizing that their own immediate deaths had been averted.

From then on, it was easy—almost.

Planoforming ships always carried telepaths. Telepaths had their sensitiveness enlarged to an immense range by the pin-sets, which were telepathic amplifiers adapted to the mammal mind. The pin-sets in turn were electronically geared into small dirigible lightbombs. Light did it.

Light broke up the Dragons, allowed the ships to reform three-dimensionally, skip, skip, skip, as they moved from star to star.

The odds suddenly moved down from a hundred to one against mankind to sixty to forty in mankind's favor.

This was not enough. The telepaths were trained to become ultra-sensitive, trained to become aware of the Dragons in less than a millisecond.

But it was found that the Dragons could move a million miles in just under two milliseconds and that this was not enough for the human mind to activate the light-beams.

Attempts had been made to sheathe the ships in light at all times. This defense wore out.

As mankind learned about the Dragons, so, too, apparently, the Dragons learned about mankind. Somehow they flattened their own bulk and came in on extremely flat trajectories very quickly.

Intense light was needed, light of sunlike intensity. This could be provided only by light-bombs. Pinlighting came into existence.

Pinlighting consisted of the detonation of ultra-vivid miniature photonuclear bombs, which converted a few ounces of a magnesium isotope into pure visible radiance.

The odds kept coming down in mankind's favor, yet ships were being lost.

It became so bad that people didn't even want to find the ships because the rescuers knew what they would see. It was sad to bring back to Earth three hundred bodies ready for burial and two hundred or three hundred lunatics, damaged beyond repair, to be wakened, and fed, and cleaned, and put to sleep, wakened and fed again until their lives were ended.

Telepaths tried to reach into the minds of the psychotics who had been damaged by the Dragons, but they found nothing there beyond vivid spouting columns of fiery terror bursting from the primordial id itself, the volcanic source of life.

Then came the Partners.

Men and Partner could do together what Man could not do alone. Men had the intellect. Partners had the speed.

The Partners rode their tiny craft, no larger than footballs, outside the spaceships. They planoformed with the ships. They rode beside them in their six-pound craft ready to attack.

The tiny ships of the Partners were swift. Each carried a dozen pinlights, bombs no bigger than thimbles.

The pinlighters threw the Partners—quite literally threw—by means of mind-to-firing relays direct at the Dragons.

What seemed to be Dragons to the human mind appeared in the form of gigantic Rats in the minds of the Partners.

Out in the pitiless nothingness of space, the Partners' minds responded to an instinct as old as life. The Partners attacked, striking with a speed faster than Man's, going from attack to attack until the Rats or themselves were destroyed. Almost all the time, it was the Partners who won.

With the safety of the interstellar skip, skip, skip of the ships, commerce increased immensely, the population of all the colonies went up, and the demand for trained Partners increased.

Underhill and Woodley were a part of the third generation of pinlighters and yet, to them, it seemed as though their craft had endured forever.

Gearing space into minds by means of the pin-set, adding the Partners to those minds, keying up the mind for the tension of a fight on which all depended—this was more than human synapses could stand for long. Underhill needed his two months' rest after half an hour of fighting. Woodley needed his retirement after ten years of service. They were young. They were good. But they had limitations.

So much depended on the choice of Partners, so much on the sheer luck of who drew whom.

THE SHUFFLE

Father Moontree and the little girl named West entered the room. They were the other two pinlighters. The human complement of the Fighting Room was now complete.

Father Moontree was a red-faced man of forty-five who had lived the peaceful life of a farmer until he reached his fortieth year. Only then, belatedly, did the authorities find he was telepathic and agree to let him late in life enter upon the career of pinlighter. He did well at it, but he was fantastically old for this kind of business.

Father Moontree looked at the glum Woodley and the musing Underhill. "How're the youngsters today? Ready for a good fight?"

"Father always wants a fight," giggled the little girl named West. She was such a little girl. Her giggle was high and childish. She looked like the last person in the world one would expect to find in the rough, sharp dueling of pinlighting.

Underhill had been amused one time when he found one of the most sluggish of the Partners coming away happy from contact with the mind of the girl named West.

Usually the Partners didn't care much about the human minds with which they were paired for the journey. The Partners seemed to take the attitude that human minds were complex and fouled up beyond belief, anyhow. No Partner ever questioned the superiority of the human mind, though very few of the Partners were much impressed by that superiority.

The Partners liked people. They were willing to fight with them. They were even willing to die for them. But when a Partner liked an individual the way, for example, that Captain Wow or the Lady May liked Underhill, the liking had nothing to do with intellect. It was a matter of temperament, of feel.

Underhill knew perfectly well that Captain Wow regarded his, Underhill's, brains as silly. What Captain Wow liked was Underhill's friendly emotional structure, the cheerfulness and glint of wicked amusement that shot through Underhill's unconscious thought patterns, and the gaiety with which Underhill faced danger. The words, the history books, the ideas, the science—Underhill could sense all that in his own mind, reflected back from Captain Wow's mind, as so much rubbish.

Miss West looked at Underhill. "I bet you've put stickum on the stones."

"I did not!"

Underhill felt his ears grow red with embarrassment. During his novitiate, he had tried to cheat in the lottery because he got particularly fond of a special Partner, a lovely young mother named Murr. It was so much easier to operate with Murr and she was so affectionate toward him that he forgot pinlighting was hard work and that he was not instructed to have a good time with his Partner. They were both designed and prepared to go into deadly battle together.

One cheating had been enough. They had found him out and he had been laughed at for years.

Father Moontree picked up the imitation-leather cup and shook the stone dice which assigned them their Partners for the trip. By senior rights, he took first draw.

He grimaced. He had drawn a greedy old character, a tough old male whose mind was full of slobbering thoughts of food, veritable oceans full of half-spoiled fish. Father Moontree had once said that he burped cod-liver oil for weeks after drawing that particular glutton, so strongly had the telepathic image of fish impressed itself upon his mind. Yet the glutton was a glutton for danger as well as for fish. He had killed sixty-three Dragons, more than any other Partner in the service, and was quite literally worth his weight in gold.

The little girl West came next. She drew Captain Wow. When she saw who it was, she smiled.

"I *like* him," she said. "He's such fun to fight with. He feels so nice and cuddly in my mind."

"Cuddly, hell," said Woodley. "I've been in his mind, too. It's the most leering mind in this ship, bar none."

"Nasty man," said the little girl. She said it declaratively, without reproach.

Underhill, looking at her, shivered.

He didn't see how she could take Captain Wow so calmly. Captain Wow's mind *did* leer. When Captain Wow got excited in the middle of a battle, confused images of Dragons, deadly Rats, luscious beds, the smell of fish, and the shock of space all scrambled together in his mind as he and Captain Wow, their consciousness linked together through the pin-set, became a fantastic composite of human being and Persian cat.

That's the trouble with working with cats, thought Underhill. It's a pity that nothing else anywhere will serve as Partner. Cats were all right once you got in touch with them telepathically. They were smart enough to meet the needs of the fight, but their motives and desires were certainly different from those of humans.

They were companionable enough as long as you thought tangible images at them, but their minds just closed up and went to sleep when you recited Shakespeare or Colegrove, or if you tried to tell them what space was.

It was sort of funny realizing that the Partners who were so grim and mature out here in space were the same cute little animals that people had used as pets for thousands of years back on Earth. He had embarrassed himself more than once while on the ground saluting perfectly ordinary non-telepathic cats because he had forgotten for the moment that they were not Partners.

He picked up the cup and shook out his stone dice.

He was lucky—he drew the Lady May.

The Lady May was the most thoughtful Partner he had ever met. In her, the finely bred pedigree mind of a Persian cat had reached one of its highest peaks of development. She was more complex than any human woman, but the complexity was all one of emotions, memory, hope and discriminated experience—experience sorted through without benefit of words.

When he had first come into contact with her mind, he was astonished at its clarity. With her he remembered her kittenhood. He remembered every mating experience she had ever had. He saw in a half-recognizable gallery all the other pinlighters with whom she had been paired for the fight. And he saw himself radiant, cheerful and desirable.

He even thought he caught the edge of a longing—

A very flattering and yearning thought: *What a pity he is not a cat.*

Woodley picked up the last stone. He drew what he deserved—a sullen, scarred old tomcat with none of the verve of Captain Wow. Woodley's Partner was the most animal of all the cats on the ship, a low, brutish type with a dull mind. Even telepathy had not refined his character. His ears were half chewed off from the first fights in which he had engaged.

He was a serviceable fighter, nothing more.

Woodley grunted.

Underhill glanced at him oddly. Didn't Woodley ever do anything but grunt?

Father Moontree looked at the other three. "You might as well get your Partners now. I'll let the Scanner know we're ready to go into the Up-and-Out."

THE DEAL

Underhill spun the combination lock on the Lady May's cage. He woke her gently and took her into his arms. She humped her back luxuriously, stretched her claws, started to purr, thought better of it, and licked him on the wrist instead. He did not have the pin-set on, so their minds were closed to each other, but in the angle of her mustache and in the movement of her ears, he caught some sense of gratification she experienced in finding him as her Partner.

He talked to her in human speech, even though speech meant nothing to a cat when the pin-set was not on.

"It's a damn shame, sending a sweet little thing like you whirling around in the coldness of nothing to hunt for Rats that are bigger and deadlier than all of us put together. You didn't ask for this kind of fight, did you?"

For answer, she licked his hand, purred, tickled his cheek with her long fluffy tail, turned around and faced him, golden eyes shining.

For a moment, they stared at each other, man squatting, cat standing erect on her hind legs, front claws digging into his knee. Human eyes and cat eyes looked across an immensity which no words could meet, but which affection spanned in a single glance.

"Time to get in," he said.

She walked docilely into her spheroid carrier. She climbed in. He saw to it that her miniature pin-set rested firmly and comfortably against the base of her brain. He made sure that her claws were padded so that she could not tear herself in the excitement of battle.

Softly he said to her, "Ready?"

For answer, she preened her back as much as her harness would permit and purred softly within the confines of the frame that held her.

He slapped down the lid and watched the sealant ooze around the seam. For a few hours, she was welded into her projectile until a workman with a short cutting arc would remove her after she had done her duty.

He picked up the entire projectile and slipped it into the ejection tube. He closed the door of the tube, spun the lock, seated himself in his chair, and put his own pin-set on.

Once again he flung the switch.

He sat in a small room, *small, small, warm, warm,* the bodies of the other three people moving close around him, the tangible lights in the ceiling bright and heavy against his closed eyelids.

As the pin-set warmed, the room fell away. The other people ceased to be people and became small glowing heaps of fire, embers, dark red fire, with the consciousness of life burning like old red coals in a country fireplace.

As the pin-set warmed a little more, he felt Earth just below him, felt the ship slipping away, felt the turning Moon as it swung on the far side of the world, felt the planets and the hot, clear goodness of the Sun which kept the Dragons so far from mankind's native ground.

Finally, he reached complete awareness.

He was telepathically alive to a range of millions of miles. He felt the dust which he had noticed earlier high above the ecliptic. With a thrill of warmth and tenderness, he felt the consciousness of the Lady May pouring over into his own. Her consciousness was as gentle and clear and yet sharp to the taste of his mind as if it were scented oil. It felt relaxing and reassuring. He could sense her welcome of him. It was scarcely a thought, just a raw emotion of greeting.

At last they were one again.

In a tiny remote corner of his mind, as tiny as the smallest toy he had ever seen in his childhood, he was still aware of the room and the ship, and of Father Moontree picking up a telephone and speaking to a Scanner captain in charge of the ship.

His telepathic mind caught the idea long before his ears could frame the words. The actual sound followed the idea the way that thunder on an ocean beach follows the lightning inward from far out over the seas.

"The Fighting Room is ready. Clear to planoform, sir."

THE PLAY

Underhill was always a little exasperated the way that Lady May experienced things before he did.

He was braced for the quick vinegar thrill of planoforming, but he caught her report of it before his own nerves could register what happened.

Earth had fallen so far away that he groped for several milliseconds before he found the Sun in the upper rear right-hand corner of his telepathic mind.

That was a good jump, he thought. This way we'll get there in four or five skips.

A few hundred miles outside the ship, the Lady May thought back at him, "O warm, O generous, O gigantic man! O brave, O friendly, O tender and huge Partner! O wonderful with you, with you so good, good, good, warm, warm, now to fight, now to go, good with you. . . ."

He knew that she was not thinking words, that his mind took the clear amiable babble of her cat intellect and translated it into images which his own thinking could record and understand.

Neither one of them was absorbed in the game of mutual greetings. He reached out far beyond her range of perception to see if there was anything near the ship. It was funny how it was possible to do two things at once. He could scan space with his pin-set mind and yet at the same time catch a vagrant thought of hers, a lovely, affectionate thought about a son who had had a golden face and a chest covered with soft, incredibly downy white fur.

While he was still searching, he caught the warning from her.

We jump again!

And so they had. The ship had moved to a second planoform. The stars were different. The Sun was immeasurably far behind. Even the nearest stars were barely in contact. This was good Dragon country, the open, nasty, hollow kind of space. He reached farther, faster, sensing and looking for danger, ready to fling the Lady May at danger wherever he found it.

Terror blazed up in his mind, so sharp, so clear, that it came through as a physical wrench.

The little girl named West had found something—something immense, long, black, sharp, greedy, horrific. She flung Captain Wow at it.

Underhill tried to keep his own mind clear. "Watch out!" he shouted telepathically at the others, trying to move the Lady May around.

At one corner of the battle, he felt the lustful rage of Captain Wow as the big Persian tomcat detonated lights while he approached the streak of dust which threatened the ship and the people within.

The lights scored near-misses.

The dust flattened itself, changing from the shape of a sting-ray into the shape of a spear.

Not three milliseconds had elapsed.

Father Moontree was talking human words and was saying in a voice that moved like cold molasses out of a heavy jar, "C-A-P-T-A-I-N." Underhill knew that the sentence was going to be "Captain, move fast!"

The battle would be fought and finished before Father Moontree got through talking.

Now, fractions of a millisecond later, the Lady May was directly in line.

Here was where the skill and speed of the Partners came in. She could react faster than he. She could see the threat as an immense Rat coming direct at her.

She could fire the light-bombs with a discrimination which he might miss.

He was connected with her mind, but he could not follow it.

His consciousness absorbed the tearing wound inflicted by the alien enemy. It was like no wound on Earth—raw, crazy pain which started like a burn at his navel. He began to writhe in his chair.

Actually he had not yet had time to move a muscle when the Lady May struck back at their enemy.

Five evenly spaced photonuclear bombs blazed out across a hundred thousand miles.

The pain in his mind and body vanished.

He felt a moment of fierce, terrible, feral elation running through the mind of the Lady May as she finished her kill. It was always disappointing to the cats to find out that their enemies whom they sensed as gigantic space Rats disappeared at the moment of destruction.

Then he felt her hurt, the pain and the fear that swept over both of them as the battle, quicker than the movement of an eyelid, had come and gone. In the same instant, there came the sharp and acid twinge of planoform.

Once more the ship went skip.

He could hear Woodley thinking at him, "You don't have to bother much. This old son of a gun and I will take over for a while."

Twice again the twinge, the skip.

He had no idea where he was until the lights of the Caledonia space board shone below.

With a weariness that lay almost beyond the limits of thought, he threw his mind back into rapport with the pin-set, fixing the Lady May's projectile gently and neatly in its launching tube.

She was half dead with fatigue, but he could feel the beat of her heart, could listen to her panting, and he grasped the grateful edge of a thanks reaching from her mind to his.

THE SCORE

They put him in the hospital at Caledonia.

The doctor was friendly but firm. "You actually got touched by that Dragon. That's as close a shave as I've ever seen. It's all so quick that it'll be a long time before we know what happened scientifically, but I suppose you'd be ready for the insane asylum now if the contact had lasted several tenths of a millisecond longer. What kind of a cat did you have out in front of you?"

Underhill felt the words coming out of him slowly. Words were such a lot of trouble compared with the speed and the joy of thinking, fast and sharp and clear, mind to mind! But words were all that could reach ordinary people like this doctor.

His mouth moved heavily as he articulated words, "Don't call our Partners cats. The right thing to call them is Partners. They fight for us in a team. You ought to know we call them Partners, not cats. How is mine?"

"I don't know," said the doctor contritely. "We'll find out for you. Meanwhile, old man, you take it easy. There's nothing but rest that can help you. Can you make yourself sleep, or would you like us to give you some kind of sedative?"

"I can sleep," said Underhill. "I just want to know about the Lady May."

The nurse joined in. She was a little antagonistic. "Don't you want to know about the other people?"

"They're okay," said Underhill. "I knew that before I came in here."

He stretched his arms and sighed and grinned at them. He could see they were relaxing and were beginning to treat him as a person instead of a patient.

"I'm all right," he said. "Just let me know when I can go see my Partner."

A new thought struck him. He looked wildly at the doctor. "They didn't send her off with the ship, did they?"

"I'll find out right away," said the doctor. He gave Underhill a reassuring squeeze of the shoulder and left the room.

The nurse took a napkin off a goblet of chilled fruit juice.

Underhill tried to smile at her. There seemed to be something wrong with the girl. He wished she would go away. First she had started to be friendly and now she was distant again. It's a nuisance being telepathic, he thought. You keep trying to reach even when you are not making contact.

Suddenly she swung around on them.

"You pinlighters! You and your damn cats!"

Just as she stamped out, he burst into her mind. He saw himself a radiant hero, clad in his smooth suede uniform, the pin-set crown shining like ancient royal jewels around his head. He saw his own face, handsome and masculine, shining out of her mind. He saw himself very far away and he saw himself as she hated him.

She hated him in the secrecy of her own mind. She hated him because he was—she thought—proud, and strange, and rich, better and more beautiful than people like her.

He cut off the sight of her mind and, as he buried his face in the pillow, he caught an image of the Lady May.

"She *is* a cat," he thought. "That's *all* she is—a *cat!*"

But that was not how his mind saw her—quick beyond all dreams of speed, sharp, clever, unbelievably graceful, beautiful, wordless and undemanding.

Where would he ever find a woman who could compare with her?

THE DECISION MAKERS

Joseph Green

I

The Decision Maker swam leisurely just beneath the surface, listening to the vast pulsebeat that was the life of his people. It had been some time since he had eaten last and his eyes, obedient to that primal command, were alert for prey; but hunting did not interfere with the more mental functions which occupied the group part of his mind.

He angled to the surface for air, glancing briefly at the humans' Gathering-Place while his head was above water. The round gray buildings squatted like overlarge toadstools on the rock shore a hundred body-lengths away, dimly seen through the snow that a driving wind had brought down off the mountains.

As he dipped beneath the surface he caught a glimpse of something dark and sleek to his left and turned that way. The fish saw him and tried, too late, to flee. He bit off its head while still in motion, swallowed it, then seized the body in his webbed fingers and disposed of it in two bites.

The fish-which-flies comes, Decision Maker, came a strong projection from the south. It was a composite voice made by many individuals, and accompanying it was a clear image of a small winged ship.

He swam to the surface and turned his eyes to the southern sky. The ship itself was too small to be visible, but he located it by the brightness of its flaring retrorockets.

Then the fires winked out as it sank below the horizon.

He called for strength from all people in his immediate area, received it, and projected. He found the ship immediately, now moving swiftly toward him. And yes, the humans' Decision Maker was inside.

"I've put us in a polar orbit, Conscience Odegaard," said the shuttle pilot to his only passenger. "Ground Control says the blow-storm should clear up by the time we make a round. I'll de-polarize the floor viewplate and let you look Sister over direct while we wait."

He touched a control and the floor between their seats grew milky, then transparent. The harsh, xanthic light of Capella G flooded in. Below them, stretching endlessly to the horizons, was mile after mile of deep blue water.

The pilot made a few final adjustments on the attitude gyros, then relaxed and said, "Atlantis is on the other side, and we'll pass over the station in a minute."

Allan Odegaard stared with weary disinterest at the watery landscape. They were moving toward the planet's northern pole, and the edge of the north polar continent soon came in sight. He saw a narrow ledge of ice hugging a low and rocky shore.

"The station's under those," said the pilot, pointing. Allan gazed where the finger indicated, but saw only the white-tinged clouds of the blowstorm. As they moved inland the clouds fell behind, and he saw great mountains rearing craggy heads in an immense annular formation, the dominant feature of the continent. A thin sheet of ice covered most of the lower land between the peaks, sparkling and glittering in the sunlight. Like a rather flat diamond in a Tiffany setting, Allan thought. Then they were over the sea once more.

"There's the first peaks of Atlantis," said the pilot, pointing again, and Allan saw three small islands floating like green jewels on the blue water, the last two curving sharply away to the left. Then the view was monotonous until they reached the southern polar continent, where the mountains seemed taller and the icecap even thinner.

Allan sat back and relaxed, knowing he had seen the planet's entire land area. Sister, or Capella G Eight as it was more properly known, was visually less interesting than most, and nowadays even the best bored him. He had been too long away from home. After this assignment he was going to *insist* on returning to Earth, if only for a vacation. A Practical Philosopher could not afford to lose contact with the people he represented.

The pilot was good, the touchdown scarcely jarring the little shuttle. A big, smiling man in cold weather clothes met Allan at the ship's base and helped him loosen his helmet. The fresh air was so cold he almost strangled on his first breath.

"I'm Station Manager Zip Murdock, Conscience Odegaard," said the big man in a hearty voice. "And this is Phyllis Roen, our biologist."

The tiny woman by the big man's side said, "I'm afraid I'm responsible for getting you here, Conscience Odegaard. Zip and the others don't feel a question even exists."

Murdock glanced up at the cargo hatch, where the pilot was already rigging the small crane. "They don't need us for the unloading. Let's get inside and get you settled, and then Phyllis can bring you up to date on our problem—if we have one."

The sun had moved behind a high cirque in the west, and deep shadows were creeping across the field. Allan started with them toward the foamfab buildings, which huddled at the base of a rocky ridge two hundred yards inland. From the ridge to the sea the ground had been cleared of loose rock, the debris forming two long piles of heaped boulders. Half of the cleared area nearest the beach was used for a landing field.

They had taken only a few steps when there was a loud yell of warning behind them. Allan turned, to see that the scene had suddenly and dramatically changed. From behind the rock walls near the water, and from the sea itself, fist-sized rocks were appearing and flying toward the Earthmen. The unloading crew was scrambling for shelter, yelling wildly and drawing their laser guns.

"It's the seals!" said Phyllis, and there was fear in her voice. Murdock had already drawn a laser pistol, its dark red jewel glinting in the fading light. There were no attackers in sight, just the rocks appearing from nowhere and arcing toward them. After a moment, Murdock, in apparent frustration, fired toward a cluster of rocks near at hand. The hit boulder sparkled briefly, absorbing the heat but not all the light. Other beams began to flash as the unloading crew got into action. The little landing area became a weird tangle of multicolored lights, shifting shadows and coruscating rocks. The net effect was to provide a flickering but adequate illumination.

Allan saw his first seal clearly as it left the shelter of the rocks and ran for the water, dragging a wounded comrade. They were tiny creatures, only half his height, and they moved with an odd, stiff-jointed swing from one leg to the other that looked awkward but was marvelously fast. Murdock saw them also and lifted his gun, but the beam hissed through the air where they had been as they dove together into the sea. And abruptly the creatures were gone. It was quiet again and the darkness was creeping swiftly over the narrow beach.

"The little devils are getting bolder," said Murdock, holstering his gun. "That's the first daylight attack on dry land."

Allan stooped and picked up one of the stones which had just been flung at them. It was apparently obsidian, and had been hand-chipped until it had several sharp edges, each capable of penetrating a spacesuit. Primitive—but deadly.

"How did they propel them so far?" he asked Phyllis, but before she could answer an excited voice called, "Miss Roen! Miss Roen, I've found a dead one in the rocks! Do you want the body?"

Allan saw the small woman visibly hesitate before she called back, "Yes, please. Take it into the lab."

"I'd better stay here a moment and assess the damage," said Murdock, moving toward a man who was lying on the ground holding a bloody arm. "If you'll go with Phyllis, Conscience Odegaard . . ."

As they approached the buildings Allan saw two sentries standing on rocky eminences, where they could observe the entire area. Large floodlights brightly illuminated the ground around the buildings. Evidently these civilians had learned to take some rather military precautions on Capella G Eight.

There was no airlock, but the station personnel had built an anteroom where both spacesuits and cold weather gear were hung. Allan shed his suit with thanksgiving, and turned to find Phyllis Roen already out of her heavy clothes and waiting for him.

The tiny woman was obviously Eurasian, with very black hair streaked with gray and features which were delicate without being pretty. He estimated her age at around thirty-five. She still looked very good to him, and this was another indication that he had been too long away from Earth.

"Do you like what you see, Conscience Odegaard?" Phyllis asked, and though she was smiling there was an edge in her voice. He realized he had been staring.

"I'm sorry," he said quickly. "And please, call me Allan." He paused, not wanting to explain that "Conscience" was a popular term rather than an actual title, and he had grown very tired of hearing it. A doctorate in philosophy was the highest academic achievement on his record, but to qualify as a Practical Philosopher master's degrees were required in political science, alien psychology, sociology and biology. The public, when it learned of the unique responsibilities of the Practical Philosophers, had swiftly christened them the "Consciences of Mankind," and the name had stuck.

Mankind needed a conscience, these days. His swiftly expanding exploration and colonization of the galaxy was bringing him into contact with dozens of completely new lifeforms, and seemingly limitless variations of those already familiar. Time and again the question had arisen of whether alien creatures on habitable worlds were animals or intelligent beings, and some wrong decisions had been made before the P.P. corps had been established. The exhaustive academic routine deterred all but the most hardy, and there were less than a dozen "Consciences" to date, but they had brought the problem somewhat under control. At least romantic Space Service captains were no longer declaring a planet unfit for colonization because its overlarge ants had unusually well-developed instinctual patterns.

This time her smile was more sincere. "All right, Allan, and the same. Now if you'll come with me I'll take you on the penny tour, and after dinner we'll have a look at the dead seal."

II

The Decision Maker's body had relaxed into the state of lazy somnolence which was the nearest his kind approached sleep, but his group mind was still active. As he moved automatically toward the dark surface for air he turned to the matter of his opposite among the humans, and finally concluded that there were too many unknowns at present. He was unable to perform his function.

He could, and did, reach one conclusion, and communicated it to those individuals whose added consciousness within his mind enabled him to be a Decision Maker. It was that the people would make no further attacks at present. The next move would be left to the humans.

At dinner Allan met about half the station's complement of forty scientists, and discovered there was a general air of cheerful optimism prevalent. On some tiny stations on bitterly hostile worlds he had seen isolation and confinement sour personal relations until the whole crew was ready to commit murder. He was surprised, as Phyllis kept rattling off names and professions, to find meteorologists, geologists and glacialists dominating the group. Usually it was chemists, biologists, and the new "Environmental Adjusters."

Zip Murdock did not appear for dinner. Apparently he and the unloading crew were still busy outside.

The departing thunder of the shuttle's rockets penetrated the aerated walls as Phyllis led Allan into the lab. The seal was lying on a table in the cold room, an area ventilated to outside atmosphere. Phyllis produced light but warm clothing for them and they went inside.

Allan looked down at the prone form on the table, the sleek skin marred by a deep-burned hole in the neck. It was the head that gave the first strong impression of seal. The face had a black, square-cut nose, long whiskers, a rounded ridge of forehead rising abruptly above the muzzle; but the body ruined the illusion. The lower abdomen split into two short legs, each ending in a large flat pad. The upper members, though equally short, had a jointed section, and the ends terminated in long ridged fingers of cartilage, with a thin membrane between.

Allan ran trained fingers over the musculature of a leg. The large muscles on the front and back were equal in size, a wonderful arrangement for swimming but somewhat awkward for walking. Yet he had seen two of them actually running when they had retreated after that brief attack on the landing field.

He asked Phyllis how they did it. She grinned, an impish grimace on her small face. "They fool you, Allan. A bit more adaptable than they look. Watch."

She lifted one pad clear of the table, held the leg with her other hand and slowly forced the pad to move. It revolved until it was perpendicular to the body, and he saw that it was set in a very flexible bone socket. She dropped the leg, rolled the creature on its side and twisted the other pad in the opposite direction. It also moved to the perpendicular.

"One pad before, one behind. A very stable arrangement," said Phyllis. "It gets around with relative ease on land, even though it looks awkward to us, and you saw how they threw stones with those arms."

"Not with the arms. Look what they found with this fellow." Allan stepped to another bench, picked up a long flat strip of hide she had not noticed, and folded the ends together. A wide section in the center formed a pouch.

"A sling! Of all weapons." There was a touch of awe in Phyllis' voice. "Well, *this* should convince Zip, if he still needs convincing!"

"That the seals are intelligent? I doubt it. Animals have used tools before."

"Yes, but—they didn't have these earlier, you see. They live an almost entirely aquatic existence, and the only artifacts we've seen have been sharpened basalt spears. This is a dry land weapon. They just *invented* it, to use in fighting us."

"That's interesting, but still no proof. This continent you're trying to raise has been dry land several times, I understand. Quite possibly these creatures have used the sling in the past and retained an instinct of how to build it."

"A far more sensible explanation than intelligence," said a new voice.

Allan turned, to see Murdock entering the cold room from outside. The big man stamped some clinging snow off his feet and walked to the table. "H-m-m-m, a nice fat one. Let's have him for dinner tomorrow, Cissy."

"Zip! Please, I have a hard enough time living with the memory that we *did* eat a few!"

"And they were a little fishy tasting, but not bad," said Murdock cheerfully. "Beats the concentrates every time. Look, I've got to change and go eat. Don't let this dizzy female fill your head full of nonsense, Conscience Odegaard."

"I do not form premature conclusions," said Allan carefully. Murdock, and most of the scientists here, were university employees, the result of a steadily increasing trend for large universities to contract colonization evaluations. They had almost edged out the competing private companies, and the government had long ago settled for supervision of the contracts. These people had a strong vested interest in seeing that his decision went against the seals. When intelligence was established it was standard policy to abandon the planet to its native owners.

"Fine. Cissy is unabashedly prejudiced on the question. I'll see you later in the evening, then."

As the big man closed the door behind him Allan turned to the woman and asked, "Even in an unmilitary organization such as this, isn't that manner of speaking to you a little familiar?"

She gave him a cool glance. "Perhaps, but that's because he feels familiar. We've entered into a trial marriage contract, and plan on full matrimony when we get back to Earth."

"Oh, I see. That's odd; I wouldn't have thought you compatible types."

She shrugged. "Who says we are? Perhaps it's just sex drive and propinquity on both sides. But in any case we're living together, and were perfectly happy until we started quarreling about the seals. I had to go over his head to get you in here, and he's going to be a long time forgiving me for that."

Allan found himself wishing heartily he had not ventured into such personal ground. It was presumptuous of him, and her answer had brought back his own deep-seated loneliness, twisting the knife of bitterness again. Kay had quickly divorced him when he had announced he was going into space; there would be no "widow's wait" for her. She had married again before he finished his final studies and left Earth, and when he visited his children his little daughter was already calling another man father.

The life of a regular spaceman was bad enough, but at least he returned to Earth an average of once every two years. Allan had not been home in eight. Planet after planet raised the unique problem which called for a P.P.'s special authority, and the swiftly spreading network of exploration brought in new ones faster than decisions could be made. Unless he rebelled he might spend the rest of his days hopping from world to world, with never a life of his own.

Allan beat a hasty retreat. "I'd like to see your notes, if you've already performed a dissection," he said, turning toward the door. "Tomorrow I'll run one on this chap myself."

"Of course," said Phyllis, reverting to business as easily as he. "I ran several, and I've never seen a body better adapted for both swimming and walking. But the brain is—very odd. You'll have to see it for yourself."

She escorted him to his cubicle, then left with word that she would see him later in the lounge. He found his luggage stacked on the bunk, and an hour later, showered, depilated and dressed in clean clothes, he headed for the lounge. Most of the station's off-duty personnel were there, including Murdock.

"Come sit by me, Allan," the big man called. "I'll split my shaker with you."

Murdock was drinking *maquella,* a mildly intoxicating beverage from Centaurus Four that had no after-effects. Allan accepted a glass and sat down.

"What do you think of our operation so far?" asked Murdock pleasantly.

"I hardly know enough about it to think at all. Can you give me a general run-down on your plans? I was amazed to find Phyllis the only biologist here, and this is the first time I've seen an evaluation team with a high percentage of glacialists."

"He can talk about it all night," said Phyllis, who was sitting on Murdock's other side. "But the basic fact is that Sister is so nearly Earth-type that chemists and biologists aren't really needed. The only genuine problem is raising Atlantis, and the general opinion is that this can be accomplished by a slight change in the weather."

"Yes, all it requires is a new ice age," said Murdock with a chuckle. "But to give you some background—the median temperature on Sister is somewhat higher than humans prefer, and the open land area almost nonexistent. Offhand it looks very unpromising. But this planet has a very fortunate peculiarity. All three major land masses, the two poles and Atlantis, have the same distinguishing feature, a great circle of volcanic mountains surrounding a lower inland area. Atlantis is the largest and lowest of the three, and almost entirely under water. We propose, not to raise the continent, but to lower the ocean level.

"The means of accomplishing this is relatively simple. Sister, despite the high concentration of water vapor in the air, has a low precipitation rate. The atmosphere is exceptionally clean, due to the tiny exposed land surface and low volcanic activity, and there is very little dust to serve as sublimation nuclei for raindrops. Precip is almost entirely dependent on giant condensation nuclei, and that too is small because the oceans have a low salinity rate and there is very little sodium chloride in the air. Briefly, we propose to stimulate the precip rate by blowing up the smallest of the four moons, in such a fashion that most of the material turns to dust. We will slow it below orbital speed with the explosions, and create a rain of dust into the upper atmosphere which will continue for many years. Precip will rise to several thousand percent of normal. Over both polar regions this will come down as snow, and the rapid accumulation in the two enclosed continents will swell the existing ice-fields until a sizable percentage of the planet's water is locked up in ice. The world ocean level will drop, we estimate slightly over three-hundred feet, and that will bring all the ring of mountains and about half the interior of Atlantis above the surface. In addition, the temperature will drop to bearable limits. And then you can send in the colonists."

"It sounds almost too simple," said Allan wonderingly.

"That's an explanation in very broad terms. There are a few relevant details to be worked out, such as the large sunmirrors we'll have to post above each pole, to artificially stimulate the firm fields and turn snow to ice by continuous melting and refreezing, the four mirrors we plan to place above what will be the largest lakes on the continent, both to help dry them up and stimulate the precip rate, the river shaping that will have to be done when the dropping ocean level starts them flowing, and a few thousand smaller details, some of which we can't even imagine yet. This will be the first attempt to terraform an entire planet by weather control. But if plans work out, within a hundred years nine-tenths of Atlantis will be growing grass, and that's a land area of almost eight million square miles. The farming activities of the colonists should keep the dust level high and make the new precip rate self-perpetuating."

"It's a big undertaking, but everyone thinks it can be done," said Phyllis earnestly. "When you compare that much surface to those tiny areas on some of the new planets, where every square foot of soil has to be treated and retreated before it will take Earth plants, you can begin to see what a wonderful opportunity this is."

"Yes, we've taken at least two thousand cores out of the higher areas in Atlantis," resumed Murdock. "They show it's been raised and inundated three times within the past hundred thousand years, obviously a result of volcanic activity causing a temporary increase in the dust level. Plant growth was extensive each time the water receded, and we have a fairly thick layer of humus-rich soil on which to plan an economy. The sea has both animal and plant life in great quantities, including many species, like the seals, which can live on either land or water. I think Sister, within two hundred years, can support a hundred million people."

"Weather control is still not an exact science, even on Earth. Can you really be this sure of how your dust and mirrors will affect this planet?"

"No, but we're certain enough to recommend going ahead with it once we've finished our current job of assessing the ice-carrying capacity of this pole. After all, there's no intelligent life to be harmed if we blunder."

Phyllis glared angrily at Murdock, but did not answer the implied derision. Most of the people in the lounge had been drifting out as they talked, suppressing yawns. The tiny Eurasian rose, said goodnight to Allan, and left also.

"I'm prepared to offer you any assistance within my power, Allan," said Murdock, rising. "Just let me know what you need."

"Thanks. I'll probably call on you. Phyllis and I are going to dissect that seal in the morning and see what we can learn."

They learned very little Phyllis had not already known. Allan pushed back from the table after four hours of intense work, and turned off the recorder into which he had been making a running commentary. The seal was basically a variation of its distant cousins on Earth. There was nothing of unusual interest about its bodily processes, with the exception of that baffling brain. The pan was small, the cranium narrow, the actual size less than a quarter that of a human. But it was like nothing he had ever seen.

They washed up and went to lunch. Phyllis had been a competent but not brilliant helper, and the notes she had taken on what little she had observed of the seals' behavior were no help. Her belief that the creatures were intelligent was apparently based on woman's intuition rather than accumulated data.

"I think we've learned as much as we can from a dead specimen," he said after the meal. "What we need is a *live* seal. How do we go about getting one?"

"That's a tough question. They carry away their wounded after an attack, and it's almost impossible to catch them in the water. Several of the men tried, when we were"—she made a moue of distaste—"eating them."

"I'll discuss it with Murdock tonight," said Allan.

I should be the one! the Decision Maker projected into the night, his individuality for once overriding the group consciousness and speaking clearly. *Mine is the risk, let mine be the body!* . . . But the soft, insistent voices of the individuals comprising the race memory cried *No! No! It may not be! No danger to the Decision Maker. No danger. No danger* . . . and he yielded, letting the desire to offer himself for the trap the humans were setting fade from his mind. With its passing came the need for decisions.

The humans were establishing a work party near the edge of the water, the work to continue after dark in hopes of luring the seals into an attack. Men with stun-guns were hidden throughout the rocks, and three large lights had been concealed at high points overlooking the area. The seals' movements must be planned to insure that the humans captured only the one individual the group selected. Also, the attack must look real, must seem to involve a large party while actually exposing the smallest possible number to danger.

The word "tactics" appeared in his mind, and almost immediately there was an answering pulse. One of the new memory carriers, containing only the human knowledge. . . . He scanned the word and its associated meanings, leaped to three other memorybank units checking out inferences and related data, and had his plan. One of the humans had been an ardent follower of a game played on Earth, one which involved deceptive movement of bodies, concerted displays of an object called a ball to a specified section of the playing area. . . . He formulated the necessary details, and swiftly communicated them to the selected units of the people.

III

Allan crouched low in the rocks and watched the water. The two larger moons were passing slowly through the clear sky and the beach was well-lighted. He turned away a second to rub his eyes, and when he looked again the beach was swarming with short figures. It was almost as if he had signaled them to attack by looking away.

The seals came running upright out of the water and scurried behind the two walls of rock, moving stiff-legged but swiftly across the open area. From his vantage point Allan could see the leaders starting to twirl their slings. He drew his laser pistol and sent a red beam flaring into the sky.

Instantly the searchlights came on, brightly illuminating the areas behind the rocks where the seals were gathering. The work gang dropped their tools and drew stun-guns, and the men hidden in the rocks rose to their feet, searching for targets.

The abortive attack stalled. The seals broke for the sea, fleeing what was obviously a trap. Allan saw the hurrying line of sleek forms plunging into the water, and rubbed his eyes. He would have sworn there had been many more of them than now seemed visible.

"Got one!" came an exultant yell, and "Me too!" said another voice. But Allan's attention was abruptly distracted. A seal popped into view less than twenty feet away, twirling a sling and looking directly at him.

He hastily drew his stun-gun, fired and missed, cursed himself for a bungling professor who belonged in a classroom, fired again, and saw the small figure drop. The sharp-edged missile clattered to the rock at his feet.

The floodlights abruptly went out. There were wild yells as the humans, their eyes slow to adjust back to moonlight, found themselves blinded.

Allan groped his way to the seal he had shot and crouched over the body. They should have gotten several prisoners, but remembering the creatures' habit of carrying off their wounded he was taking no chances.

After a moment someone found the outlet where the power cable had been disconnected, and the lights came back on. The noises of fighting had died away in the darkness, and now Allan saw there were no attackers in sight.

"Hey! My seal's gone!" called the first man who had claimed a hit, as though he could hardly believe it.

"Mine too!" said another voice, and other men began to climb among the rocks, looking for seals they had been certain they saw fall. When the confusion subsided Allan discovered they had exactly one captive . . . his.

The small creature in the cage twitched its long whiskers, stirred, and after a moment raised its head. The eyelids moved, and Allan found himself staring into a slightly protuberant pair of golden eyes. The thick black lips opened as the seal gave an almost human yawn, showing the long incisors of a carnivore's dentition. The mouth closed with an audible click of teeth, and it moved to the bars separating them.

"At close range it even *looks* intelligent," said Phyllis softly, and the captive turned the golden eyes on her. They were alone in the cold room.

I am not intelligent as you humans use the term, said a clear, cold voice in both their minds, in perfect World English. *As a separate entity I exist as an animal, directed primarily by inherited instincts. But I am a member of a mentally interlocked race, and the combined minds which merge in my brain possess the quality of intelligence.*

The two humans turned toward each other simultaneously, and each saw that the other had received the message. There was a brief silence while the stunning implications sank in, and then Phyllis opened her rosebud mouth in a yell of high glee. "I told him! Oh, the thick-headed oaf, I told him, I told him!"

Her enthusiasm was contagious, but Allan forced himself to be calm. A sense of steadily mounting excitement was building up and his breath was ragged—these unexpected discoveries were one of the rewarding parts of his job—but this was no time to become emotional.

There was an odd quality to the mental voice. It gave a strong impression of a group speaking in chorus, but with the voice of this individual dominating the rest.

"How may I best communicate with you?" he asked aloud.

As you are now doing. Your immediate thoughts are unclear when you do not vocalize.

"Then first"—his mind shifted into high gear, many events of the past few hours clicking together into a coherent pattern—"first I want to know why you only pretended to attack the work party and deliberately let us capture you."

Because we wish to establish face-to-face communication. It is our understanding that you will decide whether these humans now here will leave or stay and be joined by many more.

"That is my responsibility, yes. But why are you interested in my decision?"

There was a brief silence. Allan felt Phyllis' hand clinging tightly to his arm, and he stared into the unblinking golden eyes, waiting. The creature finally projected, *It would be best if you would accompany this unit to a Gathering-Place. I am only a messenger. The Decision Maker wishes to meet you face-to-face, in the presence of a complete memory.*

Allan turned to look at Phyllis. She was staring at him, wide-eyed. Her expression asked, Trap?

He shook his head, turned back to the seal. It had closed its mouth, and the heavy lips hid the sharp teeth. For the first time he saw how the large eyes, the downward curve of the mouth, the jutting whiskers, gave the seal a tragic-comic look, like the sad clowns of an ancient circus. "I will go with you," he said aloud.

"Your safety while you are here is my responsibility!" said Murdock angrily. "I couldn't possibly permit it!"

"You have no way of preventing me." Allan made a strong effort and kept his voice down. Despite the man's bluff friendliness he had not liked Murdock from the first, and this unexpected opposition was too ill-timed to be anything but deliberate obstruction. "I have the authority to take command of this or any other civilian-operated station, and I will summarily remove you as manager if that becomes necessary."

Murdock jumped to his feet, stood towering over the smaller man. His face was a fiery red, his big hands clenched into fists. Allan found himself wondering if Murdock would actually be foolish enough to hit him.

"Removing me may not be as easy as you seem to think!" the big man bellowed. They were alone in his private office, and the sound was almost deafening.

"Don't be childish. The station personnel are thoroughly familiar with the authority of a Practical Philosopher. They aren't going to risk a prison sentence by supporting you."

"You talk pretty rough for such a small man!"

"Please. Will you simply supply me with the needed equipment without further argument?"

Murdock supplied it. An hour after daybreak Allan and the seal were swimming through the blue water, about twenty feet below the surface, heading northwest along the ice shelf. The station's standard underwater gear was a spacesuit with a ducted propeller mounted on the back, with a simple variable speed control installed between the first two fingers of the right hand. At maximum he could move less than ten miles an hour, and keeping his head tilted back for vision and his arms rigidly ahead for guidance was tiring.

Surrounding them, but keeping at a respectful distance, were fighting seals, all carrying basalt spears. Phyllis had assured him she had seen a team of seals kill the largest fish in this fresh-water ocean with those sharpened rocks.

It was another long and weary hour before his escort projected, *Move toward the ice and descend slightly. Slow your speed.*

He obeyed, and after a moment he saw a dark shadow in the white wall of ice, a shadow that swiftly grew larger. He angled slowly toward it and it became a jagged tunnel. The seal moved ahead to guide him.

After a few yards the roof began to recede and he angled upward; he rose until he broke the surface, to find himself in a scene of strange but compelling beauty.

It was a large grotto in the ice, at the head of a glacier that had reached the shore and lost its momentum. It had calved in a peculiar way, leaving this great hollow opening, and the sides had grown together again at the top. The ceiling was thin, sunlight pouring in through several long cracks where the joint was not perfect. The yellow beams struck one ice wall and rebounded in glittering fantasms of color, springing from surface to surface in a deceptive brightness that concealed more than it revealed. The massive walls were rough and jagged, with many sharp protruding edges.

It was a fairy palace of crystal and glass, of reflected light and softened shadow, and Allan Odegaard thought it the most beautiful spot he had ever seen.

Lying on the little beach and watching him with unblinking attention were about thirty adult seals. As he waded out of the water Allan saw that they formed a semi-circle, and at its center was the one who could only be the Decision Maker.

IV

The two Decision Makers faced each other, the golden eyes of the seal meeting and matching the brown eyes of the small Earthman. Allan lowered his gaze to check his environmental indicator, then undid his helmet. The air had a slightly fishy smell, but was crisp and cold.

We welcome you to this Gathering-Place, came a projection, strong and commanding, and again it was compounded of many minds, though the overriding personality was that of the Decision Maker. *We have brought you here to prove that within the meaning of your terms defining "race" and "intelligent" we are an intelligent race. We want you to declare this planet unlawfully occupied by Earthmen, and order those present to leave and all others to stay away.*

"I have no choice but to grant that as a race you are intelligent," said Allan slowly. "But if this mental ability is achieved by grouping minds, and as individuals you are something much less than the unified whole, then you are a unique lifeform and will require further study. But for now I would like to know why you want us to leave the planet."

We know what the other Earthmen, those who understand the ways of wind, water and ice, seek to do here. Three times from the year our racial memory came into being the ice has grown, the sea lowered, the area you call Atlantis become half land and half water, the land green with growing things. Three times within memory our people have moved in great numbers onto the land, only to be driven back into the sea when the ice melted once more. We have confirmed, from knowledge found in the minds of Earthmen, what we already felt to be true, that we as a race cannot progress until we have freed ourselves of the environment of the sea. In another eight thousand of our seasons the ice will begin to form, as it has before. We will move onto the land, as we have before. But this time we will apply what we have taken from the minds of your companions and stored in our memory; we shall master the physical sciences, develop the necessary technology, learn to control the weather as you do. There will be no more flooding of the land.

Listening to the calm, relentless way the words formed themselves and beat slowly through the neural passages of his brain, Allan accepted the fact these people could do exactly what they said.

"You have taken all the knowledge of all the humans here and stored it in your racial memory?"

All except yourself. Yours we will have in a few more nights.

"Since you can read my mind you know that I have a difficult decision to make. It would help me if I knew what your 'racial memory' is, and how it works. I would also like to know your goals as a race once you are on the land, and how you plan to achieve them."

Those questions are easily answered. Our group memory is an accumulated mass of knowledge which is impressed on the memory area of young individuals at birth, at least three such young ones for each memory segment. We are a short-lived race, dying of natural causes after eight of our years. As each individual who carries a share of the memory feels death approaching he transfers his part to a newly born child, and thus the knowledge is transmitted from generation to generation forever.

As for our aims, they are similar to your own. We have achieved—there was a brief pause—*economic plenty. We have none of the conflicts between individuals which characterize your society. But this is not enough. We seek to improve the life of the individual within the race, and this entails increasing the natural lifespan, eliminating enemies, perfecting a science of medicine—a concept new to us—and achieving the ability to enjoy pleasure, which we now know to be lacking in our lives. All this we can accomplish by means of the knowledge now stored in our memory, once the land is again ours.*

And the Earthman has corrupted another innocent race, thought Allan with wry bitterness.

We can read your thoughts when you project that strongly. You define "corruption" as increased knowledge of the choices open to an intelligent being, and an inclination to make those choices which lead toward greater pleasure in life. Why do you consider this a retrogressive quality?

"I'm afraid it would be too complicated to explain, and perhaps I don't fully understand myself," said Allan grimly. "For now, it's enough to know I must make a decision which will vitally affect your future, and I freely admit I'm going to find it hard to do."

Since you state we qualify as an intelligent race your path should be clear. If you are now ready another unit will guide you back to your base. When you have made your decision, speak it aloud, and we will hear. Bear in mind that if you decide to stay we will harass and fight you in every manner within our power.

Allan slowly replaced his helmet and turned toward the water. He felt like a man who has eaten too large a meal and wants nothing more than to crawl into a corner and estivate while it digests. But his meal had been mental, and he might be a long time in torpor before he fully understood all that he had learned.

The trip back was uneventful, and by noon he found himself in Murdock's office, with only Phyllis and the base manager present. He gave them a brief report, and watched the incredulous expression form on Murdock's face. Phyllis, too, seemed a little stunned.

"Do I understand you have definitely decided an individual seal is not intelligent?" asked Murdock when he regained his composure.

"I've made no decisions. This ability to group minds is new to us, and requires study."

"Because their group intelligence is a unique phenomena is no reason to consider the individuals within the group as weak," said Phyllis heatedly.

"I'll probably want to talk to you again later." Murdock's voice was carefully expressionless. "In the meantime why don't you get a bite of lunch. Phyllis, can you stay a moment?"

Allan took the implied dismissal at face value and rose. He was hungry, but when he sat down to eat, the concentrates seemed curiously tasteless. He kept thinking of the refreshing coolness of the air in the grotto, of the beauty of the sun on the sparkling ice, the strange and ancient wisdom he had found in a group of seals. How odd, that as a race they had achieved the goals that had dominated the thinking of Earth's best philosophers for thousands of years, and then had formed the conviction that the needs of the individual were as important as those of the race. There were *still* social planners on Earth who were unable to think of people in any terms except "groups" and "masses."

After lunch he put on cold weather gear and went outside. He walked the beaches all afternoon, hating his responsibility and the necessity for it. When he returned to the station at dusk his thinking had degenerated to vagrant thoughts: loose fragments, impressions and partial memories swirled through his mind . . . *we have achieved economic plenty, but this is not enough . . . corruption is increased knowledge of the choices open to an intelligent being . . . we will harass and fight you in every manner within our power* . . . The memory of blood oozing from the bitten body of a fish before the seal gulped it down without chewing, the sad-clown faces, the overwhelming inclination to think of them as lovable pets. . . . What would it be like, to share your thoughts, emotions and desires with your fellows, to form a composite being greater than the sum of its parts? There was a clear, reasoning power in the Decision Maker, an intellect of great strength.

When he stepped inside the door the p.a. was calling his name. He walked to Murdock's office as requested.

"Sit down, Allan." The bluff heartiness, the easy, friendly attitude had been discarded, as though the big man knew they no longer served a purpose. His voice was brisk and impersonal. "I'm going to give you some information about Sister you won't find in the regular reports. All personnel who are aware of it have been sworn to strict secrecy. Not that that's necessary in your case, of course."

"Thanks," said Allan stiffly.

"You are aware, I'm sure, that Earth's supply of uranium is almost exhausted. In the excitement over this new 'sunlight diffusion' method of power generation and propagation the public has tended to forget the thousands of other industrial and medical applications of atomic science. They think that virtually unlimited power, available anywhere at any time, will solve all problems. Actually, the need for uranium grows every day, and it has proven hard to find in commercial quantities. Sister is a very rich planet. The cores we have taken from Atlantis show extensive deposits of uranite and davidite, as well as some pitchblende, carnotite and tobernite. The primary concentration of davidite is on a rather high plateau, one which will be above water in five years. I predict that within ten there will be a refining plant there, shipping ore to Earth. I can't over-emphasize how important this is." ·

"That's interesting information, Zip, but I fail to see the direct connection. I'm sure you are aware economic considerations never play any part in a P.P.'s decision."

"Oh, come off it! That garbage about being the 'conscience of Mankind' won't wash with me. When word of these deposits reaches certain ears on Earth they'll have your credentials withdrawn in a minute if you give us trouble."

"Do you really think so?" asked Allan. His voice was soft, almost gentle.

"I'm certain of it. Idealism has its uses, but it can't stand in the way of a geniune need."

"Would this sudden disbelief in a P.P.'s authority be connected in any way with the royalties your university will lose if I rule against you?"

Murdock's face flushed, and he rose to his feet.

"Can't you understand that I'm thinking of the good of *all* mankind?"

Allan sighed tiredly. "Perhaps you are. And the needs of all mankind influence me, in a way you might not understand. But you're a little late with your information. I've already made up my mind. And I'll require that underwater gear again in the morning."

When he was standing in his own cubicle after dinner he spoke into the air. "You said that you could hear me. Acknowledge that you do."

There was a sudden electric sense of awareness, as though someone had picked up a telephone and stood holding it without speaking. He waited, and after a moment the calm multiple voice asked, *What is your wish?*

"I would like to speak to the Decision Maker again, in person. Would you send someone at daylight to take me to the Gathering-Place?"

There was another brief silence, and he could almost hear the ether stirring with the hurried conference.

Then the voice said, *It shall be done.*

The beautiful grotto seemed unchanged, except that there were several more of the spear-carrying warriors present. They did not trust him, which indicated that their mind-reading abilities were limited. He had prepared no treachery.

The Decision Maker regarded him sadly from the center of his race's memory bank, the golden eyes unblinking. *This time you have summoned us.*

Allan took a deep breath of the cold air and paced back and forth on the small beach as he spoke, not looking at the seals. "You said you had no concept until our arrival of the science of medicine. Do you understand the meaning of the term 'gamble'? Because I am gambling with your future, and I can't possibly know how it will turn out. Let me give you my reasons and then my decision, which I have already sent to Earth."

The guards nearest him moved closer, their spears perceptibly rising. He sensed the air of menace in the room, and wondered if he had made a mistake in coming here in person. It would be strange to die in this ice palace, when he had many times felt himself to be in far greater danger and escaped alive.

"If you are left alone it will be eight thousand years before a seal again walks the land, but then it will be a safe and certain thing. If we occupy your planet and war comes, you will kill many Earthmen before you are finally hunted down and killed. But make no mistake about it, you will be exterminated. Man is a capable, ruthless, relentless foe, and if he sets out to destroy you he will succeed. Your cooked bodies will grace his table, and it will not matter that the brains he shatters contain a racial memory that reaches farther into the past than his own.

"I cannot endure the thought that another thousand generations of your kind should follow the tortuous road of the sea, gaining nothing but the day's sustenance. Neither do I wish war between us. My decision has been to report that you are definitely an intelligent race . . . but that I recommend completing the terraforming operation and starting colonization."

There was an instant stir among the seals, a silent shifting of position as the guards nearest him raised their spears and advanced, stood poised, ready to thrust him through. He glanced to the waiting warriors and back to the Decision Maker, and knew that his life hung on his next words.

He had not known how they would react, and his meager knowlege of hive-minds did not justify guesses, but somehow he had not thought they'd take an immediate and personal revenge.

"I am an Earthman," he said slowly and clearly. "Sometimes I have been proud of my people, and sometimes ashamed. But the gamble I am taking is based on a knowledge of them, of other races, of your own, that you cannot match even with your long memory. If the colonists will follow my recommendation—cooperate with you, help you on land and be helped by you in the sea—there is no reason the two races cannot progress together. Despite our past history I have enough faith in man to think he will fulfill his share of the bargain. Will you match my faith, and pledge your race to work with mine?"

The Decision Maker faced him silently, and he felt a secret tug of knowing sympathy for an individual who must decide the course of his entire race. The silence stretched out; the guards standing by him did not lower their spears.

The Earthman stood waiting for the word that would decide his personal fate. The decision that the two races could work together had been reached by reasoning, the one to tell the seals in person by a sudden impulse.

Now he would learn the truth of both.

A DEATH IN THE HOUSE

Clifford Simak

Old Mose Abrams was out hunting cows when he found the alien. He didn't know it was an alien, but it was alive and it was in a lot of trouble and Old Mose, despite everything the neighbors said about him, was not the kind of man who could bear to leave a sick thing out there in the woods.

It was a horrid-looking thing, green and shiny, with some purple spots on it, and it was repulsive even twenty feet away. And it stank.

It had crawled, or tried to crawl, into a clump of hazel brush, but hadn't made it. The head part was in the brush and the rest lay out there naked in the open. Every now and then the parts that seemed to be arms and hands clawed feebly at the ground, trying to force itself deeper in the brush, but it was too weak; it never moved an inch.

It was groaning, too, but not too loud—just the kind of keening sound a lonesome wind might make around a wide, deep eave. But there was more in it than just the sound of winter wind; there was a frightened, desperate note that made the hair stand up on Old Mose's nape.

Old Mose stood there for quite a spell, making up his mind what he ought to do about it, and a while longer after that working up his courage, although most folks offhand would have said that he had plenty. But this was the sort of situation that took more than just ordinary screwed-up courage. It took a lot of foolhardiness.

But this was a wild, hurt thing and he couldn't leave it there, so he walked up to it and knelt down, and it was pretty hard to look at, though there was a sort of fascination in its repulsiveness that was hard to figure out—as if it were so horrible that it dragged one to it. And it stank in a way that no one had ever smelled before.

Mose, however, was not finicky. In the neighborhood, he was not well known for fastidity. Ever since his wife had died almost ten years before, he had lived alone on his untidy farm and the housekeeping that he did was the scandal of all the neighbor women. Once a year, if he got around to it, he sort of shoveled out the house, but the rest of the year he just let things accumulate.

So he wasn't as upset as some might have been with the way the creature smelled. But the sight of it upset him, and it took him quite a while before he could bring himself to touch it, and when he finally did, he was considerably surprised. He had been prepared for it to be either cold or slimy, or maybe even both. But it was neither. It was warm and hard and it had a clean feel to it, and he was reminded of the way a green corn stalk would feel.

He slid his hand beneath the hurt thing and pulled it gently from the clump of hazel brush and turned it over so he could see its face. It hadn't any face. It had an enlargement at the top of it, like a flower on top of a stalk, although its body wasn't any stalk, and there was a fringe around this enlargement that wiggled like a can of worms, and it was then that Mose almost turned around and ran.

But he stuck it out.

He squatted there, staring at the no-face with the fringe of worms, and he got cold all over and his stomach doubled up on him and he was stiff with fright—and the fright got worse when it seemed to him that the keening of the thing was coming from the worms.

Mose was a stubborn man. One had to be stubborn to run a runty farm like this. Stubborn and insensitive in a lot of ways. But not insensitive, of course, to a thing in pain.

Finally he was able to pick it up and hold it in his arms and there was nothing to it, for it didn't weigh much. Less than a half-grown shoat, he figured.

He went up the woods path with it, heading back for home, and it seemed to him the smell of it was less. He was hardly scared at all and he was warm again and not cold all over.

For the thing was quieter now and keening just a little. And although he could not be sure of it, there were times when it seemed as if the thing were snuggling up to him, the way a scared and hungry baby will snuggle to any grown person that comes and picks it up.

Old Mose reached the buildings and he stood out in the yard a minute, wondering whether he should take it to the barn or house. The barn, of course, was the natural place for it, for it wasn't human—it wasn't even as close to human as a dog or cat or sick lamb would be.

He didn't hesitate too long, however. He took it into the house and laid it on what he called a bed, next to the kitchen stove. He got it straightened out all neat and orderly and pulled a dirty blanket over it, and then went to the stove and stirred up the fire until there was some flame.

Then he pulled up a chair beside the bed and had a good, hard, wondering look at this thing he had brought home. It had quieted down a lot and seemed more comfortable than it had out in the woods. He tucked the blanket snug around it with a tenderness that surprised himself. He wondered what he had that it might eat, and even if he knew, how he'd manage feeding it, for it seemed to have no mouth.

"But you don't need to worry none," he told it. "Now that I got you under a roof, you'll be all right. I don't know too much about it, but I'll take care of you the best I can."

By now it was getting on toward evening, and he looked out the window and saw that the cows he had been hunting had come home by themselves.

"I got to go get the milking done and the other chores," he told the thing lying on the bed, "but it won't take me long. I'll be right back."

Old Mose loaded up the stove so the kitchen would stay warm and he tucked the thing in once again, then got his milk pails and went down to the barn.

He fed the sheep and pigs and horses and he milked the cows. He hunted eggs and shut the chicken house. He pumped a tank of water.

Then he went back to the house.

It was dark now and he lit the oil lamp on the table, for he was against electricity. He'd refused to sign up when REA had run out the line and a lot of the neighbors had gotten sore at him for being uncooperative. Not that he cared, of course.

He had a look at the thing upon the bed. It didn't seem to be any better, or any worse, for that matter. If it had been a sick lamb or an ailing calf, he could have known right off how it was getting on, but this thing was different. There was no way to tell.

He fixed himself some supper and ate it and wished he knew how to feed the thing. And he wished, too, that he knew how to help it. He'd got it under shelter and he had it warm, but was that right or wrong for something like this? He had no idea.

He wondered if he should try to get some help, then felt squeamish about asking help when he couldn't say exactly what had to be helped. But then he wondered how he would feel himself if he were in a far, strange country, all played out and sick, and no one to get him any help because they didn't know exactly what he was.

That made up his mind for him and he walked over to the phone.

But should he call a doctor or a veterinarian? He decided to call the doctor because the thing was in the house. If it had been in the barn, he would have called the veterinarian.

He was on a rural line and the hearing wasn't good and he was halfway deaf, so he didn't use the phone too often. He had told himself at times it was nothing but another aggravation and there had been a dozen times he had threatened to have it taken out. But now he was glad he hadn't.

The operator got old Doctor Benson and they couldn't hear one another too well, but Mose finally made the doctor understand who was calling and that he needed him and the doctor said he'd come.

With some relief, Mose hung up the phone and was just standing there, not doing anything, when he was struck by the thought that there might be others of these things down there in the woods. He had no idea what they were or what they might be doing or where they might be going, but it was pretty evident that the one upon the bed was some sort of stranger from a very distant place. It stood to reason that there might be more than one of them, for far traveling was a lonely business and anyone—or anything—would like to have some company along.

He got the lantern down off the peg and lit it and went stumping out the door. The night was as black as a stack of cats and the lantern light was feeble, but that made not a bit of difference, for Mose knew this farm of his like the back of his hand.

He went down the path into the woods. It was a spooky place, but it took more than woods at night to spook Old Mose. At the place where he had found the thing, he looked around, pushing through the brush and holding the lantern high so he could see a bigger area, but he didn't find another one of them.

He did find something else, though—a sort of outsize birdcage made of metal lattice work that had wrapped itself around an eight-inch hickory tree. He tried to pull it loose, but it was jammed so tight that he couldn't budge it.

He sighted back the way it must have come. He could see where it had plowed its way through the upper branches of the trees, and out beyond were stars, shining bleakly with the look of far away.

Mose had no doubt that the thing lying on his bed beside the kitchen stove had come in this birdcage contraption. He marveled some at that, but he didn't fret himself too much, for the whole thing was so unearthly that he knew he had little chance of pondering it out.

He walked back to the house and he scarcely had the lantern blown out and hung back on its peg than he heard a car drive up.

The doctor, when he came up to the door, became a little grumpy at seeing Old Mose standing there.

"You don't look sick to me," the doctor said. "Not sick enough to drag me clear out here at night."

"I ain't sick," said Mose.

"Well, then," said the doctor, more grumpily than ever, "what did you mean by phoning me?"

"I got someone who is sick," said Mose. "I hope you can help him. I would have tried myself, but I don't know how to go about it."

The doctor came inside and Mose shut the door behind him.

"You got something rotten in here?" asked the doctor.

"No, it's just the way he smells. It was pretty bad at first, but I'm getting used to it by now."

The doctor saw the thing lying on the bed and went over to it. Old Mose heard him sort of gasp and could see him standing there, very stiff and straight. Then he bent down and had a good look at the critter on the bed.

When he straightened up and turned around to Mose, the only thing that kept him from being downright angry was that he was so flabbergasted.

"Mose," he yelled, "what *is* this?"

"I don't know," said Mose. "I found it in the woods and it was hurt and wailing and I couldn't leave it there."

"You think it's sick?"

"I know it is," said Mose. "It needs help awful bad. I'm afraid it's dying."

The doctor turned back to the bed again and pulled the blanket down, then went and got the lamp so that he could see. He looked the critter up and down, and he prodded it with a skittish finger, and he made the kind of mysterious clucking sound that only doctors make.

Then he pulled the blanket back over it again and took the lamp back to the table.

"Mose," he said, "I can't do a thing for it."

"But you're a doctor!"

"A human doctor, Mose. I don't know what this thing is, but it isn't human. I couldn't even guess what is wrong with it, if anything. And I wouldn't know what could be safely done for it even if I could diagnose its illness. I'm not even sure it's an animal. There are a lot of things about it that argue it's a plant."

Then the doctor asked Mose straight out how he came to find it and Mose told him exactly how it happened. But he didn't tell him anything about the birdcage, for when he thought about it, it sounded so fantastic that he couldn't bring himself to tell it. Just finding the critter and having it here was bad enough, without throwing in the birdcage.

"I tell you what," the doctor said. "You got something here that's outside all human knowledge. I doubt there's ever been a thing like this seen on Earth before. I have no idea what it is and I wouldn't try to guess. If I were you, I'd get in touch with the university up at Madison. There might be someone there who could get it figured out. Even if they couldn't they'd be interested. They'd want to study it."

Mose went to the cupboard and got the cigar box almost full of silver dollars and paid the doctor. The doctor put the dollars in his pocket, joshing Mose about his eccentricity.

But Mose was stubborn about his silver dollars. "Paper money doesn't seem legal, somehow," he declared. "I like the feel of silver and the way it clinks. It's got authority."

The doctor left and he didn't seem as upset as Mose had been afraid he might be. As soon as he was gone, Mose pulled up a chair and sat down beside the bed.

It wasn't right, he thought, that the thing should be so sick and no one to help—no one who knew any way to help it.

He sat in the chair and listened to the ticking of the clock, loud in the kitchen silence, and the crackling of the wood burning in the stove.

Looking at the thing lying on the bed, he had an almost fierce hope that it could get well again and stay with him. Now that its birdcage was all banged up, maybe there'd be nothing it could do but stay. And he hoped it would, for already the house felt less lonely.

Sitting in the chair between the stove and bed, Mose realized how lonely it had been. It had not been quite so bad until Towser died. He had tried to bring himself to get another dog, but he never had been able to. For there was no dog that would take the place of Towser and it had seemed unfaithful to even try. He could have gotten a cat, of course, but that would remind him too much of Molly; she had been very fond of cats, and until the time she died, there had always been two or three of them underfoot around the place.

But now he was alone. Alone with his farm and his stubbornness and his silver dollars. The doctor thought, like all the rest of them, that the only silver Mose had was in the cigar box in the cupboard. There wasn't one of them who knew about the old iron kettle piled plumb full of them, hidden underneath the floor boards of the living room. He chuckled at the thought of how he had them fooled. He'd give a lot to see his neighbors' faces if they could only know. But he was not the one to tell them. If they were to find it out, they'd have to find it out themselves.

He nodded in the chair and finally he slept, sitting upright, with his chin resting on his chest and his crossed arms wrapped around himself as if to keep him warm.

When he woke, in the dark before the dawn, with the lamp flickering on the table and the fire in the stove burned low, the alien had died.

There was no doubt of death. The thing was cold and rigid and the husk that was its body was rough and drying out—as a corn stalk in the field dries out, whipping in the wind once the growing had been ended.

Mose pulled the blanket up to cover it, and although this was early to do the chores, he went out by lantern light and got them done.

After breakfast, he heated water and washed his face and shaved, and it was the first time in years he'd shaved any day but Sunday. Then he put on his one good suit and slicked down his hair and got the old jalopy out of the machine shed and drove into town.

He hunted up Eb Dennison, the town clerk, who also was the secretary of the cemetery association.

"Eb," he said, "I want to buy a lot."

"But you've got a lot," protested Eb.

"That plot," said Mose, "is a family plot. There's just room for me and Molly."

"Well, then," asked Eb, "why another one? You have no other members of the family."

"I found someone in the woods," said Mose. "I took him home and he died last night. I plan to bury him."

"If you found a dead man in the woods," Eb warned him, "you better notify the coroner and sheriff."

"In time I may," said Mose, not intending to. "Now how about that plot?"

Washing his hands of the affair entirely, Eb sold him the plot.

Having bought his plot, Mose went to the undertaking establishment run by Albert Jones.

"Al," he said, "there's been a death out at the house. A stranger I found out in the woods. He doesn't seem to have anyone and I aim to take care of it."

"You got a death certificate?" asked Al, who subscribed to none of the niceties affected by most funeral parlor operators.

"Well, no, I haven't."

"Was there a doctor in attendance?"

"Doc Benson came out last night."

"He should have made you out one. I'll give him a ring."

He phoned Doctor Benson and talked with him a while and got red around the gills. He finally slammed down the phone and turned on Mose.

"I don't know what you're trying to pull off," he fumed, "but Doc tells me this thing of yours isn't even human. I don't take care of dogs or cats or—"

"This ain't no dog or cat."

"I don't care what it is. It's got to be human for me to handle it. And don't go trying to bury it in the cemetery, because it's against the law."

Considerably discouraged, Mose left the undertaking parlor and trudged slowly up the hill toward the town's one and only church.

He found the minister in his study working on a sermon. Mose sat down in a chair and fumbled his battered hat around and around in his work-scarred hands.

"Parson," he said, "I'll tell you the story from first to last," and he did. He added, "I don't know what it is. I guess no one else does, either. But it's dead and in need of decent burial and that's the least that I can do. I can't bury it in the cemetery, so I suppose I'll have to find a place for it on the farm. I wonder if you could bring yourself to come out and say a word or two."

The minister gave the matter some deep consideration.

"I'm sorry, Mose," he said at last. "I don't believe I can. I am not sure at all the church would approve of it."

"This thing may not be human," said Old Mose, "but it is one of God's critters."

The minister thought some more, and did some wondering out loud, but made up his mind finally that he couldn't do it.

So Mose went down the street to where his car was waiting and drove home, thinking about what heels some humans are.

Back at the farm again, he got a pick and shovel and went into the garden, and there, in one corner of it, he dug a grave. He went out to the machine shed to hunt up some boards to make the thing a casket, but it turned out that he had used the last of the lumber to patch up the hog pen.

Mose went to the house and dug around in a chest in one of the back rooms which had not been used for years, hunting for a sheet to use as a winding shroud, since there would be no casket. He couldn't find a sheet, but he did unearth an old white linen table cloth. He figured that would do, so he took it to the kitchen.

He pulled back the blanket and looked at the critter lying there in death and a sort of lump came into his throat at the thought of it—how it had died so lonely and so far from home without a creature of its own to spend its final hours with. And naked, too, without a stitch of clothing and with no possession, with not a thing to leave behind as a remembrance of itself.

He spread the table cloth out on the floor beside the bed and lifted the thing and laid it on the table cloth. As he laid it down, he saw the pocket in it—if it was a pocket—a sort of slitted flap in the center of what could be its chest. He ran his hand across the pocket area.

There was a lump inside it. He crouched for a long moment beside the body, wondering what to do.

Finally he reached his fingers into the flap and took out the thing that bulged. It was a ball, a little bigger than a tennis ball, made of cloudy glass—or, at least, it looked like glass. He squatted there, staring at it, then took it to the window for a better look.

There was nothing strange at all about the ball. It was just a cloudy ball of glass and it had a rough, dead feel about it, just as the body had.

He shook his head and took it back and put it where he'd found it and wrapped the body securely in the cloth. He carried it to the garden and put it in the grave. Standing solemnly at the head of the grave, he said a few short words and then shoveled in the dirt.

He had meant to make a mound above the grave and he had intended to put up a cross, but at the last he didn't do either one of these. There would be snoopers. The word would get around and they'd be coming out and hunting for the spot where he had buried this thing he had found out in the woods. So there must be no mound to mark the place and no cross as well. Perhaps it was for the best, he told himself, for what could he have carved or written on the cross?

By this time it was well past noon and he was getting hungry, but he didn't stop to eat, because there were other things to do. He went out into the pasture and caught up Bess and hitched her to the stoneboat and went down into the woods.

He hitched her to the birdcage that was wrapped around the tree and she pulled it loose as pretty as you please. Then he loaded it on the stoneboat and hauled it up the hill and stowed it in the back of the machine shed, in the far corner by the forge.

After that, he hitched Bess to the garden plow and gave the garden a cultivating that it didn't need so it would be fresh dirt all over and no one could locate where he'd dug the grave.

He was just finishing the plowing when Sheriff Doyle drove up and got out of the car. The sheriff was a soft-spoken man, but he was no dawdler. He got right to the point.

"I hear," he said, "you found something in the woods."

"That I did," said Mose.

"I hear it died on you."

"Sheriff, you heard right."

"I'd like to see it, Mose."

"Can't. I buried it. And I ain't telling where."

"Mose," the sheriff said, "I don't want to make you trouble, but you did an illegal thing. You can't go finding people in the woods and just bury them when they up and die on you."

"You talk to Doc Benson?"

The sheriff nodded. "He said it wasn't any kind of thing he'd ever seen before. He said it wasn't human."

"Well, then," said Mose, "I guess that lets you out. If it wasn't human, there could be no crime against a person. And if it wasn't owned, there ain't any crime against property. There's been no one around to claim they owned the thing, is there?"

The sheriff rubbed his chin. "No, there hasn't. Maybe you're right. Where did you study law?"

"I never studied law. I never studied nothing. I just use common sense."

"Doc said something about the folks up at the university might want to look at it."

"I tell you, Sheriff," said Mose. "This thing came here from somewhere and it died. I don't know where it came from and I don't know what it was and I don't hanker none to know. To me it was just a living thing that needed help real bad. It was alive and it had its dignity and in death it commanded some respect. When the rest of you refused it decent burial, I did the best I could. And that is all there is to it."

"All right, Mose," the sheriff said, "if that's how you want it."

He turned around and stalked back to the car. Mose stood beside old Bess hitched to her plow and watched him drive away. He drove fast and reckless as if he might be angry. Mose put the plow away and turned the horse back to the pasture and by now it was time to do chores again.

He got the chores all finished and made himself some supper and after supper sat beside the stove, listening to the ticking of the clock, loud in the silent house, and the crackle of the fire.

All night long the house was lonely.

The next afternoon, as he was plowing corn, a reporter came and walked up the row with him and talked with him when he came to the end of the row. Mose didn't like this reporter much. He was too flip and he asked some funny questions, so Mose clammed up and didn't tell him much.

A few days later, a man showed up from the university and showed him the story the reporter had gone back and written. The story made fun of Mose.

"I'm sorry," the professor said. "These newspapermen are unaccountable. I wouldn't worry too much about anything they write."

"I don't," Mose told him.

The man from the university asked a lot of questions and made quite a point about how important it was that he should see the body.

But Mose only shook his head. "It's at peace," he said. "I aim to leave it that way."

The man went away disgusted, but still quite dignified.

For several days there were people driving by and dropping in, the idly curious, and there were some neighbors Mose hadn't seen for months. But he gave them all short shrift and in a little while they left him alone and he went on with his farming and the house stayed lonely.

He thought again that maybe he should get a dog, but he thought of Towser and he couldn't do it.

One day, working in the garden, he found the plant that grew out of the grave. It was a funny-looking plant and his first impulse was to root it out.

But he didn't do it, for the plant intrigued him. It was a kind he'd never seen before and he decided he would let it grow, for a while at least, to see what kind it was. It was a bulky, fleshy plant, with heavy, dark-green, curling leaves, and it reminded him in some ways of the skunk cabbage that burgeoned in the woods come spring.

There was another visitor, the queerest of the lot. He was a dark and intense man who said he was the president of a flying saucer club. He wanted to know if Mose had talked with the thing he'd found out in the woods and seemed terribly disappointed when Mose told him he hadn't. He wanted to know if Mose had found a vehicle the creature might have traveled in and Mose lied to him about it. He was afraid, the wild way the man was acting, that he might demand to search the place, and if he had, he'd likely have found the birdcage hidden in the machine shed back in the corner by the forge. But the man got to lecturing Mose about withholding vital information.

Finally Mose had taken all he could of it, so he stepped into the house and picked up the shotgun from behind the door. The president of the flying saucer club said good-by rather hastily and got out of there.

Farm life went on as usual, with the corn laid by and the haying started and out in the garden the strange plant kept on growing and now was taking shape. Old Mose couldn't believe his eyes when he saw the sort of shape it took and he spent long evening hours just standing in the garden, watching it and wondering if his loneliness were playing tricks on him.

The morning came when he found the plant standing at the door and waiting for him. He should have been surprised, of course, but he really wasn't, for he had lived with it, watching it of eventide, and although he had not dared admit it even to himself, he had known what it was.

For here was the creature he'd found in the woods, no longer sick and keening, no longer close to death, but full of life and youth.

It was not the same entirely, though. He stood and looked at it and could see the differences—the little differences that might have been those between youth and age, or between a father and a son, or again the differences expressed in an evolutionary pattern.

"Good morning," said Mose, not feeling strange at all to be talking to the thing. "It's good to have you back."

The thing standing in the yard did not answer him. But that was not important; he had not expected that it would. The one important point was that he had something he could talk to.

"I'm going out to do the chores," said Mose. "You want to tag along?"

It tagged along with him and it watched him as he did the chores and he talked to it, which was a vast improvement over talking to himself.

At breakfast, he laid an extra plate for it and pulled up an extra chair, but it turned out the critter was not equipped to use a chair, for it wasn't hinged to sit.

Nor did it eat. That bothered Mose at first, for he was hospitable, but he told himself that a big, strong, strapping youngster like this one knew enough to take care of itself, and he probably didn't need to worry too much about how it got along.

After breakfast, he went out to the garden, with the critter accompanying him, and sure enough, the plant was gone. There was a collapsed husk lying on the ground, the outer covering that had been the cradle of the creature at his side.

Then he went to the machine shed and the creature saw the birdcage and rushed over to it and looked it over minutely. Then it turned around to Mose and made a sort of pleading gesture.

Mose went over to it and laid his hands on one of the twisted bars and the critter stood beside him and laid its hands on, too, and they pulled together. It was no use. They could move the metal some, but not enough to pull it back in shape again.

They stood and looked at one another, although looking may not be the word, for the critter had no eyes to look with. It made some funny motions with its hands, but Mose couldn't understand. Then it lay down on the floor and showed him how the birdcage ribs were fastened to the base.

It took a while for Mose to understand how the fastening worked and he never did know exactly why it did. There wasn't, actually, any reason that it should work that way.

First you applied some pressure, just the right amount at the exact and correct angle, and the bar would move a little. Then you applied some more pressure, again the exact amount and at the proper angle, and the bar would move some more. You did this three times and the bar came loose, although there was, God knows, no reason why it should.

Mose started a fire in the forge and shoveled in some coal and worked the bellows while the critter watched. But when he picked up the bar to put it in the fire, the critter got between him and the forge and wouldn't let him near. Mose realized then he couldn't—or wasn't supposed to—heat the bar to straighten it and he never questioned the entire rightness of it. For, he told himself, this thing must surely know the proper way to do it.

So he took the bar over to the anvil and started hammering it back into shape again, cold, without the use of fire, while the critter tried to show him the shape it should be. It took quite a while, but finally it was straightened out to the critter's satisfaction.

Mose figured they'd have themselves a time getting the bar back in place again, but it slipped on as slick as could be.

Then they took off another bar and this one went faster, now that Mose had the hang of it.

But it was hard and grueling labor. They worked all day and only straightened out five bars.

It took four solid days to get the bars on the birdcage hammered into shape and all the time the hay was waiting to be cut.

But it was all right with Mose. He had someone to talk to and the house had lost its loneliness.

When they got the bars back in place, the critter slipped into the cage and starting fooling with a dingus on the roof of it that looked like a complicated basket. Mose, watching, figured that the basket was some sort of control.

The critter was discouraged. It walked around the shed looking for something and seemed unable to find it. It came back to Mose and made its despairing, pleading gesture. Mose showed it iron and steel; he dug into a carton where he kept bolts and clamps and bushings and scraps of metal and other odds and ends, finding brass and copper and even some aluminum, but it wasn't any of these.

And Mose was glad—a bit ashamed for feeling glad, but glad all the same.

For it had been clear to him that when the birdcage was all ready, the critter would be leaving him. It had been impossible for Mose to stand in the way of the repair of the cage, or to refuse to help. But now that it apparently couldn't be, he found himself well pleased.

Now the critter would have to stay with him and he'd have someone to talk to and the house would not be lonely. It would be welcome, he told himself, to have folks again. The critter was almost as good a companion as Towser.

Next morning, while Mose was fixing breakfast, he reached up in the cupboard to get the box of oatmeal and his hand struck the cigar box and it came crashing to the floor. It fell over on its side and the lid came open and the dollars went free-wheeling all around the kitchen.

Out of the corner of his eye, Mose saw the critter leaping quickly in pursuit of one of them. It snatched it up and turned to Mose, with the coin held between its fingers, and a sort of thrumming noise was coming out of the nest of worms on top of it.

It bent and scooped up more of them and cuddled them and danced a sort of jig, and Mose knew, with a sinking heart, that it had been silver the critter had been hunting.

So Mose got down on his hands and knees and helped the critter gather up all the dollars. They put them back into the cigar box and Mose picked up the box and gave it to the critter.

The critter took it and hefted it and had a disappointed look. Taking the box over to the table, it took the dollars out and stacked them in neat piles and Mose could see it was very disappointed.

Perhaps, after all, Mose thought, it had not been silver the thing had been hunting for. Maybe it had made a mistake in thinking that the silver was some other kind of metal.

Mose got down the oatmeal and poured it into some water and put it on the stove. When it was cooked and the coffee was ready, he carried his breakfast to the table and sat down to eat.

The critter still was standing across the table from him, stacking and restacking the piles of silver dollars. And now it showed him with a hand held above the stacks, that it needed more of them. This many stacks, it showed him, and each stack so high.

Mose sat stricken, with a spoon full of oatmeal halfway to his mouth. He thought of all those other dollars, the iron kettle packed with them, underneath the floor boards in the living room. And he couldn't do it; they were the only thing he had—except the critter now. And he could not give them up so the critter could go and leave him too.

He ate his bowl of oatmeal without tasting it and drank two cups of coffee. And all the time the critter stood there and showed him how much more it needed.

"I can't do it for you," Old Mose said. "I've done all you can expect of any living being. I found you in the woods and I gave you warmth and shelter. I tried to help you, and when I couldn't, at least I gave you a place to die in. I buried you and protected you from all those other people and I did not pull you up when you started growing once again. Surely you can't expect me to keep on giving endlessly."

But it was no good. The critter could not hear him and he did not convince himself.

He got up from the table and walked into the living room with the critter trailing him. He loosened the floor boards and took out the kettle, and the critter, when it saw what was in the kettle, put its arms around itself and hugged in happiness.

They lugged the money out to the machine shed and Mose built a fire in the forge and put the kettle in the fire and started melting down that hard-saved money.

There were times he thought he couldn't finish the job, but he did.

The critter got the basket out of the birdcage and put it down beside the forge and dipped out the molten silver with an iron ladle and poured it here and there into the basket, shaping it in place with careful hammer taps.

It took a long time, for it was exacting work, but finally it was done and the silver almost gone. The critter lugged the basket back into the birdcage and fastened it in place.

It was almost evening now and Mose had to go and do the chores. He half expected the thing might haul out the birdcage and be gone when he came back to the house. And he tried to be sore at it for its selfishness—it had taken from him and had not tried to pay him back—it had not, so far as he could tell, even tried to thank him. But he made a poor job of being sore at it.

It was waiting for him when he came from the barn carrying two pails full of milk. It followed him inside the house and stood around and he tried to talk to it. But he didn't have the heart to do much talking. He could not forget that it would be leaving, and the pleasure of its present company was lost in his terror of the loneliness to come.

For now he didn't even have his money to help ward off the loneliness.

As he lay in bed that night, strange thoughts came creeping in upon him—the thought of an even greater loneliness than he had ever known upon this runty farm, the terrible, devastating loneliness of the empty wastes that lay between the stars, a driven loneliness while one hunted for a place or person that remained a misty thought one could not define, but which it was most important one should find.

It was a strange thing for him to be thinking, and quite suddenly he knew it was no thought of his, but of this other that was in the room with him.

He tried to raise himself, he fought to raise himself, but he couldn't do it. He held his head up a moment, then fell back upon the pillow and went sound asleep.

Next morning, after Mose had eaten breakfast, the two of them went to the machine shed and dragged the birdcage out. It stood there, a weird alien thing, in the chill brightness of the dawn.

The critter walked up to it and started to slide between two of the bars, but when it was halfway through, it stepped out again and moved over to confront Old Mose.

"Good-by, friend," said Mose. "I'll miss you."

There was a strange stinging in his eyes.

The other held out its hand in farewell, and Mose took it and there was something in the hand he grasped, something round and smooth that was transferred from its hand to his.

The thing took its hand away and stepped quickly to the birdcage and slid between the bars. The hands reached for the basket and there was a sudden flicker and the birdcage was no longer there.

Mose stood lonely in the barnyard, looking at the place where there was no birdcage and remembering what he had felt or thought—or been told?—the night before as he lay in bed.

Already the critter would be there, out between the stars, in that black and utter loneliness, hunting for a place or thing or person that no human mind could grasp.

Slowly Mose turned around to go back to the house, to get the pails and go down to the barn to get the milking done.

He remembered the object in his hand and lifted his still-clenched fist in front of him. He opened his fingers and the little crystal ball lay there in his palm—and it was exactly like the one he'd found in the slitted flap in the body he had buried in the garden. Except that one had been dead and cloudy and this one had the living glow of a distant-burning fire.

Looking at it, he had the strange feeling of a happiness and comfort such as he had seldom known before, as if there were many people with him and all of them were friends.

He closed his hand upon it and the happiness stayed on—and it was all wrong, for there was not a single reason that he should be happy. The critter finally had left him and his money was all gone and he had no friends, but still he kept on feeling good.

He put the ball into his pocket and stepped spryly for the house to get the milking pails. He pursed up his whiskered lips and began to whistle and it had been a long, long time since he had even thought to whistle.

Maybe he was happy, he told himself, because the critter had not left without stopping to take his hand and try to say good-by.

And a gift, no matter how worthless it might be, how cheap a trinket, still had a basic value in simple sentiment. It had been many years since anyone had bothered to give him a gift.

It was dark and lonely and unending in the depths of space with no Companion. It might be long before another was obtainable.

It perhaps was a foolish thing to do, but the old creature had been such a kind savage, so fumbling and so pitiful and eager to help. And one who travels far and fast must likewise travel light. There had been nothing else to give.

Technology

Much science fiction has explored the possibilities of technology with a somewhat jaundiced eye. It is technology which has given us robots and other "frankenscience" monsters alluded to in the headnote to the section on robots. It is technology which has made World War III the horrible concept that it is. And it is technology which has enabled us to produce the many goods and services with which we are now littering the globe and adjacent space. But to be fair, it is also technology which has enabled man to go into space and thereby fulfill the earliest dreams of science fiction writers. It is technology which has helped develop so many cures and preventatives that, if enough time and money were devoted to it, much sickness and pain could be banished. And it is technology which, according to recent projections, will free us from the menial so that we may enjoy the pleasant.

What technology does for us, or to us, then, is going to be a result of our attitude toward it and control of it. The problem of control is not so simple as environmentalist vs. industrialist or dictator vs. elected official, although these conflicts are important. The larger problem is whether man is going to control technology or whether technology is going to control man. John Brunner's *The Squares of the City* presents an example of how a man could use modern technology. In this case, chessboard strategy is combined with subliminal television suggestioning to enable a power group to control a whole city. Brunner's *Stand on Zanzibar* also examines, among many things, technology in the not-too-distant future. Frederik Pohl and Cyril Kornbluth's *The Space Merchants* depicts a society in which production and advertising control everything. In fact, the industrial and advertising magnates are only in partial control, as all cultural forces are geared for consumption. And, of course, there are such stories as Harlan Ellison's "I have no Mouth and I must Scream" involving the ultimate computer and what it does to man.

Each of the four stories which follows focuses on a particular aspect —the city, service facilities, advertising and production, or time scheduling—of the present technological society and speculates about that aspect as it might develop into the future. J. G. Ballard's "Build-up" examines the city as a total, and perhaps self-contained, living unit and, extrapolating on the growth of cities and present life in them, depicts life in a city so large that few realize that there might be something outside the city limits. "Build-up" illustrates some of the ways in which life would have to change if such an environment were developed and points out how such things as airplanes as well as the knowledge of them would simply disappear.

Alvin Toffler maintains that as our needs are met we will be offered more services, but he doesn't speculate on the outcome of increased services as does Will Worthington in "Plenitude." The two groups in this story are reminiscent of the Eloi and the Moorlocks in H. G. Wells' *The Time Machine,* and although the comparison of what they represent is hardly one-to-one, the social process through which the division could have come about is strikingly similar. The symbolism of the grape-like dwellings and of the boy's hunt which ends the story lead the reader to a conclusion, if not a moral judgement, which Worthington's main character continually refuses to make.

"The Wizards of Pung's Corners," by Frederik Pohl, focuses on electronic and technological complexity and applies its speculations to the military. Interestingly enough, as more and more becomes known about modern military methodology, the army portrayed in this story seems less and less bizarre. As a sidelight, the explanation of how a society can come to be dominated by production and sales, besides being an ironic comment of the ever-present governmental concern with the Gross National Product (GNP), can serve as a good introduction to Pohl and Kornbluth's *The Space Merchants.*

Any modern folklorist would support the contention that Western man is extremely time-conscious, and most folklorists would probably admit that Harlan Ellison's " 'Repent, Harlequin!' Said The Ticktockman" is a logical extrapolation on that sense of time. At the beginning of the story, Ellison quotes a passage from Thoreau which could serve as the keynote for all four stories. Ellison's story and all the others involve an attempted rejection of what the society has been made into by its technology.

The question is not whether or not to have a technological society. We have come too far to stop now. The question is how are we to order our priorities so that we remain in control of the technology rather than allowing the reverse to happen.

BUILD-UP

J. G. Ballard

Noon talk on Millionth Street:

"Sorry, these are the West millions. You want 9775335d East."

"Dollar five a cubic foot? Sell!"

"Take a westbound express to 495th Avenue, cross over to a Redline elevator and go up a thousand levels to Plaza Terminal. Carry on south from there and you'll find it between 568th Avenue and 422nd Street."

"There's a cave-in down at KEN county! Fifty blocks by twenty by thirty levels."

"Listen to this—'PYROS STAGE MASS BREAK-OUT! FIRE POLICE CORDON BAY COUNTY!' "

"It's a beautiful counter. Detects up to .005 per cent monoxide. Cost me $300."

"Have you seen those new intercity sleepers? Takes only ten minutes to up 3,000 levels!"

"Ninety cents a foot? Buy!"

"You say the idea came to you in a dream?" the voice jabbed out. "You're sure no one else gave it to you."

"No," M. said flatly. A couple of feet away from him a spotlamp threw a cone of dirty yellow light into his face. He dropped his eyes from the glare and waited as the sergeant paced over to his desk, tapped his fingers on the edge and swung round on him again.

"You talked it over with your friends?"

"Only the first theory," M. explained quietly. "About the possibility of flight."

"But you told me the other theory was more important. Why keep it quiet from them?"

M. hesitated. Outside somewhere a trolley shunted and clanged along the elevated. "I was afraid they wouldn't understand what I meant."

The sergeant laughed sourly. "You mean they would have thought you really were crazy?"

M. shifted uncomfortably on the stool. Its seat was only six inches off the floor and his thighs and lumbar muscles felt like slabs of inflamed rubber. After three hours of cross-questioning logic had faded and he groped helplessly. "The concept was a little abstract. There weren't any words for it."

The sergeant snorted. "I'm glad to hear you say it." He sat down on the desk, watched M. for a moment and then went over to him.

"Now look," he said confidentially. "It's getting late. Do you still think both theories are reasonable?"

M. looked up. "Aren't they?"

The sergeant turned angrily to the man watching in the shadows by the window.

"We're wasting our time," he snapped. "I'll hand him over to Psycho. You've seen enough, haven't you, Doc?"

The surgeon stared thoughtfully at his hands. He was a tall heavy-shouldered man, built like a wrestler, with thick coarsely-lined features.

He ambled forward, knocking back one of the chairs with his knee.

"There's something I want to check," he said curtly. "Leave me alone with him for half an hour."

The sergeant shrugged. "All right," he said, going over to the door. "But be careful with him."

When the sergeant had gone the surgeon sat down behind the desk and stared vacantly out of the window, listening to the dull hum of air through the huge ninety-foot ventilator shaft which rose out of the street below the station. A few roof lights were still burning and 200 yards away a single policeman slowly patrolled the iron catwalk running above the street, his boots ringing across the darkness.

M. sat on the stool, elbows between his knees, trying to edge a little life back into his legs.

Eventually the surgeon glanced down at the charge sheet

Name .... Franz M.
Age .... 20.
Occupation .... Student.
Address .... 3599719 West 783rd Str.,
                                          Level 549-7705-45 KNI
                                          (Local).
Charge .... Vagrancy.

"Tell me about this dream," he said slowly, idly flexing a steel rule between his hands as he looked across at M.

"I think you've heard everything, sir," M. said.

"In detail."

M. shifted uneasily. "There wasn't much to it, and what I do remember isn't too clear now."

The surgeon yawned. M. waited and then started to recite what he'd already repeated twenty times.

"I was suspended in the air above a flat stretch of open ground, something like the floor of an enormous arena. My arms were out at my sides, and I was looking down, floating—"

"Hold on," the surgeon interrupted. "Are you sure you weren't swimming?"

"No," M. said. "I'm certain I wasn't. All around me there was free space. That was the most important part about it. There were no walls. Nothing but emptiness. That's all I remember."

The surgeon ran his finger along the edge of the rule.

"Go on."

"Well, the dream gave me the idea of building a flying machine. One of my friends helped me construct it."

The surgeon nodded. Almost absently he picked up the charge sheet, crushed it with a single motion of his hand and flicked it into the waste basket.

"Don't be crazy, Franz!" Gregson remonstrated. They took their places in the chemistry cafeteria queue. "It's against the laws of hydrodynamics. Where would you get your buoyancy?"

"Suppose you had a rigid fabric vane," Franz explained as they shuffled past the hatchways. "Say ten feet across, like one of those composition wall sections, with hand-grips on the ventral surface. And then you jump down from the gallery at the Coliseum Stadium. What would happen?"

"You'd make a hole in the floor. Why?"

"No, seriously."

"If it was large enough and held together you'd swoop down like a paper dart."

"Glide," Franz said. "Right." Thirty levels above them one of the inter-city expresses roared over, rattling the tables and cutlery in the cafeteria. Franz waited until they reached a table and sat forward, his food forgotten.

"And say you attached a propulsive unit, such as a battery-driven ventilator fan, or one of those rockets they use on the Sleepers. With enough thrust to overcome your weight. What then?"

Gregson shrugged. "If you could control the thing, you'd, you'd . . ." He frowned at Franz. "What's the word? You're always using it."

"Fly."

"Basically, Matteson, the machine is simple," Sanger, the physics lector, commented as they entered the Science Library. "An elementary application of the Venturi Principle. But what's the point of it? A trapeze would serve its purpose equally well, and be far less dangerous. In the first place consider the enormous clearances it would require. I hardly think the traffic authorities will look upon it with any favour."

"I know it wouldn't be practical here," Franz admitted. "But in a large open area it should be."

"Allowed. I suggest you immediately negotiate with the Arena Garden on Level 347-25," the lector said whimsically. "I'm sure they'll be glad to hear about your scheme."

Franz smiled politely. "That wouldn't be large enough. I was really thinking of an area of totally free space. In three dimensions, as it were."

Sanger looked at Franz curiously. "Free space? Isn't that a contradiction in terms? Space is a dollar a cubic foot." He scratched his nose. "Have you begun to construct this machine yet?"

"No," Franz said.

"In that event I should try to forget all about it. Remember, Matteson, the task of science is to consolidate existing knowledge, to systematize and reinterpret the discoveries of the past, not to chase wild dreams into the future."

He nodded and disappeared among the dusty shelves.

Gregson was waiting on the steps.

"Well?" he asked.

"Let's try it out this afternoon," Franz said. "We'll cut Text 5 Pharmacology. I know those Fleming readings backwards. I'll ask Dr. McGhee for a couple of passes."

They left the library and walked down the narrow, dimly-lit alley which ran behind the huge new Civil Engineering laboratories. Over 75 per cent of the student enrolment was in the architectural and engineering faculties, a meagre 2 per cent in pure sciences. Consequently the physics and chemistry libraries were housed in the oldest quarter of the University, in two virtually condemned galvanized hutments which once contained the now closed Philosophy School.

At the end of the alley they entered the university plaza and started to climb the iron stairway leading to the next level a hundred feet above. Half-way up a white helmeted F.P. checked them cursorily with his detector and waved them past.

"What did Sanger think?" Gregson asked as they stepped up into 637th Street and walked across to the Suburban Elevator station.

"He's no use at all," Franz said. "He didn't even begin to understand what I was talking about."

Gregson laughed ruefully. "I don't know whether I do."

Franz took a ticket from the automat and mounted the Down platform. An elevator dropped slowly towards him, its bell jangling.

"Wait until this afternoon," he called back. "You're really going to see something."

The floor manager at the Coliseum initialled the two passes.

"Students, eh? All right." He jerked a thumb at the long package Franz and Gregson were carrying. "What have you got there?"

"It's a device for measuring air velocities," Franz told him.

The manager grunted and released the stile.

Out in the centre of the empty arena Franz undid the package and they assembled the model. It had a broad fan-like wing of wire and paper, a narrow strutted fusilage and a high curving tail.

Franz picked it up and launched it into the air. The model glided for twenty feet and then slithered to a stop across the sawdust.

"Seems to be stable," Franz said. "We'll tow it first."

He pulled a reel of twine from his pocket and tied one end to the nose.

As they ran forward the model lifted gracefully into the air and followed them round the stadium, ten feel off the floor.

"Let's try the rockets now," Franz said.

He adjusted the wing and tail settings and fitted three firework display rockets into a wire bracket mounted above the wing.

The stadium was four hundred feet in diameter and had a roof two hundred and fifty high. They carried the model over to one side and Franz lit the tapers.

There was a burst of flame and the model accelerated off across the floor, two feet in the air, a bright trail of coloured smoke spitting out behind it. Its wings rocked gently from side to side. Suddenly the tail burst into flames. The model lifted steeply and looped up towards the roof, stalled just before it hit one of the pilot lights and dived down into the sawdust.

They ran across to it and stamped out the glowing cinders. "Franz!" Gregson shouted. "It's incredible! It actually works."

Franz kicked the shattered fuselage.

"Of course it works," he said impatiently, walking away. "But as Sanger said, what's the point of it?"

"The point? It flies! Isn't that enough?"

"No. I want one big enough to hold me."

"Franz, slow down. Be reasonable. Where could you fly it?"

"I don't know," Franz said fiercely. "But there must be somewhere. Somewhere!"

The floor manager and two assistants, carrying fire extinguishers, ran across the stadium to them.

"Did you hide that match?" Franz asked quickly. "They'll lynch us if they think we're pyros."

Three afternoons later Franz took the elevator up 150 levels to 677-98, where the Precinct Estate Office had its bureau.

"There's a big development between 493 and 554 in the next sector," one of the clerks told him. "I don't know whether that's any good to you. Sixty blocks by twenty by fifteen levels."

"Nothing bigger?" Franz queried.

The clerk looked up. "Bigger? No. *What* are you looking for? A slight case of agoraphobia?"

Franz straightened the maps spread across the counter.

"I wanted to find an area of more or less continuous development. Two or three hundred blocks long."

The clerk shook his head and went back to his ledger. "Didn't you go to Engineering School?" he asked scornfully. "The City won't take it. One hundred blocks is the maximum."

Franz thanked him and left.

A south-bound express took him to the development in two hours. He left the car at the detour point and walked the 300 yards to the end of the level.

The street, a seedy but busy thoroughfare of garment shops and small business premises running through the huge ten mile thick BIR Industrial Cube, ended abruptly in a tangle of ripped girders and concrete. A steel rail had been erected along the edge and Franz looked down over it into the cavity, three miles long, a mile wide and 1,200 feet deep, which thousands of engineers and demolition workers were tearing out of the matrix of the City.

Eight hundred feet below him unending lines of trucks and railcars carried away the rubble and debris, and clouds of dust swirled up into the arc-lights blazing down from the roof.

As he watched a chain of explosions ripped along the wall on his left and the whole face suddenly slipped and fell slowly towards the floor, revealing a perfect cross-section through fifteen levels of the City.

Franz had seen big developments before, and his own parents had died in the historic QUA County cave-in ten years earlier, when three master-pillars had sheared and two hundred levels of the City had abruptly sunk 10,000 feet, squashing half a million people like flies in a concertina, but the enormous gulf of emptiness still made his imagination gape.

All around him, standing and sitting on the jutting terraces of girders, a silent throng stared down.

"They say they're going to build gardens and parks for us," an elderly man at Franz's elbow remarked in a slow patient voice. "I even heard they might be able to get a tree. It'll be the only tree in the whole County."

A man in a frayed sweat-shirt spat over the rail. "That's what they always say. At a dollar a foot promises are all they can waste space on."

Below them a woman who had been looking out into the air started to simper nervously. Two bystanders took her by the arms and tried to lead her away. The woman began to thresh about and an F.P. came over and dragged her away roughly.

"Poor fool," the man in the sweat-shirt commented. "She probably lived out there somewhere. They gave her ninety cents a foot when they took it away from her. She doesn't know yet she'll have to pay a dollar ten to get it back. Now they're going to start charging five cents an hour just to sit up here and watch."

Franz looked out over the railing for a couple of hours and then bought a postcard from one of the vendors and walked back thoughtfully to the elevator.

He called in to see Gregson before returning to the student dormitory.

The Gregsons lived up in the west million on 985th Avenue, in a top three-room flat right under the roof. Franz had known them since his parents' death, but Gregson's mother still regarded him with a mixture of sympathy and suspicion, and as she let him in with her customary smile of welcome he noticed her glancing quickly at the detector mounted in the hall.

Gregson was in his room, happily cutting out frames of paper and pasting them on to a great rickety construction that vaguely resembled Franz's model.

"Hullo, Franz. What was it like?"

Franz shrugged. "Just a development. Worth seeing."

Gregson pointed to his construction. "Do you think we can try it out there?"

"We could do." Franz sat down on the bed, picked up a paper dart lying beside him and tossed it out of the window. It swam out into the street, lazed down in a wide spiral and vanished into the open mouth of a ventilator shaft.

"When are you going to build another model?" Gregson asked.

"I'm not."

Gregson swung round. "Why? You've proved your theory."

"That's not what I'm after."

"I don't get you, Franz. What are you after?"

"Free space."

"Free?" Gregson repeated.

Franz nodded. "In both senses."

Gregson shook his head sadly and snipped out another paper panel. "Franz, you're crazy."

Franz stood up. "Take this room," he said. "It's twenty feet by fifteen by ten. Extend its dimensions infinitely. What do you find?"

"A development."

"*Infinitely!*"

"Non-functional space."

"Well?" Franz asked patiently.

"The concept's absurd."

"Why?"

"Because it couldn't exist."

Franz pounded his forehead in despair. "*Why* couldn't it?"

Gregson gestured with the scissors. "It's self-contradictory. Like the statement 'I am lying'. Just a verbal freak. Interesting theoretically, but it's pointless to press it for meaning." He tossed the scissors on to the table. "And anyway, do you know how much free space would cost?"

Franz went over to the bookshelf and pulled out one of the volumes. "Let's have a look at your street atlas."

He turned to the index. "This gives a thousand levels. KNI County, one hundred thousand cubic miles, population 30 million."

Gregson nodded.

Franz closed the atlas. "Two hundred and fifty counties, including KNI, together form the 493rd Sector, and an association of 1,500 adjacent sectors comprise the 298th Local Union."

He broke off and looked at Gregson. "As a matter of interest, ever heard of it?"

Gregson shook his head. "No. How did—"

Franz slapped the atlas onto the table. "Roughly 4×10^{15} cubic Great-

Miles." He leaned on the window ledge. "Now tell me: what lies beyond the 298th Local Union?"

"Other Unions, I suppose," Gregson said. "I don't see your difficulty."

"And beyond those?"

"Farther ones. Why not?"

"Forever?" Franz pressed.

"Well, as far as forever is."

"The great street directory in the old Treasury Library on 247th Street is the largest in the County," Franz said. "I went down there this morning. It occupies three complete levels. Millions of volumes. But it doesn't extend beyond the 598th Local Union. No one there had any idea what lay further out. Why not?"

"Why should they?" Gregson asked. "Franz, what are you driving at?"

Franz walked across to the door. "Come down to the Bio-History Museum. I'll show you."

The birds perched on humps of rock or waddled about the sandy paths between the water pools.

" 'Archaeopteryx,' " Franz read off one of the cage indicators. The bird, lean and mildewed, uttered a painful croak when he fed a handful of beans to it.

"Some of these birds have the remnants of a pectoral girdle," Franz said. "Minute fragments of bone embedded in the tissues around their rib cages."

"Wings?"

"Dr. McGhee thinks so."

They walked out between the lines of cages.

"When does he think they were flying?"

"Before the Foundation," Franz said. "Three hundred billion years ago."

When they got outside the Museum they started down 859 th Avenue. Half-way down the street a dense crowd had gathered and people were packed into the windows and balconies above the Elevated, watching a squad of Fire Police break their way into a house.

The bulkheads at either end of the block had been closed and heavy steel traps sealed off the stairways from the levels above and below. The ventilator and exhaust shafts were silent and already the air was stale and soupy.

"Pyros," Gregson murmured. "We should have brought our masks."

"It's only a scare," Franz said. He pointed to the monoxide detectors which were out everywhere, their long snouts sucking at the air. The dial needles stood safely at zero.

"Let's wait in the restaurant opposite."

They edged their way over to the restaurant, sat down in the window and ordered coffee. This, like everything else on the menu, was cold. All cooking appliances were thermostated to a maximum 95°F., and only in the more expensive restaurants and hotels was it possible to obtain food that was at most tepid.

Below them in the street a lot of shouting went up. The f.p.s seemed unable to penetrate beyond the ground floor of the house and had started to baton back the crowd. An electric winch was wheeled up and bolted to the girders running below the kerb, and half a dozen heavy steel grabs were carried into the house and hooked round the walls.

Gregson laughed. "The owners are going to be surprised when they get home."

Franz was watching the house. It was a narrow shabby dwelling sandwiched between a large wholesale furniture store and a new supermarket. An old sign running across the front had been painted over and evidently the ownership had recently changed. The present tenants had made a half-hearted attempt to convert the ground floor room into a cheap stand-up diner.

The f.p.s appeared to be doing their best to wreck everything, and pies and smashed crockery were strewn all over the pavement.

"Crowd's pretty ugly," Franz said. "Do you want to move?"

"Hold on."

The noise died away and everyone waited as the winch began to revolve. Slowly the hawsers wound in and tautened, and the front wall of the house bulged and staggered outwards in rigid jerky movements.

Suddenly there was a yell from the crowd.

Franz raised his arm.

"Up there! Look!"

On the fourth floor a man and woman had come to the window and were looking down frantically. The man helped the woman out onto the ledge and she crawled out and clung to one of the waste pipes.

The crowd roared: "Pyros! You bloody pyros!"

Bottles were lobbed up at them and bounced down among the police. A wide crack split the house from top to bottom and the floor on which the man was standing dropped and catapulted him backwards out of sight.

Then one of the lintels in the first floor snapped and the entire house tipped over and collapsed.

Franz and Gregson stood up involuntarily, almost knocking over the table.

The crowd surged forward through the cordon. When the dust had settled there was nothing left but a heap of masonry and twisted beams. Embedded in this was the battered figure of the man. Almost smothered by the dust he moved slowly, painfully trying to free himself with one hand and the crowd started roaring again as one of the grabs wound in and dragged him down under the rubble.

The manager of the restaurant pushed past Franz and leant out of the window, his eyes fixed on the dial of a portable detector.

Its needle, like all the others, pointed to zero.

A dozen hoses were playing on the remains of the house and after a couple of minutes the crowd shifted and began to thin out.

The manager switched off the detector and left the window, nodding to Franz.

"Damn Pyros. You can relax now, boys."

Franz pointed at the detector.

"Your dial was dead. There wasn't a trace of monoxide anywhere here. How do you know they were Pyros?"

"Don't worry, we knew." He smiled obliquely. "We don't want that sort of element in this neighbourhood."

Franz shrugged and sat down. "I suppose that's one way of getting rid of them."

The manager eyed Franz unpleasantly. "That's right, boy, This is a good five-dollar neighbourhood." He smirked to himself. "Maybe a six dollar now everybody knows about our safety record."

"Careful, Franz," Gregson warned him when the manager had gone. "He may be right. Pyros do take over small cafés and food bars."

Franz stirred his coffee. "Dr. McGhee estimates that at least 15 per cent of the City's population are submerged Pyros. He's convinced the number's growing and that eventually the whole City will flame-out."

He pushed away his coffee. "How much money have you got?"

"On me?"

"Altogether."

"About thirty dollars."

"I've saved fifteen," Franz said thoughtfully. "Forty-five dollars; that should be enough for three or four weeks."

"Where?" Gregson asked.

"On a Supersleeper."

"Super—!" Gregson broke off, alarmed. "Three or four weeks! What do you mean?"

"There's only one way to find out," Franz explained calmly. "I can't just sit here thinking. Somewhere there's free space and I'll ride the Sleeper until I find it. Will you lend me your thirty dollars?"

"But Franz—"

"If I don't find anything within a couple of weeks I'll change tracks and come back."

"But the ticket will . . ." Gregson searched ". . . billions. Forty-five dollars won't even get you out of the Sector."

"That's just for coffee and sandwiches," Franz said. "The ticket will be free." He looked up from the table. "You know . . ."

Gregson shook his head doubtfully. "Can you try that on the Super-sleepers?"

"Why not? If they query it I'll say I'm going back the long way round. Greg, will you?"

"I don't know if I should." Gregson played helplessly with his coffee. "Franz, how can there be free space? How?"

"That's what I'm going to find out," Franz said. "Think of it as my first physics practical."

Passenger distances on the transport system were measured point to point by the application of $a = \sqrt{b^2 + c^2 + d^2}$. The actual itinerary taken was the passenger's responsibility, and as long as he remained within the system he could choose any route he liked.

Tickets were checked only at the station exits, where necessary surcharges were collected by an inspector. If the passenger was unable to pay the surcharge—10 cents a mile—he was sent back to his original destination.

Franz and Gregson entered the station on 984th Street and went over to the large console where tickets were automatically dispensed.

Franz put in a penny and pressed the destination button marked 984. The machine rumbled, coughed out a ticket, and the change slot gave him back his coin.

"Well, Greg, good-bye," Franz said as they moved towards the barrier. "I'll see you in about two weeks. They're covering me down at the dormitory. Tell Sanger I'm on Fire Duty."

"What if you don't get back, Franz?" Gregson asked. "Suppose they take you off the Sleeper?"

"How can they? I've got my ticket."

"And if you do find free space? Will you come back then?"

"If I can."

Franz patted Gregson on the shoulder reassuringly, waved and disappeared among the commuters.

He took the local Suburban Green to the district junction in the next county. The Green Line train travelled at an interrupted 70 m.p.h. and the ride took two and a half hours.

At the Junction he changed to an express elevator which got him up out of the Sector in ninety minutes, at 400 m.p.h.

Another fifty minutes in a Through-Sector Special brought him to the Mainline Terminus which served the Union.

There he bought a coffee and gathered his determination together. Supersleepers ran east and west, halting at this and every tenth station. The next arrived in seventy-two hours time, Westbound.

The Mainline Terminus was the largest station Franz had seen, a vast mile-long cavern tiered up through thirty levels. Hundreds of elevator shafts sank into the station and the maze of platforms, escalators, restaurants, hotels, and theatres seemed like an exaggerated replica of the City itself.

Getting his bearings from one of the information booths Franz made his way up an escalator to Tier 15, where the Supersleepers berthed. Running the length of the station were two gigantic steel vacuum tunnels, each two hundred feet in diameter, supported at thirty-foot intervals by massive concrete buttresses.

Franz walked slowly along the platform and stopped by the telescopic gangway that plunged into one of the airlocks.

Two-seventy feet true, he thought, all the way, gazing up at the curving underbelly of the tunnel. It must come out somewhere. He had forty-five dollars in his pocket, sufficient coffee and sandwich money to last him three weeks, six if he needed it, time anyway to find the City's end.

He passed the next three days nursing coffees in any of the thirty cafeterias in the station, reading discarded newspapers and sleeping in the local Red trains which ran four hour journeys round the nearest sector.

When at last the Supersleeper came in he joined the small group of fire police and municipal officials waiting by the gangway, and followed them into the train. There were two cars; a sleeper which no one used, and a day coach.

Franz took an inconspicuous corner seat near one of the indicator panels in the day coach, pulled out his notebook and got ready to make his first entry.

1st Day: West 270 feet. Union 4,350.

"Coming out for a drink?" a Fire Captain across the aisle asked. "We have a ten-minute break here."

"No thanks," Franz said. "I'll hold your seat for you."

Dollar five a cubic foot. Free space, he knew, would bring the price down. There was no need to leave the train or make too many inquiries. All he had to do was borrow a paper and watch the market averages.

2nd Day: West 270 feet. Union 7,550.

"They're slowly cutting down on these Sleepers," someone told him. "Everyone sits in the day coach. Look at this one. Seats sixty, and only four people in it. There's no need to move around. People are staying where they are. In a few years there'll be nothing left but the suburban services."

97 cents.

At an average of a dollar a cubic foot, Franz calculated idly, it's so far worth about 4×10^{27}.

"Going on to the next stop, are you? Well, good-bye young fellow."

Few of the passengers stayed on the Sleeper for more than three or four hours. By the end of the second day Franz's back and neck ached from the constant acceleration. He got a little exercise walking up and down the narrow corridor in the deserted sleeping coach, but had to spend most of his time strapped to his seat as the train began its long braking runs into the next station.

3rd Day: West 270 feet. Federation 657.

"Interesting, but how could you demonstrate it?"

"It's just an odd idea of mine," Franz said, screwing up the sketch and dropping it in the disposal chute. "Hasn't any real application."

"Curious, but it rings a bell somewhere."

Franz sat up. "Do you mean you've seen machines like this? In a newspaper or a book?"

"No, no. In a dream."

Every half day's run the pilot signed the log, the crew handed over to their opposites on an Eastbound sleeper, crossed the platform and started back for home.

125 cents.

8×10^{33}.

4th Day: West 270 feet. Federation 1,225.

"Dollar a cubic foot. You in the estate business?"

"Starting up," Franz said easily. "I'm hoping to open a new office on my own."

He played cards, bought coffee and rolls from the dispenser in the washroom, watched the indicator panel and listened to the talk around him.

"Believe me, a time will come when each union, each sector, almost I might say, each street and avenue will have achieved complete local independence. Equipped with its own power services, aerators, reservoirs, farm laboratories . . ."

The car bore.

6×10^{75}.

5th Day: West 270. 17th Greater Federation.

At a kiosk on the station Franz bought a clip of razor blades and glanced at the brochure put out by the local chamber of commerce.

"12,000 levels, 98 cents a foot, unique Elm Drive, fire safety records unequalled . . ."

He went back to the train, shaved, and counted the thirty dollars left. He was now ninety-five million Great-Miles from the suburban station on 984th Street and he knew he couldn't delay his return much longer. Next time he'd save up a couple of thousand.

7×10^{127}.

7th Day: West 270. 212th Metropolitan Empire.

Franz peered at the indicator.

"Aren't we stopping here?" he asked a man three seats away. "I wanted to find out the market average."

"Varies. Anything from fifty cents a—"

"Fifty!" Franz shot back, jumping up. "When's the next stop? I've got to get off!"

"Not here, son." He put out a restraining hand. "This is Night Town. You in real estate?"

Franz nodded, holding himself back. "I thought . . ."

"Relax." He came and sat opposite Franz. "It's just one big slum. Dead areas. In places it goes as low as five cents. There are no services, no power."

It took them two days to pass through.

"City Authority are starting to seal it off," the man told him. "Huge blocks. It's the only thing they can do. What happens to the people inside I hate to think."

He chewed on a sandwich. "Strange, but there are a lot of these black areas. You don't hear about them, but they're growing. Starts in a back street in some ordinary dollar neighbourhood; a bottleneck in the sewage disposal system, not enough ash cans, and before you know it—a million cubic miles have gone back to jungle. They try a relief scheme, pump in a little cyanide, and then—brick it up. Once they do that they're closed for good.

Franz nodded, listening to the dull humming air.

"Eventually there'll be nothing left but these black areas. The City will be one huge cemetery. What a thought!"

10th Day: East 90 feet. 755th Greater Metropolitan—

"Wait!" Franz leapt out of his seat and stared at the indicator panel.

"What's the matter?" someone opposite asked.

"East!" Franz shouted. He banged the panel sharply with his hand but the lights held. "Has this train changed direction?"

"No, it's eastbound," another of the passengers told him. "Are you on the wrong train?"

"It should be heading west," Franz insisted. "It has been for the last ten days."

"Ten days!" the man exclaimed. "Have you been on this sleeper for ten days? Where the hell are you going?"

Franz went forward and grabbed the car attendant.

"Which way is this train going? West?"

The attendant shook his head. "East, sir. It's always been going east."

"You're crazy," Franz snapped. "I want to see the pilot's log."

"I'm afraid that isn't possible. May I see your ticket, sir?"

"Listen," Franz said weakly, all the accumulated frustration of the last twenty years mounting inside him. "I've been on this . . ."

He stopped and went back to his seat.

The five other passengers watched him carefully.

"Ten days," one of them was still repeating in an awed voice.

Two minutes later someone came and asked Franz for his ticket.

"And of course it was completely in order," the police surgeon commented.

He walked over to M. and swung the spot out of his eyes. "Strangely enough there's no regulation to prevent anyone else doing the same thing. I used to go for free rides myself when I was younger, though I never tried anything like your journey."

He went back to the desk.

"We'll drop the charge," he said. "You're not a vagrant in any indictable sense, and the Transport authorities can do nothing against you. How this curvature was built into the system they can't explain. Now about yourself. Are you going to continue this search?"

"I want to build a flying machine," M. said carefully. "There must be free space somewhere. I don't know . . . perhaps on the lower levels."

The surgeon stood up. "I'll see the sergeant and get him to hand you over to one of the psychiatrists. He'll be able to help you with that dream."

The surgeon hesitated before opening the door. "Look," he began to explain sympathetically, "you can't get out of time, can you? Subjectively it's a plastic dimension, but whatever you do to yourself you'll never be able to stop that clock—" he pointed to the one on the desk "—or make it run backwards. In exactly the same way you can't get out of the City."

"The analogy doesn't hold," M. said. He gestured at the walls around them and the lights in the street outside. "All this was built by us. The question nobody can answer is: what was here before we built it?"

"It's always been here," the surgeon said. "Not these particular bricks and girders, but others before them. You accept that time has no beginning and no end. The City is as old as time and continuous with it."

"The first bricks were laid by someone," M. insisted. "There was the Foundation."

"A myth. Only the scientists believe in that, and even they don't try to make too much of it. Most of them privately admit that the Foundation Stone is nothing more than a superstition. We pay it lip service out of convenience, and because it gives us a sense of tradition. Obviously there can't have been a first brick. If there was, how can you explain who laid it, and even more difficult, where they came from?"

"There must be free space somewhere," M. said doggedly. "The City must have bounds."

"Why?" the surgeon asked. "It can't be floating in the middle of nowhere. Or is that what you're trying to believe?"

M. sank back limply. "No."

The surgeon watched M. silently for a few minutes and paced back to the desk. "This peculiar fixation of yours puzzles me. You're caught between what the psychiatrists call paradoxical faces. I suppose you haven't misinterpreted something you've heard about the wall?"

M. looked up. "Which wall?"

The surgeon nodded to himself. "Some advanced opinion maintains that there's a wall around the City, through which it's impossible to penetrate. I don't pretend to understand the theory myself. It's far too abstract and sophisticated. Anyway I suspect they've confused this wall with the bricked-up black areas you passed through on the Sleeper. I prefer the accepted view that the City stretches out in all directions without limits."

He went over to the door. "Wait here, and I'll see about getting you a probationary release. Don't worry, the psychiatrists will straighten everything out for you."

When the surgeon had left M. stared emptily at the floor, too exhausted to feel relieved. He stood up and stretched himself, walking unsteadily round the room.

Outside the last pilot lights were going out and the patrolman on the catwalk under the roof was using his torch. A police car roared down one of the avenues crossing the street, its rails screaming. Three lights snapped on along the street and then one by one went off again.

M. wondered why Gregson hadn't come down to the station.

Then the calendar on the desk riveted his attention.

The date exposed on the fly leaf was 12 August.

That was the day he had started off on his journey.

Exactly three weeks ago.

Today!

Take a west-bound Green to 298th Street, cross over at the intersection and get a Red elevator up to Level 237. Walk down to the station on Route 175, change to a 438 suburban and go down to 795th Street. Take a Blue line to the Plaza, get off at 4th and 275th, turn left at the roundabout and

You're back where you first started from. $HELL \times 10.

PLENITUDE

Will Worthington

"Why can't we go home now, Daddy?" asked Mike, the youngest, and the small tanned face I saw there in the skimpy shade of the olive tree was mostly a matter of eyes—all else, hair, cheeks, thumb-sized mouth, jelly-bean body and usually flailing arms and legs, were mere accessories to the round, blue, endlessly wondering *eyes.* (*"The Wells of 'Why'"* . . . It would make a poem, I thought, if a poem were needed, and if I wasn't so damned tired. And I also thought, "Oh, God! It begins. Five years old. No, not quite. Four.")

"Because Daddy has to finish weeding this row of beans," I said. "We'll go back to the house in a little while."

I would go back to the house and then I would follow the path around the rocks to the hot springs, and there I would peel off what was left of my clothes and I would soak myself in the clear but pungent water that came bubbling—perfect—from a cleft in the rocks to form a pool in the hollow of a pothole—also perfect. And while I steeped in the mineral water I could think about the fish which was soon to be broiling on the fire, and I could think of Sue turning it, poking at it and sprinkling herbs over it as though it was the first or perhaps the last fish that would ever be broiled and eaten by human creatures. She would perform that office with the same total and unreserved dedication with which, since sun-up, she had scraped deerskin, picked worms from new cabbage-leaves, gathered firewood, caulked the walls of the cabin where the old chinking had fallen away or been chewed or knocked away by other hungry or merely curious creatures, and otherwise filled in the number-less gaps in the world—trivial things mostly which would not be noticed and could not become great things in a man's eyes unless she were to go away or cease to be. I don't think of this because, for all immediate purposes—there are no others—she is the first Woman in the world and quite possibly—the last.

"Why don't we live in the Old House in the valley, Daddy?"

It is All-Eyes again. Make no mistake about it; there is a kind of connectedness between the seemingly random questions of very small kids. These are the problems posed by an *Ur*-logic which is much closer to the pulse of reality than are any of the pretentious, involuted systems and the mincing nihilations and category-juggling of adults. It is we who are confused and half-blinded with the varieties of special knowl-edge. But how explain? What good is my experience to him?

"There are too many old things in the Old House which don't work," I say, even as I know that I merely open the floodgates of further questions.

"Don't the funny men work, Daddy? I want to see the funny men! Daddy, I want . . ."

The boy means the robots. I took him down to see the Old House in the valley once before. He rode on top of my haversack and hung on to my hair with his small fingers. It was all a lark for him. I had gone to fetch some books—gambling that there might be a bagful of worthwhile ones that had not been completely eaten by bugs and mice; and if the jaunt turned out depressing for me, it was my fault, which is to say the fault of memory and the habit of comparing what has been with what is—natural, inevitable, unavoidable, but oh, God, just the same . . . The robots which still stood on their size-thirty metal feet looked like grinning Mexican mummies. They gave me a bad turn even though I knew what they were, and should have known what changes to expect after a long, long absence from that house, but to the kid they were a delight. Never mind transphenomenality of rusted surfaces and uselessly dangling wires; never mind the history of a senile generation. They were the funny men. I wish I could leave it at that, but of course I can't. I hide my hoe in the twigs of the olive tree and pick up Mike. This stops the questions for a while.

"Let's go home to Mummy," I say; and also, hoping to hold back the questions about the Old House long enough to think of some real answers, "Now aren't you glad we live up here where we can see the ocean and eagles and hot springs?"

"Yeth," says Mike firmly by way of making a querulous and ineffectual old man feel better about his decision. What a comfort to me the little one is!

I see smoke coming from the chimney, and when we round the last turn in the path we see the cabin. Sue waves from the door. She has worked like a squaw since dawn, and she smiles and waves. I can remember when women would exhaust themselves talking over the phone and eating bonbons all day and then fear to smile when their beat husbands came home from their respective nothing-foundries lest they crack the layers of phony "youthful glow" on their faces. Not like Sue. Here is Sue with smudges of charcoal on her face and fish-scales on her leather pants. Her scent is of woodsmoke and of sweat. There is no artificial scent like this—none more endearing nor more completely "correct." There was a time when the odor of perspiration would have been more of a social disaster for a woman than the gummata of tertiary pox. Even men were touched by this strange phobia.

Sue sees the question on my face and she knows why my smile is a little perfunctory and strained.

"Chris . . . ?" I start to ask finally.

"No. He took his bow and his sleeping-bag. Muttered something about an eight-point buck."

We do not *need* the venison. If anything has been made exhaustively and exhaustingly clear to the boy it is that our blessings consist in large part of what we do not need. But this is not the point, and I know it is not the point.

"Do you think he'll ever talk to me again, Sue?"

"Of course he will." She pulls off my sweaty shirt and hands me a towel. "You know how twelve is. Everything in technicolor and with the throbbiest possible background music. Everything drags or jumps or swings or everything is Endsville or something else which it actually isn't. If it can't be turned into a drama it doesn't exist. He'll get over it."

I can think of no apt comment. Sue starts to busy herself with the fire, then turns back to me.

"You did the best thing. You did what you had to do, that's all. Go take your bath. I'm getting hungry."

I make my way up the path to the hot springs and I am wearing only the towel and the soles of an ancient pair of sneakers held on with thongs. I am thinking that the hot water will somehow dissolve the layers of sickly thought that obscure all the colors of the world from my mind, just as it will rid me of the day's accretion of grime, but at once I know that I am yielding to a vain and superstitious hope. I can take no real pleasure in the anticipation of my bath.

When I emerge from the underbrush and come in sight of the outcroppings of rock where the springs are, I can see Sato, our nearest neighbor and my oldest friend, making his way along the path from his valley on the other side of the mountain. I wave at him, but he does not wave back. I tell myself that he is concentrating on his feet and simply does not see me, but myself answers back in much harsher terms. Sato knows what happened when I took my older son to the City, and he knows why my son has not spoken more than a dozen coherent words since returning. He knows what I have done, and while it is not in the man's nature to rebuke another or set himself above another or mouth moral platitudes, there are limits.

Sato is some kind of a Buddhist. Only vaguely and imperfectly do I understand what this implies; not being unnecessarily explicit about itself is certainly a part of that doctrine. But there is also the injunction against killing. And I am—notwithstanding every meretricious attempt of my own mind to convert that fact into something more comfortable—a killer. And so . . . I may now contemplate what it will mean not merely to have lost my older son, but also the priceless, undemanding and yet immeasurably rewarding friendship of the family in the next valley.

"It was not intentional," I tell myself as I lower my griminess and weariness into the hot water. "It was necessary. How else explain why we chose . . . ?" But it isn't worth a damn. I might as well mumble Tantric formulae. The water feels lukewarm—*used*.

I go on flaying myself in this manner. I return to the house and sit down to supper. The food I had looked forward to so eagerly tastes like raw fungus or my old sneakers. Nothing Sue says helps, and I even find myself wishing she would go to hell with her vitamin-enriched cheerfulness.

On our slope of the mountain the darkness comes as it must come to a lizard which is suddenly immured in a cigar box. Still no sign of Chris and so, of course, the pumas are more vocal than they have been all year. I itemize and savor every disaster that roars, rumbles, creeps, slithers, stings, crushes or bites: everything from rattlers to avalanches, and I am sure that one or all of these dire things will befall Chris before the night is over. I go outside every time I hear a sound—which is often—and I squint at the top of the ridge and into the valley below. No Chris.

Sue, from her bunk, says, "If you don't stop torturing yourself, you'll be in no condition to *do* anything if it *does* become necessary." She is right, of course, which makes me mad as hell on top of everything else. I lie on my bunk and for the ten-millionth time reconstruct the whole experience:

We had been hacking at elder bushes, Chris and I. It had been a wet winter and clearing even enough land for garden truck out of the encroaching vegetation began to seem like trying to hold back the sea with trowels. This problem and the gloomy knowledge that we had about one hatful of beans left in the cabin had conspired to produce a mood in which nothing but hemlock could grow. And I'd about had it with the questions. Chris had started the "Why" routine at about the same age as little Mike, but the questions, instead of leveling off as the boy began to exercise his own powers of observation and deduction, merely became more involved and challenging.

The worst thing about this was that I could not abdicate: other parents in other times could fluff off the questions of their kids with such hopeless and worthless judgments as "Well, that's how things *are*," thereby implying that both the questioner and the questioned are standing passively at the dead end of a chain of historical cause, or are existentially trapped in the eye of a storm of supernal origin, or are at the nexus of a flock of processes arising out of the choices of too many other agencies to pinpoint and blame definitively . . . *our* life, on the other hand, was clearly and in every significant particular our own baby. It did not merely proceed out of one particular historical choice, complete with foreseeable contingencies, but was an entire fabric of choices—*ours*. Here was total responsibility, complete with crowding elder bushes, cold rain, chiggers, rattlers, bone-weariness and mud. I had elected to live it—even to impose it upon my progeny—and I was prepared for its hardships, but what galled me was having to justify it.

"The people in the City don't have to do *this*, do they?" ("This" is grubbing out elder bushes, and he is right. The people in the City do not have to do *This*. They do not have to hunt, fish, gather or raise their own food. They do not have to build their own cabins, carry their own water from springs or fashion their own clothes from the skins of beautiful, murdered—by me—animals. They do not have to perspire. One of these days I will have to explain that they do not even have to sleep with their own wives. *That* of itself should be the answer of answers, but twelve is not yet ready; twelve cares about things with wheels, things which spin, roar, roll, fly, explode, exude noise and stench. Would that twelve were fourteen!)

In the meantime it is *dig—hack—heave; dig—hack—heave!* "Come on, Chris! It isn't sundown yet."

"Why couldn't we bring an old tractor up here in pieces and put it together and fix it up and find oil and . . ." (I try to explain for the fifty-millionth time that you do not simply "fix up" something which is the outgrowth of an enormous Organization of interdependent Organizations, the fruit of a dead tree, as it were. The wheel will not be turned back. The kid distrusts abstractions and generalities, and I don't blame him, but God I'm tired!) "Let's just clear off this corner by the olive tree, Chris, and then we'll knock off for the day."

"Are we *better* than the City-People?"

(This one hit a nerve. "Better" is a judgment made by people after the fact of their own decisions. Or there isn't any "Better." As for the Recalcitrants, of which vague class of living creatures we are members, they were and are certainly both more and less *something* than the others were—the City people—the ones who elected to Go Along with the Organization. Of all the original Recalcitrant families, I would guess that not ten per cent are now alive. I would if I had any use for statistics. If these people had something in common, you would have to go light-years away to find a name for it. I think it was a common lack of something—a disease perhaps. Future generations will take credit for it and refer to their origins as Fine Old Stock. I think most of them were crazy. I am glad they were, but most of them were just weird. Southern California. I have told Chris about the Peters family. They were going to make it on nothing but papaya juice and stewed grass augmented by East Indian breathing exercises. Poor squittered-out souls! Their corpses were like balsa wood. Better? What is Better? Grandfather was going to live on stellar emanations and devote his energies to whittling statues out of fallen redwoods. Thank Nature his stomach had other ideas! And God I'm tired and fed up!)

"Dammit, boy! Tomorrow I'll *take* you to the City and let you answer your own questions!"

And I did. Sue protested and old Sato just gave me that look which said, "I'm not saying anything," but I *did.*

The journey to the City is necessarily one which goes from bad to worse. As a deer and a man in the wilderness look for downward paths and lush places if they would find a river, the signs which lead to the centers of human civilization are equally recognizable.

You look for ugliness and senselessness. It is that simple. Look for places which have been overlaid with mortar so that nothing can grow or change at its will. Look for things which have been fashioned at great expense of time and energy and then discarded. Look for tin and peeling paint, for rusted metal, broken neon tubing, drifts and drifts of discarded containers—cans, bottles, papers. Look for flies and let your nose lead you where it would rather not go.

What is the difference between the burrow of a fox and a huge sheet-metal hand which bears the legend, in peeling, garish paint: THIS WAY TO PERPETUAL PARMENIDEAN PALACES . . . ? I do not know why one is better than the other, or *if* it is. I know that present purposes—purposes of intellect—lead one way, and intuition leads the other. So we resist intuition, and the path of greatest resistence leads us from one vast, crumbling, frequently stinking artifact or monument to another.

Chris is alternately nauseated and thrilled. He wants to stay in the palatial abandoned houses in the outskirts, but I say "no." For one thing, the rats look like Doberman Pinschers and for another . . . well, never mind what it is that repels me.

Much of the city looks grand until we come close enough to see where cement and plaster, paint and plastic have sloughed away to reveal ruptured tubes and wires which gleam where their insulation has rotted away, and which are connected to nothing with any life in it. We follow a monorail track which is a silver thread from a distance, but which has a continuous ridge of rust and bird droppings along its upper surface as far as the eye can see. We see more of the signs which point to the PERPETUAL PARMENIDEAN PALACES, and we follow them, giving our tormented intuition a rest even while for our eyes and our spirits there is no relief.

When we first encounter life we are not sure that it *is* life.

"They look like huge grapes!" exclaims Chris when we find them, clustered about a central tower in a huge sunken place like a stadium. The P. P. Palaces are indeed like huge grapes—reddish, semitransparent, about fifteen feet in diameter, or perhaps twenty. I am not used to measuring spaces in such terms any more. The globes are connected to the central tower, or stem, by means of thick cables . . . their umbilicals. A high, wire-mesh fence surrounds the area, but here and there the rust has done its work in spite of zinc coating on the wire. With the corn-knife I have brought to defend us from the rats and God knows what, I open a place in the fence. We are trespassing, and we know this, but we have come this far.

"Where are the people?" asks Chris, and I see that he looks pale.

He has asked the question reluctantly, as though preferring no answer. I give none. We come close to one of the spheres, feeling that we do the wrong thing and doing it anyway. I see our objective and I point. It is a family of them, dimly visible like floating plants in an uncleaned aquarium. It is their frightened eyes we first see.

I do not know very much about the spheres except from hearsay and dim memory. The contents, including the occupants, are seen only dimly, I know, because the outer skins of the thing are filled with a self-replenishing liquid nutrient which requires the action of the sun and is augmented by the waste-products of the occupants. We look closer, moving so that the sun is directly behind the sphere, revealing its contents in sharper outline.

"Those are not real people," says Chris. Now he looks a little sick. "What are all those tubes and wires for if they're real people? Are they robots or dolls or what?"

I do not know the purpose of all the tubes and wires myself. I do know that some are connected with veins in their arms and legs, others are nutrient enemata and for collection of body wastes, still others are only mechanical tentacles which support and endlessly fondle and caress. I know that the wires leading to the metal caps on their heads are part of an invention more voracious and terrible than the ancient television—direct stimulation of certain areas of the brain, a constant running up and down the diapason of pleasurable sensation, controlled by a sort of electronic kaleidoscope.

My imagination stops about here. It would be the ultimate artificiality, with nothing of reality about it save endless variation. Of senselessness I will not think. I do not know if they see constantly shifting masses or motes of color, or smell exotic perfumes, or hear unending and constantly swelling music. I think not. I doubt that they even experience anything so immediate and yet so amorphous as the surge and recession of orgasm or the gratification of thirst being quenched. It would be stimulation without real stimulus; ultimate removal from reality. I decide not to speak of this to Chris. He has had enough. He has seen the wires and the tubes.

I have never sprung such abstractions as "Dignity" upon the boy. What good are such absolutes on a mountainside? If there is Dignity in grubbing out weeds and planting beans, those pursuits must be more dignified *than* something, because, like all words, it is a meaningless wisp of lint once removed from its relativistic fabric. The word does not exist until he invents it himself. The hoe and the rocky soil or the nutrient enema and the electronic ecstasy: He must judge for himself. That is why I have brought him here.

"Let's get away from here," he says. "Let's go home!"

"Good," I say, but even as I say it I can see that the largest of the pallid creatures inside the "grape" is doing something—I cannot tell what—and to my surprise it seems capable of enough awareness of us to become alarmed. What frightening creatures we must be—dirty, leather clothes with patches of dried animal blood on them, my beard and the small-boy grime of Chris! Removed as I am from these helpless aquarium creatures, I cannot blame them. But my compassion was a short-lived thing. Chris screamed.

I turned in time to see what can only be described as a huge metal scorpion rushing at Chris with its tail lashing, its fore-claws snapping like pruning shears and red lights flashing angrily where its eyes should have been. A guard robot, of course. Why I had not foreseen such a thing I will never know. I supposed at the time that the creature inside the sphere had alerted it.

The tin scorpion may have been a match for the reactions and the muscles of less primitive, more "civilized" men than ourselves, or the creators of the Perpetual Parmenidean Palaces had simply not foreseen barbarians with heavy corn-knives. I knocked Chris out of the way and dispatched the tin bug, snipping off its tail-stinger with a lucky slash of the corn-knife and jumping up and down on its thorax until all its appendages were still.

When the reaction set in, I had to attack something else. I offer no other justification for what I did. We were the intruders—the invading barbarians. All the creatures in the spheres wanted was their security. The man in the sphere set the scorpion on us, but he was protecting his family. I can see it that way now. I wish I couldn't. I wish I was one of those people who can always contrive to have been Right.

I saw the frightened eyes of the things inside the sphere, and I reacted to it as a predatory animal reacts to the scent of urea in the sweat of a lesser animal. And they had menaced my son with a hideous machine in order to be absolutely *secure!* If I reasoned at all, it was along this line.

The corn-knife was not very sharp, but the skin of the sphere parted with disgusting ease. I heard Chris scream, "No! Dad! No!" . . . but I kept hacking. We were nearly engulfed in the pinkish, albuminous nutritive which gushed from the ruptured sac. I can still smell it.

The creatures inside were more terrible to see in the open air than they had been behind their protective layers of plastic material. They were dead white and they looked to be soft, although they must have had normal human skeletons. Their struggles were blind, pointless and feeble, like those of some kind of larvae found under dead wood, and the largest made a barely audible mewing sound as it groped about in search of what I cannot imagine.

I heard Chris retching violently, but could not tear my attention away from the spectacle. The sphere now looked like some huge coelenterate which had been halved for study in the laboratory, and the hoselike tentacles still moved like groping cilia.

The agony of the creatures in the "grape" (I cannot think of them as People) when they were first exposed to unfiltered, unprocessed air and sunlight, when the wires and tubes were torn from them, and especially when the metal caps on their heads fell off in their panicky struggles and the whole universe of chilly external reality rushed in upon them at once, is beyond my imagining; and perhaps this is merciful. This and the fact that they lay in the stillness of death after only a very few minutes in the open air.

Memory is merciful too in its imperfection. All I remember of our homeward journey is the silence of it.

"Wake up! We have company, old man!"

It is Sue shaking me. Somehow I did sleep—in spite of Chris and in spite of the persistent memory. It must be midmorning. I swing my feet down and scrub at my gritty eyes. Voices outside. Cheerful. How cheerful?

It is Sato and he has his old horse hitched to a crude travois of willow poles. It is Sato and his wife and three kids and my son Chris. There trussed up on the travois is the biggest buck I have seen in ten years, its neck transfixed with an arrow. A perfect shot and one that could not have been scored without the most careful and skillful stalking. I remember teaching him that only a bad hunter . . . a heedless and cruel one . . . would risk a distant shot with a bow.

Chris is grinning and looking sheepish. Sato's daughter is there, which accounts for the look of benign idiocy. I was wondering when he would notice. Then he sees me standing in the door of the cabin and his face takes on about ten years of gravity and thought, but this is not for the benefit of the teen-age female. Little Mike is clawing at Chris and asking *why* he went away like that and *why* he went hunting without Daddy, and several other *whys* which Chris ignores. His answer is for his old man:

"I'm sorry, Dad. I wasn't mad at you . . . just sort of crazy. Had to do . . . this. . . ." He points at the deer. "Anyhow, I'm back."

"And I'm glad," I managed.

"Dad, those elder bushes . . ."

"To hell with them," say I. "Wednesday is soon enough."

Sato moves in grinning, and just in time to relieve the awkwardness. "Dressed out this buck and carried it down the mountain by himself." I think of mountain lions. "He was about pooped when I found him in a pasture."

Sue holds open the cabin door and the Satos file in. Himself first, carrying a jug of wine, then Mrs. Sato, grinning greetings. She has never mastered English. It has not been necessary.

I drag up what pass for chairs. Made them myself. We begin talking about weeds and beans, and weather, bugs and the condition of fruit trees. It is Sato who has steered the conversation into these familiar ways, bless his knowing heart. He uncorks the wine. Sue and Mrs. Sato, meanwhile, are carrying on one of their lively conversations. Someday I will listen to them, but I doubt that I will ever learn how they communicate . . . or what. Women.

I can hear Chris outside talking to Yuki, Sato's daughter. He is not boasting about the deer; he is telling her about the fight with the tin scorpion and the grape-people.

"Are they blind . . . the grape-people?" the girl asks.

"Heck no," says Chris. "At least one of them wasn't. One of them sicced the robot bug on us. They were going to kill us. And so, Dad did what he had to do. . . ."

I don't hear the details over the interjections of Yuki and little Mike, but I can imagine they are as pungent as the teen-age powers of physiological description allow. I hear Yuki exclaim, "Oh how utterly *germy!*" and another language problem occurs to me. How can kids who have never hung around a drugstore still manage to evolve languages of their own . . . characteristically adolescent dialects? It is one more mystery which I shall never solve. I hear little Mike asking for reasons and causes with his favorite word. *"Why, Chris?"*

"I'll explain it when you get older," says Chris, and oddly it doesn't sound ridiculous.

Sato pours a giant-size dollop of wine in each tumbler.

"What's the occasion?" I ask.

Sato studies the wine critically, holding the glass so the light from the door shines through.

"It's Tuesday," he says.

THE WIZARDS
OF PUNG'S CORNERS

Frederik Pohl

1

This is the way it happened in the old days. Pay attention now. I'm not going to repeat myself.

There was this old man. A wicked one. Coglan was his name, and he came into Pung's Corners in a solid-lead car. He was six feet seven inches tall. He attracted a lot of attention.

Why? Why, because nobody had ever seen a solid-lead car before. Nobody much had ever seen a stranger. It wasn't usual. That was how Pung's Corners was in the old days, a little pocket in the middle of the desert, and nobody came here. There weren't even planes overhead, or not for a long time; but there had been planes just before old man Coglan showed up. It made people nervous.

Old man Coglan had snapping black eyes and a loose and limber step. He got out of his car and slammed the door closed. It didn't go *tchik* like a Volkswagen or *perclack* like a Buick. It went woomp. It was heavy, since, as I mentioned, it was solid lead.

"Boy!" he bellowed, standing in front of Pung's Inn. "Come get my bags!"

Charley Frink was the bell-boy at that time—yes, the Senator. Of course, he was only fifteen years old then. He came out for Coglan's bags and he had to make four trips. There was a lot of space in the back of that car, with its truck tyres and double-thick glass, and all of it was full of baggage.

While Charley was hustling the bags in, Coglan was parading back and forth on Front Street. He winked at Mrs Churchwood and ogled young Kathy Flint. He nodded to the boys in front of the barber shop. He was a character, making himself at home like that.

In front of Andy Grammis's grocery store, Andy tipped his chair back. Considerately, he moved his feet so his yellow dog could get out the door. "He seems like a nice feller," he said to Jack Tighe. (Yes, *that* Jack Tighe.)

Jack Tighe stood in the shelter of the door and he was frowning. He knew more than any of the rest of them, though it wasn't time to say anything yet. But he said: "We don't get any strangers."

Andy shrugged. He leaned back in his chair. It was warm in the sun.

"Pshaw, Jack," he said. "Maybe we ought to get a few more. Town's going to sleep." He yawned drowsily.

And Jack Tighe left him there, left him and started down the street for home, because he knew what he knew.

Anyway, Coglan didn't hear them. If he had heard, he wouldn't have cared. It was old man Coglan's great talent that he didn't care what people had to say about him, and the others like him. He couldn't have been what he was if that hadn't been so.

So he checked in at Pung's Inn. "A suite, boy!" he boomed. "The best. A place where I can be comfortable, *real* comfortable."

"Yes, sir, Mister—"

"Coglan, boy! Edsel T. Coglan. A proud name at both ends, and I'm proud to wear it!"

"Yes, *sir*, Mr Coglan. Right away. Now let's see." He pored over his room ledgers, although, except for the Willmans and Mr Carpenter when his wife got mad at him, there weren't any guests, as he certainly knew. He pursed his lips. He said: "Ah, good! The bridal suite's vacant, Mr Coglan. I'm sure you'll be very comfortable there. Of course, it's eight-fifty a day."

"The bridal suite it is, boy!" Coglan chucked the pen into its holder with a fencer's thrust. He grinned like a fine old Bengal tiger with white crew-cut hair.

And there was something to grin about, in a way, wasn't there? The bridal suite. That was funny.

Hardly anybody ever took the bridal suite at Pung's Inn, unless they had a bride. You only had to look at Coglan to know that he was a long way from taking a bride—a long way, and in the wrong direction. Tall as he was, snapping-eyed and straight-backed as he was, he was clearly on the far side of marrying. He was at least eighty. You could see it in his creepy skin and his gnarled hands.

The room clerk whistled for Charley Frink. "Glad to have you with us, Mr Coglan," he said. "Charley'll have your bags up in a jiffy. Will you be staying with us long?"

Coglan laughed out loud. It was the laugh of a relaxed and confident man. "Yes," he said. "Quite long."

Now what did Coglan do when he was all alone in the bridal suite?

Well, first he paid off the bell-boy with a ten dollar bill. That surprised Charley Frink, all right. He wasn't used to that kind of tipping. He went out and Coglan closed the door behind him in a very great good humour.

Coglan was happy.

So he peered around, grinning a wolf's grin. He looked at the bathroom, with its stall shower and bright white porcelain. "Quaint," he murmured. He amused himself with the electric lights, switching them on and off. "Delicious," he said. "So *manual.*" In the living-room of the suite, the main light was from an overhead six-point chandelier, best Grand Rapids glass. Two of the pendants were missing. "Ridiculous," chuckled old Mr Coglan, "but very, very sweet."

Of course, you know what he was thinking. He was thinking of the big caverns and the big machines. He was thinking of the design wobblators and the bomb-shielded power sources, the self-contained raw material lodes and the unitized distribution pipelines. But I'm getting ahead of the story. It isn't time to talk about those things yet. So don't ask.

Anyway, after old man Coglan had a good look around, he opened one of his bags.

He sat down in front of the desk.

He took a Kleenex out of his pocket and with a fastidious expression picked up the blotter with it, and dumped it on the floor.

He lifted the bag on to the bare desk top and propped it, open, against the wall.

You never saw a bag like that! It looked like a kind of electronic tool kit, I swear. Its back was a panel of pastel lucite with sparks embedded in it. It glittered. There was a cathode screen. There was a scanner, a microphone, a speaker. All those things and lots more. How do I know this? Why, it's all written down in a book called *My Eighteen Years at Pung's Hall,* by Senator C. T. Frink. Because Charley was in the room next door and there was a keyhole.

So then what happened was that a little tinkly chime sounded distantly within the speaker, and the cathode screen flickered and lit up.

"Coglan," boomed the tall old man. "Reporting in. Let me speak to V. P. Maffity."

2

Now you have to know what Pung's Corners was like in those days.

Everybody knows what it is now, but then it was small. Very small. It sat on the bank of the Delaware River like a fat old lady on the edge of a spindly chair.

General "Retreating Johnnie" Estabrook wintered there before the Battle of Monmouth and wrote pettishly to General Washington: "I can obtain no Provision here, as the inhabitants are so averse to our Cause, that I cannot get a Man to come near me."

During the Civil War, a small draft riot took place in its main square, in which a recruiting colonel of the IXth Volunteer Pennsylvania Zouaves was chased out of town and the son of the town's leading banker suffered superficial scalp wounds. (He fell off his horse. He was drunk.)

These were only little wars, you know. They had left only little scars. Pung's Corners missed all the big ones.

For instance, when the biggest of all got going, why, Pung's Corners had a ticket on the fifty-yard line but never had to carry the ball.

The cobalt bomb that annihilated New Jersey stopped short at the bank of the Delaware, checked by a persistent easterly wind.

The radio-dust that demolished Philadelphia went forty-some miles up the river. Then the drone that was spreading it was rammed down by a suicide pilot in a shaky jet. (Pung's Corners was one mile farther on.)

The H-bombs that scattered around the New York megalopolis bracketed Pung's Corners, but it lay unscathed between.

You see how it was? They never laid a glove on us. But after the war, we were marooned.

Now that wasn't a bad way to be, you know? Read some of the old books, you'll see. The way Pung's Corners felt, there was a lot to be said for being marooned. People in Pung's Corners were genuinely sorry about the war, with so many people getting killed and all. (Although we won it. It was worse for the other side.) But every cloud has its silver lining and so on, and being surrounded at every point of the compass by badlands that no one could cross had a few compensating features.

There was a Nike battalion in Pung's Corners, and they say they shot down the first couple of helicopters that tried to land because they thought they were the enemy. Maybe they did. But along about the fifth copter, they didn't think that any more, I guarantee. And then the planes stopped coming. Outside, they had plenty to think about, I suppose. They stopped bothering with Pung's Corners.

Until Mr Coglan came in.

After Coglan got his line of communication opened up—because that was what the big suitcase was, a TV communications set—he talked for a little while. Charley had a red dent on his forehead for two days, he pressed against the doorknob so hard, trying to see.

"Mr Maffity?" boomed Coglan, and a pretty girl's face lighted up on the screen.

"This is Vice President Maffity's secretary," she said sweetly. "I see you arrived safely. One moment, please, for Mr Maffity."

And then the set flickered and another face showed up, the blood brother to Coglan's own. It was the face of an elderly and successful man who recognized no obstacles, the face of a man who knew what he wanted and got it. "Coglan, boy! Good to see you got there!"

"No sweat, L.S.," said Coglan. "I'm just about to secure my logistics. Money. This is going to take money."

"No trouble?"

"No trouble, Chief. I can promise you that. There isn't *going* to be any trouble." He grinned and picked up a nested set of little metallic boxes out of a pouch in the suitcase. He opened one, shook out a small disc-shaped object, silver and scarlet plastic. "I'm using this right away."

"And the reservoir?"

"I haven't checked yet, Chief. But the pilots said they dumped the stuff in. No opposition from the ground either, did you notice that? These people used to shoot down every plane that came near. They're softening. They're ripe."

"Good enough," said L. S. Maffity from the little cathode screen. "Make it so, Coglan. Make it so."

Now, at the Shawanganunk National Bank, Mr LaFarge saw Coglan come in and knew right away something was up.

How do I know that? Why, that's in a book too. *The Federal Budget and How I Balanced It: A Study in Surplus Dynamics,* by Treasury Secretary (Retired) Wilbur Otis LaFarge. Most everything is in a book, if you know where to look for it. That's something you young people have got to learn.

Anyway, Mr LaFarge, who was then only an Assistant Vice-President, greeted old man Coglan effusively. It was his way. "Morning, sir!" he said. "Morning! In what way can we serve you here at the bank?"

"We'll find a way," promised Mr Coglan.

"Of course, sir. Of course!" Mr LaFarge rubbed his hands. "You'll want a checking account. Certainly! And a savings account? And a safety deposit box? Absolutely! Christmas Club, I suppose. Perhaps a short-term auto loan, or a chattel loan on your household effects for the purpose of consolidating debts and reducing—"

"Don't have any debts," said Coglan. "Look, what's-your-name—"

"LaFarge, sir! Wilbur LaFarge. Call me Will."

"Look, Willie. Here are my credit references." And he spilled a manila envelope out on the desk in front of LaFarge.

The banker looked at the papers and frowned. He picked one up. "Letter of credit," he said. "Some time since I saw one of those. From Danbury, Connecticut, eh?" He shook his head and pouted. "All from outside, sir."

"I'm from outside."

"I see." LaFarge sighed heavily after a second. "Well, sir, I don't know. What is it you wanted?"

"What I want is a quarter of a million dollars, Willie. In cash. And make it snappy, will you?"

Mr LaFarge blinked.

You don't know him, of course. He was before your time. You don't know what a request like that would do to him.

When I say he blinked, I mean, man, he *blinked*. Then he blinked again and it seemed to calm him. For a moment, the veins had begun to stand out in his temples; for a moment, his mouth was open to speak. But he closed his mouth and the veins receded.

Because, you see, old man Coglan took that silvery scarlet thing out of his pocket. It glittered. He gave it a twist and he gave it a certain kind of squeeze, and it hummed, a deep and throbbing note. But it didn't satisfy Mr Coglan.

"Wait a minute," he said, offhandedly, and he adjusted it and squeezed it again. "That's better," he said.

The note was deeper, but still not quite deep enough to suit Coglan. He twisted the top a fraction more, until the pulsing note was too deep to be heard, and then he nodded.

There was silence for a second.

Then: "Large bills?" cried Mr LaFarge. "Or small?" He leaped up and waved to a cashier. "Two hundred and fifty thousand dollars! You there, Tom Fairleigh! Hurry it up now. What? No, I don't care where you get it. Go out to the vault, if there isn't enough in the cages. But bring me two hundred and fifty thousand dollars!"

He sank down at his desk again, panting. "I am really sorry, sir," he apologized to Mr Coglan. "The clerks you get these days! I almost wish that old times would come back."

"Perhaps they will, friend," said Coglan, grinning widely to himself. "Now," he said, not unkindly, "shut up."

He waited, tapping the desk top, humming to himself, staring at the blank wall. He completely ignored Mr LaFarge until Tom Fairleigh and another teller brought four canvas sacks of bills. They began to dump them on the desk to count them.

"No, don't bother," said Coglan cheerfully, his black eyes snapping with good humour. "I trust you." He picked up the sacks, nodded courteously to Mr LaFarge, and walked out.

Ten seconds later, Mr LaFarge suddenly shook his head, rubbed his eyes and stared at the two tellers. "What—"

"You just gave him a quarter of a million dollars," said Tom Fairleigh. "You made me get it out of the vault."

"I *did?*"

"You did."

They looked at each other.

Mr LaFarge said at last: "It's been a long time since we had any of *that* in Pung's Corners."

3

Now I have to tell a part that isn't so nice. It's about a girl named Marlene Groshawk. I positively will not explain any part of it. I probably shouldn't mention it at all, but it's part of the history of our country. Still—

Well, this is what happened. Yes, it's in a book too—*On Call,* by One Who Knows. (And we know who "One Who Knows" is, don't we?)

She wasn't a bad girl. Not a bit of it. Or, anyway, she didn't mean to be. She was too pretty for her own good and not very smart. What she wanted out of life was to be a television star.

Well, that was out of the question, of course. We didn't use live television at all in Pung's Corners those days, only a few old tapes. They left the commercials in, although the goods the old, dead announcers were trying to sell were not on the market anywhere, much less in Pung's Corners. And Marlene's idol was a TV saleslady named Betty Furness. Marlene had pictures of her, dubbed off the tapes, pasted all over the walls of her room.

At the time I'm talking about, Marlene called herself a public stenographer. There wasn't too much demand for her services. (And later on, after things opened up, she gave up that part of her business entirely.) But if anybody needed a little extra help in Pung's Corners, like writing some letters or getting caught up on the back filing and such, they'd call on Marlene. She'd never worked for a stranger before.

She was rather pleased when the desk clerk told her that there was this new Mr Coglan in town, and that he needed an assistant to help him run some new project he was up to. She didn't know what the project was, but I have to tell you that if she knew, she would have helped anyhow. Any budding TV star would, of course.

She stopped in the lobby of Pung's Inn to adjust her make-up. Charley Frink looked at her with that kind of a look, in spite of being only fifteen. She sniffed at him, tossed her head, and proudly went upstairs.

She tapped on the carved oak door of Suite 41—that was the bridal suite; she knew it well—and smiled prettily for the tall old man with snapping eyes who swung it open.

"Mr Coglan? I'm Miss Groshawk, the public stenographer. I understand you sent for me."

The old man looked at her piercingly for a moment.

"Yes," he said, "I did. Come in."

He turned his back on her and let her come in and close the door by herself.

Coglan was busy. He had the suite's television set in pieces all over the floor.

He was trying to fix it some way or another, Marlene judged. And that was odd, mused Marlene in her cloudy young way, because even if she wasn't really *brainy*, she knew that he was no television repairman, or anything like that. She knew exactly what he was. It said so on his card, and Mr LaFarge had shown the card around town. He was a research and development counsellor.

Whatever *that* was.

Marlene was conscientious, and she knew that a good public stenographer took her temporary employer's work to heart. She said: "Something wrong, Mr Coglan?"

He looked up, irritably. "I can't get Danbury on this thing."

"Danbury, Connecticut? Outside? No, sir. It isn't supposed to get Danbury."

He straightened up and looked at her. "It isn't supposed to get Danbury." He nodded thoughtfully. "This forty-eight-inch twenty-seven tube full-colour suppressed sideband UHF-VHF General Electric wall model with static suppressors and self-compensating tuning strips, it isn't supposed to get Danbury, Connecticut."

"That's right, sir."

"Well," he said, "that's going to be a big laugh on the cavern in Schenectady."

Marlene said helpfully: "It hasn't got any antenna."

Coglan frowned and corrected her. "No, that's impossible. It's got to have an antenna. These leads go somewhere."

Marlene shrugged attractively.

He said: "Right after the war, of course, you couldn't get Danbury at all. I agree. Not with all those fission products, eh? But that's down to a negligible count now. Danbury should come in loud and clear."

Marlene said: "No, it was after that. I used to, uh, date a fellow named Timmy Horan, and he was in that line of business, making television repairs, I mean. A couple years after the war, I was just a kid, they began to get pictures once in a while. Well, they passed a law, Mr Coglan."

"A *law*?" His face looked suddenly harsh.

"Well, I think they did. Anyway, Timmy had to go around taking the antennas off all the sets. He really did. Then they hooked them up with TV tape recorders, like." She thought hard for a second. "He didn't tell me why," she volunteered.

"I know why," he said flatly.

"So it only plays records, Mr Coglan. But if there's anything you want, the desk clerk'll get it for you. He's got lots. Dinah Shores and Jackie Gleasons and *Medic*. Oh, and Westerns. You tell him what you want."

"I see." Coglan stood there for a second, thinking. Not to her but to himself, he said: "No wonder we weren't getting through. Well, we'll see about that."

"What, Mr Coglan?"

"Never mind, Miss Groshawk. I see the picture now. And it isn't a very pretty one."

He went back to the television set.

He wasn't a TV mechanic, no, but he knew a little something about what he was doing for sure, because he had it all back together in a minute. Oh, less than that. And not just the way it was. He had it improved. Even Marlene could see that. Maybe not *improved*, but different; he'd done something to it.

"Better?" he demanded, looking at her.

"I beg your pardon?"

"I mean does looking at the picture do anything to you?"

"I'm sorry, Mr Coglan, but I honestly don't care for *Studio One*. It makes me think too hard, you know?"

But she obediently watched the set.

He had tuned in on the recorded wire signal that went out to all of Pung's Corners TV sets. I don't suppose you know how we did it then, but there was a central station where they ran off a show all the time, for people who didn't want to bother with tapes. It was all old stuff, of course. And everybody had seen all of them already.

But Marlene watched, and funnily, in a moment she began to giggle.

"Why, Mr *Coglan*," she said, though he hadn't done anything at all.

"Better," he said, and he was satisfied.

He had every reason to be.

"However," said Mr Coglan, "first things come first. I need your help."

"All right, Mr Coglan," Marlene said in a silky voice.

"I mean in a business way. I want to hire some people. I want you to help me locate them, and to keep the records straight. Then I shall need to buy certain materials. And I'll need an office, perhaps a few buildings for light industrial purposes, and so on."

"That will take a lot of money, won't it?"

Coglan chuckled.

"Well, then," said Marlene, satisfied, "I'm your girl, Mr Coglan. I mean in a business way. Would you mind telling me what the business is?"

"I intend to put Pung's Corners back on its feet."

"Oh, sure, Mr Coglan. But how, I mean?"

"Advertising," said old man Coglan, with a devil's smile and a demon's voice.

Silence. There was a moment of silence.

Marlene said faintly: "I don't think they're going to like it."

"Who?"

"The bigwigs. They aren't going to like that. Not advertising, you know. I mean I'm for *you*. I'm in favour of advertising. I *like* it. But—"

"There's no question of liking it!" Coglan said in a terrible voice. "It's what has made our country great! It tooled us up to fight in a great war, and when the war was over, it put us back together again!"

"I understand that, Mr Coglan," she said. "But—"

"I don't want to hear that word from you, Miss Groshawk," he snapped. "There is no question. Consider America after the war, ah? You don't remember, perhaps. They kept it from you. But the cities all were demolished. The buildings were ruins. It was only advertising that built them up again—advertising, and the power of research! For I remind you of what a great man once said: 'Our chief job in research is to keep the customer reasonably dissatisfied with what he has.' "

Coglan paused, visibly affected. "That was Charles F. Kettering of General Motors," he said, "and the beauty of it, Miss Groshawk, is that he said this in the Twenties! Imagine! So clear a perception of what Science means to all of us. So comprehensive a grasp of the meaning of American Inventiveness!"

Marlene said brokenly: "That's beautiful."

Coglan nodded. "Of course. So, you see, there is nothing at all that your bigwigs can do, like it or not. We Americans—we *real* Americans—know that without advertising there is no industry; and accordingly we have shaped advertising into a tool that serves us well. Why, here, look at that television set!"

Marlene did, and in a moment began again to giggle. Archly she whispered: "Mr Coglan!"

"You see? And if that doesn't suffice, well, there's always the law. Let's see what the bigwigs of Pung's Corners can do against the massed might of the United States Army!"

"I do hope there won't be any fighting, Mr Coglan."

"I doubt there will," he said sincerely. "And now to work, eh? Or—" he glanced at his watch and nodded—"after all, there's no real hurry this afternoon. Suppose we order some dinner, just for the two of us. And some wine? And—"

"Of course, Mr Coglan."

Marlene started to go to the telephone, but Mr Coglan stopped her. "On second thought, Miss Groshawk," he said, beginning to breathe a little hard, "I'll do the ordering. You just sit there and rest for a minute. Watch the television set, eh?"

4

Now I have to tell you about Jack Tighe.

Yes, indeed. Jack Tighe. The Father of the Second Republic. Sit tight and listen and don't interrupt, because what I have to tell you isn't exactly what you learned in school.

The apple tree? No, that's only a story. It couldn't have happened, you see, because apple trees don't grow on upper Madison Avenue, and that's where Jack Tighe spent his youth. Because Jack Tighe wasn't the President of the Second Republic. For a long time, he was something else, something called V.P. in charge of S.L. divison, of the advertising firm of Yust and Ruminant.

That's right. Advertising.

Don't cry. It's all right. He'd given it up, you see, long before—oh, *long* before, even before the big war; given it up and come to Pung's Corners, to retire.

Jack Tighe had his place out on the marshland down at the bend of the Delaware River. It wasn't particularly healthy there. All the high-lands around Pung's Corners drained into the creeks of that part of the area, and a lot of radio-activity had come down. But it didn't bother Jack Tighe, because he was too old.

He was as old as old man Coglan, in fact. And what's more, they had known each other, back at the agency.

Jack Tighe was also big, not as big as Coglan but well over six feet. And in a way he looked like Coglan. You've seen his pictures. Same eyes, same devil-may-care bounce to his walk and snap to his voice. He could have been a big man in Pung's Corners. They would have made him mayor any time. But he said he'd come there to retire, and retire he would; it would take a major upheaval to make him come out of retirement, he said.

And he got one.

The first thing was Andy Grammis, white as a sheet.

"Jack!" he whispered, out of breath at the porch steps, for he'd run almost all the way from his store.

Jack Tighe took his feet down off the porch rail. "Sit down, Andy," he said kindly. "I suppose I know why you're here."

"You do, Jack?"

"I think so." Jack Tighe nodded. Oh, he was a handsome man. He said: "Aircraft dumping neoscopalamine in the reservoir, a stranger turning up in a car with a sheet-lead body. And we all know what's outside, don't we? Yes, it has to be that."

"It's him, all right," babbled Andy Grammis, plopping himself down on the steps, his face chalk. "It's him and there's nothing we can do! He came into the store this morning. Brought Marlene with him. We should have done something about that girl, Jack. I knew she'd come to no good—"

"What did he want?"

"Want? Jack, he had a pad and a pencil like he wanted to take down *orders*, and he kept asking for—asking for—'Breakfast foods,' he says, 'what've you got in the way of breakfast foods?' So I told him. Oatmeal and corn flakes. Jack, he *flew* at me! 'You don't stock Coco-Wheet?' he says. 'Or Treets, Eets, Neets, or Elixo-Wheets? How about Hunny-Yummies, or Prune-Bran Whippets, The Cereal with the Zip-Gun in Every Box?' 'No, sir,' I tell him."

"But he's mad by then. 'Potatoes?' he hollers. 'What about potatoes?' Well, we've got plenty of potatoes, a whole cellar full. But I tell him and *that* doesn't satisfy him. '*Raw*, you mean?' he yells. 'Not Tater-Fluff, Pre-Skortch Mickies, or Uncle Everett's Converted Spuds?' And then he shows me his card."

"I know," said Jack Tighe kindly, for Grammis seemed to find it hard to go on. "You don't have to say it, if you don't want to."

"Oh, I can say it all right, Jack," said Andy Grammis bravely. "This Mr Coglan, he's an adver—"

"No," said Jack Tighe, standing up, "don't make yourself do it. It's bad enough as it is. But it had to come. Yes, count it that it had to come, Andy. We've had a few good years, but we couldn't expect them to last forever."

"But what are we going to *do*?"

"Get up, Andy," said Jack Tighe strongly. "Come inside! Sit down and rest yourself. And I'll send for the others."

"You're going to fight him? But he has the whole United States Army behind him."

Old Jack Tighe nodded. "So he has, Andy," he said, but he seemed wonderfully cheerful.

Jack Tighe's place was a sort of ranch house, with fixings. He was a great individual man, Jack Tighe was. All of you know that, because you were taught it in school; and maybe some of you have been to the house. But it's different now; I don't care what they say. The furniture isn't just the same. And the grounds—

Well, during the big war, of course, that was where the radio-dust drained down from the hills, so nothing grew. They've prettied it up with grass and trees and flowers. Flowers! I'll tell you what's wrong with that. In his young days, Jack Tighe was an account executive on the National Floral account. Why, he wouldn't have a flower in the house, much less plant and tend them.

But it was a nice house, all the same. He fixed Andy Grammis a drink and sat him down. He phoned down-town and invited half a dozen people to come in to see them. He didn't say what it was about, naturally. No sense in starting a panic.

But everyone pretty much knew. The first to arrive was Timmy Horan, the fellow from the television service, and he'd given Charley Frink a ride on the back of his bike. He said, breathless: "Mr Tighe, they're on our lines. I don't know how he's done it, but Coglan is transmitting on our wire TV circuit. And the stuff he's transmitting, Mr Tighe!"

"Sure," said Tighe soothingly. "Don't worry about it, Timothy. I imagine I know what sort of stuff it is, eh?"

He got up, humming pleasantly, and snapped on the television set. "Time for the afternoon movie, isn't it? I suppose you left the tapes running."

"Of course, but he's interfering with it!"

Tighe nodded. "Let's see."

The picture on the TV screen quavered, twisted into slanting lines of pale dark, and snapped into shape.

"I remember that one!" Charley Frink exclaimed. "It's one of my favourites, Timmy!"

On the screen, Number Two Son, a gun in his hand was backing away from a hooded killer. Number Two Son tripped over a loose board and fell into a vat. He came up grotesquely comic, covered with plaster and mud.

Tighe stepped back a few paces. He spread the fingers of one hand and moved them rapidly up and down before his eyes.

"Ah," he said, "yes. See for yourself, gentlemen."

Andy Grammis hesitatingly copied the older man. He spread his fingers and, clumsily at first, moved them before his eyes, as though shielding his vision from the cathode tube. Up and down he moved his hand, making a sort of stroboscope that stopped the invisible flicker of the racing electronic pencil.

And, yes, there it was!

Seen without the stroboscope, the screen showed bland-faced Charlie Chan in his white Panama hat. But the stroboscope showed something else. Between the consecutive images of the old movie there was another image—flashed for only a tiny fraction of a second, too quick for the conscious brain to comprehend, but, oh, how it struck into the subconscious!

Andy blushed.

"That—that girl," he stammered, shocked. "She hasn't got any—"

"Of course she hasn't," said Tighe pleasantly. "Subliminal compulsion, eh? The basic sex drive; you don't know you're seeing it, but the submerged mind doesn't miss it. No. And notice the box of Prune-Bran Whippets in her hand."

Charley Frink coughed. "Now that you mention it, Mr Tighe," he said, "I notice that I've just been thinking how tasty a dish of Prune-Bran Whippets would be right now."

"Naturally," agreed Jack Tighe. Then he frowned. "Naked women, yes. But the female audience should be appealed to also. I wonder." He was silent for a couple of minutes, and held the others silent with him, while tirelessly he moved the spread hand before his eyes.

Then *he* blushed.

"Well," he said amiably, "that's for the female audience. It's all there. Subliminal advertising. A product, and a key to the basic drives, and all flashed so quickly that the brain can't organize its defences. So when you think of Prune-Bran Whippets, you think of sex. Or more important, when you think of sex, you think of Prune-Bran Whippets."

"Gee, Mr Tighe. I think about sex a lot."

"Everybody does," said Jack Tighe comfortingly, and he nodded.

There was a gallumphing sound from outside then and Wilbur LaFarge from Shawanganunk National came trotting in. He was all out of breath and scared.

"He's done it again, he's done it again, Mr Tighe, sir! That Mr Coglan, he came and demanded more money! Said he's going to build a real TV network slave station here in Pung's Corners. Said he's opening up a branch agency for Yust and Ruminant, whoever they are. Said he was about to put Pung's Corners back on the map and needed money to do it."

"And you gave it to him?"

"I couldn't *help* it."

Jack Tighe nodded wisely. "No, you couldn't. Even in my day, you couldn't much help it, not when the agency had you in its sights and the finger squeezing down on the trigger. Neo-scop in the drinking water, to make every living soul in Pung's Corners a little more suggestible, a little less stiff-backed. Even me, I suppose, though perhaps I don't drink as much water as most. And subliminal advertising on the wired TV, and subsonic compulsives when it comes to man-to-man talk. Tell me, LaFarge, did you happen to hear a faint droning sound? I thought so; yes. They don't miss a trick. Well," he said, looking somehow pleased, "there's no help for it. We'll have to fight."

"Fight?" whispered Wilbur LaFarge, for he was no brave man, no, not even though he later became the Secretary of the Treasury.

"Fight!" boomed Jack Tighe.

Everybody looked at everybody else.

"There are hundreds of us," said Jack Tighe, "and there's only one of him. Yes, we'll fight! We'll distil the drinking water. We'll rip Coglan's little transmitter out of our TV circuit. Timmy can work up electronic sniffers to see what else he's using; we'll find all his gadgets, and we'll destroy them. The subsonics? Why, he has to carry that gear with him. We'll just take it away from him. It's either that or we give up our heritage as free men!"

Wilbur LaFarge cleared his throat. "And then—"

"Well you may say 'and then,'" agreed Jack Tighe. "And then the United States Cavalry comes charging over the hill to rescue him. Yes. But you must have realized by now, gentlemen, that this means war."

And so they had, though you couldn't have said that any of them seemed very happy about it.

5

Now I have to tell you what it was like outside in those days.

The face of the Moon is no more remote. Oh, you can't imagine it, you really can't. I don't know if I can explain it to you, either, but it's all in a book and you can read it if you want to . . . a book that was written by somebody important, a major, who later on became a general (but that was *much* later and in another army) and whose name was T. Wallace Commaigne.

The book? Why, that was called *The End of the Beginning,* and it is Volume One of his twelve-volume set of memoirs entitled: *I Served with Tighe: The Struggle to Win the World.*

War had been coming, war that threatened more, until it threatened everything, as the horrors in its supersonic pouches grew beyond even the dreads of hysteria. But there was time to guesstimate, as *Time* Magazine used to call it.

The dispersal plan came first. Break up cities, spread them apart, diffuse population and industry to provide the smallest possible target for even the largest possible bomb.

But dispersal increased another vulnerability—more freight trains, more cargo ships, more boxcar planes carrying raw materials to and finished products from an infinity of production points. Harder, yes, to hit and destroy, easier to choke off coming and going.

Then dig in, the planners said. Not dispersal but bomb shelter. But more than bomb shelter—make the factories mine for their ores, drill for their fuels, pump for their coolants and steams—and make them independent of supplies that may never be delivered, of workers who could not live below ground for however long the unpredictable war may last, seconds or forever—even of brains that might not reach the drawing boards and research labs and directors' boards, brains that might either be dead or concussed into something other than brains.

So the sub-surface factories even designed for themselves, always on a rising curve.

Against an enemy presupposed to grow smarter and slicker and quicker with each advance, just as we and our machines do. Against our having fewer and fewer fighting men; pure logic that, as war continues, more and more are killed, fewer and fewer left to operate the killer engines. Against the destruction or capture of even the impregnable underground factories, guarded as no dragon of legend ever was—by all that Man could devise at first in the way of traps and cages, blast and ray—and then by the slip-leashed invention of machines ordered always to speed up—more and more, deadlier and deadlier.

And the next stage—the fortress factories hooked to each other, so that the unthinkably defended plants, should they inconceivably fall, would in the dying message pass their responsibilities to the next of kin—survivor factories to split up their work, increase output, step up the lethal pace of invention and perfection, still more murderous weapons to be operated by still fewer defenders.

And another, final plan—gear the machines to feed and house and clothe and transport a nation, a hemisphere, a world recovering from no one could know in advance what bombs and germs and poisons and—name it and it probably would happen if the war lasted long enough.

With a built-in signal of peace, of course: the air itself. Pure once more, the atmosphere, routinely tested moment by moment, would switch production from war to peace.

And so it did.

But who could have known beforehand that the machines might not *know* war from peace?

Here's Detroit: a hundred thousand rat-inhabited manless acres, blind windows and shattered walls. From the air, it is dead. But underneath it—ah, the rapid pulse of life! The hammering systole and diastole of raw-material conduits sucking in fuel and ore, pumping out finished autos. Spidery passages stretched out to the taconite beds under the Lakes. Fleets of barges issued from concrete pens to match the U-boat nests at Lorient and, unmanned, swam the Lakes and the canals to their distribution points, bearing shiny new Buicks and Plymouths.

What made them new?

Why, industrial design! For the model years changed. The Dynaflow '61 gave place to the Super-Dynaflow Mark Eight of 1962; twin-beam headlights became triple; white-wall tyres turned to pastel and back to solid ebony black.

It was a matter of design efficiency.

What the Founding Fathers learned about production was essentially this: It doesn't much matter what you build, it only matters that people should want to buy it. What they learned was: Never mind the judgematical faculties of the human race. They are a frail breed. They move no merchandise. They boost no sales. Rely, instead, on the monkey trait of curiosity.

And curiosity, of course, feeds on secrecy.

So generations of automotivators created new cosmetic gimmicks for their cars in secret laboratories staffed by sworn mutes. No atomic device was half so classified! And all Detroit echoed their security measures; fleets of canvas-swathed mysteries swarmed the highways at new-model time each year; people talked. Oh, yes—they laughed; it was comic; but though they were amused, they were piqued; it was good to make a joke of the mystery, but the capper to the joke was to own one of the new models oneself.

The appliance manufacturers pricked up their ears. Ah, so. Curiosity, eh? So they leased concealed space to design new ice-tray compartments and brought them out with a flourish of trumpets. Their refrigerators sold like mad. Yes, like mad.

RCA brooded over the lesson and added a fillip of their own; there was the vinylite record, unbreakable, colourful, new. They designed it under wraps and then, the crowning touch, they leaked the secret; it was the trick that Manhattan Project hadn't learned—a secret that concealed the real secret. For all the vinylite programme was only a façade; it was security in its highest manifestation; the vinylite programme was a mere cover for the submerged l.p.

It moved goods. But there was a limit. The human race is a blabbermouth.

Very well, said some great unknown, eliminate the human race! Let a *machine* design the new models! Add a design unit. Set it, by means of wobblators and random-choice circuits, to make its changes in an unforeseeable way. Automate the factories; conceal them underground; programme the machine to programme itself. After all, why not? As Coglan had quoted Charles F. Kettering, "Our chief job in research is to keep the customer reasonably dissatisfied with what he has," and proper machines can do *that* as well as any man. Better, if you really want to know.

And so the world was full of drusy caverns from which wonders constantly poured. The war had given industry its start by starting the dispersal pattern; bomb shelter had embedded the factories in rock; now industrial security made the factories independent. Goods flowed out in a variegated torrent.

But they couldn't stop. And nobody could get inside to shut them off or even slow them down. And that torrent of goods, made for so many people who didn't exist, had to be moved. The advertising men had to do the moving, and they were excellent at the job.

So that was the outside, a very, very busy place and a very, very big one. In spite of what happened in the big war.

I can't begin to tell you how busy it was or how big; I can only tell you about a little bit of it. There was a building called the Pentagon and it covered acres of ground. It had five sides, of course; one for the Army, one for the Navy, one for the Air Force, one for the Marines, and one for the offices of Yust & Ruminant.

So here's the Pentagon, this great building, the nerve centre of the United States in every way that mattered. (There was also a "Capitol", as they called it, but that doesn't matter much. Didn't then, in fact.)

And here's Major Commaigne, in his scarlet dress uniform with his epaulettes and his little gilt sword. He's waiting in the anteroom of the Director's Office of Yust & Ruminant, nervously watching television. He's been waiting there for an hour, and then at last they send for him.

He goes in.

Don't try to imagine his emotions as he walks into that pigskin panelled suite. You can't. But understand that he believes that the key to all of his future lies in this room; he believes that with all his heart and in a way, as it develops, he is right.

"Major," snaps an old man, a man very like Coglan and very like Jack Tighe, for they were all pretty much of a breed, those Ivy-League charcoal greys, "Major, he's coming through. It's just as we feared. There has been trouble."

"Yes, sir!"

Major Commaigne is very erect and military in his bearing, because he has been an Army officer for fifteen years now and this is his first chance at combat. He missed the big war—well, the whole Army missed the big war; it was over too fast for moving troops—and fighting has pretty much stopped since then. It isn't *safe* to fight, except under certain conditions. But maybe the conditions are right now, he thinks. And it can mean a lot to a major's career, these days, if he gets an expeditionary force to lead and acquits himself well with it!

So he stands erect, alert, sharp-eyed. His braided cap is tucked in the corner of one arm, and his other hand rests on the hilt of his sword, and he looks fierce. Why, that's natural enough, too. What comes in over the TV communicator in that pigskin-panelled office would make any honest Army officer look fierce. The authority of the United States has been flouted!

"L.S.," gasps the image of a tall, dark old man in the picture tube, "they've turned against me! They've seized my transmitter, neutralized my drugs, confiscated my subsonic gear. All I have left is this transmitter!"

And he isn't urbane any more, this man Coglan whose picture is being received in this room; he looks excited and he looks mad.

"Funny," comments Mr Maffity, called "L.S." by his intimate staff, "that they didn't take the transmitter away too. They must have known you'd contact us and that there would be reprisals."

"But they *wanted* me to contact you!" cries the voice from the picture tube. "I told them what it would mean L.S., they're going crazy. They're spoiling for a fight."

And after a little more talk, L.S. Maffity turns off the set.

"We'll give it to them, eh, Major?" he says, as stern and straight as a ramrod himself.

"We will, sir!" says the major, and he salutes, spins around and leaves. Already he can feel the eagles on his shoulders—who knows, maybe even stars!

And this is how the punitive expedition came to be launched; and it was exactly what Pung's Corners could have expected as a result of their actions—could have, and did.

Now I already told you that fighting had been out of fashion for some time, though getting *ready* to fight was a number-one preoccupation of a great many people. You must understand that there appeared to be no contradiction in these two contradictory facts, outside.

The big war had pretty much discouraged anybody from doing anything very violent. Fighting in the old-fashioned way—that is, with missiles and radio-dust and atomic cannon—had turned out to be expensive and for other reasons impractical. It was only the greatest of luck then that stopped things before the planet was wiped off, nice and clean, of everything more advanced than the notochord, ready for the one-celled beasts of the sea to start over again. Now things were different.

First place, all atomic explosives were under *rigid* interdiction. There were a couple of dozen countries in the world that owned A-bombs or better, and every one of them had men on duty, twenty-four hours a day, with their fingers held ready over buttons that would wipe out for once and all whichever one of them might first use an atomic weapon again. So that was out.

And aircraft, by the same token, lost a major part of their usefulness. The satellites with their beady little TV eyes scanned every place every second, so that you didn't dare drop even an ordinary HE bomb as long as some nearsighted chap watching through a satellite relay might mistake it for something nuclear—and give the order to push one of those buttons.

This left, generally speaking, the infantry.

But what infantry it was! A platoon of riflemen was twenty-three men and it owned roughly the firepower of all of Napoleon's legions. A company comprised some twelve hundred and fifty, and it could single-handed have won World War One.

Hand weapons spat out literally sheets of metal, projectiles firing so rapidly one after another that you didn't so much try to shoot a target as to slice it in half. As far as the eye could see, a rifle bullet could fly. And where the eye was blocked by darkness, by fog, or by hills, the sniperscope, the radar-screen, and the pulse-beam interferometer sights could locate the target as though it were ten yards away at broad noon.

They were, that is to say, very modern weapons. In fact, the weapons that this infantry carried were so modern that half of each company was in process of learning to operate weapons that the other half had already discarded as obsolete. Who wanted a Magic-Eye Self-Aiming All-Weather Gunsight, Mark XII, when a Mark XIII, With Dubl-Jewelled Bearings, was available?

For it was one of the triumphs of the age that at last the planned obsolescence and high turnover of, say, a TV set or a Detroit car had been extended to carbines and bazookas.

It was wonderful and frightening to see.

It was these heroes, then, who went off to war, or to whatever might come.

Major Commaigne (so he says in his book) took a full company of men, twelve hundred and fifty strong, and started out for Pung's Corners. Air brought them to the plains of Lehigh County, burned black from radiation but no longer dangerous. From there, they journeyed by wheeled vehicles.

Major Commaigne was coldly confident. The radioactivity of the sands surrounding Pung's Corners was no problem. Not with the massive and perfect equipment he had for his force. What old Mr Coglan could do, the United States Army could do better; Coglan drove inside sheet lead, but the expeditionary force cruised in solid iridium steel, with gamma-ray baffles fixed in place.

Each platoon had its own half-track personnel carrier. Not only did the men have their hand weapons, but each vehicle mounted a 105-mm explosive cannon, with Zip-Fire Auto-Load and Wizardtrol Safety Interlock. Fluid mountings sustained the gimbals of the cannon. Radar picked out its target. Automatic digital computers predicted and outguessed the flight of its prey.

In the lead personnel carrier, Major Commaigne barked a last word to his troops:

"This is it, men! The chips are down! You have trained for this a long time and now you're in the middle of it. I don't know how we're going to make out *in there*—" and he swung an arm in the direction of Pung's Corners, a gesture faithfully reproduced in living three-dimensional colour on the intercoms of each personnel carrier in his fleet—"but win or lose, and I know we're going to win, I want every one of you to know that you belong to the best Company in the best Regiment of the best Combat Infantry Team of the best Division of—"

Crump went the 105-mm piece on the lead personnel carrier as radar range automatically sighted in and fired upon a moving object outside, thus drowning out the tributes he had intended to pay to Corps, to Army, to Group, and to Command.

The battle for Pung's Corners had begun.

6

Now that first target, it wasn't any *body*.

It was only a milch cow, and one in need of freshening at that. She shouldn't have been on the baseball field at all, but there she was, and since that was the direction from which the invader descended on the town, she made the supreme sacrifice. Without even knowing she'd done it, of course.

Major Commaigne snapped at his adjutant: "Lefferts! Have the ordnance sections put the one-oh-fives on safety. Can't have this sort of thing." It had been a disagreeable sight, to see that poor old cow become hamburger, well ketchuped, so rapidly. Better chain the big guns until one saw, at any rate, whether Pung's Corners was going to put up a fight.

So Major Commaigne stopped the personnel carriers and ordered everybody out. They were past the dangerous radioactive area anyway.

The troops fell out in a handsome line of skirmish; it was very, very fast and very, very good. From the top of the Presbyterian Church steeple in Pung's Corners, Jack Tighe and Andy Grammis watched through field glasses, and I can tell you that Grammis was pretty near hysterics. But Jack Tighe only hummed and nodded.

Major Commaigne gave an order and every man in the line of skirmish instantly dug in. Some were in marsh and some in mud; some had to tunnel into solid rock and some—nearest where that first target had been—through a thin film of beef. It didn't much matter, because they didn't use the entrenching spades of World War II; they had Power-Pakt Diggers that clawed into anything in seconds, and, what's more, lined the pits with a fine ceramic glaze. It was magnificent.

And yet, on the other hand—

Well, look. It was this way. Twenty-six personnel carriers had brought them here. Each carrier had its driver, its relief driver, its emergency alternate driver, and its mechanic. It had its radar-and-electronics repairman, and its radar-and-electronics repairman's assistant. It had its ordnance staff of four, and its liaison communications officer to man the intercom and keep in touch with the P.C. commander.

Well, they needed all those people, of course. Couldn't get along without them.

But that came to two hundred and eighty-two men.

Then there was the field kitchen, with its staff of forty-seven, plus administrative detachment and dietetic staff; the headquarters detachment, with paymaster's corps and military police platoon; the meteorological section, a proud sight as they began setting up their field teletypes and fax receivers and launching their weather balloons; the field hospitality with eighty-one medics and nurses, nine medical officers and attached medical administrative staff; the special services detachment, prompt to begin setting up a three-D motion-picture screen in the lee of the parked personnel carriers and to commence organizing a hand-ball tournament among the off-duty men; the four chaplains and chaplains' assistants, plus the Wiseham Counsellor for Ethical Culturists, agnostics and waverers; the Historical officer and his eight trained clerks already going from foxhole to foxhole bravely carrying tape recorders, to take down history as it was being made in the form of first-hand impressions of the battle that had yet to be fought; military observers from Canada, Mexico, Uruguay, the Scandinavian Confederation, and the Soviet Socialist Republic of Inner Mongolia, with their orderlies and attachés; and, of course, field correspondents from *Stars & Stripes,* the New York *Times,* the *Christian Science Monitor,* the Scripps-Howard chain, five wire services, eight television networks, an independent documentary motion-picture producer, and one hundred and twenty-seven other newspapers and allied public information outlets.

It was a stripped-down combat command, naturally. Therefore, there was only one Public Information Officer per reporter.

Still . . .

Well, it left exactly forty-six riflemen in line of skirmish.

Up in the Presbyterian belfry, Andy Grammis wailed: "*Look* at them, Jack! I don't know, maybe letting advertising back into Pung's Corners wouldn't be so bad. All right, it's a rat race, but—"

"Wait," said Jack Tighe quietly, and hummed.

They couldn't see it very well, but the line of skirmish was in some confusion. The word had been passed down that all the field pieces had been put on safety and that the entire fire-power of the company rested in their forty-six rifles. Well, that wasn't so bad; but after all, they had been equipped with E-Z Fyre Revolv-a-Clip Carbines until ten days before the expeditionary force had been mounted. Some of the troops hadn't been fully able to familiarize themselves with the new weapons.

It went like this:

"Sam," called one private to the man in the next foxhole. "Sam, listen, I can't figure this something rifle out. When the something green light goes on, does that mean that the something safety is off?"

"Beats the something hell out of me," rejoined Sam, his brow furrowed as he pored over the full-coloured glossy-paper operating manual, alluringly entitled, *The Five-Step Magic-Eye Way to New Combat Comfort and Security.* "Did you see what it says here? It says, 'Magic-Eye in Off position is provided with postive Fayl-Sayf action, thus assuring Evr-Kleen Cartridge of dynamic ejection and release, when used in combination with Shoulder-Eez Anti-Recoil Pads.' "

"What did you say, Sam?"

"I said it beats the something hell out of me," said Sam, and pitched the manual out into no-man's-land before him.

But he was sorry and immediately crept out to retrieve it, for although the directions seemed intended for a world that had no relation to the rock-and-mud terra firma around Pung's Corners, all of the step-by-step instructions in the manual were illustrated by mock-up photographs of starlets in Bikinis—for the cavern factories produced instruction manuals as well as weapons. They had to, obviously, and they were good at it; the more complicated the directions, the more photographs they used. The vehicular ones were downright shocking.

Some minutes later: "They don't seem to be doing anything," ventured Andy Grammis, watching from the steeple.

"No, they don't, Andy. Well, we can't sit up here for ever. Come along and we'll see what's what."

Now Andy Grammis didn't want to do that, but Jack Tighe was a man you didn't resist very well, and so they climbed down the winding steel stairs and picked up the rest of the Pung's Corners Independence Volunteers, all fourteen of them, and they started down Front Street and out across the baseball diamond.

Twenty-six personnel carriers electronically went *ping*, and the turrets of their one-oh-fives swivelled to zero in on the Independence Volunteers.

Forty-six riflemen, swearing, attempted to make Akur-A-C Greenline Sighting Strip cross Horizon Blue True-Site Band in the Up-Close radar screens of their rifles.

And Major Commaigne, howling mad, waved a sheet of paper under the nose of his adjutant. "What kind of something nonsense is *this*?" he demanded, for a soldier is a soldier regardless of his rank. "I can't take those men out of line with the enemy advancing on us!"

"Army orders, sir," said the adjutant impenetrably. He had got his doctorate in Military Jurisprudence at Harvard Law and he knew whose orders meant what to whom. "The rotation plan isn't my idea, sir. Why not take it up with the Pentagon?"

"But, Lefferts, you idiot, I can't get through to the Pentagon! Those something newspapermen have the channels sewed up solid! And now you want me to take every front-line rifleman out and send him to a rest camp for three weeks—"

"No, sir," corrected the adjutant, pointing to a line in the order. "Only for twenty days, sir, *including* travel time. But you'd best do it right away, sir, I expect. The order's marked 'priority'."

Well, Major Commaigne was no fool. Never mind what they said later. He had studied the catastrophe of Von Paulus at Stalingrad and Lee's heaven-sent escape from Gettysburg, and he knew what could happen to an expeditionary force in trouble in enemy territory. Even a big one. And his, you must remember, was very small.

He knew that when you're on your own, everything becomes your enemy; frost and diarrhoea destroyed more of the Nazi Sixth Army than the Russians did; the jolting wagons of Lee's retreat put more of his wounded and sick out of the way than Meade's cannon. So he did what he had to do.

"Sound the retreat!" he bawled. "We're going back to the barn."

Retire and regroup; why not? But it wasn't as simple as that.

The personnel carriers backed and turned like a fleet in manoeuvres. Their drivers were trained for that. But one P.C. got caught in Special Service's movie screen and blundered into another, and a flotilla of three of them found themselves stymied by the spreading pre-fabs of the field hospital. Five of them, doing extra duty in running electric generators from the power take-offs at their rear axles, were immobilized for fifteen minutes and then boxed in.

What it came down to was that four of the twenty-six were in shape to move right then. And obviously that wasn't enough, so it wasn't a retreat at all; it was a disaster.

"There's only one thing to do," brooded Major Commaigne amid the turmoil, with manly tears streaming down his face, "but how I wish I'd never tried to make lieutenant colonel!"

So Jack Tighe received Commaigne's surrender. Jack Tighe didn't act surprised. I can't say the same for the rest of the Independence Volunteers.

"No, Major, you may keep your sword," said Jack Tighe kindly. "And all of the officers may keep their Pinpoint Levl-Site No-Jolt sidearms."

"Thank you, sir," wept the major, and blundered back into the officer's club which the Headquarters Detachment had never stopped building.

Jack Tighe looked after him with a peculiar and thoughtful expression.

William LaFarge, swinging a thirty-inch hickory stick—it was all he'd been able to pick up as a weapon—babbled: "It's a great victory! Now they'll leave us alone, I bet!"

Jack Tighe didn't say a single word.

"Don't you think so, Jack? Won't they stay away now?"

Jack Tighe looked at him blankly, seemed about to answer and then turned to Charley Frink. "Charley. Listen. Don't you have a shotgun put away somewhere?"

"Yes, Mr Tighe. And a .22. Want me to get them?"

"Why, yes, I think I do." Jack Tighe watched the youth run off. His eyes were hooded. And then he said: "Andy, do something for us. Ask the major to give us a P.O.W. driver who knows the way to the Pentagon."

And a few minutes later, Charley came back with the shotgun and the .22; and the rest, of course, is history.

"REPENT, HARLEQUIN!"
SAID THE TICKTOCKMAN

Harlan Ellison

There are always those who ask, what is it all about? For those who need to ask, for those who need points sharply made, who need to know "where it's at," this:

> The mass of men serve the state thus, not as men mainly, but as machines, with their bodies. They are the standing army, and the militia, jailors, constables, posse comitatus, etc. In most cases there is no free exercise whatever

of the judgment or of the moral sense; but they put themselves on a level with wood and earth and stones; and wooden men can perhaps be manufactured that will serve the purpose as well. Such command no more respect than men of straw or a lump of dirt. They have the same sort of worth only as horses and dogs. Yet such as these even are commonly esteemed good citizens. Others—as most legislators, politicians, lawyers, ministers, and office-holders—serve the state chiefly with their heads; and, as they rarely make any moral distinctions, they are as likely to serve the Devil, without intending it, as God. A very few, as heroes, patriots, martyrs, reformers in the great sense, and *men*, serve the state with their consciences also, and so necessarily resist it for the most part; and they are commonly treated as enemies by it.

Henry David Thoreau
Civil Disobedience

That is the heart of it. Now begin in the middle, and later learn the beginning; the end will take care of itself.

But because it was the very world it was, the very world they had allowed it to *become*, for months his activities did not come to the alarmed attention of The Ones Who Kept The Machine Functioning Smoothly, the ones who poured the very best butter over the cams and mainsprings of the culture. Not until it had become obvious that somehow, someway, he had become a notoriety, a celebrity, perhaps even a hero for (what Officialdom inescapably tagged) "an emotionally disturbed segment of the populace," did they turn it over to the Ticktockman and his legal machinery. But by then, because it was the very world it was, and they had no way to predict he would happen—possibly a strain of disease long-defunct, now, suddenly reborn in a system where immunity had been forgotten, had lapsed—he had been allowed to become too real. Now he had form and substance.

He had become a *personality*, something they had filtered out of the system many decades before. But there it was, and there *he* was, a very definitely imposing personality. In certain circles—middle-class circles—it was thought disgusting. Vulgar ostentation. Anarchistic. Shameful. In others, there was only snickering, those strata where thought is subjugated to form and ritual, niceties, proprieties. But down below, ah, down below, where the people always needed their saints and sinners, their bread and circuses, their heroes and villains, he was considered a Bolivar; a Napoleon; a Robin Hood; a Dick Bong (Ace of Aces); a Jesus; a Jomo Kenyatta.

And at the top—where, like socially attuned Shipwreck Kellys, every tremor and vibration threatening to dislodge the wealthy, powerful and titled from their flagpoles—he was considered a menace; a heretic; a rebel; a disgrace; a peril. He was known down the line, to the very heartmeat core, but the important reactions were high above and far below. At the very top, at the very bottom.

So his file was turned over, along with his time card and his cardioplate, to the office of the Ticktockman.

The Ticktockman: very much over six feet tall, often silent, a soft purring man when things went timewise. The Tickockman.

Even in the cubicles of the hierarchy, where fear was generated, seldom suffered, he was called the Ticktockman. But no one called him that to his mask.

You don't call a man a hated name, not when that man, behind his mask, is capable of revoking the minutes, the hours, the days and nights, the years of your life. He was called the Master Timekeeper to his mask. It was safer that way.

"This is *what* he is," said the Ticktockman with genuine softness, "but not *who* he is. This time-card I'm holding in my left hand has a name on it, but it is the name of *what* he is, not *who* he is. The cardioplate here in my right hand is also named, but not who named, merely what named. Before I can exercise proper revocation, I have to know who this what is."

To his staff, all the ferrets, all the loggers, all the finks, all the commex, even the mineez, he said, "Who is this Harlequin?"

He was not purring smoothly. Timewise, it was jangle.

However, it *was* the longest single speech they had ever heard him utter at one time, the staff, the ferrets, the loggers, the finks, the commex, but not the mineez, who usually weren't around to know, in any case. But even they scurried to find out

Who is the Harlequin?

High above the third level of the city, he crouched on the humming aluminum-frame platform of the air-boat (foof! air-boat, indeed, swizzle-skid is what it was, with a tow-rack jerry-rigged) and stared down at the neat Mondrian arrangement of the buildings.

Somewhere nearby, he could hear the metronomic left-right-left of the 2:47 P.M. shift, entering the Timkin roller-bearing plant, in their sneakers. A minute later, precisely, he heard the softer right-left-right of the 5:00 A.M. formation, going home.

An elfin grin spread across his tanned features, and his dimples appeared for a moment. Then, scratching at his thatch of auburn hair, he shrugged within his motley, as though girding himself for what came next, and threw the joystick forward, and bent into the wind as the air-boat dropped. He skimmed over a slidewalk, purposely dropping a few feet to crease the tassels of the ladies of fashion, and—inserting thumbs in large ears—he stuck out his tongue, rolled his eyes and went wugga-wugga-wugga. It was a minor diversion. One pedestrian skittered and tumbled, sending parcels everywhichway, another wet herself, a third keeled slantwise and the walk was stopped automatically by the servitors till she could be resucitated. It was a minor diversion.

Then he swirled away on a vagrant breeze, and was gone. Hi-ho.

As he rounded the cornice of the Time-Motion Study Building, he saw the shift, just boarding the slidewalk. With practiced motion and an absolute conservation of movement, they sidestepped up onto the slowstrip and (in a chorus line reminiscent of a Busby Berkeley film of the antideluvian 1930's) advanced across the strips ostrich-walking till they were lined up on the expresstrip.

Once more, in anticipation, the elfin grin spread, and there was a tooth missing back there on the left side. He dipped, skimmed, and swooped over them; and then, scrunching about on the air-boat, he released the holding pins that fastened shut the ends of the homemade pouring troughs that kept his cargo from dumping prematurely. And as he pulled the trough-pins, the air-boat slid over the factory workers and one hundred and fifty thousand dollars' worth of jelly beans cascaded down on the expresstrip.

Jelly beans! Millions and billions of purples and yellows and greens and licorice and grape and raspberry and mint and round and smooth and crunchy outside and soft-mealy inside and sugary and bouncing jouncing tumbling clittering clattering skittering fell on the heads and shoulders and hardhats and carapaces of the Timkin workers, tinkling on the slidewalk and bouncing away and rolling about underfoot and filling the sky on their way down with all the colors of joy and childhood and holidays, coming down in a steady rain, a solid wash, a torrent of color and sweetness out of the sky from above, and entering a universe of sanity and metronomic order with quite-mad coocoo newness. Jelly beans!

The shift workers howled and laughed and were pelted, and broke ranks, and the jelly beans managed to work their way into the mechanism of the slidewalks after which there was a hideous scraping as the sound of a million fingernails rasped down a quarter of a million blackboards, followed by a coughing and a sputtering, and then the slidewalks all stopped and everyone was summarily dumped thisawayandthataway in a jackstraw tumble, still laughing and popping little jelly bean eggs of childish color into their mouths. It was a holiday, and a jollity, an absolute insanity, a giggle. But . . .

The shift was delayed seven minutes.

They did not get home for seven minutes.

The master schedule was thrown off by seven minutes.

Quotas were delayed by inoperative slidewalks for seven minutes.

He had tapped the first domino in the line, and one after another, like chik chik chik, the others had fallen.

The System had been seven minutes worth of disrupted. It was a tiny matter, one hardly worthy of note, but in a society where the single driving force was order and unity and promptness and clocklike precision and attention to the clock, reverence of the gods of the passage of time, it was a disaster of major importance.

So he was ordered to appear before the Ticktockman. It was broadcast across every channel of the communications web. He was ordered to be *there* at 7:00 dammit on time. And they waited, and they waited, but he didn't show up till almost ten-thirty, at which time he merely sang a little song about moonlight in a place no one had ever heard of, called Vermont, and vanished again. But they had all been waiting since seven, and it wrecked *hell* with their schedules. So the question remained: Who is the Harlequin?

But the *unasked* question (more important of the two) was: How did we get *into* this position, where a laughing, irresponsible japer of jabberwocky and jive could disrupt our entire economic and cultural life with a hundred and fifty thousand dollars' worth of jelly beans . . .

Jelly for God's sake *beans!* This is madness! Where did he get the money to buy a hundred and fifty thousand dollars' worth of jelly beans? (They knew it would have cost that much, because they had a team of Situation Analysts pulled off another assignment, and rushed to the slidewalk scene to sweep up and count the candies, and produce findings, which disrupted *their* schedules and threw their entire branch at least a day behind.) Jelly beans! Jelly . . . *beans?* Now wait a second—a second accounted for—no one has manufactured jelly beans for over a hundred years. Where did he get jelly beans?

That's another good question. More than likely it will never be answered to your complete satisfaction. But then, how many questions ever are?

The middle you know. Here is the beginning. How it starts:

A desk pad. Day for day, and turn each day. 9:00—open the mail. 9:45—appointment with planning commission board. 10:30—discuss installation progress charts with J.L. 11:15—pray for rain. 12:00—lunch. *And so it goes.*

"I'm sorry, Miss Grant, but the time for interviews was set at 2:30, and it's almost five now. I'm sorry you're late, but those are the rules. You'll have to wait till next year to submit application for this college again." *And so it goes.*

The 10:10 local stops at Cresthaven, Galesville, Tonawanda Junction, Selby and Farnhurst, but not at Indiana City, Lucasville and Colton, except on Sunday. The 10:35 express stops at Galesville, Selby and

Indiana City, except on Sundays & Holidays, at which time it stops at . . . *and so it goes.*

"I couldn't wait, Fred. I had to be at Pierre Cartain's by 3:00, and you said you'd meet me under the clock in the terminal at 2:45, and you weren't there, so I had to go on. You're always late, Fred. If you'd been there, we could have sewed it up together, but as it was, well, I took the order alone . . ." *And so it goes.*

Dear Mr. and Mrs. Atterley: In reference to your son Gerald's constant tardiness, I am afraid we will have to suspend him from school unless some more reliable method can be instituted guaranteeing he will arrive at his classes on time. Granted he is an exemplary student, and his marks are high, his constant flouting of the schedules of this school make it impractical to maintain him in a system where the other children seem capable of getting where they are supposed to be on time *and so it goes.*

YOU CANNOT VOTE UNLESS YOU APPEAR AT 8:45 A.M.

"I don't care if the script is *good.* I need it Thursday!"

CHECK-OUT TIME IS 2:00 P.M.

"You got here late. The job's taken. Sorry."

YOUR SALARY HAS BEEN DOCKED FOR TWENTY MINUTES TIME LOST.

"God, what time is it, I've gotta run!"

And so it goes. And so it goes. And so it goes. And so it goes goes goes goes goes tick tock tick tock tick tock and one day we no longer let time serve us, we serve time and we are slaves of the schedule, worshippers of the sun's passing, bound into a life predicated on restrictions because the system will not function if we don't keep the schedule tight.

Until it becomes more than a minor inconvenience to be late. It becomes a sin. Then a crime. Then a crime punishable by this:

EFFECTIVE 15 JULY 2389, 12:00:00 midnight, the office of the Master Timekeeper will require all citizens to submit their time-cards and cardioplates for processing. In accordance with Statute 555-7-SGH-999 governing the revocation of time per capita, all cardioplates will be keyed to the individual holder and—

What they had done was devise a method of curtailing the amount of life a person could have. If he was ten minutes late, he lost ten minutes of his life. An hour was proportionately worth more revocation. If someone was consistently tardy, he might find himself, on a Sunday night, receiving a communiqué from the Master Timekeeper that his time had run out, and he would be "turned off" at high noon on Monday, please straighten your affairs, sir.

And so, by this simple scientific expedient (utilizing a scientific process held dearly secret by the Ticktockman's office) the System was maintained. It was the only expedient thing to do. It was, after all, patriotic. The schedules had to be met. After all, there *was* a war on!

But, wasn't there always?

"Now that is really disgusting," the Harlequin said, when pretty Alice showed him the wanted poster. "Disgusting and *highly* improbable. After all, this isn't the day of the desperado. A *wanted* poster!"

"You know," Alice noted, "you speak with a great deal of inflection."

"I'm sorry," said the Harlequin, humbly.

"No need to be sorry. You're always saying 'I'm sorry.' You have such massive guilt, Everett, it's really very sad."

"I'm sorry," he repeated, then pursed his lips so the dimples appeared momentarily. He hadn't wanted to say that at all. "I have to go out again. I have to *do* something."

Alice slammed her coffee-bulb down on the counter. "Oh for God's *sake*, Everett, can't you stay home just *one* night! Must you always be out in that ghastly clown suit, running around annoying people?"

"I'm—" he stopped, and clapped the jester's hat onto his auburn thatch with a tiny tingling of bells. He rose, rinsed out his coffee-bulb at the tap, and put it into the drier for a moment. "I have to go."

She didn't answer. The faxbox was purring, and she pulled a sheet out, read it, threw it toward him on the counter. "It's about you. Of course. You're ridiculous."

He read it quickly. It said the Ticktockman was trying to locate him. He didn't care, he was going out to be late again. At the door, dredging for an exit line, he hurled back petulantly, "Well, *you* speak with inflection, *too*!"

Alice rolled her pretty eyes heavenward. "You're ridiculous." The Harlequin stalked out, slamming the door, which sighed shut softly, and locked itself.

There was a gentle knock, and Alice got up with an exhalation of exasperated breath, and opened the door. He stood there. "I'll be back about ten-thirty, okay?"

She pulled a rueful face. "Why do you tell me that? Why? You *know* you'll be late! You *know* it! You're *always* late, so why do you tell me these dumb things?" She closed the door.

On the other side, the Harlequin nodded to himself. *She's right. She's always right. I'll be late. I'm always late. Why* do *I tell her these dumb things?*

He shrugged again, and went off to be late once more.

He had fired off the firecracker rockets that said: I will attend the 115th annual International Medical Association Invocation at 6:00 P.M. precisely. I do hope you will all be able to join me.

The words had burned in the sky, and of course the authorities were there, lying in wait for him. They assumed, naturally, that he would be late. He arrived twenty minutes early, while they were setting up the spiderwebs to trap and hold him, and blowing a large bullhorn, he frightened and unnerved them so, their own moisturized encirclement webs sucked closed, and they were hauled up, kicking and shrieking, high above the amphitheater's floor. The Harlequin laughed and laughed, and apologized profusely. The physicians, gathered in solemn conclave, roared with laughter, and accepted the Harlequin's apologies with exaggerated bowing and posturing, and a merry time was had by all, who thought the Harlequin was a regular foofaraw in fancy pants; all, that is, but the authorities, who had been sent out by the office of the Ticktockman, who hung there like so much dockside cargo, hauled up above the floor of the amphitheater in a most unseemly fashion.

(In another part of the same city where the Harlequin carried on his "activities," totally unrelated in every way to what concerns us here, save that it illustrates the Ticktockman's power and import, a man named Marshall Delahanty received his turn-off notice from the Ticktockman's office. His wife received the notification from the gray-suited minee who delivered it, with the traditional "look of sorrow" plastered hideously across his face. She knew what it was, even without unsealing it. It was a billet-doux of immediate recognition to everyone these days. She gasped, and held it as though it was a glass slide tinged with botulism, and prayed it was not for her. Let it be for Marsh, she thought, brutally, realistically, or one of the kids, but not for me, please dear God, not for me. And then she opened it, and it *was* for Marsh, and she was at one and the same time horrified and relieved. The next trooper in the line had caught the bullet. "Marshall," she screamed, "Marshall! Termination, Marshall! OhmiGod, Marshall, whattl we do, whattl we do, Marshall, omigodmarshall . . ." and in their home that night was the sound of tearing paper and fear, and the stink of madness went up the flue and there was nothing, absolutely nothing they could do about it.

(But Marshall Delahanty tried to run. And early the next day, when turn-off time came, he was deep in the forest two hundred miles away, and the office of the Ticktockman blanked his cardioplate, and Marshall Delahanty keeled over, running, and his heart stopped, and the blood dried up on its way to his brain, and he was dead that's all. One light went out on his sector map in the office of the Master Timekeeper, while notification was entered for fax reproduction, and Georgette Delahanty's name was entered on the dole roles till she could remarry. Which is the end of the footnote, and all the point that need be made, except don't laugh, because that is what would happen to the Harlequin if ever the Ticktockman found out his real name. It isn't funny.)

The shopping level of the city was thronged with the Thursday-colors of the buyers. Women in canary yellow chitons and men in pseudo-Tyrolean outfits that were jade and leather and fit very tightly, save for the balloon pants.

When the Harlequin appeared on the still-being-constructed shell of the new Efficiency Shopping Center, his bullhorn to his elfishly-laughing lips, everyone pointed and stared, and he berated them:

"Why let them order you about? Why let them tell you to hurry and scurry like ants or maggots? Take your time! Saunter a while! Enjoy the sunshine, enjoy the breeze, let life carry you at your own pace! Don't be slaves of time, it's a helluva way to die, slowly, by degrees . . . down with the Ticktockman!"

Who's the nut? most of the shoppers wanted to know. Who's the nut oh wow I'm gonna be late I gotta run . . .

And the construction gang on the Shopping Center received an urgent order from the office of the Master Timekeeper that the dangerous criminal known as the Harlequin was atop their spire, and their aid was urgently needed in apprehending him. The work crew said no, they would lose time on their construction schedule, but the Ticktockman managed to pull the proper threads of governmental webbing, and they were told to cease work and catch that nitwit up there on the spire with the bullhorn. So a dozen and more burly workers began climbing into their construction platforms, releasing the a-grav plates, and rising toward the Harlequin.

After the debacle (in which, through the Harlequin's attention to personal safety, no one was seriously injured), the workers tried to reassemble and assault him again, but it was too late. He had vanished. It had attracted quite a crowd, however, and the shopping cycle was thrown off by hours, simply hours. The purchasing needs of the system were therefore falling behind, and so measures were taken to accelerate the cycle for the rest of the day, but it got bogged down and speeded up and they sold too many floatvalves and not nearly enough wagglers, which meant that the popli ratio was off, which made it necessary to rush cases and cases of spoiling Smash-O to stores that usually needed a case only every three or four hours. The shipments were bollixed, the trans-shipments were misrouted, and in the end, even the swizzleskid industries felt it.

"Don't come back till you have him!" the Ticktockman said, very quietly, very sincerely, extremely dangerously.

They used dogs. They used probes. They used cardioplate crossoffs.

They used teepers. They used bribery. They used stiktytes. They used intimidation. They used torment. They used torture. They used finks. They used cops. They used search&seizure. They used fallaron. They used betterment incentive. They used fingerprints. They used Bertillon. They used cunning. They used guile. They used treachery. They used Raoul Mitgong, but he didn't help much. They used applied physics. They used techniques of criminology.

And what the hell: they caught him.

After all, his name was Everett C. Marm, and he wasn't much to begin with, except a man who had no sense of time.

"Repent, Harlequin!" said the Ticktockman.

"Get stuffed!" the Harlequin replied, sneering.

"You've been late a total of sixty-three years, five months, three weeks, two days, twelve hours, forty-one minutes, fifty-nine seconds, point oh three six one one one microseconds. You've used up everything you can, and more. I'm going to turn you off."

"Scare someone else. I'd rather be dead than live in a dumb world with a bogey man like you."

"It's my job."

"You're full of it. You're a tyrant. You have no right to order people around and kill them if they show up late."

"You can't adjust. You can't fit in."

"Unstrap me, and I'll fit my fist into your mouth."

"You're a nonconformist."

"That didn't used to be a felony."

"It is now. Live in the world around you."

"I hate it. It's a terrible world."

"Not everyone thinks so. Most people enjoy order."

"I don't, and most of the people I know don't."

"That's not true. How do you think we caught you?"

"I'm not interested."

"A girl named pretty Alice told us who you were."

"That's a lie."

"It's true. You unnerve her. She wants to belong, she wants to conform, I'm going to turn you off."

"Then do it already, and stop arguing with me."

"I'm not going to turn you off."

"You're an idiot!"

"Repent, Harlequin!" said the Ticktockman.

"Get stuffed."

So they sent him to Coventry. And in Coventry they worked him over. It was just like what they did to Winston Smith in *1984*, which was a book none of them knew about, but the techniques are really quite ancient, and so they did it to Everett C. Marm, and one day quite a long time later, the Harlequin appeared on the communications web, appearing elfish and dimpled and bright-eyed, and not at all brainwashed, and he said he had been wrong, that it was a good, a very good thing indeed, to belong, and be right on time hip-ho and away we go, and everyone stared up at him on the public screens that covered an entire city block, and they said to themselves, well, you see, he was just a nut after all, and if that's the way the system is run, then let's do it that way, because it doesn't pay to fight city hall, or in this case, the Ticktockman. So Everett C. Marm was destroyed, which was a loss, because of what Thoreau said earlier, but you can't make an omelet without breaking a few eggs, and in every revolution, a few die who shouldn't, but they have to, because that's the way it happens, and if you make only a little change, then it seems to be worthwhile. Or, to make the point lucidly:

"Uh, excuse me, sir, I, uh, don't know how to uh, to uh, tell you this, but you were three minutes late. The schedule is a little, uh, bit off."

He grinned sheepishly.

"That's ridiculous!" murmured the Ticktockman behind his mask: "Check your watch." And then he went into his office, going mrmee, mrmee, mrmee, mrmee.

Population

Population is not a problem which will wait a few more decades while man decides what solution to employ. A counter to over-population must be employed immediately or it will be too late. In fact, some scientists predict great famines before the end of this century no matter what we do. It is becoming obvious that countries like the United States will be placed, whether they like it or not, in the position of deciding who lives and who dies. As population continues to increase over food supply, the United States will find its surpluses dwindling to the point at which it is no longer possible to give food as foreign aid. After that comes the question of who gets fed and who doesn't in this country. But the population problem involves more than food supply. Various university experiments have shown that, even with an abundance of food, over-crowding can produce a form of insanity. Are people fated to become lemmings and rush headlong to their own destruction through over-population?

John Brunner has written two novels which depict the problems that over-population might bring. In *Jagged Orbit* and *Stand on Zanzibar*, Brunner plays down the problem of food supply to focus on such things as the housing of all these people, the distribution of wealth, and the psychological effects of so much crowding. Harry Harrison, in *Make Room! Make Room!*, discusses what New York City may be like in the year 1999 when the population there could be as high as 35 million people. In order to alert more people to the dangers of over-population, Zero Population Growth and Ballantine Books have published *Voyages: Scenarios for a Ship Called Earth,* edited by Bob Sauer. This book is an anthology of science fiction short stories dealing with Earth of the future, especially over-populated Earth. There is a foreword by the Ehrlichs, factual headnotes to each of the sections, and a fairly complete bibliography of nonfiction dealing with population and resources.

Ursula Le Guin's "Nine Lives" makes some references to world-wide famine and indicates that over-population was a contributing factor. The main topic of the story, however, is cloning. If individual cells can be stored and later made to grow into a duplicate of the human form from whom they were taken, who decides who gets cloned, and does cloning take precedence over natural reproduction? This sort of question concerning the ordering of priorities is a part of each of these four stories if not the whole Science Fiction and the Future section. Besides being able to present important issues through the medium of science fiction, Ursula Le Guin also has the ability to visualize and render believable strange worlds and different beings (physical and psychological).

In "Golden Acres" Kit Reed offers a possible way to help alleviate the problem of over-population, and the ease with which the aged are shoved aside by the young is not unlike what happened to the poor in Ron Goulart's "Calling Dr. Clockwork." Reed's description of the room in which Hamish and Nelda will live epitomizes a room in almost any institution—function over form. In addition, the idea that an institution can assign each member a specific quantity of life can easily be a metaphor for any resource which over-population threatens to deplete.

"Population Implosion" by andrew j. offutt can be read on one level as a whimsical statement about a serious topic, but on another level, this story, too, can be read as a metaphor about the nature of our resources. The idea of balance which offutt introduces here is crucial to any plan for population and resource control.

The final and perhaps culminating statement on over-population in this group of stories is made by Alice Glaser in "The Tunnel Ahead." This story shows how far man can retreat from moral responsibility or, from another viewpoint, how much responsibility the government will have to take—not to mention the means they will have to use—if people refuse to accept personal responsibility. Apart from the moral question, the reader must ask why these people will use such a tunnel week after week.

This group of stories—and most especially Alice Glaser's—provides this book with a conclusion which is highly charged with moral considerations; however, the ethical problems explicit in these stories are at least implicit in all the stories in the Science Fiction and the Future section. Moreover, an awareness of the moral considerations implicit in this second section points out the fact that the neat categories into which this book is divided are not mutually exclusive. Man's self-concept, for example, will be central to the way in which he structures his educational system, builds and reacts to robots, and directs his technology. What should the educational system be educating for? What status should robots be accorded? What should we direct our technology to provide for us? The answers to these questions depend upon man's self-concept (which, in turn, depends upon his morals or ethics) and man's imagination or speculative vision.

NINE LIVES

Ursula K. Le Guin

She was alive inside, but dead outside, her face a black and dun net of wrinkles, tumors, cracks. She was bald and blind. The tremors that crossed Libra's face were mere quiverings of corruption: underneath, in the black corridors, the halls beneath the skin, there were crepitations in darkness, ferments, chemical nightmares that went on for centuries. "Oh the damned flatulent planet," Pugh murmured as the dome shook and a boil burst a kilometer to the southwest, spraying silver pus across the sunset. The sun had been setting for the last two days. "I'll be glad to see a human face."

"Thanks," said Martin.

"Yours is human to be sure," said Pugh, "but I've seen it so long I can't see it."

Radvid signals cluttered the communicator which Martin was operating, faded, returned as face and voice. The face filled the screen, the nose of an Assyrian king, the eyes of a samurai, skin bronze, eyes the color of iron: young, magnificent. "Is that what human beings look like?" said Pugh with awe. "I'd forgotten."

"Shut up, Owen, we're on."

"Libra Exploratory Mission Base, come in please, this is *Passerine* launch."

"Libra here. Beam fixed. Come on down, launch."

"Expulsion in seven E-seconds. Hold on." The screen blanked and sparkled.

"Do they all look like that? Martin, you and I are uglier men than I thought."

"Shut up, Owen. . . ."

For twenty-two minutes Martin followed the landing-craft down by signal and then through the cleared dome they saw it, small star in the blood-colored east, sinking. It came down neat and quiet, Libra's thin atmosphere carrying little sound. Pugh and Martin closed the head-pieces of their imsuits, zipped out of the dome airlocks, and ran with soaring strides, Nijinsky and Nureyev, toward the boat. Three equipment modules came floating down at four-minute intervals from each other and hundred-meter intervals east of the boat. "Come on out," Martin said on his suit radio, "we're waiting at the door."

"Come on in, the methane's fine," said Pugh.

The hatch opened. The young man they had seen on the screen came out with one athletic twist and leaped down onto the shaky dust and clinkers of Libra. Martin shook his hand, but Pugh was staring at the hatch, from which another young man emerged with the same neat twist and jump, followed by a young woman who emerged with the same neat twist, ornamented by a wriggle, and the jump. They were all tall, with bronze skin, black hair, high-bridged noses, epicanthic fold, the same face. They all had the same face. The fourth was emerging from the hatch with a neat twist and jump. "Martin bach," said Pugh, "we've got a clone."

"Right," said one of them, "we're a tenclone. John Chow's the name. You're Lieutenant Martin?"

"I'm Owen Pugh."

"Alvaro Guillen Martin," said Martin, formal, bowing slightly. Another girl was out, the same beautiful face; Martin stared at her and his eye rolled like a nervous pony's. Evidently he had never given any thought to cloning, and was suffering technological shock. "Steady," Pugh said in the Argentine dialect, "it's only excess twins." He stood close by Martin's elbow. He was glad himself of the contact.

It is hard to meet a stranger. Even the greatest extrovert meeting even the meekest stranger knows a certain dread, though he may not know he knows it. Will he make a fool of me wreck my image of myself invade me destroy me change me? Will he be different from me? Yes, that he will. There's the terrible thing: the strangeness of the stranger.

After two years on a dead planet, and the last half year isolated as a team of two, oneself and one other, after that it's even harder to meet a stranger, however welcome he may be. You're out of the habit of difference, you've lost the touch; and so the fear revives, the primitive anxiety, the old dread.

The clone, five males and five females, had got done in a couple of minutes what a man might have got done in twenty: greeted Pugh and Martin, had a glance at Libra, unloaded the boat, made ready to go. They went, and the dome filled with them, a hive of golden bees. They hummed and buzzed quietly, filled up all silences, all spaces with a honey-brown swarm of human presence. Martin looked bewilderedly at the long-limbed girls, and they smiled at him, three at once. Their smile was gentler than that of the boys, but no less radiantly self-possessed.

"Self-possessed," Owen Pugh murmured to his friend, "that's it. Think of it, to be oneself ten times over. Nine seconds for every motion, nine ayes on every vote. It would be glorious!" But Martin was asleep. And the John Chows had all gone to sleep at once. The dome was filled with their quiet breathing. They were young, they didn't snore. Martin sighed and snored, his hershey-bar-colored face relaxed in the dim afterglow of Libra's primary, set at last. Pugh had cleared the dome and stars looked in, Sol among them, a great company of lights, a clone of splendors. Pugh slept and dreamed of a one-eyed giant who chased him through the shaking halls of Hell.

From his sleeping-bag Pugh watched the clone's awakening. They all got up within one minute except for one pair, a boy and a girl, who lay snugly tangled and still sleeping in one bag. As Pugh saw this there was a shock like one of Libra's earthquakes inside him, a very deep tremor. He was not aware of this, and in fact thought he was pleased at the sight; there was no other such comfort on this dead hollow world, more power to them, who made love. One of the others stepped on the pair. They woke and the girl sat up flushed and sleepy, with bare golden breasts. One of her sisters murmured something to her; she shot a glance at Pugh and disappeared in the sleeping-bag, followed by a giant giggle, from another direction a fierce stare, from still another direction a voice: "Christ, we're used to having a room to ourselves. Hope you don't mind, Captain Pugh."

"It's a pleasure," Pugh said half-truthfully. He had to stand up then, wearing only the shorts he slept in, and he felt like a plucked rooster, all white scrawn and pimples. He had seldom envied Martin's compact brownness so much. The United Kingdom had come through the Great Famines well, losing less than half its population: a record achieved by rigorous food-control. Black-marketeers and hoarders had been executed. Crumbs had been shared. Where in richer lands most had died and a few had thriven, in Britain fewer died and none throve.

They all got lean. Their sons were lean, their grandsons lean, small, brittle-boned, easily infected. When civilization became a matter of standing in lines, the British had kept queue, and so had replaced the survival of the fittest with the survival of the fair-minded. Owen Pugh was a scrawny little man. All the same, he was there.

At the moment he wished he wasn't.

At breakfast a John said, "Now if you'll brief us, Captain Pugh—"

"Owen, then."

"Owen, we can work out our schedule. Anything new on the mine since your last report to your Mission? We saw your reports when *Passerine* was orbiting Planet V, where they are now."

Martin did not answer, though the mine was his discovery and project, and Pugh had to do his best. It was hard to talk to them. The same faces, each with the same expression of intelligent interest, all leaned toward him across the table at almost the same angle. They all nodded together.

Over the Exploitation Corps insignia on their tunics each had a nameband, first name John and last name Chow of course, but the middle names different. The men were Aleph, Kaph, Yod, Gimel, and Samedh; the women Sadhe, Daleth, Zayin, Beth, and Resh. Pugh tried to use the names but gave it up at once; he could not even tell sometimes which one had spoken, for the voices were all alike.

Martin buttered and chewed his toast, and finally interrupted: "You're a team. Is that it?"

"Right," said two Johns.

"God, what a team! I hadn't seen the point. How much do you each know what the others are thinking?"

"Not at all, properly speaking," replied one of the girls, Zayin. The others watched her with the proprietary, approving look they had. "No ESP, nothing fancy. But we think alike. We have exactly the same equipment. Given the same stimulus, the same problem, we're likely to be coming up with the same reactions and solutions at the same time. Explanations are easy—don't even have to make them, usually. We seldom misunderstand each other. It does facilitate our working as a team."

"Christ yes," said Martin. "Pugh and I have spent seven hours out of ten for six months misunderstanding each other. Like most people. What about emergencies, are you as good at meeting the unexpected problem as a nor . . . an unrelated team?"

"Statistics so far indicate that we are," Zayin answered readily. Clones must be trained, Pugh thought, to meet questions, to reassure and reason. All they said had the slightly bland and stilted quality of answers furnished to the Public. "We can't brainstorm as singletons can, we as a team don't profit from the interplay of varied minds; but we have a compensatory advantage. Clones are drawn from the best human material, individuals of IIQ 99th percentile, Genetic Constitution alpha double A, and so on. We have more to draw on than most individuals do."

"And it's multiplied by a factor of ten. Who is—who was John Chow?"

"A genius surely," Pugh said politely. His interest in cloning was not so new and avid as Martin's.

"Leonardo Complex type," said Yod. "Biomath, also a cellist, and an undersea hunter, and interested in structural engineering problems, and so on. Died before he'd worked out his major theories."

"Then you each represent a different facet of his mind, his talents?"

"No," said Zayin, shaking her head in time with several others. "We share the basic equipment and tendencies, of course, but we're all engineers in Planetary Exploitation. A later clone can be trained to develop other aspects of the basic equipment. It's all training; the genetic substance is identical. We *are* John Chow. But we were differently trained."

Martin looked shell-shocked. "How old are you?"

"Twenty-three."

"You say he died young— Had they taken germ cells from him beforehand or something?"

Gimel took over: "He died at twenty-four in an aircar crash. They couldn't save the brain, so they took some intestinal cells and cultured them for cloning. Reproductive cells aren't used for cloning since they have only half the chromosomes. Intestinal cells happen to be easy to despecialize and reprogram for total growth."

"All chips off the old block," Martin said valiantly. "But how can . . . some of you be women . . . ?"

Beth took over: "It's easy to program half the clonal mass back to the female. Just delete the male gene from half the cells and they revert to the basic, that is, the female. It's trickier to go the other way, have to hook in artificial Y chromosomes. So they mostly clone from males, since clones function best bisexually."

Gimel again: "They've worked these matters of technique and function out carefully. The taxpayer wants the best for his money, and of course clones are expensive. With the cell-manipulations, and the incubation in Ngama Placentae, and the maintenance and training of the foster-parent groups, we end up costing about three million apiece."

"For your next generation," Martin said, still struggling, "I suppose you . . . you breed?"

"We females are sterile," said Beth with perfect equanimity; "you remember that the Y chromosome was deleted from our original cell. The males can interbreed with approved singletons, if they want to. But to get John Chow again as often as they want, they just reclone a cell from this clone."

Martin gave up the struggle. He nodded and chewed cold toast. "Well," said one of the Johns, and all changed mood, like a flock of starlings that change course in one wingflick, following a leader so fast that no eye can see which leads. They were ready to go. "How about a look at the mine? Then we'll unload the equipment. Some nice new models in the roboats; you'll want to see them. Right?" Had Pugh or Martin not agreed they might have found it hard to say so. The Johns were polite but unanimous; their decisions carried. Pugh, Commander of Libra Base 2, felt a qualm. Could he boss around this superman-woman-entity-of-ten? and a genius at that? He stuck close to Martin as they suited for outside. Neither said anything.

Four apiece in the three large jetsleds, they slipped off north from the dome, over Libra's dun rugose skin, in starlight.

"Desolate," one said.

It was a boy and girl with Pugh and Martin. Pugh wondered if these were the two that had shared a sleeping-bag last night. No doubt they wouldn't mind if he asked them. Sex must be as handy as breathing, to them. Did you two breathe last night?

"Yes," he said, "it is desolate."

"This is our first time Off, except training on Luna." The girls's voice was definitely a bit higher and softer.

"How did you take the big hop?"

"They doped us. I wanted to experience it." That was the boy; he sounded wistful. They seemed to have more personality, only two at a time. Did repetition of the individual negate individuality?

"Don't worry," said Martin, steering the sled, "you can't experience no-time because it isn't there."

"I'd just like to once," one of them said. "So we'd know."

The Mountains of Merioneth showed leprotic in starlight to the east, a plume of freezing gas trailed silvery from a vent-hole to the west, and the sled tilted groundward. The twins braced for the stop at one moment, each with a slight protective gesture to the other. Your skin is my skin, Pugh thought, but literally, no metaphor. What would it be like, then, to have someone as close to you as that? Always to be answered when you spoke, never to be in pain alone. Love your neighbor as you love yourself. . . . That hard old problem was solved. The neighbor was the self: the love was perfect.

And here was Hellmouth, the mine.

Pugh was the Exploratory Mission's ET geologist, and Martin his technician and cartographer; but when in the course of a local survey Martin had discovered the U-mine, Pugh had given him full credit, as well as the onus of prospecting the lode and planning the Exploitation Team's job. These kids had been sent out from Earth years before Martin's reports got there, and had not known what their job would be until they got here. The Exploitation Corps simply sent out teams regularly and blindly as a dandelion sends out its seeds, knowing there would be a job for them on Libra or the next planet out or one they hadn't even heard about yet. The Government wanted uranium too urgently to wait while reports drifted home across the light-years. The stuff was like gold, old-fashioned but essential, worth mining extraterrestrially and shipping interstellar. Worth its weight in people, Pugh thought sourly, watching the tall young men and women go one by one, glimmering in starlight, into the black hole Martin had named Hellmouth.

As they went in their homeostatic forehead-lamps brightened. Twelve nodding gleams ran along the moist, wrinkled walls. Pugh heard Martin's radiation counter peeping twenty to the dozen up ahead. "Here's the drop-off," said Martin's voice in the suit intercom, drowning out the peeping and the dead silence that was around them. "We're in a side-fissure; this is the main vertical vent in front of us." The black void gaped, its far side not visible in the headlamp beams. "Last vulcanism seems to have been a couple of thousand years ago. Nearest fault is twenty-eight kilos east, in the Trench. This region seems to be as safe seismically as anything in the area. The big basalt-flow overhead stabilizes all these substructures, so long as it remains stable itself. Your central lode is thirty-six meters down and runs in a series of five bubble-caverns northeast. It is a lode, a pipe of very high-grade ore. You saw the percentage figures, right? Extraction's going to be no problem. All you've got to do is get the bubbles topside."

"Take off the lid and let 'em float up." A chuckle. Voices began to talk, but they were all the same voice and the suit radio gave them no location in space. "Open the thing right up. —Safer that way. —But it's a solid basalt roof, how thick, ten meters here? —Three to twenty, the report said. —Blow good ore all over the lot. —Use this access we're in, straighten it a bit and run slider-rails for the robos. —Import burros. —Have we got enough propping material? —What's your estimate of total payload mass, Martin?"

"Say over five million kilos and under eight."

"Transport will be here in ten E-months. —It'll have to go pure. —No, they'll have the mass problem in NAFAL shipping licked by now; remember it's been sixteen years since we left Earth last Tuesday. —Right, they'll send the whole lot back and purify it in Earth orbit. —Shall we go down, Martin?"

"Go on. I've been down."

The first one—Aleph? (Heb., the ox, the leader)—swung onto the ladder and down; the rest followed. Pugh and Martin stood at the chasm's edge. Pugh set his intercom to exchange only with Martin's suit, and noticed Martin doing the same. It was a bit wearing, this listening to one person think aloud in ten voices, or was it one voice speaking the thoughts of ten minds?

"A great gut," Pugh said, looking down into the black pit, its veined and warted walls catching stray gleams of headlamps far below. "A cow's bowel. A bloody great constipated intestine."

Martin's counter peeped like a lost chicken. They stood inside the epileptic planet, breathing oxygen from tanks, wearing suits impermeable to corrosives and harmful radiations, resistant to a two-hundred-degree range of temperatures, tear-proof, and as shock-resistant as possible given the soft vulnerable stuff inside.

"Next hop," Martin said, "I'd like to find a planet that has nothing whatever to exploit."

"You found this."

"Keep me home next time."

Pugh was pleased. He had hoped Martin would want to go on working with him, but neither of them was used to talking much about their feelings, and he had hesitated to ask. "I'll try that," he said.

"I hate this place. I like caves, you know. It's why I came in here. Just spelunking. But this one's a bitch. Mean. You can't ever let down in here. I guess this lot can handle it, though. They know their stuff."

"Wave of the future, whatever," said Pugh.

The wave of the future came swarming up the ladder, swept Martin to the entrance, gabbled at and around him: "Have we got enough material for supports? —If we convert one of the extractor-servos to anneal, yes. —Sufficient if we miniblast? —Kaph can calculate stress."

Pugh had switched his intercom back to receive them; he looked at them, so many thoughts jabbering in an eager mind, and at Martin standing silent among them, and at Hellmouth, and the wrinkled plain. "Settled! How does that strike you as a preliminary schedule, Martin?"

"It's your baby," Martin said.

Within five E-days the Johns had all their material and equipment unloaded and operating, and were starting to open up the mine. They worked with total efficiency. Pugh was fascinated and frightened by their effectiveness, their confidence, their independence. He was no use to them at all. A clone, he thought, might indeed be the first truly stable, self-reliant human being. Once adult it would need nobody's help. It would be sufficient to itself physically, sexually, emotionally, intellectually. Whatever he did, any member of it would always receive the support and approval of his peers, his other selves. Nobody else was needed.

Two of the clone stayed in the dome doing calculations and paperwork, with frequent sled-trips to the mine for measurements and tests. They were the mathematicians of the clone, Zayin and Kaph. That is, as Zayin explained, all ten had had thorough mathematical training from age three to twenty-one, but from twenty-one to twenty-three she and Kaph had gone on with math while the others intensified other specialties, geology, mining engineering, electronic engineering, equipment robotics, applied atomics, and so on. "Kaph and I feel," she said, "that we're the element of the clone closest to what John Chow was in his singleton lifetime. But of course he was principally in biomath, and they didn't take us far in that."

"They needed us most in this field," Kaph said, with the patriotic priggishness they sometimes evinced.

Pugh and Martin soon could distinguish this pair from the others, Zayin by gestalt, Kaph only by a discolored left fourth fingernail, got from an ill-aimed hammer at the age of six. No doubt there were many such differences, physical and psychological, among them; nature might be identical, nurture could not be. But the differences were hard to find. And part of the difficulty was that they really never talked to Pugh and Martin. They joked with them, were polite, got along fine. They gave nothing. It was nothing one could complain about; they were very pleasant, they had the standardized American friendliness. "Do you come from Ireland, Owen?"

"Nobody comes from Ireland, Zayin."

"There are lots of Irish-Americans."

"To be sure, but no more Irish. A couple of thousand in all the island, the last I knew. They didn't go in for birth-control, you know, so the food ran out. By the Third Famine there were no Irish left at all but the priesthood, and they were all celibate, or nearly all."

Zayin and Kaph smiled stiffly. They had no experience of either bigotry or irony. "What are you then, ethnically?" Kaph asked, and Pugh replied, "A Welshman."

"Is it Welsh that you and Martin speak together?"

None of your business, Pugh thought, but said, "No, it's his dialect, not mine: Argentinean. A descendant of Spanish."

"You learned it for private communication?"

"Whom had we here to be private from? It's just that sometimes a man likes to speak his native language."

"Our is English," Kaph said unsympathetically. Why should they have sympathy? That's one of the things you give because you need it back.

"Is Wells quaint?" asked Zayin.

"Wells? Oh, Wales, it's called. Yes. Wales is quaint." Pugh switched on his rock-cutter, which prevented further conversation by a synapse-destroying whine, and while it whined he turned his back and said a profane word in Welsh.

That night he used the Argentine dialect for private communication. "Do they pair off in the same couples, or change every night?"

Martin looked surprised. A prudish expression, unsuited to his features, appeared for a moment. It faded. He too was curious. "I think it's random."

"Don't whisper, man, it sounds dirty. I think they rotate."

"On a schedule?"

"So nobody gets omitted."

Martin gave a vulgar laugh and smothered it. "What about us? Aren't we omitted?"

"That doesn't occur to them."

"What if I proposition one of the girls?"

"She'd tell the others and they'd decide as a group."

"I am not a bull," Martin said, his dark, heavy face heating up. "I will not be judged—"

"Down, down, *machismo*," said Pugh. "Do you mean to proposition one?"

Martin shrugged, sullen. "Let 'em have their incest."

"Incest is it, or masturbation?"

"I don't care, if they'd do it out of earshot!"

The clone's early attempts at modesty had soon worn off, unmotivated by any deep defensiveness of self or awareness of others. Pugh and Martin were daily deeper swamped under the intimacies of its constant emotional-sexual-mental interchange: swamped yet excluded.

"Two months to go," Martin said one evening.

"To what?" snapped Pugh. He was edgy lately and Martin's sullenness got on his nerves.

"To relief."

In sixty days the full crew of their Exploratory Mission were due back from their survey of the other planets of the system. Pugh was aware of this.

"Crossing off the days on your calendar?" he jeered.

"Pull yourself together, Owen."

"What do you mean?"

"What I say."

They parted in contempt and resentment.

Pugh came in after a day alone on the Pampas, a vast lava-plain the nearest edge of which was two hours south by jet. He was tired, but refreshed by solitude. They were not supposed to take long trips alone, but lately had often done so. Martin stooped under bright lights, drawing one of his elegant, masterly charts: this one was of the whole face of Libra, the cancerous face. The dome was otherwise empty, seeming dim and large as it had before the clone came. "Where's the golden horde?"

Martin grunted ignorance, crosshatching. He straightened his back to glance around at the sun, which squatted feebly like a great red toad on the eastern plain, and at the clock, which said 18:45. "Some big quakes today," he said, returning to his map. "Feel them down there? Lot of crates were falling around. Take a look at the seismo."

The needle jigged and wavered on the roll. It never stopped dancing here. The roll had recorded five quakes of major intensity back in mid-afternoon; twice the needle had hopped off the roll. The attached computer had been activated to emit a slip reading, "Epicenter 61' N by 4'24"·E."

"Not in the Trench this time."

"I thought it felt a bit different from usual. Sharper."

"In Base One I used to lie awake all night feeling the ground jump. Queer how you get used to things."

"Go spla if you didn't. What's for dinner?"

"I thought you'd have cooked it."

"Waiting for the clone."

Feeling put upon, Pugh got out a dozen dinnerboxes, stuck two in the Instobake, pulled them out. "All right, here's dinner."

"Been thinking," Martin said, coming to the table. "What if some clone cloned itself? Illegally. Made a thousand duplicates—ten thousand. Whole army. They could make a tidy power-grab, couldn't they?"

"But how many millions did this lot cost to rear? Artificial placentae and all that. It would be hard to keep secret, unless they had a planet to themselves. . . . Back before the Famines when Earth had national governments, they talked about that: clone your best soldiers, have whole regiments of them. But the food ran out before they could play that game."

They talked amicably, as they used to do.

"Funny," Martin said, chewing. "They left early this morning, didn't they?"

"All but Kaph and Zayin. They thought they'd get the first payload aboveground today. What's up?"

"They weren't back for lunch."

"They won't starve, to be sure."

"They left at seven."

"So they did." Then Pugh saw it. The air-tanks held eight hours' supply.

"Kaph and Zayin carried out spare cans when they left. Or they've got a heap out there."

"They did, but they brought the whole lot in to recharge." Martin stood up, pointing to one of the stacks of stuff that cut the dome into rooms and alleys.

"There's an alarm signal on every imsuit."

"It's not automatic."

Pugh was tired and still hungry. "Sit down and eat, man. That lot can look after themselves."

Martin sat down, but did not eat. "There was a big quake, Owen. The first one. Big enough, it scared me."

After a pause Pugh sighed and said, "All right."

Unenthusiastically, they got out the two-man sled that was always left for them, and headed it north. The long sunrise covered everything in poisonous red jello. The horizontal light and shadow made it hard to see, raised walls of fake iron ahead of them through which they slid, turned the convex plain beyond Hellmouth into a great dimple full of bloody water. Around the tunnel entrance a wilderness of machinery stood, cranes and cables and servos and wheels and diggers and robocarts and sliders and control-huts, all slanting and bulking incoherently in the red light. Martin jumped from the sled, ran into the mine. He came out again, to Pugh. "Oh God, Owen, it's down," he said. Pugh went in and saw, five meters from the entrance, the shiny, moist, black wall that ended the tunnel. Newly exposed to air, it looked organic, like visceral tissue. The tunnel entrance, enlarged by blasting and double-tracked for robocarts, seemed unchanged until he noticed thousands of tiny spiderweb cracks in the walls. The floor was wet with some sluggish fluid.

"They were inside," Martin said.

"They may be still. They surely had extra air-cans—"

"Look, Owen, look at the basalt flow, at the roof; don't you see what the quake did, look at it."

The low hump of land that roofed the caves still had the unreal look of an optical illusion. It had reversed itself, sunk down, leaving a vast dimple or pit. When Pugh walked on it he saw that it too was cracked with many tiny fissures. From some a whitish gas was seeping, so that the sunlight on the surface of the gas-pool was shafted as if by the waters of a dim red lake.

"The mine's not on the fault. There's no fault here!"

Pugh came back to him quickly. "No, there's no fault, Martin. Look, they surely weren't all inside together."

Martin followed him and searched among the wrecked machines dully, then actively. He spotted the airsled. It had come down heading south, and stuck at an angle in a pothole of colloidal dust. It had carried two riders. One was half sunk in the dust, but his suit-meters registered normal functioning; the other hung strapped onto the tilted sled. Her imsuit had burst open on the broken legs, and the body was frozen hard as any rock. That was all they found. As both regulation and custom demanded, they cremated the dead at once with the laser-guns they carried by regulation and had never used before. Pugh, knowing he was going to be sick, wrestled the survivor onto the two-man sled and sent Martin off to the dome with him. Then he vomited, and flushed the waste out of his suit, and finding one four-man sled undamaged followed after Martin, shaking as if the cold of Libra had got through to him.

The survivor was Kaph. He was in deep shock. They found a swelling on the occiput that might mean concussion, but no fracture was visible.

Pugh brought two glasses of food-concentrate and two chasers of aquavit. "Come on," he said. Martin obeyed, drinking off the tonic. They sat down on crates near the cot and sipped the aquavit.

Kaph lay immobile, face like beeswax, hair bright black to the shoulders, lips stiffly parted for faintly gasping breaths.

"It must have been the first shock, the big one," Martin said. "It must have slid the whole structure sideways. Till it fell in on itself. There must be gas layers in the lateral rocks, like those formations in the Thirty-first Quadrant. But there wasn't any sign—" As he spoke the world slid out from under them. Things leaped and clattered, hopped and jigged, shouted Ha! Ha! Ha! "It was like this at fourteen hours," said Reason shakily in Martin's voice; amidst the unfastening and ruin of the world. But Unreason sat up, as the tumult lessened and things ceased dancing, and screamed aloud.

Pugh leaped across his spilled aquavit and held Kaph down. The muscular body flailed him off. Martin pinned the shoulders down. Kaph screamed, struggled, choked; his face blackened. "Oxy," Pugh said, and his hand found the right needle in the medical kit as if by homing instinct; while Martin held the mask he struck the needle home to the vagus nerve, restoring Kaph to life.

"Didn't know you knew that stunt," Martin said, breathing hard.

"The Lazarus Jab; my father was a doctor. It doesn't often work," Pugh said. "I want that drink I spilled. Is the quake over? I can't tell."

"Aftershocks. It's not just you shivering."

"Why did he suffocate?"

"I don't know, Owen. Look in the book."

Kaph was breathing normally and his color was restored, only the lips were still darkened. They poured a new shot of courage and sat down by him again with their medical guide. "Nothing about cyanosis or asphyxiation under 'shock' or 'concussion.' He can't have breathed in anything with his suit on. I don't know. We'd get as much good out of *Mother Mog's Home Herbalist*. . . . 'Anal Hemorrhoids,' fy!" Pugh pitched the book to a crate-table. It fell short, because either Pugh or the table was still unsteady.

"Why didn't he signal?"

"Sorry?"

"The eight inside the mine never had time. But he and the girl must have been outside. Maybe she was in the entrance, and got hit by the first slide. He must have been outside, in the control-hut maybe. He ran in, pulled her out, strapped her onto the sled, started for the dome. And all that time never pushed the panic button in his imsuit. Why not?"

"Well, he'd had that whack on his head. I doubt he ever realized the girl was dead. He wasn't in his senses. But if he had been I don't know if he'd have thought to signal us. They looked to one another for help."

Martin's face was like an Indian mask, grooves at the mouth-corners, eyes of dull coal. "That's so. What must he have felt, then, when the quake came and he was outside, alone—"

In answer Kaph screamed.

He came up off the cot in the heaving convulsions of one suffocating, knocked Pugh right down with his flailing arm, staggered into a stack of crates and fell to the floor, lips blue, eyes white. Martin dragged him back onto the cot and gave him a whiff of oxygen, then knelt by Pugh, who was just sitting up, and wiped at his cut cheekbone. "Owen, are you all right, are you going to be all right, Owen?"

"I think I am," Pugh said. "Why are you rubbing that on my face?"

It was a short length of computer-tape, now spotted with Pugh's blood. Martin dropped it. "Thought it was a towel. You clipped your cheek on that box there."

"Is he out of it?"

"Seems to be."

They stared down at Kaph lying stiff, his teeth a white line inside dark parted lips.

"Like epilepsy. Brain damage maybe?"

"What about shooting him full of meprobamate?"

Pugh shook his head. "I don't know what's in that shot I already gave him for shock. Don't want to overdose him."

"Maybe he'll sleep it off now."

"I'd like to myself. Between him and the earthquake I can't seem to keep on my feet."

"You got a nasty crack there. Go on, I'll sit up a while."

Pugh cleaned his cut cheek and pulled off his shirt, then paused. "Is there anything we ought to have done—have tried to do—"

"They're all dead," Martin said heavily, gently.

Pugh lay down on top of his sleeping-bag, and one instant later was wakened by a hideous, sucking, struggling noise. He staggered up, found the needle, tried three times to jab it in correctly and failed, began to massage over Kaph's heart. "Mouth-to-mouth," he said, and Martin obeyed. Presently Kaph drew a harsh breath, his heartbeat steadied, his rigid muscles began to relax.

"How long did I sleep?"

"Half an hour."

They stood up sweating. The ground shuddered, the fabric of the dome sagged and swayed. Libra was dancing her awful polka again, her Totentanz. The sun, though rising, seemed to have grown larger and redder; gas and dust must have been stirred up in the feeble atmosphere.

"What's wrong with him, Owen?"

"I think he's dying with them."

"Them— But they're dead, I tell you."

"Nine of them. They're all dead, they were crushed or suffocated. They were all him, he is all of them. They died, and now he's dying their deaths one by one."

"Oh pity of God," said Martin.

The next time was much the same. The fifth time was worse, for Kaph fought and raved, trying to speak but getting no words out, as if his mouth were stopped with rocks or clay. After that the attacks grew weaker, but so did he. The eighth seizure came at about four-thirty; Pugh and Martin worked till five-thirty doing all they could to keep life in the body that slid without protest into death. They kept him, but Martin said, "The next will finish him." And it did; but Pugh breathed his own breath into the inert lungs, until he himself passed out.

He woke. The dome was opaqued and no light on. He listened and heard the breathing of two sleeping men. He slept, and nothing woke him till hunger did.

The sun was well up over the dark plains, and the planet had stopped dancing. Kaph lay asleep. Pugh and Martin drank tea and looked at him with proprietary triumph.

When he woke Martin went to him: "How do you feel, old man?" There was no answer. Pugh took Martin's place and looked into the brown, dull eyes that gazed toward but not into his own. Like Martin he quickly turned away. He heated food-concentrate and brought it to Kaph. "Come on, drink."

He could see the muscles in Kaph's throat tighten. "Let me die," the young man said.

"You're not dying."

Kaph spoke with clarity and precision: "I am nine-tenths dead. There is not enough of me left alive."

That precision convinced Pugh, and he fought the conviction. "No," he said, peremptory. "They are dead. The others. Your brothers and sisters. You're not them, you're alive. You are John Chow. Your life is in your own hands."

The young man lay still, looking into a darkness that was not there.

Martin and Pugh took turns taking the Exploitation hauler and a spare set of robos over to Hellmouth to salvage equipment and protect it from Libra's sinister atmosphere, for the value of the stuff was, literally, astronomical. It was slow work for one man at a time, but they were unwilling to leave Kaph by himself. The one left in the dome did paperwork, while Kaph sat or lay and stared into his darkness, and never spoke. The days went by silent.

The radio spat and spoke: the Mission calling from ship. "We'll be down on Libra in five weeks, Owen. Thirty-four E-days nine hours I make it as of now. How's tricks in the old dome?"

"Not good, chief. The Exploit team were killed, all but one of them, in the mine. Earthquake. Six days ago."

The radio crackled and sang starsong. Sixteen seconds lag each way; the ship was out around Planet 11 now. "Killed, all but one? You and Martin were unhurt?"

"We're all right, chief."

Thirty-two seconds.

"*Passerine* left an Exploit team out here with us. I may put them on the Hellmouth project then, instead of the Quadrant Seven project. We'll settle that when we come down. In any case you and Martin will be relieved at Dome Two. Hold tight. Anything else?"

"Nothing else."

Thirty-two seconds.

"Right then. So long, Owen."

Kaph had heard all this, and later on Pugh said to him, "The chief may ask you to stay here with the other Exploit team. You know the ropes here." Knowing the exigencies of Far Out Life, he wanted to warn the young man. Kaph made no answer. Since he had said, "There is not enough of me left alive," he had not spoken a word.

"Owen," Martin said on suit intercom, "he's spla. Insane. Psycho."

"He's doing very well for a man who's died nine times."

"Well? Like a turned-off android is well? The only emotion he has left is hate. Look at his eyes."

"That's not hate, Martin. Listen, it's true that he has, in a sense, been dead. I cannot imagine what he feels. But it's not hatred. He can't even see us. It's too dark."

"Throats have been cut in the dark. He hates us because we're not Aleph and Yod and Zayin."

"Maybe. But I think he's alone. He doesn't see us or hear us, that's the truth. He never had to see anyone else before. He never was alone before. He had himself to see, talk with, live with, nine other selves all his life. He doesn't know how you go it alone. He must learn. Give him time."

Martin shook his heavy head. "Spla," he said. "Just remember when you're alone with him that he could break your neck one-handed."

"He could do that," said Pugh, a short, soft-voiced man with a scarred cheekbone; he smiled. They were just outside the dome airlock, programming one of the servos to repair a damaged hauler. They could see Kaph sitting inside the great half-egg of the dome like a fly in amber.

"Hand me the insert pack there. What makes you think he'll get any better?"

"He has a strong personality, to be sure."

"Strong? Crippled. Nine-tenths dead, as he put it."

"But he's not dead. He's a live man: John Kaph Chow. He had a jolly queer upbringing, but after all every boy has got to break free of his family. He will do it."

"I can't see it."

"Think a bit, Martin bach. What's this cloning for? To repair the human race. We're in a bad way. Look at me. My IIQ and GC are half this John Chow's. Yet they wanted me so badly for the Far Out Service that when I volunteered they took me and fitted me out with an artificial lung and corrected my myopia. Now if there were enough good sound lads about would they be taking one-lunged shortsighted Welshmen?"

"Didn't know you had an artificial lung."

"I do then. Not tin, you know. Human, grown in a tank from a bit of somebody; cloned, if you like. That's how they make replacement-organs, the same general idea as cloning, but bits and pieces instead of whole people. It's my own lung now, whatever. But what I am saying is this, there are too many like me these days, and not enough like John Chow. They're trying to raise the level of the human genetic pool, which is a mucky little puddle since the population crash. So then if a man is cloned, he's a strong and clever man. It's only logic, to be sure."

Martin grunted; the servo began to hum.

Kaph had been eating little; he had trouble swallowing his food, choking on it, so that he would give up trying after a few bites. He had lost eight or ten kilos. After three weeks or so, however, his appetite began to pick up, and one day he began to look through the clone's possessions, the sleeping-bags, kits, papers which Pugh had stacked neatly in a far angle of a packing-crate alley. He sorted, destroyed a heap of papers and oddments, made a small packet of what remained, then relapsed into his walking coma.

Two days later he spoke. Pugh was trying to correct a flutter in the tape-player, and failing; Martin had the jet out, checking their maps of the Pampas. "Hell and damnation!" Pugh said, and Kaph said in a toneless voice, "Do you want me to do that?"

Pugh jumped, controlled himself, and gave the machine to Kaph. The young man took it apart, put it back together, and left it on the table.

"Put on a tape," Pugh said with careful casualness, busy at another table.

Kaph put on the topmost tape, a chorale. He lay down on his cot. The sound of a hundred human voices singing together filled the dome. He lay still, his face blank.

In the next days he took over several routine jobs, unasked. He undertook nothing that wanted initiative, and if asked to do anything he made no response at all.

"He's doing well," Pugh said in the dialect of Argentina.

"He's not. He's turning himself into a machine. Does what he's programmed to do, no reaction to anything else. He's worse off than when he didn't function at all. He's not human any more."

Pugh sighed. "Well, good night," he said in English. "Good night, Kaph."

"Good night," Martin said; Kaph did not.

Next morning at breakfast Kaph reached across Martin's plate for the toast. "Why don't you ask for it," Martin said with the geniality of repressed exasperation. "I can pass it."

"I can reach it," Kaph said in his flat voice.

"Yes, but look. Asking to pass things, saying good night or hello, they're not important, but all the same when somebody says something a person ought to answer. . . ."

The young man looked indifferently in Martin's direction; his eyes still did not seem to see clear through to the person he looked toward. "Why should I answer?"

"Because somebody has said something to you."

"Why?"

Martin shrugged and laughed. Pugh jumped up and turned on the rock-cutter.

Later on he said, "Lay off that, please, Martin."

"Manners are essential in small isolated crews, some kind of manners, whatever you work out together. He's been taught that, everybody in Far Out knows it. Why does he deliberately flout it?"

"Do you tell yourself good night?"

"So?"

"Don't you see Kaph's never known anyone but himself?"

Martin brooded and then broke out, "Then by God this cloning business is all wrong. It won't do. What are a lot of duplicate geniuses going to do for us when they don't even know we exist?"

Pugh nodded. "It might be wiser to separate the clones and bring them up with others. But they make such a grand team this way."

"Do they? I don't know. If this lot had been ten average inefficient ET engineers, would they all have been in the same place at the same time? Would they all have got killed? What if, when the quake came and things started caving in, what if all those kids ran the same way, farther into the mine, maybe, to save the one that was farthest in? Even Kaph was outside and went in. . . . It's hypothetical. But I keep thinking, out of ten ordinary confused guys, more might have got out."

"I don't know. It's true that identical twins tend to die at about the same time, even when they have never seen each other. Identity and death, it is very strange. . . ."

The days went on, the red sun crawled across the dark sky, Kaph did not speak when spoken to, Pugh and Martin snapped at each other more frequently each day. Pugh complained of Martin's snoring. Offended, Martin moved his cot clear across the dome and also ceased speaking to Pugh for some while. Pugh whistled Welsh dirges until Martin complained, and then Pugh stopped speaking for a while.

The day before the Mission ship was due, Martin announced he was going over to Merioneth.

"I thought at least you'd be giving me a hand with the computer to finish the rock-analyses," Pugh said, aggrieved.

"Kaph can do that. I want one more look at the Trench. Have fun," Martin added in dialect, and laughed, and left.

"What is that language?"

"Argentinean. I told you that once, didn't I?"

"I don't know." After a while the young man added, "I have forgotten a lot of things, I think."

"It wasn't important, to be sure," Pugh said gently, realizing all at once how important this conversation was. "Will you give me a hand running the computer, Kaph?"

He nodded.

Pugh had left a lot of loose ends, and the job took them all day. Kaph was a good co-worker, quick and systematic, much more so than

Pugh himself. His flat voice, now that he was talking again, got on the nerves; but it didn't matter, there was only this one day left to get through and then the ship would come, the old crew, comrades and friends.

During tea-break Kaph said, "What will happen if the Explorer ship crashes?"

"They'd be killed."

"To you, I mean."

"To us? We'd radio SOS all signals, and live on half rations till the rescue cruiser from Area Three Base came. Four and a half E-years away it is. We have life-support here for three men for, let's see, maybe between four and five years. A bit tight, it would be."

"Would they send a cruiser for three men?"

"They would."

Kaph said no more.

"Enough cheerful speculations," Pugh said cheerfully, rising to get back to work. He slipped sideways and the chair avoided his hand; he did a sort of half-pirouette and fetched up hard against the dome-hide. "My goodness," he said, reverting to his native idiom, "what is it?"

"Quake," said Kaph.

The teacups bounced on the table with a plastic cackle, a litter of papers slid off a box, the skin of the dome swelled and sagged. Underfoot there was a huge noise, half sound half shaking, a subsonic boom.

Kaph sat unmoved. An earthquake does not frighten a man who died in an earthquake.

Pugh, white-faced, wiry black hair sticking out, a frightened man, said, "Martin is in the Trench."

"What trench?"

"The big fault line. The epicenter for the local quakes. Look at the seismograph." Pugh struggled with the stuck door of a still-jittering locker.

"Where are you going?"

"After him."

"Martin took the jet. Sleds aren't safe to use during quakes. They go out of control."

"For God's sake, man, shut up."

Kaph stood up, speaking in a flat voice as usual. "It's unnecessary to go out after him now. It's taking an unnecessary risk."

"If his alarm goes off, radio me," Pugh said, shut the headpiece of his suit, and ran to the lock. As he went out Libra picked up her ragged skirts and danced a bellydance from under his feet clear to the red horizon.

Inside the dome, Kaph saw the sled go up, tremble like a meteor in the dull red daylight, and vanish to the northeast. The hide of the dome quivered; the earth coughed. A vent south of the dome belched up a slow-flowing bile of black gas.

A bell shrilled and a red light flashed on the central control board. The sign under the light read Suit Two and scribbled under that, A.G.M. Kaph did not turn the signal off. He tried to radio Martin, then Pugh, but got no reply from either.

When the aftershocks decreased he went back to work, and finished up Pugh's job. It took him about two hours. Every half hour he tried to contact Suit One, and got no reply, then Suit Two and got no reply. The red light had stopped flashing after an hour.

It was dinnertime. Kaph cooked dinner for one, and ate it. He lay down on his cot.

The aftershocks had ceased except for faint rolling tremors at long intervals. The sun hung in the west, oblate, pale-red, immense. It did not sink visibly. There was no sound at all.

Kaph got up and began to walk about the messy, half-packed-up, overcrowded, empty dome. The silence continued. He went to the player and put on the first tape that came to hand. It was pure music, electronic, without harmonies, without voices. It ended. The silence continued.

Pugh's uniform tunic, one button missing, hung over a stack of rock-samples. Kaph stared at it a while.

The silence continued.

The child's dream: There is no one else alive in the world but me. In all the world.

Low, north of the dome, a meteor flickered.

Kaph's mouth opened as if he were trying to say something, but no sound came. He went hastily to the north wall and peered out into the gelatinous red light.

The little star came in and sank. Two figures blurred the airlock. Kaph stood close beside the lock as they came in. Martin's imsuit was covered with some kind of dust so that he looked raddled and warty like the surface of Libra. Pugh had him by the arm.

"Is he hurt?"

Pugh shucked his suit, helped Martin peel off his. "Shaken up," he said, curt.

"A piece of cliff fell onto the jet," Martin said, sitting down at the table and waving his arms. "Not while I was in it, though. I was parked, see, and poking about that carbon-dust area when I felt things humping. So I went out onto a nice bit of early igneous I'd noticed from above, good footing and out from under the cliffs. Then I saw this bit of the planet fall off onto the flyer, quite a sight it was, and after a while it occurred to me the spare aircans were in the flyer, so I leaned on the panic button. But I didn't get any radio reception, that's always happening here during quakes, so I didn't know if the signal was getting through either. And things went on jumping around and pieces of the cliff coming off. Little rocks flying around, and so dusty you couldn't see a meter ahead. I was really beginning to wonder what I'd do for breathing in the small hours, you know, when I saw old Owen buzzing up the Trench in all that dust and junk like a big ugly bat—"

"Want to eat?" said Pugh.

"Of course I want to eat. How'd you come through the quake here, Kaph? No damage? It wasn't a big one actually, was it, what's the seismo say? My trouble was I was in the middle of it. Old Epicenter Alvaro. Felt like Richter Fifteen there—total destruction of planet—"

"Sit down," Pugh said. "Eat."

After Martin had eaten a little his spate of talk ran dry. He very soon went off to his cot, still in the remote angle where he had removed it when Pugh complained of his snoring. "Good night, you one-lunged Welshman," he said across the dome.

"Good night."

There was no more out of Martin. Pugh opaqued the dome, turned the lamp down to a yellow glow less than a candle's light, and sat doing nothing, saying nothing, withdrawn.

The silence continued.

"I finished the computations."

Pugh nodded thanks.

"The signal from Martin came through, but I couldn't contact you or him."

Pugh said with effort. "I should not have gone. He had two hours of air left even with only one can. He might have been heading home when I left. This way we were all out of touch with one another. I was scared."

The silence came back, punctuated now by Martin's long, soft snores.

"Do you love Martin?"

Pugh looked up with angry eyes: "Martin is my friend. We've worked together, he's a good man." He stopped. After a while he said, "Yes, I love him. Why did you ask that?"

Kaph said nothing, but he looked at the other man. His face was changed, as if he were glimpsing something he had not seen before; his voice too was changed. "How can you . . . ? How do you . . . ?"

But Pugh could not tell him. "I don't know," he said, "it's practice, partly. I don't know. We're each of us alone, to be sure. What can you do but hold your hand out in the dark?"

Kaph's strange gaze dropped, burned out by its own intensity.

"I'm tired," Pugh said. "That was ugly, looking for him in all that black dust and muck, and mouths opening and shutting in the ground. . . . I'm going to bed. The ship will be transmitting to us by six or so." He stood up and stretched.

"It's a clone," Kaph said. "The other Exploit team they're bringing with them."

"Is it, then?"

"A twelveclone. They came out with us on the *Passerine*."

Kaph sat in the small yellow aura of the lamp seeming to look past it at what he feared: the new clone, the multiple self of which he was not part. A lost piece of a broken set, a fragment, inexpert at solitude, not knowing even how you go about giving love to another individual, now he must face the absolute, closed self-sufficiency of the clone of twelve; that was a lot to ask of the poor fellow, to be sure. Pugh put a hand on his shoulder in passing. "The chief won't ask you to stay here with a clone. You can go home. Or since you're Far Out maybe you'll come on farther out with us. We could use you. No hurry deciding. You'll make out all right."

Pugh's quiet voice trailed off. He stood unbuttoning his coat, stooped a little with fatigue. Kaph looked at him and saw the thing he had never seen before: saw him: Owen Pugh, the other, the stranger who held his hand out in the dark.

"Good night," Pugh mumbled, crawling into his sleeping-bag and half asleep already, so that he did not hear Kaph reply after a pause, repeating, across darkness, benediction.

GOLDEN ACRES

Kit Reed

"I can walk, dammit." After a scuffle Hamish threw off the bellboy's hand and went into the elevator himself. It troubled him that Nelda rode serenely, submitting to the roller chair. The bellhops pushed him in the corner of the elevator, crowding him with the second chair; they had it full of the Scofields' luggage, and when the elevator let them out on Four they took off with a look of spite, rolling the chairs down corridors so fast that Hamish had to run to keep up. His frail lungs failed him finally and he lost them; he came round the last corner to find himself alone on a long cement porch. The pale stucco building seemed to go all the way around a court, or square, and when Hamish looked over the porch rail he saw a pool and a garden below. He would have waved or called out but they were both empty, except for the California sunlight and a few improbable flowers. He turned back to the porch and a series of identical doors, all louvered, all closed.

"Nelda? Nelda?" He hated his voice; it sounded old and thin.

He was breathing heavily, whirling in indecision, when a door opened down the way; one of the bellhops beckoned with a condescending grin.

They had arranged Nelda in the middle of the suitcases and hatboxes, tableau: woman arriving at a resort. Her hand fluttered at the bosom of her best voile dress; in a minute her smile would fly apart. "Hamish," she said, "isn't it beautiful?"

The bellboys were lingering. "That will be all," Hamish said, but they were waiting. He made a little rush at them and then, because Nelda was pale and tremulous, he went on, trying not to look around him, "Just beautiful," and when he looked up this time the bellboys were gone.

"Look, they've put the TV where you can see it from the bed."

He was looking out the door; when he had watched the bellhops around the last corner he closed the door and turned to her, full of misgivings:

"Nelda, I don't know about this place, I just don't *know.*"

"Honey, you're going to love it; it's all we ever dreamed." She had her hat off now and she was beginning to make a little tour of the room, touching the metal bedsteads, running her fingers over the glass on the dresser tops. "Look," she said, "you can see the TV from your bed, just like they said in the brochure."

"Those look like hospital beds."

"You can crank yourself up any way you want." She quoted from memory: "Everything for safety and comfort." But she was running her fingers along the walls now, they were Formica, and when she spoke again her voice was slightly off key. "My knickknack shelf—I don't see any place for my knickknack shelf."

"I don't see any place for *anything.*"

"They said I could hang my knickknack shelf."

But Hamish wasn't listening; he was moving restlessly, taking in the no-color drapes and bedspreads, the oatmeally peach Formica on the walls. The furniture was institutional and sparse: two luggage racks, one for each of them; two beds, two dressers, two straight chairs bolted into place; at waist height all the way around, there was a rail. He snarled, in sudden resentment: "I don't need any goddam rail."

" . . . *and the hot plate.* I don't see the hot plate."

"In here," Hamish said from the tiny bathroom. "On the toilet tank. Say, where in hell are all the mirrors?"

Nelda's voice rose in a tiny wail. "Where can I plug in my hairdrier? How can I do my hair?"

Hamish was out of the bathroom before she finished. He had his arm around her, saying, "Honey, are you sure this is what you want? I mean, it's not too late to change our minds. . . ."

She wavered. "Oh, Hamish."

"We could be back in Waukegan before you know it. We could be *home.*"

But he had lost her. As he spoke her arms dropped and in the next second she was tugging at one of the suitcases, wrestling it onto the bed. She took out a sun hat and put it on. "Hamish, Hamish, *this* is home."

"It's a damn motel."

"We sold everything to buy in here." She had a printed beach dress by the shoulders; she was shaking it out. "We're going to love it here."

"Nelda. . . ."

But it was already too late. She had her sunshade on the bed and on top of that her sneakers and her aqua Capri pants. "It cost us ten thousand dollars. There are thousands on the waiting list. Do you think I'm going to back out now?"

He went on patiently. "I. Just. Don't. Like. What. I've. Seen."

She turned, brandishing a purple sweater. "What would we tell the neighbors when we got back? What would we tell Albert and Lorraine?"

He knew what he wanted to say, he wanted to say "To hell with the neighbors, to hell with Albert and Lorraine," but something put him off; it wasn't the neighbors, it wasn't anybody who had been at the farewell party; he wasn't afraid of any of the rest of them, just Albert and Lorraine.

"We're going to love it here," Nelda said firmly. "It says so in the brochure." She had the children's pictures now; she was setting them on her dresser. "Albert. Eddie. Lorraine. There, that's lovely. Isn't it lovely, Spike?"

He jumped at the sound of the old name.

She came closer and her face had dropped years. "You'll see, Spike. It's going to be just like a second honeymoon. . . ."

He would have kissed her then, he would have taken her old bones in his but there was a knock on the door and before either of them could answer a young man came in, leading a bearded old man who leaned heavily on a cane.

"Mr. and Mrs. Scofield?"

Hamish stepped in front of Nelda. "I'm Hamish Scofield, of Waukegan, Illinois, and I'd like you to meet . . ."

The young man walked on past; he ran a quick finger around the carnation in his lapel and said, under his breath: "Clutter. We don't like our people to live in clutter."

Working quickly, he folded Nelda's family pictures and swept them into the dresser drawer. Albert. Eddie. Lorraine. Hamish knew he ought to protest and he would have, too, if it had been her silver dresser set, or her velvet lined vanity. . . .

"There. I'm Mister Richardson." He was neat as a scissors in his pin-striped suit. "I'm the manager here, and this is Cletus Ford, our Second Oldest Resident."

The Second Oldest Resident raised a hand from under his beard; he and Hamish touched fingers just before Richardson brushed him aside, saying. "I came to be sure you were settled happily here at Golden Acres. And if there's anything. . . ."

Hamish and Nelda both began:

"Mirror, need a damn shaving mirror."

"My knickknack shelf, I need a place for. . . ."

Richardson was still talking—". . . if there's anything we can do to make you happier, you have only to get in touch with any of our several attendants. You will know them because they wear white, the color of Hope. And now. . . ."

"I *would* like. . . ."

"If you could just. . . ."

". . . a few simple rules."

Hamish stiffened. *"Rules."*

"Rules. Then Cletus here. . . ."

Cletus said, hopelessly, *"Mis-*ter Ford."

"Cletus here will tell you about the golden opportunities waiting for you, but first. . . ."

"Well," said Cletus, "there's the Rotary and the Golden Agers and. . . ."

"Cletus. . . ."

". . . and the Close Shave Club, I'm a charter member, and the Am-vets. . . ."

Richardson had him by the shoulders. *"Cletus. . . ."*

"Mis-ter Ford?"

"Cletus, I want you to go over to that chair and sit quietly with your knees together and try and remember your place." The manager went on, through his teeth, "And if you can't remember your place, you know what will happen, don't you?"

Hamish couldn't be sure, but he thought he heard a distant rumble, as if of a gigantic grocery cart. If he heard it, then Cletus heard it too; the old man shrank, diminishing before their eyes, folding himself into a chair and clasping his hands neatly under his beard.

"Y-yessir. Yes *sir*."

Hamish had his mouth open. He was listening hard but the rumble, or whatever it was, was gone.

"First, a little about our many benefits. Of course many of them are obvious, the swimming, the sun, the happy companionship of people your own age, parties in the moonlight, dancing on the esplanade. . . ."

Nelda said, dreamily: ". . . dancing on the esplanade."

"But there is much, much more. Did you know, for instance, that there is a dispensary on every floor, or that the Tower of Hope . . ." Richardson smiled over his carnation ". . . that's what we call our hospital . . . the Tower of Hope is only three minutes away? Did you know there is an attendant on duty on every terrace twenty-four hours a day?"

Hamish stiffened. "A*tten*dant."

"To answer the cry of distress. The fall in the night. The sudden seizure at dawn."

"The doctors," Nelda said. "Tell Spike about the doctors."

"Specialists in every ailment of the human flesh." Richardson smoothed plump hands over his dark suit. "You are safe in our hands."

"Safe. See, Spike, I told you it would be wonderful."

"Reveille at seven sharp, marches over the intercom. . . ." Richardson was growing lyric. "Breakfast at eight, after you clean your room."

Nelda frowned. "Clean?"

"Walks and therapy until noon, then lunch. Then naps. Then clubs. Dinner at five-thirty, bed by nine. Cooking on special days, with permission from the desk."

"Permission from the desk my ass." Hamish advanced on him. "Dinner at five-thirty. Bed by nine. . . ."

"Bed by nine," Richardson said firmly. "You are safe in our hands. Safe to live out your golden years in this California paradise. Now Cletus here. . . ." Cletus was asleep; Richardson kicked him sharply, perforating one ankle. *"Cletus, here. . . ."*

"Huh? Whuh. Osteotomy club, cribbage teams, the. . . ."

"Cletus here is a living testimony to the good life. When he first came in here he was a hollow wreck. Weren't you, Cletus?"

". . . Progress Study Club, Great Grandmothers' Club. . . ." Cletus became aware of an ugly silence. "Sir? Oh, yes. Yessir."

Richardson went on, gratified. "A few days in our hospital, a few months in the sun, and look at him now. He's our Second Oldest Resident, loved by everybody in the place."

Nelda's face was naked. "Loved."

Hamish wanted to push the others out and take her in his arms but they were too many and he was too old; he said, in an undertone, "You'll always be loved."

Richardson had put his hands on old Cletus, trundling him into the spotlight. "O.K., Cletus, you're on." Stifling a yawn, he bowed himself out, barely remembering to say: "Remember, you are safe in our hands."

Hamish counted to sixty, and when Cletus still hadn't said anything he stood over the old man. "Well?"

Cletus was scratching his head. "Well . . . oh, the clubs. Well. Well, we have the biggest Sunshine Booster group in the whole United States and a Masonic Lodge second to none. And we have the largest Kiwanis membership in the world. . . ." He was still talking, but he was distracted, drifting away on a distant sound. "And the Lions . . . and. . . ."

Hamish said, sharply, "You were telling us about the clubs."

"The clubs." Cletus came to with a little jerk. He looked around furtively, whispering. "Do you have any idea how *big* this place is?"

"Tiny," Nelda said. "Exclusive. It says so in the brochure."

"It's a boneyard." His voice dropped even further. "It's *vast.*"

"Only a few well-chosen couples," Nelda said doggedly. "It says so in the brochure."

Hamish hushed her. "Let him talk."

"I tried to walk to the edge of this place one day. Maybe I wanted to see if the world was still there; maybe I just wanted to know there *was* an edge. I walked and walked. You want to know something?" he went on in awe. "I walked for miles."

Nelda said, crossly, "It only seemed like miles."

Hamish was leaning forward. "And you finally made it to the edge."

Cletus shook his head sadly. "Walked until m'legs gave out. They come and got me in a rolling chair. Probably just as well, come to think of it. M'blood pressure was giving me hell."

Nelda said, anxiously, "The clubs. Please. You were telling us about the clubs."

"Hell with the clubs. I always hated clubs."

"But the companionship. All the Golden Agers, just like you. . . ."

"Fossils," Cletus snorted. "Bunch of bones."

"You don't really mean it." Nelda turned to Hamish. "He doesn't really mean it. If he did, he wouldn't stay."

"Hate the buildings, too. All smell of mildew and Argyrol."

"The pool, how about the pool?"

"I'm too damn *old* to swim."

Hamish squinted at him, puzzled. "But you stay. . . ."

"Damn right I stay." Cletus drew them to the window. "Look out there. See that white thing sticking up, taller than anything else? That's the Tower of Hope. Hospital round here."

Hamish said, "What's that tall *black* thing?"

"Hospital around here," Cletus repeated, not answering. "The facings are made of Corning Glass."

He drew the shutters and faced them belligerently. "Damn right I stay. Where else could I get round-the-clock medical care? B-one shot every morning, all the hormones I can take. Doctors, nurses, guys to catch me if I fall." He was squinting at Hamish now; something he saw seemed to anger him. "Don't knock it, buddy. This place is keeping me alive."

"If that's all you get, it isn't worth it," Hamish said angrily. "If that's all. . . ."

Nelda cut him off. "That can't be all."

"All? That's *plenty*." Cletus paused, listening to something they could not make out.

Hamish was on him in a flash. "What's that noise?"

The old man was crafty, insolent. "There isn't any noise." But there was, it was coming closer, and Cletus leaped like a spider. "Archie, M'God, I bet it's for Archie." Hamish tried to hold him but he was too late. "See you," he said, and scuttled out, slamming the door.

It took Hamish a couple of minutes to get it open and when he did he saw only the cement porch receding, the regular march of the posts. He turned back to Nelda then, wondering how he could get her to come away with him, how he could begin. She was already busy with the suitcase, pulling out clothes and spreading them on the bed.

"Nelda."

She wouldn't look at him; instead she picked up a mimeographed paper from the bedside table. "Look, the newspaper. It's called the *Golden Blade*."

"Nelda, please, we have to get out of here."

"It says here they're having a Shipwreck Party Friday; and there are shuffleboard lessons today at four. . . ."

Outside someone was calling faintly, "Cletus, Cletus. . . ."

"We don't belong here, Nelda, I thought we might but we don't."

She turned on him in sudden spite. "Then where *do* we belong?"

"Cletus . . . I know you're in here, Cletus. Come on out." The old lady came skidding into the room in white Ground Grippers and a white lawn dress. "Excuse me," she said when she saw them. "Where's he hiding this time, in the shower?"

Nelda put on her best air. "Beg your pardon?"

"He loves to curl up on the seat . . . come on," she said impatiently. "They're looking for him and I've got to let him know."

"Well, he *was* here, but he. . . ."

"Just like him to run out, just when the pressure is so. . . ."

Hamish took her elbow. "What pressure?"

She shook him off. "Oh, you know. Being the Oldest Living Resident. Sorry I bothered you. . . ."

Nelda stepped forward, intercepting her with a smile so bright that Hamish was embarrassed for her. "Don't go. We were just hoping we'd get to meet some of the people here."

"Look, I have to. . . ."

"I'm Nelda Scofield and this is Hamish. . . ." Nelda's voice went up, quavering. Couldn't you sit down for a minute?"

"I really ought to. . . ." The old lady seemed to see the need in Nelda's face because she said, "Oh hell, sure. Name's Lucy Fortmain," and plopped in one of the chairs.

The silence was ragged, embarrassing; Hamish saw Nelda going through her purse, mentally sizing up the larder, realizing she had nothing to offer her guest. He had come this far for her so he fished in his pockets. "Have a Life Saver?"

The old lady turned with a gracious smile. "Hell, sure."

"I'm sorry we don't have anything more exciting to offer," Nelda said. Hamish saw she was on the verge of tears.

Lucy patted her hand. "Lemon was always my favorite."

"That collar," Nelda said. "That's a lovely looking collar."

"Daughter made it. Tatting. I taught her when she was a kid."

"It's lovely," Nelda said.

"Margaret, m'oldest. Do you know, I have seven kids?"

Nelda touched her flat bosom. "We have two—a boy and a girl."

"Oh, how old are they?"

"Thirty-nine and forty-three. Lost our youngest when he was in his teens."

"Forty-three," Lucy said thoughtfully. "That's just about the cutest age."

"You should have seen ours when they found out we were leaving," Nelda said. "They were fit to be tied."

"Oh, so were mine," Lucy said. "You know how kids are."

"They begged us to stay with them in Waukegan, but when I showed them the brochure, how beautiful it was, well, they just had to give in gracefully; Mother, they said, we'll just have to give in gracefully."

Lucy said, "Well, *my* kids said, if it was any place but here they'd come and drag me out, but they know I'm in such good hands. . . ."

"I know." Nelda was gaining confidence. "I sensed that about the place as soon as we came in. All the attendants, the doctors. . . ."

". . . All the help," Lucy said. "It's as close as the buzzer by your bed." She lowered her head, brooding. After a while she said, with determined cheer: "And there are lots of parties and stuff, clubs and dances and all. My kids could never give me all that."

"It's all so friendly," Nelda said.

"Well. Uh. Yes. They have people to pick you up if you fall and people to come in the night if you have a bad dream, and people on the terrace, they're paid to talk to you, and people to bring you shots you don't even want. . . ." Lucy was beginning to sound depressed. "It's all just great. If only. . . ."

Nelda pressed her. "If only?"

Lucy shook herself. "Well. I'll say one thing. We all have a lot in common here. Same problems, same regrets. We've all come the same distance, and we're all going the same way." She snorted. "All in the same damn boat."

Hamish said quietly, "What do you mean, going the same way?"

"I can't explain. It's just that for everything they give you in this place they take something away." She went on bleakly, "Some mornings I get up and don't know who I am. There isn't even any mirror, so I can check."

"You were telling us about the people," Nelda said with bright determination. "Interests, friends, all the things that keep you here."

"I'd leave in a minute if they'd let me." Lucy stood like a small ramrod. "Kids don't want me. *That's* why I'm here."

Nelda's voice rose. "No."

"Well, I'm off. Thanks for the Life Saver. If you see Cletus, tell him they're after him."

"Wait a minute. . . ."

She was in the doorway. "How many charms you got on your grand-mother bracelet?"

Nelda said, defensively: "Five."

"You lose. I've got twenty-four." The door closed on her.

"Damn jail," Hamish said, testing for a reaction; Nelda had her head turned so he couldn't see her face. "Just like a damn jail. Even the damn chairs are bolted down."

"Now, now, settle down."

"Damn jail," he said again. "Prison furniture. Prison rules."

She put down the nightie she was unpacking and turned. "I suppose there weren't any rules at Albert's house? Or when we were living with Lorraine? 'Don't use that chair, Daddy. . . .' " Her voice was ugly, but he recognized the inflections. " 'We're going to have some people in for dinner, Mommy. I wonder if you and Daddy would mind. . . .' "

"Don't." He knew it was already too late to head her off.

"You used to have to smoke in the coal room at Albert's; Lucy made you stop tying flies. And how about all those mornings when you had to go down cellar at five or six, so you wouldn't wake up anybody when you coughed?"

"They're our *kids,* Nelda. You'll put up with a lot of things for kids. Nelda, we were born in Waukegan, and that's where we belong."

"So you want to go back and let them go on hurting us. They don't need us anymore, Spike, don't you see? They passed us one day when we weren't looking, they outgrew us, and every day since then they have been getting bigger and stronger, and the two of us. . . ." She took his hand. "We had to get out of there before we just faded away."

"Dammit, Nelda, they're our past. They're all the future we've got." Hamish freed himself without even noticing what he was doing. He was at the window now, tired and thoughtful. "I read somewhere about how they used to handle it in New Hampshire, or maybe it was Vermont. Put the old people out in the barn every winter, stacked 'em like cordwood, and left 'em to freeze until spring." He pressed his forehead against the shutters, dreaming. "Then one sunny day in spring all the children and grandchildren would come for them; they'd lay the old bodies out in the sun to thaw so they could help with the planting. There they were, out of the way until somebody needed them. And when they woke up they were home where they belonged, all warmed up, with plenty to do."

"Hamish, that's *terrible.*"

"They were *needed.* What's so terrible about that?" From where he stood he could see part of the porch and the fringes of the court below; he could not see but imagined a hundred thousand identical quadrangles stretching beyond, all quiet, all orderly, all crammed with bodies full of pills and injections. The old people were all in their places, hooked up to intravenous tubes, and around them the rooms were neat and tidy with no junk in sight; someone had swept out all the fragments of their past and there they were, laid out with their hair brushed smoothly and all the character laundered out of their clothes. He and Nelda would be just like them soon. They would be. . . . He turned to Nelda, breathing hard. "They were *needed.* Who needs us here?"

When Nelda spoke her voice was so low he hardly heard her. Straining, he made it out: "I need you, Hamish."

He couldn't help himself; his mouth filled with tears.

"Please, for me. Remember how it was. . . ." She didn't go on; she didn't have to, her tone struck echoes, and winter was in the room; he was at her bedside, nursing her after her fall and promising anything just to make her live; winter was in the room and he was keeping her alive on promises, feeding her on gaudy, color-shot brochures.

He sighed heavily. "I remember." Then, on a last hope. "You were sick, you *needed* to think. . . ."

"I still need. I need to be safe. I'm sick to death of being tired and sick and being afraid of being sick. Promise you'll stay, Hamish. For me?"

He wasn't ready to face her; he didn't have to because the door slapped wide and Cletus was in the room like a lightning bolt, with limbs flailing and electricity crackling in his beard. Before they could stop him he slammed the door and headed into the tiny bathroom; he was burrowing in the shower. When Hamish went in after him and tried to pull him out he turned and spat like a cat.

"Let go, you son of a bitch, they're after me."

Lucy was next, crowding into the tiny bathroom, and the three of them went round and round, Cletus flapping and blubbering, Lucy trying to pull him off the shower seat. "Come on, Clete, no use fighting. The cart's outside."

"Let go, dammit."

Hamish found himself crowded against the basin; he hunkered up on it, trying to stay out of the way. He was conscious of Nelda whimpering just outside the bathroom door.

"Come on, Clete," Lucy was wheedling. "Come on boy, come on. Tchum on."

He poked his head out. "Have they gone?"

"You know damn well they haven't gone." She grabbed quickly, before he could duck back into the shower; she nodded to Hamish and together they began maneuvering him back into the room.

He pulled back, saying sullenly, "Why did you have to come along and ruin everything?"

The old man couldn't see her face but Hamish could; it was lined with pain. She said, "God knows I didn't want to. I just thought it might make it a little easier."

He was whimpering. "I want my shot; it's past time for my shot."

"You've had so *many* shots, Clete, and angiograms, and vitamin pills, and X-rays, and IVs. Come on, baby, they'll take you along all neat and tidy, and maybe. . . ."

He snuffled hopefully. "Maybe?"

"Maybe they'll even give you a shot before you go."

He bounded away from her, howling. "I don't want to go."

Hamish stepped in front of the old man: he could feel his back hairs going stiff and he had to clear his throat twice before his voice would work properly. "Look here," he said to Lucy, "You have no right. If he doesn't want to go with you . . ."

She looked at him without passion. "He has to go. It's time."

Cletus was blubbering. "But I've only been here for a *minute*. . . ."

"Fourteen years. Fourteen mortal years." She moved past Hamish, putting her arm around the old man's shoulder. "You smoothed the way for me when I came in, knew it was hard for me, being shoved in here. If I'd known then that I was going to have to come for you. . . ." She jammed her fist into her mouth, trying not to cry. When she was able she said to Hamish, "He wasn't always like this. Used to put up a hell of a fight. He got us napkins at dinner, and later lights. . . ."

"It can't be time, I haven't had my shot. I'll be good, I promise I will. . . ." Cletus was wiping his nose on his beard.

"Come on, Clete. Brace up. Take it like a man."

"I won't go. It's not my turn." He wrenched out of her grip, grinning slyly. "It's not my turn at all. It's your turn."

"Oh, Clete, you're a caution."

He giggled, falling into an old pattern of banter. "Or maybe you're so ugly they won't take you."

"You old goat. . . ." She brightened. "Hey, that sounds more like my old Clete. Now go on out there and show those guys you can take it like a man."

"Oh Lucy, I'm afraid."

Lucy looked over his head at the Scofields. "Would you believe he was the best linotypist in the East? *That's* what this place does to you."

He was weeping, wiping his eyes with her hand. "Please don't let them take me, please."

"Takes it right out of you."

"Lucy, Lucy, Ma. Mom. Mom. *Mommy*. . . ."

She still stood proudly but her old face was glazed with tears. "You see?" She patted Cletus on the shoulder. "There there, baby. You'll be all right. . . ."

Hamish said, quietly, "Maybe you'd better tell us about it."

But she wasn't listening. She was patting Cletus, saying, "You'll be all right, I'll take care of you. . . ." Hamish would have shaken an answer out of her but she was busy with her own thoughts, planning. "Well," she said abstractedly, "I'll show *them*." Then she was busy with her buttons and in the next second her dress fell to the floor and she stood, straight and proud of her stiff white muslin underslip. "Here," she said to Cletus. "You just slip into my frock."

"Lucy. . . ." The old man should have been protesting. Hamish wanted to take him by the shoulders and shake him and scream into his face until he turned and went outside and *fought.* . . .

It was too late. Cletus took the dress and shimmied into it, stuffing his beard into the bodice, not caring that his hairy arms and black trouser legs stuck out incongruously. When he was ready Lucy held him off at arm's length, revolving him with one hand.

"Yes," she said finally, "you'll do. Now you go on out, and if they try and stop you duck into the Ladies Room. I don't think they'll follow you into the Ladies Room."

"Lucy, I . . . I don't know what to say."

"Never mind. Let's just say you're not up to it, and I am." She gave him a shove. "You go wait in the Ladies Room until you hear them leave."

He danced on the doorsill for a minute, looking as if he would thank her, or apologize, or beg her to change her mind, but it was apparent to all of them that he didn't really want her to change her mind; in the end, he wasn't even able to thank her. Instead he said, dully, "It's time for my shot."

Lucy watched out the window, turning back to the Scofields with a grim smile. "He made it." She smoothed her slip and put a hand to her hair. "Well. . . ."

Hamish moved toward her. "You're not going out there. . . ."

She was cool and proud. "Why not?"

"You know what's out there."

"Hell yes. The dead cart. From the Tower of Sleep."

Nelda's voice went up and up. "It isn't even your *turn.* . . ."

"I'd rather go now, while I still have some choice. After all, I've still got my pride. Pride's all I have left." She looked past Nelda, talking directly to Hamish. "You understand. If I'd just held out, you know, when they tried to put me in this place. I could have sold flowers or something, to earn my keep."

Hamish said, "Or camped in the train station."

"Or gone on relief," Lucy said wistfully. "Anything but this. I gave up everything when I let myself be suckered into this. Well, it's been nice knowing you." She raised one hand in a gladiator's salute.

"Hang on, dammit. Hang *on.*"

She turned to Hamish. "You're still your own man. Better get out before it's too late."

The door slammed behind her. There was a second of silence from outside, then the sound of a scuffle, the rattle of bodies against metal and the crash of heels on the cement. Hamish could hear the sounds of arms and heads in desperate friction and over it, Lucy's voice rising: "Let go of me, you bastards. I'll climb on by my*self.*"

There was a long pause and then the rattle, or rumble, receding as the cart took her away.

Before the sound faded Hamish was at the suitcase, stuffing Nelda's resort clothes in willy-nilly, putting sneakers in on top of her Capri pants and finishing off with the sunshade, not minding that clothes stuck out of all the cracks when he sat on top and tried to close the thing. "Come on," he said, assuming she was with him. "If you want those damn kids' pictures, you'd better get their pictures. I'll sneak the suitcases out the back and wait in the bushes by the gate. . . ."

"No."

". . . You can tell them you're going out for a little walk. . . ." He climbed off the suitcase slowly, seeing that she had taken the family pictures to her bosom. She was sitting quietly in one of the two straight chairs. "Give me those damn things. Don't you want to take them home?"

"I'm not going."

"The dead cart, Nelda." He tugged at the pictures. He had to get her moving. "The Tower of Sleep."

She let go of the pictures unexpectedly. "I already knew."

The pictures fell between them with a little crash. "You *knew*?"

"Of course I did. It's in the back of the brochure. The tiny print."

He was backing away from her. "But you didn't *tell* me."

"I was hoping you'd get to like it here first. It's perfectly fair," she said matter-of-factly. "When you've used up your quota of medicine they come for you. The funerals here are beautiful, I've seen the card; it doesn't hurt at all and in the meantime you have everything you want."

"Nelda, its monstrous."

She stood now, looking at him, so steadily that he backed into a bed and sat down. "It's better than anything we *had*—all those damn fights with the kids; being sick, being afraid. They have drugs to take care of that kind of thing, they have everything you need over in the Tower of Hope, and if you fall—there's somebody there. There wasn't anybody there last winter. . . ."

He winced. "Never mind."

"I lay in the alley for twelve hours. I just ducked around a corner to get out of the cold and there I was in the dirt with slush running under me and blood in my mouth. I couldn't even call for help. I don't want to go through that again. I don't even want to be *afraid* of going through it, and I don't. . . ."

She was near tears; she opened the suitcase again, taking out the Capri pants, and when she had collected herself she took a deep breath and began again.

"I don't want to be dependent on the kids. They're at us all the time,

Don't this, Don't that, and as soon as company comes they scrub us and prop us up in the living room, Exhibit A. Well I'm not up to it anymore, Hamish. I'm just not up to it."

He saw an opening. "Are you any better off here? You know what we are? Vegetables, goddam vegetables. They'll tend us and water us and cart us off before we can even die on the vine. . . ."

"It's worth it for a little comfort and safety." She was pushing him away from the suitcase, trying to unpack. After a little scuffle she gave up, saying sadly, "I was hoping you'd get to like it here. If only you'd get to like it here. . . ." She changed her tone, accusing him. "You promised you'd give it a chance."

"I didn't promise to drop dead. I'm going home."

"You'd rather go back there and suffer. . . ."

"Hell yes. At least I'll know I'm still alive." He had the suitcase to himself now; he was jamming things in again, wrestling it shut. "Look, I'd rather be hurt and sick *and* afraid, I'd rather be living with those damn kids. . . ."

"Don't make me tell you. Promise you'll stay."

Something in her voice arrested him. "Tell me what?"

"I don't want to have to tell you. Hamish, the kids. . . ."

"I've just got to get out of here." He was already in motion, trying not to listen. "If I can just get going before it gets dark. . . ."

"The kids." The words popped into the room. Nelda hushed him gently, saying, "It was right after my fall, I was laid up in bed and in they came, Albert and Lorraine. They were so damn sympathetic, all about how awful winters were for us, how we deserved better than that, that and living in back rooms. . . . I was too sick to make any sense of it. Then they started bringing folders, pictures of swimming pools and people playing in the sun . . . I don't know, it all looked sort of good, and after they left I looked at some of the folders. I began to dream a little bit."

"You don't have to tell me anymore, Nelda. Just remember me when I'm gone."

"Let me finish." She had him by the arm now; her fingers were like iron bands. "Then one day they came back, they said, how would we like to try Golden Acres, and I thought about it. I told them it was probably all right for people without *folks* but we'd just as soon stay home, with them, and then. . . ."

She didn't have to finish, he didn't want to have to finish, but she seemed bound to go on. He tried to stop her; he said, "Nelda. . . ."

"Then I found out. It was all arranged; they'd sold off our stocks for the down payment. I was supposed to break the news." She went on grimly. "I sat there in that iron bed with my back hurting and those damn smug kids staring at me and I thought, I thought. Nothing can be worse than this. It was the kids, Hamish. The kids wanted to get rid of us."

"I know."

"You didn't know."

"I didn't want to admit it, but I knew it all along."

"So here we are." She managed a brave little smile. "Might as well make the best of it."

"I can't do it, Nelda. I have to go." He was desperate to be away, to have her come with him before the manager or the bellboys came along and locked them in; he tugged at her, saying, "Come on, come *on*," and when she wouldn't move he said, "Do you want to sit and wait for them? They'll come with the cart and after that they'll put our clothes in a box to be burned and then they'll scrub everything and change the linens and disinfect the room. Nelda, when I go I want to leave something behind, even if it's only a—a *smell*."

She disengaged herself. "I'll miss you so much."

"I've always been my own man, Nelda; I've got to go where somebody cares."

"Do you think anybody out *there* cares?" They were having a little battle over the suitcase; she made him put it down and she had it open again.

"At least they'll feel *some*thing about me, even if it's only dislike." He tried to lift her with his voice. "Maybe I'll go back to Waukegan and get a job."

"Waukegan doesn't want us, Hamish. Nobody does."

"I was born in that town. My past is in the streets, my past and my future, if I've got any future. I've got to go and see."

She shook her head. "You're only fooling yourself."

"Then *let* me fool myself."

They were both crying; there was a little silence while he fumbled in the tiny closet and put on his coat. Nelda brushed his shoulders and turned down his collar and she spoke, finally, saying: "You'll need a few things. You can't go off without a few things."

He tried to steady his voice. "The overnight bag, if you don't need it."

She said, quietly, "I'm not going anywhere."

"I'll get a job. I used to be a pretty good bricklayer. Then I'll find us a place and I'll send for you." He took her hand, lingering. "You will come, won't you?"

She said, with love, "We'll be together soon."

He wrapped his dry bones around her in a fierce embrace. "I'll find a place and then I'll send for you. It won't be long." He let her go and now he was in the doorway; he had to break away or he would never be free.

Her voice was so low he could hardly make out what she was saying: "It doesn't matter where we are . . . it won't be for long."

He might have turned. He might have gone back inside the room to plead with her but the sun was on its way down and in the distance there began a subtle rumble and he knew without stopping to think about it that it was coming his way.

POPULATION IMPLOSION

andrew j. offutt

I

Nobody mentioned it for a while. Not on a large scale, I mean. A couple of years actually passed before it was noticed as a definite trend. I'd heard other doctors comment, of course. Merely that they seemed to be losing a lot of old patients all of a sudden, for no particular reason. But physicians are so used to death we didn't get excited. It was a hard-working insurance actuary who saw it for what it was.

People were just . . . dying. Old people. Doctors and coroners wouldn't admit to perplexity.

They would put down "heart attack" or "stroke" or "heart failure" or "cardiac arrest," or the like. Mostly cardiac arrest. Good old catchall. Think about it. Means the patient's heart stopped beating. Well, I should smile, it did! Did you ever hear of anyone's being dead and his heart still beating? That's an *effect*, not a cause. When you're dead your heart stops pumping. But something causes *that*.

A bullet. A fall. An illness: cancer, or cerebral hemorrhage. Or a plague. That is, a Plague.

The insurance actuary pointed out that the death rate was up—way up—among old people. Everything else was still there, of course; men murdering each other with automobiles and slipping in the bathtub and so on. But old people were dying. The oldest.

Well, there wasn't anything unusual about that, and I remember even I chuckled. Sure, we knew old age was a disease. We called its cause a virus, which meant we didn't know what it was. A *filterable* virus . . . which means the organism was *not* filterable. We hadn't *found* it. And since we hadn't found the cause, we certainly hadn't done much about the effect. We had lengthened the lifespan. We could keep a man alive and we were proud of it. Oh, maybe he was a vegetable, but hurray and so what, we were keeping him alive. The family usually found the money, somehow.

But the actuary was one hundred per cent on the beam. The death rate was up among the oldest people, and it was increasing. Today thirty, tomorrow thirty-one, this day next month forty, this day next year sixty-two. I'm using relative figures, you realize. No need to start spouting precise ones. Just consider that in City A, on May 1st of 1979, twenty people died. In 1985 twenty-six died on that same day. In 1992, thirty-three. All in accord with the population increase; no cause for alarm. You have ten people, one dies. You have a hundred, ten die, *et cetera*.

But then it began curving up.

That actuary was shaken, I'll tell you. He shook the company president, too, and the board of directors. And there's where I came in. I had just been made a director. You know how it goes: you don't mind working, which puts you in a class by yourself. You make money and become pretty well known and make some more money, and all of a sudden you're successful. People think you're pretty smart. They want you to be a director of the United Fund and the school board and a bank and the country club and a hospital and Kiwanis and this and that. Doesn't matter if you're an executive in an aircraft company or a plumbing and heating contractor or a distiller or even an M.D. So I had a chunk of stock and a chunk of permanent life insurance and somehow wound up a director of the Great Coastal Life Insurance Company of America.

No, I didn't attend the meetings. Lord, I knew about as much about the life insurance business as I do about quantum mechanics . . . I can define "quantum" and I can come close to defining "mechanics"—I think. Anyhow, this actuary's report was mentioned in the minutes I received in the mail and I read it and chuckled. So he had discovered that old people were dying! Just tell me if they start dying of scarlet fever or botulism or chicken pox, I thought. Or puerperal fever.

Well, then the article showed up in *Newsweek* five months later. A lot of people still thought it didn't make sense, but it was the second time I'd seen it and there I was a professional and . . . well, I called

Roger Calkin at Great Coastal and asked him to send that nutty young actuary of his over.

And there it was. The actuary—Ike Hill—had by that time started collecting figures from all over the world. All you had to do was look at them. All deaths were up, naturally. Way up. But . . . the increase that reached up and slapped you in the eyeball and squeezed the pit of your stomach was in the over-75 group. It hadn't struck anyone as particularly odd that the Russian Premier, the West German Chancellor and the Speaker all had died within a few months of each other. But they'd had plenty of company. Those three had all been past eighty, and their group was dying by the score, by the thousand, by the tens of thousands. We'd prolonged their lives for them; now they were cashing in one after the other, as if they were crowding each other to prove or disprove their particular faith's belief or disbelief in afterlife. As if they were tired of life, or as if they were trying to make us look bad. Sure, I had that thought.

I remember saying, "Hell, Ike Hill, at this rate there won't be anyone over 75 alive anywhere!"

And I was right. It took less than a year. In the meanwhile the world lost seventy or eighty assorted senators, representatives, MP's and what-have-you lawmakers. A king. An even ten presidents, premiers and the like, and one dictator. Several generals. A potful of judges. The Pope. Two-thirds of the Roman Curia. And every Cardinal Archbishop in the world but eleven. Oh, it was great for promotions, and pageants!

People were taking notice by then, of course. Someone used the word "plague" in a newspaper story one day, and after that it was The Plague. A lot of people did a lot of theorizing. There was religious gabble and atheist gabble and medical gabble and political gabble-gabble. Over a dozen different men announced over a dozen different causes. One even announced a cure.

They were all wrong.

Then I found it, and I couldn't think of anyone to call save Ike Hill.

II

We got our heads and our figures together. We barely had to glance at them. Of course they weren't completely accurate. It's impossible to learn exactly how many people in the world died or were born last year, or for that matter even twenty years ago. The ladies of Africa and India and China don't publish announcements every time they have a kid, whether they expose it to die or not, and they don't file death certificates, either.

We took the figures over to Ike's office and turned on some lights and fed them into the Iron Brain, and it told us what we already knew, which is about all Iron Brains are good for anyhow.

The death rate matched the birth rate.

In the United States it exceeded the birth rate.

Every time somebody popped a kid on the tail and made him suck up that first highly addictive drag of air, someone, somewhere, gasped his last one. And whatever the cause, it didn't know anything about fair play or national boundaries. The birthrate was highest in Asia. You know which country had the longest life expectancy, don't you? The largest percentage of old people? Uh-huh. The U.S. of A. was rapidly running out of the euphemism I've always hated: "Senior Citizens." (I don't like any euphemism that indicates I'm junior.) Even then an extraneous thought went creeping across my mind like a guilty cat: something or somebody—capitalize that if you want—was solving the Medicare problem. In a few years, maybe months, I wouldn't be filling out so many of those government forms for aged patients any more. The AHA wouldn't be hollering about all the paperwork involved in Medicare admissions. And my sons wouldn't have the 21% social security tax I was paying!

Frankly, Ike Hill and yours truly M.D. didn't know what the hell to do. We just stared at each other and the machine and then went out and found a quiet, dark place to talk. I forgot to call my answering service for the first time in five years. First time I'd got drunk in fifteen years, since I was a freshman in pre-med.

Whom do you tell? For maybe three years a plague had been raging across the world, a plague which obligingly passed over people who had lives to live and knocked on the doors of those who'd lived a fair-sized one already. Whom do you tell? No one else knew there was no one, not one single person, anywhere in the world, older than 75—maybe 74 by then. No one knew that every time an OB checked in at Admittance some oldster checked out of the world. And . . . if it went on . . . then by this time next year, there wouldn't be anyone over 73, or 72, depending upon the international birthrate and the number of people in that age group. Or maybe 71, or 70. And the *next* year . . . whom do you tell? Call Washington and say "Mister President, this is Thomas Jefferson McCabe, M.D., in Atlanta, and pretty soon our country is going to be out of business, populationwise, and by the way you're 69, aren't you? Have you arranged disposal of your papers?"

Ike Hill and I didn't know. So we drank too many gimlets and had to be poured into a couple of taxis and sent home to unundetstanding wives.

In the morning I prescribed the usual ineffectual old wives' tales for myself and held my head carefully as I called A. T. Griffin, M.D., Chief at Good Samaritan Hospital. And I called Michael Rosen, M.D., head of the U of G Med School and I managed to get them together in Doctor Griff's office at Good Sam. And I took poor Ike Hill with me and I told them. We told them. Then we showed them. It meant a lot more to them than to us, I assure you . . . Doctor Griff was sixty-four and Doctor Mike admitted to sixty-seven. And they bought it. They had to. Oh, we thought, and we postulated, and we opined, and we theorized and hoped out loud. But we had the answer.

Swell. What to do with it? I felt relieved—I'd shared it. I'd transferred the weight and the responsibility of the knowledge onto the shoulders of the best two medical father-images I had. I was out of it!

Well, I took my first plane ride to Washington. Doctor Mike's doctor said he shouldn't travel—you think *we* don't have doctors? Physician, heal thyself!—or try. And Doctor Griff just wouldn't-couldn't. So Mister Ike Hill, B.S., M.S., and T. J. McCabe, M.D., flew up to the big town with introductions from those two Big Men—Doctor Griff was also president of the Georgia Medical Association and a director of the AMA—and papers and graps and reports and analyses and a few inches of computer tape.

We got in amazingly fast. My medical friends had done a good job, working personally and through senators and what not. I think it was the President's secretary got us in; he was a Georgian. It's pretty hard for mere people to get an audience with the President of, by, and for the people.

Sorry. Getting old, as things go now. I'll be forty-five next month.

Naturally we wound up with the Surgeon General (first time he'd had anything to do in years!) and some fellow from Bethesda and a couple of hotrods from Johns H. and somebody else I later found out was a psychiatrist. Watching us! Ike and me!

They had to buy it, too. It's tough to buy truth you don't like. But it's tougher to turn your back on it, and not too smart, either, as Galileo, among others, proved.

You can't imagine how they looked. How we felt. What to do? There was the evidence. Now they were in the same leaky dinghy I'd been hand-paddling the past several days. What to do?—and how? I was relieved, I can tell you that. I'd unshouldered the burden. I had gently laid it at the feet of the boss, the proverbial Authorities, and now I was out from under.

And that's how Ike Hill and I got put in charge of Project Methuselah. That's how I got to be one of the Jaycee's Ten Most that year. I think it would have—and should have—been Ike, but there was a choice, and I was a member.

Funny thing about the Government Mind. You tell them you know where there's a problem, they right away treat you with respect—especially if you're in the American Magician's Association and have the initials after your name. The schools translate them Medical Doctor. I've always figured they stand for Me Dunno. But everybody else automatically assumes Magic Dispenser.

Back to that government mind. It assumes that if you've been smart enough to point out a problem, obviously you're the man to tackle it. Tell the Feds you've found something wrong and they say fine, work on a cure, here's some money (we have lots and lots) and some papers to order some more and a title and some blank progress reports for you to file in triplicate, triweekly. I did have enough sense at least to get a commitment from the President, and get it in writing, my way.

Then . . . funny thing about the human mind (as opposed to the one just mentioned). Somebody gives you a problem, and you right away do one of three things. Punch the nearest panic button. Fake it. Or find that your mind is hurtling off in ten directions to Get the Job Done. That's what happened to me. Oh, obviously I had no solution. But I had thought of Step One, how to study the problem.

We got ourselves ten volunteers, Controls, seven male and three female human beings, aged 74. We put 'em in a hospital, third floor of Good Sam, and cleared the rest of the floor. In reverse order; I was *careful* with those people. My Personal Responsibilities. Sure, there were a lot more women of that age, but the reason I wound up with seven men was the men we interviewed weren't as touchy about giving their birthdates. We recorded them. I felt a monster, grisly, ghoulish, as I put them down, one under the other, in order: earliest birthdate at the top.

Then I did everything. Ran tests. X-rays, EKG's. EEG's. Taps. Smears. Basal Metabolisms. Those ten people were *delighted*. Free room service, lots of attention and no cost. And furthermore they could *enjoy* it; they weren't sick! I'd deliberately picked them in good health (as well as could be expected, considering, as we're fond of saying). I supervised their diets as if they were the first septuplets and I had a movie contract riding on them. Decuplets, I guess, under the circumstances—perish the thought. They lived in near-sterile conditions. Daily checks. Blood pressure. Sistolics. Reactions. Put-out-your-tongue-and-say-ah. All of it.

They died. Very neatly, from the top of the list. And I felt ghoulish and grisly, crossing off their names, one by one, from the top, with ugly satisfaction that they were proving me right. Cause of death: cardiac arrest.

It was enough to give me back the religion I'd outgrown in med school when I first realized there's no justice in nature. Really. I felt like putting down "God" after Cause of Death. I didn't. But I didn't write cardiac arrest or natural causes or any of that rot, either. I put "PLAGUE," in block letters. And plague it was, The Plague. The one we couldn't cure, because it didn't make anyone sick or have any symptoms whatever, and we haven't found a cure for death yet.

None of these old people had any symptoms. They just died, peacefully and quietly. Patient Rested Comfortably To The End. We had permission, and we autopsied to shame all previous autopsies. We examined those cadavers more carefully than Leonardo had. Nothing. No bugs. No . . . well, just nothing. I'd have welcomed a little note: "I decided his time had come and there's nothing you can do about it so go on back to prescribing the Pill and delivering the ones who don't use it and Wednesday-afternoon golf. Yours very truly, (signed) Prime Mover."

And about that time I had the insane thought. The answer. The only one. Crazy.

The aforementioned Pill.

III

There are more things in heaven and earth, Horatio, than you and I will ever dope out, so let's start by talking about something we do know. At the beginning of the Christian Era there were about 250,000,000 people in the world. By the middle of the 17th Century there were a half-billion; it took some 1650 years to double. By the 1800s there were a billion. By 1960 the world's population had doubled again, to two billion, and indications were that there would be six billion by AD 2000. Momentum. Snowball effect. Like compound interest.

People didn't have enough sense to stop breeding in the face of over-population. It wasn't personal enough. So who's Julian Huxley? Yes, well, how about if it's good and personal? Or bad and personal.

Look: every time a baby's born, someone dies.

No population explosion, no problem of food and water and *lebensraum*, or *liebensraum* either. We could've saved a lot of worry and palaver over that one. Somebody—go ahead, capitalize that: Somebody had decided the world was full enough. So he—I mean big h, *He* had either to stop the income or accelerate the outgo. He chose the second. I had to admit: it was the first time I'd witnessed justice in nature. Population implosion.

Oh Lord. The announcement. You remember it. It was . . . it was awful. Uncle Charlie died yesterday . . . my God, I'm responsible! . . . the baby . . . Uh-huh. Granddad began to look at his expectant daughter as if she were some sort of monster. She wasn't a monster, not really. No. But she *was* killing him. Or working on it. Just as soon as she went into the delivery room.

That's *personal*. It was horrible.

It was elsewhere, too. Oh, everybody corroborated, all over the world. It was simple enough. All the evidence was there, it was just that Ike and I collated it first. I published the results of Control Group 1 and saw that copies were sent to the USSR and everywhere else. By that time I was into Control Group 3: 73-and-a-half-year-olds, and I was advertising for a long-term observation: 70-year-olds. I tried to think ahead.

Take China. The leaders were delighted (until they remembered how old they were). They didn't have to worry about us any more. Not when The Plague would solve their problem. Simple matter of numbers. Mathematics. And there weren't a lot of old people over there to start with (a lot of those pictures you saw of Asian women who looked about 90 were women with *infants*, remember?). But . . . Communist or not, those people hadn't got completely over venerating the old. For the first time in history Chinese women had a good reason to practice a little *conception*-control, stopping pregnancies, rather than using the time-honored method of family-size control: merely exposing the infants to die. Getting oneself *enceinte* was murdering one's venerable grandfather.

Same thing in Japan, of course, and Thainambodia and the rest.

But we had the worst problem. The Land of Opportunity. We were strong . . . but outnumbered by all sorts of countries. Mostly enemies. Russia (which really hadn't been an active enemy since the fifties, but . . . they were always ready) and China. Chou said about mid-century that after World War III there would remain ten million Americans and fifteen million Russians and 300 million Chinese. Nice mind Chou had! But now he didn't need WW III. All he had to do was reproduce us right out of business. He had more children to have more babies, and the old Asian Long View. (Not Chou; he was long dead. I'm talking about Huing, of course.)

It became patriotic not to have babies. People damn near stopped. Little Debbie and Jeff—everybody born in the fifties and sixties was named Debbie and Kevin and Jeffrey—married and bit their lips and didn't have babies, for poor old Grandpop's sake. Pill business boomed as Geritol sales began to dwindle. But poor old Grandpop hit the magic age and his heart stopped just the same. Debbie and Jeff got mad. It was all very well for us to support the world; to ship wheat to Russia whilst she called us the same old names; to support the UN almost single-handedly; to send all those goodies to our enemies; to steal Jeff's money to put into Grandpop's pocket—or rather his physician's pocket. But not having babies was *personal*. And when it didn't do any good anyhow . . . well, I used to think we were due for a revolution around 1970, until I grew up and realized people *wanted* socialism. But we darned near had one in Year One of The Plague, and not over socialism, either.

Over making babies!

There wasn't any way to cover up. Somebody, somewhere, wasn't holding up his end. When oldsters continued to die, when age 72 became the barrier, everybody knew we were being conned. *We* weren't having babies. But somebody was. And as soon as Grandpop died—heck with 'em. Debbie and Jeffrey couldn't be worried about the Grandpop next door. There was a, as the clicheists say, hue and cry. Meaning one hell of a lot of loud noise. Oh, the noises in the UN! The accusations! Here we'd just grown up enough to admit we'd been covering our pride for an old mistake all these decades, we'd just let China in . . . and bang! Right off the bat we're jumping all over them in the UN! Mister Krishnapur swore his country was cooperating. Mister Vorlonishev said quietly and smugly that his country hadn't begun cheating now. But Mister Li said the same thing.

Somebody was lying. A few African ladies here and there who hadn't got the word couldn't be affecting things the way they were being affected.

We had a celebration in the hospital the night of Henry Clark's 72nd birthday. Tea and cake in his room. Booze in dixicups in the resident's lounge later. Henry Clark didn't wake up the next morning.

The story got itself put together later, but here's how it happened, in sequence: The Russians had been shook. Really shook. Trigger fingers had never been so itchy before. They were scared we didn't believe them. So for the first time in Lord knows when they invited us—se-cretly—to come in and have a look. They were on the level. Our observers confirmed that the Soviet government had proclaimed re-production a crime against one's fellow man and, *ergo,* the State. What was more important, our spies confirmed the observers. . . .

Meanwhile Stephen Levee had got out of China, somehow, and brought back photographs and stories.

The Chinese were breeding like crazy. Practically at gunpoint. Told that the Americans were doing so. Patriotism: breed, that China may realize her destiny in the world. That sort of thing and threats were stamping out the oldster-veneration which had moved over to the U.S. sometime around 1930.

We didn't even announce it to the UN.

For the first time since World War Two, Washington and Moscow joined hands and said let's get together and do it together. Secretly, China has been a common threat for years; now it's far worse. Some people just can't be got on with. For the first time since . . . 1941, I guess, the United States announced honestly that it was embarking on a war of aggression. Oh, it was self-defense, of course, and therefore a Holy War. All wars are Holy Wars, to somebody. This one was for Granddad and Grandma and Uncle Elmer. Except it wasn't even a war.

Stephen Levee came out of China on April 11th. On the 16th the President announced that on May 1 he would make a major speech, and all the Lippmans and Huntley-Brinkleys wondered aloud and in print what he would have to say. Of course they pointed out that he had chosen to speak on the biggest day in the Communist World. What he did was to review the problem, the pleas, the agreements. The UN brawl. Then he displayed Stephen Levee's films and read his reports, word for word, and introduced Levee and Mister Vorlonishev and talked awhile and then announced that the governments of the United States and the Union of Soviet Socialist Republics had declared war on the People's Government of China.

Retroactively: the buttons had been pushed and the planes had swung Chinaward *before* his speech began.

IV

The Chinese were busily celebrating May Day, Peking was full of aircraft and missiles and troops and tanks, parading under the eyes of Huing and hundreds of thousands of people, all of whom had of course gathered spontaneously; one assumed the Red Guards were directing traffic. Just as spontaneously they went to join their revered ancestors before Huing even heard about the President's speech. Peking wasn't hit with *one* bomb. The Chinese missile bases weren't hit with one bomb each. The missiles came from half-a-dozen different directions and the bombs came from aircraft whose white stars and red stars had been effaced and replaced with big UN insignia. The whole operation was unbelievably successful, mainly because China had always known we'd never do it.

A missile got through and removed Colorado Springs and a tremendous chunk of mountain from our map. Two submarines sent four missiles streaming in toward Washington and New York, and miracle of miracles all that propaganda from Denver was on the level; we *were* able to stop them! Not to mention the submarines.

Rand-McNally started working on new maps; the old ones, showing China, were obsolete. Norad began reorganizing. Re-aiming. The Russians were terribly sorry they'd goofed and sent Formosa down to join Atlantis, but little mistakes will happen, as we used to say when we napalmed our own troops every now and again. There was one hell of a—sorry, here comes the cliche again—*hue and cry* in the UN. Then there were a lot of very big goggle eyes when Mister Vorlonishev and Mister Davis and the President stood up and said okay, we attacked them and we damn near destroyed China and what are you going to do about it? There were plenty of warheads and planes and silos left, and the allied nations of USASR were willing to use them if forced.

They weren't forced. The Aussie—funny—was the first to jump up and say he was going to call home and recommend his government broaden the alliance to three. By the time he was through there were so many delegates clamoring for recognition to climb aboard that the Secretary-General had to call for a general motion to save time. He got it. There was amazing unity.

A month later we celebrated William Michael's 71st birthday, and he woke up the next morning, too.

But everyone seemed to have celebrated the "war" in the same way. Nine months later, on approximately February 1, Granddads started dropping dead again.

And in a few months it was all back again and in a few years life expectancy (certainly!) was below 65, and Senator Martin—age 63—introduced a bill to cut Social Security takeouts by two-thirds. He even managed to smile and say he'd never collect anyway.

As far as we can see now the population of Planet Earth must remain constant at approximately five billion people or less. The nearest we've come in our figures is 4,998,987,834, and we've gotten that figure three times. Apparently either the Prime Mover didn't share our regard for numbers or he counted differently. Maybe he meant for us to have six fingers.

Somehow everybody just gave up and let it ride. For possibly the first time in history the young got their way. Twice the old managed to get us in war-shape again, and both times the young got together and said nothing doing. We learned pretty quickly that you don't have wars if the senators are invited to go, or if a few million young men, in both nations involved, say no. And when they suggest that if overgrown children insist on settling things by violence, let's try the old method: personal trial-by-combat . . . ! The President and the Prime Minister backed down pretty fast while the rest of us guffawed at the editorial cartoons.

They might as well have gone along. Within a year the Plague had got them both anyhow.

Meanwhile a lot of us were looking for answers. Why?

Okay. There was a rule: another Natural Law; really a restatement of the old one: survival, after all, of the fittest. This law said there shall not be more than approximately 5×10^9 personnel in existence on Planet Earth at any one time. Fine. *Why?* I figured once again we had ourselves an effect, not a cause. Effect: the Plague. Causative effect: our having reached such-and-such a population figure. Causative effect: There Shall Not be more than such-and-such many people. But it was an effect, not a cause.

Okay. Why?

Well, here's a theory. If it doesn't happen to agree with your religion, that's tough; make up your own theory. Plenty of people have made up their own religions. This one represents the thinking of a lot of people over a lot of centuries. It's been the basis for a lot of religions both before and since Christianity. There was some truth to the Mystery Religions—certainly Paul respected them highly. There is some, too, in Christianity, in Judaism, Buddhism and Islam. Mostly Buddhism, I guess. It was in Christianity, too, originally; called Gnosticism. The early Christians stamped it out. Too hard to sell. Isn't that just like Man, trying to interpret God? Those first several centuries were mostly salesmanship centuries, and the Roman state religion and Mithraism were tough foes. Even so the original concepts may have remained if the Empress Theodora hadn't so adamantly stamped them out. And even so the whole new faith might have gone by the board if the Emperor Julian hadn't got himself killed in battle just when he was starting to stamp out Christianity. *(There's a death I'd like to investigate!)*

Reincarnation. The ring of return. You die, but your life-force or soul or whatever you wish to call it keeps coming back. Oh, not as bugs or cattle; your life-force is a mind, and enters only human beings. Without memories, usually. Except people who have funny dreams in full color . . . or wind up nuts on some period of history without knowing why. Easy. You were there, once.

Look, just keep your mind on Hamlet's words that there are more things in heaven and earth than are dreamt of in your philosophy. And try to remember that a closed mind is pretty much like a closed door . . . there can't be much traffic, either way.

The idea is we have to try, over and over, no matter how long or how many corporate lives it takes, to be "good enough to retire" (I'm simplifying, naturally). If you commit six crimes (let's keep it straight and say "against nature," and I'm not talking about that implied definition of "Crimes against Nature" lurking like rattlesnakes in our lawbooks either. Men pretend to be so horrified by Sodom and Gomorrah they won't even use the words . . . yet nowhere in that old book does it say *what* the crime of those two cities was! For all we know it may have been over-defoliation or water or air pollution; those are crimes against nature, aren't they?)

Anyhow, if you committed six crimes in life #1 while you were Babble-babble of Memphis in 6,000 BC, you've got to compensate/atone for them somewhere, somewhen else. Your life-force seeks at/one/ment, whether you as Babble-babble do or not. As B-b you died and your life-force (go ahead and use soul if you feel you must) hung around without drawing a new body until 1,000 BC. There weren't many bodies around then, remember; there was a long wait between assignments. You became a Hellenic peasant. You "atoned" for three of the crimes, but committed two new ones before you died. You've moved up one notch. You've got five bad deeds to wipe off the master ledger. But . . . you will have the opportunity; the man *said* you would be born again, didn't he? You think he meant by being splashed a little?

As a Pfc. under Titus you held your own. You died. Your ego waited around some more, still with five black marks. Back in Memphis you had killed without mercy and had died of old age as a lot of killers do . . . they do NOT die by the sword . . . *that* time. Sometime. Someplace. As a serf or maybe as a woman accused of witchcraft in the Middle Ages you had such a hard time you cut the tally down to two. Surely there are special rules for those murdered in the name of God. Maybe you were lucky enough to be sworded.

You came back as Rudolf Schickner, say chief gas man at Auschwitz. Oops. Back to the end of the line. Next time you came back as . . . well, that's the system, anyhow. And of course you're coming back a lot more frequently now. That's the whole point.

At the beginning, whatever and whenever that "is," all life-forces were made. All the souls. All of them. None has been created/activated since.

Yes. You get the point. There aren't six billion in AD 2000. And there won't be six billion people in the world by 2500, either, or AD 5000. There never will be.

All the souls have been used up.

Don't call me a mystic. Try to open up your mind a little, let the light shine on the cobwebs of preconceptions. And remember I've had no religion save *Ad majorem hominis gloriam* since I was 23 years old. And, if you don't like that theory, think up another.

So here we are. No more interviews with Mrs. 101-years-old. The wastebaskets at the bank aren't full of unstamped brown envelopes at the first of the month any more. There aren't any old folks sitting around barberships or on the courthouse steps or post-office steps any more. The old folks' homes with the cute names are closed down. You can buy Geritol stock with nickels and dimes. Companies have to advertise for night watchmen, and some of them don't have gray hair. In another fifty years, maybe, the Social Security Administration will be out of the red. Right now they're sending out a fourth of the checks they were thirteen years ago.

Do? Nothing. I don't think you can. Oh, I may be wrong, but I've got plenty of agreement. Sure, maybe you can find a way out of it. Maybe if a million people leave Earth to colonize another planet we can add a million human beings to the ledger and stop writing PLAGUE on death-certificates for a while . . . while we get more ships ready. I don't think so. I think we're at five billion, give or take a few, for keeps. Holding, situation no-go. It's up to you. Sure, there'll be a stop. A temporary one, anyhow. When it reaches the point that parents give birth and both die the instant twins are born, it will be over for a while. And maybe somebody will start acting sensibly. But unless you stop horsing around you're going to have a life expectancy of twenty and then fifteen and then Lord knows what, eventually.

Meanwhile I intend playing a lot of golf and doing a lot more reading. I'll be forty-five next month, and life expectancy's down to fifty-seven this month.

THE TUNNEL AHEAD

Alice Glaser

The floor of the Topolino was full of sand. There was sand in Tom's undershorts, too, and damp sand rubbing between his toes. Damn it, he thought, here they build you six-lane highways right on down to the ocean, a giant three-hundred car turntable to keep traffic moving over the beach, efficiency and organization and mechanization and cooperation and what does it get you? Sand. And inside the car, in spite of the air-conditioning, the sour smell of sun-dried salt water.

Tom's muscles ached with their familiar cramp. He ran his hands uselessly around the steering wheel, wishing he had something to do, or that there were room to stretch in the tiny car, then felt instantly ashamed of his antisocial wish. Naturally there was nothing for him to do because the drive, as on all highways, was set at "Automatic". That was the law. And although he had to sit hunched over so that his knees were drawn nearly to his chin, and the roof of the car pressed down on the back of his neck like the lid of a box, and his four kids crammed into the rear seat seemed to be breathing down his shirt collar—well, that was something you simply had to adjust to, and besides, the Topolino had all the five-foot wheelbase the law allowed. So there was nothing to complain about.

Besides, it hadn't been a bad day, all things considered. Five hours to cover the forty miles out to the beach, then of course a couple of hours waiting in line *at* the beach for their turn in the water. The trip home was taking a little longer: it always did. The Tunnel, too, was unpredictable. Say ten o'clock, for getting home. Pretty good time. As good a way as any of killing a leisureday, he guessed. Sometimes there seemed to be an awful lot of leisuretime to kill.

Jeannie, in the seat beside him, was staring through the windshield. Her hair, almost as fair as the kids', was pulled back into pigtails, and although she was pregnant again she didn't look very much older than she had ten years before. But she had stopped knitting, and her mind was on the Tunnel. He could always tell.

"Ouch!" Something slammed into the back of Tom's neck and he ducked forward, banging his forehead on the windshield.

"Hey!" He half-turned and clutched at the spade that four-year old Pattie was waving.

"I swimmed", she announced, blue eyes round. "I swimmed good and I din't hit nobody."

"Anybody", Tom corrected. He confiscated the spade, thinking tiredly that "swim" these days meant "tread water", all there was room to do in the crowded bathing-area.

Jeannie had turned too, and was glowing at her daughter, but Tom shook his head.

"Over and out", he said briefly. He knew a car ride was an extra strain on kids, and lord knew he saw them seldom enough, what with their school-shifts and play-shifts and his own job-shift. But his brood was going to be properly brought up. See a sign of extroversion, squelch it at the beginning, that was his theory. Save them a lot of pain later on.

Jeannie leaned forward and pressed a dashboard button. The tranquillizer drawer slid open; Jeannie selected a pink one, but by the time she had turned around Pattie had subsided with her hands folded patiently in her lap and her eyes fixed on the rear seat TV screen. Jeannie sighed and slipped the pill into Pattie's half-open mouth anyway.

The other three hadn't spoken for hours which, of course, was as it should be. Jeannie had fed them a purposely heavy lunch in the car, steakopop and a hot, steaming bowl of rehydrated algaesoup from the thermos, and they had each had an extra dose of tranquillizers for the trip. Six-year old David, who was having a particularly hard time learning to introvert, was watching the TV screen and breathing hard. David, his first-born son, born in the supermarket delivery booth in the year twenty-one hundred on the third of April at 8:32 in the morning. The year the population of the United States hit the billion mark. And the fifth child to arrive in that booth that morning. But his own son. The tow-headed twins, Susan and Pattie, sat upright and watched the screen with expressions of great seriousness on their faces, and the baby, two-year old Betsy, had her fat legs stuck straight out in front of her and was obviously going to be asleep in minutes.

The car crawled forward at its allotted ten mph, just one in a ribbon of identical bright bubble cars, like candy buttons, that stretched along the New Pulaski Skyway under a setting sun. The distance between them, strictly rationed by Autodrive, never changed.

Tom felt the dull ache of tension settled behind his eyes. All of his muscles were protesting now with individual stabs of cramp. He glanced apologetically at Jeannie, who disliked sports, and switched on the dashboard TV. Third game in the World Series, and the game had already begun. Malenkovsky on red. Malenkovsky moved a checker and sat back. The cameras moved to Saito, on black. It was going to be a good game. Faster than most.

They were less than a mile from the Tunnel when the line of cars came to a halt. Tom said nothing for a minute. It might just be an accident, or even somebody, driving illegally on Manual, out of line. Another minute passed. Jeannie's hands were tense on the yellow blanket she was knitting.

It was a definite halt. Jeannie regarded the motionless lines of cars, frowning a little.

"I'm glad it's happening now. That gives us a better chance of getting through, doesn't it?"

Her question was rhetorical, and Tom felt his usual stir of irritation. Jeannie was an intelligent girl; he couldn't have loved her so much otherwise. But explaining the laws of chance to her was hopeless. The Tunnel averaged ten closings a week. All ten could happen within seconds of each other, or on the hour, or not at all on a given day. That was how things were. The closing now affected their own chance of getting through not one iota.

Jeannie said, thoughtfully, "We'll be caught sometime, Tom."

He shrugged without answering. Whatever might happen in the future, they were obviously going to be held up for a good half hour now.

David was wriggling a little, his face apologetic.

"Can I get out, Daddy, if the Tunnel's closed? I *ache*."

Tom bit his lip. He could sympathize as well as anyone, remembering the cramped misery of the years when his own body was growing and all he wanted to do was run fast, just run headlong, anyplace. Kids.

Extros, all of them. Maybe you could get away with that kind of wildness back in the Twentieth century, when there were no crowds and plenty of space, but not these days. David was just going to have to learn to sit still like everybody else.

David had begun to flex his muscles rhythmically. Passive exercise, it was called, one of the new pseudo-sports that took up no room, and it was very scientifically taught in the playshifts. Tom eyed his son enviously. Great to be in condition like that. No need to wait in line to get your ration of gym time when you could depend on yourself like that.

"Dad, no kidding, now I gotta go." David wriggled in his seat again. Well, that sounded valid. Tom looked through the windshield. The thousands of cars in sight were still motionless, so he swung the door open. Luckily there was a chemjohn a few yards away, and only a short line in front of it. David slid quickly out of the car. Tom watched him start to stretch his arms over his head, released from the low roof, then sheepishly remember decent behavior and tighten into the approved intro-walk. "He's getting tall", Tom thought, with a sudden accession of hopelessness. He had been praying that David would inherit Jeannie's height instead of his own six feet. The more area you took up the harder everything was, and it was getting worse: Tom had noticed that, already, people would sometimes stare resentfully at him in the street.

There was an Italian family in the bright blue Topolino behind his own; they too had a car full of children. Two of the boys, seeing David in front of the chemjohn, burst out and dashed into the line behind him. The father was grinning; Tom caught his eye and looked away. He remembered seeing them pass a large bottle of expensive reclaimed-water around the car, the whole family guzzling it as though water grew on trees. Extros, that whole family. Almost criminal, the way people like that were allowed to run loose and increase the discomfort of everyone else. Now the father had left the car too. He had curly black hair; he was very plump. When he saw Tom watching him he grinned broadly, waved towards the Tunnel and lifted his shoulders with a kind of humorous resignation.

Tom drummed on the wheel. The extros were lucky. You'd never catch them worrying unduly about the Tunnel. They had to get the kids out of the city, once in a while, like everybody else; the Tunnel was the only way in and out, so they shrugged and took it. Besides, there were so many rules and regulations now that it was hard to question them any more. You can't fight City Hall. The extros would neither dread the trip, the way Jeannie did, nor . . . Tom's fingers were rigid on the wheel. He clamped down, hard, on the thought in his mind. He had been about to say, *needed* it, the way he did.

David emerged from the chemjohn and slid back into his seat. The cars had just begun to move; in a moment they had resumed their crawl.

On the left of the Skyway they were coming to the development that was already called, facetiously, "Beer Can Mountain." So far there was nothing there except the mountainous stacks of shiny bricks, the metal bricks that had once been tin cans, and would soon be constructed into another badly-needed housing development. Probably with even lower ceilings and thinner walls. Tom winced, involuntarily. Even at home, in a much older residential section, the ceilings were so low that he could never stand up without bending his head. Individual area-space was being cut down and cut down, all the time.

On the flatlands, to the right of the Skyway, stretched mile after garish mile of apartment buildings, interspersed with gasoline stations and parking lots. And beyond these flatlands were the suburbs of Long Island, cement-floored and stacked with gay-colored skyscrapers.

Here, as they approached the city, the air was raucous with the noise of transistor radios and TV sets. Privacy and quiet had disappeared everywhere, of course, but this was a lower-class unit and so noisy that the blare penetrated even the closed windows of the car. The immense apartment buildings, cement block and neon-lit, came almost to the edge of the Skyway, with ramps between them at all levels. The ramps, originally built for cars, were swarming now with people returning from their routine job-shifts or from marketing, or just carrying on the interminable business of leisuretime. They looked pretty apathetic, Tom thought. You couldn't blame them. There was so much security that none of the work anybody did was really necessary, and they knew it. Their jobs were probably even more monotonous and futile than his own. All he did, on his own job-shift, was verify figures in a ledger, then copy them into another ledger. Time-killing, like everything else. These people looked as though they didn't care, one way or the other.

But as he watched there was a quick scuffle in the crowd, a sudden, brief outbreak of violence. One man's shoe had scraped the heel of the woman ahead of him; she turned and swung her shopping bag, scraping a bloody gash down his cheek. He slammed his fist at her stomach. She kicked. A man behind them rammed his way past, his face contorted. The pair separated, both muttering. Around them other knots of people were beginning to mutter. The irritation was spreading, as it seemed to do from time to time, as though nobody wanted anything so much as the chance to strike out.

Jeannie had seen the explosion too. She gasped and turned away from the window, looking quickly back at the children, who were all asleep now. Tom pulled one of her pigtails, gently.

The skyline loomed ahead of them, one vast unified glass-walled cube of Manhattan. Light rays shot from it into the sunset; the spots of foliage that were the carefully planned block gardens, one at each level of the ninety-eight floors of the Unit, glowed dark green. Tom, as he always did, blessed the foresight that had put them there. Each one of his children had been allotted his or her weekly hour on the grass and a chance to play near the tree. There was even a zoo on each level, not the kind of elaborate one they had in Washington and London and Moscow, of course, but at least it had a cat and a dog and a really large tank of goldfish. When you came down to it, luxuries like that almost made up for the crowds and the noise and tiny rooms and feeling that there was never quite enough air to breathe.

They were just outside the Tunnel. Jeannie had put her knitting down; she was looking intently ahead, but as though she were listening rather than looking. In spite of his own arguments, Tom felt his fingers thudding on the dashboard. On the TV screen, Malenkovsky triumphantly moved a king.

They had reached the Tunnel entrance. Jeannie was silent. She glanced at her watch, irrationally. Tom pressed the tranquillizer button and the drawer shot out, but Jeannie shook her head.

"I hate this, Tom. I think it's an absolutely *lousy* idea."

Her voice sounded almost savage, for Jeannie, and Tom felt a little shocked.

"It's the fairest thing", he argued. "You know it perfectly well."

Jeannie's mouth had set in a stubborn line. "I don't care. There must be another way."

"This is the only fair way", Tom said again. "We take our chances along with everybody else."

His own heart was pounding, now, and his hands felt cold. It was the feeling he always had on entering the Tunnel, and he had never decided whether it was dread or elation, or both. He was no longer bored. He glanced at the children on the back seat. David was watching television again and gnawing on a fingernail; the three little ones were still asleep, sitting up as they had been taught to do, hands folded properly in their laps. Three blind mice.

The Tunnel was echoing and cold. White light slipped off the white tile walls that were clean and polished and air-tight. Wind rushed past, sounding as though the car were moving faster than it actually was. The Italian family was still behind them, following at a constant speed. Huge fans were set into the Tunnel ceiling; their roar reverberated over the roar of the giant invisible air-conditioning units, over the slow wind of the moving cars.

Jeannie had put her head down on the seat back as though she were asleep. The cars stopped for an instant, started again. Tom wondered if Jeannie felt the same vivid thrill that he felt. Then he looked at the line of her mouth and saw the fear.

The Tunnel was 8500 feet long. Each car took up seven feet, bumper to bumper. Allow five feet between cars. About seven hundred cars in the tunnel, then: more than three thousand people. It would take each car about fifteen minutes to go through. Their car was halfway through now.

They were three-quarters of the way through. Automatic signal lights were flashing at them from the catwalk under the Tunnel roof. Tom's foot moved to the gas pedal before he remembered the car was set on Automatic. It was an atavistic gesture: his hands and feet wanted a job to do. His body, for a minute, wanted to control the direction of its plunge. It was the way he always felt, in the Tunnel.

They were almost through. His scalp felt as though tiny ants were running along the hairs. He moved his toes, feeling the scratch of sand on the nerves between them. He could see the far end of the Tunnel. Maybe two minutes more. A minute.

They stopped again. A car, somewhere ahead, had swerved out of line to search for the right exit. Once out of the Tunnel it was legal to switch back to Manual drive, since it was necessary to pick the right exit out of ten, and all too easy to find yourself carried to the top level of Manhattan Unit before finding a place to turn off.

Tom's hand drummed at the wheel. The maverick ahead had edged back into line. They started movement again. They picked up speed. They were out of the Tunnel.

Jeannie picked up her knitting and shook it, sharply. Then she dropped it as though it had bitten her fingers. A bell was clanging over their heads, not too loud, but clear. Just behind their rear bumper a gate swung smoothly into place.

Jeannie turned to look back at the space behind them where the Italian family in the bright blue car, and others, had been. There were no cars there now. She turned back, to stare whitely through the windshield.

Tom was figuring. Two minutes for the ceiling sprays to work. Then the seven hundred cars in the Tunnel would be hauled out and emptied. Ten minutes for that, say. He wondered how long it was supposed to take for the giant fans to blow the cyanide gas away.

"Depopulation without Discrimination", they called it at election time. Nobody would ever admit voting for it, but almost everybody did. Aloud, you had to rationalize: it was the fairest way to do a necessary thing. But in the unadmitted places of your mind you knew it was more than that. A gamble, the one unpredictable element in the long, dreary process of survival. A game. Russian Roulette. A game you played to win? Or, maybe, to lose? The answer didn't matter, because the Tunnel was excitement. The only excitement left.

Tom felt, suddenly, remarkably wide awake. He switched to Manual Drive and angled the round nose of the Topolino over to the Fourth Level exit.

He began to whistle between his teeth. "Beach again next weekend, sweetie, huh?"

Jeannie's eyes were on his face. Defensively, he added, "Good for all of us, get out of the city, get a little fresh air once in a while."

He nudged her and pulled a pigtail gently, with affection.

Afterword

Each of the stories included in this book and each of the novels and short stories briefly mentioned in the headnotes is applicable to more categories than the one under which it is included or discussed. The novels especially have been done an injustice as one or two sentences is not enough to indicate more than one of the many possible themes.

I apologize to the authors and urge the readers of this book to familiarize themselves with those novels they have not yet read.

C.W.S.

Bibliography

The books in the following bibliography are divided into two sections. The first group is composed of science fiction criticism, and the second is composed of nonfiction books focused on the future. There is no bibliography of fiction for several reasons. First, Alexi Panshin has provided an excellent one in *Library Journal,* XCV, 12 (June 15, 1970). Second, the critical works included below mention a great deal of science fiction and place it in several contexts. And third, there are over fifty books listed in the headnotes of this book.

I. SELECTED CRITICISM

Ackerman, Forrest J., *The Frankenscience Monster.* New York: Ace Books, 1970.

Amis, Kingsley, *New Maps of Hell.* New York: Harcourt, Brace, & Co., 1960.

Atheling, William, Jr. (James Blish), *The Issue at Hand.* Chicago: Advent Publishers, 1964.

Bailey, J.O., *Pilgrims through Space and Time.* West Los Angeles, Calif.: Argus Publishers Corp., 1947.

Bretnor, Reginald, ed., *Modern Science Fiction—Its Meaning and its Future.* New York: Coward-McCann, 1953.

Clareson, Thomas, ed., *Extrapolation: A Science Fiction Newsletter.* (The newsletter of the MLA conference on science fiction. For copies write the English Department, Box 2515, College of Wooster, Wooster, Ohio 44691.)

———, *Science Fiction Criticism: An Annotated Checklist.* Kent, Ohio: Kent State University Press, 1972.

———, *Science Fiction: The Other Side of Realism.* Garden City, N.Y.: Doubleday & Co., Inc., 1972.

Davenport, Basil, ed., *The Science Fiction Novel: Imagination and Social Criticism.* Chicago: Advent Publishers, 1964.

de Camp, L. Sprague, *Science Fiction Handbook.* Hermitage, 1953.

Franklin, H. Bruce, *Future Perfect: American Science Fiction of the 19th Century.* Oxford, 1966.

Green, Roger Lancelyn, *Into other Worlds.* New York: Abelard-Schuman, Ltd., 1957.

Hillegas, Mark R., *The Future as Nightmare: H.G. Wells and the Anti-Utopians.* Oxford, 1967.

Huxley, Aldous, *Science and Literature.* New York: Harper & Row, Publishers, 1963.

Knight, Damon, *In Search of Wonder.* Chicago: Advent Publishers, 1967.

Lerner, Fred, *An Annotated Checklist of Science Fiction Bibliographical Works.* Privately printed, 1969.

Lewis, C. S., *Of other Worlds.* New York: Harcourt, Brace, & World, 1966.

Lundwall, Samuel J., *Science Fiction: What It's all About.* New York: Ace Books, 1971.

Moore, Patrick, *Science and Fiction.* London: George G. Harrap & Co., Ltd., 1957.

Moskowitz, Sam, *Explorers of the Infinite.* New York: World Publishing Co., 1963.

———, *Seekers of Tomorrow.* New York: Ballantine Books, Inc., 1967.

Nicolson, Marjorie Hope, *Science and Imagination.* Great Seal, 1956.

———, *Voyages to the Moon.* New York: The Macmillan Co., 1948.

Panshin, Alexi, *Heinlein in Dimension.* Chicago: Advent Publishers, 1968.

Rogers, Alva, *Requiem for Astounding.* Chicago: Advent Publishers, 1964.

Warner, Harry, Jr., *All our Yesterdays.* Chicago: Advent Publishers, 1969.

Williamson, Jack, *Science Fiction Comes to College: A Preliminary Survey of Courses Offered.* Privately printed, 1971. (Information may be obtained by writing Jack Williamson, Box 761, Portales, New Mexico 88130.)

Wollheim, Donald, *The Universe Makers.* New York: Harper & Row, Publishers, 1971.

II. SELECTED WORKS ON THE FUTURE

Asimov, Isaac, *Is Anyone There?* New York: Ace Books, 1970.

Calder, Nigel, ed., *The World in 1984* (2 vols.). Gretna, La.: Pelican Publishing Co., Inc., 1964.

Clarke, Arthur C., *Profiles of the Future.* New York: Bantam Books, Inc., 1964.

———, *Report on Planet Three.* New York: Harper & Row Publishers, 1972.

DeBell, Garrett, ed., *The Environmental Handbook.* New York: Ballantine Books, Inc., 1970.

Ehrlich, Paul, *The Population Bomb.* New York: Ballantine Books, Inc., 1968.

———, and Anne Ehrlich, *Population, Resources, Environment, Issues in Human Ecology.* San Francisco: W. H. Freeman & Co., Publishers, 1970.

Eurich, Alvin C., ed., *Campus 1980: The Shape of the Future in American Higher Education.* New York: Delacorte Press, 1968.

Fairbrother, Nan, *New Lives, New Landscapes: Planning for the 21st Century.* New York: Alfred A. Knopf, Inc., 1970.

Feinberg, Gerald, *The Prometheus Project: Mankind's Search for Long Range Goals.* Garden City, N.Y.: Doubleday & Co., Inc., 1969.

Ferkiss, Victor C., *Technological Man: The Myth and the Reality.* New York: New American Library Inc., 1969.

Greeley, Andrew M., *Religion in the Year 2000.* New York: Sheed & Ward, 1969.

Gutkind, Erwin A., *The Twilight of Cities.* New York: Free Press, 1962.

Marx, Wesley, *The Frail Ocean.* New York: Ballantine Books, Inc., 1969.

Mitchell, John G., and Constance L. Stallings, eds., *Ecostatics: The Sierra Club Handbook for Environmental Activists.* New York: Pocket Books, Inc., 1970.

Paddock, William, and Paul Paddock, *Famine 1975! America's Decision: Who will Survive?* Boston: Little, Brown & Co., 1967.

Sullivan, Walter, *We are not Alone: The Search for Intelligent Life on Other Worlds.* Signet, 1966.

Toffler, Alvin, *Future Shock.* New York: Bantam Books, Inc., 1970.

World Future Society, *The Futurist: A Journal of Forecasts, Trends, and Ideas about the Future.* (P.O. Box 19285, Twentieth Street Station, Washington, D.C. 20036)

Zero Population Growth, *National Reporter.* (A monthly magazine included with membership. Write ZPG, 330 2nd Street, Los Altos, California 94022.)